LIKE CHAFF TO THE WIND

LIKE CHAFF TO THE WIND

A novel based on true happenings

Robert Morgan

iUniverse, Inc.
New York Lincoln Shanghai

Like Chaff to the Wind

iUniverse, Inc.

For information address:
iUniverse, Inc.
2021 Pine Lake Road, Suite 100
Lincoln, NE 68512
www.iuniverse.com

Cover painting by Stefan Oliver.

ISBN: 0-595-32925-X

Printed in the United States of America

Dramatis Personae

Robert George Henery	**Amateur jockey**
Lord & Lady Shotley (Honest Ned)	**Racehorse owner**
Cock Sparrow	Head stable lad for John Smith
John Smith	Race horse trainer.
Bill Carter & Wally Jones	Jockeys
Mrs Dennis	Race horse owner
Lillian Mary Henery	A nurse. First wife of Robert
Hotel lady. (London)	
Count August Ramoskie	**Hungarian race horse owner**
J B Smith	A Police Inspector
Man in sausage shop	
Herr Schmitt	Secretary to Count Ramoskie
Joseph	Coachman to Count Ramoskie
Innkeeper and Elly his granddaughter	
Franc	Butler to Count Ramoskie
Elisabet "Graffinflein"	**Daughter of Count Ramoskie**
Soldo	Head stable lad to Ramoskie
Countess Helga Ramoskie	Wife of Count Ramoskie

Emil, Count von Zelletall, Prince von Tauber, Cousin of Helga Ramoskie

Maria Von Zelletall	Wife of Emil.
'Boy'	Stable lad for Count Ramoskie
Anna	Cook for Robert Henery
Dr Hoffman	Village Doctor.
German officer	Rounding up deserters.
Doctor's wife	Wife of Hoffman
An Ostler	Ostler to Inn
A Coachman	Coachman to Maria Von Zelletall
A Soldier	Soldier on station, going to the war.
Captain of the guard	Red guard.
Priest	A member of the Clergy at Cologne Cathedral
Lady with room	A 'good Samaritan' in Cologne
Boarding house woman	Boarding house keeper in Rotterdam
Dock Superintendent	Port Official in Rotterdam
Dutch fisherman	Trawler skipper at Den Haag
Ticket Clerk	Railway ticket clerk at Lowestoft
Station Master	At Newmarket.
Cabbie	At Newmarket
Vicar	Anglican clergy at Newmarket
Bank manager	At Newmarket

Various other waiters, cabbies, chamber maids and boys, soldiers and guards.

Introduction

This story is based on true events and is so compelling that it must be told. It tells of the circumstances of two people trying to make their way and seek true happiness through a series of disastrous events that are not of their making and over which they have no control. I have pieced the story together, in the belief that the main events are true, gathered from many conversations that I have had, over a long period of time, with the three daughters. All of them were reluctant to talk about the happenings in this story, which had such a dramatic effect on their lives, but now that they are all dead I feel that this could and should be written.

Robert Morgan

CHAPTER 1

The police had been very insistent! They had made it quite plain they did not believe a word he had said.

Robert lay back in his seat, his head lolling back and forth as the train sped south. Its billowing smoke whisked away with the wail of its whistle in the steamy vortex of its passing. His ear brushed on the rough fabric of the seat cover as it kept an uneven beat to the time of the wheels on the track. His mouth went dry as he thought about that interview.

Beyond the grimy window of the train there seemed another world. Light spangled hills slowly pirouetted past in the dark night. Small villages rattled by as the speeding train thundered through their dark closed stations—a cluster of lights, gone in an instant. Out there people, ordinary people, lived out their ordinary lives, resenting the brief incursion upon their peace as the train sped past, leaving only the smell of damp soot in the air to mark that he, Robert Henery, had passed that way.

Luckily the whole business had been kept out of the newspapers. Even if people had seen him, they would not have known who he was, nor would they have cared.

Robert watched a runnel of condensation jog down the glass. Was it only last month? His unseeing eye watched the water drip onto the floor of the carriage where it shimmered rhythmically to the pounding of the wheels, flickering and twinkling as the train jolted along.

He stared again into the blackness beyond the steamy window. As though reflecting the images of his mind, he could see himself again, standing in the dimly lit Police Station. He could plainly remember the gas lamps hissing in the background. There had been several people there—he could see them all clearly. Now, as it had then, everything seemed grey. The Sergeant, the Constables, the Inspector, even the furniture and the walls, everything seemed grey. He could recall the pain of his grip on the greasy wood as the Sergeant read out the charge from a piece of paper.

"Robert George Henery, you—is that your full name?"

"Yes, Officer," he had mumbled.

"Don't you have a proper surname, like ordinary people?"

"Yes, Officer," he had replied wearily. He had long since learned to ignore that jibe and to give a flat factual reply. He ruefully remembered the painful kicks he had received when, as a new boy at school, he had been tormented because he had not got a 'proper surname'.

"Henery. My surname is Henery."

The Sergeant looked at him for a while suspiciously, then began again…

"Robert George 'enry, you are charged this day, 30th June, 1882, that at a place, on a day unknown, you did on your own or with other persons, unlawfully kill, or have conspired to kill, your wife, Lillian Mary 'enry! You will be remanded in custody whilst further inquiries is made. You are not obliged to say nuffin, but anything that you do say, will be writ down and might be used in evidence against you." The Sergeant put his papers down and looked at Robert with a gleam of triumphant satisfaction in his eye.

Say anything?

Robert could not think, let alone say anything.

As he had been led away, his mind was blank. He was pushed, none too gently, into a dark, damp cell, lit only by the feeble light that filtered in through the grimy heavily barred window from the gas street-light outside. The hard bunk onto which he fell had on it a musty smelling, mouldy blanket. He had lain numb with despair. The Constable had lingered for a while, then, with some gesture of sympathy, had left the cell. The door had slammed with a crash.

Robert's reverie was broken by the mournful whistle of the train as it shrieked into the night. The next minute it exploded into a tunnel. The sound of the train hammered back off the rocky walls. The smoke and steam billowed eerily around them, forced into the carriage by the pressure trapped by the confines of the tunnel. The roar and clatter was intense as it burrowed through the hill. Just as suddenly it burst out into the night. The noise and pressure in the carriage vanished. Once again distant clusters of lights could be seen spangling some unseen hill in the inky blackness. Robert eased back into his seat and loosened his collar. The smell of the smoke, forced into the carriage as they sped through the tunnel, was all pervading.

It reminded Robert of his vile cell, so recently vacated. He wrinkled his nose in disgust.

He tried to think of how it had all begun. There were so many loose ends. He did not know which one to pick up first. The stark truth was that Lillian had disappeared. After months of searching and inquiry that had been totally fruitless, he had been arrested and charged with her murder. Just as suddenly, before he had come to trial, he had been released. The Inspector had handed him a card, asking him to call upon Lord Shotley as soon as convenient. *Good old 'Honest Ned'*, Robert thankfully thought to himself. *Always there when he was needed*. How on earth had he become involved? Robert did not know, but he would find out when he arrived in London and met him.

Lord Shotley had proved to be a good friend as well as benefactor. Robert, through his present gloom, was forced to admit it had been a lucky day for him when their paths had first crossed. But that was another loose end in the chain of events—not a very apt expression, really. You did not have loose ends in a chain, just links, each inescapably joined to the next—your life, each event, sometimes unconnected, yet somehow tied to the other events, as they too were tied to those before and after them. There must be just one link some-where upon which all those that were subsequently added could be hung. As the train sped through the dark night, Robert pondered...

Perhaps it was the fall? No. In a way, the fall was the end of the beginning, not the beginning of the end. It was the episode that had completely changed his life. Perhaps he could use it as a peg upon which to hang things that had happened before and afterwards.

Even now, he could remember the horse going over. He was riding one of Lord Shotley's fillies in a race for three year olds She had taken off too early, being pressed hard by the rest of the field and had just clipped the top of the fence with her forefeet. Even as he sat in his seat he could feel her cartwheeling beneath him.

He could not understand how people who had bad accidents could recall nothing afterwards. He could remember every agonising detail.

He felt her feet strike the fence. He knew that she was going to fall! Grace-fully and slowly, she began to cartwheel. His instinct was to fall off, but he knew he would be under the feet of the other horses if he did. He felt the shock of her nose hitting the ground. Then his own head. Then the crushing weight of her body as she fell down on top of him. He felt with awful agony, his mus-cles tearing and heard his bones breaking. Then all was still, the dead weight of her body pressing his crumpled form into the ground. Mercifully blackness came over him! He saw and felt no more. People ran to try to help. Some tried to pull the inert horse, others tried to pull the pathetic rag doll that lay beneath her, but for all the hope and shouting, nothing was achieved. The horse lay still, only able to raise its head with feeble wickerings. Two people came running down the course, carrying a hurdle between them, upon which they had hastily thrown a horse blanket. The Veterinary Officer galloped up on his horse, closely followed by the Clerk of the Course.

Robert gazed into the steamy window. He could clearly see the Veterinary Officer look at his horse. He exchanged quick glances with the Steward. He took a heavy revolver out of his bag. The flat sound of the shot was whipped away with the smoke from the revolver, in the wind. The Drag horses were led up, two ageing Suffolk geldings. Quickly a chain had been fastened round a dead foot, a tarpaulin was thrown over the carcass and the greatest three year old, never to be, was pulled away, leaving his twisted body, inert on the ground like some discarded pile of dirty laundry.

He remembered pain. Dreadful, searing, grating, jarring pain, and as they lifted him onto the hurdle, he cried out in anguish.

He looked at his reflection in the steamy window and shuddered at the horror of the memory. He groped for his handkerchief to wipe the sweat from his top lip.

He remembered dimly seeing Lord Shotley bending over him, as it were, through a misty pink haze. He remembered the look of surprised relief that appeared on that fine face, when he had cried out. Lord Shotley had turned to his wife, peering white-faced from their still rocking carriage.

"He's still alive. Thank God he's still alive! Quick, my dear, please step down. You there! Help Lady Shotley alight! Look lively, you men! Put him on the stretcher. Be careful there. Lift him in to my carriage. You, you, get in first. Tilt the bloody thing." Robert cried out in anguish. "Oh, be careful, man! I'm sorry. I did not mean to snap at you—here, let me help…For goodness sake open the other bloody door and get out that side…I'm sorry…I'm sorry, but we must make haste."

Gradually the unwieldy hurdle was manoeuvred into the carriage, balanced precariously across the two seats, and Lord Shotley had squeezed in beside it.

"Steward, please assist Lady Shotley back to the enclosure. I will ride with Henery. Drive on, Coachman, but for God's sake drive carefully." Lord Shotley wedged himself into the corner and braced the hurdle with his foot.

Mercifully Robert remembered only dimly the journey to the Hospital. He could recall crying out at every lurch of the carriage as it carefully made its way off the Heath, jolting and bumping over every rut. He vaguely remembered hearing, as if in the far distance, Lord Shotley's voice urging the coachman to greater speed but cursing him at every bump. He had taken off his coat and had thrown it over Robert, who was shaking uncontrollably from cold and shock. All the time Lord Shotley was talking to Robert, encouraging him, urging him to hang on to consciousness, cajoling him when he seemed to be failing, shouting at him when he seemed to have gone.

"Damn it, Henery, don't you dare die. You haven't got time to die! You ride for me, not the Devil!" He struggled to his feet in the cramped, swaying confines of the coach. He took out his pocket knife and stuck it into Robert's hand. The pain roused him.

"Come back, I say!" he roared with all the authority he could muster, as it seemed that Robert was sliding down that long dark tunnel from which there was no return. Robert faintly heard the voice, as if echoing from the depths of a deep cave.

"Come back. Damn it! I need you here now. Come back, I say! Come back!" Robert's slide away from pain and agony stopped. "Come back!" urged Lord Shotley with every ounce of force that he could produce.

Slowly Robert turned away from defeat and the welcoming oblivion that beckoned him and struggled his mind back to the pain and agony of reality. Somehow in that terrible journey Lord Shotley managed to keep Robert's body and soul together by the sheer strength of his will.

Robert dimly remembered being carried into the Hospital. He was aware of the terrible pains as his bones were reset and his body bound to allow them to knit. He had dim recollections of white sheets and of people washing him. He could vaguely remember seeing misty figures moving around him and hearing far away muffled voices. He could not remember how long he had remained in that state, languishing between life and death. But gradually he became aware of light and dark and of a voice. The voice kept calling for Robert, whoever he was. It kept on calling—on and on it went.

"Robert, Robert, are you there, Robert? Come back to us, Robert." The voice kept on calling.

"Robert, Robert, come back to us, Robert." He moved the idea round in his head. *Strange that Robert never answered. If someone kept calling him like that, he would answer. You had to answer. You could not ignore someone calling you like that, on and on.*

Presently the darkness was getting lighter. He could see a figure sitting beside him. He made a great effort. He could see that it was a nurse. She was sitting by him, gently rubbing his hand, and as she did so she was softly calling "Robert, Robert, come back Robert." It was then that he realised that *he* was Robert—the voice was calling *him*.

"I'm here, I'm here. Can't you see me? It is me! I am Robert." His spirit cried out. His voice made a barely audible croak.

"I'm here, I'm here," he whispered.

The nurse let go of his hand and ran to the door.

"Matron, Matron!" she called out excitedly. "Mr. Henery, he's back, he's back!" She ran to the bedside, tears streaming down her face.

"Oh! Robert, Mr Henery, you've returned to us. We have all been trying so hard, we have been willing you back for so long. Where have you been?"

Robert tried a weak smile and even that hurt. Every part of his body seemed to have its own special pain.

"I don't know," he had feebly whispered. "I don't know; wherever it was, it's been a bloody long way."

His rehabilitation had been long and painful. He soon found that the nurse who looked after him was called Lillian. She had nursed him virtually night and day, ever since he had been brought into the Hospital. Because of her, he recovered. Without her determination, he would have died. He studied his reflection in the train window, shocked to realise that it had taken him until now to understand that.

It has been months before he had been allowed to take his first steps on crutches, but eventually he became strong enough to stagger outside with them, so that he was able to sit in the garden. The summer was fine and bright. He flourished in the fresh air and the warm sun. Lillian used to take him out and stay with him as long as she dared.

He remembered with a bitter taste in his mouth how he had finally plucked up courage to ask the Doctor when he would be able to ride again. And his stunned shock at the Doctor's harsh laugh and his curt reply.

"Ride? You will never be able to ride again! You will be lucky if you can ever walk straight without crutches, let alone ride!"

Robert had spent weeks in an inner ferment. Riding was his be-all an end-all. The very breath of his life. If he couldn't ride, his life in racing was over! Even a lad had to be able to ride. Any hope that he might have had of being a trainer was gone, shattered. If he couldn't ride, he would be condemned for-ever to be an odd-job hand round the stable, mucking out, sweeping, rubbing down for the rest of his life, watching them riding out every morning, leaving him behind. No! He would rather be dead than that!

It had taken Lillian all her patience, tact and guile to talk him out of the state of lethargy into which he fell after that blow. It had taken him weeks to come to terms with this devastating news. His whole life was riding. He had been riding ever since he was fourteen.

Robert had been determined that he would one day become a trainer, but first he must make a name for himself as an amateur jockey. He worked hard in the hope that he would be noticed and be given a chance for his first 'ride'. Perhaps through the illness or indisposition of a jockey, he might get a chance as a last minute stand-in in a race. He could remember the day when that chance came as if it were yesterday.

It was the third day of the June meeting. The yard had only one horse running that day, 'Corn Dolly', a hot hope belonging to Mrs. Dennis that was to run in the Heath Cup. It was still dark when they had left the stable. He and the head lad, who was known to everyone as 'Cock Sparrow', both mounted, leading 'The Dolly' between them. Wally Jones who was to ride 'The Dolly' in the afternoon race, followed on another horse. Robert normally looked after 'The Dolly' and rode her out at exercise. It was to be his job to look after her and take charge of the other horses during the day.

The little cavalcade had set out at first light. It clattered through the back streets, its breath hanging in little puffs in the chill air, punctuating their passage. A cat, which had been sitting on a cottage wall, took fright as they suddenly rounded the corner and, with a feline shriek of terror, had leapt off the wall and fled across the street right under 'The Dolly's' feet. She shied sideways. A considerable mêlée developed as the highly strung horses, already a bit nervy because of the earliness of the hour, shied and jostled. 'Corn Dolly', hemmed in by the other three horses, reared and plunged. She shied sideways and cannoned into Cock Sparrow who by then was letting out a string of oaths that would follow all cats and that one in particular, to their graves. He was unseated. He fell heavily to the ground and was only saved from injury by the tenacity of his grip on 'The Dolly's' leading rein. 'The Dolly' reared again but he hung on like a monkey to an organ grinder's braces. Robert by now had his horse under control. He had managed to hang on to 'The Dolly's' other leading rein. Between them they managed to calm her down and subdue her plunging. Wally Jones had also been unseated. He was leaning limply against the cottage wall, clutching his elbow, struggling with his horse which was still exceedingly restless.

"Oh my God, Wally, whatever's wrong wiv you?" cried Cock Sparrow, scuttling over to him.

"I fink it's me bleedin' collar bone!" he moaned weakly. Cock Sparrow had been doing a non-too-gentle inspection. An anguished cry from Wally had told him that his probing fingers had found the sharp edges of the broken bone.

"Oh, for Gawd's sake, shut your racket!" replied Cock Sparrow angrily, the furrowed look of a man suddenly confronted by one of life's greater problems etched on his wizened face.

"Well, one thing's certain, you ain't ridin' in no race today! What the 'ell am I goin' to do na'?" Cock Sparrow pulled off his cloth cap and clawed his sparse hair in desperate panic. He chewed the end off his riding crop anxiously. The horses were becoming restless again. He had to make his mind up quickly.

"All right," he said, decisively. "Get your silks off. Give us your cap. Get back on your 'orse. Ride back to the stables. Wake up Bill Carter. Tell 'im to get 'is self up 'ere as quick as 'e can and 'e can take your ride. If 'e don't make it on time, the boy, 'e'll 'ave to take your ride, that's all. Get back on your horse and get going."

"I can't!" wailed the unfortunate Wally.

"Oh my God, give me bleedin' strengf!" moaned Cock Sparrow. "'Ere boy, 'old me 'orse!"—and with that he flung the reins over to Robert, leaving him to struggle with the three horses, and went to help Wally. Despite his wretched cries of pain, Cock Sparrow soon had him back up on his horse and pointed round the way that they had come. He caught the horse a frustrated crack across the rump with his crop and it set off down the road as it if had been stung by a bee.

"Make 'aste!" he called after it, "or Carter will be too late to get to us in time for the race." He swung himself back into his saddle. "Come on boy, or we'll be too late an' all!"

The horses soon settled down again, once they were on the move. They set off at a fast trot, the sound of their hoof beats echoing off the walls of the cottages as they passed.

The day was just dawning. A magnificent rose red light lit the clouds on the edge of the distant sky. A row of gnarled twisted pine trees stood out in stark indigo silhouette against the morning's early glow, gaunt sentinels who had witnessed the passing of Boedecea across this heath. The pale sky, primrose yellow on the horizon, shaded through the purest tones of iridescent blue as the sun just lifted up past the edge of the earth.

Robert looked sleepily out through the steamy window as, with his thoughts, the sun raised itself over the flat countryside and blazed upon them, striking long black shadows and streaking the sky red when it shone on the high clouds. Robert marvelled. The colour of the clouds faded as the sun rose and gathered strength. The colours had faded that day, too, to show a beautiful morning, the air crisp and fresh, the grass thick with dew, caught in a myriad of tiny cobwebs, sparking and twinkling in the morning light like some magical fairy quilt.

As he and Cock Sparrow trotted across the heath with 'Corn Dolly' between them, he felt a strange thrill of exhilaration. This was the magic hour. Of all the beauties of the natural world, this first hour of a summer's day must surely be the best. He breathed in great lungfulls of the sweet crisp air. He turned his face to receive the first welcome warmth of the dawn sun. He shivered slightly. It was only then that he realised how chilly it had been. A Lark was already lifting into the sky, pouring out his song like some heavenly libation upon the earth. Cock Sparrow, who had said nothing since the incident, looked at him.

"Boy, do you reckon you could?" Robert came back to earth with a jolt.

"Could? Could what?"

"Ride—'The Dolly'." Robert looked at the chestnut head rising and falling between them as they trotted along. He noticed the ears flattened slightly back. He knew what that meant. He had ridden 'The Dolly' enough times out on the gallops. He knew how she went when those ears went back!

"Yes, Mister," he replied. "I've ridden out on her enough times; I reckon I know how she goes."

"This ain't goin' to be like ridin'her out and knowin' how she goes. If you rides her today, you've got to bloomin' well win!"

"Well, I'll do my best," replied Robert.

"No," said Cock Sparrow vehemently. "Ain't good enough! She could beat all of them what's against 'er today, if she's rid right! She's got to win! There's a lot of money on 'er head today!"

Robert looked a little puzzled. Promising horse though she undoubtedly was, she had not run too well this season and though Wally had ridden her for every race, the best he had managed was second. To put a lot of money on her in the hope of pulling off a win seemed to be an act of folly.

"But she's never won, not this season, at least," he ventured. "There isn't one of them running that hasn't beaten her at least once this season!"

"They might 'ave beaten 'er once, but I'm tellin' you, she can beat them all." Robert's look of disbelief obviously showed. "You won't never win no race if you don't believe you can," scolded Cock Sparrow. "I'm tellin' you, 'old 'er 'ard for the first four furlongs and then give 'er 'er head. She'll win."

They threaded their way to the enclosure at the back of the Stewards tent. Robert was soon busy rubbing down 'The Dolly' and looking after the other horses. Cock Sparrow had hurried off to find Mr Smith, the trainer, to tell him what had happened and what he had done. Robert's main task was to make sure that no one could injure or interfere with 'The Dolly' before the race.

Presently Cock Sparrow returned with Mr Smith. They both had worried looks on their faces.

"Well, boy, Cock Sparrow has told me what happened. Do you think that you could ride 'The Dolly' today, if Carter is not here on time? Though heavens knows what Mrs. Dennis is going to say!"

"Yes, Mr. John," replied Robert with more confidence than he felt.

"So be it then, we've got no other choice. With luck Carter will get here, but be ready in case he cannot. If you ride, listen to what Cock Sparrow has to say and make damn sure you win!"

With that, he turned on his heel and strode off.

Robert spent the next hour in a ferment of anxiety, excitement and apprehension. He desperately wanted his first 'ride' in a 'real' race, but he knew that this would not be like some apprentice boy stakes; he would be up against top horses and jockeys—this would be the real thing. He would get a hard race. The others would capitalise on his youth and inexperience. If he was going to win, he would have to fight the whole way, but anyway, Carter would arrive in time.

As time went by and Carter did not arrive, Robert's feeling of unease gradually turned to acute anxiety. When Cock Sparrow called out to him "Better get ready, it will be weighin' in soon an' it don't look as if Carter is goin' to get 'ere!" he felt physically sick. As Robert pulled on Mrs. Dennis' colours, the knot in his stomach tightened with a knuckly grip.

"I don't like this," he said to Cock Sparrow. "I don't like this one little bit."

"Oh, shut up and get on. You'll be late for weighin' in," he growled unsympathetically. "'Ere, take your saddle. And your bleedin' bridle—'ere, you've forgotten your whip." Robert grabbed all his tackle and ran through into the Steward's tent. Weighing-in seemed to pass in a blur. Some of the other jockeys objected, so the Stewards hastily conferred. Mr Smith was summoned. There was a prolonged and somewhat heated discussion. In the end, Robert was allowed to ride but had to carry full weights, up to the average of the others. He had to wait until everyone else had been weighed, the average calculated and the weights added to his pouches. Finally everything was settled. He was allowed out to the saddling enclosure.

He was stunned by the brightness after the gloomy tent. The sun was shining. The owners and jockeys were standing around looking at the horses being paraded round. It made a wonderful and colourful scene—the jockeys' colours, the ladies' bright dresses, hats and parasols. The men, mostly in silk top hats. The magnificent horses, turned out to look their best, were groomed and brushed until their coats shone like polished wood. Each with a brightly coloured rug, having been paraded round, was now saddled. Robert searched for 'The Dolly.' He saw her on the far side of the ring being held by Cock Sparrow. Mr. Smith and Mrs. Dennis stood talking together. They saw him and beckoned him over.

"Well, Henery!" She looked at him imperiously, her fierce blue eyes untouched by the smile on her face. "Your Master has explained the situation. I am not at all happy. I expect my horses to be ridden by the best jockeys, not by some mere lad from the yard!"

"But, Madam…" protested Mr Smith.

"No buts, Mr. Er-er…, I know it cannot be helped, but it's not good enough; I mean, look at him. He's not big enough. Surely you've got a bigger one somewhere." She wrung her hands.

"His small size is to our advantage, Madam; but it is not the size of his biceps that count, it is the size of his brain."

Mrs. Dennis inspected Robert as though she were examining a cut of meat on the butcher's slab.

"You mean to tell me that he has a brain in there somewhere? I hope then that this small boy with the large brain has been properly instructed. Corn Dolly simply *has* to win. I have some very important friends who have come to watch her run. If she does not win, we will all look such fools. I am sure that you now what that will mean!" Mr. Smith went red in the face at the obvious threat. His knuckles shone white as he gripped his cane in anger and frustration.

"I am sure, Madam," he said as icily as he dared, "young Henery is a most promising lad. I have every faith in him. I would have chosen him from among all the lads in my yard." He hoped the lie would calm her down. She looked down on Robert, her misgiving still apparent. Robert felt as though he were a toad that she had suddenly espied in her path. He writhed in discomfort. Suddenly she was distracted. A beaming smile cut off the threat that she was about to utter.

"My dear Lord Shotley!" she simpered obsequiously. "*There* you are. Isn't it terribly exciting? Jones has had a terrible accident. Young er, em…er…, here is going to ride the Dolly in his place." She beamed encouragingly at Lord Shotley whilst contriving to throw desperate glances at John Smith and Robert. Lord Shotley, a tall well-built man in his late fifties, dressed in an immaculate dove grey frock coat, doffed his shiny black top hat to reveal a thick head of silver hair. His sun-tanned face flashed a dazzling white smile.

"Dear lady, charming to see you. Yes, I heard the slight altercation in the Stewards' tent at the weigh-in. I had to attend. I am so glad I am able to be here today to see your horse run. Your enthusiastic invitation and glowing forecast even prompted me to have a modest wager." He chuckled. "I'm sorry to hear about Jones, though. Is my money going to be safe in your young hands?" He turned abruptly to Robert. Robert frantically sought for words. He knew of Lord Shotley. Most respected by all and sundry, his one passion in life was horses. He had led a crusade to clean up racing and although he had made many enemies, he had earned with grudging respect the nickname of 'Honest Ned'. Robert tried to splutter an answer. Lord Shotley took his confusion for embarrassment.

"Don't worry lad. If your Master here thinks you are up to it, I am sure you will do your best."

"Yes, sir…Yes, my lord," Robert hastily corrected himself as that well-known eyebrow rose. Robert quailed under the stare and was suddenly seized with a desperate desire to have a piddle. Luckily Mr Smith stepped in to his rescue…

"He will do well enough, My Lord. He's ridden out on the Dolly. He looks after her. He knows well enough how she goes and how to handle her. I have every…er…confidence in him, even though he is small." He added the last observation as an afterthought.

"Mount up!" called the steward and suddenly there was Cock Sparrow giving him a leg up.

"Go on, Robert, just you get on down there and you show them. That won't 'urt to 'ave 'is Lordship watch yew neither. 'E is always on the lookout for new lads to ride for 'im." And with that, he threw Robert up into the saddle and led him out on to the course, catching the rug off Dolly as he slipped the leading rein. Dolly, who was an old hand at this, set off for the start at a furious gallop to stretch all her sinews.

Robert pulled her back to a steady canter. His mind had been in a ferment. His first race. His real chance to show what he could do, in front of Lord Shotley as well. What a chance! What a dream! If he lost, he would have to face Cock Sparrow and Mrs Dennis!

. He wrestled with the Dolly, to try and get her into line. She was much stronger than he remembered. She pulled and snatched at the reins in her eagerness to be off.

At last, after what seemed an age of swearing, struggling and jostling, they were lined up. The starter raised his flag. He whipped it down with a flourish. They were off.

The Dolly seemed to be hanging back a little. It was not long before he was well and truly boxed in against the rail. There was nothing for it but to go along in the press, until an opening might present itself.

At the first bend, the horse in front of him ran a little wide. He saw a chance. He gave The Dolly a smart crack with his whip and a couple of vicious digs with his heels. The Dolly, unused to such treatment, leapt forward. She took the bit between her teeth and set off, determined this time she would show who had the fastest heels.

He did not remember much about the rest of the race. He might as well have tried to stop the tide as hold her back for four furlongs, as he had been instructed. His back ached to breaking, sweat stood out on his forehead. His arms felt as if they were being pulled out of their sockets. The Dolly knew who had the fastest legs and the bravest heart! She was going to show them. Her pride had taken a severe battering from those earlier encounters. Now was the time for retribution.

Robert had hung on as well as he could but the race passed in a confusion of flying mud, pounding hoofs and heaving flanks. He had vaguely heard the swelling roar of the crowd, then he had flashed past the post. At last Dolly slowed to a walk. He could regain his breath. He reined her round and headed back towards the unsaddling enclosure. It was then the truth dawned. The rest of the field were still straggling in. He had won. He had WON! HE HAD WON!

He stood up in the stirrups and waved his cap in the air in excitement. His first race and he had won!

Not some tin pot apprentices' race, but The Cup!

He, a mere lad, had won The Cup. He fell forward on the neck and kissed the sweating mane.

"Oh, you big beautiful winner of races, you!" He sat up and patted her flank. "You marvellous, wonderful horse. You showed them."

He was surrounded by the course stewards, who led him through the cheering, shouting crowd to the unsaddling enclosure. Tears of excitement flowed down his face. He slid off the horse and was immediately swallowed up by the excited crowd, all eager to pat him on the back. Somehow, Cock Sparrow had managed to wriggle his ferret way through the press.

"Bleedin' brilliant!" he shouted excitedly as he jumped up and down and clapped him on the back.

"I told you would bloomin' well do it and you bloomin' well 'as." He hugged Robert with excitement. "I had a bleedin' packet on your nose and you've bleedin' well done it! I've made a bloomin' fortune...well, a few quid, anyhow. Didn't I say what you would always do it? Didn't I?" His excitement was interrupted by the arrival of Lord Shotley, Mrs. Dennis on his arm, and Mr Smith following beaming in their wake.

"Oh, darling boy, you have no idea how excited I feel at this moment," she gushed excitedly at Robert. "Oh, well done! Oh splendid! Oh, I am so excited! My little mare has won The Cup. It is so exciting. Oh, well done, little mare—and little jockey," she added as a hasty afterthought. Lord Shotley grabbed Robert by the hand and pumped his arm vigorously. He, too, was in a high state of excitement.

"Henery, well done, my fine fellow. Fantastic ride. You showed them! I knew that Dolly had got it in her. Always said so. Only needed the right person to ride her, then there would be no one to touch her. You beat my horse, fair and square. Well done, well ridden, young man, I am delighted for you. My dear Mrs. Dennis, this is so exciting, let me be the first to congratulate you and to praise your courage in using this young man, as it turned out, so successfully. I think you have found quite a treasure there! This is magnificent, you have won The Cup, excellent, excellent!"

Even as he spoke, the crowd was parted by some policemen and they stood in the middle of a circle of people, with the Chief Steward holding The Cup. Mrs. Dennis flushed bright red to her hairline and, unable to compose herself, dropped an embarrassed curtsey.

"Madam, allow me to congratulate you on a splendid victory. I present The Cup to a most worthy winner." The Steward shook her hand and then handed her The Cup. She dropped a quick curtsey She clasped The Cup to her and turned to face the enthusiastic crowd, who cheered and yelled with delight. Cock Sparrow clapped Robert on the back. The Steward stood in the middle of it all, thoughtfully stroking The Dolly's nose.

"Fantastic ride!" he said out loud. He searched the crowd and spotted Robert. "You had a brilliant ride, young man." He looked at him more closely. "I do not think I know you, do I?" He turned and asked the crowd at large. Mr Smith hastily stepped forward.

"Allow me to present Master Robert Henery, your grace. He is one of my lads and stepped in to ride The Dolly at the last moment, because her jockey had an accident this morning."

"Last minute, you say, Smith?" He looked at Robert. "Well done, my boy," he smiled benignly. "If you can ride like that at the last minute, how will you be able to go when you are properly prepared? Allow me to shake you by the hand, Sir." Robert held out his hand as if in a slow motion-like trance and felt the firm grip on his own! He bowed stiffly from the waist. Suddenly the crowd vanished in search of a new hero as the next race was called.

A groom led The Dolly away and Robert was left standing there with Cock Sparrow hopping up and down beside him.

"Is'nt this the best bloomin' day? The best thing what ever 'appened?" He capered around with excitement. "I've won enough today to buy my own bleedin' 'ouse. I'm pretty sure that our Boss 'ad a good bit on and all. Mrs Dennis, I think she 'ad a packet on it an' all. You should have seen the look on 'er face at the start, when you came off the tapes last! If she'd 'ad a pound of cheese in 'er 'and, she'd have squeezed it flat. She went white when you winned! She nearly fainted."

"Stop!" Robert managed to stop him. "What would have happened if I had lost?"

"Oh my God, don't ask! Don't even think of it" Cock Sparrow replied with anguish. "Did you ride a blinder? Yes! Did the 'orse go like the Devil 'is self? Yes! Did you bleedin' well win? Yes! Didn't bleedin' Lord Shotley 'is self shake your bleedin' 'and? Yes, 'e bleedin' did! And the Duke too. Ain't there thousands of bleedin' jockeys what 'as never won nothing in their bleedin' lives, what would give their right 'and to do all that? Yes! What do you bleedin' well do? Stand there moaning away about what would 'ave 'appened if you'd lost, like some Salvation Army girl what 'as just been caught behind the pub with her knickers down. For God's sake, Robert, you are a bloomin' hero, mate. You are made, mate! Lord Shotley, 'e 'as got 'is eye on you. 'E 'as seen you ride a winner. There isn't no one in racin' what won't know who you are after today and that's what counts. You got to be known. Some takes all their bleedin' lives and fails—you've done it in one day, you lucky sod!"

Robert looked at him in astonishment. He had never heard him say so much in one go and he was surprised at the tinge of envy in his voice. But he was right. Everything he said was true. He had done his best, the horse had done her best. Cock Sparrow was right, he had dared and he had won! Suddenly, he was overcome with the excitement of it all and he turned round and was violently sick.

"Oh my God," cried Cock Sparrow, "give me strengf, 'ave I got to be a bleedin' nurse, now and all!"

The train stopped with a jerk. The others in the carriage gathered up their possessions and left. Robert sat there; he had not even noticed that they had reached London. He stood up and took his case down from the rack. In his pocket he had a note with the address of a hotel Lord Shotley's secretary had sent him. He shrugged. *Well, tomorrow is another day.* He stepped out of the carriage and set off into the smoky gloom.

CHAPTER 2

❀

The station was a bustle of clanking metal, billowing steam, shouting people and smoky gloom. People hustled and jostled in the dark. The gas lamps hissed in foggy solitude, serving to draw attention to the gloom rather than lighting it. The trains were drawn up in dirty sulky rows, hissing and gasping their displeasure at being so confined in those sooty environs. All this passed unnoticed by Robert who, head down, was allowing himself to be carried on by the press of people as they spilled on the platform.

"Porter, Sir?" a bored voice inquired at his elbow. Robert turned to see a wizened little man with a large barrow, a stained home-rolled cigarette sticking to his top lip.

"No…er…thank you, this is all I have." He raised his battered case.

"Cor, a body ain't goin' to earn a livin' off o' you then gov'," replied the porter, turning away. "Porter! Anyone want a porter?" He called and was soon hurrying off to a large lady in a red coat who was frantically waving from a carriage window. *Funny*, thought Robert, *he reminded me of Cock Sparrow. Wonder what has happened to him? Haven't seen him for….*

"Ticket please," a voice abruptly interrupted him.

"What? Oh yes, here you are." Robert searched his pockets and eventually found and produced his ticket.

"Runnin' away from the Misses then, are we?" asked the ticket collector in bored levity.

"What?" said Robert in disbelief.

"Only a joke, sir," said the ticket inspector. "Cabs over there, sir." He waved his clippers towards the exit. "Got somewhere to stay, 'as yer, sir?" he inquired, more by way of an apology than from interest.

"Yes, thank you," said Robert, mentally checking the piece of folded paper in his coat pocket. Why did he want to know? Surely he was not police? Surely they weren't checking on him already. *I suppose if they want to know where I am they will have to watch me all the way,* he thought to himself. The idea that he might be watched everywhere he went was irritatingly repugnant. He hated London anyway. The thought that he might be tailed and spied on made him quite angry.

"I'm sure you have enough to do, checking tickets, without worrying yourself about my affairs," he snapped irritably.

"Sorry, guv, I'm sure. Only passin' the time of day," the man replied apologetically. Robert wrapped his coat round himself with a show of injured dignity and stumped off towards the exit.

"Stupid geeser!" mumbled the ticket inspector with some glee. "He's going the wrong way!"

Robert, having found himself in a luggage bay and retraced his steps, eventually discovered the exit and stood waiting for a cab.

"I say," said an angry voice, "there's a queue here, if you don't mind!" Robert looked. He saw a group of impatient, angry-looking people. He shrugged his apology and went to the end. There did not seem to be a cab in sight. The people were grumbling and stamping in the cold. *If I knew where to go,* thought Robert, *I would walk. It cannot be that far.* He stared out into the fog, but he definitely did not relish the thought of being lost, wandering around in the gloom. He felt the paper in his pocket with the address of the hotel on it, which Lord Shotley had sent him and decided to wait.

Presently three cabs came clattering down the ramp together. Only one more and it would be his turn. Then he could be on his way.

At last his turn came. He handed the piece of paper up to the driver.

"Do you think you can find that?" he asked.

"Yer, we might just about make it, Guv," said the driver, snapping shut the hatch and whipping up his horse. The horse made a good effort up the ramp and they were soon in the press of cabs, carriages and carts that thronged the road outside the station. The driver dextrously threaded his way through the traffic and stopped at the pavement on the other side of the road, opposite to the station. He opened the hatch.

"Here we are, guv," he called down cheerily. "That will be two bob."

"What?" Said Robert. "This is it? I'm not going to pay two shillings to be taken across the road. I could have walked."

"Well, you didn't, guv! Did ye? Two bob, if you please!"

"But this is ridiculous! I waited twenty minutes in the freezing fog. If I had known, I would have walked!"

"Well, you should'av asked, shouldn't you?" laughed the cabby. "Two bob."

"I'm not going to pay two shillings just for that!"

The cabby's good humour vanished in an instant. "Are you refusing to pay the lawful fare, guv?" he growled. "Two bob."

Robert rummaged in his pocket and gave him the coin.

"What abart my tip?" inquired the cabby.

"Be off with you," said Robert angrily. "You have got your fare, now be off with you!" Luckily at that moment two men came up and, seeing the cab empty, jumped in.

"Sloane Street, please cabby, as quick as you can." So the cab drove off.

Robert briefly watched it depart, until it became lost in the mêlée of other vehicles.

He turned and studied the brown painted door with the unpolished brass knocker that confronted him. *Well,* he thought, *Honest Ned might have done better than this.* He shrugged and stepping forward, he wrapped the knocker. Nothing happened. He waited in the street. Presently he knocked again, more firmly. Still nothing. He waited, then knocked again, this time loud and long. Still no reply. *Now what on earth do I do?* He stamped his feet up and down on the pavement, but soon stopped when he noticed he was splashing the filth onto his trouser leg. He hadn't noticed until then, but the road and pavement were covered with filth and muck of all kinds, mostly horse manure. He stood around uncertainly for a while, then decided there was nothing he could do but wait a while and try again later.

He wandered aimlessly up the road. Presently he came to a pub, the "Cross Keys" by the sign. He marvelled at the design etched and cut into the glass of the window. It was wonderful how they could do such things on such a seemingly fragile and unresponsive substance. He went in. At least it was warm inside. He could wait in here for a while, then return to see if he could gain admittance to his hotel. The pub was packed. It was full of people obviously having a drink before they went home. The talk, loud and jocular, was about money and the rise and fall of stocks and shares. All totally meaningless to Robert. About horses he was something of an authority, but in this company he felt totally alien and lost. He ordered a pint of bitter from the local brewery from the pert girl behind the bar and took himself off to the only seat he could find, in a quiet corner.

When he had ordered his beer, the barmaid asked him if he would like anything to eat. It was then that he realised how hungry he was. He chose a pie but
now as he sat regarding the unappetising looking confection with some trepidation, his hunger waned. The pastry was a pale grey colour! He was sure that
he could still see fingerprints in it. Robert eyed it with failing enthusiasm, but
when he noticed a long black hair trailing from it, his hunger vanished completely.

He took a cautious sip at his beer. It was cold, thin and wet. He shuddered
as the harsh liquid flowed down his throat and into his empty stomach. He
looked over towards the fire. On the hearth, between the legs of the people
standing round, he saw a large poker. Before he knew it he had the poker and
had thrust it into the fire. Presently it was red hot. Taking it out of the fire he
thrust it into his beer. The red hot metal was immediately quenched with a hiss
of steam. Those by the fire had parted when he had pushed his way through.
He became aware that the conversation had stopped and that all eyes were on
him. Robert took his now warm beer and, abandoning his pie to whoever
might be desperate enough to eat it, settled himself in another chair, now
vacated, nearer the fire.

He was near enough to the fire to feel its warmth and his hot beer was
warming him up. He felt his cheeks begin to glow. Gradually the buzz of conversation started up again.

"How could you put that filthy thing in your beer and then drink it?"
inquired a small red-faced man standing at his shoulder.

"Most pure thing on earth, fire," replied Robert. "If you want to clean a
wound, what is the best way of doing it?" Robert did not wait for a reply but
turned his back on the man and buried his nose in his mug. It was a trick he
had learned as a lad, when they regularly used to heat their ration of small beer
from a poker thrust into the iron stove, which provided the only warmth in the
'Bothy' on a winter's night. Robert was glad of the glow that spread inside him
from the warm liquid, but began to feel hungry again. He even contemplated
the evil-looking pie, but when he looked over to where he had left it, he saw to
his dismay that it had already disappeared. He did not know whether to be
angry or sorry for the thief.

Robert made his pint last as long as he could, but reluctantly, when it was
finished, he left the warmth of the fireside and decided it was time to try his
lodgings again.

This time he knocked with more purpose, but still he got the same result.
He rattled the door. It came open in his hand. After a brief hesitation, he

pushed it open and entered. He found himself in a little dingy hall, which smelt damp. Another door confronted him, so pushing this open he entered what was obviously an inner hall. Everything was brown. The walls were painted a light but dirt-stained brown. All the woodwork was painted dark brown. The carpet was dirty brown. Even the faded prints on the wall were brown. The notice saying 'ring for service' that drew his attention to an unpolished brass bell on the sill of a closed hatch was also brown. The air was redolent with the smell of boiled cabbage. Robert, who up to now had been a little uncertain about entering unbidden, realised this was indeed expected. He rang the bell. Presently, after a prolonged rattle and struggle, the hatch slowly opened. A small owl-faced woman in her late sixties looked out. She too was dressed in brown. Her small round spectacles that so contributed to the owl-like appearance, had brown frames. She wore brown mittens from which her gnarled arthritic fingers poked like the ancient twisted claws of some prehistoric beast.

"Yes? What do you want?" she demanded with a thrust of her red tipped nose in Robert's direction.

"Excuse me," he said with as little enthusiasm as he felt. "Your door was open, so I walked in. I hope I did the right thing."

"Oh, yes," replied the little old lady, "the children knock so often on the knocker, then run away, that we do not bother to answer the door any more. What do you want?"

Robert drew the paper out of his pocket and handed it over.

"Oh yes," she said after she had minutely perused its every jot, "…Lord Shotley sent a message round by hand to tell us to expect you. You must be Mr. Henery." Robert nodded. "Your room is reserved for two nights. Please sign the register, then I will show you up. Breakfast is at 8 o'clock and the evening meal is at 6 o'clock. If you wish to take lunch you must sign in at breakfast time. How do you like your eggs? Turned?"

"What?" asked Robert in puzzlement.

"Your eggs at breakfast. How do you like them? Do you like them turned when they are fried?" She gestured a flipping motion with her hand.

"Oh, no, not turned, I like to see the nice yellow yoke, thank you," replied Robert is some surprise—as if it mattered. Robert filled in his name and address in the dog-eared register on its opened proffered brown page. It was fairly old, so they obviously did not have too many guests.

"I will show you to your room," she said, shutting the hatch again with some difficulty. Robert waited in the hall. After what seemed an age, she emerged from a side door and offered to show him the way. She was even smaller than she had appeared in the hatch. Her skirt and wrinkled wool stockings were also brown. Robert felt that if she stood still, in that hallway, she could remain there all day and no one would notice her!

She led him up the narrow dark stairs, then along the narrow landing. She pointed to a door:

"Bathroom," she said. "If you want a bath you must sign for it the day before. It is extra. You must say what time you want it. The water will be brought up in jugs for you."

"Oh," said Robert. "I was rather hoping that I might have a bath tonight. I have been in the train all day and feel rather dirty."

"That is all right. Lord Shotley reserved a bath for you when he booked your room. Here you are." She opened a door at the end of the corridor. She showed him into a—*let me guess…a brown room*, thought Robert, as he walked in. It was. Brown bedspread, brown walls, brown carpet, brown paintwork. Only the basin and jug on the washstand showed a splash of white and blue. Well, Honest Ned had thought of everything for him, but his money certainly was not being wasted on luxuries!

"You have a cupboard there for your clothes. I must tell you that we do not allow visitors of any kind in the rooms." And with that, she left him. It was on the tip of Robert's tongue to ask if there was any chance of some food, but fearing a rebuff, he refrained. At least he could have a bath.

Unpacking his case he took himself down to the bathroom. He was not surprised to find that it was also brown. His water stood ready in three big brass jugs, from each of which a plume of steam arose. As it was very cold in the room, he was not long over his bath. The water was none too hot, so he was soon back in his room and in bed, trying as well as he could to get warm.

It was not long before he became aware of the noise of the trains. His room was on the front of the house. Immediately across the road was the station. *Wonderful*, he thought, bitterly, *cold and hungry in a brown room! Now I shall not be able to sleep at all because of the noise of the engines*. As if to confirm his thought an engine started a vociferous burst of shunting. Robert turned over and buried his head under the brown blankets.

It would not be fair to say that he did not sleep a wink, but the night was very long. He slept only fitfully, being continually woken by a steamy cacophony from the station and painfully vivid dreams about food.

He was woken by a loud knocking on his door. A cheery voice called: "Time to get up, Sir. I'll leave your water outside for you."

"Thank you," mumbled Robert from under his sheets.

"Are you awake, Sir?" called the cheery voice more loudly.

"Yes, thank you!" shouted back Robert.

"I'll leave your water outside," repeated the voice.

"Yes, thank you!" shouted back Robert. He stretched out in bed. He felt jaded and tired. He ached all over. Then, throwing off the blankets, he went to the door to retrieve his water. Another, though smaller brass jug stood there. His room was not very warm so he was soon shaved and downstairs. It did not take him long to locate the dining room. He sat down at a table set for one in the corner. He waited—nothing happened, no one came. He looked round for a bell. Spying one he gave it a good ring. Nothing happened. He looked at his watch. 7.48. *Oh dear. I suppose I will have to wait until 8 o'clock.*

Presently a man came in and sat at one of the other tables.

"Good morning. I see you have a paper—is it possible to buy a paper nearby?" The man looked at him, opened his paper and settled down behind it to read. He said nothing. Robert was slightly unnerved by the rebuff. Presently another man walked in, reading his paper as he walked. He came right up to Robert.

"Good morning," said Robert. The man looked up, startled.

"You are sitting in my place," he said, in some surprise.

"I beg your pardon?"

"This is my place. You are sitting in my place," repeated the man with rising indignation.

"I am very sorry," said Robert, hastily standing up. "I did not know. Where shall I sit then?" he asked, as he stood aside. The man sat down and started reading his paper as if Robert was not there. Robert stood uncertainly, not quite knowing what to do. *Well, if I cannot beat them, I might as well join them,* he thought. He walked out into the street, to the corner where he found a news boy. He bought himself a paper. Returning to the hotel, he stayed in the hall reading his paper.

At eight o'clock precisely the little lady of the night before, still clad in brown, appeared bearing a tray with plates of steaming porridge.

"Here we are, Mr. Henery. The dining room is this way." He followed her. "You can sit here," she said, indicating the table nearest the door.

To his surprise the room had filled up. The table indicated was the only one available.

"Good morning," Robert said again to the room at large. Again no one replied, not a single paper even fluttered. Clearly silence was the order of the day, he thought as he sat down. Immediately a bowl of steaming porridge was placed before him.

"Would you like tea or coffee?" the little lady earnestly asked him.

"Coffee, thank you," he replied, giving his porridge a liberal sprinkling of sugar and savouring the smell. It was then that he realised how hungry he was. He spooned his porridge with a will and felt more himself as the warm glow of it spread through his stomach. Presently a smell of eggs and bacon wafted into the room. A young girl of about eighteen wearing a simple black dress came bustling in with another large tray of plates. Though he was nearest to the door, he was the last to be served. By the time she got to him, his mouth was watering.

"Here you are, sir." Robert recognised the cheery voice of the bearer of his early morning water can. "Your eggs is done just as you like 'em, nicely turned. And I'll just bring you your tea."

"Coffee," said Robert. "I asked for coffee."

"Yes, sir," she smiled at him. "I'll bring it in a minute. Would you like some toast?"

"Yes, please," said Robert brightening. That was the first smile he had received since he arrived in this God-awful place.

"One piece, or two?"

"Two please," said Robert. If he did not soon eat his eggs they would get cold. He looked at his plate and his spirits rose. Whatever else the shortcomings of this place, breakfast was not one of them. Four long rashers of bacon, three sausages, two fried eggs, turned, admittedly, a large slice of fried bread and a fried tomato. The proprietors obviously believed that the well-being of the working man depended on a good breakfast. Robert set to with a will. Never mind the turned eggs. His world was rapidly beginning to look rosier. If the little lady had seen him polishing the shovel that was used to clean out the horse box, then use it to fry his eggs over an open fire, which he had done on many an occasion when he had been away at a Race Meeting and had, for security reasons, slept in the stable with the horse, she would have known that he did not really mind how his eggs were done.

As if conjured up by his thoughts, she stood at his elbow.

"Here is your tea." She placed a pot on the table.

"But I asked for coffee."

"Yes, that's right," she said. "You said coffee."

"But this is tea," said Robert.

"Yes, that's right," said the little lady earnestly. *Oh! I give up*, thought Robert. *What the heck. I do not mind if I have tea or coffee, as long as it is hot.* Robert poured himself out a cup—hot and strong.

"Everything all right for you?" she inquired earnestly. Robert looked at the small size of the pot.

"Could I have a jug of hot water to top up my pot with?" he inquired. She gave him a long hard stare. "Please." He added as an afterthought.

"I'll have one brought in for you." Robert tackled his breakfast with enthusiasm. Presently the girl came back with his toast and water. By the time he had finished his meal he was feeling very much better.

After his breakfast he collected his hat and coat. Going out into the street he hailed a cab. Handing the driver a note with the name of Lord Shotley's club on it, he settled down to enjoy the drive and the sights. He was always full of awe at the way the cabbies drove through all that traffic. The roads were filled with horse-drawn vehicles of every kind, all intent on their business, weaving in and out of the traffic. He marvelled that there were not more accidents than there were. The drivers seemed to be so nonchalant about it all, talking cheerfully to each other as they drove along. He would not want to drive in traffic like that, but they all seemed quite happy. He looked at the horses. *However many were going round London at this moment?* he wondered. *I wouldn't want to find oats for this lot*, he thought, *or clear up behind them! That must be a major problem.* The streets were in a filthy condition. There must be hundreds of tons of muck lying around. He wondered what happened to it. Getting rid of the muck was one of the major problems of a stable, so what must it be like in London? It must be a nightmare.

They threaded their way through the City and up into the West End. It was just before 11 o'clock when he was set down outside the club. He paid the cabby and went inside.

As he walked inside he was greeted by the doorman.

"Good morning, Sir, can I help you?"

"Good morning, yes, Lord Shotley expects me at 11 o'clock. I wonder if you would be kind enough to inform him that I am here."

"You Mr 'Enerey, sir?" Robert nodded. "His Lordship is expecting you. If you would be good enough to step this way, sir, this gentleman will take you to him." As Robert followed the footman he could not help noticing the contrast between the hotel where he was staying and the opulence here. Every piece of wood shone from careful polishing. The walls, panelled in polished maple. The polish on the furniture reflected the items, vases, flowers, silver trophies,

standing on it, with a rich lustre. The paintwork on walls, ceilings and mouldings was clean and fresh. The pictures on the wall, mostly portraits and racing
scenes, glowed out from within gilt frames. The floors were polished, the carpets thick. The air smelt of cigar smoke. Robert had been here several times
before, but he was always impressed when he walked in.

The footman led the way into an anti-room.

Lord Shotley was sitting in front of a coal fire. On the table in front of him
was a silver tray with a large dark fruit cake, a jug of claret and some glasses,
which evidently he had been enjoying. As soon as Lord Shotley saw him, he
put down the paper that he had been reading. He rose from his chair and came
over to greet him. The two men had grown to know and respect each other
over the years. There was real pleasure on his face and warmth in his greeting
as they shook hands.

"Henery, my dear fellow, what a pleasure to see you here again. I hope you
were comfortable enough last night."

"Hello, my Lord. Yes, sir, thank you, sir. It was very kind of you to arrange it
all for me."

"Don't mention it. We will talk of it later. Come and sit by the fire. Have
some of this claret. It is really very good." He continued talking as he filled both
their glasses. "A piece of this cake. I think this is a splendid idea, just the job to
keep the wolf at bay until luncheon. First saw the idea at my wine merchants. I
was soon sat down with a lusty slice of cake and some of his claret. Thought it
was a pretty nasty idea at first, but I didn't want to be rude to the man. It wasn't
long before I had ordered a dozen cases. He knew how to sell something."

Robert gave a wan smile, wondering what Lord Shotley was trying to sell
him.

"Mind you," continued Lord Shotley, "I don't mind doing business like that.
Damn good claret it was, too. I've still got a few bottles left, actually. I ought to
drink them up. Here, my dear fellow, your glass in empty." Robert held out his
glass appreciatively. He smiled wryly and wished he'd had as many pound
notes as bottles of claret he'd drunk with Honest Ned. It was indeed a lucky day
for him when Lord Shotley had seen him ride his first winner.

"Do you remember when we first met?" chuckled Lord Shotley. "You were
so young and scared out of your skin of blowing your chance to do well in your
first ride." Robert had an uncomfortable shock, realising they had both been
thinking of the same thing.

"I did not do much," said Robert, with a smile. "I could not do much; the
Dolly got the bit between her teeth. All I could do was hang on."

"Well, I made a fortune on that race. I won't tell you how much I put on you, but suffice to say, I felt I would forever be in your debt—still do, as a matter of fact." Robert stared at him with astonishment.

"It sounds as if you took an enormous risk on the first ride of a mere lad!"

"Well," said Lord Shotley, "being successful with horses is about assessing risks. Being able to keep a cool head when the stakes are high. I knew that the Dolly had been beaten by all the other horses in that race at different times, but only narrowly. I felt it must be due to the way she was ridden. I knew she was always ridden by the same man. That somehow, he did not suit her. He somehow rode her in a way that prevented her from giving that little extra. So I concluded that with a young lad up, if you will excuse me, less wise, less experienced, less strong, she would get the bit between her teeth. The rest of the field would not see her heels for dust. So it was not a risk at all, really. John Smith did pretty well, as well," he added with a quick smile.

"What about Mrs. Dennis?" Robert asked.

"No, silly cow," Lord Shotley laughed at the recollection. "Excuse me, I shouldn't refer to the fairer sex in those ungallant terms, but this is one of those occasions when the term seems so apt." He laughed again. "No, she was so put out that her horse was being ridden by a mere lad, she didn't back you. Can you believe it? An owner not having a bet on her own horse! Both Smith and I tried to persuade her, but she would not. She put her money on the favourite. If only she had had faith in us all, she would have been all right. She lost! Eventually she had to sell out of racing.

"I don't believe in fate much, Robert, but it was a damn fine day when our two lives came together. You have always been good luck for me. I don't remember how many winners you rode for me before your accident, but I know that through you I was one of the most successful owners."

"Well, it has been lucky for me, too," said Robert. "I had some good horses to ride, I could not go wrong. By all accounts, if it had not been for you I would have died after the accident. So I owe you more than I can ever repay." Lord Shotley looked acutely embarrassed as he vividly remembered that terrible ride off the heath to the hospital.

"No more than anyone else would have done." He tried to shrug it off.

"Maybe, maybe not," said Robert, "but that doesn't alter the fact. Not many people would have taken me on as assistant trainer afterwards, though. Nor allowed me to take over when the trainer retired."

"Oh, yes. I was being entirely philanthropic!" said Lord Shotley sarcastically. "Chose you because I knew you would be as good a trainer as you were a jockey! I've been proved right. You've done very well for me over the past few years. I have done extremely well from it."

Over the years they had become close friends, as close as the master/man relationship would allow. They had spent many an hour together talking of horses and putting the world to rights generally. There had grown between them a mutual affection and respect—an empathy so strong that that the one almost seemed to know what the other was going to say before it was said. A great bond of friendship had grown between them, cemented by the episodes where each felt he owed his all to the other.

Lord Shotley called for another bottle of claret and the two of them chatted about this and that.

Lord Shotley stood in front of the fire, his hands thrust into his pockets, a large cigar clamped between his teeth. Robert like the smell of cigar smoke but did not like smoking them himself. Lord Shotley looked ill at ease. He removed the cigar from his mouth and looked intently at its glowing end. *Good heavens,* thought Robert, *the old boy is embarrassed.*

"Robert, I must speak plainly." *He's never called me Robert—what's coming up now?*

"I was very sorry to hear of your present troubles. Terrible business." He looked at Robert with intense blue eyes.

"Thank you, sir. Thank you for getting me out of prison and for everything you have done."

"Fortunately I knew the Sheriff, so I was able to get you out on bail."

"You paid bail for me? How much did you have to pay?"

"The amount does not matter. But it was a lot. I cannot afford to let you disappear." He silenced Robert's thanks. "I will do everything that I can to help you, but first I need to hear the truth from you. I am going to put you on your honour to tell me all about the whole business. If I can, I will help you in any way possible. But I need to hear the truth from you. No sworn oaths, no having it drawn out of you by a cross-examination in Court. Just on the strength of what exists between us, you must tell me the truth." Robert was a little taken back by his earnestness.

"Of course I will tell you the truth. Ask me what you like."

"All right," resumed Lord Shotley, "did you kill her?"

Robert was completely taken aback by the blunt question. "Of course not," he replied hotly.

"The police are quite convinced you did," said Lord Shotley calmly.

"They have no evidence," said Robert, considerably flustered. "They have no evidence at all. Nothing. I wish they would find something. This just not knowing is very trying." Lord Shotley looked at him with warm sympathy. He sat down again, by the fire.

"Don't you think it would be a good thing if you started from the beginning and told me everything. If it is not too painful."

"Well, I can't tell you anything. We had been to Doncaster for the meeting there. We were late home. By the time we had the horses back in their boxes and settled down it was 2 o'clock in the morning. When I got home, she was not there. I crept quietly to bed so as not to wake her and she was not there. She was not in the house anywhere! There was no note. Nothing. Her coat was still on the peg. I did not know what to do. I took my horse and rode down to the police station. There had been no reports of any accidents. I went up to the hospital. No one had been brought in. I went home again. I searched the whole place. I could not find anything. Nothing out of place, or anything that might give a clue. As soon as I could the next morning, I sent word round to all her family and our friends. I myself rode over to her mother. No one had seen her or heard from her for days. The police helped make inquiries far and wide. We circulated her description and put up posters. I have asked everyone that I can think of who might know her or recognise her—nothing. Nothing. She has simply disappeared."

"How long ago was this?" asked Lord Shotley.

"Eleven weeks," said Robert. "It has been terrible. The police have turned the place upside down. They have had the floors up. They have searched the whole stud. Every bit of recently dug ground has been dug up again. They have dredged the ponds. They have put someone down the wells. They have even turned over the muck heap and taken all the ashes away from the fires to analyse them. They are quite convinced I have done away with her. They insist that people just do not disappear. They say it is impossible to just disappear. Someone somewhere would spot you. I am afraid that I am as mystified as you. I do not know where she is or what has happened to her. It seems that no one has seen her after she disappeared. Any ship that left within a fortnight of her disappearance has now put into port. All the passengers have been questioned. It has not produced anything. It is the uncertainty, the not knowing."

Lord Shotley listened with thoughtful concentration.

"I don't know what to do. I cannot think of anything that I have not done that I could do. It is bad enough that my wife has simply disappeared without any trace, but I wish the police would leave me alone. If I knew anything, I would tell them. Anything rather than have them accuse me of her murder." Robert buried his head in his hands.

Lord Shotley had been watching the look of abject misery on Robert's face as he told his story. He was convinced he spoke the truth.

"It is quite plain to me that you are telling the truth, but was there anything between you? Some small thing the police might construe as a motive?"

"Well, you know what it's like, sir, every marriage has its bumpy moments."

Yes, and don't I know it, Lord Shotley thought to himself, nodding. "Don't say that to the police—they will seize upon it and interpret all kinds of mischief into it." Lord Shotley was thoughtful for a while. "Let the police finish their searches and inquiries. Be as co-operative as you can. When they have finished, I do not think there will be too many problems persuading them to drop their charges. In the meantime it's up to you to persuade her family and all your friends and acquaintances that you certainly did not do away with her. See what you can find out, if anything, that can throw some light on the mystery. I am sure that you will be able to carry on with your employ for me. You may take off whatever time you need to try to bring this very bad business to a rapid conclusion."

Robert felt a surge of gratitude to his employer—not only for what he had done and would do to try and help, but because he had not lost his faith in him and had accepted what he had to say as the absolute truth.

"I don't know how to thank you, sir; your support and help mean so much."

Lord Shotley stopped him. "I will hear no more of it," he said. "I have already told you that I feel that I am so much in your debt that this is very little that I do in return. Come on, fill you glass, you are embarrassing me. I know a few people; I will have a word or two in a few ears. Perhaps they might come up with something."

They sat in companionable silence for a while. Eventually after a brief discussion about the affairs of the stud, Robert rose to leave. They shook hands affectionately.

"Good luck, Henery," Lord Shotley said. "Keep me informed of the least development. You can always leave a message here at the Club or at home. If anything of importance arrives and I am not there, my secretary is very efficient in making sure that it catches up with me."

"Goodbye, sir. Thank you so much. I will let you know of anything. I cannot tell you how much I appreciate your help."

"Oh, go on, be off with you!"

"Goodbye sir, goodbye," said Robert. And so they parted.

Robert walked slowly back to his lodgings. As he did so he contemplated his future with considerable misgivings. He was totally mystified by the whole business. Why should she go? What had happened to her? What if she never came back? He felt very depressed. He found it very difficult to imagine life without her.

When he had been discharged from hospital, following his accident, it soon became very plain to him that he had become very attached to the brown-haired nurse who had looked after him. There began between them a correspondence from which it was very soon obvious that his feelings were returned. He managed to make several visits to see her. Their love blossomed. When Lord Shotley had asked him to take the post as assistant to the trainer in his newly enlarged stud, he had jumped at the chance. When he had seen what went with the job—a small cottage at the back of the stable yard—he had asked Lillian to marry him, which she had joyfully accepted.

The wedding had been a small affair, just Lillian's mother and his immediate family with a few close friends. Lord Shotley had agreed to propose the health of the bride at the reception, much to the delight of the small number of guests. They had gone for a week's honeymoon in Scarborough. On their return, they had settled down into their new home with a sense of triumphant happiness.

Robert had thrown himself into his new position as assistant to the trainer with vigour and enthusiasm. He still felt very stiff from his accident and walked with a slight limp. If he spent too long on the saddle, he suffered extreme discomfort from his hip, but apart from that, he had made a most remarkable recovery. He worked hard at his job and kept very long hours. He felt it was important that he led by example. He was always in the yard first in the morning and last to leave at night.

They had three stallions standing at stud and a steady procession of mares coming and going all the time, in addition to the brood mares of their own. Lord Shotley had an ambition that one day he would have a Derby winner that he bred himself. Over the years he had produced a number of highly successful horses, but this ambition had as yet eluded him.

The provisions and fodder for all the horses was produced on Lord Shotley's estate. This was delivered to the stables every week and Robert used to take a great delight when the teams of matched Suffolk horses would pull into the yard with the familiar green and red wagons loaded with bags of oats and chaff or piled high with hay or straw.

The organisation of all this took a considerable effort. Lillian, who had one day stepped in to help out when the clerk to the Stud was ill, found the work both interesting and challenging. She was delighted to find a way of being involved in the whole enterprise, for she soon realised that horses were Robert's life. She was always going to have to take second place. Both of them threw all their energies into the work of the stud. She had learnt to ride and had taken over as clerk. She used to ride out with him and note down any point about the training of each horse. In their way they were very happy. Both delighted in the success of a common interest shared. The emotional sentimentality of their relationship that had grown in the hospital, had gradually changed to one of two very good friends striving together. When Robert was appointed Trainer and stud manager and they were able, with some reluctance, to move from their small cottage to the Manager's House, their lives became totally absorbed with the work. They had not time even to think about any children.

Since Lillian had disappeared, Robert had felt he had lost his right hand. He did not realise how much of the administration she had undertaken. He was hard put to keep up with it all. He needed to take on someone to help, but could not bring himself to do it, as it would be admitting that she had really gone. His house was also curiously empty, but fortunately he was far too busy to notice and too tired, when he did finally get to bed, to linger long on the idea that she was not there, before he fell asleep. Because he had always worked long hours and risen early in the morning, he had schooled himself to go to sleep as soon as he got into bed. He knew that if he were to survive, he needed to sleep. If he was going to be up at half past four in the morning, he must go to sleep now. Fortunately for him, this stood him in good stead when she disappeared; otherwise he would have lain awake all night pondering the imponderable.

Robert's walk had taken him across London and he had arrived back at his lodgings. After the sophisticated opulence of Lord Shotley's club, they looked dowdy and seedy. He was reluctant to go in. He contemplated delaying this and thought about going up to the pub for a while. He decided that if he was quick he could make a dash and catch the overnight mail train. He quickly returned to his room, hastily repacked his case and bade goodbye to his landlady and ran across the street to the station.

He caught the train with a few minutes to spare and was soon speeding north. His trick of shutting his problems out and going to sleep deserted him. He spent an uncomfortable night, fitfully dozing, whilst the events of the last weeks and his conversation with Lord Shotley churned around in disjointed segments in his mind. When he eventually alighted from the train at four thirty in the morning, he felt cold and jaded. He was in a black mood. His mood was made worse when he found that there were no cabs—the station was shut. There was nothing for him to do but walk. He left his case on the platform outside the Left Luggage Office. He turned up his collar and, thrusting his hands deep into his pocket, set out. It is one thing to be up at four thirty in the morning because you want to; it is another to have it forced on you, especially after an almost sleepless night. His eyes, usually receptive to the delights of the dawn, were fixed in a sour glower upon the road. His spirits, usually raised by the sound of a lark singing in the first rays of the sun, refused to be cheered as he felt its warmth on his back. He finally reached the stud, just as the first strings of horses were coming out for their morning gallops. He climbed up on a stile to watch them, but even that sight, which usually took every ounce of his interest and concentration, failed to lift the mood that had settled on him which was dragging his spirits down like some great smothering shroud.

CHAPTER 3

Robert found the months that followed increasingly difficult. The police were determined to prove he had murdered Lillian. He was continually being called in for more questioning. They re-searched the house and the grounds with even more thoroughness than before. They questioned everyone that worked there. They re-questioned everyone who had any contact whatever with her. Through all this Robert had to maintain the efficient running of the stud. It was not long before it was obvious to all that he was in trouble. Despite prompting from the Head Lad, Robert had forgotten to order up the farrier and one of their best horses had gone lame. To make it worse the horse belonged to a friend of Lord Shotley. She had complained bitterly about it; as it meant the horse had not run in a race where it had stood a good chance of winning. It was the acknowledged favourite and she had already placed some large bets on it, which were forfeited. Then they had run out of oats. The usual weekly delivery had not materialised. No one noticed that it had not come until the bins were empty. Robert had had to send his trap over to the mill to collect enough for that day and leave an urgent message that some be delivered in the morning.

Some entries for a race had not been sent. When the horses and lads had arrived at the course, their entries were void. They had to come home without running. The jockeys and owners were vociferous in their complaints. Then he had overlooked ordering a horse box to be added to the train. Horses that were to be taken for a race were left standing at the station.

In desperation he engaged an assistant. At least the day-to-day running of the stables was settled again in capable hands.

Robert was never much of a housekeeper. His place became dirty with piles of unwashed dishes. He was continually running out of wood for the fires and had fallen into the habit of going down to the 'King's Head' for beer and a bite. Often he would wake up in the back of his trap in the yard. How he had got himself aboard he could not remember; luckily the horse could find its own way home, but needless to say he felt like death for the rest of the day.

All these things had not escaped the attentions of Lord Shotley. At last he made it his business to call on Robert.

"I can't imagine what you are feeling," he said after greeting him with his usual warmth, "but I can guess and imagine that you are going through hell—but this cannot go on. Everything must be impeccable! We cannot have any slip-ups. No silly mistakes. Our reputation depends on it. Our success depends on our reputation."

Robert's shoulders drooped. He could not look at him. He rubbed his forehead with an anxious hand and wiped the tear that had, unbidden, filled his eye. He shook his head, not knowing what to say.

Lord Shotley saw that he was lost for words. He saw his distress. His heart went out to his friend.

"Look Robert," he said, guiding him into a chair and himself sitting on the edge of the desk. "I'm not angry with you. God forbid I should be that! I know what you can do; I know that you are beyond reproach. You're just trying to do too much. You were right to employ an assistant. He seems to have got a grip of things pretty well, but you must get some more help with the administration. If that is up the creek, then everything else is at risk." He held up his hand to stop Robert from speaking. "You will have to get someone in. Get someone on a temporary basis. If Lillian returns and would like to, she may take up her post again."

Robert looked at him, the hurt evident in his eyes. "I know that is what I should do, but I have not done it, because if I do, I will have to finally admit that she has gone." He sobbed brokenly.

Lord Shotley took his friend's hand in his own and said kindly: "Don't you think that perhaps the time has come when you did? She has been gone now for six months. Nothing has been found. Not a trace of her. Don't you think the time has come for you to face the fact that she's a missing person?"

Robert looked at him without seeing. It would be like signing her death warrant. If he formally declared her a missing person, he would first have to acknowledge to himself that she had gone. But what could have happened to her? He had thought of every possibility. She could have been injured in an accident, yet nothing had been found after exhaustive inquiries.

That was the worst part. Just nothing. The not knowing. He looked at Lord Shotley, pathetically.

"Yes, all right, I'll get someone right away." There, he had done it. "I'll go down to the Police Station and formally report her missing." Lord Shotley visibly relaxed.

"I'm sure that you're doing the right thing. You cannot go on hanging in limbo. Get the office sorted out with someone competent and then you won't feel so pressured. You will be able to think properly again. For goodness sake, don't drop any more clangours. I'm fed up with having to give disgruntled owners lunch at my club in an attempt to smooth their ruffled feathers."

Despite his gloom, Robert smiled. That was as close as he had ever come to being told off since Cock Sparrow had had a go at him when he was an apprentice, for giving one of the horses in his charge the wrong feed.

"I am sorry, my Lord," was all he could mumble. He knew the rebuke was justified. "I am afraid that the whole business has just become too much and I have allowed everything to get on top of me."

"There is no need to apologise, I quite understand. I am not trying to reprimand you. All I want to do is to help you sort yourself out—for your good as well as mine."

"Yes, thank you, sir. It is quite strange, actually. Even forcing my hand to get someone else in has made me see things more clearly. It has brought me to the brink. I can look over without fear. I can see that the jump is not as great as I had feared. I will go down to the police station this afternoon and finally settle it."

When it was all finally over, he returned home from the police station slowly, feeling like a flannel that had been wrung out. He felt totally drained of everything. Feelings and emotions had been exhausted.

When he arrived, it was nearly dark and Tom the stable lad was standing anxiously in the stable doorway, with a lantern in his hand, waiting for his master's return.

"I'm sorry, Tom, I've kept you waiting." Tom often had to wait for his master's return—it was part of his duties. Robert could remember when he was a lad. He could bitterly recall the hours he had spent hanging about waiting for his Master's late return. He tried not to do it without giving prior notice.

"I'm afraid the police kept me longer than I had expected." He was annoyed. He knew that by tomorrow morning everyone in the village would know that the police had kept him all afternoon. It would add fuel to the fire that was already smouldering there. Lillian had been popular. She had that touch that made people feel she was really interested in them and their problems. The people in the village liked her. So did the workers in the stud. Everyone was quite convinced he had done away with her. The landlord of the 'King's Head' was running a small book on the outcome of the police inquiries.

Robert handed over the horse and walked into the house. He walked into the study and made up the fire. It had burned so low that it would be some time before it got up. He looked disconsolately at its smoking embers. He found the bellows and poked and bellowed some reluctant life into the hissing logs. Unfortunately he filled the room with smoke but produced only a tiny flame. He poured himself out a large glass of whisky and flopped down into his favourite leather-covered chair. Since Lillian had gone he used this room all the time. He did not bother to light the fire in the drawing room.

It was no good; the fire was going to be ages before it got up and gave any heat. It was too cold to sit there until it did. He wandered around the house in the gloom, seeing things, as it were, for the first time. He stopped here and there, picking up this object, looking at that. Looking at the pictures, the furnishings, the flowers. There was no doubt it was a beautiful house, but he realised with a start, he had never really felt at home in it. Well, that was natural. It was not his anyway. It went with the job. When the job went, the house would go with it. Knowing this, he had never put down any roots. Anyway, a house was where you lived, it was just a house. Of course, you needed to make yourself as comfortable as you could, but when it came down to it, it was only a roof over your head. When the time came, you packed up and moved on.

Robert returned to the study, to the warmth of the now blazing fire. He put the decanter near his chair and settled down, his feet on the hearth. He sat in the dark, just in the light of the flickering flames. How long he sat there he did not remember, but in those flickering flames he saw his life flicker past, almost as if he were leafing through a book. Somehow, being forced to confront the fact that Lillian was missing, was almost like coming to the end of a chapter. He knew in his heart that if nothing had been heard from her now, she would never come back. It was an idea that he had had in his head for a long time, but every time it came to the front of his mind he had pushed it back. Now, however, it had come to the front. Like a dumpling in a stew, it had somehow floated to the top and would not sink again.

He gazed into the fire. He unseeingly, watched the sap bubbling out of the end of a log, boiling in the heat, then dripping into the hot ashes, to disappear in a spurt of steam. Life was a bit like that—you spent most of it going quietly about your business and then suddenly some outside influence sent you bubbling and seething into activity, until you dropped exhausted; and if you were not careful, you, too, disappeared in a puff of steam. These past few months had certainly reduced him to boiling activity. Had it not been for Lord Shotley's timely intervention, he too might have suffered the same fate.

The fire was burning low. He watched a plume of smoke curl lazily up the chimney. He was going to have to get used to the idea of life without Lillian. He shuddered with cold and the apprehension that this idea provoked in him. He was just about to throw another log on the fire when he heard the rattle of a bucket out in the yard and a cheery thin whistle.

He sat up with a start. *Good grief!* he thought to himself, stiffly getting out of his chair and stretching, realising that he had sat there all night. He pulled on his coat and cap and went out to start the day.

The air felt chilly and his unrested body shivered at its unwelcome cold. Robert went the rounds of the boxes as he always did. By the time he had finished, the lads had come down from the Bothy; he had discussed the day's events with the Head Lad and his cob had been brought out for him, saddled ready. Ten minutes later he was riding out at the head of his string of horses. Robert's whole mood changed. This was why he was in the game. They walked on up the street, across the road, up under the trees and on to the heath. The sun was just slanting misty beams through the branches. Occasionally when there was a bigger gap in the trees, he could feel its warmth strike his back. The air held that magic clear pale, pale blue quality of the dawn and the myriad cobwebs sparkled and twinkled as the sun caressed their dew-spangled threads. High above, a lark was singing, a pure torrent of joy cascading on the earth in a silver tumbling jubilance of song. At the top of a tall beech tree, a missal thrush was shouting his excitement at the top of his voice, a robust challenge, defying the sigh of the gentle breeze that softly rustled the leaves. As they walked along, rabbits hopped unconcernedly out of their way. On the heath three hares were cavorting together and a cock pheasant, splendid in his spring finery, drew himself up to his full height, and with a boisterous flapping of his wings that nearly lifted him off the ground, crowed his happy claim to the wood through which they walked.

When they emerged from the wood onto the grass of the heath, the whole string broke into a canter and then a headlong gallop that took them to the top of the hill. *This is what it is all about,* thought Robert, *this is what bloody well makes the hard work bearable, just the sheer joy of being out on a morning like this*. They pulled up, a steaming cavalcade, whilst Robert sorted them out into their various pairs and groups for their gallop. Then he cantered down so that he could watch them. He saw that there were several horsedrawn traps pulled up along the road. He noticed the glint of eyeglasses. The racecourse touts were out, looking to see how the horses performed. Robert felt like a king as each group of horses came thundering past. His old cob, who had seen all this every day for several years, cropped the grass disinterestedly. Robert quietly made mental notes about each horse as they went by. These would affect the feed regime, exercise pattern and the racing aspirations of each of them. When they returned to the stables, he would go round each box, whilst each horse was being done down. With the Head Lad and the assistant, he would review the treatment of each horse in the light of what he had seen and their racing plans and entries. Everything would be logged down in the work book. Granted, the administration of the whole enterprise was interesting and there was considerable excitement and glamour at the race meetings, but this was the part he liked the most—working with these magnificent creatures, carefully preparing them so that each reached the peak of its fittest condition for its next race. This filled him with a great satisfaction and delight.

When they had returned to the yard and his rounds had been completed, then and only then, could he go inside for his breakfast. This was the meal he enjoyed the most. He usually went out at half past four in the morning. By the time he had completed his tasks, he had a keen appetite. He was looking forward to his bowl of hot porridge, his eggs and bacon and his pot of hot coffee. When he had lived on his own he had the production of this feast down to a fine art. He could have the whole meal ready in ten minutes—his toast propped up on a fork, roasting in front of the kitchen fire whilst he ate his porridge, the oats for which had been soaking overnight. His eggs and bacon, and perhaps some mushrooms if he had found some out on the heath, would be sizzling in a pan.

When he got married, Lillian had engaged a housekeeper. It was her job to make sure that everything was ready when the Master came in.

He went into the house this morning, still feeling pretty jaded after his sleepless night. The ride out had not lifted his spirits as it usually did; one of his good hopes had not performed as well as he had expected, and there was some doubt that it would be ready for its scheduled race in five weeks time. When they had returned, he had had a difference of opinion with his Head Lad about feed for one of the horses. He had been pretty sharp with one of the lads because of the slipshod way he was grooming his horse.

Robert was not in the best of moods when he went into the house for breakfast. His mood was made worse by finding he had forgotten to put the oats for his porridge to soak the previous night. He found he had only one small rasher of bacon left when he unwrapped the paper and two of the three eggs he had in the larder were bad. They stank with a sickening reek when he broke them into an exploratory cup. Disgusted, he threw them into the sink. He had no coffee ground so, laboriously, he ground up some beans whilst the kettle boiled. His spirits lifted a little with the aromatic smell of the coffee but it made him feel hungrier. In desperation he went into the larder to see what he could find to augment his small meal. He found a piece of cold mutton that had grown a mould on one end. Carefully scraping this off, he cut three good slices and tossed them into the pan with the bacon. He put some bread to toast in front of the fire and found a pot of honey. In the end he had quite a good breakfast but decided that fried slices of mutton, whilst better than nothing, were not to be recommended. He sat over his hot steaming coffee and contemplated his domestic arrangements with some dismay. Three weeks after Lillian had gone his housekeeper had left his employ. She was a very prim lady. She felt it was not proper that she should be expected to be in a house alone with a man. She also complained that though she had meals prepared on time, they were often spoilt, her efforts wasted because he was late. She could see no excuse that was good enough for being late for one of her meals. She felt she could not cope with that slight to her cooking. Robert was at first very glad to see the back of her, for the continual confrontations had got on his nerves. However, as time went by he found he missed having his household well ordered. As he looked at the remains of his far from satisfactory breakfast, he decided the time had come to try and find someone else.

He was interrupted by a loud knock at the door. It was repeated and the bell jangled demandingly. At length he got up and went to answer it.

"Yes, Officer?" he asked resignedly when he had opened the door and found a fresh-faced young Constable standing there.

"The Inspector asked me to give you this, sir," he said.

"Give the Inspector my compliments," said Robert "and thank him for his letter," he added as he checked that it was addressed to him.

"Yes, righto, sir. Thank you, sir." The Constable mounted his bicycle and peddled erratically out of the yard.

Robert took the letter into his office and opened it. He read:

For the personal attention of Mr. Robert George Henery.

ભ

Dear Sir,

Pursuant of our inquiries into the disappearance of Lillian Mary Henery on or about 30th June 1882 we do now write to inform you that following exhaustive inquiries, both in the country and abroad we can find no trace of her. According to your request, we have posted her a 'missing person' as of that date. We further state that we have found no evidence whatever to support any allegations against you. All charges against you in connection with her disappearance and possible murder are herewith dropped. We thank you for your co-operation and will keep you informed of any developments in the future.

On behalf of Her Majesty's Police force, I have the honour to remain, Your humble and obedient servant

J B Smith, Inspector

Robert stood at the door with the letter in his hand, his eyes seeing nothing. No message reached his brain. It was swamped with a feeling of relief. He felt he was growing physically taller. It was as if a great crushing weight had been removed from his shoulders. At the same time he felt a great sadness. This would mean that they had finally given up. This was the end of hope. They would be in touch if anything transpired, though they obviously felt this was unlikely, or they would have kept the case open. Robert went inside and shut the door.

Later in the morning, he walked down to the little village church and, going in, sat on a pew at the back. He was not a particularly religious man and only went to church on the occasion of the main festivities. However, he found here a place of peace, the quiet, the ancient stone, witness to more than their share of human joy and sadness.

He wandered round, looking at the windows that remained—mostly a hotchpotch selection, some of them placed there quite recently. As he walked up the aisle, his eye fell on a small niche on the wall, the wall round it pockmarked with musket ball holes. Obviously the soldiers of the Commonwealth had used the figure of the saint that had stood there as target practice.

He walked through the choir stalls and knelt at the altar rail. Slowly the anxiety, the frustration and the worry of the last few months crept over him. Try as he might, he could not stop the tears welling up and dropping on the rail between his elbows. Great hot salty tears filled his eyes and ran down his cheeks and he sobbed, head in hands, uncontrollably.

"Wherever you are, Lillian, may God look after you," he said in a low voice. "Our life together here, started with our wedding in this church. This is the right place for it to end. I cannot even give you a decent funeral. What am I talking of funerals for? You see, one day you will just come walking back again." But in his heart he knew she would not. He rose and walked slowly down the aisle. When he got to the door, he turned. "Look after her, wherever she is." And opening the door he passed out into the sunshine.

He was surprised how warm it felt and he shuddered as he realised he had become quite chilled in the time that he had been inside. In a large chestnut tree in the corner of the churchyard a wood pigeon was cooing loudly. He listened to it and his spirits lifted slightly. They always seemed to coo when it was raining. Robert always took it as a sign that it was about to stop. Robert listened. He thought it a good omen.

The lifting of his spirits on receipt of the letter did not last long. If the police had decided he was innocent, it was evident that everyone else disagreed. He found himself increasingly isolated. A terrible paranoia was creeping over him. Everywhere he went people seemed to be talking to each other about him. Wherever he went people, who had been talking animatedly together, suddenly stopped. Robert did his best to avoid meeting people that he knew and grew more and more despondent and introverted. Some of his friends tried inviting him out for lunch or dinner, but in the end they gave up, because he always refused to come.

Thankfully he had made successful appointments of an administrator and a housekeeper. At least the affairs of the stud were running smoothly again. His housekeeper, too, soon had his domestic arrangements organised and so the petty worries of everyday life were lifted from him. But still his gloom deepened. Everywhere he went, there was Lillian's presence. He had not been able to decently bury her and have, as it were, a final exorcism. She was still just missing. Everywhere he felt her there. He felt too that he was losing concentration on his work, that he was letting Lord Shotley down.

Gradually it dawned on him that for his own sanity he was going to have to leave and find himself another position somewhere else, a long way away from here. At first he shut the idea out of his head. It was unthinkable that he should leave Lord Shotley. Their lives had been inextricably linked for so long, they had almost become part of each other. However the idea, once planted, would not go away and in fact grew, until he felt sure there was no other course.

Accordingly, it was with a heavy heart that he sat down one evening and wrote to Lord Shotley:

⚬

My Lord,

It has taken me many days to come to the point when I am sitting down and writing this letter to you. I sought hard and long for the right things to say but can find no fine words or eloquent phrases to help me and so I will write in plain English, in the way that we have always talked with each other.

Your help and support to me over the past months has been a wonderful prop and enabled me to carry on when it seemed that I should be overwhelmed by my problems. As you know, these last few months have been very difficult for me but thanks to your generosity and kind concern, I have been able to endure them.

However it is now plainly clear to me that I can no longer continue here in this position. I face this decision with a heavy heart, bearing in mind what I owe you and your generosity to me over the years that I have had the good fortune to know you.

I have decided therefore to ask your assistance in finding another situation far away from here, where perhaps, removed from these surroundings and their associations, I may begin to regain some sense in my life. There is no power that would be able to persuade me to leave your service or give up this exceptional position. Your generosity has allowed me to be a part of building something that is admired and envied throughout the land. I am afraid, however, that for the time being, I feel that I have met my match and I must bow to the circumstances that are not of my making, or of my choice. It is with great sadness that I write this letter, trusting as I do always, in your generosity.

I remain your humble and obedient servant.

Robert read it through and finally signed it, Robert Henery. When the ink had dried, he folded and sealed it.

For two days the letter lay on the table, but finally Robert's resolve overcame his hesitation. He took it out to the yard and called the lad.

"Boy, take the roan mare and deliver this letter to Lord Shotley. He is at his club. Look, I have written directions on this piece of paper, so you should be able to find it all right."

"But, Mister, I cannot read," whined the boy, a look of terror in his eyes. Robert looked at him in amazement. That was the last thing he had thought of. He went into the yard. The lads were busily grooming and mucking out.

"Can any one of you read?" he called out. All work stopped and everyone looked somewhat surprised at the question. Two or three voices called.

"Yes, I can, Mister," a tow-headed lad called. He walked over.

"Read this out to me, so that I am sure," Robert said. The boy read it.

"Yes, sir. I know where this is. Before I came out here to work in the stables, I was groom for a toff in London. I often used to go there as footman on 'is coach. Yes, I can get that there alright, but even if I ride 'ard, I won't get there and back before night; I shall 'ave to put up somewhere for the night."

Now that Robert had made up his mind, he did not want to be thwarted.

"All right. Come to the house and I'll give you some money. I most particularly want that letter delivered today. Give the letter to his Lordship in person and wait for a reply."

The boy was delighted at this chance of a break in the routine and now the sudden possibility of a night in London.

"Now who's a sissy for being able to read?" he jeered at the sullen jealous faces round him. What any one of them would not have given for the chance of a night in London with some of Mister Robert's money in their pocket!

"Be off with you," called Robert. "Get on your way."

Robert found it difficult to contain his impatience and when the boy returned late the next evening, he was beside himself with frustration.

"Well, where have you been? Did you deliver my letter? Have you got a reply?"

"Yes, Mister. I gave the letter into his Lordship's hand."

"Did he read it?" asked Robert anxiously.

"No, he just took it and said 'thank you'. I said that beggin' 'is pardon but that you was 'oping for a reply. 'E just looked at me and 'e said 'e would reply as soon as 'e could and that I shouldn't wait."

Robert had to possess himself with patience for two whole days until the reply came, and when it did, he tore it open in the yard and read it there and then.

ℭ

Dear Henery,

I cannot tell you how sad I was to read your letter and the contents thereof. I must be honest and say that I was not surprised and have in fact, been anticipating this as the inevitable outcome of your situation. How you have endured for so long, I do not know and I can only admire your courage and fortitude in tolerating for so long what must have become for you an impossible situation.

I have for some time, as I say, been expecting this letter and so I have quietly presumed to make a few inquiries on your behalf.

It has occurred to me that you would find it difficult to make a clean break because the racing fraternity make contacts far and wide. I have, however, an idea and I would be very grateful if you would wait on me here at the Club in the forenoon on the 27th of this month when I might have some interesting news for you. Perhaps you would care to join me for a spot of lunch.

Yours sincerely,

Shotley

On the appointed day Robert was again being ushered through the familiar rooms. Lord Shotley rose to greet him and was horrified by how thin and gaunt he looked.

"You've not been looking after yourself," he said as they shook hands.

"Nothin' but vot the care of a good vomans would not cure," chuckled a rubicund figure boisterously, as he emerged from within a big wing chair that had at first hidden him from view when Robert had entered. "Mien Gott man! Look at you! If my hunting dogs found you, they vould search somevere else for the piece of good meats!" He roared with laughter. "That is vot you need, a good voman to cook you dam fine food and varm your bed at night." He grabbed Robert's hand and pumped it vigorously. Robert was too taken aback to say anything. He stared open-mouthed at the strange little man, with his almost incomprehensible accent, who was pumping his hand for all he was worth.

"Now, Henery," continued Lord Shotley, "I particularly want you to meet Count Ramoskie. August, allow me to present to you one of the most successful young trainers that we have. I am very glad to say he works for me!"

"Arr, Mister 'Enerey. I have heared many talkings about your exploits. Your fame, it goes in front of you." They shook hands and as they did so, the Count's heels clicked together. Robert regarded the little man. Robert himself was short. It was unusual to meet anyone outside of racing who was his height. But this little man was the same height as himself. What looked so odd, was that he was very broad, so he looked like a little cube. He was dressed in a loudly chequed suit with exaggerated his width. He appeared to have two moustaches. One on his top lip and one below. Both bristled outwards in an alarming and ferocious way. *I bet they bristle when he gets cross*, thought Robert to himself. He had to bite his lip to stop himself from laughing.

Lord Shotley ushered them into chairs. The waiter poured out some claret and handed round the cake, then departed.

"Damn fine idea, this the eatin' cake vith the claret." The Count beamed enthusiastically and took a huge bite from his slice of cake, then washed it down with a long draught, which drained his glass in one gulp. He waved it hopefully in Lord Shotley's direction. Lord Shotley winced at the cavalier dispatch of his finest claret, but nonetheless refilled the proffered glass.

"Vell," said the Count, his mouth still full of cake, "Lord Shotley he say you vill come and to the vork for me!" Lord Shotley tried to stop him.

Too late, the cat was out of the bag.

"What...?" Robert's eyebrows shot up. He flashed an inquiring glance at Lord Shotley, who spoke quickly and seriously, trying to quieten the Count.

"I don't think we have got as far as that." He might as well have tried to turn off a waterfall. The Count had helped himself to a third slice of cake and was not to be diverted.

"Lord Shotley, he say you are best damn fine trainer and that I am very lucky to get you. Then that is fixed. I am damn lucky to get you! You are damn lucky to get me!"

Robert looked appealingly at Lord Shotley.

"I am terribly sorry." He looked wretched. "I had not meant it to happen like this at all! I am sorry, Robert, I wanted you to meet the Count and then over lunch I had planned to explore the possibilities."

"You mean he did not know?" inquired the Count, realising he had spoken out of turn and that Robert as yet did not know anything of the idea.

"Look, I am terribly sorry, Robert." Lord Shotley was wringing his hands in embarrassment. "It seemed such a wonderful idea. It seemed the complete solution to everything. Had you heard the whole plan carefully explained, you would have seen at once how perfect it was." Lord Shotley looked at him appealingly.

Tell me what to say, thought Robert frantically. *I don't know what to say. This is ridiculous. I wouldn't work for that stupid little man if he were the last person on earth.* He looked at them both. No help was forthcoming from Lord Shotley.

"Well…er…I don't know what to say."

"This is that paragon of yours. I offer to him the splendid chance to vork for me and he does not know vot to say…?" The Count took another large gulp at his claret in disbelief.

"I think that the whole idea has been a bit of a surprise," said Lord Shotley, in an attempt to smooth his ruffled feathers. "When Henery has had time to think about it, he might be better able to consider the proposal. Come on. Let's go and discuss it over lunch." He ushered them towards the dining room, the Count clutching the last slice of cake in his hand.

"Is this for real?" Robert whispered to Lord Shotley as they went through.

"Yes" he hissed back. "I am sorry it has happened like this."

"Who the hell is he?" asked Robert, urgently.

"Shh. I will tell you later. Ah! Count. Will you sit here? Henery, there?"

They sat down and the menus passed round. The Count eyed his with ill-concealed glee. He chose oxtail soup, a grilled turbot steak, a roast partridge with runner beans, followed by roast beef and vegetables; then apple pie and whipped cream; then herring roes on toast for savoury and the cheese board to follow, with perhaps "just a few fresh fruits to finish."

Robert looked at Lord Shotley round the corner of his menu. "I could not keep up with that—I cannot eat that much."

Lord Shotley looked at him with a weak smile. "Be brave, dear boy, be brave." He was worrying how he was going to choose suitable wines to go with this vast feast. *If he is going to eat everything off the menu*, he thought to himself, *I will floor him with the wine!*

The waiter noted it down without a flicker of his eyelid. Lord Shotley looked at Robert with a look of triumphant expectation.

"Your turn," he said softly from behind his wine list. Robert had been dreading this moment. It would be rude to the Count not to choose from the same selection and he certainly did not want to embarrass Honest Ned, so he chose his way through the menu, hoping he had selected the items that would be served in the smallest or lightest portions. He was gratified to see that Lord Shotley did the same.

The Count hugely enjoyed his lunch. He ploughed through every course with happy dedication. Lord Shotley had to call for a second bottle of the claret to go with the roast. He and Robert were getting slower and slower and Robert was in severe difficulties with his main course. He was pushing roast potatoes round his plate, desperately wondering how many of them he could leave, when the Count, understanding that he was defeated, and with a gleam in his eye, spoke.

"'Enery, you do not eat enough," he said. "No vonder so ill you look. Those potatoes, you not vant?" Before Robert could answer, he, with the sureness of a heron securing its prey, leant across the table and impaled one of them on his fork. The others followed in quick succession. "It is a pity to vaste good food when there are hungry people at the table to eat it." Robert and Lord Shotley exchanged glances. It was not until they had reached the fruit and Port that the pace of eating and small talk slackened enough for serious conversation. The Count had eaten everything that had been placed before him, attacking each course as if he had not seen food for a month. Robert and Lord Shotley struggled on in his wake as best they could. Both had now thankfully reached that stage when they sat with distended stomachs and that lethargic feeling that left them incapable of any serious thought or action. During the course of the meal Robert had gathered that the Count had a passion for his horses, of which he had a large number. He had a stud and large estate in Hungary, but spent most of his time in Budapest, Vienna or Prague. He was always at race meetings and spent much of his energy travelling round from one race meeting to another. His first passion was food. He gave glowing accounts of the excellence of the food to be had in this restaurant or that. He spoke of the skill of his chefs with an admiration and tenderness that brought tears to his eyes. Whilst he loved racing, it appeared that he had not been very successful. When Lord Shotley had suggested that Henery might be interested in considering training for him, he had been filled with excitement and, in the way of such people, the idea had no sooner entered his head than it was fact.

He was very surprised to gather that Lord Shotley had not spoken to Robert about it. He talked volubly and surprisingly managed to eat that enormous quantity of food with hardly an interruption in his flow of exuberant chatter. Robert ventured to compliment him on his English. He was obviously a man who responded to flattery.

"You are too kind. Vhen we vere very little, we 'ad an Eengleesh nurse. How do you say...a nanny?" They nodded. "We 'ad this nanny. She taught us to speak the best Eengleesh. To her it is that I must thank." He smiled at them from behind his next forkful of food, which was already on its way to meet its brothers before he had finished speaking.

"How very fortunate," muttered Lord Shotley, shutting his eyes and forcing down another small mouthful.

Thank goodness for that, thought Robert, *I could not work for someone who had no English. What do you mean?* He corrected himself in alarm. *Work for him? I don't* think so. Robert looked at the strange little man and thought what a volatile, unpredictable and hazardous career anyone might have with this strange person.

"Henery," said Lord Shotley, absentmindedly twiddling the stem of his glass. "The Count would be quite keen for you to start straight away, if you would consider going."

"Well, sir. I am not at all sure…" Robert began.

"Oh, you do not vant to vork for me, is that right?" the Count asked belligerently.

"No, sir, your Excellency…I don't mean, no. I mean no, it is not right." Robert felt himself getting too flustered. This was too sudden. He needed to think about it. He had not even thought of leaving England and the thought of burying himself somewhere out in the middle of nowhere, working for this eccentric little man with this rapacious appetite and atrocious accent was too much. "No. It is not that, your Excellency, it is just that I had not really thought about what sort of move I should make."

"Vell, it is time you think. It is not every day you vill have the chance to work for damn fine place like mine, I tell you!"

"But I cannot speak the language," said Robert, desperately seeking to stall the situation.

"That is easy," said the Count, helping himself to an enormous cigar from the box being offered him. "Everyone speak German."

"But I don't" said Robert in mounting alarm.

"You *don't?*" asked the Count in curt surprise. "*Everyone* speak German." He looked at Lord Shotley. "You speak German, do you not?" Lord Shotley shook is head. "No? I thought everyone spoke German."

"No August, we do not have much need of it here. If anyone wants to get on in England they have to speak English." The Count nodded. He had found this to be true and was glad he had learned a smattering of the language when he was young. In fact, he had worked quite hard at learning the language and was justly proud of his progress. He looked at Robert.

"Vell, you vill have to learn."

"But, your Excellency, this might take me rather a long time," ventured Robert.

"Herr 'Enery," replied the Count, "do not prevaricate vith me! I am not to be prevaricated. If you vish to vork for me you vill not prevaricate."

Robert was a little taken aback; as far as he knew, at that moment he was not working for the Count and not likely to, according to the way the present conversation was developing.

"But how would I manage, where would I live?"

"Oh, Herr 'Enery, always these questions. Do you not trust me that little bit? I have a little house vich you can have and you vill manage very vell. Anything Lord Shotley give you I give you more. It is easy. It is fixed. Come to my Hotel tomorrow and my secretary vill draw up papers."

All eyes were now on Robert. He did not know what to say—this was far too sudden for him.

"I am very sorry, Your Excellency." (That seemed to by the style of address that pleased the old boy) "I cannot make up my mind about this off the cuff like this. Will you allow me to think about it for a while?"

"Vell, if you going to vork for me, you got to damn vell learn to make up your mind."

"Now, come on, August," Lord Shotley interjected. "You are asking him to uproot himself, leave his country and everything he knows and go to some place far away that he has never heard of, where he cannot even speak the language and you expect him to answer you straight away? I think you are being a little unfair. To allow him at least a day or two to answer you would not be unreasonable." The Count clearly did not like this, even from an English Lord:

"Oh, you Eengleesh, always you must think things over. Never do you do things from the heart. Always from the head. After you have had a cold shower." It was on the tip of Lord Shotley's tongue to ask who was a major world power and who was a decaying Empire in the middle of Europe, but fortunately he held his peace.

"Well, I have had an excellent lunch, Lord Shotley, as alvays you have look after me very vell." He leaned back. "All right, to show I do listen to vot you say, you think it over and let me know. I leave on the afternoon train for Paris, tomorrow. If you do not come to my hotel, I vill know that you are not coming. I vill have my secretary prepare papers. They vill be ready in the morning. If you have not come vhen ve are ready to go, they go on the fire. Goodbye Herr 'Enery, I see you tomorrow, I hope. Goodbye Lord Shotley, my dear friend. I hope that you vill talk the sense into his head!"

Robert made to go, but Lord Shotley motioned to him to stay. He ushered the Count out with many mutual expressions of goodwill and returned.

"Come on, I've ordered some brandy. Let's go through into the smoke room. We can sit by the fire and I need to talk to you."

I should think you do, thought Robert, *and I need to talk to you!*

They were soon settled down in front of the fire, a glass of brandy each from the decanter of the Club's best Hine, which was placed between them.

"Robert, I cannot apologise enough," began Lord Shotley. "I just wanted you to meet him today and get to know him a little first before raising the subject of you going to work for him, but the silly old ass blurted it out. I am very sorry."

"Well, sir, I know you mean well and that you have always had my best interests at heart, but you cannot seriously suggest that I go and work for that comic opera character?"

"Well, yes! actually." Lord Shotley looked at him intently. "Don't you see, it's the perfect solution. He's looking for someone. You would be absolutely ideal. You are young, you work hard. You know what you're talking about. His whole enterprise is run down. He has a big stud, but it has not been doing well. It's a wonderful chance for anyone to make a real name for themselves. He likes to race his horses all over Europe. You would become well known if you were successful. You have no ties—in fact, you want to get away. You would be able to work out there. No one would know about what had happened here. When I heard that he wanted someone, I took the liberty of speaking to him at once. You must seriously consider it, and if you want my advice, I would suggest that it's a wonderful opportunity and that you should take it." Robert looked at him.

"But it would mean leaving my loved ones. My hearth and home and going off to foreign parts and…"

"I don't believe I'm hearing this! You have got no loved ones!" Lord Shotley snapped brutally. "You haven't got a hearth and home. Of all the people I know, you are the one who can just pack up at a minute's notice and go. As for going to foreign parts, where is your sense of adventure, man?"

"I think I've had quite enough adventure in the last few months, thank you."

"Look, please, Robert, I've got to go now. Please promise me you will think about it. It's a wonderful chance. Don't just not go and see him tomorrow because you feel too sorry for yourself." They both got up to leave.

"All right, sir, I will give it some little thought this evening. And thank you. I know you meant well and I have always respected your judgement and taken your advice. It was just a little sudden, coming like that."

"That's all right, Robert. Actually I thought you were extremely calm, under the circumstances. Anyway, good luck. Let me know what you decide."

"Yes, of course, tomorrow afternoon. Goodbye, sir, thank you." They shook hands and Robert walked out into the street.

Robert walked and walked. Eventually he found himself down by the river. He lent on the Embankment parapet watching the river traffic go by. He was amazed at the number of vessels, the coming and goings of skiff, water taxis, barges and lighters. The whole river seemed a bustle of activity. In his walk he had got over his anger at having the plan thrust at him. He was even beginning to see the sense in what Lord Shotley had said. The question that was uppermost in his mind was, could he work for that strange little man? Eventually he walked back to his hotel and, still full from his enormous lunch, he declined to go down for dinner; instead, he spent the evening in his room lying on the brown bed, trying to consider the proposition from every angle. Honest Ned was right—it seemed the almost perfect solution. A clean break. A real challenge. Doing what he liked best. A real adventure. A chance to make a name for himself. And yet, and yet…He woke with a start. The chambermaid was hammering on his door.

"I'll leave your 'ot water outside," she called.

"Thank you," he called back. *Oh God! Look at me!* He glowered into the mirror at his unshaved, unwashed self. He had slept on his bed, still in his clothes. He felt stiff, crumpled and dirty. He retrieved his water and washed and shaved.

Suddenly, as he looked at his lathered face in the mirror, he realised he still had not made up his mind.

When he was dressed he went down to breakfast. He was hungry now and soon demolished a bowl of porridge and a pair of kippers. He felt very much better. *Never do battle on an empty stomach*, he thought to himself. The battle was within. The real trouble was that he felt he just did not have the courage. He buttered a slice of toast and took a long drink of his coffee, hot and strong. What had he got to lose? Nothing! What could he gain? Lots! Why did he not go for it? He was afraid! No-one ever accused Robert Henery of being afraid! But it was the truth. They could only see the outside. He was the only one who could see the inside. But they were right. He had a reputation for courage when he was a jockey, and no whimperer had survived that fall. What was he afraid of? Strange places? Foreign people? Different languages? He watched the vortex in his coffee as he stirred it. Going round and round, into the dark abyss. That is what would happen to him, unless he could break away. As he contemplated falling down the ever spinning chasm, he made up his mind.

"I *will!*" he said out loud. "I damn well will!" The other people in the dining room stopped eating as a man, and stared at him. He did not care! He had decided. All those black days were suddenly behind. There was a new world out there waiting to be conquered, and he, by God, was going to conquer it! He felt ten feet tall. All that burden of self doubt and self pity fell off him like a sack of wheat. It was as if the sun had come out inside of him. He went outside. The sun was shining. He could not believe it, after all those grey, wet days when he had felt so depressed. Now the sun was shining. He turned slowly round and felt its warmth through his jacket.

He hailed the first cab.

"Take me to the Count!" he cried dramatically as he jumped in. The cabby whipped up his horse and they joined the throng of traffic. He opened the hatch.

"Where did you say, guv?" He looked down at Robert with a puzzled expression on his face. Robert laughed—and laughed. He had not laughed for days.

"I said take me to the Count!" and he roared with laughter. The cabby looked at him in astonishment.

Aw my Gawd, got a right one 'ere, he said to himself. "That's wot I fought you said, guv; where is this bleedin' Count then, guv?"

Robert was still laughing. "'E 's in the bleedin' Barchester Hotel!" he shouted up in his best cockney accent, "and get a bleedin' move on!"

The cabby looked pained. "How was I supposed to know that, then? There's no need to take the bleedin' Mick."

"I'm very sorry, cabby. It's just that I feel a bit light-headed. I've finally managed to shut a door, you know, that one where all the eebijeebies are, and someone has opened another one for me, the one that leads the way to milk and honey, excitement and adventure!"

"Aw, my Gawd! It's too early in the bleedin' morning for bleedin' nuts." He shut the hatch with a snap.

CHAPTER 4

Robert's feeling of light-headed euphoria continued all the way to the Barchester Hotel. He felt exhilarated by the press of traffic and the throng of horse drawn vehicles. He delighted at the hustle and bustle of it all. He called greetings to people in other vehicles as they became stuck in the inevitable traffic confusion.

At last the cab pulled up outside the Barchester. With a flourish he jumped out, tossing a half sovereign up to the cabby.

"Keep the change," he called flamboyantly as he ran up the steps, the cabby's surprised thanks lost as he flung open the door of the foyer.

He found himself in a very large and ornate room, decorated in vying shades of blue, embellished with much over-ornate gilding. Behind a large mahogany desk an aged receptionist in a military-style uniform regarded him with a supercilious stare. Robert was frantically trying to think of a cutting remark to wipe that impertinent sneer off the man's face, when the Count himself, with a considerable retinue, scuttling along in his billowing wake, swept down the broad stairway that curved majestically round a large bay in the end wall of the room. His heavy green Loden cape swirled about him and his small curly brimmed black Homberg hat sat jauntily on his head. His bright yellow spats winked cheekily from between black patent leather shoes and grey flannel trousers. Robert went over to him.

"Your Excellency, you see, I am here!" he said, with a slight bow and broad smile.

"Here?" the Count looked bemusedly at him. "Vat you vant? Vhy you stop me like this?" He peered at Robert without any sign of recognition. "Who are you? Vat you vant? Out of my vay! I have this train to fetch! Vait, it vill not!"

Robert felt stunned. He couldn't believe what he heard. He could feel the colour draining out of his face. He clenched his hands until the knuckles went white.

"Yesterday, Your Excellency! At the Club! With Lord Shotley!" He prompted desperately. This was a bad dream. Were all his hopes, his new-found interest in life, to be dashed before they had barely taken root? He thought of the huge mental struggle he had fought yesterday and won. Had it all been in vain? The black hole of the abyss loomed large in his mind. He tried again.

"Over lunch, Sir, you offered me a position as your trainer—in Hungary." His confidence waned with every word. His mouth went dry with the effort. The worm of doubt was slowly writhing in his stomach. The Count peered at him more closely.

"Ah, I now see! Herr 'Enery. He who could not make up his mind, the best damn offer he ever had, to accept! He has decided to come, has he? Vell, vith Schmidt you must speak! Come, everyone, or the train it leave vithout us!" With that he flung his cape round his shoulder with an imperious flourish and swept out of the hotel, his retinue flapping in his wake. Robert gaped after him, hopping uncertainly from foot to foot. *What the hell am I supposed to do now?* he thought to himself.

"Herr 'Enery?"

A thin cold voice startled him. He turned. He had been so preoccupied with his panic that he had not noticed the person come down the stairs behind him. He was thin and dark, his black hair smeared flat across his head, with an untidy and irregular parting. He wore an unbrushed black frock coat, his trousers saggy, his boots in need of a polish. *I bet he has got dirty nails*, thought Robert unkindly to himself.

"Herr 'Enery? I am Herr Schmidt. I am Count Ramoskie's private secretary. You vill be kind enough to follow me." With that he turned on his heel and set off up the stairs. Schmidt led the way in silence to a door on the first floor. Inside, the room was furnished like an exaggeratedly plush drawing room. Robert's senses recoiled from a sea of gold scrolls, large cord tassels and heavy fabric. Schmidt seated himself behind a large desk at the side of the room and motioned Robert to take the chair that had been placed in front of it.

"Herr 'Enery, please to be seated."

Robert started at the slight hint of impatience in the voice. As he took the chair, he stared with rising dislike at the thin white face and scraggy neck that protruded out of a greasy collar beneath the lank mass of black oily hair.

"Mr. Schmidt," Robert began uncertainly, "I don't know how much you know, but yesterday…" He was cut off in mid sentence by a raised hand.

"Yes, yes, the Count has told me," Schmidt interrupted testily. "Here are your tickets—you take the train to Paris, you change train to Vienna. You then take the steamer down the Danube to this place." He showed the paper to Robert. "There you must disembark. I vill have a carriage vaiting three days for you. If you do not arrive in that time, it vill return vithout you. You must make your own vay." Robert regarded him uneasily. The man continued: "Your train it is booked for the 23rd. That is in four days time. Overnight to Vienna, one day down the Danube, you stay the night at the landing in the inn. I have the coach there on 26th, it wait for three days. If you no come, it leave." He picked up a folder and held it out to Robert. Robert took it automatically.

"The 23rd? But it's the 19th today! That only gives me four days to pack up my things. Everything, my whole life. I can't do that in four days." He looked aghast and stuck his chin out at the greasy little man. Schmidt's eyes narrowed.

"You vant this job?" He looked coldly at Robert. "You vant this job, you be there."

Robert looked at him with rising impatience and distaste. "But all my things. Furniture, books, clothes. I cannot sort all that out in four days!"

"Vell, Herr 'Enery, if you vant this job, you vill think of something. Now let us consider the small things. You vill train all the Count's horses and have the free hand in all the affairs of the racing. You must enter vot races you think fit and you vill be responsible for all the matters of running the stud. To you vill be the hire and the fire. All you have to do is make sure you vin many races so that ve all make great monies. There is an 'ouse at the stables and there you vill live."

"But money, what do I do for money?"

"We do not talk about money, it is too vulgar."

"Race winners do not grow on trees. I need to know about money. If you are not able to sensibly inform me about this, I will talk to the Count!"

Schmidt's eyes narrowed even further. "Herr 'Enery, there is something that you must understand. The Count, he has the grand ideas. He does not concern himself vith the, how you say, the nitty gritty. He say move that mountain, and it move. I, it is, am the one who make it happen. When it come to moving of the mountain, you come to me! I make myself clear?" Robert felt himself nodding in dumb agreement.

"If you must be so vulgar," continued Schmitt archly, "as to discuss money, then, I suppose that we must. You vill have control of the account of the racing, vich is in a bank in Prague. I vill give you a letter of authorisation." Robert nodded.

"And my remuneration?"

Schmidt looked at him as if he were a toad that had just crawled out from under a stone.

Robert returned his stare, glower for glower. "It is just that it is so important that there is no misunderstanding."

Schmidt remained silent for a while and then, as if being asked to sign his life away, he wrote on a piece of paper, with a rasping steel pen and handed it to Robert. Robert took the proffered sheet and slowly unfolded it.

"But this is in Marks. How much is that in real money?" Robert immediately realised he had made a bad mistake. Schmidt positively bristled with indignation.

"You vill find that the Marks is very much real money. You vill have to get used to it if you are going to be living in the Empire." He snatched the paper fiercely from Robert's hand. Taking up the steel pen, he scrawled a figure on it with an angry scratch. He thrust it back at him. Robert hastily looked at the figure. It was considerably more than he was being offered at the moment and he tried to keep the look of pleasant surprise out of his face. Schmidt mistook his hesitation.

"You think you worth more than thiss?" he demanded angrily, with a hiss. Robert was too surprised to reply.

"You Eengleesh, all you think of is money!" He snatched the paper back from Robert again, and furiously scratched again and thrust it back. Robert's astonishment was mounting. He slowly read the poor hand. An allowance for living expenses doubled the figure. Robert was not an avaricious person. Money did not worry him. Easy come, easy go. Even as a lad, his money was no sooner paid than he had spent it. But now he suddenly perceived an opportunity to put one over on this arrogant unpleasant man, to whom he had taken an instant dislike. He looked at the paper in silence and slowly did his best imitation of Lord Shotley's raised eyebrow. Slowly and quietly he drew in his breath between his teeth in a gentle but prolonged hiss. He studied the paper in silence and waited and waited. At last Schmitt could stand it no longer. He snatched the paper again, his neck turning bright red with a sudden flush of anger.

"Mein Gott, you Eengleesh! You drive a bargain hard—we are the Master Race and we are alvays giving. You, you Eengleesh, you alvays take." He scrawled on the paper at some length and handed it back with an ill-tempered flourish. Robert carefully took it up, trying desperately not to let his hand shake. Horses and staff for his personal use. Free firewood from the estate and free milk and butter from the dairy. House and domestic staff at no charge. Free removal expenses had been added in Schmidt's angry scrawl.

Who was taking and who was having to give? he smiled to himself, keeping his face impassive. Could he try again? What more might the greasy little man offer? How far could the Master Race be pushed? Schmidt was fiddling with his pen in rising impatience. Robert decided he had pushed his luck far enough. He permitted himself a slight smile.

"You have omitted to sign it." He smiled at Schmidt as he handed the paper back. Schmidt looked at him with considerable disdain.

"In my country, Herr 'Enery, the vord of a gentleman it is enough."

"In my country, too," said Robert, the smile gone. He paused. "Please sign it."

Schmidt went white with anger at the implied insult. Some seconds passed before he had composed himself enough to sign the paper and hand it back to Robert, who folded it and put it in the inside pocket of his coat.

"I am not free to start now, because I am still beholden to Lord Shotley. I cannot just walk out at a minute's notice, on your say so."

"Herr 'Enery, it is not on my say so. Vhen I say, it is the Count who speaks; this you need to understand from the beginning. Vhen the Count he say, he expect that things happen. You are vell not to make the enemy of me. The Count he only hear vot I tell him and you only hear vot I tell you. I make myself clear?" Robert nodded his understanding, but thought privately, *We'll see about that.* Schmidt permitted himself a smile. With the air of one trumping a winning hand, he placed a letter on the table in front of Robert.

Robert picked it up. It was from Lord Shotley. He quickly read it.

ᐁ

It is with great sorrow that I allow Henery to leave my employ. He has worked hard for me. His efforts have been crowned with the success that he deserves and I seek. However his personal circumstances are such that, to our mutual regret, it is no longer possible for him to stay in his present position. I have therefore no reasonable alternative, but to let him leave my employ as soon as he can conveniently find another and suitable situation. I can only express my continued support and admiration for all that he has achieved whilst he has been with me and wish him well in his future endeavours, however soon they may come about...

Robert could not read the rest of the letter. Good old Honest Ned, loyal to the end.

"These personal circumstances? We should perhaps know about them?" simpered Schmidt.

Robert started. The whole episode of the last months instantly flashed through his mind.

"No, it is nothing to do with you at all. It was a personal domestic matter that caused considerable local feeling. From which I need to get away." Schmidt looked at him suspiciously for a minute, then a lewd grin slowly spread across his pallid features.

"Could it be that the Proper Meester 'Enery has the affair of the heart vith some lady unsuitable? The maid, perhaps, the scullion?" He noticed the scowl on Robert's face, but caught up in his own imagination, he continued: "Perhaps the daughter of the priest? A good scandal, no? Much better in our country, our priests do not marry. They have no daughters, no scandals." He shrugged his shoulders and continued magnanimously: "We are men of the vorld. We understand these things, even if narrow-minded village in Eengland does not. Their loss, it is the Count's gain." He smiled patronisingly. Robert's anger had been mounting as he expounded his ridiculous fantasy. His indignation bristled to boiling point. He was on the point of telling this smarmy and insignificant little man exactly what he could do with his lewd innuendoes, but he relaxed. *What the heck.* This was something they could understand, the idea was straightforward and uncomplicated. If he told them what had really happened, it would take a deal more patience and explanation than he was prepared to expend at the moment. He shrugged his shoulders and remained silent. If the man was so stupid that he would rather believe his own fantasies than listen to the real answer, let him. Robert was content to let him think what he liked; besides, he had more urgent problems to worry about. If Honest Ned was prepared to let him go at a moment's notice, then there was nothing that would prevent his departure in four days. He had somehow to contrive to have all his affairs tied up by then, his furniture and possessions packed and his house emptied before he went. His house went with the job. He was bound to hand it over, empty and clean when the job ended. He would have to dismiss his housekeeper and organise the smooth handover of the Stud to his assistant, for safe keeping until his successor could be appointed. Even as these ideas were going through his head, he could feel the adrenaline begin to course through his veins. He could feel excitement begin to rise in him, much as he remembered he had felt when he had been lining up for a race, years ago. Suddenly he was impatient to be away. He wanted to get on with all the things that needed his urgent attention. Decisively, he stood up. He felt that if he was to take the upper hand with this unpleasant little man, now was the time. Abruptly leaning over the desk so that he looked down on the secretary, he proffered his hand.

"Thank you, Mr Schmidt. You have made everything very clear. It all seems to be satisfactory." He collected the ticket and papers off the desk. "I will be in the inn at the landing on the 26th—God willing." Schmitt jumped to his feet and, in a fluster, turned to Robert and took his hand in a limp and brief shake.

"I vill see you ven you reach the schloss. Good day, Herr 'Enery." He hastened to open the door and show him out.

Robert went immediately to the Bank. He had some money changed into Marks. He was going to ask them to transfer his account to a bank in Hungary, but had, with some embarrassment, to admit that he did not know which would be the most convenient town. The matter would have to be left until he wrote with further instructions when he had settled into his new home. That raised another point. What was his new home to be like? Schmitt had said there was a house available, but had given no indication of what it might be like. Would he need to take furniture?

As he walked, he considered what he should do. The obvious thing, given the shortage of time and the uncertainty of the situation, was to take his personal effects in a trunk or two. He should put his furniture in store until he knew what he wanted and could decide what to do with it. Perhaps the best thing to do was to put the whole lot in auction and start again. He would not have too much time to worry about furniture—he would be too busy with the affairs of the stud. Perhaps that was the best idea. The idea of packing all his furniture and shipping it to darkest Central Europe filled him with dismay. The idea of doing anything about it in the short time he had left, seemed impossible.

He walked to Lord Shotley's club. Presently he was shown into the familiar room. Lord Shotley rose from his chair to greet him.

"Robert, how are you?" he said warmly as he took his hand and managed dextrously to usher him into a chair by the fire. He pressed into his hand a large glass of Madeira. "How did you get on? What have you decided?" Robert shortly told him all that had transpired both with his encounter with the Count and with Schmidt. Lord Shotley listened to the end.

"Typical," he said when Robert had reached the end of his story. "Ramoskie is a bit of a martinet. He is mad as a hatter. You will find working for him nothing if not invigorating. He is one of those people who's convinced he's always right, and when he wants something done, expects everyone to jump. Unfortunately his judgement is not as reliable as his faith in it. You will have to use all the tact you can muster to deal with him. His Secretary, Schmidt—I can't like him. It would be like forming an affection for an adder. I would not trust him with the takings from a village fete. He is very efficient. He feels he has a mission to realise the least of the Count's fantastic whims. Watch out for him. He's completely ruthless, without a single shred of compassion. If he feels the Count wants something done, he'll let nothing stand in his way until it's achieved. Be careful how you deal with him. He will be a powerful ally but a very dangerous adversary. Well, it all sounds most exciting, but you have omitted to say whether you will accept the position and when you will start."

Lord Shotley refilled his glass and looked at him with an inquiring expression.

Robert blenched. Up to now, events had moved so fast that he had not really thought too deeply, but now the time had come. This was the point of no return. He was going to have to look his employer in the eye and say 'Yes, I am going to go.' He looked with dismay at the enormous step he was about to take. This was his Beecher's Brook. This was his gigantic leap into the unknown. He looked at the fence, fast approaching, and he quailed. Lord Shotley noticed his hesitation and quickly caught his mood.

"Not having second thoughts are you, Robert?" he asked quietly. Robert swallowed hard.

"He wants me to leave in four days!" His throat felt dry and he had to force the voice out of himself. Lord Shotley could not disguise his shock.

"Four days! He expects you to be packed up and ready in four days?"

"Yes, Sir" nodded Robert glumly.

"What did you say to him?"

"Well, it was Schmidt who told me this. I said I had to ask you. He then produced a letter from you saying that you would release me to go whenever I was needed—sir" he added as an afterthought.

"But I mean, four days. That is a totally unreasonable demand. How on earth does he think that you can be ready to leave in four days?"

"I suppose that it is the efficient Mr. Schmidt who manages to bully everyone to make his ridiculous ideas happen."

"Yes. You look out for that one. If the Count wants it, he will make it happen!"

"But, sir, I could not possibly leave you at four days' notice."

"Robert, if you were ill, we would have to cope. If you have done your job properly, the stud should be able to carry on like clockwork without you! At the moment there is nothing serious coming on—in fact there is plenty of time to find a replacement for you before our honour is really at stake. If you want to take this position, if you feel you can put up with the Count and with Schmidt, then take it, dear boy; all I can do is to wish you the very best of luck." Robert stared into the fire for what seemed like an age. This was it. This was the moment that fate had decreed he would turn over a new page, that blank page, bare and clean, upon which the future in all its bald starkness would be written.

"Well, sir," he hesitated, unwilling even at this late stage to take that step onto the virgin ice, that might see him gliding majestically forward, or might break under his faltering weight and precipitate him, floundering, into the icy, muddy depths. "If you are certain that I will not be letting you down…"

"Of course not," interjected Lord Shotley, "this seems such a perfect solution…"

Robert looked at him for a minute. "Well, in that case, sir, the answer is…" He hesitated yet again. He twirled his glass nervously in his hand. His lips felt dry, his throat parched. The atmosphere in the room was tense and stifling. "Yes…yes, I think I would like the challenge." Lord Shotley let out a hiss of air like a steam train halting at the buffers. The atmosphere in the room dissipated like mist in the morning sun.

"My God!" gasped Lord Shotley, reaching for the Madeira bottle, "I thought you were going to fall at the last fence." He poured himself a generous glassful and recharged Robert's glass. "I am so pleased. I cannot tell you how pleased I am. This is a wonderful chance for you to get away from this unhappy business, to start again where you are not known. You've got a clean slate. You have a real chance to make a name for yourself. You are young yet, who knows? You may find someone else and get married again. Who knows? Lillian may return. If she does, she is bound to come to me and I can direct her to you." A cloud of reality covered Robert. Unconsciously he had given up any chance of seeing her again, but here suddenly was the possibility, rearing up before him, that she might return. He was shocked to confront these thoughts. After all the anguish he had endured, would he welcome her back or would he tell her to go to hell? His life had been ruined. He had had to give up all he had worked for, to leave house and home, to start up in some foreign place where he did not even speak the language. What would he say to her? How would he react? Suppose he did meet and fall in love with someone else, what then? He was already married to Lillian. He could not enter into a bigamous relationship with someone else!

"But, sir, I am already married, I could not marry anyone else." Lord Shotley frowned.

"Yes. That is a difficult one. You could hardly greet her on the doorstep and say 'Hello, old girl, fancy seeing you again after all this time. Come on in and meet my new wife. Bit difficult, what!" He chuckled at the ridiculousness of the situation, but quickly resumed a serious expression when he saw Robert was definitely not amused.

"I'm sorry, old boy; I did not mean to have a cheap laugh at your expense. Actually, I have made a few enquiries. I gather that if she has not appeared after seven years, she can be declared legally dead. You would then be free to marry again, should you so wish." He noticed the pained expression on Robert's face. "I am sorry, my dear fellow, I did not mean to hurt you, but it is as well to face the facts." Robert had gone quite white. He had just not thought that far ahead.

"I am sorry, sir. That is all right. I just had not thought that far. I had just assumed that one day she would come walking in the door again and we would pick up the pieces again…" He petered out. Lord Shotley could see how distressed he had become.

"I am terribly sorry, old chap. I did not mean to open old wounds. But when you get to the fence, you have got to jump it. You cannot sit and look at it."

"No, sir. No, you are right, of course. It is just that…" He relapsed into silence and they both sat staring into the fire for a while.

"Here, old boy, let me fill you glass. When are you thinking of leaving?" Robert stared into the fire for a second or two longer. "Schmidt has given me tickets for the 23rd."

"My God! Robert, that's three days, not four. Can you get packed up and organised in time?"

"No, sir, counting today, it is four. I think that I will put all my furniture in an auction. They are mostly things that Lillian and I have collected together. Somehow, I do not think that I want them round me any more. If you agree, I will have everything moved out into the barn. It can be collected and sent to auction as soon as I can arrange it. I will attend to all that tomorrow. At least then the house will be empty, ready for my successor. Have you anyone else in mind?"

Lord Shotley looked slightly embarrassed. "Well, actually, I have taken the liberty of making a few soundings, depending of course on your decision," he added hastily. "I think that I have someone lined up to take over fairly quickly, so that will be fine. He will be able to move in as soon as he can. That will be very suitable."

"Might I ask who you have in mind, M'lord?"

"Well, if you don't mind, Robert, I would rather not say at this moment, many a slip 'twixt cup and lip…"

Robert nodded. He would not have said himself, in the same situation. He felt a great relief. He had got over the last hurdle safely, admittedly with Honest Ned's help, but thanks to him, he was clear. He could leave with a clear conscience. There was nothing more he could say. All he had to do was to take his leave of Lord Shotley and walk out of the door to prepare to start a new life. He stood up, but suddenly it was not so easy. A lump came into his throat. Tears welled up in his eyes. If it had not been for Lord Shotley he would be dead. He would not have had the chances that had come his way. He would not have gained a firm and reliable friend and ally. Lord Shotley, too, stood up. He took his proffered hand. Spontaneously the two men embraced.

"I cannot thank you enough for all you have done for me M'lord," Robert managed to blurt out between sniffs.

"Rubbish, man. Look what you have been able to do for me. I do not think that anyone else could have brought my horses up to the standard that they are now."

Robert managed to disentangle himself. He blew his nose noisily on a large handkerchief, managing at the same time to wipe his eyes.

"Well, good luck, Robert. I shall not see you again before you leave. Take care of yourself. Remember your friend, here in England." Robert's eyes were filled with tears.

"Good-bye, My Lord. Thank you again. Good luck to you, too, sir." They shook hands, then he abruptly turned on his heel and walked out into the night without looking back.

CHAPTER 5

On the train home he was running through his mind what had to be done in the next few days. He would have to get his Head Lad and his Assistant together in the morning. They would have to spend the greater part of the day organising the affairs of the stud before he could begin to think about his own things.

What should he do about his Housekeeper? He pondered the matter for a while. Finally, he decided that he should offer her a month's wages and suggest that she stay in the house until his successor arrived.

What would she do about furniture? That reminded him. He must see the auctioneers about the sale of his things. He must get some of the lads to help carry everything into the barn.

He pulled out his notebook and started to jot down a list of things he needed to remember. If he moved all his furniture out, what was the House-keeper going to do? She could not remain in an empty house with no furni-ture. She had her own things in her room, but apart from that everything in the house belonged to him. He would have to talk to her. Perhaps he could put a few things, a chair, a table, a lamp and so on into the study. She could use that as her sitting room for the time being. She could have it as a 'thank you' present. It would, after all, fetch precious little in auction.

It was late by the time the train had dropped him at the station and he had walked to the Kings Head. It took some time to rouse the Ostler and have his horse harnessed into his gig. It was moonlight when he finally began the five mile drive back to the stud. The countryside was bathed in an unearthly blue light. The trees threw their gaunt shadows across the road. The countryside was displayed all around him in its stark and simple beauty. At the top of the hill, he reigned in his horse and sat and looked. Slowly tears filled his eyes. In the distance on the other side of the valley he could see his house, the single lamp burning in the hall, waiting his return. This was his place. This part of the country was where he had put down his roots. The idea of packing up and leaving never to come back, suddenly seemed too awful to contemplate. As he sat and brooded, he came as near as he ever had to changing his mind.

Suddenly, on some urgent nocturnal quest of its own, a large hare sprang from the gateway at the side of the road. Startled by the apparition of the gig standing there, it dashed across the silvery road with a spurt of scattered gravel and a flash of its white tail. His horse, equally startled, shied a few steps sideways. Robert was jerked from his reverie.

Quickly he had the horse under control and was on his way again. No, the die was cast. There was no turning back now. In three days time he was gong to leave this beautiful place, most probably for ever. All he would have would be the treasured memories of the good times and some horrible ghosts to haunt him when the nights were long and dark and his spirits were low.

The next three days passed in a whirl of activity and feverish preparation. There seemed no way that he could be ready in time, but somehow on the evening of the third day he stood by his carriage, three enormous trunks and some stout wooden boxes packed on to the yard cart. All the staff were gathered round. Robert felt that a speech was required. He walked round the group, shaking hands as he went. He climbed on to the step of the carriage and turned to face them all.

"I cannot thank you enough," he began, but he could not continue; a lump welled up in his throat and hot tears scalded his eyes. He tried again. "Your support and help has meant so much…" Again he was forced to stop. He drew a large handkerchief from his pocket and tried to hide his emotion with a loud and prolonged blow. He was lost for words. He did not know what to say.

"Thank you all," he managed to force out, his voice sounding like the steam escaping from a kettle on the fire. "Thank you all. Good luck. God bless you all." He swung himself inside and slammed the door. The coachman whipped up the horses and the little cavalcade swung out of the yard.

Robert's return journey to London and his arrival at the small brown hotel had none of the air of the start of a great new adventure. He felt totally depressed. The situation, however fortuitous it may be, was being forced on him. It was not one of his choosing. He had had to leave behind that which he loved the most. In a week or two he would have a new string of horses to worry about.

He spent the rest of the noisy night worrying about his new charges. What would they be like? Would he have any chance of the success that everyone seemed to be expecting? What were the stable lads like? What were the stables and gallops like? How would people take to him? How would he cope with the language problem? Would there be problems with vets? Feed? Jockeys? Officials? Rivals? Nobblers? Yes, he had no doubt he would be the Aunt Sally when it came to nobbling. How would he get on with the Count and Schmidt? What would it be like living there? His head streamed with questions. A new chain of thought started up with every train that chuffed and clanked in the station over the road from his Hotel. He tossed and turned and groaned the night away. It seemed no time at all before the cheerful voice was calling him from outside the door, that his water was ready for him. He sat up instantly, and swinging his legs out of bed, with his feet on the bare boards, sat shivering in the cold dawn light, his head in his hands. God, he felt awful. His eyes felt as if they were full of hot cinders. His head swam with a persistent blinding ache that all but shut his left eye.

"Oh, it's not fair!" he groaned to himself.

By the time he had washed and shaved in the tepid water he felt, though slightly fresher, no better. He packed his case and went down the narrow staircase feeling as if he had just been spawned from the inside of a threshing machine. He automatically walked into the dining room. It was in darkness. There was no one there. He shrank from the thought. He simply could not face breakfast. He knocked on the hatch. Presently it opened with a wheezy rattle.

"Oh, hello. Er, er, I mean, good morning, I won't have any breakfast today thank you. Let me pay for the night and I will be on my way."

"But Mr. Henery, you can't possibly go out at half past six in the morning without any breakfast."

"No, thank you, no really, I don't want anything."

"You must have something. How would it be if I made you a nice pot of tea and a round of hot toast? Your poor stomach, you could not be so unkind as to make it to go out in the cold morning air with nothing to sustain it!"

Robert realised that it would be easier to agree than to resist.

"Well, yes, perhaps a pot of tea would be nice. Thank you very much. I'll sit in the dining room, shall I?" Robert waited in the dark room. Presently the little lady scuttled in with the tea and toast and a smoky oil lamp on a tray.

"Thank you so much," said Robert, anxious only to be on his way. "You are too kind. You have looked after me with every consideration, I am extremely grateful."

"Fie on you, Mr. Henery, anyone might think that you are leaving us."

"Well, yes. I am. I am going now to catch the boat train at Victoria Station this morning. I shall not be coming back."

"Not come back? Not never?" She clutched her tray to her chest in shock.

"No. Not ever. Well, not until I retire. Well, who knows, not for a long time anyway."

"Oh, Mr. Henery, I'll be really sad to see you go. You have been one of our regular gentlemen. I will get your reckoning and I'll tell the others, I am sure that they would like to say goodbye to you." With that she went. Robert resigned himself to an embarrassing round of handshakes, half-mumbled thanks and good wishes. Presently the staff came trooping in. He shook hands and thanked them, one by one. Last of all, the little lady brought in a cracked plate bearing a tatty scrap of paper—his account for the stay. Robert thanked them all. He was glad to be able to finish his tea and toast in peace.

Presently with his coat thrown over his shoulder and his case in his hand, he shut the faded door firmly behind him for the last time. He stood alone in the street. At last, that final gesture, that firm shutting of the door was the simple act that closed what had been a long and harrowing chapter in his life. Suddenly that chapter was ended. Everything that had gone before was now in the past. He was tempted to open the door and see if it would all be brought into the present again, but did not. He hailed a cab and was soon on his way to Victoria Station.

The station was a bustle of people arriving and departing, waiting and meeting. His mood was soon captured by the atmosphere of subdued excitement. Everywhere hawkers and vendors called their wares, porters shouted for custom and newsboys, shrilly proclaimed their headlines. Robert bought a bag of pieces of barley sugar, which he dropped in his pocket and a small nosegay of violets, which he carefully threaded into his buttonhole. He felt quite cheered. This simple gesture awoke in him a touch of excitement. The bustling mood was infectious. He felt his step quicken and his pulse rate increase. He should first go to inquire that his luggage had arrived and was being placed on the train. Then he ought to find the time that his train departed.

There were all sorts of people standing around, or sitting on their luggage, all studiously ignoring each other, in the way that those who are travelling do when they are expecting to be met by someone else. He did not want to become part of that disinterested-looking gathering, so he walked slowly round the group, stopping to purchase a newspaper. A train that was standing just the other side of the barrier let out a Titanic cacophony of barking, hissing smoke and hot steam. Everyone was engulfed in the swirling clouds and the roar and hiss of the engine. Gradually the noise subsided. The choking clouds dispersed.

Robert, although he would not admit it, was feeling very apprehensive about the whole journey. He was already brewing up a small panic in case his luggage should be mislaid, or worse still, he should get on to the wrong train and find himself in Barnstable or somewhere else instead of Dover. Luckily Robert spied the conveniences. The tea and toast at the Hotel was already beginning to weigh noticeably heavy. If he had not seen the sign, he would have jumped on to the train and felt uncomfortable for the rest of the journey. As he came out, he was feeling decidedly more cheerful. A grubby face thrust up at him.

"Shoe shine, Guv?" Robert looked at the urchin and then at his shoes. He hated having dirty shoes. Why not? When the boy had finished, he gave him a shilling.

He discovered from where his train departed and, walking to the barrier, he presented his ticket. He always felt like a criminal at a ticket barrier. He was sure that his ticket would be rejected and he would be humiliated in front of everyone else. The inspector checked though the sheets.

"All seems in order, Sir. Change trains in Paris, Sir. Have a good journey, Sir. 'Ope you don't find too much trouble, when you gets there, Sir. Your carriage is the fifth one along, Sir.—Yes Sir," he replied to Robert's anxious enquiry, "your luggage has come, Sir. It has been put in the guard's van." He waved his clipboard towards the back of the train where a pile of luggage could be seen, being loaded on by some porters.

Robert walked down the platform to his carriage. He opened the door and climbed in. This was a much smarter train than he was used to on his more rural line. It still had the same smell, damp soot and warm steam, but the upholstery was plush, the trim elegant, the mahogany woodwork deeply hued and well-polished. The floor was cleanly swept. The antimacassars were newly white, freshly laundered. He settled himself into his seat. Exactly on time the guard's whistle blew. The train slowly moved out of the station.

Robert sat looking out of the window as London's southern suburbs slowly slid past. *Well*, he thought, *this is it. I am finally on my way*. So much had happened over the last few weeks that it seemed incredible that he was finally actually on his way. It did not seem possible that a life could take such a change so suddenly…

"Breakfast, Sir?" A cheerful steward in a white jacket thrust his head in the compartment. "The Restaurant Car is that way, Sir." He pointed and moved on. Robert could hear him at the next compartment. He must get bored doing that all down the train. Robert considered the idea. It seemed a good one. The more he thought about it, the hungrier he felt. He always felt hungry when he was travelling. It was a very good idea. The Rail was renowned for its breakfast. He jumped up and followed the direction of the steward's pointed finger along the gently swaying corridor. He was soon seated at a table, a clean white cloth and Railway china clinking rhythmically to the beat of the wheels.

Robert picked up the menu. He practically drooled as the scent of fried bacon wafted through the car from the galley.

"Yes Sir, what can I get you?" The steward hovered before him.

He ordered a bowl of porridge, a pair of kippers, followed by fried eggs and bacon with tomato, kidneys and a sausage and some toast and marmalade. He also ordered two pots of coffee. Robert thought of the countless frosty dawns when as a lad he had galloped over the heath, his breath and the breath and steam of the horses hanging in a little vapour trail behind him. He recalled, so vividly that the saliva swam in his mouth, the great bowls of steaming porridge and the mountains of fried bacon, ready for them in the Yard tack room when they returned from their morning exercise.

He had always started the day with a good breakfast, especially when he had been out and going for three or four hours before getting some. That was when it is a feast for the Gods. Nothing like a good gallop in the frosty dawn to give you a good appetite.

"Yes Sir, having a last English breakfast, are we Sir?" said the Steward, noting it all down. "When you lands on the Continent, it is all Croissants, so they tell me."

"Croissant? What are they?"

"Sir? You have never had a croissant?"

Robert nodded negatively.

"Croissant, Sir, served hot, with apricot jam and hot coffee make a breakfast conceived in heaven, so I have been led to believe."

Robert looked at him with disbelief. "Well, each to his own. That does not sound like my idea of a perfect breakfast. You keep you croissants, I will stick with my eggs and bacon!"

"I fear not, Sir."

Robert raised a quizzical eyebrow.

"I am afraid, Sir, that it is almost universal custom, Sir, once you cross the Channel, Sir. I am afraid that you will have to get used to croissants, Sir."

"If I cannot get a decent breakfast, I shall get on the first train back to London when we reach Dover. If I cannot get a civilised breakfast, I'm not going."

"Come, Sir, it is very civilised and indeed very good. If I might venture to suggest, Sir, there are some who might regard your breakfast as positively barbaric. They might equate the consumption of such, if I might make so bold, a gruesome selection of food at this early hour of the day, as being a habit expected only from Atilla the Hun."

Robert looked at him in astonishment. "No one can begin a hard day without a good breakfast."

The waiter shut his notebook with a snap. He presently returned with the toast, the porridge and the coffee. Robert sprinkled his porridge with a little salt and drowned it in a sea of creamy milk. Sinking the now floating island with a mound of white sugar, he ate it with relish. When Robert's kippers arrived, they were steaming hot and firm, though tender. Robert savoured their aroma before consigning them, with considerable satisfaction, to join the porridge. Presently his eggs and bacon were brought, the eggs with their yolk yellow and soft; the bacon filling the whole carriage with its aroma, was fried to perfection, just turning crispy round the edges. This consumed, Robert fell upon the toast and marmalade and his second pot of coffee with the satisfaction of knowing that whatever else happened, his last breakfast in England was going to be truly memorable.

All the time that he was eating the Kent countryside had been slowly rolling past outside the window. When he finally finished his toast and poured out his last cup of coffee, he wiped his mouth with his napkin and sat back in his chair.

"I hope your breakfast was to your satisfaction, Sir?" The steward deftly collected up his plates.

"Yes thank you, I feel a new man. I haven't had a breakfast like that for months. There is nothing like a good meal to make you feel in tune with the world." Perhaps *that is what is wrong*, he mused to himself. *Perhaps that is why I have been such a miserable devil lately. I haven't been eating properly.*

He sat watching the country unfolding as the train sped south.

"It is very beautiful. I am going to Hungary."

"Yes, Sir, very green, very fertile looking, prosperous."

"Do you know what is it like in Hungary?"

"Well, Sir, I do not know, really. I have never been that far East, but I believe that it is mountainous."

"Oh, I always thought that Hungary was flat. A big plain, steppes and all that."

"Yes, Sir, that is correct, in the main, so I believe, but up to the North, it is in the foothills of the Carpathian mountains, but what it is like, I cannot say, Sir, I have never been there. Look, Sir, I can see the sea!"

They both looked out of the window as the Channel came into view. The train presently pulled into the harbour, right alongside the steamer. Robert hurried back to his compartment. He collected his hand luggage and joined the other passengers walking through the Customs and Excise Offices, on their way to board the ship. They waited in a rather grubby lounge whilst the passengers were ushered one by one through the Office where their papers were inspected. After their passports were stamped, they were ushered straight onto the boat. He could see the luggage from the train was being unloaded onto trolleys and wheeled through the Customs shed. He had to assume that it would be safely stowed in the hold. He enquired anxiously about it and was assured that he need not worry. It would be safely conveyed and would arrive with him in Paris.

As soon as he was on board the ferry, Robert set out on a tour of inspection of the boat. He had never been on a vessel of this size before. He was interested in every detail. The polished brass and the salt-stained woodwork. The ropes and chains and all the paraphernalia of combating the wiles of an unpredictable sea, all had a fascination for him. The great paddle wheels, either side, the masts and flags, all added a mysterious glamour.

The saloon was quite small, furnished with deep buttoned leather seats and mahogany wood. There was considerable bustle as passengers secured for themselves some sheltered or favoured place to sit. Robert stayed on deck, anxious not to miss any detail of their departure. They were five minutes late in leaving but suddenly the horn let out a strident mournful wail, which made everyone jump and the children on board shriek with terror. As the lines were cast off the great wheels churned in the water. The boat slowly made its way across the harbour and out into the sea. As they left the harbour, they met a strong cross stream. The boat reared and plunged in a most alarming fashion, but it soon settled down as it met the open sea.

Finally he was on his way!"

CHAPTER 6

The little steamer travelled up the coast for some distance before cutting through the gap in the Goodwin Sands, made too grisly obvious by the gaunt masts of wrecked ships sticking up through the brown surge that washed round them. It was a grey day. The sea churning over the shallow sands was a dirty yellow. The muddy spume blew in frothy bubbles in the chill wind that was blowing with some purpose up the Channel. Robert wrapped his coat tightly round him. He stood by the stern rail, watching the cliffs of Dover gradually fade into the mist, their whiteness glowing through the murk long after the port had become invisible in the gloom.

Robert felt the cold edge of the wind blowing through him, but he was determined to stay at the rail at least until the last loom of England faded from sight. Overhead the seagulls wheeled in the turbulence of the steamer with hardly a flicker of either wing. Robert watched for a long time, fascinated by their ability seemingly to hang in the air without any obviously effort, yet maintain their station just behind the boat. They floated there so gracefully, so effortlessly, as if drawn along by some invisible thread. Some of them were so close that he could almost touch them. He looked at the fragile beauty of their tiny feathers, each flattened to make the perfect aerodynamic shape. They seemed so smooth it was almost impossible to tell one feather from the next. He gazed in wonder into their liquid eyes staring fearlessly into his.

He looked back towards England and saw that it had disappeared into the mist. He had been so intent on watching the gulls, he had not noticed it had gone. All at once he felt vulnerable, very alone, cut off. Who knew what was going to be in store for him? He might die in some foreign place never to see England again. He stood silent for some long while. That was a serious thought. He might never return to his home, ever! He brooded this possibility for some while. That was not very good. In everything that had happened up to now, he had never come to the point when he might go never to return!

He suddenly felt very fragile and mortal.

"What on earth am I doing?" he demanded angrily, out loud, to the seagulls. They only shrieked in reply, their strange musical, yet raucous cries snatched away on the wind. Embarrassed, he hastily looked round, in case anyone else had heard him, but there was no one in sight. Everyone else had long since sought refuge from the cruel wind in the small cabins. He shivered violently. Noticing the flags of the little vessel standing out stiffly in the wind, he realised how cold he had become. He turned and sought the shelter of the cabin. It was only when he started to walk that he realised how much the boat was pitching. He reached the cabin in an involuntary staggering run.

He entered the saloon, shutting the door with some difficulty against the wind. The hot stuffy atmosphere hit him like a blast from an oven. All round there were people sitting huddled together with that pale sweaty look that betokened a determination not to be seasick. In the middle of it all there sat at a swaying table a small girl of about eight years old, who had before her on a plate, a large creamy confection which she was eating with gusto and an enthusiasm that made him feel queasy just to watch.

He found the steamy heat of the enclosed, crowded cabin oppressive; if he stayed there any longer he might regret the breakfast he had so recently enjoyed.

He went out onto the cold windy deck again, shutting, with some difficulty, the door behind him. The wind felt decidedly bitter after the fug of the cabin. Leaning on its icy blast, wrapping his coat round him as best he could, he decided that staying outside was preferable to the hot unpleasant cabin. He walked round the deck, seeking a sheltered spot where he could enjoy watching the many other boats that dotted the horizon. When he got to the bow, he paused, standing like some gaunt figurehead, gazing ahead with a fixed earnestness. The cold wind made the tears stream down his face. He hastily wiped them away with the back of his hand.

He could just make out a thin narrow line of coast, low and grey on the distant horizon. That was a bit of a letdown after the towering cliffs of Dover that had so recently disappeared in the gloom astern. He had to smile to himself at the vision of himself standing sadly in the stern watching England disappear into the murk, whilst now he stood straining his eyes, his heart too full to speak, to catch a glimpse of this low coastline. This small stretch of water was

half a world wide. Once it is crossed, huge continents were there to be travelled, country upon country spread out to explore. It was this small stretch of
sea that divided the English from most of the rest of the world! He was surprised by the thought. He had met many foreign people in his dealings with
racing, but to him they were all vaguely foreigners who lived the other side of
the Channel. He had never though of them as being denizens of 'half of the
world'. He could not imagine half the world spread out before him. Somehow,
the idea was too big to encompass. That was a pretty terrifying notion. Half the
world spread out for him to explore. It made his little incursion seem trivial.

He stood watching the coast come closer. He was amazed by the amount of
shipping to be seen. Everywhere he looked, there were sails and smoky steam-
ers ploughing their way through the Channel.

Robert could just make out the mole that marked the entrance to the harbour. He was eager to see the ship enter the port and to watch the business of
docking. He had never had anything to do with boats. He had been surprised
by the seemingly casual attitude of the crew when they had embarked. There
seemed to be no shouting or confusion; the whole business of getting under
way and leaving the harbour had been conducted with a silent familiar ease
which had surprised him.

The boat entered the harbour and was secured with several ropes without,
as far as he could observe, any instructions being given at all. The blue clad
workers on the dock received the tossed ropes without a word and dropped the
eyes over the bollards on the dock. The gangplank was lowered and people
were already going ashore, before, it seemed, the boat had even stopped.

A train was drawn up on the quayside the other side of the small Customs
building. People who had passed through were already climbing into their
seats. Robert was surprised to see there was no elevated platform, as in
England. Everyone, even the ladies, had to climb up the steps to board the
train.

He felt a little cheated. He had not really known what to expect, but this
didn't look a bit foreign. It almost looked the same as the dock in England. *Perhaps we have just gone round in a circle and we are back in Dover again,* he
mused.

He could already see the luggage sliding down the conveyor and being
loaded on to the train.

He quickly joined the rest of the passengers. He was suddenly beginning to
feel apprehensive. In the Customs post, where the inspection of their papers

was almost casual, the officer stamped them with a big rubber stamp and, muttering something in French, ushered the passengers through.

What did he say? wondered Robert, when he had recovered from the overpowering smell of garlic and pungent tobacco that had assailed them in the Customs Office. He walked down the station. He selected an empty compartment, keenly watching the other people that he saw. He noticed they all seemed to talk volubly. They all seemed to be smoking the most foul-smelling cigarettes. The pungent smell of the tobacco was noticeable even over the smell of the engines.

He climbed up into his compartment. He noticed at once the all-pervading smell of the French tobacco in the carriage. The seats were well-sprung and comfortable. It was certainly a considerable improvement on the train at home.

The train began to move imperceptibly and presently they were making a good time through open farmland. Robert was determined not to miss anything! He sat by the window, watching, fascinated, as the countryside went by. The farm houses for the most part were painted white. The fields seemed to be fairly small with high straggly hedges. With the few small cattle, there were sheep, pigs and goats. Poultry and duck and geese seemed to roam about anywhere. The cattle seemed to be a mixture, though mostly white or mottled grey in colour. There were also some draught horses that looked like grey Percherons. There seemed to be a lot of people working their small plots. He saw one man ploughing with a pair of enormous white bullocks. There were many children about, either herding geese or goats and sheep, or just playing. They seemed to be a fairly ragged bunch. Most were without shoes.

Robert enjoyed watching the flat landscape going past. He was pleased at the brief glimpses of French rural life that unfolded as they sped through. A few people rested on their hoes, or looked up as they passed—one even waved his hat lazily—but for the most part they took no notice of the train at all.

It was late afternoon before they reached Paris and some time before it had passed through the squalid suburbs to reach the station.

The train came to a halt. He alighted into the gloom of a Paris evening. There seemed to be a confused throng of people milling around the station; they all seemed to be talking at the top of their voices, taking no notice whatever of anything that anyone else was saying. They seemed to be talking extremely fast. Robert could not understand one syllable of what was being said. He stood by the railway carriage, wondering if he could obtain a porter and felt very alone indeed. He tried to make himself as inconspicuous as possible. As he became engulfed in a tide of voluble French people engrossed in what seemed to him to be a violent argument, he shrank against the carriage. Eventually they moved on up the station. He was petrified that someone would speak to him so he tried his best to put on his 'go away, I'm out' face, in the hope that he might repel any aspirant conversation. Presently, to his enormous relief, he saw a scruffy little man clad in dirty blue overalls, pushing a large old barrow in front of him. Like a snowplough he cleaved a path through the crowd. Robert looked at the porter.

"Come with me—we will collect the luggage!" he commanded with as much authority as he could muster. He set off for the back of the train, beckoning purposefully to the porter, urging him to follow. The porter made a wide gesture with his hands. He muttered something completely incomprehensible, then pushed his barrow in the opposite direction. Robert turned and ran after him in exasperation. He stopped in front of the barrow. He pointed excitedly at the back of the train.

"The luggage!" He pantomimed with exaggerated waving of his hands. "There are three trunks and five wooden boxes." He held up his fingers, mouthing deliberately, knowing that he was getting louder and louder. The man had stopped—he had to. Robert was blocking has path. He looked at Robert, muttering something that Robert could not understand. Deftly avoiding Robert, he carried on towards the front of the train.

"Stop!" cried Robert, louder than ever; he was getting very hot and flustered. He felt that everyone was watching him. "Bloody foreigners. Why can't they speak English like everyone else?" He tried again, very slowly and carefully: "Look, my baggage, we must collect it, three trunks and five boxes." He waved his hands in front of the man's face. The porter stopped. He said something angrily to Robert. Robert did not understand, but he did not like his tone. "Now, look here," he said crossly, for he was more than a little exasperated. "You have been retained to collect my baggage. Will you please come and get it." He pointed angrily at the back of the train. The porter waived his arms up and down a lot. He poured out a great long speech that was totally lost on Robert. It seemed to involve a lot of pointing and exaggerated gestures, which seemed alternately to be aimed at a large pile of horse manure and at Robert. When he had finished, the man took off his hat and threw it on the ground. Grabbing Robert's arm, he pointed to the front of the train. There, Robert could see a growing pile of luggage as the baggage was unloaded onto the station.

"Why on earth don't they have the luggage van at the back, like civilised trains?" he asked angrily as the fact dawned on him. He managed to smile an apology at the porter, who sighed an exaggerated sigh of relief, picked up his hat, put it on and made an exaggerated pantomime of asking Robert's permission, in mime, if he might continue. Robert waved him forward, stepping aside to let him pass. He felt very embarrassed. His embarrassment was heightened when he realised that people who had been watching the whole episode were enjoying a good laugh at his expense. Eventually after much shouting, gesticulating and sweat, he managed to have all the luggage loaded precariously onto the handcart and pushed to the barrier.

Robert paced up and down wringing his hands in an extremity of anxiety. How on earth was he going to cope? If he could not organise his baggage from the train onto a handcart to have it deposited at the barrier without breaking into a shouting, sweating panic, how on earth was he going to manage to run a racing stable? He could picture himself trying to explain to an uncomprehending stable lad, in a mixture of gesticulation and shouting, that the brown mare, the one with the star on its forehead, not the one with the white sock, nor the one with grey hairs in its tail, was due to go to the stallion in ten days time, that she ought to be prepared for the event. He could not even deal with this villainous-looking porter, who was rolling a brown stained cigarette round in his mouth and showing every sign of increasing impatience at the non-appearance of his money. Robert was not going to produce his purse in case he was robbed on the spot. The porter certainly looked as if he might have a lethal knife secreted about his person, which at the sight of Robert's purse, he might whip out. He looked evil enough for anything, with his thin unshaven face and pallid complexion beneath his floppy black beret.

Robert turned to the porter and by beckoning and pointing, managed to persuade him to follow him. He led the way through the crowded concourse. Robert marvelled at the variety of humanity crammed into the station. There were many who looked as if they lived there and there were several untidy piles of old blankets and torn discarded tarpaulins, that looked as if they contained nests of these wretched people. There were several groups of people sitting round braziers and on one there were some small creatures roasting on a stick. As far as Robert could see, they looked for all the world like rats. There were many more peddlers than in London, all pressing round trying to persuade Robert to buy their wares. Robert felt quite flustered by all the confusion. Eventually he threaded his way through the throng and after several inquiries, found himself at his train. He looked at the list of names on the destination board. Vienna, Budapest, Constantinople. Exotic names that sounded to him like places from a fairy story. Shortly, he himself would be going there—it all seemed too fantastic to be true. There were no officials attendant on the train, and from the board he discerned that it was going to leave at 23.35 hours. Robert looked at it with some bafflement.

"Twenty-three thirty-five? What on earth time is that?" He persuaded the porter to leave the luggage with a pile that was rapidly growing by the luggage van and offered him a handful of coins. The man selected the biggest one and, muttering under his breath, trundled his barrow away in search of more fares. Robert stood around wondering what he should do next. He had finally worked out what the time was. He had heard that they used the twenty-four hour clock on the continent, but this was the first time he had actually met one in action. He realised that he had a couple of hours to wait and so decided to go in search of some food. Suddenly, at the thought of food, he felt almost faint with hunger.

Robert had a horror of station restaurants as he had had to frequent many in England. He had endured innumerable rounds of curly sandwiches, dubious pies and cups of cold black tea. He looked uncertainly at the shabby paint of the station restaurant. The grimy steamy windows obscured the view inside and allowed only a dim light to escape. He pushed open the door and went in. He hesitated on the threshold. The gust of hot air that rushed out the moment the door was opened, pungent with the hot smell of garlic, tobacco smoke and the smell of gas lamps, practically bowled him over. He recoiled gasping.

An ancient waiter approached him and led him to a table in the corner, relieved him of his coat and sat him down in a chair. He produced a menu with a flourish. Robert looked at it in complete bafflement. There seemed to be a variety of different set meals, written in some indecipherable script, one on each page. Robert hesitated for some time, then pointed to the middle one. The waited nodded and made a jot on his pad. Robert mimed pouring from a bottle into a glass and he nodded, noted and departed. He soon returned and placed a carafe of red wine and a glass on the table. Robert poured out a glass of the bright purple liquid and cautiously sniffed its sharp aromas. It was not at all like the claret and burgundy he had experienced at home. It smelt rather sharp and astringent, but somehow the pervading smell of garlic disappeared. He took a sip. Sharp and fresh, but strange, too, the taste of garlic also went. He was left with a clean vinous taste in his mouth and a warm sensation in his stomach. It had a youthful freshness that added charm to the thin texture and bright purple colour. His feelings about the restaurant that had been confirmed when he had walked in, began to mellow. The satisfyingly fresh taste of the wine revived his spirit. He looked around curiously. The low large room, supported by iron pillars which seemed to be placed in a haphazard fashion and upon which were hung the patrons' coats, was lit by gas lamps that hissed noisily, audible even about the clatter of crocks and cutlery and the loud conversation. It was obvious to Robert that the French talked with a voluble enthusiasm. They obviously had strong opinions about everything. Even as they argued vociferously together they managed to eat their food with enthusiastic gusto, whilst gesticulating wildly with whatever was in their hand, be it a roll, a glass, a napkin, a forkful of food, or even a chicken bone. They obviously had a zest for life, even in a railway restaurant that was somehow missing in the way that the English behaved.

A large brown bowl of golden soup was placed in front of him, interrupting his reverie. Suspiciously he stirred its yellow globules cautiously with his spoon. He helped himself to a large roll from a basket that had been set on the table. He addressed himself to his soup, from which a strong smell of garlic wafted round him like some magician's spell. He cautiously tasted a spoonful. It was piping hot and scalded his mouth. He hastily took a roll and broke off a portion to eat quickly, to put out the fire that was raging within him. The soup was the product of a magician's hand. It was followed by a bowl of mussels, the aroma of their garlic sauce announcing their arrival even before they had left the kitchen door. Robert eyed them suspiciously. He had never eaten mussels. He was none too anxious to start now. They gaped at him aggressively from within their blue and pearly shells.

Robert carefully prized one out of its shell and glowered at the yellow object on his fork. Deliberately, he put it in his mouth. It was firm and chewy, a little gritty. It tasted of garlic, mud, seawater and was totally delicious. He ate two or three more—they were delicious. Well, to think that something so insignificant could be so good! Robert was soon hard at work mopping the garlicky creamy sauce up for all he was worth with a bread roll. No sooner had the mussels been finished than some breasts of chicken in a green sauce appeared, followed by a dish that he took to be baby marrows. Robert had never eaten these before and was surprised by their subtle bitterness cleverly masked by a light cheese sauce. He was then presented with a generous slice of what appeared to be apricot tart. He was brought a cup of coffee and his bill on a scrap of scruffy paper was placed on the table. He sat back with considerable satisfaction. He had eaten well. He had enjoyed his meal and he had enjoyed watching the natives as they ate! It had been vastly different to the Railway restaurants at home. The waiter was trying to attract his attention, hovering behind his shoulder with a small plate. Robert turned and saw him.

"What? Oh, yes, I'm sorry." He pulled out his wallet and drew out a handful of French notes. He rifled through them, puzzled by their unfamiliar look and figures. He looked at the bill and rifled again through his notes. He could not decipher what was written on the bill and none of the notes seemed to look anything like the amount scrawled on the paper. In any event, the figures on the notes gave him no clue as to their value. In desperation he handed the whole lot to the waiter. He selected two small notes and, bowing his thanks, offered Robert his coat.

When he left the restaurant, Robert was feeling much more kindly disposed to the French. He was well warmed and satisfied by his meal. He had been astonished that such a good meal could be had so cheaply from such an unpromising-looking place. He looked forward to many such gastronomic encounters in the future.

Robert pulled out his ticket and presented himself at the barrier. With a mixture of gesticulation and pigeon, he managed to discover where his reserved compartment was. His baggage had already been loaded on to the train, though he insisted that he check it himself, to make certain.

The train started exactly on time. He hung out of the window so as not to miss anything he might be able to see. He was quite disappointed that he had not been able to have a look at Paris, so he was determined to make the most of whatever glimpses he might get from the train. Their way at first, like probably every other train route from a major city, lay through grimy smoke-blackened, squalid factory and slum areas, but gradually, as they went through the suburbs, the skyline of Paris revealed itself against the fading light of the western sky. The spires and towers stood out in black silhouette against the vivid primrose cloudless evening. Presently he was speeding through flat open countryside dotted with small farms surrounded by poplar trees. As the train picked up speed, it became very cold in the evening air, so Robert shut the window and sat down, but sill continued to watch the countryside as it rolled by.

Presently the countryside changed to flat chalky hills. The low hills were covered in row upon row of neat low bushes stretching in regimental order in all direction. Robert looked out in the fading light with considerable interest. Eventually he decided they must be vines. He had never imagined fields full of vines. He had no clear idea in his head of what a vineyard might be like, but it certainly was not like this. He had imagined some walled garden, with the cosseted vines growing in sheltered luxury, nurtured with devotion and tender care by generations of hooded monks. To see them like this, spreading over large hillsides, was something of a shock.

It was not long before it was too dark to see, so he put on the lights in the compartment and dozed fitfully in his seat.

"Pardon Monsieur." Robert must have dozed off, for an attendant was standing in his compartment. He motioned to Robert to move out of the way and, reaching up, pulled down the bunk. Robert surveyed it with its inviting white sheets, already turned down.

"Well, that's clever. I hope we do not go over a bump. I would hate it to shut up with me inside, like some giant oyster shell!"

"Bon nuit momseiur, bein dormir." The attendant left.

Robert slept only fitfully. His mind was too full of the things he might be missing out there in the dark. Every now and then the train would roar through a tunnel, some long, some short. Just as suddenly they would burst out into the open again. Occasionally he would see a distant light, high up. It must be some mountain dwelling. He wished he could see. The train stopped several times in the night, he was not sure how many, and after a short spell in the station with banging doors and shouting porters, they would get underway again.

Robert awoke just as dawn was breaking. He pulled back the corner of the curtain and looked out of the window. He pressed his face against the glass to see out, but a bend in the track had filled his view with black mountains and all he could see was darkness. He opened the window and leaned out. The air cut him like a knife. It was bitterly cold, but fresh and keen. The cold air made his eyes stream. The train went round another bend and there were the mountains, more clearly now, etched against the dawn sky.

Wow! They towered above him, as it were, layer upon layer, their soaring snow-clad pinnacles shining pink in the first rays of the dawn sun high, high above him, whilst he, in the depths of the valley, was still in darkness. Robert was spellbound at the sight. All around were those towering peaks. Suddenly, with a shriek of its whistle, the train plunged into another tunnel. Robert hastily ducked his head in and heaved on the strap to pull the window shut as steam and smoke billowed in, in great choking clouds.

He shivered slightly at the thought of those towering peaks over their heads. There would not have to be much movement in those billions of tons of rock for them to be crushed out of existence. He shuddered again at the thought. The train was still roaring in the tunnel so he decided to go and wash and shave and freshen up. He rubbed his hand round his chin and felt his bristly growth. He hated being unshaven. He somehow felt dirty and untidy. He found shaving in the minute compartment with his cut-throat razor extremely difficult. There was not room for him to lift his arms up high enough to wield his razor and still see what he was doing in the looking glass. And to compound his difficulties, the train was obviously on a downward incline as it was gathering speed and was joggling and swaying in a most inconsistent manner. However, ignoring the risk of cutting off the tip of his nose, he finally managed to finish reasonably successfully. He washed and towelled his face and felt a new man. The train was still roaring in the tunnel as he made his way back to his compartment. A steward was knocking on everyone's door.

"Bonjour, Mesdames et Messieurs. Petit dejeuner est servis," he said to Robert as he passed.

"Oh, thank you," said Robert, wondering what he had said to him.

"Breakfast, Monsieur. Eet ees waits you," said the Steward, realising that he was English.

Robert decided to make haste before the restaurant car should become too crowded. Presently his breakfast was brought to him. A pot of coffee, a plate of hot croissants and some butter and apricot jam. Robert scowled at the offending pastries with an ill-disguised distaste.

"They call that breakfast? At least the coffee is hot." He poured himself a steaming cup. Preparing a small bonbouche, he quickly chewed on it. There was no doubt it was good. Very good. His automatic aversion to the idea of apricot jam at breakfast vanished with the first mouthful. He realised they must be eaten hot to be good. He became so engrossed in his breakfast that he had not noticed they had come out of the high mountains and the hills were much lower. Ahead in the distance he could see the spires of Vienna and, stretching like a thin serpentine thread of silver into the distance, he could make out a river.

CHAPTER 7

❀

Vienna station was as busy as it had been in Paris. But somehow there was a cleaner, more prosperous look. Even the urchins looked as if they had had a good wash and the beggars were not so ragged. The street vendors looked as if they might have washed their hands that morning. Their wares looked more appetising. There were an astonishing variety of bakery and confectionery goods being offered, as well as cooked and smoked meats, fruit and vegetables. Robert was bewildered by the noise and variety of it all and the heady cooking smells coming from those stalls selling hot food. His attention was taken by a stall selling marzipan sweetmeats cleverly made to look like cold sausage. The vendor offered a small piece to Robert, who selected the smallest piece that he could see and cautiously put it in his mouth; his senses, fooled into thinking it was meat, were surprised to find a sweet almondy taste. Robert bought a small selection to take with him.

He found a porter and by dint of gesticulation and showing him the boat ticket, managed to make him understand what he needed. The porter quickly found a carrier with a small pony and a little cart. All the trunks and boxes were piled on the little conveyance. It was dispatched to make what haste it could through the mêlée of traffic, to the quayside. Robert watched it depart with some apprehension. He might never see his possessions again!

He realised that the river must be down hill from the station and the Porter indicated that the distance was not too far, so Robert decided to walk in order to see as much as possible. He was very impressed with Vienna, with the elegance of the buildings and the prosperous-looking shops. Everywhere there seemed to be elegant restaurants and coffee houses. The smell of fresh coffee and delicious cooking smells that wafted round him as he walked made him feel acutely hungry. He had to pause to allow a young girl with an impossible number of large foaming tankards of a pale coloured beer, push her way backwards through some swing doors, into a small crowded restaurant. The smell of cooked sausage that escaped into the street when she did so was so tantalising that he could resist no longer and followed her inside. There seemed to be a queue of people waiting to be served. Each was receiving three steaming boiled sausages and a lump of brown bread. It seemed that they then took them and, standing against the bar that was placed all round the walls, ate them, washed down by the pale beer. Even as he watched, another girl came struggling in through the door with two more handfuls of foaming tankards, which was evidently collected from next door. Robert's turn came to be served. He gestured three fingers to the white-clad girl behind the bar. At that moment another girl came in carrying an impossible number of enormous tankards of a light golden ale, the froth spilling over as she walked. Everyone around was earnestly eating their sausages. The ale was rapidly delivered to people who had obviously paid previously. Robert was handed his sausages and bread on a plate. He moved along the counter. A large madam in a black dress with a lace jabot elegantly spread over her ample bosom, sat at the end of the counter to collect the money. Robert handed her one of his notes and, espying an empty tankard standing near, picked it up and waved it at her hopefully. She handed him his change and gave him a small pink ticket. Robert found a space at the wall bar and placed his pink ticket down in obvious view. One of the girls placed a tankard of beer beside him and deftly took the ticket away. Robert was feeling very hungry and the deficiencies of croissant as a sustaining breakfast for a travelling man were becoming painfully obvious. He had never eaten boiled sausage like this before and regarded them suspiciously. His first tentative taste revealed them to be spicy with an agreeable meaty texture. The beer looked pale and thin. He had seen more interesting looking specimens in the veterinary officer's laboratory at home, but its light agreeable flavour of hops went well with the bread and sausages.

He became aware of a steam hooter that was blowing repeatedly somewhere in the distance.

"What is that?" he asked out loud, to no one in particular. The man next to him looked at him.

"Englander?" he asked, with a smile.

"Yes," said Robert, thankful at last to find someone who might speak English. "What is that hooting?"

"Der boot, she…" The man tried to gesture with his hand the boat leaving the quayside and bouncing on the water. Robert understood.

"The boat? It leaves?" He pulled out his watch. Indeed, if it left on time he had only ten minutes! He swallowed the rest of his beer and, cramming his bread in his pocket and with a sausage in each hand, he made for the door.

Down the street he ran, a hot greasy sausage in each hand and his beer slopping noisily in his stomach. He ran, taking his direction downhill. Suddenly he turned a corner and there was the river. The steamer was moored a short way along the quay. Robert collapsed against the rail by the quayside, fighting and gasping for breath, still with his sausages clutched in each hand. He was desperately unfit.

At that moment the steamer let out another long, mournful hoot. He ran for the gangplank. A member of the crew, standing at its head, said something to him that he did not understand, but it was obvious from his demeanour that they were not going to let him get on board without paying. He stood hesitantly, a sausage in each hand. There was nothing for it. He put one of the sausages into his mouth, like a ridiculous fat cigar and, fishing in his inner pocket with greasy fingers, pulled out the papers and handed them to the man, who rifled though them and extracted the ticket for the steamer. The man tore it in half and, replacing the other half, folded up the papers and gave them back to Robert, motioning him on board. As he passed he said something that Robert did not understand. Taking the sausage out of his mouth, he turned.

"What did you say?"

"Rauchen verboten, mein Herr." Robert looked at him in surprise.

"What do you mean, Rauchen? What is *Rauchen*?" The man pantomimed smoking a fat cigar.

"The sausage!" Robert understood and he too laughed. Sticking it back between his teeth, he marched on board. He walked along the deck to the bow. He was amazed by the great width and sweep of the river, with ancient buildings crowding to the water's edge and backed by green hills. In the far distance the mountains loomed. Suddenly he panicked.

"The baggage! What has happened to it?" Even as he spoke he felt the boat move and the ropes were cast off. "The luggage, I forgot about the luggage." He looked round in desperation. He was greatly relieved to see it piled on deck and that deck hands were even then putting it in the hold. The cart that brought it from the station stood on the quayside. The driver returned his wave. Robert relaxed.

And so it came about that he found himself leaning on the rail of a steamer, sailing down the Danube, taking in the new and strange sights with the eagerness of a schoolboy, munching contentedly on two cold sausages and a large chunk of brown bread in the warm morning sun. This must be the most perfect way to travel, he thought after he had licked his greasy fingers. Hardly any sound. No bumps and jolts. No jostling crowds. Just sitting in the sun. They passed two small black tarred rowing boats. The crews with their shirts off, brown in the hot sun, were hauling in a long net that bowed out between the two boats. One man in each boat was rowing for all he was worth, so that the boats gradually converged making a trap with the net. Robert sat up to watch with considerable interest. Might they catch a sturgeon? Caviar! He had eaten caviar and had not liked it. Somehow this made him feel very far away from home. Caviar was so exotic. It came from so far away. It was so expensive but here he was. In front of him fishermen were trying to catch the fish before his very eyes. He watched hoping that he might see one of these exotic creatures hauled from the river, even as he watched. The fishermen had been working with some speed and at last the end of the net was pulled in. Robert jumped to his feet. He could see the silvery flash of flapping fish as they were hauled over the side. There was nothing very big. Probably perch. They were good to eat. Nothing big enough to be a mighty sturgeon.

Robert leaned over the rail and watched the waters of the river flowing. As the boat was going downstream, with the flow, they were going at quite a speed. The water hardly seemed to be moving. It was only when he looked at the bank that he could see how much current there really was.

They stopped a couple of times at small towns, each visit accompanied with much hooting and shouting. Some people had got on and some off and the boat was soon on its way again. Boxes and crates were swung upon deck, from the hold, ready to be unloaded as quickly as possible when they reached the next village.

There was a steady stream of traffic in both directions, mostly barges going up and down the river and ferries crossing from one side to the other.

On practically every bend there were groups of fishing boats. Robert was quite sad that he did not see a mighty sturgeon being hauled struggling from the depths. There were flat punts loaded high with hay or reeds slowly crossing crabwise across the river. Craft of all kinds were always in sight and it was obvious how vital this route was to the people who lived along its banks. Of them, there was not much sign. The occasional roof could be seen behind the tall reeds that fringed the edge. Or the glimpse of a church spire or a windmill showed over the top of the luxuriant growth that lined the banks. He saw a small village perched on the edge of a low hill. They passed people fishing from the river bank with enormously long poles. Groups of cattle or horses were watering in the shallows, with some small children looking over them and once a group of women, completely naked, were swimming and washing their hair.

Robert could not remember when he had enjoyed a journey as much as this. This was total relaxation. He sat in the warm sun absorbing all these strange sights—listening to the strange languages being spoken around him, absorbing the new smells and atmosphere with which he was surrounded. Presently a vendor came round selling rolls, sausages and sweetmeats. He purchased some smoked sausage, some rolls and some apricot pastries and sat on the scrubbed deck of the ancient old steamer, facing the late afternoon sun, his back against a rusty windlass and contentedly ate the smoky pungent sausage and the crusty roll, paring off slices with his pocket knife.

He had lost some of his earlier anxiety. The journey was full of new things to claim his attention. He was beginning to realise his life was going to undergo a great change. Things were going to be quite different out here in this deeply rural spot.

One of the crew came and shook his shoulder and pointed. "Journeys end?" Robert stood up and went to the bow. The boat was just rounding a bend in the river and there ahead was a group of low roofs. The river was swinging round a great bend and was now swinging south. The landing stage was just beyond the bite of the bend. This was as far as he could go on the river. Besides, if Herr Schmidt was as good as his word, the coach would be waiting for him. It was due to depart in the morning, whether he turned up or not.

Robert was pleased to see that his baggage had already been brought up on deck and a quick count showed he still had everything. The little steamer quickly moored at the ancient quay and he had hardly walked ashore before it was blowing its hooter, telling everyone that it was about to sail. The luggage was quickly manhandled onto the quay. The steamer cast off and was soon gone down the river. He stood, with his baggage, uncertain as to what to do next. There was a porter sitting on a barrow nearby. He stood up and pushed his barrow over.

He was an old man dressed in old and tatty clothes. His teeth were stained and broken and he had a grizzled, dirty, unshaved look. It seemed he had been sent to meet Robert off the boat His spat a squirt of brown tobacco juice between his feet.

"Englander?"

Robert nodded. The man made to lift one end of one of the heavy trunk onto his rickety barrow. Robert quickly helped him. He indicated that he would return for the others and, beckoning Robert to follow, he trundled off towards the village.

Of all the places that had punctuated his journey, this was the full stop! There were a few small houses—a place that looked like a smithy, a small shop that appeared to be shut. Everything was shut. The houses had shutters at their windows and they were shut. Apart from the aged porter, the only living thing in sight was a small white dog, rough and ragged, that ran up to them with a great show of excitement, wagging its tail enthusiastically. He bent and stroked it.

"Hello scruffy dog. At least you have come to say hello." The dog wagged its tail and ran round in excited circles, barking happily.

The old man kept up a continual torrent of grumbling and complaining all the way in a language that Robert could not understand. He shrugged. He had heard it all before, though usually from old stable hands. He turned a deaf ear. He followed him up the dusty dirty street, if indeed, the dusty rutted gap between the ramshackled buildings could be dignified with the name 'street'. They came to a low building in need of considerable repair. It had rickety unpainted windows and a rough sign on the wall, so worn he could not read it. The old man tipped the trunk off the barrow onto the ground and returned the way he had come, still grumbling. Robert entered. The room was dark and low, with wooden benches and low tables that stood haphazardly around. The floor was boarded, though it was such a long time ago since it had been swept that it was difficult to tell the difference between it and the road outside. There were a group of men sitting round the brightly burning fire that was giving off more smoke than heat. They had glasses in their hands and some bottles on a table between them. They were rugged and unshaven and looked rough and scruffy. They had been talking loudly together when he entered, but they immediately stopped and stared at him in sullen silence. Robert noticed a small brass bell sitting on a shelf by an opposite door and so he gave it a tentative ring. Immediately a shrill voice scolded loudly from a back room.

Robert started back in alarm. She sounded fairly angry. The biggest man by the fire, a large shaggy fellow in a rough grey coat and massive boots, got up and came towards him with a big roar. Robert instinctively grabbed a chair which was handy. He was about to pick it up and crash it down in the man's head. He had been in pub brawls before and he knew that surprise was the best weapon. The big man, seeing his move, had stopped. He threw his head back and roared with laughter. He held out an enormous hand.

"Englander. You come!" Robert could see that he was none too steady on his feet. The man stood towering above him. He dropped his glass on the floor and clapped Robert on the back with a blow that shook every bone in his body. With his other massive paw, he grabbed Robert's hand and started shaking it as a terrier would a rat.

"Err 'Enery. Ve vait free." He waved three grimy fingers under Robert's nose. "Vait free days. Tomorrow ve go. You are come. It is good. I am Josef. The Count 'e say 'You speak English good, go vait free days. Ven Count 'e say, ve do." He roared with laughter again. "Elly, Elly!" he roared towards the back room and then a torrent of some rough dialect. The same shrill voice poured forth a violent vitriolic reply. Joseph shrugged his shoulders.

"She feed baby." He shambled back to the fire, ushering Robert before him. The other men all stood up and shuffled sheepishly backwards. They stood in a hesitant ring, holding their hats awkwardly in front of their chests.

"Your Excellency," began Joseph, swaying slightly, "these too verk for Count." They all bowed solemnly and shook hands, bobbing as they did so.

Joseph motioned him to sit and, throwing another great log on the fire, roared again for Elly. He poked the fire again with a charred stick and sent a shower of sparks erupting up the chimney. "Elly! Elly! Elly! Elly!" he bellowed. This time he was rewarded. A small tousle-headed blonde girl of about 13 or 14 came in from the back room. She wore a green floral print cotton dress and had nothing on her feet. Her bare arms and legs were a golden brown from the sun. She had a fat brown baby in her arms, which was eagerly suckling her breast through the open front of her dress. She started an immediate and violent tirade at Joseph, who wilted under its onslaught. He bowed his head until it was all over, then spoke to her sharply and pointed at Robert and the empty wine jug that quite plainly said even to Robert's uncomprehending ear, 'For goodness sake shut up and bring more glasses and another jug of wine.' Robert was fascinated by her brown legs and feet. She seemed only a child. Far too young to have a baby. Robert was fascinated by how white her breast appeared against the brown of the baby's skin and her own suntanned arms and face. She smiled at him and returned to the back room. Presently she returned, the baby clutched on her hip and in her other hand a jug and some none-too-clean glasses, which she set down on the table between them. Then she sat on the small stool with the baby on her lap. The baby, now that it had been fed, was gurgling happily on her knee. It was obviously her child, for it looked just like her. It, too, was very brown from being out in the sun.

"Joseph, ask her if she has a room for me for the night." He obviously did not understand. Robert tried again. "Me sleep here tonight?"

Joseph grinned and spoke rapidly to Elly. She smiled and nodded her head and pointed to the room above.

"Ya. she say you sleep zere." He pointed to the ceiling. "She say, you eat?"

"Yes please." He nodded his head. He was hungry, though a bit dubious about what might be produced from this seedy looking establishment.

Elly smiled at him. Settling the fat baby on her hip, she hurried out.

Joseph and his colleagues had stood up and were giving every sign of leaving.

"Ve go…" He held up seven grubby fingers. "In the morning. You be ready your Excellency." Joseph and his colleagues shook his hand and unsteadily staggered out.

Elly came struggling in with a large iron pot that she hooked on to the chain hanging down the chimney and gave the contents a vigorous stir with an iron ladle that had been hanging on a nail by the side of the fireplace. She smiled at him and ran upstairs, her bare feet pattering on the boards above.

He heard a creaky door open and then bang shut. A shower of soot rained down the chimney, fortunately missing the pot. She pattered across the room and come down the stairs carrying on a wooden board a small ham and a sausage. There was evidently a door in the chimney so that meat could be hung there to smoke. She then brought bread, butter, cheese and a bowl of salad with radishes, chopped onions and peppers from the back room and hurried off again. She returned with a bowl of pickled gherkins and a bowl of fresh apricots and figs. She refilled the wine jug and gestured to him to help himself, whilst she stirred the stew on the fire. He poured out some of the pale yellow wine, then carefully carved some thin slices off the ham and the sausage with the wicked-looking knife provided. Elly ladled a large wooden bowl full with the stew from the pot and, flashing him a smile, her teeth brilliantly white in her tanned face, pattered off to the back room, from where the baby was noisily demanding her attention. The stew was hot and fiery and filled with chunks of spicy meat. There was no doubt that the meat was very good. Succulent and tender.

The wine had a bitter-sweet taste but a delicious freshness that went well with the supper. A man appeared, short and bald, wearing a white apron. He was obviously the innkeeper. He smiled at Robert and gestured at all the food.

"Gut, Gut, Ya?"

"Yes, thank you." Robert nodded vigorously and smiled. "Very good, thank you." He held up his wine glass. "Good, very good. Thank you." The innkeeper smiled and after putting another log on the fire, left. Presently Elly returned with a three-branched log that did duty as a candlestick. On the end of each short branch, melted in to the encrusted wax, was a burning candle. He enjoyed his supper by its rustic light and the flicker of the fireside and was well content to linger by the hearth. Eventually Elly came to clear away the dishes and the remains of the food. She ran upstairs again with the ham and the sausage and he could hear her put it back in the chimney. Another cascade of soot when she shut the door, confirmed it. The innkeeper returned and taking up the candles, motioned him to follow. He led the way to some stairs leading downwards, evidently to some sort of cellar, below the stairs to the first floor. He led the way down to a room that must be the whole size of the inn. There was a row of ancient gnarled wooden posts that held up the heavy floor beams of the rooms above. Because of the fall of the ground the cellar had a door in the end, that opened out into the back yard of the inn. The innkeeper proudly walked Robert round and pointed out everything. A massive wine press stood in the middle of the floor. At the other end of the cellar, above it, in the top of the end wall, was another door. This was at ground level at the front of the Inn. Through this door the grapes could be tipped directly into the receiving hopper for the press. There was room to roll one of the barrels directly under the spout from the press. The contraption was constructed of stout wooden beams to withstand the force exerted by the wooden screw that was turned by a robust wooden pole. A basket of wooden slats held with several bands of rope contained each load of grapes as they were pressed. In the receiving hopper there was a heavy pair of fluted rollers that crushed the grapes as they fell into the press. The juice, squeezed out through the slatted basket, ran out of a spout and into a funnel directly into the barrels for fermentation. When this was finished, the wine was siphoned off into barrels at a lower level, for storage and to mature. Wine was drawn off these barrels and bottled to be used in the Inn and any that was left over at the end of the year was placed in the back cellar, which was through another door, which Robert had not noticed. This was cut directly into the living rock and was cool and dark. It contained stack upon stack of dusty bottles. The innkeeper went to the end of the cellar and came back with a very dusty bottle.

He led the way back to the fireside and quickly produced two small glasses from the back room. He carefully opened the bottle and carefully poured out two glasses of a golden viscous wine. He handed one to Robert. Raising his own he muttered an unintelligible toast. Robert raised his own glass.

"Your very good health, Sir" he laughed. He might as well have said 'fly to the moon'. Hopefully the man understood the sentiment. Robert took a gentle sniff. Ripe sun-drenched raisins? Apricots? Peaches? He shut his eyes and his mind was filled with a sensation of sun-drenched hillsides, brown arms and luscious ripe fruits. He tasted it gingerly. The image in his mind was confirmed—the wine had a honeyed viscosity reminiscent of peaches, ripe, still sun warmed, that was balanced with a slight and refreshing acidity that lifted its wonderful flavour from out of the cloying into the realms of pure poetry. He allowed his mouthful to trickle slowly down his throat. His mouth was filled with a full raisiny, honeyed sweetness that enveloped his tongue with lingering delight. His eyebrows shot up—he had never tasted anything like it in his life. He had met quite a lot of fine port. This was not like that. Not so cedery. Sweeter. More viscous. This was heaven. He saw the innkeeper looking at him expectantly.

"Stunning," was all he could say. "Absolutely stunning." The man did not know what he said, but could tell by his expression and demeanour what he meant. His look of anxiety quickly changed to a beaming smile. Robert did not know how to convey his pleasure to the man, so he stepped forward and shook him warmly by the hand.

They sat by the fire until the small hours of the morning when the last drops of the heavenly liquid had been consumed.

The first streaks of the dawn light were appearing in the sky when they finally went to bed. His bed was huge with immaculate white sheets and a deep feather mattress. It was not long before he was sound asleep. It seemed no time at all before there was a loud hammering on his door and Elly came pattering in, on her bare feet, carrying a large tray on which was a pot of coffee, strong and black, a cup, some bread and a lump of hard cheese, a pot of apricot jam and a large jug of hot water. She put the heavy tray thankfully down on the table and opened the curtains. Grinning all over her face, she dropped him a little curtsey and ran out giggling. Robert swung his feet to the floor and sat on the bed with his head in his hands. He felt awful. His mouth was dry, his eyes ached and his head swam. With grim determination, he gritted his teeth and stood up. The room swayed so violently that he had to sit down again quickly. He tried again. Luckily there was a china chamber pot under the bed so he was able to solve his most pressing problem straight away. He splashed some water into the basin, but decided not to shave—the effort was too much. He looked out of the window and saw the coach drawn up outside. His luggage was tied precariously on the back and top but of the men there was no sign. He ate a hurried breakfast and went downstairs. The Count's men were all seated round the fire, as before, this time eating bread and cheese and cold meat, all washed down with the hot strong coffee. They all jumped up when they saw him. Joseph shook him again by the hand.

"Excellency, we go in five minutes." He held up five big fingers, still unwashed from yesterday. The Inn keeper came with two bills. One he gave to Robert and the other to Joseph. Robert handed some money over and looked at Joseph.

"Joseph, quick, quickly pay and then we can go."

Joseph looked at him. "I no pay."

"Herr Schmidt, he give you money?"

"No! He says you pay when you come!"

"No! I do not believe you. He didn't tell me to pay. You pay!"

"I no money. Herr Schmidt say you pay! You pay. I no pay!"

Robert hesitated. He could see no other way. He would have to pay the whole bill and get it back from Schmidt later, though he guessed that that would be like trying to get limpets off a rock with a playing card.

Robert shook the Innkeeper by the hand and went outside. He stood on the step and looked at the coach. *If 'Onest Ned could see this*, he thought, *he'd have a purple fit!* The coach was in urgent need of attention. The paintwork was shabby, some of the wood trim had come detached and stuck out at a dangerous angle. Some was missing altogether. He shook one of the wheels. It was loose and wobbly. The hub bush and the stub axle were so worn the wheel was in danger of falling off. It had had no grease for months and it was rusty and dry, as were all the others. Robert jumped on the step and bounced. The springs had hardly any resilience left in them. The weight of the luggage had pressed them down practically to their stops. They were going to have a pretty rough ride. He looked inside. The upholstery was worn and shabby with several holes in it. The cushions had deep dents in them; the springing had obviously long given up. This was not going to be a good journey. He groaned at the prospect.

He turned his attention to the horses. From a distance, they looked fairly well-matched. They were all of a uniform dark chocolate colour, with white socks. But to the experienced eye, they were a rag-tail bunch. The experienced eye surveyed them and did not like what it saw. *For heavens sake*, Robert thought to himself, *if this is a sample of the Count's horses, God help us all.* The harness was in an equally sad state. The leather was unpolished and in some places so badly cracked that it was in danger of breaking. The brass had not been cleaned for weeks, months more likely, and the chains were rusty and clang with mud. Tethered to the back of the coach, there were four more horses, two saddled and two on halters and leading reins. They were in an equally sorry state. Robert rubbed his gloved hand over their flanks, and it came away black with accumulated dirt and grease. They had not been properly groomed for weeks. At that moment the others came out of the inn. Robert rounded on Joseph.

"Who coachman?"

Joseph pointed to himself.

"Who horseman?"

Joseph pointed at a swarthy individual with a strange white steak of hair in his beard.

"This is a disgrace! Terrible. Dirt. Look!" He slapped the nearest horse on the rump. A cloud of dust rose in the air. He glowered at them both fiercely. Joseph shrugged his shoulders and spat on the ground.

"Herr Schmidt he say nothing. Count, he say nothing," he mumbled. Robert looked up at him, a fierce anger in his eyes.

"This is bad! Bad! Bad for Count! Bad for horses! Bad for you! Next week I Captain of Horse. Then if it bad for me, it very very bad for you!" Robert glowered up at the man. He was not intimidated by his size. He had tangled with bigger men than him before. Joseph would not meet his eye. He climbed up onto his box. One of the men climbed up with him and the horseman and the other mounted the spare horses. Robert climbed into the coach.

This is going to be a journey to Hell. Look at the state of this thing. Robert bounced on the seats. *As I thought, the springing has gone.* Robert stuck his head out of the window.

"Joseph, what is this sack?" he demanded, pointing to a dusty sack that took up half the carriage.

"Feed, Excellency, for the horses."

"Get it out of here. Quick, quick. Out!"

"Where put? Boxes take all."

"I could tell you! I don't care. Out, quick." Robert climbed out. It was true, every space was taken up by his luggage. It could go right on top, but already the coach was dangerously high.

"Ah," he pointed, "under your seat. There, look!"

Joseph unwillingly climbed down and hoisted the offending bag out of the carriage and stuffed it beneath his seat pushing alongside a basket that Robert assumed carried his food for the journey.

"Break. It stop break." Robert looked.

"Push it over a little more, then it will not be in the way. I don't suppose that the break works anyway, by the look of it." Joseph climbed back onto his seat and looked at Robert with an expression that said 'Can we be off now?' Robert climbed onto the step.

"Drive on," he said as he swung inside and slammed shut the door. It did not shut.

That would be too much to expect. He opened the door again and slammed it with a lift. This time it shut.

"Stay. You brute," he glowered at it. *Look, the hinge has dropped, that is why it won't shut. What a shambles. Did you ever see such a disaster? It is not fit to be used as a chicken coop, let alone go out on the road with people inside. And the turnout. Look at the state of the harness and the horses! Haven't been groomed for weeks. None of those men have a uniform. Did you ever see such a motley lot? Those horses. I wouldn't buy them for dog food. I hope all his horses are not like that.* Robert's mental tirade was cut short by a particularly violent jolt. *If we have any more of those, the blessed coach will fall to pieces and we will have to walk!*

The protection from the springs was almost non-existent and the seat cushions were hard and unsprung. He felt every jolt. To make matters worse, because of the weight of the luggage on the roof, the carriage rolled like a ship in a rough sea.

The day wore on and their journey progressed at a steady trot. He was feeling somewhat woebegone from the night before. He pulled out his watch; it was half past twelve. He leaned out of the window and called up to Joseph.

"Stop. Next inn."

Joseph laughed "Inn? No Inn. Stop soon." Half an hour later, they still had not stopped. Robert leaned out again.

"Joseph, we must stop."

"Water, Excellency. Soon. Water for horses. Look, by trees we stop." He pointed with his whip at a distant clump of trees. Robert sat back in the coach.

Robert had been caught too often when he had been going to race meetings with nothing to eat all day, to leave uneaten food behind on the table when he was going on a long journey. He had packed the remains of his breakfast into a handkerchief and put it in his pocket. Just as they were leaving, the Innkeeper and handed him a parcel. Robert retrieved it from under the seat. It contained a loaf, some radishes, slices of cold meat, some hard boiled eggs and a bottle of wine.

Presently the coach pulled off the road by the clump of trees. They all alighted. This was evidently a spot that was regularly used for this purpose. There was a good-sized pond and the horseman and the coachman had soon unhitched the horses and taken them to drink. The third man was preparing their nosebags and the fourth man disappeared into the bushes. He soon returned with an armful of firewood and by the time the horses had all been tethered to the coach, with their nosebags on, he had made a good fire which was now reduced to glowing embers. The others joined him and squatting on their haunches round the fire, were soon grilling lumps of fatty bacon which they cut off a large piece from a bag. They also had a loaf of bread and some cheese and a bottle of wine. Robert settled with his back against a tree with his food spread out beside him. He felt the world was not such a bad place after all. He watched the Count's men. They squatted comfortably on their heels. In their left hand they had a lump of cheese, their piece of bacon and a chunk of bread. In their right hand, they held their knives. They cut alternative slices off their foods and popped them straight into their mouths. When the bottle was passed round, they put their knife down, took the bottle with their right hand, wiped the neck on their sleeve and took a drink before passing it on.

There were several fire circles dug in the ground and ringed with stones and there was also a clay oven and a crude wooden table.

They rested for about a half hour and then the horses were re-harnessed, after they had all been changed. The harness and coach may be shabby, but the men certainly knew what they were doing. All was ready very efficiently, with hardly a word spoken by any of them. The horses were quietly but firmly handled. Robert was impressed. As Robert climbed back into the coach, he called up to Joseph.

"I watch you. Very good. Very good." Joseph looked at him and muttered under his breath.

"Stupid. You think you tell us about horses." He swung his whip with a vicious crack just over the horses' heads and they were off again. The afternoon was long and tedious. Robert dozed through most of it. There seemed to be very little other traffic on the road. It was not made-up and was for the most part not wide enough for another vehicle to pass. The countryside seemed to be mostly grazing. Occasionally they would see a distant roof, with a patch of maize beside it. There were big herds of cattle and on the higher ground, sheep.

They passed a large flock of geese, apparently in the middle of nowhere, being driven along by some children. The landscape was dotted with clumps of trees and always in the background, higher hills covered with forest. They saw the occasional village clustered round its little church and they drove through two little towns, with a few shops. As they passed, the people stopped to stare at the little cavalcade.

In the background there were the ever-present mountains covered with thick forest. Robert took more interest in the countryside, especially in the afternoon, as this was going to be his home. He wanted to try and develop a feel of 'place'. They passed through the odd village and they saw the odd roof-top, the odd church spire, even a distant castle, high on a crag, but by and large the country seemed to be almost deserted but getting flatter and more verdant looking.

As darkness fell, he could feel a greater urgency in their passage. Joseph was pushing the horses a little harder.

It was half past nine by his watch when they finally clattered over a wooden bridge and into a large courtyard and stopped.

For better or worse, he had arrived.

CHAPTER 8

❀

Robert looked out of the coach window. It was pitch dark. He could see nothing. Some dogs were barking furiously from somewhere close at hand, he could hear their chains rattling, so they were obviously secured somewhere in the courtyard. A lantern appeared. By the way it was bobbing up and down, it was being carried by someone running down some steps. Behind it he could see a dim light from an open door.

The door of the coach was opened by a heavily breathing boy who held the lantern. Robert climbed stiffly out. He ached in every bone of his body. They had not stopped since lunchtime. The deficiencies in the coach's springing were all too apparent. They had pushed the horses harder as it became obvious they were not going to arrive before dark.

Joseph and the three men unloaded all the luggage and disappeared into the darkness with it, carrying it up some broad stone steps that led to the lighted doorway.

Another lantern came bobbing down, carried by another boy. He was accompanied by an aged retainer who wore a blue tailcoat with yellow breeches and stockings, his grey hair tied back with a blue ribbon. He bowed respectfully and spoke to Robert in German. When it was obvious he had not understood, the old man beckoned him to follow.

Robert followed the old man up the steps into the entrance hall. The room was dimly lit by three candles in a brass candlestick placed on a central table. His luggage stood in an untidy heap to one side.

The retainer led the way though one of the doors into a small room. There was a large heavy table with heavy carved legs, set about with chairs. One place was laid in front of the fireplace, in which a cheerful fire burnt, throwing a flickering light into the room. The walls were hung with pictures of horses and the chase and the three windows were closed with heavy burgundy coloured curtains.

The retainer ushered Robert into his chair and left the room by a side door. With the fire warming his back, Robert sat there contemplating this development. Presently the retainer returned, followed by a footman wearing a slightly less important version of the same uniform and bearing a large tray. This was placed on a side table. The retainer, who managed to convey to Robert that he was called Franc, proceeded to wait on Robert.

Robert felt so uneasy with this new situation that he had no idea what he ate. He just wanted to be finished as quickly as possible, for he felt very embarrassed at this personal attention. At last it was finished. Franc beckoned him to follow and led the way.

They crossed the hall and ascended the great stairway. He knocked on a door and, opening it, gave a little cough and announced, "Herr Emery, Excellencies." The room was in partial darkness. The wall covering, the drapes, the furniture covers, all were blue. The woodwork was a pale cream and gold. Every space on the wall was taken up with gilt framed mirrors and pictures. The ceiling was heavily moulded with intricate plasterwork. Robert stood uncertainly just inside the door, mesmerised by a sea of furniture. Occasional tables covered with ornaments and flowers made islands in the room. Gilt chairs, all with their backs to the door, connected them all together.

A bright fire was burning in the grate and between two candelabra on the mantelpiece; a large ormolu clock was supported by a pair of struggling cherubs.

"Come in 'Enery, do not just stand there, come in so that we may see you," the Count's voice called out. Robert peered towards the fire but could not see anyone. Then he noticed the Count's hand beckoning to him from within one of the deep wing chairs by the fireside. Whatever else the Count's faults may or may not be, you could not accuse him of being wasteful with his candles. There was hardly enough light to cross the room without falling over the furniture and only those chairs by the fire received any kind of light at all. Robert made his way over to them, being careful not to knock anything over.

"Ah, 'Enery, you have finally arrived. We have been expecting you these last three days. I do not like to have my coach kept vaiting, it cost money to keep the coach vaiting." Robert did not think this was the moment to agree with him and point out that the money had come from his own pocket. He would take that up with Schmidt when he had an opportunity. The Count, who was wearing a red velvet smoking jacket, a pair of red slippers with pointed turned up toes and a small pillbox embroidered hat with a large black tassel, sat in a deep armchair. He had in one hand a large cigar and on a small table conveniently placed by his other hand, stood a large brandy glass and decanter.

Opposite to him, on a deep sofa, sat in regal posture, a lady of about the same age. She wore an all-enveloping black dress and a pair of black lace mittens. Over her head and shoulders she had a black lace shawl. She had on her lap some embroidery that she had just put down. She had a small triangular face with pale, pale blue eyes, which were regarding him with some interest from behind small gold-rimmed spectacles.

"Ah, so you are Mr 'Enery, of whom I am heard so much. Come to make our 'orses run faster." Her English was spoken very easily but with a strong accent, so that Robert had to listen very attentively to make out what she said. He bowed stiffly to her.

"Yes, Madam. That is the plan. I look forward to working with them."

"Meester 'Enery, we have a beautiful place here. I hope that you enjoy your vork and that you have great successes.

"It is good that he does. I not spend all these moneys and not have successes. If my horses can learn to run a little faster we make good money." He added as an afterthought: "That is my vife."

Robert again bowed to her. She spoke better English than the Count and was obviously of a more refined disposition than he. She smiled at him kindly. The smile took ten years off her age.

"I vish you every success. There is the great delights in making the horses run faster."

Robert bowed to her again. "Thank you, Madam. I am looking forward to it with great excitement."

She smiled kindly at him again. "Meester 'Enery, come. Sit here and tell me all your journeys. Tell me about Eengland. They say it rains a lot."

Robert sat on the sofa beside her and regaled her with the details of the journey across Europe. She was an attentive listener. She elicited from him, by careful questioning, details that he did not know that he had observed. She was most interested to know about England. She had never been there. Her husband, it seemed, went there quite often, but she stayed here. She went to Budapest, Vienna and Prague occasionally, but to England she had never been. She was particularly interested to know about fashion. Robert had to search his memory to give an account of what English Ladies were wearing, how they behaved and what they did. Robert had to confess that he was remarkably poorly informed about such things! For the most part he lived a rural life, concerned with the affairs of his horses. But at race meetings, she insisted, what did the women wear? Did they wear feathers in their hats? Did they still wear bustles? What colours were popular? Robert had to confess that he really had not noticed. He could give no reliable information.

"Did you hear that, Elizabet!" she scolded lightly. "The vomen in Eengland make the great trouble to make themselves look attractive but the oh so gallant mans take so much interest in the 'orses, they do not even notice!"

Robert looked round. He had not noticed anyone else in the room. Elizabet? He saw in the opposite corner, sitting at a small grand piano, with a single candle for light, the object of this remark. She had been obscured from view by the table full of flowers when he came into the room, for his attention had been taken by the Count and Countess. She now rose and came over to join them. She was wearing a blue evening dress with a very tightly laced bodice that emphasised her petiteness and slim waist. She had over her shoulders a white crocheted shawl. Round her rather short neck she had a black choker ribbon with a small broach in the middle. Her fair hair was coiled up on her head. She had a longish face with a determined chin and her blue eyes had a fierce greyish tinge to them. Her full mouth with its pale lips smiled fleetingly at Robert, who had stood up as she walked across the room.

"Meester 'Enery, this is our daughter, Elizabet." She smiled briefly again and held out her hand. Robert shook it solemnly, bowing as he did so.

"How do you do-er—Miss?" He smiled in return into those bold eyes. He let go her hand and was surprised to see a slight look of hurt followed by irritation on her face. *What happened?* he thought to himself, *what have I done? What went wrong?* Fortunately the Countess was more perceptive.

"Meester 'Enery, is it not the Eengleesh custom to kiss the hand of the lady ven you meet?"

Robert understood. He felt very embarrassed. He felt himself blush.

"Mother, a shame on you, you have made the good Captain of the Horse blush." Elizabet looked at him with a mock smile on her face.

"Countess, Mademoiselle, I must apologise. I mean…I did not know. No. In England it is not the custom. I am so sorry, I meant no offence…it is just that it is not our custom…" He trailed off.

Elizabet looked at him with her nose in the air.

"What a nasty rude place Eengland must be," and she sat down beside her mother with her back turned slightly towards Robert.

"Meester 'Enery, I think that you vill find life a little different here. Here the romantic idea of women is still important. Our gentlemen still have the ideas of chivalry and 'old vomen in great respect. It is very good. It is sad if Eengland has lost this. Elizabet, child, it is time you vent to your bed. We have vaited up very late to meet Meester 'Enery. Go along vith you." She leant across and offered her cheek to her daughter. Elizabet too, leaned across and kissed her mother. "Good night mother. It is late. I am tired." She rose "Good night Father."

The Count who was fast asleep in his chair, let out a tuneless snore.

"Good night Mr 'Enery, we shall meet in the morning, no?"

Robert jumped to his feet in a panic. *Oh my goodness! If she offers me her hand, do I kiss it?* Thankfully she did not. His alarm subsided.

"Goodnight-er-Mademoiselle." He bowed stiffly and she was gone from the room.

"Meester 'Enery, please be seated. I am sorry we have made you uncomfort tonight. We do not have many visitors and it is so good for us to see vhat is going on in the world outside of here. I have been never to Eengland. Alvays my husband he talk about Eengland and alvays I long to see It. You must be patient. We vant to hear all we can about Eengland. You vill be a great attraction here. Everyone, they vish to hear about Eengland and your great Queen Victoria, the aunt, I think, of Villiam the king of Prussia."

Robert blenched at the thought. His mind had been full of his duties with the Count's stud. It had not occurred to him that he might be a social curiosity as well. He did the best that he could to convince the Countess that he was not actually personally acquainted with Queen Victoria, but being used to attending Court herself, in Budapest and Vienna, she could not conceive that there were people who were not on familiar terms with their Sovereign.

"I'm sorry, Meester 'Enery, you must have the great fatigue after the journey. You have come so far and seen so much, in such discomfort. For tonight, I have had ready made a room for you. You may sleep vell. Tomorrow is plenty time to talk of what is to happen." Robert, who had been wondering what he was expected to do, was relieved.

"That is very kind of you."

There was an awkward pause in the conversation, punctuated only by the crackling of the fire and the sonorous snoring of the Count. Robert shifted uncomfortable in his seat.

"Madam, I must congratulate you on your English."

"You are too kind. Ever since my husband he have the interest in Eengland, we have made great effort to speak it, in 'ope that one day we go to London. My husband, he was taught Eengleesh as a child. He have this Eengleesh nanny. He have made a rule vhen we at home together are, we talk Eengleesh. Now you are here, you vill be able to help us." Robert was startled. Here was another aspect of the situation that he had not considered. He accepted that he was going to have to learn at least a smattering of German and Hungarian, but that he was going to have to act as English tutor had not even occurred to him. He digested this new facet of his employment with considerable misgivings. This was something for which he was not prepared.

"Meester 'Enery, I think we vill meet a lot, it vill be good if you call me Countess. Now I think, I retire. You no doubt have the many things to talk vith my husband." She rose. "Good night, Meester 'Enery. I shall see you tomorrow. Breakfast it is served in the Breakfast Room, from eight until nine in the morning. If you are not there by nine o'clock it is too late. It is cleared avay. Vould you be so kind as to pass that poker?"

"Poker, Countess?"

"That one, vith the big brass knob." Robert, bewildered, picked it up.

"This one? My La…. Countess.

"Yes, pass it here." Apprehensively, Robert handed it over. She declined to take it. Rapidly, Robert changed his grip and offered her the brass handle. She accepted this and, wielding it with obvious practise, gave the Count a viscous dig in the ribs. He let out a cry of agony, roused so cruelly from his deep sleep. He struggled to sit up. His face went red with the effort of dragging his senses back to reality. He slobbered down his chin, gasping and wheezing as he rubbed his side. He let out a torrent of swearing, none of which Robert could understand. The Countess obviously did, for she answered him sharply. The Count opened his eyes. His wits returned enough for him to recollect where he was. He rubbed his eyes and his side simultaneously.

"Are you avake?" demanded the Countess imperiously.

"Of course I have the damn vell avake. I vas avake. Vhy you poke me? he asked angrily.

"You were not avake. You sleep like the pigs in the sty. Vake up!" she commanded.

"I am avake, you stupid voman. Vat you think, you poke a man like that, he is avake." He rubbed his side again tenderly.

"I am going to retire. Do not sit half the night vith Meester 'Enery, he has had a long day."

"'Enery? 'Enery, who in devil's name is he? Oh it is you! Oh go to bed! It is too damn late to talk tonight. Go to bed. I see you in the morning." His head lolled on his chest. He sat up with a jerk. "Good night 'Enery. I see you in the morning."

Robert held open the door for the Countess. As she swept out, her long black gown rustled softly as she walked.

"I vill find someone to show you to your room." She reached for the bell pull on the landing. A footman appeared and took up one of the candles.

"Goodnight, Meester 'Enery. Follow this man. He vill show you to your room." With that she sailed off round the gallery with a majestic rustle and disappeared through a door.

The footman led the way, round the gallery and through a different door. This one did not lead to a room, but into another corridor that soon led to a flight of narrow steps. Here the walls were of whitewashed stone and the floor less even. This was obviously an older part of the house. They followed the way up a curving narrow set of stairs, and came into a round room. The room was quite large, and protruding into it, its head against one wall, was a large four poster bed with faded scarlet drapes. There was a wardrobe, a chest of drawers and a marble-topped washstand. All made of light-coloured wood, unstained, but highly polished. Robert was not an expert on wood, but these were really nice. Solidly constructed and tactile. He ran his hand over the polished surface and marvelled at its robust smoothness. In the middle panel of each door on each piece was a heraldic device, beautifully inlaid in the most exquisite marquetry. The room had a stone vaulted ceiling and a thick rug on the floor. Either side of the bed were rugs of some long thick fur. There was a fireplace with a cheerful fire burning. In front of the fire an easy chair stood. The room was obviously in a tower of some kind. It was a splendid room.

The footman placed the candle on the bedside table and withdrew from between the sheets a large brass pan on a long handle and opened the lid to show the hot charcoal inside, as proof. He pushed it back, further down the bed. He said something in German and departed.

There was another door. Robert opened it and looked in. It was a small room, serving as a toilet. There was a wooden bench across the end wall, with three lids in it, one large, one small and one middle sized. Robert opened the large one. A howling gale blew through it. It opened straight into the moat. Robert shut the lid with a bang. "Ye gods, that would bring tears to your eyes." Thankfully he noticed a china chamber pot under the bed.

Suddenly he froze in silence, the hairs on the back of his neck rising and goose pimples running up his arms and legs. The wind whistled eerily through the window frame. "What in hells name is that?"

Robert felt his body tingling all over. In the distance could be heard a mournful howling, wavering on the night air. Eery and spine-chilling, it seemed to reverberate round the room. It seemed to grow louder and softer, nearer and further away. It went on and on, a terrible howl as if from the depths of the occult. Robert felt his nails cutting into his palms as he gripped his hands tightly together. Another replied, nearer, louder and more quavering than the first. The first one joined in and one further away. The dogs in the yard started up a ferocious barking whilst the unearthly chorus echoed off the ancient walls. Robert ran to the window and threw open the curtains. Outside, the moon was shining brightly and beyond the roof tops, nothing could be seen under the moonlight but the low mountains, covered with the black forest that surrounded them. Somewhere someone fired a gun. The chorus stopped as if a box lid had been firmly shut and a stark silence filled the air. The dogs in the yard rattled their chains as they went back into their kennels. *Wolves? Those must be wolves. They must have wolves here.*

"Wolves!" Robert uttered aloud.

The shock on his face was evident. *I thought wolves only existed in fairy stories and Gothic horror books. I thought they were extinct in Europe!*

Robert got undressed quickly in front of the fire. He put on his warmed night-dress and taking the warming pan out of his bed and laying it in the hearth, he was soon tucked up between the fresh linen sheets. He sank into the luxury of the deep feather filled mattress, almost floating in the warm cocoon of the bed. He had shut the curtains over the windows, but did not blow out his candle. Presently the wolves started howling again—there seemed to be several of them. Now that he realised what they were and had got over his initial chill, there seemed to be a primitive beauty in their sounds.

He slept only fitfully and kept waking with dreams of slavering jaws and bloody fangs sinking into his neck. He tossed and turned all night and felt tired and unrested when a cockerel on a rooftop below his window started to crow its daily salute to the first warming rays of the sun. Robert rose and dressed carefully. He was very apprehensive about going down to breakfast. He sat for some time on his bed before screwing up the necessary courage to go downstairs to find the breakfast room. A footman stood at the bottom of the stairs, obviously posted there to guide him when he should rise. He collected Robert and ushered him into the room where he had had supper the previous night.

Robert stood inside the room. He looked round with some apprehension. The heavy curtains had been drawn and the sun streamed in through the large windows. Seated at the table were the Count, Elizabet and Schmidt. Apart from a few discarded cups and plates, the table was bare but there was an array of dishes on the sideboard. Everyone looked up when he entered. Elizabet smiled.

"I hope you sleep vell?"

"Yes, thank you…though…"

"Ah, 'Enery, you are not dead, after all! We began to vonder vhat had happened to you. Our fears are allayed, you valk through the doorvay." The Count resumed reading the newspaper behind which he had been enveloped and Elizabet smiled at him.

"Good morning, Herr 'Enery!" Schmidt called from across the room. "I hope that your journey vas goot."

"Yes, thank you, Herr Schmidt, everything went very smoothly. Thank you for organising it all so thoroughly."

Her Schmidt permitted himself the thinnest smile. "That ees goot." He resumed reading the papers that he had spread out on the table round him. Robert still hovered uncertainly by the door. Seeing his hesitation, Elizabet smiled again and beckoned him to the sideboard, as she stood up.

"Herr 'Enery, we do not vait on ceremony in this house. At breakfast, it is all mans to himself. Take for yourself a plate." She lifted a large silver lid. A concoction of rice sizzled as she turned it with a spoon, the spirit lamp beneath keeping it warm. "You like?" She proffered him a spoonful.

"What is it?" asked Robert, eyeing it suspiciously.

"Carp." She found a tender flake and held it up for his inspection.

"From the moat?"

"Oh yes! We have good carp in the moat, very good. Very fat."

I bet you do! thought Robert. "No, thank you. What is in that dish?"

She opened lid after lid and eventually Robert had selected for himself some wild mushrooms, some scrambled eggs, some rashers of fried fatty bacon and some funny little sausages, tied up with a small piece of stick between each one and some kidneys. Taking his plateful and a cup of steaming coffee from the samovar at the end of the sideboard, he sat down at the table in the only remaining seat, between Elizabet and the Count.

As Robert spread his voluminous napkin over his lap, he mentally gave thanks that the Count at least had a civilised idea about what constituted a good breakfast and that he was not going to have to make do with the eternal croissant. He noticed with some satisfaction that Elizabet had obviously also had a good breakfast—no effeminate pecking at a half-eaten roll for her. There were several little sausage sticks left on her plate. She was just finishing the remains of some scrambled egg. She looked up, the fork poised halfway to her mouth and flushed slightly as she realised he was looking at her. She smiled with slight embarrassment and he noticed with pleasure her strong even white teeth. He looked away quickly and began his own breakfast. Despite the alarms of the night, he was feeling quite hungry. Silence seemed to be the order of the day, so he devoted his attention to his food. So engrossed was he, that he started when Elizabet spoke.

"Herr 'Enery. Today you vill be very busy. You must see your house. You must see too the stables and the horses. Papa, Papa?"

"Do you not see, I read the paper, child."

"But Papa, Herr 'Enery, he must see his house and the horses. He vill vant to see the stables and the gallops…"

"Shush child…I read the paper." The paper rustled fiercely but he did not put it down. Elizabet looked crestfallen, but she brightened.

"Herr Schmidt, Herr 'Enery vishes to see his house and everything else. I vill show him. Please give to me the keys of the house so that we may look inside."

Schmidt, obviously did not like this idea. "Frauline, there is no need for you to make the trouble. At ten o'clock I vill be free. I can show Herr 'Enery all he has to see. You vill be busy vith the arrangements for tonight."

Her eyes lit up. She turned to Robert, both hands clasped to her mouth in excitement. She flushed again, the firelight flashing in her eyes.

"Herr 'Enery, I forgot," she lightly touched his arm. "We heard that you arrive in Vienna and that you would soon be here, we have plan a small party for people to meet with you. It is tonight." Her face, alight with excitement, glowed with animation. "It is so excitement. We do not have many the party. Everyone vill be so excited to meet vith you."

"But how did you know that I had arrived in Vienna?" interrupted Robert, puzzled by the idea.

"Do not vorry, we know everything!"

"But how? I came as fast as I could—how could news come faster?"

"Ah! We have our vays." She smiled conspiratorially. "We have the spies everywhere. Beware, Herr 'Enery, vot you do, we vill know about it before you have done it. Now, tonight—Herr Schmitt be so good as to ask Franc and the Chef to come now; I vish to make sure that everything is for tonight ready." She turned and smiled at Robert, her eyes alight with excitement. "Then we can go and look at Herr 'Enery's house and the horses." She turned back to Schmidt who was just leaving the room. "Please have my little carriage brought to the door."

"Miss Elizabet," said Robert. She held up her hand.

"Herr 'Enery." The excited laughter in her eyes had changed to a stern glint. "All here call me Graffinflein, and to save confusion, it is goot if you do the same. After a while, maybe, we see."

Robert smiled. "What on earth does that mean?"

She looked at him seriously. "It mean 'Little Countess'. I am not Countess, not yet. When Papa is dead, then I am Countess. I have, you see, no brothers, just me. When Papa is dead, I am Count...Countess. Now my mother, she is Countess, but she take no part in affairs. I it is who do all things. They call me 'Little Countess—Graffinflein."

Robert pushed his chair back and made a deep bow. "Graffinflein." He took her hand and gallantly raised it to his lips. With this young lady he felt totally at ease. "Graffinflein, the Captain of the Horse bids you a most loyal and convivial good day." He sat down, slightly flushed. *What on earth did I do that for?* he thought, alarmed. *I have never kissed a lady's hand in my life. What on earth is going on? It must be this place getting to me!*

She snatched her hand away and a look of anger flashed across her face.

"You mock me! I am the mistress in this house, I vill not be mock." She stood looking at him a smouldering anger in her eyes.

My God! thought Robert. *Like father, like daughter.*

Luckily the situation was saved by the return of Schmidt ushering the Chef and Franc. She turned away from him with a flounce and, seating herself in her chair, proceeded to subject the three to a barrage of questions. Robert had no idea what was said, but from the look of everyone and their replies, he deduced that they were being grilled about the evening's arrangements. Herr Schmidt made copious notes on a pad, the Chef gesticulated wildly and argued exhaustively about everything that was said to him, whilst Franc maintained a dignified silence, only occasionally nodding and interjecting the odd "Ja Graffinflein". Robert was impressed by the way Elizabet was in complete control of the three men. Although she spoke to each with authority, at no time did she talk down to them. At last she sprang to her feet and clapped both her hands together. She turned to Robert, her good humour restored.

"It is vonderful, it is all fixed. The food will be so vonderful."

God! Not more stew, Robert groaned inwardly.

"The flowers and trees are being brought in, the furniture, it is being put out. The orchestra, it arrive this morning. The people, extra, for the kitchen and the ballroom, are come this afternoon. The clothes, they are made ready for them." She clapped her hands together again and skipped an excited pirouette.

"Ice. Herr Schmidt. Ice? Have we plenty left? We must have ice. We cannot have a party if we have no ice." She saw his hesitation. "Send to the ice house at once!"

"Graffinflein, we have ice enough for twenty parties. The ice house, it was filled only two months ago. There vill be ice enough yet for months." Herr Schmidt had been conferring briefly with Franc and was able to relay this report with relief.

"Is that everything? Can any of you think of anything that we have forgot?"

Herr Schmidt sucked his pencil and looked vague. She turned to Franc and the Chef. Both looked nonplussed. She hastily translated into German and then French. Franc nodded assuredly, but the Chef launched into a voluble torrent of totally, to Robert, incomprehensible, hysterical sounding talk which Elizabet cut off with a gesture. The three left the room, the Frenchman still talking volubly to the air. She turned to Robert again.

"In ten minutes we go. Meet me then in the Hall"—and she swept out.

Robert who had jumped up as she swept out, sat down in his chair again with a bump. He now realised who was the boss in the household. He was half in admiration and awe and half puzzled. There was no denying that she was pretty, young, attractive, even desirable, but it would be a little like keeping a volcano under a meat dish—fine until you took the lid off...But then, there was nothing he hated more in a woman than a wishy-washy simpering disposition; well, here was the very opposite. She was self-assured Master in her own hose—well, Mistress. Heaven help anyone who got in the way. He mused a little. How could someone so small generate such a whirlwind? He had heard it said that the troubles in the world came from little people and, being small himself, had ignored the idea; but here, perhaps, was the personification of the phrase.

The Breakfast room door flew open.

"Vell, Herr 'Enery, shall we go?" She stood imperiously in the doorway. "Vhat is the problem? Are you not ready?"

Robert leapt to his feet, sending his chair crashing to the floor and scattering the discarded coffee cups and breakfast dishes in all directions.

"I am sorry, Graff-in-flein." He fitted his tongue awkwardly round the unfamiliar word. "I did not think that you would be ready so quickly."

"How can you measure me? You do not know how quick I am. How can you guess?"

"I am very sorry; at home no lady could be ready to go out as quickly as this."

"Vell, Herr 'Enery, you are far away from your home. Things are different here. If you are quite ready, we go."

"I must quickly get my hat and put on my boots."

"Herr 'Enery, I do not vait for mans to get their hats and put on their boots. This is not goot enough. Be so kind as to be quickness."

"I shall be very quickness, you see if I am not." Robert ran from the room and was soon struggling into his boots. He grabbed his hat and ran back downstairs.

"Herr 'Enery, thiss is not goot. When I am ready to go, I go. I do not vait while some Captain of 'Orse he run for his boots."

"I am very sorry," puffed Robert breathlessly. He was definitely out of training. "When I know what to expect, I shall be prepared."

She laughed at his breathlessness.

"I hope you learn quick. I do not wait for fat men who puff! Come, we vaists enough time."

She strode outside. Robert followed. Drawn up outside the door was a smart gig, a neat chocolate brown horse pawing the ground quietly, held by a groom dressed in what he later learned was the traditional costume of the area—black boots, white pantaloons, long white shirt, black waistcoat that hung open and a black felt hat.

He handed Elizabet up into the little carriage. He climbed in beside and sat down. The instant the groom let go of the horse's head, it started off at a brisk trot for the archway. The groom had to run and jump to gain his seat in front of them. Elizabet seemed not the least disconcerted. This was obviously usual and Robert allowed his rising alarm to subside.

They clattered through the arch at great speed and rattled over the wooden bridge. Elizabet called out something to the driver and he took the left-hand fork in the road. They passed through an orchard. Robert looked at the trees and could not decide what they were.

"What are those trees?"

"Apricots. And those," she pointed, "cherries. Do you not have these in Eengland?"

"Well, yes. They are usually grown in walled gardens. I have not seen them grown in orchards like this. It is too cold for them to grow in the open. Although I believe they do grow cherries in Kent," he added as an afterthought.

They clattered across a stone bridge and turned to pass in front of the water mill, its heavy wooden wheel cascading silver streams of water that twinkled in the morning sun as it turned ponderously. The stream that had been dammed at this point ran fast and clear from the distant hills. Robert peered speculatively at its deep willow-fringed pool. He had been introduced to the delights of trout fishing by Lord Shotley. Robert had at first found the sport frustrating and pointless, but had been, one day, hooked after he had managed to net and drag onto the grass a two and a half pound brown trout after an eventful struggle. As he unhooked the fly, he was totally captivated by the sheer glistening beauty of the creature as it lay on the lush bank at his feet, its powerful yet graceful lines and the crimson and black spots upon the shiny deep greenish ochre skin. He recalled the powerful fins and the creamy yellow belly. It had seemed to him that everything had contrived to compose a creature of such magnificence, for surely no one beholding it could doubt for one minute the beneficent hand of the bountiful creator. He had sat on the river bank in the soft evening light, the air redolent with the heavy smell of the crushed water mint beneath his feet and filled with the buzzing of a myriad insects. He had been quite overcome by the beauty of his surroundings and his wonderful capture.

He peered hopefully at the reedy fringes of the pool to see if he might see a trout rise to a fly. It looked a very likely stretch and every bone in his body told him there must be trout there.

"Are there any trout in this river?" he asked, eagerly scanning the pool.

"Trout?"

Robert did the best he could be gesture and sign to explain. She looked at him, puzzled, and then as she understood burst into peals of laughter.

"Ah, ja. Die forelle und die languite."

It was Robert's turn to be baffled. She pantomimed a small lobster with her two hands pincering the air. It was his turn to laugh. He caught both her hands and they laughed together.

"Crawfish." He laughed again, as he understood.

"How wonderful. Does anyone fish for them? It would be such fun to catch some fat trout and have some crawfish to go with them."

He tried to explain to her the thrill of fishing, but she looked more and more astonished. At last she held up her hand to stop him.

Herr 'Enery, we do not make the fishing." She looked horrified. "It is the peasant which make the fish." She poked the driver with her umbrella and shouted to him. He pulled up the carriage outside the mill, dismounted and ran inside. He presently reappeared with a very dusty man, obviously the miller. He tried to dust himself off as best he could and raised a cloud of white flour from his coat that blew away in the morning air. He made a little bow and tugged his forelock. Elizabet spoke to him rapidly and he bobbed again and again, tugging his forelock, and returned to the mill.

"There you are. You vant trout, you have trout. He vill bring them in the morning."

Robert did not know what to say. He did not want trout as such. He certainly enjoyed eating them and it was true he would not bother to fish at all if he could not eat them afterwards. It was the thrill of the hunt, the patient stalk, the beautiful surroundings, the artfully contrived fly and the delicately placed cast, the drama of the fish taking and the triumphant flick of the net, that landed the beautiful fish on the bank that thrilled him. He tried to explain this to her but she would not understand. The peasants did the fishing, it was part of their livelihood and that was that. She would not hear of Robert fishing and could not imagine that anyone would want to do this for sport.

They were trotting through a small village. Several wooden boarded huts with heavy thatched roofs stood in a cluster by the side of the road. A large flock of white geese ambled along, minded by some ragged children, and some noisily barking dogs. Elizabet waved to them as they passed, but they only stood and stared, open-mouthed.

"They are so rude. They have no manners," she said in disgust.

"Do these people work for you?" asked Robert.

She tried to explain how the people had been released from serfdom and given the land that they worked by revolutionary resolutions forced through Parliament, even though it belonged to her father. Many of them had been unable to make a living and had had to sell the land back to the original landowners. Although this meant that her father had been able to recover most of the land that he had lost, it had not been without cost. Although the peasants now had to work for him again, because there was no other employment in the area, it meant that they were serfs no longer and he now had to pay them. This made a huge expense and was seriously jeopardising the economic future of the estate. Robert listened without comment.

"How many people does your father employ?"

She shrugged. "I have not knowing." She paused and thought. "There are those who vork on the farms. There are the villages. The village where the cows for the milk, the butter and der kafe…" She hesitated, searching her mind for the English word "…cheese. Then there are those that vork in the forest; the woodmen, the 'unters, the charcoal burners. There are people who catch the fishes and vork the fish farms and vatch the river and make the baskets. There is the man in the mill and the man who make the leathers, shoes, harnesses and all such things. There are many, many. There are those who vork vith the horses and the carriages. There are many in the garden and the house."

"But all that must mean many families. What do the women and children do?"

"They do sowing and they vork with their men in the fields."

"Even the children?"

"Oh yes. As soon as they can walk, they help too. There are small little vorks that they can do. They mind the gooses, pick the nuts and the berries, find the mushrooms. As they get bigger, they can vork in the fields vith their fathers. The good girls come and vork in the castle, we need plenty there."

"But do they not go to school? How do they learn to read and write?"

"School? No, there is no school. Vhy do they need to read and write? They have no need to know these things. These are for educated people. They vould be unsettled if they had this."

"But everyone needs to learn to read and write. How else are they going to get on in the world and better themselves, if they cannot read and write?"

"Why make them unhappy? They are content. If the children vork, they are paid more. If they learn, then they get the big ideas and then they vant to go away. Then who vill do the vorks here?"

"But education is a basic human right. You are denying them their basic rights."

"Herr 'Enery, I do not know how things are in your country, but here things are different. What is better? To have them lead the simple life here. They have the good life. We provide all they need. They have their own houses and we pay them vell. We make vith them the big feasts and holidays. We have for them doctors, who live in the village. There is always enough vork for them and their children. They have secure and happy. Or is it better to educate them—then they spend the rest of there lives vanting always what they cannot have? We are keeping them happy. We have had the small revolutions. We have seen what has happened in France and Germany when there are educated peasants. We do not vant it to happen here to us. Even now there is troubles in Russia. We are very anxious that they do not travel here." She looked at him like a mother trying to explain something to a persistent child.

"But do you not see, it is just your attitude that is causing the troubles that you most fear? You are denying your people any chance of making up their own minds. You are condemning them to be second class citizens."

"They are not citizens, they are peasants!" she snapped petulantly. "It is when they *think* they are citizens, that the trouble it start."

They had been passing through a deep wood, the massive trees shading over the road, but now they came out into a wide valley made more spectacular by the sudden sunlight as they emerged from the shade of the wood. The valley had been formed by a stream that ran down the middle. It was about a mile and a half long and in its broadest part about three quarters of a mile wide. It was surrounded in perfect shelter on all sides by massive oak woods, like the one they had just passed through. The whole valley was one vast lush green meadow. In the middle, under a clump of willows and poplars, was a cluster of low reed thatched buildings.

"Vell, Herr 'Enery, what do you think? These are your gallops and stables. This is where you vill vork and live." She pointed. Beyond the roof of the barn he could see the turreted roof of a house. Robert looked in awe.

"Stop the carriage. Ask him to stop!"

She called out and the carriage slowed to a halt. He stood up and looked out over the valley.

"What a truly perfect place!" He beamed down at her and she was surprised to see tears in his eyes. Robert stood in the carriage and drank in the view. The air thrilled with the sound of larks singing, too numerous to count. From the woods came the fat throaty cooing of wood pigeons and the higher soft purring of some turtle doves. He let the beauty of it sink into him. Gradually he could feel a lump rising in his throat. After all those months of bitter frustration and anxiety, this was like coming to heaven. This beautiful place. Doing the work he loved most. All his troubles behind him. A new start. What more could a man ask? He looked down at her again, unable to speak and she, sensing the emotion in him, pulled off her glove and reaching up, took his hand in her own. She called out to the driver and the carriage started up again. Robert sat down with a bump as it lurched forward. She looked at him searchingly.

"Vell, Herr 'Enery, what vas that about?" She sat forward in her seat, still holding his hand and staring intently into his eyes. Robert felt choked with emotion and could not meet her eyes. A tear slid out of the corner of his eye and rolled down his cheek. She shook his hand with both of hers. "You must tell me. It is not goot to keep all in. The hurts they ferment like the rotten vine in the bottle, until it burst." Robert managed to regain his composure.

"Well, it is all behind now. One day, perhaps, I will tell you all about it. When I left England, things were not happy for me. Your father's offer, in the end, seemed like the wonderful chance to start a new life, begin again. And now…" He hesitated, the lump rising in his throat again, "…and now, here we are in this perfect place, it all seems too good to be true."

"Vell, Herr 'Enery, I hope that it is so."

As they drove up the valley, Robert could see groups of horses out grazing on the grass. There were mares and yearlings, and older horses all seemingly running together. They were all a very uniform dark chocolate colour and in conformation, slightly small for racing, Robert thought. Suddenly five horses, close harnessed together, three and two, thundered past them at a fast canter. The driver, if he could be called that, stood one foot on the rumps of each of the two rear horses and thus balanced, drove the five at a majestic pace. Five more thundered past and then five more behind. Robert stood up in the carriage to watch. He had never seen such a sight. He stood swaying precariously in the jolting cart as he watched them.

"What on earth is going on?"

"Do not vorry. They hear you are coming, they vish to put on the spectacle for you."

Robert watched the three teams make a wide circle to the right and was taken completely unawares as two more teams thundered past from behind, causing him to lose his balance and sit down with a bump. The five teams performed some breathtaking circles at speed round the carriage, before taking up position, two on either side and one in front. They escorted them the rest of the way into the stable yard, through an impressive wrought iron gateway.

"I thought that I had come to take charge of race horses, not run a ruddy circus!"

"You vorry too much about things. Do not vorry, this is a traditional way of riding. It is very goot. It mean that one man can vork five horses at once."

Robert gaped open-mouthed. He was about to say that that was a ridiculous idea—each horse needed to be worked individually. If they always worked in a group like that they would get used to going at the speed of the slowest! No wonder the Count's horses never won races! However, he decided to keep his council, so instead he took a studious interest in his surroundings.

The five teams had come to a halt. The riders remained standing on the rear two horses. Some boys came running out and took the heads of the lead horses. Several other men appeared from the building and one, a wizened little bandy-legged man, came hurrying towards them. They were all dressed alike, in black boots, waistcoats and felt hats with a voluminous white shirt and skirt with baggy white breeches.

"This is Soldo. He is head man, he in charge."

Robert looked at the little man. Short, thin, wizened, bandy-legged, wiry and tough, his face and hands tanned a deep mahogany. His teeth, stained and broken, were all a startling contrast to the canny blue eyes that were now peering at him with some curiosity from beneath craggy grey whiskered eyebrows. *My God!* thought Robert, *they are the same wherever you go. Change the costume and this could be Cock Sparrow!*

"Vell, they vait!" Elizabet pushed him up to stand in the carriage.

"You think I should say something?"

"Vhy, yes, of course. They have made for you the show, you must thank the honour." She smiled encouragingly up at him.

He was seized with panic. He could not speak their language. What could he do? The horses were getting restless! Every face was looking at him. *What the hell can I do?* he implored silently. Elizabet was looking at him expectantly. Soldo stood by the carriage, his hat in his hand. He had to do something.

"Of course, you could just say nothing and become known as 'Enery the Silent." Elizabet laughed.

Robert stood uncertainly. Suddenly inspiration came to him. He clapped his hands. Loudly and wildly, he clapped and he smiled. He jumped down from the carriage and shook Soldo by the hands. Still clapping, he walked to the nearest team. The rider jumped lightly down. He shook his hand. He went round everyone, clapping as he went and shook all their hands in turn. Everyone joined in. Even Elizabet stood up in the carriage and joined in the clapping. From the smiles on their faces he could see he had done the right thing. He walked back to the carriage and with a flamboyant gesture, threw open the door and offered to hand Elizabet down. She alighted with a graceful curtsey, and spoke rapidly to Soldo.

"I ask him to show us round."

Soldo, with an exaggerated flourish of his hat that bade them follow, led the way.

They were in a large courtyard formed by four lengthy low buildings, thatched ponderously with reed that in some places came down to the ground. In the middle of the yard was a large stone water trough, which seemed to be fed from a spring. Water was welling up in the middle and flowing over the sides. Even now the teams of horses were being taken over to drink. In the middle of the long barn, opposite the entrance, there was an archway.

They entered the first building through a low door. After the bright sunlight outside, it seemed very dark. As his eyes became accustomed to the gloom, he could make out rows of stalls, many of them occupied.

"Ask him why these horses are here."

"He says that they have been vorking and that now they come in for their feed and rub down."

Robert nodded. He would see about that, but now was not the time. If he was going to get anything out of this man he needed first to win him over. He was obviously going to resent having a new and, what was worse, a foreign person who could not speak the language, put over him; so it was very important that Robert did nothing to antagonise him. At the end of the building there was a ladder fixed to the wall.

"Ask him what they do with the loft."

"It is where the families of the men live."

"May I see?" Robert began climbing the ladder without waiting for an answer. When he reached the top, he pushed the closed hatch open with his head and peered cautiously in. He was met by two malevolent yellow slit eyes set in a scarred and battered face that gazed for a long stare into his own. Then the cat, for cat it was, the mangiest, most moth-eaten sample that was ever seen, its ears torn from countless fights and a sardonic sneer spread over its bristling bewhiskered face, struck out a steel-tipped paw at the face that had so rudely invaded its territory. The claws ripped his nose and Robert, letting out an anguished cry of pain, ducked down, blood streaming down his face. This caused the hatch to drop onto his fingers and he lost his footing on the ladder and he hung there crying out with pain, trapped by his fingers. Someone in the loft ran to lift the hatch and, thus released, he fell with a sickening thud to the floor below. He lay there in a dazed state, the blood from his nose running down his face and dripping off his chin onto his shirt. He was so winded by his fall that he did not feel the pain or the hurt in his fingers. He became dimly aware of a circle of faces peering down at him from the hatchway and Elizabet, tears streaming down her face, was convulsed with laughter. Soldo scuttled over and tried to help him up, attempting to dust him down as he did so. The grinning faces above disappeared and the hatch crashed shut. Soldo pulled him to his feet and continued flapping at him with his hat. Elizabet had regained her composure, but stifling her giggles behind a handkerchief, had hurried over to make sure he was all right.

"Vell, Herr 'Enery, we have no fear that you fly away! I see you cannot fly!" She collapsed again into helpless laughter.

"Ha, bloody, ha! Very funny, I'm sure. I could have been badly hurt, broken my neck or something. It was not bloody funny!"

"Herr 'Enery," she scolded in mock anger, "you do not use the stable vords in front of me. I do not hear such things. It is very bad. I have the shock." She turned her back on him in an exaggerated flounce, but her shaking shoulders and barely suppressed giggles belied her anger. Robert walked stiffly round to face her. He stood in front of her and stared into her eyes.

"I was hurt once. Badly hurt. But for two people, I would have died. People tell you they do not remember anything of when they were badly hurt, but I do. I remember every terrible sweating bit of it and I can tell you it is not bloody funny."

She stepped back, taken aback by the ferocity of what he said, all feelings of mirth instantly gone.

"I am sorry," she reached out and held his arm. "I am sorry, but you looked so funning hanging there. Die Fledermaus himself." She looked at his non-comprehension. "Die Fledermaus, it flies." She crossed her hands, hooked her thumbs together and fluttered them in front of his face. "Die fledermaus."

"Die fledermaus?" Robert watched the pantomime. Comprehension dawned. "Bat! You mean bat."

"Die fledermaus. Bat. Oh Bat!" They looked into each others eyes. "Oh Bat!" They both roared with laughter. "Bat!"

"I think die fledermaus is better!" They both laughed again. Robert's nose had stopped bleeding and he realised that nothing but his dignity had been hurt.

"Well, if I am to be the cabaret, I might as well go for the encore." He turned to the ladder and climbed again. When he reached to top, he threw open the hatch with a crash. *Any mangy moggy lurking there is going to know who is boss*, he thought as he pulled himself through the opening and stood upon the floor. He was not prepared for what he saw. He had lived in many Bothies, but none like this. The thatched roof was low and so there was very little standing room. The end of the reed bundles hung down in cobwebby dusty festoons and even he had difficulty standing in the middle of the floor under the apex of the roof. The air was filled with smoke from a fire lit on a stone slab in the middle of the loft. Sunlight shafted through the many holes in the thatch. There were about thirty people in the loft, women and children of mixed ages, all with ill-concealed mirth on their faces. An old crone slept on a grubby pile of blankets under the eve, out of the way. Some completely naked children played round the fire and on a box a young girl suckled a fat baby as she looked at him, amusement sparkling in her eyes and at the corner of her mouth. From the rafters hung some dead rabbits and a pot, on a black chain, hung from a beam over the fire. Even as he watched, sparks from the fire rose into the thatch. *Ye Gods!* he thought, *how do they not burn the place down?* Suddenly everyone jumped up and looked past him. He turned and saw Elizabet's head and shoulders protruding through the hatch.

"What on earth are you doing? It is far too…"

"Not like the lady?" she interrupted, with an amused look on her face. "I have vondered what is up here. Now I see." All the women were curtseying to her.

"Graffinflein," they twittered nervously.

"For goodness sake, be careful. It would not do for you to fall as well. They would say that die fledermaus has found a mate." He laughed, but she did not.

"Don't be so ridiculous!" and she was gone from the hatch. Robert looked at his audience and now that all attention was focused on him again, to the delighted shrieks of laughter from all round, he pantomimed the fluttering bat and climbed down the ladder. At the bottom, he brushed himself off, and readjusted his hat.

"Well, is there anything else to see?" Soldo led them through the buildings that made up the surrounds of the courtyard. They consisted of yards and horse boxes of all kinds, most in a fairly shabby and unkempt condition. At last they had completed their inspection and came out into the welcome sunlight again. It was then that Robert noticed the air was filled with the heady smell of horse beans on flowers. Obviously there was a field of the crop nearby and the heady erotic sweet smell of the flower filled the air. On the roof of the buildings there was the customary crowd of pigeons and their cooing added an exotic orchestration to the surroundings. Soldo pointed and led the way.

"This is the vay to your house." Elizabet took his arm and purposely led him through the archway in the middle barn, after the departing servant.

CHAPTER 9

Soldo led the way through the arch to the back of the yard area.

"I would really like to see the horses," Robert protested as he was ushered along through a narrow path with beds of angry-looking stinging nettles, shoulder high on either side. He looked longingly back at the yard. Soldo, who could not understand, waved encouragingly onward and determinedly led them on, thrusting his way through the undergrowth without hesitation. Robert followed and Elizabet came behind, her hand in the small of his back, determinedly propelling him onward. He did the best he could to trample the nettles down for her, but she did not seem to notice them and indeed, the length of her grey worsted skirt probably armoured her against them. The whole place was completely overgrown and untouched. Quite plainly no one had lived there for several years. The house was extremely shabby and in desperate need of a coat of paint. The door hung ajar on a broken hinge and chickens ran in and out at will. A small hen with a brood of black chicks was scratching round on the doorstep, trying to find some small titbits. Many of the wooden tiles had fallen off the roof. Pigeons were flying in and out of the gaping holes. Much of the glass was missing from the windows. There were festoons of weeds from the sagging guttering. Soldo, who had arrived first, dragged the trailing creepers aside and put his shoulder to the door. Its remaining rusty hinge gave way under the shock. It crashed to the floor amidst a cloud of dust, flying feathers and squawking chickens. Undaunted, Soldo took off his hat and waved them in with an exaggerated bow.

Robert stepped over the wreckage of the front door. With some misgivings he entered a large hall where, opposite the front door, a splendid flight of stairs with imposing banisters stretched up to the first floor. The spacious hall was panelled with shoulder-high wooden mouldings, painted dark brown. Everywhere was festooned with black cobwebs. Because of the mud that the chickens had brought in, it was impossible to see of what the floor was constructed. All was covered with a uniform layer of grime and feathers. The previous coats of paint from the ceiling hung down in grimy layers and scattered on the floor in chalky flakes. A dusty ray of sun illuminated the scene from a hole in the roof. From the floor above, the whole house was filled with the sound of the cooing of doves that had made their homes in the exposed rafters.

They made their way from room to room and everywhere the sorry picture was the same. Years of neglect had left their pathetic toll. In the kitchen at the back, a broken window had allowed some swallows entrance. They had made their nest, the mud thick and encrusted, on a beam. The spiky chicks crouched low in their nest, trying not to be seen as they observed their unexpected visitors. Robert threw open the lid of a flour bin and out jumped a large and indignant rat. He leaped aside and let the lid fall with a clatter. Elizabet screamed and picked up a large piece of wood that lay handy. Soldo, with the agility of a pouncing puma, grabbed the darting creature by the scaly tail and before it knew what had happened had swung it with such force that he dashed its brains out on the hearth. Elizabet dropped her piece of wood and, deathly white, she turned on Soldo. She began a ferocious torrent of anger and disgust at the poor man that set him cowering under its vehement wrath. She threw the occasional word of English in Robert's direction.

"This beautiful house. Not fit for pigs! How could it be in such a state?" She ranted on and on and Soldo positively wilted under the onslaught. Robert stepped forward and catching her gesticulating hand in his own, he placed his other arm round her shoulders and gave her a gentle but firm shake.

"Shush. Shush. It is only a house! I do not mind about a house. I want to see the horses—they are why I am here. I don't mind about the house. It can be repaired. I can live in the Bothy if I have to." He hugged her and tried to calm her down.

"It vas such a beautiful house! So comfortable. Now look! Look at it! How could they let it get to such a state? It vill take an army of mans to put it right." She looked up at him and for once he saw a crack in her strong facade. Her eyes were filled with tears of anger and frustration. "It was such a beautiful house," she repeated. "It vould have been so perfect for you. You vould have been so happy here." She buried her tear-stained face in his shoulder and he enveloped her in a conciliatory hug.

"Shush. Shush. Don't worry about it. I am sure it can be restored. Look what fun we will have doing it up again and bringing it back to life." She lifted her tear-stained face to him.

"We?"

"I could not possibly undertake such a thing on my own. There are the horses to be seen to and your father's business to take my attention. I could not possibly see to the restoration of this house in the way that it needs and deserves. I just would not have the time or the energy. I would need the help of one with an eye for such things. One with the imagination to restore the house to what it had previously been. One who could change it from a wreck to a home. I know that I presume, but I wonder, Graffinflein, perhaps I could solicit your help and expertise in the project? I know that through you, we could work a sympathetic restoration." She looked up at him, the beginning of a smile on her face.

"You think that we could do thiss?"

"Yes, of course, we could have such fun!" *Thank God I have the gift of the silver tongue of the Irish!* he thought to himself. Already she was cheered and was beginning to look around with a new interest.

"We could clean this room out and make some paint. Mend the vindow. A table, some chairs. We could take these from the castle. Why, it would be the good fun! I would enjoy this…" She paused. "Is it always that the Eenglish hold the daughters of the people for whom they vork, so tightly?" She smiled up at him. Robert realised he still held her in a tight hug. He hastily let her go.

"I am sorry; I didn't mean to squeeze you."

"Squeeze? Vot is squeeze?"

"Hold you tightly. I was holding you rather tightly."

"Do not have sorry. If you me squeeze some more, I vill come again."

Robert laughed, but blushed. That was not such a bad idea. "Come on then. Let's see what else needs doing. I'm afraid it will need more than a bit of paint and a few sticks of furniture from the Castle." He took her hand and together they explored the rest of the rooms. Clambering up the decaying staircase they looked into the bedrooms and at the roof. Elizabet had recovered her spirits. She was full of excitement at the possibilities of each room. Robert, however, was getting impatient. He could see that the day was wearing on, and he wanted to see the horses.

"Come on, it is obvious that I cannot live here for the time being. I will sleep with a horse rug in the stable, if I have to, until it is fixed. We have got plenty of time to discuss what is to be done later. I want to have a look at the horses now. Please tell Soldo that I wish to see them."

Elizabet looked at him with a surprised smile.

"Who is become so masterful?" She tuned to Soldo and, judging from the crestfallen and cringing expression on his face, she had not yet had the last word on the state of the house. However, her tone changed and so did his expression. His look of terror changed to one of panic. He launched into a long reply, which seemed to involve a great deal of pointing in different directions and much wringing of the unfortunate black hat.

"Well?" said Robert. "What was that all about?"

"There are only the horses that you have seen which is here. The mothers and the little ones are down by the river, they are too far, it is not possible for us to see them today. We have to be home in time for the soiree. The young ones are out on the meadows. We can drive to them on the way home. There are only some mothers in here in the boxes and the papa and the young papa. Soldo will show you these if you vish."

"Good, we will see what we can, it will be a start. Tomorrow I can ride round and see the rest."

"Oh, I cannot come tomorrow. Tomorrow we go to Vienna, for the week."

"Well, I will have to ride round on my own. I must make a start."

"Oh, but you vill come too. It is the meeting of June. Papa has the horses entered. "He vill be expecting you to make them win."

"How can I make them win? I have not worked with them. I have not even seen them. I do not know anyone. What race is it anyway? What is the distance? Who is the jockey? Who will be going with the horses?"

"Questions, always questions! You worry too much. Just do not worry. Just make the horse win, that is all, it is simple."

"Shall I fly to the moon at the same time? I mean, no task, be it ever so difficult, is impossible. Just bring it to Henery, he will solve all your problems, I don't think!" Robert added with a bitter taste in his mouth.

"Herr 'Enery, I think you are making the dumpling out of the breadcrumb!. Do not make the complainings. I hate the men who make the complainings."

Robert groaned inwardly. "Ask Soldo about the horse for the race. When will it go? How will it get there? Who is going to go with it? Who is the jockey? What about the food, the blacksmith, the vet? Have the entries been correctly made?"

Elizabet looked at him, open mouthed. "This is very complicated. I see that horses run past the winning post. I do not think of these things. I do not want to think of these things. You have to think of these things, there are so many. I make the small bet, and I watch them and I have the champagne and the caviar. I have no idea there are so many worries." She questioned Soldo at length. "It is that the horses have already gone, three days. They go by box to the river and then on the boat to Vienna. They arrive tomorrow. There are three men who have gone with them. The jockey, he arrive of Tuesday. Soldo he come with us tomorrow. He is only here now to velcome to you. Soldo he does not know about the forms and the entries. Schmitt he see to all that."

Robert listened to all this with slightly slowing pulse rate. At least it looked as if things were in train, but as for winning, that was in the lap of the Gods. He realised that there was absolutely nothing he could do about any of it. Events would just have to take their turn.

"Come on, let's have a look at what we can then."

Soldo led the way to a range of boxes that they had not yet seen. There were some of the mares. Robert minutely inspected each one. By and large they were in good condition and were very uniform in conformation and colour. They seemed a little on the small side but size was not everything. Robert inspected their feed troughs and ran his hand under their rugs. He was not too impressed with the standard of grooming and noticed that the state of the litter showed they had not been cleaned out as often as might be expected. The tack, the bridles and halters and the rugs, were not that clean and the mangers obviously had not been washed out since they were built. Robert took up a handful of food and brought it to his nose. It had a sour musty smell to it and he wrinkled up his nose in disgust. There was an almost bald yard broom standing by the door and beside it a rusty shovel caked with hard dung, that had seen neither use or polishing for a long time. He was annoyed that these small details, which suggested slack management, were so obvious. At the same time, they were improvements that, although they would make him unpopular, would make a difference to the running of the animals.

He soon realised he too was under scrutiny. Both Elizabet and Soldo watched his every move and reaction like hawks. The various lads that they saw were watching, too, to see if he knew anything about horses at all. He could detect an air of resentment and hostility, with which he could sympathise. He would not have liked a total stranger and a foreigner who did not speak the language, to have been placed over him. He would have to tread carefully if he was to secure the co-operation of these people. He could not afford to bully these men. Their life was horses. They almost certainly knew more about them than he did, but if he were to succeed, he needed their willing co-operation and enthusiasm for what he was trying to do. To try to impose his will by pulling rank and showing his fangs would simply alienate them and stultify their enthusiasm. He finished the inspection.

"Let's have a look at the stallions." Elizabet looked puzzled. "The papas." Elizabet translated and with a slight shrug, Soldo led the way. The stallions' boxes were in the corner of the barn and were as heavily fortified as a siege barricade. Heavy oak doors supported by iron hinges and bolts were held secure with a massive oak beam passed through some heavy wrought iron hoops. Robert had seen many stallion boxes before, but this one took the prize for the weight of its fortifications. It would have contained a rampaging rhinoceros. He peered through the barred aperture. Inside it was totally dark and he could see nothing at all. Suddenly a pair of white, flared, snorting nostrils blew angrily right into his face and a hoof pounded on the door, shaking it to its foundations. He involuntarily started backwards. Elizabet and Soldo both cried out. Gingerly he returned to the opening. This time he was ready. When the horse snorted in his face and lashed at the door with his hoof, he stood his ground and when it had stopped he blew long and hard into its nostrils. It stood quietly. He reached through the bars and stroked its nose. It stood still, gently tossing its head against the pressure of his hand. He stood back and gestured to Soldo to open the door. A look of panic spread over the aged retainer's face. He spoke rapidly to Elizabet.

"He say do not go in, the horse, he is danger."

"So would you be if you were shut in this hell hole. Tell him to open the door."

Soldo looked defiant and hesitated. Robert was just about to tell him again when he reluctantly drew the clanking bolts and shifted the massive bar. Robert pulled the door, which opened stiffly. Stepping quickly inside, he shut it behind him. The stallion stood looking at him, with his ears back and his lips curled showing his yellow teeth. Robert quickly blew into its nostrils again, and though it shook its head its lip relaxed and its ears twitched. Robert gently took hold of its halter and softly stroked its neck and shoulder. Robert's hand gradually and quietly explored the creature. He suddenly came across a great weal and the animal flinched as he touched it. He found another and another, each as tender as the first. Someone had been fiercely beating the horse. No wonder they were afraid of it. It would react badly to savage treatment! No wonder! Robert quietly let himself out of the box. Soldo rapidly locked the door with a look of total disbelief on his face. He was white and trembled as he pushed home the big bar. Ashen faced, he spoke rapidly to Elizabet.

"He say you very, very foolish to enter his stable. He is very dangerous. They snare him from the rafters and tie him up before they dare enter. You vere lucky he did not kill you. You must not take again the risks."

"No wonder he is savage if they treat him like that. How would you like it, kept in this dark hole and cruelly treated? I bet the only excitement that he gets is when a mare is brought to him. I should not be surprised that he is shy. Ask Soldo how he is with the mares." A rapid conversation ensued.

"It seem that he is very difficult with the mares."

"I bet, poor animal. He probably knows that the thing he wants to do most, will simply earn him stress and a beating. I bet he is so frustrated and confused that he doesn't know what he is doing. I don't like this at all. This has got to be changed. No wonder the poor creature reacts so badly. What is in the next box?"

"Apparently ziss…"

"Ziss? Why do you always keep saying 'ziss'? If you want to learn to speak English properly, you must say this, *th, th, th, th*is." Robert eyed her irritably. He had been becoming more and more despondent as his tour of inspection had found the organisation sadly lacking, according to his standards. The condition of the unfortunate stallion had been the last straw. She looked at him in surprised alarm, as if her pet dog had suddenly turned round and bitten her.

"Herr 'Enery, I think the feet are in the other boot—it is *you* who are here to learn German." A glint of annoyed astonishment flashed across her eyes. "You make no effort. You do not speak the vord of German. How you learn if you do not speak?" She glowered at him. Robert was not the least repentant.

"I am starting from nothing. I have to get used to hearing it spoken and then learn some words and then become bold enough to utter them, but you, you are well advanced. You speak English very well. I was only seeking to help you improve your accent, so that you can speak it better, as your mother suggested that I should." She looked at him, eye for eye and the expression on her face softened somewhat.

"I am sorry. Yes, it is good that you help me to improve and I vill help you with your German." She carefully formed the sound. "This is the home of the young stallion." Robert looked at her quizzically.

This box had more light and Robert could see that it contained a well built but rather evil looking brute, but decided that further inspection could wait until another time. They had gathered quite a retinue of stable lads and their families, who seemed intent on watching everything that happened.

They left the dark confines of the horse barns and went outside again into the bright sun and warmth of the central yard. After the gloom within, the sunlight was almost overpoweringly dazzling. Elizabet took out her small gold watch that was hung round her neck on a slim gold chain.

"Herr 'Enery, it is time ve—we"—she spoke carefully—"vent back to the Castle, as there are many things that must be done for the soiree tonight."

"But what about the young stock, the racing horses, the mares and foals, where are they? I would like to at least see them, before we go home."

"We can drive home by the river and see them as we go, now come, we must go." She turned and walked swiftly across to the carriage. She allowed herself to be handed in by one of the stable lads who had run to open the door. Robert did not quite know what to do. He felt he wanted to say something, make some gesture. He turned and shook the hand of Soldo who seemed quite surprised and, waving to everyone else, he quickly hopped into the carriage. Elizabet called to the driver and with a snap of his whip, they set off round the yard and out through the arched gate at a furious pace, scattering chickens and people in all directions as they went.

As they sped through the arch, they came face to face with a small cart piled high with a tottering heap of luggage. Both attempted to pull to the side, but in the narrow confines there was little room. Their wheels crashed together with a sickening crunch and their carriage was pushed sideways with a crash against the stone arch. The cart was pushed against the other side and the pile of luggage cascaded onto the ground. The horses were rearing and plunging, the traces and harness broken by the sudden impact. The driver had been jerked off his seat and from the ground he was doing the best that he could to calm them. Robert and Elizabet had been thrown in a heap together on the floor of the carriage. She struggled to her feet and let out a torrent of words at the other driver, her own man and the stable hands, who had come running from the yard. Robert struggled to his feet.

"I am glad that I could not understand any of that. It was not his fault, we were going too fast."

She turned on him, anger in her eyes. "You Eengleesh, you are always so bloody fair."

Robert was shocked both at the language and the intensity of her fury.

"The stupid man has wrecked the carriage and the harness. How we now get to home in time for this evening?" She stamped her foot and started shouting and gesticulating at everyone again with renewed fury.

Robert took her arm and tried to restrain her. "For goodness sake, calm down. I am sure that we can sort it all out."

She looked at him, like a tigress deprived of its prey, her hat awry and a long wisp of hair blowing wild.

"Herr 'Enery, you do not tell me vhat to do!" she snapped angrily at him. "Get off and make some helpings, instead of standing there and telling me vhat to do!"

Robert climbed down and was surprised to find that all the luggage that had been piled so precariously on the little cart and which now lay scattered all over the road, was his own. The driver staggered to his feet and, still holding on to his horses' reins, handed Robert a letter. Robert quickly broke the seal and unfolded the paper. It was from the Countess

Herr Henery,

I convey to you my best greeting and hope that you passed a comfortable and restful night last night. Now that you have seen your new home, you will be anxious to move in straight away, so that you can become settled before you depart with us tomorrow for Vienna. I have therefore commanded Schmidt to have a man prepare your luggages and arranged for them to be transported to you, as unfortunately we need your room tonight for my cousin who is staying with us, for the little soirée that we are holding tonight in your honour. I have taken the liberty of asking for a small hamper of provisions to be sent as well, so that you will not starve until you can make your own arrangements. Please give the enclosed letter to my daughter.

We will expect you at the Castle tonight at 7 o'clock.

Countess von Ramoskie

He handed the folded and sealed piece of paper to Elizabet. She read it in silence, her lips forming the words as she read.

"It is redicule. You can not stay here. What does my mother think? They must find room for you somewhere."

"I have slept in worse places, not often, admittedly, but I can manage. It is only for one night after all. Tomorrow we go to Vienna." They argued for some time about what to do, until Robert noticed that Soldo was hovering in the background.

"Yes?" asked Robert.

He pointed, indicating that they had been able to repair the harness. If Graffinflein's carriage could back a little, it could be freed from the gatepost and could continue on its way. Robert had been so busy with Elizabet that he had not noticed that the activity had stopped round them. His luggage was back on the cart, the horses reharnessed. Elizabet's driver was back on his box and the group of people who had come to help stood quietly together watching the proceedings with considerable interest.

Robert made up his mind. He handed Elizabet back into her carriage.

"Just ask your man to back a little and then you can go. I will stay here and come over later." He heard nothing of her protests and as the driver backed the horses a little, he and Soldo and some of the stable hands manhandled the carriage wheel round the gatepost. As soon as it was free, which was not effected without some considerable exertion and shouting in a variety of languages, he waved the driver off. As they departed down the road he saw Elizabet standing in her carriage, her anxious face peering at them over the back. He waved.

He became aware that he had become the centre of a group of onlookers, who, now that Elizabet had departed, had turned their undivided attention on him.

Robert stood undecided. What should he do now? Elizabet had by now disappeared behind the large cloud of dust raised by her passing. There was obviously not going to be a chance to see the young stock now. That would have to wait for another day. The most pressing question was where was he going to spend the night. The house was obviously out of the question. Despite the brave boast, Robert did not relish spending the night in the Bothy. His mind's eye ran through the remaining buildings. The tack room, he recalled, had been cleaner than most. There was a pile of horse blankets, and he could sleep in he clothes, if he had to. He pointed to the tack room and made them understand that was where his luggage was to be taken. If he was to be back at the Castle in time, he needed to start getting ready. He was fairly sure he could remember in which trunk he had packed his evening cloths.

Eventually he was changed and sitting in the small cart that had brought his luggage, bouncing his way back to the Castle.

CHAPTER 10

Thus it was that some hours later, Robert, dressed to kill, with Soldo precariously perched on the box, drove into the castle yard in a ridiculously small cart. The place was a bustle of activity. The yard was crowded with carriages that had been pushed to the side by the waiting grooms. The horses had been led off to stables at the rear. Even as they arrived, a magnificent four in hand team of Lippizaners was being led away.

As soon as they had stopped, Soldo leapt off the box and disappeared. He obviously had duties in the stables. Robert was left sitting in the little cart, feeling abandoned and crestfallen. Some boys ran to him and, handing him down, led the little cart away. He stood on the foot of the steps, uncertain as to what to do. It had been a bit of a shock to him to hear that he had been thrown out, only a few hours earlier. Now here he was again, a guest, indeed the guest of honour, returning alone, not sure of his audience. He hovered uncertainly, but was galvanised into action as a coach and four hurtled through the arch, the sound of their arrival crashing round the enclosed courtyard in a clattering of iron shod hooves, clanking harness and creaking, scrunching wheels. The splendid equipage pulled up at the foot of the steps. *I cannot stop here, they will think I am a bloody footman,* thought Robert to himself. As the splendid vehicle scrunched to a stop, the horse scattering gravel, sparks and steam as they clattered to a halt. He took his courage in both hands. Mounting the stone steps, he approached the front door. Even as he stretched out his hand to the handle, it swung open and he was able to enter. The sombre hall of the night before had been transformed. The bronze figures that he had hardly noticed, either side of the fireplaces, were a blaze of light from the many branched candelabra that they carried. On every piece of furniture, glittering candelabra shed their bountiful light into the room. The fireplaces were ablaze with fire and a small boy posted at each continually fed the flames with tinder dry fuel, so that they constantly flared and flashed their warmth, giving light and life into the hall. The heat after the bone chilling drive in the small cart, was intense. The effect was like the pulsating heat of some throbbing volcano, generating energy for its last cataclysmic outburst.

Franc stood in the hallway and greeted him with a long and obsequious salutation. It was plain that Robert had not understood and so with a sweep of his arm and a gentle shove, he propelled Robert through the massive door on the left of the hall. With a deep breath, Robert entered.

The whole room was a sea of light. Enormous glittering chandeliers, festooned with a king's ransom of flaming candles, filled the ceiling. On the many tables candles flamed in myriad profusion. In the wall sconces flaming torches cast their flickering light into even the darkest recesses of the room. The vaulted ceiling disappeared into celestial blackness. This must be the Great Hall of which he had heard slight mention.

He became aware of the Countess standing before him.

"Ah Herr 'Enery, I hope that you have found your new house to your satisfaction. I am sorry that I had to ask you to leave, but you see we are a little full tonight. I do hope that you enjoy this little soiree, that we have planned especially to honour your arrival. Oh, Gustaff!" She threw herself in a familiar embrace into the arms of the person who had entered behind Robert and he, feeling rather superfluous, moved on. He felt his hand taken and pumped vigorously.

"Ah! 'Enery!" boomed the Count, who was standing next to his daughter. "You are settled into your house and now ready to start vork in the morning?" Robert felt a flash of anger—of course he was not settled in. The house was not fit for pigs and would not be for some weeks. Stupid man! Did he not know about the condition of the place? Robert was about to give voice to a modified edition of his thoughts.

"We velcome you to our humble household. This little party is to celebrate the many victories that you vill make with the horses." The Count took a deep breath and bellowed at the company a long address in German. Robert grinned, but did not understand a word. He turned to the Countess.

"What does he say?" She quickly translated.

"He says you vill make many victories with the horses. If they all back our horses, you vill make their fortunes."

There was a roar of approval from the room and Robert, full of confusion and misgivings and not a little awestruck by the idea that these people might be expecting him to make their fortunes, turned to face the room. He was confronted with a sea of faces and nodding ostrich feathers. As he turned, they all burst into applause. Robert felt embarrassed and vulnerable. However, with an uncomfortable smile, he waved and bowed to them all. Instantly a loud and prolonged round of applause broke out from the assembled company and rang round the room.

The Count stamped his foot and clapped his hands. With much gesticulating and bellowing in German, the room fell silent and he addressed the gathering again.

"He is telling everyone…" Elizabet was translating for him "…vhat a jolly fine trainer you are and how the English Milord Shotley was so keen to recommend you. From now on everyone should bet on 'is 'orses, for once you took charge of them, there would be no other to touch them." The room erupted into a burst of clapping and good humoured cheering. "Herr 'Enery, you must make the speech!" There was an expectant hush and Robert could see a sea of eager faces peering at him. Robert went white at the prospect.

"I cannot speak to them," he hissed between his teeth in panic. "I cannot speak German for a start." He writhed in anguish.

"But I vill make the translate for you." She smiled encouragingly at him.

"But how can I?" He could see that he was trapped. The guests were still looking at him expectantly but a gentle buzz of conversation had started. A few were beginning to shuffle. It was now or never; if he did not speak, he would be seen to be a failure. He might as well pack his bags and go home. He took a deep breath and, summoning up his courage, began.

"Count and Countess, Ladies and Gentlemen, I must apologise for not being able to speak to you in your own language. I hope that soon I shall learn. In the meantime, I ask your patience. I feel very fortunate in being able to come to this, your beautiful country and I look forward to beginning work with the Count's splendid horses. Once I have had time to work with them, then might be the time for a few small bets, but until that time, my best advice is to keep your money in your pocket."

Elizabet translated and there was a ripple of laughter round the room. Robert, encouraged, continued. "I am most grateful for the kind welcome that I have received and for the generous support that I have received from those who have tried to help me." He smiled at Elizabet and was gratified to see her blush and cast a lingering glance at him. Their eyes met. His spine tingled as he met that stare. He continued: "I am most flattered that you are met here tonight. I hope that the horses of the Count will win many races to the enrichment of us all." Elizabet translated and there was a spontaneous burst of applause and cheering.

Robert wiped his brow with his handkerchief and turned with a sense of elation to Elizabet. "Well, how did I do? That was the first speech that I have made in a foreign language!"

"Vot? You did the speech, I did the language." Elizabet smiled at him.

Robert laughed. "Of course, without you I would be unable to do anything other than gesticulate. You are wonderful."

"Ah Gustaff! You have come in time." The Count turned from Robert and enveloped the person behind him in a benign bear hug. Robert turned to Elizabet.

"Herr 'Enery, the little cart brought you here safely, then?"

Robert turned and as their eyes met an electric moment passed. Elizabet smiled at him and offered him her hand. He took it and slowly raised it to his lips, all the while their eyes together. The transformation from her work-a-day grey pin-striped worsted, to this dazzling apparition in pearl cream satin, was overwhelming. Her hair was piled up in a creation of cream coloured rosebuds on the top of her head, one slender ringlet falling casually behind her left ear. The pale pearl coloured dress emphasised the slimness of her waist and the figure-hugging bodice gave lift to her elegant posture and framed her bare shoulders that glowed a soft sheen in the flickering light. As their eyes met they were both tongue-tied. Robert was the first to recover.

He still held her hand and again their eyes met, for just that lingering look longer than casual conversation deemed necessary.

"Herr 'Enery, perhaps we might dance later. My card it is full at the moment, but perhaps one will become too tired or too drunk and we have the dance?"

Robert could feel the warmth vibrating through her hand. He abruptly let it drop.

"Graffinklein, you don't know what you ask!" he laughed. "The last time that I danced, everyone thought that I was doing an imitation of a carthorse with a wooden leg!" She laughed too.

"I am the frisky filly too, vhen I get going!" They both laughed and enjoyed that intimate moment of a joke unknown to others, shared between them. He moved on, as other arrivals claimed her attention. "You must go to the buffet and 'ave some food." She pointed with her fan to a long table, which was already attracting a crowd of people.

His passage to the buffet did not prove to be as easy as he hoped. His way was barred by a sea of starched white shirt fronts, heaving cleavages and nodding ostrich feathers, as people pressed to shake his hand and make him feel welcome. Most were anxious to show him how good their English was and he fought his way through a succession of garbled conversations that mostly consisted of "God Bless Queen Victoria" or "Does it rain today?" or "'Oo ees going to vin next veek?" As Robert had not a clue who was even running, he felt himself hardly qualified to reply. A plate was thrust into his hand and he was swept along the long serving tables by a throng of happy freeloading people all anxious to pile titbits onto his plate. Before he knew it, someone had cut a huge slice off the great glazed carp that was the centrepiece of the display and placed it on his pate with a triumphant smile. Robert tried to refuse it, but he was too late, the deed was done and his language was not up to the situation. In desperation he looked up and saw Elizabet at the other end of the table. She was on the arm of a sallow, greasy-looking Guard's officer, as he plied her plate with delicacies from the proffered dishes. A pang of jealousy flashed through him and in some state of disgruntlement, he took a glass of red wine and with his loaded plate, set off for the only vacant place that he could see, amongst the side tables provided. He placed his plate on the table and gratefully sat down. Immediately the men seated round it, opposite him, leapt to their feet. Then began a prolonged introduction. They each introduced themselves and the ladies they were with and then they introduced each other. As far as Robert could see, they repeated this at least three times. It became apparent that he could not understand a word they said, so they lapsed into an embarrassed silence. Robert sought refuge in his food. Driving his fork in the mountainous contents he came up with a large flake of carp.

"Ah, carp," he chuckled nervously, "from the moat." He eyed it with terror. No one else appeared to have any. He gingerly put it in his mouth. It was firm, yet tender and succulent. He tried not to think of the flavour, but considering its diet, it was really quite agreeable. *Don't think of the diet, just enjoy the flavour.* He was conscious that everyone was looking at him. A decanter of wine appeared over his shoulder and poured into a glass a pale white wine. He tasted the astringent bitter-sweet liquid. It was agreeably fragrant, yet tart. It cut a clear thrust through any thoughts that he had of the moat and developed in his mouth the subtle flavours of the fish. Stupid people! The fish was really rather fine. They did not know what they were missing!

He stood up. "Excuse me," he said. The fish was rally rather good. The moat be damned, he was going to have another piece to finish with his wine. He returned to the buffet and to his relief found that there was plenty left. In fact it seemed that the small portion that he had had, was the only piece removed. He helped himself to another large slice, taking care to avoid the needle sharp bones.

"It seems that I have been instrumental in turning you out of your room!"

Robert turned to the person behind him who had spoken. A tall, well-built young man, dressed in immaculate evening dress, his hair brushed straight back, smiled down at him. Robert's look of surprise made him laugh.

"Your room! You had to get out of your room to make way for me. I gather that you have moved into the house of the Captain of the Horse."

Robert laughed out loud. "I would hardly say that I had moved in. Tonight I am sleeping in the Tack Room as it is the only place with anything that looks like a roof in the whole place." The man's eyebrows shot up.

"It is not that bad surely?"

"Do you know the place?"

"Well, some years ago, I have been there with Elizabet, but not for some time."

"Well," said Robert, taking an instant liking to the man. "Let me tell you that the chickens have been going in and out for so long that there is so much mud and feathers on the floor, you cannot see where the yard ends and the floorboards begin. The front door has fallen off its hinges. Most of the windows are broken and the swallows fly in and out to the nests that they have built on the beams. Pigeons fly in through the holes in the roof where the tiles have fallen off! The stairs are so rotten that even a mouse would be in danger of falling through and breaking its neck. The cobwebs are so long and plentiful that you could cast them into the moat and catch all the carp in one haul. Apart from that, it is fine!" Robert laughed ruefully. The look on the man's face was a picture.

"My dear fellow! This is terrible. It is typical of Cousin August. I would be prepared to bet that he has not been near it for years. I am very sorry that I have put you to this inconvenience! It is unthinkable that you should be put to such an unpleasant situation. I will speak to Cousin Helga at once. She must find a room. She cannot just turn you out to sleep in the stable, for the sake of Heaven!"

"No, don't worry! It is only for one night, for we are going to Vienna tomorrow for the races."

The man smiled. "Good, we look forward to seeing your horses win. Cousin August has assured us that once you are here, all his horses will sweep the board!"

"Steady on!" Robert protested. "I have not even seen any of the horses yet. Whether they win or not tomorrow, or in the week, is in the lap of the Gods. I certainly cannot influence things at this stage." He smiled. The man's look darkened slightly.

"Cousin August assured us that as soon as you are here, his horses will win." He paused, a slight frown spreading over his face. "They will win tomorrow, won't they?" He looked at Robert in an appealing way. Robert understood. *Oh my God!* He thought to himself, *he has bet more on them than he can afford. Why won't people bet with their heads, not their hearts?*

"No matter what the Count says, how on earth do you think that I can have done anything with the horses? I have only been here two days and have not yet even seen the racing stock. Most of the field will be strange to me, though I may have seen some of them in England. It takes weeks to know about a horse and perhaps several months of careful feeding, handling and training to bring a horse to its best condition. Only then is it possible to make some assessment about its likely form or how it might do against any possible rivals." His companion looked crestfallen. "I hope that you have not ventured too much money on it on the say-so of your-a—Cousin?"

"He has done nothing but say how wonderful his horses are going to be—how there will be nothing to beat them now that you are here. I think everyone has been backing them."

"Well, I hope that they are not too disappointed. They should know better than to expect miracles the first day. You should know better than to get too carried away by the enthusiasms of your Cousin." Robert laughed at the crestfallen look on his face. "Don't worry, perhaps if we have a look at the other runners, you can find the possible winner. Maybe a small amount on that will cover your potential loss on your Cousins horse."

He brightened a little. "That is good. With you to advise me, perhaps all is not lost. You are right. My Cousin is an ass, I should have known better. Forgive me, I should have introduced myself. I am Emil, Count von Zelletall, Prince von Tauber. I am a cousin of Countess Helga Ramoskie. The Count, therefore, is only my cousin by marriage." He offered his hand and as he did so, he clicked his heels and bowed slightly. Robert too bowed and took his hand.

"I am very glad to meet you Sir. I am Robert Henery. I am newly appointed Captain of your Cousin's horses." They both shook hands solemnly and laughed together at the formality.

"Ah! Waiter!" Count Emil did a neat pirouette and diverted a tray of drinks in front of Robert. "A glass of champagne, Captain, and I will have one too, to drink a toast to your new appointment, success and happiness."

They raised their glasses, clinked them together. As he savoured the refreshing effervescence and the rich toasty flavour of the chilled wine, Robert saw in this man a friend and ally. There are times when you meet people that you detect in them a kindred spirit, someone with whom you are instantly at ease. Robert felt sure that here was just such a one.

"I must congratulate you, Count, on your excellent English. I wish that I could speak even a little German. I am feeling a little lost at the moment and completely alienated."

"Do not worry, my friend, you will soon pick it up. You will soon be speaking like a native. Yes, thank you, I was for a while at school in England and spent some time at the University of Cambridge. By the way, when we are together, I would like it if you were to call me Emil and with your permission, I will call you Robert."

"Of course, I should be delighted." They shook hands again and laughed together.

"Robert, here we stand in front of this magnificent buffet—what about some food?"

Robert looked about him. He had put his plate down and now it seemed to have disappeared. Oh well, perhaps it was no bad thing. No one else seemed to have eaten any of the huge carp.

"That huge fish, there, look, in the middle. No one seems to have taken any. What is it?"

Emil looked to where Robert was pointing.

"Don't eat any of that. That is a carp from the moat. My Cousin Helga always has one prepared as a centre piece, but everyone knows that it has come from the moat; as we all know what goes in there, no one eats it." He looked more closely. "Oh! I see some poor unfortunate has taken some." He laughed. "I hope he does not have a sleepless night." Robert began to feel queasy.

"Oh, is it that bad?"

"Well, when you think what its diet is, it is a little off-putting."

Robert laughed and his gastronomic unease subsided. "What is going to happen to it then? It seems a waste to kill the poor creature just for display?"

"Do not worry. Anything that is left over will be given to the servants. They will take it home. Some family will no doubt make a feast of it."

Robert wrinkled his nose. "Won't they mind where it has come from, eating it, I mean?"

Emil laughed "Good heavens no! They are peasants. They do not mind, they eat that sort of thing."

Robert was shocked at this callous and indifferent view that again brought home to him the great gulf that existed between master and man.

"Come on. Let's attack the food or there will be none left." Even as they had stood talking, they had been continually jostled by a succession of people as they made their way along the table collecting huge platefuls of food. *There's not going to be much left for the peasants tonight*, thought Robert as they joined the throng. Under Emil's guidance he left the table with a plate overflowing with food. He had a cold stuffed roasted quail, some pike quenelles, neatly rolled in breadcrumbs. Some fat white asparagus, some slices of home smoked ham, some cold salt beef and a great slice off the ham of a wild boar. On top of this was perched a mound of pickled cabbage, some pickled gherkins and a prettily cut tomato. He hovered uncertainly at the end of the table, wondering where to sit. Emil caught his eye. He too was struggling to balance a similarly laden plate.

"Follow me, we can go and sit over there." The two of them weaved their way across the room, Robert following Emil.

"Here we are, Robert, you sit here, I will sit there." He put his plate down and placed a kiss on the cheek of the very large lady beside him. He half turned to Robert.

"My dear, let me introduce to you Herr Robert Henery, the new Captain of the Horse. Robert, allow me to introduce you to my wife, Maria."

Robert bowed low over the proffered hand and was completely mesmerised by the sea of pink cleavage that heaved effusively beneath his nose as he did so. He bit his lip to suppress a giggle.

"Enchanted, Madame," he murmured to try to hide his mirth. Luckily Emil called to her and distracted her attention. Robert turned to the lady on the other hand. It was Elizabet. She sat smiling up at him. The light gleamed on her bare shoulders with a soft warm glow and he had to restrain himself from reaching out and touching them. Her dress, too, in the fashion of the time, was cut low, but no sea of wobbling pink blancmange here. Her iridescent white skin was emphasised to perfection by the cut of her gown, which gave fullness to her slender figure. He contained himself no longer and burst out laughing as he sat down. With a look of alarm, she touched his arm.

"What have I done, which make you so laugh?" The look of earnest apprehension on her face made him laugh the more.

"No, Graffinflein," he managed to say between gasps. "I was not laughing at you. The contrast between you with your beautiful elegant figure and the mountainous heap of heaving pink blancmange on my left was too much. I had to laugh."

She looked surprised, then pleased, as she worked out what he had said, then puzzled.

"Blancmange, vhat is this?"

Before Robert could stop her, she had called across the table. "Emil, vhat is 'blancmange'"?

He looked back at her, slightly puzzled. "Das blancmanger?" It was his turn to look puzzled. "Why do you ask?"

Elizabet looked at Emil and Robert and then at the majestically heaving figure of Emil's wife, who was happily enjoying her food as if it were the last meal that she would see for several weeks, totally oblivious of the conversation going on around her. At last Elizabet understood. She hid her face in her hands and her shoulders shook in hopeless laughter. At last she recovered enough to scold Robert.

"You must not say these unkind things about my cousin, you are very naughty!" However, the smile on her face and the look of amusement in her eyes told him that this was only a protest, not a rebuke.

He felt very embarrassed. This was obviously the top table. He could see seated further down, the Count and Countess who were being waited on by a procession of girls in traditional costume, brought in for the evening. There was, too, an army of men, dressed in a variety of liveries, who were carrying the heavier dishes. The food was being brought from the buffet table and the dishes were being offered round the tables.

"Graffinflein, I feel very embarrassed, this seems to be the top table, but Emil insisted that I should sit here."

"Herr 'Enery, you are embarrassed to be sitting next to me?" she playfully mocked him.

"No, that is not what I meant. It just does not seem right that the mere Captain of the Horse should be seated at the top table, with the family."

"Herr 'Enery, tonight you are the guest of honour. This party is to celebrate the fact that you are come and that you are going to make our fortunes vith the winnings of the horses. Are you not satisfied vith seated here? You can move. Look, there is a chair over there, all alone in the corner. You could go and be there if you vish"

"No, no. That is not what I meant. There is nowhere in the whole world where I would rather be at this moment." Their eyes met and she held his gaze, a slight smile on her lips. They were interrupted by a dish of stuffed quails being offered between them. She accepted one and so did he. Suddenly he realised he meant what he said. He glanced quickly at her and their eyes met again and she blushed and busied herself with the quail. She unbuttoned her long white gloves at the wrist and, having gently eased her hand out of the fingers, tucked them back. She quickly cut off the small leg of the bird which she proceeded to eat with her fingers.

"These quails are so good. They are a speciality of our cook. You see, when you have eaten the little legs, he has taken out the bones, made in the stuffing of the frois gras and sticked it together again. You can cut with the knife a slice, like so." She popped it in her mouth. "So good." Robert did not like to admit that he had already had one and attacked his with fervour.

"Excellent, what a skill. How could anyone do that and here it is, cooked and looking complete?"

"Ah, he have the such skill."

"You said 'the'"

"The? What are you talking about Herr 'Enery, you talk in riddles! I find it hard to follow what you mean!"

"Graffinflein, I would deem it a great favour, if you would call me Robert. It is my name after all and Herr Henery does not seem quite appropriate in this situation. What I meant was that you said 'the'. That is excellent. Up to now you have been saying 'zee'. You have a quick ear." She smiled at him and flushed slightly.

"Yes, I have zee—the good ear. I am lucky, I can make," she paused and frowned slightly "...the singing and zee—the music."

"Oh, do you play an instrument?"

"Yes, I can play the pianoforte. And you, Herr," she hesitated and smiled uncertainly, "...Robert, do you play any instrument, or sing? Are you musical?" Robert laughed.

"Musical? No, Graffinklein. When I sing, the frogs in the pond sink for refuge into the slimy depths. As for music, I am afraid that I do not play any instrument. I have been known to play the spoons in a pub of an evening, but

it is not an accomplishment that I would recommend for the Drawing Room."
She looked puzzled.

"I do not understand. What is 'the spoons'? What are a pub?" Robert
explained, but refrained from giving a demonstration.

"Oh!" she said, "I do not go to such low places."

Luckily they were interrupted by a succession of dishes that were being carried round. Robert noticed that they were not being replaced on the buffet
table and that this was gradually being cleared. After being passed round the
tables, the dishes were taken out. Waiters kept up a continual round topping
up the glasses and the noise of talking and laughter became louder and louder.
On the gallery at the end of the room, a small string orchestra was preparing its
music and instruments. Gradually the dishes off the buffet table were being
removed. At last the table itself was quickly taken away, leaving the centre of
the room clear. Suddenly amidst a round of applause and cheering a procession of people entered the room, four men bearing an enormous coloured
confection, between them, on a huge tray. This was paraded round the room
for all to see and admire. It appeared to be like a huge castle, tower piled on
tower, made of meringue and what looked like whipped cream, decorated with
a profusion of flowers. Following this amazing confection came a procession of
jellies, tortes and lesser creations, a selection of which were placed on each
table. The mighty castle, after it had done its lap of honour was taken to a side
table and in a very short time plates were being distributed round the tables.
Robert found himself presented with a plate of meringue battlements and
amidst a pile of whipped cream, an army of wild strawberries and raspberries.

A glass of amber coloured wine was poured out for him. He was beginning
to feel a little light headed. He had long ago lost count of how many glasses of
wine he had had and his recollection of what he had drunk with what was, to
say the least, a little hazy. It seemed that there had been a different wine for all
the many different things that he had had on his plate. Whenever he had
helped himself from the many dishes that were offered him, a different wine
was poured into his glass. He surveyed the bank of used glasses in front of him,
but realised that that would give him no clue, as some had been taken away
and been replaced by others. Some had been used twice.

He took a sip of the heavy gold wine. Its aroma immediately took him back
to the room in the Inn where he had spent the night on their journey before
arriving at the Castle. He could see in his mind's eye the young peasant girl, her
bare feet and her bare brown legs. He could almost smell the fireside and could
vividly recall the almost reverent way in which the innkeeper poured out the

wine from the dust-encrusted bottle that he had brought up from the cellar. This was a wine for savouring, for lingering, for remembering. He wondered if he ever had such a glassful again if he would remember this evening. He looked round the room, trying to store it in his memory. He took in the heavy wooden beams, the ornate gilding on the massive picture frames, the uniforms of the men and the elegant table silver and flowers, the beautiful dresses of the ladies. He looked at Elizabet, so elegant; her skin so white, her face slightly flushed, she was in animated conversation with the person on her other side, the fair ringlet hanging down behind her ear springing lightly as she talked, the long pendant earrings dancing in the candlelight, the pearls glowing with a rich lustre in their flickering glow. She was a very beautiful young lady and her animation and excitement added an intense warmth to her personality that radiated from her and seemed to illuminate the room.

He looked at the women on his left, the wife of Emil, the vibrating pink blancmange. He realised he had not spoken a word to her all night. If anything, the pink had turned to pale red and heaved and billowed with more determination as she addressed her best attentions to a huge plate of cream and meringue, which she was demolishing with the relish of one who had eaten nothing all night. She became aware of him looking at her, and smiled a huge red-faced grin at him, her chin well sprinkled with crumbs of the succulent confection. She said something to him in German through a great spoonful of whipped cream. Robert picked up his glass and waved it cheerily at her. She beamed and continued eating. Emil, luckily, had heard what she said. He laughed.

"She says, Robert, that you are a very beautiful young man and that if you are not able to charm the horses, you will certainly charm the young ladies." Robert felt quite taken aback at this.

"Is that what she said?"

"Well, not exactly verbatim, no. But that is what she meant, even if it was expressed in somewhat more rugged terms."

Robert laughed. "For God's sake, tell her I am very sorry that I cannot speak to her in German, but I shall have no time for young ladies. I am here for the horses. By the look of things they are going to demand all my attention." Emil translated for her. She roared with laughter. She took his hand and patted it.

"What does she say?"

"She says that she will believe that when she sees it. She says look at how the young ladies are looking at you."

Robert hastily looked round the room and was embarrassed to meet several pairs of eyes that hastily looked away as their gaze met.

At that moment the orchestra struck up a wheezy polka and it was not long before the room was a sea of gyrating, hopping, perspiring couples.

"Come mit Maria!" exclaimed the large lady on his left and, struggling to her feet, she seized Robert's hand in a vicelike grip and dragged him onto the floor. Her generous girth was only exceeded by her height. Seizing Robert in a hug that would have extinguished the last vestige of breath from a medium sized bear, she proceeded to pirouette round the floor like a bounding hippopotamus.

Robert, his nose firmly wedged between the mounds of pink cleavage, could only hang on and hope that if his partner fell, he might land on top. Were he underneath, he might be smothered to death before his presence was discovered. Luckily for him, they reached the end of the room, still upright. The necessity of a turn threw him outwards by centrifugal force so he was able to gasp a desperate and much needed breath. Having succeeding in breaking her grasp, he was able to maintain his distance so that at least he could breathe even though his view was limited to those heaving pink mountains. Round and round they hopped, Robert expecting at any minute to be dashed to the floor and crushed under the mighty bulk. At last the orchestra finished its piece and on a wavering chord stopped playing. Robert knew that the chances of surviving a second time were remote in the extreme. And battered and bruised though he felt, he had enough presence of mind and energy left to propel her purposefully back to her chair. Fortunately a waiter had just left a vindtorte on their table and had just poured champagne into everyone's glass. With the desperation of the starving, she accepted the large slice that Robert carefully served for her, taking care to pile as much whipped cream as he could decently scoop from the rest of the cake. Of Elizabet there was no sign, so taking a glass of champagne with him, he managed to make good his escape whilst his erstwhile partner was lost in heavenly contemplation of the sublime confection. At that moment Emil returned.

"Hello. How are you getting on? I saw you being whirled by mien frau. Come and sit here—one so bold deserves a rest." He pulled two chairs back and motioned Robert to sit beside him. He took two glasses of champagne from the table. "Here, come on, anyone who can survive a turn round the floor with the light of my life needs at least one glass of champagne to restore him." Robert sat down and accepted the proffered glass thankfully, placing the one he already had on the table behind him. Emil looked at him thoughtfully.

"How are you finding things?" He waved his hand vaguely in the air, embracing the rest of the gathering.

"Well, it has all been a little sudden, really. Everyone has been very kind and welcoming, but, well, I would not be honest if I said that everything was as I expected it. The Count is your cousin?"

"Well, he is not strictly my cousin. My wife and Elizabet are first cousins, so I call him cousin. We get on well. I come here hunting and he comes to visit me in Bavaria for the hunting in my forests. We share an interest in race horses and we have some business interests together, so we see a lot of each other, so yes, I know him well. I know he can be a bit of a tyrant, so watch out. He is not easily shaken, once he has made up his mind. You must stand up for yourself. He gets an idea in his head and there is no shifting it. Do you want me to have a word about the state of the house? I know it. We have used it as a hunting lodge, so I could make some occasion to mention it, if you like."

"No, it is very kind of you, but I have got to fight my own battles. I am on my own, so it is not that important. It is not as if I had a wife and family. I can manage, until it is refurbished. What is worrying me most is that I am expected to produce winners at the meeting in Vienna this week. We are going tomorrow. I have not even seen the horses, but I am expected to make them win!"

Emil laughed. "That is typical of August. Well, I wish you luck. But things change. I hope that you will be very careful. There are big changes in the wind and I do not like what I can see." His eyes fell on his wife, avidly helping herself to another cream-oozing slice of vindtorte. "She used to be so young, so strong, tall, athletic and beautiful." Emil drained his glass and took up another and looked round the room at the happy dancers. "Now there's a one. How have you got on with Elizabet?" He watched her as she glided round the floor in the arms of a young officer. By popular demand the orchestra was playing a waltz and she seemed to float through the press of dancers with an ethereal animation as she gracefully pirouetted round the room. "Look at that! Did you eve see such poise, such grace? What a complexion! Look at that laugh. What she can see in that idiot, I don't know."

Robert was shocked to note a touch of jealousy in his tone. But she was his cousin, surely. He felt a flash of jealousy himself. Elizabet was looking all round the room. Their eyes met and she smiled. He smiled back and she flushed slightly. Robert knew that he had blushed as well. He felt a warm feeling run through him. She had been looking for him. As he watched, she looked directly at him again, until she was lost in the swirl of dancers. Emil too had been watching and had noticed the exchange, but he kept his thoughts to himself.

"Robert, I am being serious. Things may change. If you find that your position becomes untenable, you must come and work for me. I need a good trainer for my horses. I am sure that we could get on very well together."

"Well, thank you very much…"

"Vhat is he offering?" Unnoticed by them the orchestra had stopped and Elizabet had been returned by her partner. Both men stood up.

"I was saying that when Robert had got tired of living out here in the backwoods, he could come to work for me and return to civilisation."

Elizabet, flushed from her dance, had sat down and taken up a glass of champagne. She laughed.

"He has only been here one day! Already you are trying to take him from us. We are very civilised here. He vill be very happy here. We vill make him the most happy. He vill have the many winners and many mares vill come to stand with his famous stallions. It vill be most good. You see. We vill all be most rich." She was interrupted by another young man who hovered at her elbow. She looked in her card. Smiling, she got up.

"Excuse me, I go for this dance. Robert, if you vould like to dance vith me, I have the last dance free."

"Thank you very much, I would like that."

He and Emil stood up as she went to the floor on the arm of the young man. They stood and watched them join the dancing.

"Come on. If there is anything I hate, it is watching other people dance."

"Do you not dance then?" asked Robert.

"Yes, I dance, I love to dance. Maria and I used to dance the night through. God how we used to twirl! Now she finds it too fatiguing. She does not like it if I dance with anyone else, so I dance no more. Come, let's go to the billiard room. Bring your glass." He spoke rapidly to a passing waiter. "I have asked them to bring us a bottle of champagne." He noticed that Robert hesitated. "Oh! come on. I have asked him to come to tell us when it is time for the last dance." Robert grinned sheepishly and came.

"I hope that she knows what she has let herself in for! I do not dance very well. I find it difficult to keep my balance when I move quickly." He told Emil briefly about his accident and his miraculous recovery.

"Do not worry. She dances like a fairy. She could make even a tailor's dummy dance like an angel. Come on." He led the way. Just by the door, they found that the remains of the buffet had been redressed and set out on a table just in case anyone might feel like some further sustenance. They stopped and looked at it.

"Do you fancy some more?" Emil took up a plate and offered it to Robert.

"Good heavens, no. I couldn't eat another thing." Despite his protest, he soon had a selection of titbits on his plate. Emil, too, had selected a few things and then led the way to the Billiard Room.

"Your wife, will she be all right?"

"Yes, she is fine. Do not worry about her. I put another whole windetorte in front of her. She will be well occupied until we return."

They entered the Billiard Room. There were about twenty men in there, all refugees from the dancing. The air was thick with cigar smoke. Emil took him round and introduced him. He seemed to know everyone. They attached themselves to a group at a side table and sat watching the play and picking at their food. The game was finished and they were offering Robert the chance to play. He played quite well, having spent many evenings in pubs and clubs and he was pleased of the chance to show what he could do. He stood up eagerly and took off his coat. He was just about to take his first shot, when the waiter returned. Everyone cheered and jeered his announcement. Robert looked enquiringly at Emil.

"It is the last dance." Robert threw down his cue and grabbed his coat.

"I must go. I am to dance with Graffinflein." Amidst a chorus of cheers and catcalls, he fled the room and ran back to the Ballroom. The music had already started and most of the dancers were already on the floor. He ran in and slithered to a stop by Elizabet's chair. She sat there alone, with a slight pout.

"Graffinflein, I am so sorry, I was in the Billiard Room." She smiled at him and her pout vanished.

"Robert, I am not used to being kept vaiting, especially for the last dance."

"I am very sorry, I came as quickly as I could." He took her hand and led her to the floor. "I am afraid that I have two left feet and they don't always go in the same direction." She laughed and turned to face him, so that he could take her in his arms. Now that they stood together, he could see that she was almost exactly the same height as he was. He stood, holding her hands and looking into her eyes—and the strangest sensation ran through him, such as he had never known before. She blushed slightly but did not look away.

"Come on. We cannot stand here like this, people are looking at us." Robert took her in his arms and, waiting for the beat of the music, he hesitantly began to dance. She was light and responsive in his arms and she floated round him like thistledown. His confidence grew and they sailed in stately circles round the room.

"Graffinflein, you dance most beautifully."

"Robert, do you not think that you might call me Elizabet? You dance most vell too."

"I think that you are one of those beautiful people who could make even an ancient oak tree dance with the grace of a swan." She laughed.

"You are here to make the horses run faster. We do not expect the poet as vell!" She smiled at him and they danced round laughing into each other's eyes.

"I hope you have enjoyed our little evening."

"It has been wonderful. Everyone has been too kind and the food and wine, magnificent. And this—perfect."

"Did you like our vines? We grow them all here. Our cellar man is very good."

"But this, dancing with you in my arms, is the perfect end."

"This is not the end. Now we give you the real Magyar velcome, you vatch!" The music came to an end and everyone clapped and applauded. Robert and Elizabet glided to a halt and she leant over and kissed him lightly on the cheek. Robert was both surprised and delighted and he squeezed her hand as they stood there together.

"What is going to happen now?"

"Vait, and you vill see."

Suddenly the doors at the end of the room burst open. The members of the orchestra tore off their black ties and jackets. Thus revealed in their costumes they started a furious gypsy tune on violins and guitars. A troop of dancers burst into the room and started an energetic and passionate set dance. Everyone formed a ring round them and clapped and cheered to the rhythm. Robert noticed among them the girls who had been waiting on them earlier at the table. Their furious dance came to an end and the orchestra came down into the hall and walked amongst the guests. Some more fiddlers came in and together, from wherever they were, they started a tune of such power and rhythm that no one could resist clapping, or tapping their feet. Even the mighty Maria had forsaken the table and was wobbling majestically to the beat. All at once a group of men in gypsy costume burst into the room and began a ferocious dance.

"They tell of the fights with the Turks," Elizabet whispered into his ear.

"Poor Turks!" said Robert as he swayed to the rhythm. The Turks were evidently vanquished and the group of girls formed up and began a dance together. This apparently was the demonstration set for they soon broke up and moved among the guests, forming them into other sets. The fiddlers started again and soon all the ladies with much skirt swishing and expenditure of energy were stamping their way round the room. Elizabet was joining in with gusto and stamping and swirling with the best. The dance came to an end and everyone cheered and shouted. Elizabet returned to him, red with exertion and flushed with exhilaration.

"Fetch the champagne! I burn like the bush fire," she gasped. Robert ran and brought her a glass.

"Here, put your fire out with this. That was brilliant."

"Do not laugh. Now it is your turn!"

She laughed at his look of alarm. Even as she spoke, the costumed men linked arms and started the dance. Soon, with much cheering from the ladies, they had all the men marshalled and the dance began. Round and round the room they went, in dancing, prancing lines. Luckily the steps were few and Robert soon mastered them. The ladies cheered and the men shouted a rhythmic chant as they danced. The dance ended in a confusion of cheering and clapping as the men made a concerted dive for the champagne. They formed couples again and started a succession of country dances, which seemed to consist of a lot of cheering, clapping, twirling and stamping of feet. It all ended with a mad gallop, with nearly everyone careering round the room at breakneck speed, even the Count and Countess, shedding pounds as they joined in and thundered round. The dance ended in an uproar of cheering and clapping. Elizabet collapsed into Robert's arms.

"I have not had so much fun since I don't know when."

Robert squeezed her tightly. "Thank you so much, this has been the most terrific evening. Is that the end, or have you more surprises for me?"

"Vell, one little surprise." She kissed him lightly on the lips. "Goodnight Robert, I vill see you in the morning, we leave for Vienna at 7 o'clock."

"Goodnight, Elizabet. Until tomorrow then!"

But she was gone, caught up in the throng of guests all anxious to leave and get to bed. Robert walked out into the hall in a daze, practically walking past Emil.

"Goodnight, Robert"

Robert started.

"You look like the cat that has got at the cream!"

"Oh, I am sorry, I did not see you standing there."

"Why not? I am big enough!"

"I am sorry, that last dance was a bit shattering. I just was not looking where I was going. Good night. Thank you for your kindness. If ever I need somewhere to go, I will remember your kind offer."

"Yes, you do. I meant it. I expect we will meet again at the races."

"Yes, goodnight. I will see you there, then." One of the waiters offered him his coat.

The courtyard was a confusion of coaches being wheeled out, teams of horses being led in from the stables and harnessed up. Franc stood in the doorway and as each coach was made ready, he called the name out into the hall. Those departing hurried out and clambered aboard, so that they could quickly get out of the way and make room for the next. Robert's little cart stood ready by the gateway, being the smallest vehicle in the yard. Robert climbed aboard and Soldo soon had the little horse whipped into a swift trot.

The kiss on Robert's lips tingled all the way home.

CHAPTER 11

Somewhere, a long way away, someone was shouting. The shouting got nearer. Suddenly, it was right in his ear. Robert sat up. There was a light shining right in his eyes. He tried to push it away. The shouting started again. With a great effort, he opened his eyes. He shook his befuddled head. He was cold. He was shivering. He was shaking with cold. No, it was not him that was shaking, he was being shaken violently. In front of his face, in the light, something was swinging to and fro. With a great effort he focused on it. It was a large old rusty watch. If only it would keep still, he could see what the time was. Unsteadily he caught it in his hand. Painfully, he squinted at it. It said a quarter past six. Again he was shaken violently. The shouting started up again. He turned to look and saw that it was Soldo who was both author of the shouting and cause of the violent shaking. Soldo, seeing that he had at last succeeded in waking some semblance of life into Robert, was pointing frantically at the watch and gesticulated towards the door. The last vestiges of sleep cleared from Robert's brain. Quarter past six. Quarter past six! He sat up as the import dawned on him. They were supposed to be at the Castle ready to leave at 7 am. He leapt up, and fell again as the horse blanket round his legs remained firmly wrapped. He struggled to his feet. His teeth were chattering from the cold. He had only been in bed for an hour. He was still in evening dress and he started to look round for his clothes, but Soldo shouted and again beckoned frantically towards the door.

Robert threw a horse blanket over his shoulders and staggered outside. He ran to the horse trough and dashed his face into the cold water. The icy shock wiped the last vestige of sleep from his brain. Shivering violently from cold and lack of sleep, he staggered after Soldo who ran ahead and jumped into the little cart. As he did so the horse started forward. Robert had to run to catch up and scramble in. Soldo stood up, cracking his whip over the unfortunate pony's head and, leaning back on the rains like some Roman charioteer in the arena, his coat tails flying in the wind as they careered along, he urged the little pony to greater efforts…The little pony galloped for all that it was worth, thoroughly frightened by the cracking whip, by Soldo's shouting, and by the unaccustomed creaking and rattling of the cart that was swaying and bouncing in the most alarming way. Robert was thrown into a heap on the floor. Eventually he managed to sit up and hang onto the side. He was bounced and rattled around like a pea on a drum, so had to hang on for all he was worth to save himself from being thrown out. They charged along in the dark like some mad messengers from Hades, trailing a great cloud of dust that rolled over the dewy meadows. Eventually they clattered over the wooden bridge and into the courtyard of the castle. Thankfully he scrambled out. Every muscle and joint ached. He was bruised and battered all over. Every protruding piece of bone was sore and hurt. Soldo had leapt off the cart and was banging on the door. The pony was completely blown. It stood head down, its foam-flecked flanks heaving.

At last the door opened. Frank, wrapped in a large blanket, ushered them in. He managed to make Robert understand that the Count had gone an hour ago. As he was talking he opened the breakfast room door and showed Robert in. The table was laid with the cold remnants of the previous night's supper. Coffee was steaming in the samovar. Franc gestured that he should help himself. He found some sticks to put on the glowing embers in the fire to make a cheery blaze. It was whilst he was doing this, that Robert realised he was still in his evening dress. He stank. The horse blankets had not been the best things in which to sleep. Their unwashed, horse sweaty odour had transferred to him. He appealed to Franc.

"Look, I am still in my evening dress. What am I to do? I can't spend the next few days in Vienna in my evening dress. Apart from anything else, it is dirty and crumpled. It stinks of horse sweat!" He tried again, with much mime and gesticulation. At last, it seemed that Franc understood, for he left the room.

Presently he returned with a large cloak and a long woollen scarf. With him was a young man smartly dressed in coachman's uniform. He spoke to Robert in German, but Robert could make no sense of what he said. Franc laughed and thought; then, taking some cutlery on the table, he mimed a small spoon sliding across the table to join a large serving spoon, then taking a spoon, he pointed at the coachman and Robert, and putting two cold peas in the spoon he slid it across the table to join the serving spoon. He smiled at Robert and gestured for him to be quick, quick. Robert understood. If he left now, he could catch up with the Count.

Robert wrapped the scarf round his neck and threw the cloak over his shoulders. The cloak was so voluminous that it came almost to the ground and completely hid the fact that he was still in evening dress. He thanked Frank for all he had done for him and hurried out to the front door. There, standing ready, was a plush open blue carriage with a pair of white horses. The driver held open the door for him, then climbed up onto the box.

As they left the castle, the sun rose. Robert was still feeling cold from lack of sleep. He was glad of its warmth as it struck his shoulders. The carriage flew along very easily. Cushioned by the soft plush and supported by the springs, he felt as if he floated gracefully across the countryside. It was a beautiful morning but for all his lack of sleep, Robert was enjoying the drive.

The coachman kept the horses going at a fast trot. At last, it seemed in no time at all, they reached the Inn at the river, by the landing stage. To Robert's enormous relief, he saw Elizabet and Schmidt sitting on the bench outside in the morning sun.

Robert stepped down from the coach and walked towards them. Schmidt stood up, indignation displayed in every inch of his outraged figure.

"Vot you think you are do, riding the Countess' coach? Who say that you can use it? Vot you doing?" He glowered at Robert in aggrieved fury, two red spots appearing starkly on his sallow gaunt cheeks.

"In the absence of anyone else either present or 'corpus mentus' the Captain of the Horse authorised me to use it." Robert drew himself up to his full height and bristled at him like an angry bantam cock. "The Captain of the Horse will authorise me to use whatever of the Count's horses are convenient, suitable or available if there is no one else there with better authority, to whom I can have recourse." With something like a flounce, he turned to Elizabet before Schmidt could recover from this shock. "Hello Graffinflein, I hope that you are not too tired after the party last night. It was a wonderful party—the food was magnificent and the music and dancing..." He paused as he recalled the evening again "I think I can honestly say that I have never enjoyed myself so much ever before, in all my life."

She blushed slightly and a smile lit her face with an aura of warmth and happiness. "Yes, I too. Yes, I too was more happy than ever I have ever been! I hope you slept well?"

"I would be less than honest if I said that it was the most comfortable night that I have ever had, but fortunately, I wasn't in bed long enough to really find out if I was comfortable or not!"

"Oh, why was this?"

"Well, by the time I had returned to the Stud and fallen asleep, Soldo was shouting in my ear to make haste to return to the Castle. I only had one hour's sleep. As it was, as you know, I was too late to join you on the coach." She smiled.

"Yes, my father was most angry. I hope that you have had something to eat."

"Yes, thank you. Franc organised breakfast for me when I arrived at the Castle. I really enjoyed our drive over here. The country is so peaceful and beautiful, the sun shone and the larks sang with such magic. I was very comfortable in your Mother's coach. It runs along so smoothly and those two horses, they are such a good pair. It was the most beautiful drive. I thought many times about last night." She blushed.

"Yes," she said, "so have I."

Schmidt bristled with disapproval. "It vas a very good thing your Father and Mother did not see you. They vould have had great disapproval. As too have I, Frauline Graffinflein." Schmidt pursed his lips in the best display of disgust, disapproval and dislike that he could muster.

"You, Herr Schmidt. You presume to criticise me?" Elizabet shot him a fiery glance that would have blistered paint at twenty paces. "I remind you, Herr Schmidt, that you are not my keeper. You are Herr Schmidt, you see to my Father's affairs. What I do, it is not your business. You do not tell me how to behave. You have too much the presumption." She was being her most haughty. Schmidt cringed in discomfort, but held his ground.

"Everything that happens, it is your Father's business. If I am to do my vork well, I must tell him all that I know."

"Do not be the hypercritical with me, Herr Schmidt. I know very well that you do not tell my Father many things. If I vere to tell him all the things which you have not told him, you vould have the dismiss. If you must tell my Father all things, go tell him that Herr 'Enery he has arrived." She put in every ounce of command that she could summon up. Herr Schmidt still hesitated. It was obvious that he was reluctant to leave them. Elizabet looked at him in amazement. "Herr Schmidt, when I tell go, you go! Go to your master and wag your tail like the good dog. Go and lick his hand like the fawning spaniel." Though he plainly resented these remarks he still did not move, showing both anger and resentment mingled together in a stubborn disapproval.

"Fraulein Graffinflein, I do not think it is good to speak to me in this way. I do only the best to be the loyal servant looking alvays at the best interests."

Elizabet's eyes blazed and she stood up. Robert tried to restrain her.

"The best interests of who, Herr Schmidt? Whose best interest do you serve, Herr Schmidt?"

Schmidt's eyes narrowed. He pursed his lips. "If the Graffinflein has anything to say—she should say so and not make these innuendoes. I vork hard for your Father and it is his best interests for which I vork."

Elizabet, whose anger was rising to careless pitch, was about to retort when she was fortuitously interrupted by the whistle of the boat and the plume of smoke from its funnel as it fast approached round the last bend. They all looked in its direction and as they watched, it came into view, a white wave at its bow as it stemmed the swift-flowing river. Schmidt turned on his heel and went into the inn, banging the door behind him. Robert and Elizabet sat down together on the bench.

"Oh, I hate that horrid man! I do not trust him. He is not to be trusted. He look always for his own chance. I think while he vork for my Father he help always himself." She seethed with anger and distrust.

"Don't get so excited." Robert placed a placatory hand on her arm, which she shrugged off in her anger. "Ignore the silly man, do not let him ruffle your feathers."

"Ruffle my feathers? What is 'ruffle my feathers'? I am not the chicken! What are you talking about?" she demanded with some indignation.

Robert laughed.

"Now you laugh at me!" She almost snorted at him. "Why you laugh at me? Do not laugh. Schmidt he is a dangerous man, be careful of him. He looks only for himself."

"Ha, the late Meester 'Enery!" The Count burst from the inn like a rampaging boar, his green Loden cloak flying in the wind like some battle banner. His wide-brimmed hat, crowned with its flamboyant plume, danced this way and that like some scything discus. The Count's little eyes were screwed up through lack of sleep against the harsh light. His bristling whiskers probed aggressively forward like the antennae of some preying insect.

"Always Meester 'Enery, it is that you are late. I hope you do not make my horses late! You must be early. Always you must be first to arrive, then perhaps my horses they too vill be first to arrive." His eye fell on the cloak Robert was wearing. "I see at least that you have the good idea of dress sense. I too have a cloak like that—just like that!"

The little steamer at that moment was mooring at the jetty. As if by magic a small crowd of people had assembled. The Count looked round with considerable impatience. "What are all these peasants doing? I do not vish to travel with all these peasants! Schmidt, go at once to the Captain. Present my compliments and tell him that we vill take the State Cabin." He looked round in considerable agitation. "Where is the Countess? Always we vait for the Countess! Elizabet, go inside and to your Mother—say to her hurry up!"

Schmitt and Elizabet both disappeared on their separate missions.

"'Enery, I am most displeased. Schmidt he tell me that you used the coach of the Countess to come here. Who said you use this? This is not the toy to be used by everyone to fritter around the country. It is kept at great expense so that the Countess has the suitable to make the travels. You do not use it for your travels. Who said to you to take it?" He demanded with belligerent anger. "How dare you take it?"

Robert knew that this was the time for him to make a stand. "Count, the cart that I had at my disposal was more suited to take chickens to the market than to make this journey. Had I used it, I would not have reached here in time..."

"There is other steamer, you could have taken that," the Count interrupted bombastically.

"I would not then have arrived until tomorrow afternoon, too late for the first race. I could not have looked after your horses, if I was stuck out here on a steamer. When we arrived at the Castle, Franc suggested that the coach was a possible solution and as there was no one else there to ask, the Captain of the Horse gave me permission."

The Count looked at him in some bafflement, and then as understanding dawned, he laughed.

"Vell, 'Enery, you have the cheek of the vinner. Make sure you tell this to the horses. Come now, we cannot stand here all afternoon. Where is the Countess?" He flapped his hands together in agitated impatience and strode off towards the boat. Most of the other passengers had boarded, but all stepped back and bowed and curtseyed as he strode past. The men took off their hats and held them to their chests. The Count marched into the State Cabin and sat down, totally oblivious of the fact that a mother and five small children were even then being evicted to make way for him. Schmidt had hurried back to the inn. Robert waited by the door, hopefully to see and assist Elizabet when she should come out.

A seemingly endless stream of boxes and trunks was being carried out of the inn and taken down to the steamer. Presently the Countess appeared leaning heavily on Elizabet's arm. She was followed by a retinue of maids and servants. Among them, Robert saw the French cook.

"Countess, allow me to offer you my arm," Robert managed to insert himself between her and Elizabet, to whom he offered his other arm, which, with a happy smile, she accepted.

"Herr 'Enery, you are too kind. You are the first person in this rude place who 'ave offered the help." Robert perceived that here was an ally to be cultivated. Elizabet was hanging on to his other arm in a most affectionate way. "Herr 'Enery, I 'ope that you enjoy the party last night and that you have not the too much fatigued this morning?"

"Countess, it was the most wonderful evening. It was so kind of you to arrange it for me."

She smiled weakly. She had enjoyed it too, but she was feeling very tired, especially as she had had to rise so early in the morning. She looked at him with a wry smile.

"I am glad. We love always to 'ave the party, and it is not always that there is so good excuses. I heard that you 'ad enjoyed yourself. Elizabet has been telling me vot a good dancer you are." Robert looked at Elizabet and was rewarded to see her blush through a radiant smile and feel a renewed squeeze on his arm.

The three of them crossed the road and with some difficulty mounted the narrow gangplank and boarded the small vessel.

"I think that I sleep in the cabin," said the Countess, and so they led her to the small varnished door. The Count had already taken up residence and was snoring loudly from the only bed. Robert looked at the recumbent figure with disgust. *Typical—no thought for anyone else!* The Countess looked in some dismay. Then with considerable patience and resignation she made for the settee.

"I vill make the do vith that." Robert made his excuses and left them. He stepped outside and went to the bow, where he leant on the rail to watch the departure. The last of the Count's luggage was being loaded on board.

There was also an assortment of bales and boxes and a rickety crate with some squealing piglets waiting their turn and a group of worried peasants, to whom these evidently belonged, standing apprehensively on the quayside. All was soon stowed in the little hold. The peasants had come on board and congregated at the stern in a nervous huddle. Soon the ropes were cast off and, breasting the stream, they set out for Vienna.

From his position in the bow, Robert had a superb view of all that was going on. There seemed to be far more craft on the river. Fishing skiffs, small barges piled high with mountains of reeds, small skiffs flying along on the current, a lighter full of bellowing cattle paused in it's crossing to let them pass. Over by the far bank he watched as two boats hauled the net between them and emptied the glittering cascade of flapping fish into large boxes. There seemed to be an amazing amount of bird life. Ducks swam in small rafts and white storks and egrets and heron perched on the trees or waded the margins.

Robert was so engrossed with watching all this, that he did not notice Elizabet coming and standing beside him until she spoke.

"My Mother seems to have settled all right."

Robert jumped. She laughed and placed her hand on his arm. "I did not mean to make you the fright!" She laughed again.

"No, no, that's all right! I was not frightened, I did not see you come; you made me jump, that is all."

At that moment, Schmidt also appeared and leant on the rail on the other side of Elizabet. Elizabet looked at him.

"Herr Schmidt, would you please stand up. You do not lounge about like the drunken sailor in my presence." She looked at him with her most haughty expression. Reluctantly and slowly, resentment showing in his every move, he stood up.

"Yes, Frauline Graffinflein," he said, between his teeth. The three of them stood in uneasy silence for a while. Robert noticed an empty seat in front of the varnished wheelhouse.

"Perhaps, Graffinklein, you would prefer to sit over there." Before she could reply, he had taken her arm, walked her over, sat her down and sat himself beside her. Herr Schmidt, seeing there was no room for him, could only fume impotently by the rail. In the end, he gave up his sulking vigil and disappeared aft.

Robert and Elizabet sat companionably together, watching the life of the river as they passed by. She snuggled down into Robert shoulder. She sat up suddenly.

"Poo, you smell of horse sweat!"

Robert laughed. "I am sorry, it is not entirely my fault." He told her about his night. She lifted the hem of his cloak and giggled. The smell of sweaty horse was more marked and he was still wearing his evening dress.

As the day wore on and evening approached, the sun gradually sank below the horizon throwing a path of beaten gold down the river, drawing across the sky a curtain of brilliant pink, orange and crimson. The trees stood in dark stark silhouette against the stunning display. A flight of cranes making black shapes against the vivid glow flew in silent formation on some nocturnal quest down the river.

They sat in amazed awe, watching the beauties of the evening unfold. Elizabet took hold of Robert's hand.

"This is so beautiful. It makes me feel so small." She snuggled up to Robert. Robert could not speak; he was totally overwhelmed by the brilliant spectacle and the closeness of Elizabet. Thus they sat as the light gradually faded. A velvet darkness enfolded the little boat as it pushed its way upstream against the strong current. It was late evening before they rounded the last bend and the lights of Vienna came into view. They landed with the usual hustle and bustle of disembarkation.

Schmidt handed him an envelope.

"On the front is written the name of your Hotel. Inside you vill find all the details that you vill need for the race tomorrow—the times, the horses, the jockeys, the vet."

Robert took it and thanked him. He could guess that he had been put into a hotel as far away from the Count's house as possible.

CHAPTER 12

❀

Whatever Robert felt about Schmidt, by the time the cab arrived at their hotel he had to admit that at least he was efficient. The hotel proved to be right next to the racecourse. It could not have been more convenient. It was very comfortable. He was very well accommodated.

He enjoyed a quick dinner. After a hot bath, he sent his suit down to be sponged down in the hope that the smell might lessen. It was all he had to wear and he would have to rely on the big cloak and the scarf to hide the fact that he was still in his evening dress! Then he settled down to read his instructions with a large glass of brandy that he had had sent up to his room. He read them through. He had never heard of any of the horses or jockeys. But all the weights, names and current odds were there. Also attached was a "form" sheet on each horse. He was surprised to find that the Count had four runners, not three as he had thought. However, when he had carefully read the "form" of them all, he realised the fourth was a young horse that was only out for the experience. No doubt some would back it. It was hard luck for them, but they were free to choose a more likely bet if they wished.

He studied the "form" book and tried to find out how his horses had performed against the others on the race card, but there was little to be gleaned. One of his horses seemed to have done quite well against some of the others, but there was no obvious pattern that might give him any clue or hope. He looked at the jockeys. He had never heard of any of them. One of his horses had always done well when ridden by a certain jockey. He noticed with some relief that he was to have the same ride tomorrow. He looked at the trainers. He had heard of one or two, but he had never met any of them. He was shocked to see his own name with the Count's horses. That was hardly fair. He had not even seen the horses so it was not fair to put him down as trainer!

He let the papers fall on the floor and took a thoughtful drink from his brandy. It was going to be in the lap of the Gods. There was nothing he could do about anything. Tomorrow, whatever happened, he was going to have to stand there and take it on the chin.

By four in the morning he was up, breakfasted and walked over to the stables, the long cloak borrowed from the Count's wardrobe sweeping the wet grass and flapping like the grotesque wings of some hideous bat in the breeze. The sun had not yet lifted over the horizon but there was that soft pearly colour in the light that muted all the tones and hid all the blemishes. The grass on the course was still heavy with dew. It gave off a fresh morning earthy smell with every step. The great cloak became heavier and heavier as the water gradually soaked upwards.

Robert was tired, but for the moment his tiredness had vanished in his expectations for the day ahead. When he arrived at the stables it took him some time of energetic enquiry and disinterested reply to find his horses, but eventually he spotted the shirtless figure of Soldo washing himself under a standpipe.

All around, the air was heavy with the smell of hot coffee and frying bacon. The grooms were hastily making their breakfast so that they could make an early start with their duties. The horses were accommodated in canvas stabling, specially erected for the meeting. The grooms had slept in the straw with their charges. The jockeys, who were staying in nearby inns, would come in shortly to take their rides for a short loosening up prior to weighing in.

Soldo pulled on his shirt and led the way to a tent in which their four horses were stabled. Robert's heart sank when he saw them. They stood dejectedly, their heads hung over a net of mouldy-looking hay that was tied to a post to which they were all tethered. He ran his hands all over them. No iron hard muscles here! Just soft, flabby, not very well groomed, plumpness.

None of them was in any state to race. They had not been worked and sweated enough and were all in too soft a condition, carrying too much weight. He picked up each foot in turn. All needed the attention of the blacksmith to have their shoes removed and replaced with racing plates. That, at least, he could do something about. He looked angrily at Soldo.

"These are the worst prepared horses that it has ever been my misfortune to work with. Find a blacksmith and get him here fast. I want these horses properly groomed, their hoofs and tack cleaned and polished. At least they will look well turned out. I want everyone to work now, at once. They can forget their breakfast. They can go back to that when the work is done." Soldo stared at him blankly, but something of his anger must have communicated itself, for he scuttled round and chivvied his grooms. When Robert finally made him understand, by much gesticulation and angry shouting, what he wanted, he sent a boy off for the blacksmith.

The blacksmith eventually arrived and Robert was able to make him understand what was required. There was nothing more he could do. He left instructions that the horses should be fed nothing more and went to the Steward's Tent to make sure that all the entries had been correctly made. Everything was in order there. He had again to give grudging thanks to the efficient Schmidt. Everyone appeared to be very pleased to see him. There was much handshaking and introductions all round. He felt a complete idiot in his great cloak that disguised the fact that he still had on his, by now, not at all clean evening dress. After an hour he had met all the race officials and other trainers and had been very pleased by the welcome he had received.

They were most insistent that he should join them for the pre-race lunch at 12 o'clock, so with a promise that he would return then, he went back to his horses.

Three of the jockeys had arrived, so with great difficulty he was briefly able to talk over tactics, but he had to accept what Soldo and the jockeys agreed. Just before 12 o'clock he returned to the Steward's Tent. He was regaled with the most enormous meal of cold meat and wonderfully fresh bread and champagne served with bowls of fresh radishes and pickled gherkins. Over lunch it soon became apparent that no one thought his horses had any chance at all. Though opinion was divided, there seemed to be a clear favourite in each race.

After lunch and before going to the saddling enclosure, he went round to the bookmakers. As well as placing a small loyalty bet on his own horses, he had a substantially larger wager on the horses that had emerged as the most likely at lunch.

He had not got a horse running in the first race, so he was able to watch as a spectator. There seemed to be a large crowd. The air of general excitement was infectious. The information that he had gleaned over lunch had proved correct. He was rewarded with a substantial win. After collecting his winnings he went directly to the saddling enclosure. Elizabet and the Count were already there, and so was Soldo. Their first horse with its jockey and a couple of grooms was even then being led round. To Robert it was plain to see that it carried far too much flesh. The Count waved to him as soon as he saw him.

"Ha, Herr 'Enery, late again! I hope this late is not catching. My horses vill all catch the late and we shall not vin!"

"I am afraid, Count, that none of your horses will win today. There is nothing I can do to help them at this stage. My advice to you, if you wish to win, is to place your money on number 4." The Count looked at him in amazement and horror.

"Place the bet against my own horses? Vot a suggestion! My horses they are the best! They always vin. How dare you make the suggestion?" He went red with rage. Elizabet, who was dressed in a creation of pale blue with a white hat perched on the front of her head and carrying a large white parasol, did her best to calm him down.

"Come, Papa, Herr 'Enery only came the day before yesterday. How can he make the horses win?"

He was not placated. "I pay you good moneys to make the horse vin and you say they no vin. You say bet other horses?"

"I hope, Count, that given time to work with your horses, to know them and get them into a fit condition, I will indeed be able to make them win. But I cannot walk into the stable on the morning of the race and blow some kind of magic at them to put wings on their heels. These horses are the most ill prepared, out of condition creatures that it has ever been my misfortune to see entered in a race."

"You are here to make them vin! You do not talk back to me. If they do not vin, then you can go away! I vill find someone else who can make them vin!"

Robert felt really angry and was about to answer, when a gesture from Elizabet restrained him. The Count stomped over to Soldo.

"Herr 'Enery he say my horses no good, they no vin! Why they not vin? I vant my horses to vin!"

Soldo looked at him uncomprehendingly. The Count glowered at him, then realised that Soldo had not understood. He spoke to him again in rapid German. The poor man stood there, wringing his hat in his hands, casting angry glances at Robert. Robert stood next to Elizabet and shrugged his shoulders. There was nothing he could do.

"Graffinflein, take my advice, have a small wager on number 4. At least you will go home with something."

"I cannot do that. I do not have the money. My Father he vould be very angry if he knew."

"How is he going to know?"

"Herr Schmidt, he tell him everything. If I make the bet, he vill know."

"All right, I will place it for you. I am afraid that your father is going to be disappointed today if he is not going to listen to my advice."

"He is not very good at listening to advice and he like even less people who give it. Be very careful you do not offend him. He will soon send you avay."

"If he will not listen to my advice, he would be better off sending me away and doing the training himself."

At that moment the Steward blew his horn and the horses were led off to gallop down to the start. Robert excused himself and quickly went over to the bookmakers. He placed his bets for Elizabet. He returned to the course side as the Starter's flag signalled the off. He watched in silence as the race was run. It finished as he had predicted. Robert's whole attention was on his horse, trying to get some idea of how it ran. He was agreeably encouraged by what he saw. With some work and attention to its diet it had some real promise.

The other races were equally predictable. The Count became more and more angry. At the end of the afternoon he was in such a rage he was beside himself.

"I have been made a fool of in front of all my friends. Not one of my horses 'as even had a place. I 'ave lost much moneys. I did not bring you 'ere to loose moneys but to make moneys."

"I am very sorry, Count, but if you had taken my advice you would have made much money. Two of your horses have good prospects, but if I were you I would sell these two." He pointed at the race card. "They have little hope of ever achieving anything on the race track."

"Advice, advice. I do not need your advice! I did not bring you here for advice. You are here to make my horses win. Everyone give me advice. No one ever give me vinners." He stamped his foot in frustration and rage.

"I am very sorry, Count, but if you want winners, you must accept the advice of your Captain of Horse. I know you have pride in your horses and you want to see them win. It is very important to you to have winners. I, too, want to have winners, both for you and for Graffinflein and for myself. I wish to work hard with the horses to make them win and I wish to see that happen. At the same time we must remember that we need to make money. If we cannot make money from our own efforts, we must take what chance we can from the efforts of others. If that means backing someone else's horse against your own, then so be it. If we are going to be successful, we must not be sentimental about our horses. We must be realistic about the main chance."

The Count was not used to being lectured by his employees. He was dumbstruck. He stared open mouthed as Robert uttered these heresies.

"The day will come," continued Robert, "when your horses are winning. Then we will be able to enjoy our success and take pride in your horses, but until that time, we have to survive and make what shift we can to do so."

The Count looked at him for some minutes. He was dumbstruck. He turned on his heel and strode away.

"Graffinflein, here you are. You see, my advice was not that bad." He took out of his pocket a large roll of notes, which he palmed to her and she instantly hid in her muff.

"So much?" she looked in wonder at him.

"Well, yes. I managed to find all the winners for you."

"Vell done, Herr 'Enery. I hope always you are so successful." She smiled at him encouragingly. "If it is so, we soon be very happy." She looked serious and frowned slightly. "We stay now in Vienna for two months, then we travel to our house in Prague. We do not return home until the Autumn."

Robert's first reaction was the thought: *Thank goodness, I shall be left alone to get on with it.* He was already dreading the future prospect of a daily battle with the Count over something or other, real or imaginary, and he knew that his patience would not endure for long. This would be wonderful. It would allow him time to establish himself without having to fight every inch of the way. Then, with a pang at the sight of her sad face, he realised he was going to miss her. *Don't be stupid!* he scolded himself, *you have only known her for four days*; but even in that brief time he recognised that they were kindred spirits. He would feel his pulse quicken as he waited for their next meeting. He took her hand in his.

"Graffinflein, I cannot thank you enough for the help you have been to me and for your friendship and encouragement. I will not forget when we danced together at the party."

She lowered her eyes. "No," she said, "nor I."

"What are you going to do whilst you are away?"

She shrugged. "Oh, the usual boring round of the balls and the opera and the ballet and the exhibitions and gossip and driving in the park and state banquets and things. I expect that I vill endure it."

Robert felt a pang of jealousy. Here was a whole different side of her life of which he was not a part. How he envied all those young men who would dance with her, whirling her round the floor, gazing into those blue eyes. He would not see her for several months. He was going to miss her.

"I am sure that you will have a wonderful time. I shall be very busy with the house and the horses. I shall not have time for anything else."

"No," she said. "Well, goodbye, Robert."

"Goodbye, Elizabet...until the Autumn, then."

"Yes, until the Autumn." She turned and hurried off after her father. Robert stood and watched her walk away. Herr Schmidt, who had been standing nearby watching this exchange, walked over to him.

"Herr 'Enery, vee return tomorrow. You may stay in your hotel tonight. Tomorrow we return on the steamer at 10.30."

"Thank you, Herr Schmidt for all your arrangements. Everything was done in a most efficient and excellent way. I will see you in the morning."

CHAPTER 13

The ferry left on time and it was late afternoon when they arrived. Robert found a seat on his own. He had time to think about the events of yesterday and to formulate some action plan for the next few months. However, his thoughts kept turning back to Elizabet and the fact that he would not see her again until the autumn.

By the time they arrived at the Inn on the landing he was in a very bad humour, tinged with considerable jealousy. They stayed the night there. The girl, Elly, looked after them, her baby wailing all the while from the back room. The innkeeper was pleased to see him again, but there was a considerable frostiness in his attitude towards Schmidt. Although he was perfectly civil, Robert realised that this would not be one of those evenings when one of those glorious dusty bottles of golden wine would be lovingly brought up out of the cellar.

Over their supper Robert and Schmidt discussed the practical aspect of their relationship. Robert asked about the racing programme for the summer. What commitments had been accepted? How many meetings had been entered? His immediate and present feeling was that they should withdraw from everything until he had had a chance to see and work with the horses. They were plainly not fit, if the four that he had seen were a sample. Schmitt, however, was adamant that the Count would not accept this. He would be expecting to hear news of winners! Schmidt knew that this was not likely but, if the Count expected it, then winners there should be! It would be better not to cancel any entries at the moment, but just to make sure that the horses won! He could not remember what the schedule was, but if Robert came to the office on their return, Schmidt would find him a copy so that he would know. All

Robert had to do was to let him know what horses were to run where. All the entries, travel arrangements, etc., would be made.

Robert dug his heels in. The horses definitely were not in a winning state at the moment. The Count could be as disappointed as he liked—Robert was going to withdraw all horses until he had a better feel of things. Hopefully he might have some horses ready at the end of the season, but he would save a great deal of trouble and expense if he withdrew for the time being. He was adamant. In the end, Schmidt had to concede.

Robert was impressed by Schmidt's efficient and workmanlike handling of everything, but there was a cold aloofness, an almost clinical detachment, that made him seem remote and unapproachable. Robert felt he would never like him, but if he was good at his job what did it matter?

He did not sleep at all that night and spent the dark hours tossing and turning, churning round in his head all the things that they had talked about.

They breakfasted early and were soon on the road again, back to the castle. When they arrived, it seemed that all the guests had departed and so Schmidt arranged for Robert to have a bed for the night. The next morning he was taken by Schmidt to inspect the Castle stables. He could choose for himself a riding horse and a carriage and horse. A driver would be found for him.

There were about twenty horses in the huge stone-built stables that were large enough to house several families. They were riding horses for the family and some spare ones for any guest who might need one. The carriage horses were in the other side of the stable yard in a separate range of stables. If there was a need he could use any of the spare horses or vehicles that he wanted. He had only to ask and it would be made available to him.

Robert then told Schmidt of the condition of his house. He did not mind roughing it for a few days but it was quite uninhabitable as it was. Something drastic needed to be done at once, as he was not prepared to camp in the tack room for long!

Schmidt promised to see to the house the next day. He said he would send the men from the building yard over straight away to report. He was very anxious to get Robert out of the castle. He, too, had seen Robert and Elizabet dancing. He himself had hopes in her direction and had, ever since he had worked for the Count, done whatever he could to ingratiate himself with her. He endeavoured to make sure that as far as possible he was with her and indispensable to her. He had been horrified to see the obvious attraction between her and Robert. Consequently Robert could have asked for anything and it would have been instantly granted if it got him out of the Castle.

Schmidt suggested that Robert use Soldo to get the women from the Bothy to clean the house. That would expedite things. Robert asked him about that. At home only the single lads used the Bothy. Robert had been astonished to find whole families living up there.

Schmidt replied that they were peasants—they had no home of their own. They had to live somewhere. He seemed very surprised at the idea that they might have houses. What did they need houses for? They were quite happy where they were. He laughed at Robert's indignation. Give them houses and they would want a vote; give them a vote and who knows what might happen. You could not have the great affairs of state decided by a smelly sweaty proletariat with no worldly experience or knowledge!

Robert was stunned into silence. No wonder there had been rumblings of unrest from the working classes if that was the attitude of those who felt they were their masters and betters. Robert had been constantly amazed at the casual attitude taken by those he met towards their working men and women. There was small regard for their well-being and little if any consideration given to the gulf between their relevant positions. He was surprised that by and large everyone seemed to adopt a servile and subsidiary role without apparent resentment or dissatisfaction.

He resolved, however, that he would do all he could to see that all the married men at least, had a basic cottage in which they could live a private family life with some vestige of personal dignity.

Robert felt very uneasy with Schmidt. He was far too clever and he did not trust him an inch. That he was a German was not unusual, as apparently the petty administrative posts seemed to be occupied by Germans who hoped to make a career in the Empire. The ambitious ones sought patronage from the Magyar landlords and used their positions to obtain what influence and advancement they could.

Robert considered him a creep and a climber. Such men were devious, self-seeking and dangerous and would use their position to obtain whatever personal advantage they could, totally careless of the fact that they were clawing their way over the backs of others. Robert knew that for the time being he was going to have to put up with Schmidt, but that he should be very careful of him.

Robert tried to find out from him more about the Count and his family, but apart from confirming that the Count's revenues came from the estates and that the family was expected to return to the castle sometime in the autumn, he obtained little useful information.

Supper was set for them in the breakfast room and he spent another night in the Castle.

He made an early breakfast before it was light and was on his way by dawn. The small carriage that he was given was a considerable improvement on the luggage cart he had the last time he made the journey. This Robert could keep for his own use. The driver was the broad-shouldered blond youth who had driven the Countess's carriage. His family lived in the Bothy on the stud and so he was very happy to be based there again, instead of at the castle. It appeared that he was just known as 'Boy'. He had seven sisters, all of them older than him. His parents had been so excited at finally having a son that they had never got round to actually giving him a name. He was just always known as 'the boy' and 'Boy' would do very well, thank you.

It was lunch time when they arrived back at the stud. Fortunately Franc had placed a basket of provisions in the carriage and so he ate well on cold meats and bread with a bottle of red wine to help it all down.

Robert had been worried about how he was going to manage without Soldo, but his fears were unnecessary. When they arrived at the stud, to his surprise, Soldo was already there. It appeared that Soldo, the jockeys, the grooms and the horses had travelled on the steamer with them. The horses had been in large crates in the hold. After they had been unloaded, the whole cavalcade had set out cross-country directly to the stud. They had arrived that morning, having camped overnight by the roadside.

Robert, after much gesticulation, eventually managed to make Soldo understand what he wanted, and as he sat on the stone water trough in the middle of the yard eating his lunch, he was rewarded by the sight of a stream of girls and women fetching buckets of water to the house and the cheerful sound of their clattering and chatter as they worked. Good as Schmidt's word, the team of builders arrived in a farm wagon with ladders and poles and tools. They were soon swarming over the roof, replacing the wooden shingles and repairing the guttering. One man was up on the roof, lowering a rope down the chimney. After a shout from within, he started to pull it up. After considerable effort, amid a shower of soot, twigs and feathers, he pulled out a large bunch of holly. This evidently caused something of a landslide inside because there was a chorus of shouts and shrieks from the women and a big mushroom cloud of soot puffed out of the chimney completely enveloping the poor fellow. Robert ran over to the house and found the women shouting and shrieking—the soot had fallen and billowed all over the room they had just cleaned! However, despite the noise and complaints, they soon set to and cleared up the mess.

Robert was content to let them all get on with it. So he took Soldo on an extensive inspection of the rest of the buildings. His first impressions were confirmed. The whole place had been run on a fairly slack and careless regime and things were going to have to change. The few mares that he had seen before were still in their gloomy stalls. The two stallions still snorted indignantly from their dark pens. The hay barn had only a little mouldy hay in it, but they had crossed field upon field of tall waving grass, so presumably the new season's hay would be ready before long. The stables stood mostly empty and uncleaned. The young horses for racing, it appeared, were out by the river. "Where was that?" Soldo waved his arms vaguely in the air and pointed towards some far-off trees, blue in the far distance.

After an exhausting and prolonged discussion with Soldo, Robert eventually made him understand that he wanted all the horses brought in, in the morning, so that he could see them and attempt to sort them out. The whole conversation had been conducted with much gesticulation and shouting. Robert was exhausted. He was not sure that Soldo understood what he wanted, but he led Robert through the second arch to an area at the back of the barns that had been made into a series of high pens with stout wooden stockades. These would do. They were in reasonable repair and they could sort out the animals into their different groups there. Robert went round the stockades and gates to make sure everything was secure and to work out in his own mind what he was going to do.

"How many horses are there?" This seemed to present some problem. Soldo knew that they were all there, but he did not know how many there should be. Robert would have to wait until morning so that he could count for himself. Soldo would tell him if they were all there and then he could count if he wished! Soldo himself could not count.

Meanwhile Robert set all the remaining men to work clearing all the nettles, weeds and undergrowth out of the yard and away from all the buildings. They grumbled, but Robert insisted that keeping the stables and premises clean and tidy was all part of the work of a horseman and would they please get on with it. They set to and by evening the place was transformed.

Robert was amazed to see the amount of work in the house. Everything seemed to have been done, except the replacement of the panes of glass in the windows. These were all measured up and the holes temporarily blocked with boards. The carpenter had rehung the front door and repaired the stairs. Robert was amazed at the transformation. Someone had put a big jar of wild flowers in the hall and everywhere had that clean damp fresh scrubbed smell about it. Schmidt, apparently on Elizabet's instructions, had sent over a bed and some chairs and tables and he had the basics for existence. He could move in and would not have to sleep in the tack room again that night!

One of the women had installed herself as cook with two more to act as maids. They had already taken up their duties and an appetising smell exuded from the kitchen.

As Robert sat at his dinner later that evening, lit by a candle stuck in a bottle, waited on by a girl in bare feet wearing a flowery skirt and a none too clean white blouse, with her hair tied back in a headscarf, he at last began to feel master of the situation and to look forward with some anticipation to the morrow.

CHAPTER 14

Robert woke early the next day and was soon out into the yard. He could find no one about. Frustrated, he returned at about 8 o'clock to find his breakfast being prepared.

"Where is everyone? I cannot find anyone about." The women all smiled at him, but obviously did not understand a word he said. Robert sat down to his meal. There was nothing else for him to do. Every few minutes he got up to look out of the window. Nothing came. He finished and went outside. Nothing. At 11 o'clock the carpenters arrived in their creaking wagon. They had brought a chest of drawers, a wardrobe and a desk with them and apparently there was a second wagon coming behind with more furniture. By 12 o'clock still nothing. At 1 o'clock he had become really impatient. When his cook called him to come in for lunch he snapped at her. Repentantly he was just about to go in when he saw a cloud of dust coming over the plain. Presently he could make out a large group of horseman. As they drew closer he could see they had a quantity of loose horses with them. They came flying into the yard at a running gallop and some women who had been waiting by the gates slammed them shut as the last horses poured through. The riders dismounted and stood together at the side of the yard. Gradually the horses stopped milling around and the dust began to settle.

Soldo appeared, wringing his hat. He was covered in dust and looked hot and bothered. It appeared that they had all the horses except one. They had searched for some long time, but could not find it. It was a mare, heavy in foal. It had probably hidden away to have its foal. After they had had some lunch he would send three men back to find it.

Everyone disappeared again and Robert could see that no progress could be made until everyone had had some food—so reluctantly he had to go and have his meal. The horses seemed quiet enough. As he ate his food, he tried to count them through the window. This proved impossible as they kept circling round the water tank waiting for a turn to drink.

The afternoon seemed long and dusty and it was late in the evening before he had the horses sorted out so that he could see what he had got. Soldo knew which colt or filly belonged to which mare without hesitation and Robert soon realised that he knew far more about his horses than was immediately obvious. Unfortunately, there did not appear to be any records and most of the horses had no names. As they were all of a very uniform deep chocolate colour, it was very difficult for him to tell which was which and have any idea of the breeding worth of any of them.

In the end and until he learned them all, he was reduced to numbering them with some of the white paint that had been sent to decorate the house and painting on them an 'a' or 'b' to indicate which stallion had been the sire.

Soldo was scandalised at such treatment, but until Robert could recognise them himself it was the only way. Some of the mares had progeny to the fifth generation and he needed to know them. He decided not to try and name them all at the moment—only those lines that proved to be the best.

It was obvious that these horses had had no training in the way that he understood it, so, if their performance was to improve, he would have to start anew.

All the horses that were to be in training he wanted to keep at the stud. All the mares due to foal shortly he also wanted near at hand. The mares with foals at foot, ready or due for servicing, were also to be kept close at hand. He kept a barren mare for himself to ride. All the rest returned to the river—wherever that was. Tomorrow he would be able to ride out and find out.

He wanted, if he could, to avoid having a grand muster every time he needed to look at the horses and so he resolved to start the men building paddocks so that horses could be kept together in their sorted groups for ease of handling.

That evening he made himself a big chart of all the horses to try and work out the pedigrees. He realised he was going to have to work extremely hard over the coming weeks, both to achieve what he wanted and convince the men that his ideas were good. They had been openly hostile and quite plainly thought everything he was trying to do ridiculous. However, he felt elated. However hard the task would prove, he had at last made a start.

That summer passed so quickly. He established his training routine, changed the feed and organised the men and boys into an efficient team to look after the horses and undertake the exercise schedules. He had had his paddock fencing constructed and had the horses grazing out in easily manageable groups. He had marked out some gallops and had mapped out his blood lines so that his breeding was no longer a haphazard affair but carried out with some view to producing the future winners from the best stock that he had.

He had had to work hard and lead from the front. It had proved to be very frustrating. He tried to learn the language, but he was making slow progress. He found it quicker to roll up his sleeves and show the men what he wanted rather than rely on a long and often inaccurate translation.

On the whole Robert was very pleased with the progress that had been made. He had managed to persuade Schmidt to cancel the races in the summer and he was quite looking forward to his first entries in the meeting in the autumn, the last of the season. They would show if he had managed to make any improvement in the performance of the Count's horses. He was quietly confident. His watch had shown a considerable measure of improvement in the time that the horses took to cover the marked out gallops.

The week before the meeting the selected horses and jockeys were shipped off up the Danube on the steamer and, having settled the affairs of the stud before his departure, he followed some three days later. He was desperate for success, as he had had a long hard battle all through the summer to persuade his men to do what he wanted. They made it quite plain that they thought his training ideas a complete waste of time and his feeding and rationing ideas a futile fad. Robert, however, knew that his horses were fitter and stronger. They could run faster and further and they looked lean and mean. He had done all he could—the outcome was in the lap of the Gods.

His arrival at the Steward's pre-race dinner caused quite a stir. Where had he been all summer? Could he not face the competition? Did he find the continental horses too strong for his liking? Was he afraid of a total whitewash? Could he not take a beating like a man? It must be very disappointing always being a loser. Robert took it all patiently. *I will show you arrogant buggers*, he thought to himself. After dinner they settled down to the serious business of betting amongst themselves. They laughed at Robert and offered him ridiculous odds—which he accepted. Everyone knew that Ramoskie's horses were too fat and too slow. Robert wrote the bets down in his pocket book—*you'll laugh on the other side of your faces tomorrow*, he thought with some glee and self-satisfaction, though not a little apprehension, as there was no way he could cover the bets if he lost!

He did not sleep at all that night, the brandy lay heavily on his large dinner and his anxiety churned this mixture round all night without being able to digest it. He thought through his preparations and what he had to do in the morning. He could think of nothing else that he could do. He tossed and turned. At last he fell asleep and was immediately woken up by his morning call. He struggled back to wakefulness and hastily got up. Carefully he shaved and dressed in his best dove grey suit—grey frock coat, grey trousers, grey socks and spats. He polished his black boots and brushed his top hat. When he was dressed, he looked at himself in the mirror with some satisfaction. He remembered the humiliation he had felt at the last meeting when he had appeared in a large cloak and with a scarf round his neck to hide the fact that he was still in evening dress. He had not been able to shave and he had felt like a tramp.

He adjusted his handkerchief in his top pocket. He would bloody well show them this time! Lord Shotley would have been proud of him.

He wanted to be away from the hotel before any of the others were about. He had had enough of their jibes the previous night. He was in no mood for them this morning. Now was the time for doing. He had no time for them.

CHAPTER 15

After quickly eating his breakfast and swallowing a cup of coffee, he walked over to the stable lines.

The horses were being rubbed down when they arrived. The grooms were cooking their breakfast over their stoves. Robert carefully ran his hand over every inch of his horses. Not an ounce of spare fat. Just hard rippling muscle, each sinew tuned to perfect pitch like the strings on a concert violin. There was nothing more he could do. He would see the jockeys in the saddling enclosure and would give them their last instructions then. Their every move had been rehearsed—every permutation of circumstance had been considered and worked out. They knew what to do. They only had to get out there and do it. He had three horses running today in the first three races. He had backed his horses to win and had also placed a bet on the last two races. In addition he had an accumulator on the result of the day.

He hung about nervously. Eventually it was time to weigh in. That passed without any problems. He walked out into the saddling enclosure to await the jockeys as the first horses were being paraded round. His horses were being shown at derisory odds. He had been absent from the course all the summer and the bookies had written him off.

Suddenly he was aware of Elizabet and the Count. They had entered the enclosure and were looking for him. With a sudden pang, he realised just how much he had missed her all summer—but he had been so engrossed in his work. And now, here she was. Looking as fresh as the morning dew! Somewhat older, wiser and more mature, but still exhibiting that vibrant spark of vitality that had first caught his imagination all those months ago. The Count saw him first.

"Ah, 'Enery. For once you are not late! You are instead going to tell me not to back my horses?" He glowered at Robert and brandished his stick. "I spend all this money and you tell me I will not back my own horses?" The top buttons of his waistcoat flew open with the exertion of his indignation and crumbs, refugees from his breakfast, showered in all directions.

"No, Count," said Robert with considerable satisfaction, relishing every moment. "No, today I recommend you to place as much as your prudence will allow. Today your horses will win." The Count beamed.

"You mean at last I have some return on my investment? Do not fear, Herr Schmidt he is very thorough. He keep the count of vhat is spent. These horses have got to run pretty damn fast to bring that back!"

"Well, Count, you might well see that all back today!"

He turned to Elizabet and his voice caught in his throat. She looked stunning in a pale blue outfit with a wonderful coquettish hat perched on the front of her head. She smiled at him, that warm, radiant, bewitching smile. He felt quite weak at the knees.

"I did not know that you were going to be here today."

"You do not think that we vould miss this! We have hoped all the summer to see our vinners and no horses. Now this last race, we have three horses. We must come to see them run. All our friend they laugh at us. They say we are afraid to make our horses run against theirs. They are too fat and too slow. Now we have one last chance, we vish to watch!"

Robert smiled. "I think they will change their tune today. I have needed you so much all the summer. It has been very difficult, especially with the language problem. I hope you have had a good time"

"Vell, yes, thank you. We have been very busy, but it vill be nice to be back home again. We come now and stay until the spring, except we go to Cousin Emil to his castle in Bavaria vere we do the hunting in October. When the snows come, we do not go about much, but stay home until spring. It is very beautiful in the winter, everything it is frozen and snow hang off the trees like sugar on a cake, it is all like a fairy tale." Robert interrupted her.

"Excuse me, Graffinklein, but I can see our jockey has just come into the enclosure. I must have a quick word with him. Make sure that you have a big bet on your horses today."

He doffed his hat and hurried away. As they had been talking he had been watching the other horses parading round and his confidence had grown. None of them showed the fitness of his horse. They were soon called to the saddle and to be led out. His heart was in his mouth as they went down to the start.

He scarce dare look as they started, but as he watched, the Count's horse drew steadily away from the rest of the field. By the time it passed the winning post, he was waving his hat in the air and jumping up and down like a schoolboy.

"A distance! A distance!" He ran over to Elizabet and the Count. "A distance! It could have stopped to eat some grass and still have won!" Elizabet clasped his arm and her eyes shone with excitement and pleasure.

"It is so good! Vell done, Robert! You have made the vinner. The first vinner that we have had for so long. Papa vill be so happy."

But he looked far from happy! He had a scowl on his face and he was purple with rage, despite the people who were pressing round him to shake his hand and congratulate him.

"How is it that you always cost me money?" He glowered at Robert. "Last time the race you say do not bet on my horses. I have never heard of such a thing, because my horses do not vin. So now today I bet on some dumb creature that should pull the dog cart, not run the race and my horse, on which I always bet, but did not today, because I take your advice, it finish first, which has never happened before—and so I lose my money again."

Robert was aghast.

"I am sorry Count that you lost your money—but I did tell you that you should bet on all your horses today. I suggest you hurry and make a bet on the others before the odds fall. Please excuse me—I must see to the horse and you must go and collect your cup."

The Count looked astonished. Collect a cup? He had never collected a cup!

"Come quick my dear, we must go to collect the cup."

Robert arrived just in time to lead his horse in. People cheered and shouted and patted him on the back. He felt elated, justified. All he had worked for had happened. He had shown them.

The cup was presented, which Elizabet received, her joy and excitement apparent for all to see. Then suddenly it was all over and everyone was busy with the preparations for the next race.

Robert hurried back to the saddling enclosure. He was less sure of this one. His horse had come on well in training, but it was showing a little swelling in a foreleg. He had ordered that a compress be applied early and this should have taken the swelling down. She had not come on quite as well as the other two but hopefully would be all right by the time of the race.

He watched nervously as she was led round. She was all right. He let out a large sigh of relief. Thank goodness! She walked easily, her neck well arched and a spring in her step.

"Is she going to vin too?"

He jumped. He had not noticed Elizabet coming across to him.

"I am sorry! I did not notice you coming. I was watching the horse."

"The most beautiful owner in the ring comes to talk to her clever trainer and he does not notice!" She laughed at him.

"I am sorry, Graffinflein…" he stammered, embarrassed.

"You must call me Elizabet," she said, laying her hand on his arm. "Except when we are vith the servants, that is," she added hastily. "Is my horse going to vin?" She asked eagerly. "I have made a small bettings on it."

"I think today you could safely make the large bettings," Robert mocked. "The horses have worked very hard and they are very fit. Provided that nothing goes wrong you should be in for a very successful day."

"You think the other horse vill vin?"

"Yes, I hope so. It has the best chance of all of them. It is bigger and much stronger and it has great speed. This horse however has greater heart and courage. She will win by sheer determination."

"Robert, have you missed me this summer, while we have been away?"

Robert was caught unawares by the direct question. He had been concentrating on his horse. He hesitated before answering. He had not had time to think about such things. The summer had been one unending toil. Everything had demanded his full attention. The training of the horses had been a major battle. The local Magyar horsemen thought his methods unnecessary and pointless and so had to be constantly watched that they did as he required. He had had to battle with Schmidt for everything. Despite his earlier offers of help, when it came to extracting money or materials, it was as difficult as drawing the teeth of a fully conscious Siberian tiger.

The materials for the fencing for the paddocks had just not been delivered. In the end he had had to take a wagon and some men and go down to the sawmill and get them. The carpenters working on the house had just not come and he had had to have a furious row with Schmidt to get them back. The work round the horse barns and the Stud yard had slowed right down. It appeared that the children and women he had employed to do it had gone off to work in the orchards.

Everything that he had tried to do had been frustrated.

As the house was not finished and the kitchen only half done, he became more and more unhappy. There always seemed to be a problem with his supplies. It was nearly the end of the summer before this was all sorted out and the tentacles of need had sneaked to every part of the estate to supply all the different produce and ingredients in due season, required to furnish the table of his simple household.

Had he missed her? Needed her—yes. Someone to help translate for him and make things happen when the wheels seemed to have become stuck—certainly; but missed her? He had not even had time to ask himself that question. How many times had he thought of those blue eyes smiling into his? He realised with a shock that it was the strength of their shining lustre that had sustained him and maintained his courage when he was so often on the verge of giving up. She was looking at him with some alarm.

"Yes, Elizabet, I missed you very much. More than I realised. It was only the thought of you that has kept me going this summer. Many times I have felt you in my arms as we waltzed round and round in that ball that your mother and father gave for me. Do you remember?"

"Yes, I remember it very vell. With great kindness." She still looked worried. "Why you took such a long time to answer my question?"

"I have been so busy this summer, I have not had time to think of such things, so I had to ask myself about it. Quite often, you are so busy that you do not see the obvious, even when it stares you in the face. Yes, I did miss you. I missed you very much indeed. I needed your encouragement, your help, your advice, but most of all, I missed having you by me and seeing your smile and your blue eyes and just knowing that you were there." She smiled again.

"You say the nicest things. I too have missed you. Many time I have vondered how you are getting on in that terrible house."

"You should see it now. Not a chicken in sight. When we finally scrubbed the floor clean, we found some rather nice stone tiles. We have mended the roof and evicted the pigeons and you can even walk up and down stairs without risk of breaking your neck—Look! They are mounting up." He was glad of the diversion.

The door to his heart, which had been kept firmly shut since Lillian had disappeared, was being gradually opened and he did not want it open. He could not cope with it being opened.

He gave his jockey a leg-up onto the horse and then Soldo led it out onto the course. As Robert watched it canter down to the start a little frown appeared on his face. It did seem to be going just a little tenderly. This race was a longer distance and he could not see the start.

The starter's flag went down and it was some time before the horses came into view. Robert held his breath until he could identify them. His horse was running uneasily in fourth place as they thundered past. She seemed to be all right, but they had a whole circuit to go. She made up ground steadily and was lying half a length behind the leader as they came to the final straight past the stands. The crowd was roaring and shouting. "Run, you brave little horse! Run! Run!" someone yelled. Robert realised it was him. He waved his hat in the air and jumped up and down.

"Run. Run. Just a little harder—run, you little horse!" Elizabet was also jumping up and down in her excitement, brandishing her parasol in a most unladylike way. They thundered past the winning post.

"Did we vin? Did we vin?" Elizabet squeaked, her voice completely gone. She leaned on Robert's arm, her faced flushed with excitement, breathing heavily.

"I do not know—I could not see. We will have to wait for the numbers. There—look—yes! We won! We just did it." The numbers went up on the board. They fought their way through the excited crowd to the winning enclosure just as the horses were brought in. Elizabet again accepted the trophy, this time a silver salver. The Count, for the first time that Robert had known him, was beaming.

"I have von the bet! It is the first time that one of my horses has won the money for me!" He patted the horse. "Oh, you vonderful horse. You have won me the bet. You vill come now and live at the castle. You vill race no more. You vill have many fine foals and all who come to the castle vill see you and I vill be so proud."

The presentations were soon over and the horses were brought in for the next race. Running in this race was their last horse, a big strong powerful horse. Good on speed, but not so good on endurance. This was going to be a sprint—a cavalry charge for the finishing line, hardly begun before it was over. They flashed past the post in a ragged line and again Robert had to wait for the official result before he dare be certain. At last after what seemed a very long delay, the numbers went up. He hardly dare look. To his relief he had won! He raised his eyes to heaven.

I've done it. Three in a row! I've bloody well shown them! Put that in your pipe and bloody well smoke it! He grinned with satisfaction. The Count and Elizabet came over to him.

"We've done it! Well done, Count. All your horses needed was a little work. I have done it. Everyone will watch your horses now. You will not get odds like this again." The Count was beaming all over his face. He held a huge fistful of money. He was embarrassed to be seen in public dirtying his hands on actual money, but at the same time he was surreptitiously trying to count the overflowing bundles as he stuffed them into his pockets.

"Vell done, 'Enery," he beamed. "I have made the big collection this afternoon." Even as he spoke, people who had had bets with him, certain that they would win, were thrusting bundles of notes into his pocket.

"I like this having vinners. This is very good. Ten to one, Fritz!" he beamed at a large man who was pulling notes out of his wallet and handing them over. "You said that my horse had no hope against yours and, vell, it won!" He roared with laughter. "Ten to one. Pay up, my friend, like the man! That is vhat I like to see." He thrust the notes into his inner pockets. "Vell done 'Enery! I am so pleased. I vas begin to loose heart, but no—now you have given us vinners. It is the beginning of great things. We have the big dinner tonight to make the celebrate. You must come. We celebrate and make whoopee!" Elizabet was hanging onto his arm whilst her father spoke. She jumped up and kissed Robert on the cheek in her excitement.

"Vell done, Robert. It is so good, we have not one vinners but three, it is so exciting."

"What do you think you doing?" the Count roared at his daughter, horror on his face. "What you doing? You do not kiss mans in public—what you think?" Elizabet giggled.

"You do not count your money in public, but you are doing it!"

He sheepishly stuffed his bundles of notes into his pocket.

"You do not tell me what to do," he scolded. "Behave yourself. It is most not goot. What vill people think?"

"Father, I do not care what they think—I am so happy, it is very excitement." She beamed at Robert. "Come, we must go and collect the prize!" They went down to the winners' enclosure and collected the trophy.

The rest of the afternoon passed in a golden haze. Robert failed to collect his accumulator as his choice in the last race failed to get even a place, but as he made his way back to his hotel, he felt ten feet tall.

CHAPTER 16

✿

Robert had nicked his chin whilst shaving and a smudge of blood had appeared on the starched front of his white shirt. He had sponged it off, but he was now left with a damp, soggy wet-looking patch right in the middle of his chest. He had been struggling with the gold studs and cufflinks in the starched fabric for ten minutes. He was sweating profusely from the exertion. His cufflink just would not go in. He writhed and tugged at it, but no matter how he contorted himself, it just would not go in. In desperation he took out his boot lace and, threading a loop of it through one of the holes in his cuff, he lassoed the offending link and by dextrous twisting and pulling managed to get it through the inadequate hole. Before attempting the other, he took out his pocket knife to enlarge the hole. He managed to get the first half of the link through and, resorting to the bootlace, after much tugging and twisting, managed to struggle the second half into place. He sat down on the bed and looked at his watch. He was going to be late. If he was not quick, he would be late. He could hear the Count: "Ha! the late Herr 'Enery! Always you are late!"

He stood up and looked in the mirror. His chin was still bleeding! A runnel of blood was in danger of dropping onto his shirt again. He quickly wiped it off with a flannel and walked impatiently round the room pressing the wound firmly in the hope of stopping the flow. It seemed to have worked. The bleeding had stopped. Now for the top stud and the tie. The top stud was the worst, the large inside section cut into his Adam's apple. He struggled and tugged. He could feel the sweat collecting under his lower lip and run down his chin. The shirt stuck to his shoulders and strained at the seams, in danger of bursting. At last it was in place. His neck bulged uncomfortably against the tight constriction of the collar. Despite the fact that he had worked hard all summer, he must have put on weight. He knotted his tie and tweaked it into shape. Waist-coat and jacket. He looked at himself in the mirror—he cut quite a dash! He cleaned his chin with a spit-licked finger and, quickly wetting a hairbrush, groomed some wayward hair back into shape. He adjusted his handkerchief in his top pocket. He stood back from the mirror. There was no doubt—full evening dress was very becoming. Even though he filled it more tightly than before, he still had a neat figure. He dropped his watch into his waistcoat pocket and draping his gold chain elegantly across his still fairly flat stomach, carefully placed the fob in the other pocket so that just the right amount of drape remained in the chain. Satisfied, he ran downstairs and asked the door-man to hail him a cab. Presently he was on his way to the Count's hotel.

The contrast between this place and the hotel in which he was staying could not have been greater. He mounted the marble steps between the black twisted pillars on either side of the door and entered the foyer. The whole place was a vista of baroque scrollwork in heavy gilt plaster. The floor was polished marble. Semi-draped female figures, made of gilt and white marble, held up the many-branched lights that cast a warm glow over the shining surfaces. Deep chairs covered with crimson upholstery, with gilded arms and legs, were taste-fully arranged in secluded groups. As people walked, their footfalls echoed dis-tantly off the high vaulted ceiling.

He was immediately pounced on by a flunky in an elegant dark blue uni-form, who relieved him of his hat and cape. Another conducted him across the palatial polished marble, beneath the soaring ceiling of gilded plasterwork, to a large mahogany door set in an ornate white plaster doorway enriched with intricate mouldings. The man threw open the door and, coughing slightly, announced in a sonorous tone:

"Your Highness, Count and Countess, Ladies and Gentlemen—Herr Robert Henery." He clicked his heels and bowing slightly stepped aside so that Robert could pass.

My God! thought Robert, *I'm making an entrance. I'm making a bloody entrance. I've never made an entrance before!* He drew himself up to his full height, pulled in his stomach, straightened his back and, with head held high, walked in. He was not prepared for what he saw. There was a large table at the end of the room set for dinner. It was a sea of candles, twinkling crystal and shining silver. The room was filled with candles—there seemed to be hundreds of them. Everyone was clapping.

There was a group of people round the fireplace at the other end of the room. As he walked over to them, he could hear champagne corks popping.

The Count advanced towards him, resplendent in a heavily befrogged smoking jacket.

"Here come our hero. The late hero, 'Enery." He grabbed his hand and pumped it with a vigour that threatened to dislodge his shoulder. "How did you do it? Three vinners in a row. It has never been done before. Even I have won some little monies." A tray of champagne glasses appeared at his elbow. The Count took one and thrust it into Robert's hand. "Come, come, meet my guests. Come, let me introduce you to the cousin of my vife, Prince Emil von Zellatal." Robert shook his hand.

"Congratulations. I was most impressed. I am so glad that you have had this success. From what I have heard you have worked hard for it. I am most impressed. I wish you could make my horses go like that. We must have a talk." Robert shook his hand. He liked this man: there was a genuine warmth about him—a natural charm that was both infectious and appealing. If they were all going to be formal, he could be as well.

"Thank you, Your Highness. It is very kind of you to say so. Yes, it has been a bit of a struggle, but I hope we have started something on which we can build. I hope that you are well, Sir. It has been a long summer since we last met."

"Yes, indeed. I remember well. You were then, if I recall, sleeping in the tack room. I hope that you have managed to sort yourself out better accommodation."

"Yes, thank you, Sir." Credit where credit was due. "Herr Schmidt was very helpful in restoring the house. I was soon most comfortably installed."

The Count bustled between them. "Come on, 'Enery, you cannot stand gossiping. May I present my vife."

Robert bowed and solemnly took her hand.

"Herr 'Enery," the Countess smiled, "you must not mind my 'usband. He makes so forgetful."

Robert too laughed. He had been wondering where this charade was leading.

"Countess, I am delighted to see you again. I hope you had a good summer and that you are well."

"Yes, thank you. It has been very busy." She flapped her fan languidly. "But yes, we have had the good time. I hope that you have settled in."

"Yes, thank you, Countess, we have managed to evict the chickens and the swallows; the pigeons have gone and the roof is mended—but I have been so busy, I have hardly noticed."

The Count pushed him on. "I am pleased to present you to my daughter. She causes us much grief, but she is our only child, so we have to have patient." He smiled at her indulgently. Robert looked into those blue, smiling eyes; he took her hand, which he held in his.

"Graffinflein, I am delighted to see you again. I have heard so much about you. I understand that you dance divinely." He smiled at her and was rewarded with a coy blush.

"How do you do Herr 'Enery?" She made a small curtsey with mock solemnity. "We are so pleased that you have made the horses run so vell. We have never won three races in a one meeting, look." She pointed to the table. In the middle were the three trophies, surrounded by silk ribbons of the Count's racing colours. She led him over to admire them.

"You must not mind Papa. 'E become so forgetful, he is so excited, he forget where he is, or even what day it is. He is so pleased vith you. You have given him the first winners. All his life he has wanted the winner at this meeting and now he has three! He is like the puppy dog vith the three tails. He forget all things except his three winners. He is so happy."

"Come, everyone, we stand talking when there is good food to be eated."

The Count ushered them all to the table in an excitement sharpened by the lure of food and his recent victories. As they went, Elizabet quickly introduced Robert to the other guests. The large table sagged under the weight of silver and crystal and the three imposing trophies in the middle. There was only just room for the plates, containing the first course that was even then arriving.

Robert lost count as plate after plate followed in steady succession. Wines of different hues were poured into the twinkling crystal glasses. Everyone was in a high state of excitement. The Count was in his seventh heaven. He had finally had a winner, not only one, but three. He had beaten his arch rivals and at the reception to be held tomorrow, he was jolly well going to show them, rub their noses in it and gloat over his victory. It had been long coming and he had had to endure many jibes about the failures of his horses. Tomorrow, the revenge would be his! It would be oh so sweet! They were not going to forget the race meeting today for a very long time. He had also won some money. Not a lot, admittedly, but it was such an unusual event, that he felt like a king. Even the Countess was permitting herself a thin smile. As course followed course and the ever changing rainbow hue of wines flowed through her forest of crystal glasses a glow appeared on her cheeks and a smile on her lips—as unusual as a rosebud on a glacier top in the middle of winter.

Emil von Zellatel proved to be a raconteur with an inexhaustible fund of stories and gossip told with a charming, subtle wit and humour that had those round the table reeling in their seats and weeping into their napkins. It appeared that all those present had at least a smattering of English. For the first time since Robert had arrived, he felt able to join in the conversation. Even Franc, waiting on them at table, the past master at seeing and hearing nothing, on several occasions let out a snort that had heads turning anxiously in his direction.

Elizabet was sparkling like fire reflected in a waterfall. She was animated and excited and Robert could feel the physical presence of her happiness across the table. Their eyes frequently met and when they did he felt the warmth of her affection as if it were a physical thing.

Robert felt justified. He had worked hard all summer. He had not stopped. He had felt he had to prove himself as well as restore the lost prestige of his employer. He had not spared himself. He had kept long hours and pushed with great determination. This was the first time that he had been able to relax since that first night when he had travelled home in the moonlight in the little cart after the ball.

He had succeeded! They had all felt that he was wrong. What on earth was he doing, a foreigner, coming to tell them, the Magyar, how to train horses? The Magyar practically were horses. Had not their skills on horseback conquered much of Europe whilst men in England were still dressed in woad? Robert sat back in his chair and with a smug satisfaction twirled the stem of the glass that had just been filled with a heavy amber liquid. He looked at its golden depths, the amber fire glowing like some ancient jewel catching the light from the depths of some deep hidden pool.

Three winners, he thought to himself with happy self-righteous contentment. *Three winners. Have you had three winners? Two? One?* He chuckled to himself with smug self-satisfaction. Emil had just ended a tale and everyone was laughing. The Count, his tie askew, red in the face, was gasping for breath, as if each precious inhalation would be his last. The Countess was dabbing her weeping eyes with feeble flutterings of a lace handkerchief. Elizabet was sitting back in her chair, tears streaming down her face, gasping for breath in helpless laughter. Robert laughed too, not because he knew what had just been said, but because he was caught up in the infectious spontaneous happiness of the moment. He sat back in his chair and laughed and laughed until he felt he would burst.

The Count at last recovered. Pulling a large silk handkerchief from his pocket, he wiped the sweat from his face and at the same time motioned for his glass to be refilled.

"Robert, my friend," he began in sonorous tone, taking up his glass and waving it vaguely in Robert's direction. Robert was startled and flattered to be addressed by his Christian name.

"Robert," continued the Count, "we cannot say how happy we are. That for vhich we long hoped, the impossible, has happened. You have made for us vinners, three vinners." The Count's words began to slur and he waved his glass around in the air in a wobbly way. "We are so happy for ourselves and so proud for you. It is good that you have done so well. We have most happiness. We hope for many more of vinners. If three have learned to run so fast, is it not possible that there vill be many others, who too have learnt to run as vell?" He drained his glass and with a happy satisfied smack of his lips, waved for it to be refilled. Immediately a footman, who had been standing in the shadows by a massive mahogany sideboard, stepped forward into the light bearing a heavy glittering decanter to refill his glass. "One day," continued the Count, "we may breed the wonderful stallion, which vill be the father of magnificent horses that are the greatest vinners that have ever been seen." His eyes glazed over as he was caught up in his great dream. In his mind's eye he saw a procession of brilliant horse flashing past the winning post, resplendent in his colours. "Maybe, one day perhaps, I might have the grandchildren who collect trophies and they vill remember this day as the day when Grandpapa had his first vinners." He waved his glass vaguely at Elizabet. "It is you my daughter, who vill have to carry on when I am dead. Do you think that you vill be able to manage? You are only a little girl. There are so many things for to be worried about?"

"Hush, August, you have drunk too much," the Countess lightly scolded him. "You are being maudlin. You will be telling us what hymns you want for your funeral next."

"Do not worry, Papa," interposed Elizabet. "It is very good to have vinners. I shall make sure that we have many vinners. Even after you are no more, they will run under your colours. Everyone who sees them, will know that these are the horses of August Ramoskie and his daughter, she runs them so well for him."

A beatific smile spread over the Count's face. Immortality promised. It was too much. Three winners and the promise of immortality.

"Besides, Papa, I have our worker of miracle, Herr 'Enery, to help me, to guide me…" Her voice tailed away and she looked down at the tablecloth. She looked uncertainly at Robert and then back at her father "…to look after me. When we are married, we shall have for you, both many vinners and many grandchildren."

The Countess let her knife drop with a little clatter onto her plate.

Franc, who was at that moment crossing the room with a new decanter of wine, stopped frozen in his tracks. The Count gaped at Elizabet. Robert sat bolt upright. There was a sudden deathly hush round the table. Only Emil sat back in his chair, fascinated to see what was going to happen next. Elizabet smiled for support at Robert and was horrified to see his frozen scowling face. He could not meet her eyes but stared fixedly at the massive silver trophy in front of him.

"*VHAT* is *THIS*?" roared the Count, being the first to recover from the staggering bombshell. "Vhat rubbish is this? Marry 'Enery? You cannot marry 'Enery. He is trainer of race 'orses. You do not marry a trainer. Vhat silly thing is this that you say?" He swallowed down his wine and held his glass out for a refill. Franc leapt into action from his state of shock, but in his haste clinked the decanter on the Count's glass and made him start. The wine ran all over his hand and up his sleeve.

"Take care, you clumsy man," he growled. He turned back to Elizabet. "Vhat is this silly thing?"

Elizabet had not expected this reaction. She had not planned to make any remark at all. It had just seemed the right thing to say at the moment, but it was going horribly wrong. She twirled the stem of her wineglass.

"But, Papa, I love him."

"*Love him*? You cannot love him. He is the trainer of race horses! He is not for loving."

The Countess had recovered from her shock. "Elizabet, my child, there is no question of you marrying Herr 'Enery, for he is not a Catholic."

Elizabet looked at her mother in horror and then at Robert in pleading supplication, but Robert could not look at her—he stared fixedly, unseeing, at the silver. A small tear escaped from the corner of his eye and rolled out onto his cheek. He too had been shocked.

"Herr 'Enery." He became conscious of the voice of the Countess. "I have never seen you in church, are you a Catholic?"

"'Enery!" the Count's voice bellowed before he could answer, "she says she loves you. Vhat have you done to make her think this? Do you love her?"

Robert continued to stare at the trophy. Did he love her? He had never asked himself that question. There was no doubt that he thought that she was beautiful. She had lovely skin and pretty hair. She had a chin that betokened a determined nature. Yes, he realised that he felt weak at the knees whenever he saw her. Yes, he could feel her love for him, as a tangible thing. Yes, he delighted in her company, but did he love her? Could he stand up in public and declare his love for her as boldly as she had done? Did he love her in an 'until death us do part' way, or was he feeling just a natural physical attraction for a vivacious and desirable young woman? He was conscious that all eyes were upon him. He had never asked the question, but now that it was thrust upon him, he had to acknowledge that there was only one answer.

"Yes," he said quietly. "Yes, I do love her."

There was a long silence in the room. Robert writhed in misery in his chair as the truth slowly dawned on him. Yes, he did love her, damn it, and it was so bloody unfair!

He knew then that he had loved her ever since they had first met, but all summer he had tried to put it out of his mind—to thrust it to the back of his conscious; to bury it under a deluge of work. He had worked with a feverish fanaticism that left him drained and exhausted. No time to think, just over-whelming sleep to obliterate any ideas that might float unbidden to the front of his mind. And so he had been shocked by Elizabet's declaration. As far as he knew, he had done nothing to encourage her, yet here she was expressing her-self, unasked, in a way that was shameful and wanton. He writhed in his seat in dejection and misery. He could feel her eyes upon him, imploring him for some sign, some word of comfort, some ray of warmth that would justify the bold, presumptive and extraordinary statement she had made. Robert could feel the intensity of her love reaching to him across the table, but he could not look. The stem of the glass that he was twisting in his fingers snapped in his hand and the bowl toppled onto the table spilling a stain of red across the white cloth.

"No," he said, barely audibly. "No," he repeated more loudly. Elizabet's look of supplication changed to one of horror. Every eye was upon him.

"No," he repeated. "Yes, I love Elizabet. I have not allowed myself to think how much I love her." At last he was able to look at her. She sat in her chair, her face covered by her hands, her eyes, the hurt and bafflement plainly visible in them, stared at him intently from above her fingers.

"But it cannot be. I am married already." He felt the misery well up inside him. He choked over the words. Elizabet leaped to her feet with a strangled cry. Her chair fell to the floor with a crash and she ran from the room.

The Countess rose. "I vill go to her, August." She quickly turned and followed her daughter to the anti-room, from which loud sobs could be heard.

"Mein Gott, 'Enery, I vould give you the horsewhip." The Count struggled to his feet, red in the face with furious anger. One of the footmen who had been standing in the shadows by the wall jumped forward and caught his chair, just in time to prevent it, too, crashing to the floor.

"I should give you the horse whipping vithin an inch of your life!" He groped round him wildly in the air in the hope that the instrument that he sought would miraculously appear in his hand. He continued to grope in the air, lost for words, his anger boiling over in confused fury. His evening of triumph had been turned to disaster. Somehow this man, the architect of his success, at the moment of its sweetest had contrived to ruin it. He spluttered incoherently.

"How dare you! You come to my house. You take my monies, you drink my wines. You accept my generosity, my hospitality, then you make cuckoo of my daughter. You are a trainer. You make the horses run. What do you know of love? By what right do you speak of love for my daughter? Love, it is for people, not for trainers. What have you said to her which make her think she love you? She should know better. She should know that you are for training, not for loving! You fill her head vith all ridiculous ideas and now you say that you have already the wife. How dare you make the trifle with my daughter in this way. I for it will not stand! Tomorrow, you leave my house in the morning, the first thing. I hope I never to see you again."

"August, for goodness sake, sit down before you burst a blood vessel!" Emil rose from his chair. He guided the Count back into his seat. "For goodness sake, fill his glass before he expires," he called to Franc who was hovering nearby, still holding the decanter that he had been carrying to the sideboard when he had been stopped in his tracks by Elisabet's bombshell. "You have shot the prisoner before you have heard what he has to say. Do you think that, at least, you might seek his point of view?"

"Why? Why should I hear his point of view? What has he got to say, to which I might listen? He is the married man. He admits that and he dally vith my daughter. I should whip him vith the horsewhip. He is of the horse, he understand that." Again he thrashed in the air and he let out a fierce growl of exasperation. "Throw him out. You!" He beckoned to the footmen standing round the room. "Put him out. Put him out on the street, I vish never to see him again." Stunned, no one moved. "You and you, do as I say, throw him out!" The footmen started forward.

"No!" Emil stepped forward. "No, that will not be necessary. Franc, ask these men to leave the room, please." He addressed himself to the footmen. "Not one word of this leaves this room, is that clear? If I hear that any of you has said one word to anyone, to anyone," he repeated "I will make sure that you are dismissed and that everyone knows that you are unreliable so that you do not get another job. Do I make myself clear?" The earnestness of his face and the set expression of his voice made it quite clear to everyone that this was no idle threat.

"Yes, Herr Prince." "Yes, Your Highness." One by one they assented and left the room.

"Franc, you stay, please. I know that you can be trusted."

"Yes, Herr Prince." Franc bowed slightly, deeply gratified that he was so respected and that he was not going to miss the next twist of the drama. Emil turned back to the Count.

"August, you are not being just. You cannot just throw him out. Look what he has done for you. You've got three damn great lumps of silver standing on the table there in front of you, which you would not have were it not for him. How long have you been trying to win the race this afternoon? Now you have done it because of him. Your horses are the talk of the town, thanks to him. Your carriages and teams are the smartest in the country. Thanks to him. You have become a respected and admired figure of the turf, thanks to him. Are you going to throw him out and throw all that away, just because there might be some trifling misunderstanding, which I am sure can be cleared up if only you would have the good sense to listen?"

Emil sat down in his chair again and motioned to Frank to fill his glass. Phew! He stretched his collar with his finger, as it had suddenly become very tight. It was the first time that he had stood up to his bombastic cousin, but it was time that someone told the silly old fool! Everyone else round the table sat as if frozen, enthralled to see what was going to happen next.

"It is not a trifling problem. The happiness of my daughter, it is the only thing that matter. When I am dead, what vill be left? A few horses that vill be sold, then what? There vill be nothing left to show that I was ever on this earth. All that I have done, all that for vhich I have worked, it vill be gone. Forgotten. The only monument that vill be left to me is my daughter, my Elizabet. Anyone who hurt her, hurt me. For this I vill not stand. Up vith it I vill not put!"

Robert had not been listening to this exchange. He was sunk in his own particular hell. Now that he had had to admit the true depths of his feelings for Elizabet, he felt overwhelmed with wretchedness. He had come to Hungary to get away from all the business of Lillian. Now, here it was again, leaping out of the shadows to bedevil him.

"Robert—Robert!" Emil repeated more sharply.

Robert started. He had not realised that the Prince was talking to him.

"Robert, do you not think that perhaps some explanation might be helpful? This wife of yours, how is it that we have not yet met her?"

"August, I will take Elizabet to bed, she is very distressed." The Countess swept into the room, pulling on her gloves as she entered. "As for you," she looked at Robert with a stare that would have withered an iron bar. "You see vot damage you have done? My poor Elizabet, you have broken her heart. You will call upon us tomorrow morning at 11 o'clock so that we may discuss this whole unfortunate business, but know that there is no question of you marrying our daughter. Perhaps you ladies vould come with me now, to my drawing room. Emil, be so kind as to bring my husband when you have finished. August, I will speak with you later." She swept out of the room, a lioness defending her cub. The other ladies rose and followed her. The men gathered round the Count at the head of the table and sat down again.

"Well, Robert, perhaps you have something to say about all this?" Emil passed the decanter over to Robert, so that he could fill his glass. Robert reached across and, taking the decanter, filled the only empty glass that he had left. He could see no way out—he was going to have to relive the whole wretched affair again.

"Yes, I have a wife, but she is missing."

"Missing? That sounds a bit careless. How do you mean missing?" Emil noticed Robert's flash of irritation. "I am sorry, please do continue." They all listened in silent attention whilst he told them of the whole affair, from the time of Robert's accident until the present day. Franc had silently returned and he too was listening with rapt attention, hovering close to their elbows and refilling their glasses, so that he did not miss a word. Robert drank as he talked, but such was the speed of his stressed metabolism, that the alcohol was burned up and blown away in his words. The wine gave him eloquence and the courage to speak out about things that he had long ago swept into the back corner of his subconscious. Another day and he would regret that he had not relished the wonderful and subtle aromas and tastes, but for now they were lubrication to his determination. When he had finished, his listeners sat silent for some time. Emil was the first to speak.

"This is very distressing tale and I feel most sorry for you. How long, if I can be so indelicate as to ask, will it be before you are…you are" he hesitated, searching for the right word "…free?" Robert twiddled his glass in his fingers.

"If, after seven years, she has not reappeared, she will be declared officially dead and I will be free, as you put it."

"What will happen if she returns before the time is up?"

"Then she will be my wife again and we will take up our lives together."

"But what will happen with you and Elizabet? You have both openly declared your love for each other."

"Well, if Lillian reappears, there can be no me and Elizabet and that will be the end of it."

"But if your wife returns to you after this, perhaps after six or even seven years, what will you do? You will be strangers to each other, after all that has passed; you will not be the same people that you were when you married."

"I know, I know. Do you think that I have not thought of all these things? All the time I think of them. I do not know what I will do. I don't…I don't know." His wretchedness was evident for them to see. "I don't know what I am going to do. Suppose after seven years when I am free, if I find someone to love and have married her, Lillian turns up, what am I to do then? I do not know."

Emil's heart went out to this young man, caught in this awful dilemma.

"So you have five years yet to wait. If she returns in that time you say you will take her up again as your wife, yet you have declared before us your love for Elizabet. What will you do? How can you live married to her, knowing that you love another?"

"Why not?" snapped Robert, "Plenty of people do."

The Count who up to now had remained silent banged both his fists on the table and leaned forward.

"Vell, I have to say that I am sorry for you, young man, you seem to have had the very bad misfortunes, but this does not excuse that you have made the cuckoo with my daughter. It is vorse, for you knew that you were not free to marry her. You have treated her the most cruel, for this I need the horsewhip." Robert's personal misery was giving way to anger against the obstinate old man.

"No!" He banged the table with his open hand. "No, Sir, you are not being fair! In no way, at no time, have I given your daughter any grounds or occasion to make the statement that she did. Do you think that I am forgetful of my situation? My regard for her is too high for me to risk any careless word or gesture that might bring any harm or even the slightest hurt to her. What she said came from her own fantasies, her own imagination. I was as shocked as you were when I heard them. Thrilled, flattered, delighted, but shocked that she should speak out so openly about things that we had both held secretly in our hearts. Thrilled to find that my feeling were reciprocated, but horrified to realise the implications of what she said. I would no more have my feelings for her known, than I would fly to the moon. I have not allowed myself to think of them, for I knew what the consequences would be. I would rather anything than offer her any hurt. What has happened this evening is not of my doing or of my making. I am as distressed as everyone else to see her in such a state, especially as I have, unknowingly, caused it!"

"You have never talked to her of love?"

"No, Sir, never! I have never given her word or hint that might make her think such a thing."

"You have never talked to her of marriage?"

"No, Sir. The only conversations I have had with her have been purely on business level. Talking about the horses and the affairs of the estate or the repairs and decorations to my house."

"Well, somehow she has the idea that you vill marry. This is of course quite out of the question. If you make my daughter have such silly things in her head, you do not see her again. You do not come to my house. It is best if you do not meet her again. This vill be best for both of you. It means that you vill have to finish working with my horses. I shall have to find someone else to take them over."

Robert was stunned to silence. This was not fair. Not fair! He had really begun to settle here and had at last achieved something. He had proved all his critics wrong and he was looking forward to building on what he had started. Then there was Elizabet. Up to now he would not have allowed her name to be included in the equation of this kind, but now that he had been forced to face the reality of the situation, the idea that he would be forced away from her was intolerable.

"This is most unfair, Sir. I have worked hard for your horses and we have this afternoon seen the results of that work. Now is the time to build—you have some wonderful young horses. We have shown what we can do and next season we will show everyone what we have achieved." The Count wearily held up his hand, and struggled to his feet.

"No, my mind it is made up. Good night, Herr 'Enery. I hope I never see you again. Come Emil, be so good to escort me to my room. My legs they seem to have the vobbles." He clung unsteadily to the back of his chair. His eye focused unsteadily on Franc, who had grabbed his arm and was supporting him. He looked round the room. "Go on, the rest of you, the cabaret is over. I know that we can rely on you all not to breathe a word of what has been said." He turned to Frank after they had all gone.

"Not one vord passes your lips."

"No, Excellency. Not a word. Goodnight Excellency. Goodnight Your Highness, can you manage…?"

"Yes, thank you, Franc. You get to bed. You need some sleep, you have earned it. We have all earned it tonight. Come on, my unsteady cousin, I will soon have you to your room. Goodnight Robert. I am very sorry about all this, it is terrible for you. Perhaps you will make some headway in the morning."

Robert got unsteadily to his feet. "Yes, thank you. Goodnight, we will see." He watched them stagger to the door.

"I should have give him the horsewhip."

"For goodness sake, August, just for once, bloody well shut up."

"Vhat? Vhat that you say, you do not speak to me…" Frank firmly shut the door on their staggering figures as they reeled down the hallway.

CHAPTER 17

Robert could not sleep. His nerves and pent-up frustration kept him shifting and writhing in his bed. How could she have come out with that, in that way? He had never even spoken to her of his feelings. In no way had he offered her any encouragement—had he? True, there did seem to be empathy between them. They both laughed at the same things and they could talk easily together about nothing and about everything. Clearly and in every detail, he could see again the Ball that was given for him when he arrived. He re-lived the trip on the steamer, up to Vienna. He could see her now, standing by the ship's rail, the sunlight making a halo round her face as her fair hair caught the golden light and shimmered and danced in the breeze. Was he being ridiculous? Was it absurd to think you could love someone on such a short acquaintance? He had not dared to allow such questions to enter his mind. Every time such thoughts rose in his subconscious, he had pushed them aside, not because he did not want to consider the ideas, but because he was afraid of the consequences. What would happen if Lillian should suddenly reappear? Even if she did not, he would not be free for five more years. It would be unreasonable for him to expect anyone to wait five years, before they could even discuss that which they felt between them!

But now? Now that the matter had been thrust at him, he had had to answer. He had had to face the situation. He had known the answer at once. He had not needed to think. He had only paused to assemble his thoughts before answering and to recover from the shock of Elizabet's bold statement. What had possessed her to speak out like that? She must have had too much to drink. Even if she harboured such notions, it was completely out of order to speak her thoughts in that wanton way. Even if there had been some legitimate understanding between them, it was up to him to raise the matter, to broach it as gently as he could before her parents. For her to blurt out that she loved him, in front of everyone, without even a word on the subject passing between them, was unforgivable. True, she was young and full of romantic ideas. True, she was excited because of the three winners. True, she—they—had all drunk too much; but nonetheless, look what had happened! The wonderful evening had been ruined. His moment of triumph had been totally destroyed. His dreams were shattered. He was likely to lose his job and suddenly find himself stuck in the middle of Europe without a roof over his head. Most likely, he would lose her, too, for unless the Count could be persuaded to change his mind, he was going to be unceremoniously thrown out.

. He rolled over and, burying his head in his hand, he sobbed great tears of frustration, exasperation and self-pity.

He was woken by a persistent banging that throbbed through his head. It continued. He struggled into consciousness and with an effort sat up. The room span round. He had to sit, elbows on his knees and head in hand, until it stopped. The banging continued. He realised it was from his door.

"What do you want?" he called feebly, shivering violently. Something was shouting at him in German. He did not understand, but at least the hammering stopped. He was freezing cold. He had slept on his bed in his evening clothes and had not noticed how cold it was. He struggled to his feet and opened the door. His hot water was standing outside in a china jug covered with a thick towel. He retrieved it and, bringing it in, he struggled out of his evening clothes. He was shivering so much, that he had the greatest of difficulty undoing the cufflinks and studs from his starched shirt. He poured the water into his china wash bowl, but abandoned the attempt to shave as he was shaking too much. Eventually he was dressed. Feeling tousled and unshaved, he stumbled down to the dinning room. He could not face any breakfast and ordered a pot of black coffee. The hot strong liquid, when it came, warmed him and gradually, the shaking subsided. He looked with growing apprehension at his watch. He was in no fit state to face the coming interview. He felt rough and knew that he looked it. He could not go into battle looking like the remnants of the defeated army of Napoleon. He resolved to try and smarten himself up, so returned unsteadily to his room.

Taking off his coat, his tie and his collar and tucking down the neck of his shirt, he took up his shaving mug and applied a thin coat of shaving soap. With trembling hand he took up the cut-throat razor. He remembered Lillian shaving him when he lay injured in Hospital, after the fall. Tears filled his eyes as he remembered her doing it for him, with the utmost gentleness. What would she say now to hear him openly declare his love for Elizabet? She would be hopping mad. He could imagine her eyes blazing, her angry scold. "Don't be so ridiculous. How can you love her? You don't even know her. You have hardly ever spoken to her. How can you possibly love her?" It was true. He had hardly spoken to her, but in those brief meetings he had found someone whom he knew instinctively he loved. He knew that he was drawn to her as would a fish to a light or iron to a magnet. He knew what she was thinking. When they started to speak, as like as not, they would both begin to say the same thing. They laughed at the same things. They shared a mutual dislike for Schmidt. He laughed out loud. He could not love her. It was madness to even think about it. He could not falsely raise her hopes, or his. Lillian might reappear, with some perfectly reasonable explanation for her absence. Then they would take up their lives again. What would happen to Elizabet then? She would be left desolate, broken hearted. The Count would hound him out of the Country and make sure that no one else employed him, in Europe, again. Then what would he do? He would have to go back to England with his tail between his legs. Could he re-establish himself? What if he could not, what would he do then? Perhaps he could emigrate to one of the colonies, or America?

If Lillian came back, would he feel the same for her? Could he resume their lives together, knowing that in his heart he loved Elizabet? He could not face this question, but he knew in his heart what the answer must be. It was so bloody unfair. When he had finished he struggled back into his tie and coat. Quickly sponging it down with a damp cloth, he hurried downstairs. Robert asked for a cab to be called. It was not long before he was on his way. He became increasingly nervous.

When he arrived at the Count's hotel, a footman who was obviously waiting for him, ushered him up to the Count's suite. He was shown straight in. The Count sat in a large wing chair by a bright coal fire. The Countess stood beside him. There was no doubt who was in charge.

"Herr 'Enery, please to come in," she said with studied politeness. "I 'ope you had the good night. Please to seated." She noticed his hesitation. "Do not vorry. Now I prefer to stand. Sit there." She pointed at the large sofa on the opposite side of the fire. In silence, Robert moved to where she pointed, but still did not sit.

"Herr 'Enery, it vill be easier for me to say vhat has to be said, if you sit…Sit!" She raised her voice.

Reluctantly, Robert sat on the edge of the sofa. He felt most uncomfortable. He had been brought up never to sit down if there was a lady present who was standing. He felt most ill at ease and out of place.

"Herr 'Enery, I vill say vhat I think. We have been great pleased vith you. You have vork hard and given us the three vinners. We have very pleased and happiness, but this redicule our daughter, it cannot be. You say that you love her. Is not possible! You encourage her in her stupid ideas. And then you say you have already the wife! How can that be? If you have a vife, vhere is she? She should be 'ere, by your side."

Robert told her the whole tale of Lillian again, trying as best he could to make sure she understood the whole affair.

"This is very sad. You are a very unhappy man. I feel very sorry for you," she said, when he had finished. "But you have no right to make the love to our daughter. Unhappy man. You have a vife already. This is terrible. You make a fool of our daughter and make her most unhappy too."

"For that I shall beat you!" The count rose from his chair, brandishing the poker.

"For goodness sake sit down and be quiet!" she scolded him. The Count sat down again in surprise, but still brandished the poker.

"There is no question. You do not marry our daughter. You are not free. You have still the vife and if you had not, you could not marry her. You are a trainer of horses. She is the Countess. You could not marry her. It is impossible. Already it is arranged who she is to marry. It is still more impossible. She is a Catholic. Are you a Catholic, Herr 'Enery?" She looked at him with a determination that was not to be thwarted.

At that moment, the door flew open and Elizabet came in. Her hair was dishevelled and her eyes were red. There were tear streaks on her cheeks.

"Elizabet! Vhat are you doing? You were told to stay in your room!"

Elizabet stopped dead in her tracks in the middle of the room.

"I am not a child! I will not be treated like a child! It is my happiness that you are talking about, I shall be here." She looked appealingly at Robert.

He was shocked to see her looking so distressed. He stood up, taking half a step towards her.

"Sit down. Herr 'Enery. Elizabet, my dear, return to your room."

Elizabet stood uncertainly, but did not go.

"Mother, I vill not disobey you, but I vill not go. This concerns me. I vill stay."

Robert was surprised by her boldness. The Count growled from his chair.

"Child, do vhat your mother tells you!"

"I am not a child. I vill not go." She had gone quite white. Her lip began to quiver and a tear started at the corner of her eyes. "This is about my happiness. I vill not go."

The Count struggled angrily to his feet.

"Vhen your mother says to you, go, you go. You do as you are told!"

"August, calm yourself, ve shall get nowhere vith anger. Child, you had better stay then. We vill try and discuss like sensible people. Sit down here on the sofa."

Elizabet hurried over and sat on the sofa next to Robert, tentatively putting out her hand so that their fingers just touched. The Countess, too, sat down.

"Listen to me, my daughter. We are not 'ere to talk about 'appiness, but about vhat can and cannot be. There is no question of you marrying Herr 'Enery. You are being too ridiculous. You hardly know him. How can you say you love him? The idea it is too childish and stupid!"

"But mother, you always say to me that I vould know when I met the one to love. I knew on that very first time when he came so late to our drawing room. As he stood in the door, my heart vent out to him. At the ball when I danced in his arms, I vent to heaven. We danced together on a cloud of love. Every minute of every day that we are apart, I think only of him. I know in my heart that it is only him that I vill ever love." She held Robert's hand and looked imploringly into his eyes, but he could not face her—he looked away.

"But he is a trainer of racehorses! You do not marry the trainer of racehorses! It is already arranged who you vill marry."

Elizabeth looked at her mother in astonishment.

"It is arranged? Who? Who is this person vith whom it is arranged that I marry?" Elizabet glowered with anger at her mother.

"You do not look at me like that!" she retorted sharply. "You know very vell who."

Elisabeth covered her mouth with her hands, but the look of horror in her eyes was plain for them all to see.

"You do not mean…" She stopped, the shock sounding in her voice. "You cannot mean…" She looked at her mother in disbelief, but she could see that she was right. "Never! I will never marry that fat, spotty, smelly pig, if he is the last person left in the world. If he was the last father of mankind left, I vould rather that the human race finished than marry him." She stood up and stamped her foot. "I vill never marry him! I do not even like him! He is a fat pig. I vill not marry him! I vill never marry anyone who I do not love."

The Count and Countess were shocked by the vehemence of her outburst. Robert too, was taken aback and reached up and, taking her hand, pulled her down to sit on the sofa again.

"My dear, we are talking about marriage, not about love. They are not the same thing at all. If you are lucky, perhaps, some happiness it comes. But you do not marry because you love someone, but because it has been arranged."

"Oh Mother, you have such old fashioned. I vill never marry anyone I do not love."

The Count glowered at her. "You vill do as your Mother tells you, my girl."

"Elizabet, all this argument it is pointless. Herr 'Enery, he is already married; there is no more point in this ridiculous ideas. Even if you could marry him, vich, you cannot, you could not anyway. He is already married. That is an end of it. There must be no more of this silly talk."

Elizabet took Robert's hand and stared earnestly, beseechingly, into his eyes.

"But she is gone. She is missing. Tell me she is no more."

Robert, who had sat silently through the whole exchange, now shifted nervously on his seat. His voice dried up in his throat and when he finally spoke, it was in a husky croak.

"Yes, she is missing." He paused, not knowing how to continue. "But she could one day come back"

"But it is nearly two years that she went. You surely do not think that she might come back."

"I do not know." He wiped his eye in frustration. "I do not know. How can I know? I did not know that she was going, but she is gone. Now she has gone I do not know if she will come back, or when. She may not even be still alive. For all I know, she could be lying terribly ill somewhere, her memory gone. She could have gone far away. Married someone else, living at the other end of the world. She could be dead, I do not know, I do not know." He hung his head.

"But Robert, vhat do you feel, in your heart, vhat do you feel?"

"I do not know. I dare not look in my heart. All I know is that I must wait."

"Vait, why vait?"

"I have to wait for seven years. If she has not returned in seven years, she will be declared officially dead. Then and only then, can I look in my heart."

The atmosphere in the room lightened as he said this. The Count let out a huge sigh of relief and even the Countess relaxed. Elizabet smiled, with new hope.

"But that is only five years left. I vill vait. For five years I vill vait."

"Do not be so silly. In five years you vill have met and found someone else. You vill no more remember Herr 'Enery"

"Mother, how could you be so heartless? I vill never stop loving Robert. Alvays I vill carry the love for him in my heart. If his vife comes back, I shall go to the Convent of the Little Sisters. I shall never marry anyone else. I shall never marry that fat spotty pig vhich you vish"

"Come, come, dear. Five years is a very long time. In five years we shall see then what has to be done. But for now, we will not encourage either of you. This must stop. It vill only bring sorrow."

"Stop!" The Count struggled to his feet. "This is enough. 'Enery, vith great sorry I say you go. You cannot be here like this. In five year, maybe we listen. But now, no. Now, you go. You do not return. You can stay in your hotel till you have decide what to do. Vhen you have settled, sent vord to Schmidt. He vill have your things pack and send to you. Come my dear, you must go." With that he ushered Elizabet and his wife out of the room.

Elizabet looked desperately over his arm.

"Write to me, Robert."

The Count turned at the door,

"If you write, she vill not get your letters. They vill be put in the fire."

CHAPTER 18

Robert stirred his coffee abjectly. He did not remember going to bed the previous night, nor could he recall how he had got up that morning. He looked at his jacket. He had changed. He felt his chin. He had shaved. He shrugged his shoulders. He could not remember. He resumed stirring his coffee. He must have got up, shaved, dressed and come down to breakfast. He could not remember. Sudden panic seized him. Was he in the right hotel? He looked round. Of course he was. How could he have put on his clothes if he were in the wrong Hotel! He stirred his coffee vigorously. He watched the vortex thus formed, swirling round in the middle of the cup. He felt that that was what his brain was doing, swirling round and round. It was even in danger of disappearing down the hole in the middle. Gradually, his coffee slowed down. Gradually his brain, too, began to grapple with reality. The events of the day before came back to him. He became aware of Schmidt hovering at his elbow.

"What the Hell are you doing here?" He regarded him with a hostile and nervous stair. Schmidt was equally frosty.

"So you 'ave awake and come for breakfast."

"Yes, I have awake, but how the hell did I get to bed last night? I do not remember a thing."

"No, I am not surprised. I found you—you had just been thrown out of a café. You were having considerable difficulty crossing the road. You were in danger of being run over and trampled to death..."

"Crossing the road? Surely anyone can cross the road!"

"Not the main thoroughfare. Herr 'Enery, not on your hands and knees! That ees not the best way to do it. I thought it best to bring you to your hotel and put you to bed."

Robert rubbed his eyes and supported his head on his hands. Her felt ashamed of himself and embarrassed—humiliated that Schmidt, Schmidt of all people, should have found him in this state and witnessed his degradation.

"I wasn't that far gone, was I?"

"Well, let's put it this way…If I had not happened along, you would almost certainly have been killed."

Robert found the effort of looking up at him almost too much.

"I am sorry, Herr Schmidt, but thank you, thank you for…looking after me."

"I only came because Graffinflein insisted I should follow you to see that you came to no harm."

Robert felt deeply ashamed. He burned with embarrassment. The shock of this news brought him back to his senses.

"I vas vondering vhat 'as brought about this turn of events." Schmidt sneered at Robert and rubbed his dry hands together, eagerly, like a vulture snapping its beak in expectation.

"I don't see what the hell that's got to do with you!" Robert snapped angrily.

"Herr 'Enery, of course it concern me. Everything that concern the Count, concern me."

Robert could not look at him. He shrugged his shoulders hopelessly. "Well, I expect that you will hear about it soon enough. If you must know, I have been thrown out. I have been summarily dismissed. I am not even to return to Hungary. Apparently you are to send my things, such as they are, on to me." Robert could not help notice the glint of satisfaction in Schmidt's eye.

"Vot is this? Vot 'as brought about this sudden change? After the races yesterday, you are the blue eyed boy. Then Graffinflein, who has obviously the tears, comes running to me late last night, imploring me to follow you and make sure you come to no 'arm. For 'er I would do anything, so I throw on my coat and run out into the night. I have save you. Now you say you go? Vot could make the sudden change? Vot 'as 'appened that is so dramatic?" He mused. "It can only be one thing that would do thees. The discretion with Graffinflein herself." Robert leapt to his feet and pushed Schmidt away.

"Get out, you slimy bastard, get out of my sight with you greasy innuendoes!"

Such was the fury of his demeanour that Schmidt turned and fled. Robert sank back in his chair. He leaned his elbows on the table, his head in his hand, too confused and angry to think coherently.

A page boy coughed discreetly at his shoulder. Robert looked up. The boy held out a letter and handed it to Robert.

"What is this?"

Robert opened it. The paper had a coronet heavily embossed on the top. He read:

∾

> *Robert—You may remember that at the "welcome Ball" given you at the Castle, I suggested that if you ever sought a different position, I would be very pleased indeed if you would come and train for me. Now that I can see that all your efforts have been crowned with spectacular success I am even more sure that I would like you to come. If, as I believe to be the case, you are free to consider such a move, I wonder if you would call upon me as soon as possible. If I am wrong, then please destroy this letter and know that your friend thinks enough of you to have made the offer.*
>
> *Yours sincerely—Emil von Zellatel. P von T*

Robert was speechless, he did not know what to say.

He flapped the letter. His hands shook. This was like manner from heaven, a gift from the gods. When all was lost, here was an offer to carry on the work in the kind of situation he enjoyed. He would be back in civilisation again. Emil lived near Munich.

He would be able to continue to see Elizabet. They came to stay at least twice a year for Hunting. They would be attending race meetings. He would be bound to see them then. His befuddled brain gradually slowed down as he realised the implications of this wonderful offer and he brightened considerably as the import of it penetrated his torpid mind.

"Ask at the desk for some notepaper, pen and ink and some sealing wax. I will write at once."

The boy eventually understood and soon returned with the necessary things. Robert, after some thought, quickly wrote and sealed the note. He gave it to a boy to deliver by hand as soon as he could run the distance to Emil's Hotel. Enough activity had passed for Robert to begin to feel hungry so he ordered a pot of coffee and some hot buttered rolls with some honey to be sent to the lounge, where he could wait for the return of the boy. He had not got used to the unsalted butter that was used here. He thought longingly of the soft golden salty mounds that used to be prepared in the dairy at home. However, the rolls were hot. The butter soon melted, the honey was thick and sticky. He actually enjoyed the rolls and lingered over the hot steamy rich coffee.

After about an hour, the boy breathlessly returned. He handed Robert a note.

꩜

Leaving for Munich this evening. Could you possibly call at 14.30 today? Send reply with the boy.—E von Z.

Robert scribbled on the bottom, *Yes, see you at 2.30.pm—Robert Henery*, and gave it back to the boy to redeliver. The boy looked so woebegone at the idea of having to run to the Hotel again that Robert gave him a coin that soon put wings on his feet.

At 2.30 promptly, Robert knocked at Emil's door. He was admitted by a footman who ushered him through a small hall into a small lounge. Emil, who was standing with his back to the fire, came forward to meet him. He grasped him by the hand.

"Robert, come in, come in. Warm yourself by the fire. I am so glad to see you. I was disgusted at my cousin's reaction. I told him so, but he is an obstinate old ass! Once he has made up his mind it takes more that my weight to change him."

"It is very kind of you. I was completely shattered by the whole episode. As for Elizabet speaking out like that, I could not believe my ears."

"No. That was certainly a bit of a disaster. Tell me, Robert, that was all true, was it?"

Robert looked at him quizzically.

"All that about your first wife?"

"Yes, every bit of it." Robert frowned, but would not look at him. "It is the not knowing that is the real difficult part. If I knew for certain, well, I could come to terms with it and get on with my life. But as it is, I am in Limbo! I will remain so for the next five years."

"All that about loving Elizabet—was that true, too, or was that the wine talking?" He looked at Robert sharply.

"No, it was all true. Under any other circumstance I would not let wild horses drag it out of me, but at that moment, there was no other way."

"Well, I believed you. In fact, when I saw you both at the Ball together, I could see there was something brewing." He paused. "She is a lovely girl. You know that her marriage is already arranged?"

"Yes. She told me. She is absolutely going to refuse to marry him. She described him in terms that I would not use on my worst enemy."

"Well, I should not put too much store on that, if I were you. I am sure that you are enough a man of the world to know that arranged marriages are nothing to do with feelings."

"No, I know. It all sounds cynically ruthless. I thought that such things were in the past and rightly so."

"Well, they may be in England, but out here things are still pretty feudal, as I expect you have found out."

"Yes. It has certainly been an eye opener. Well, there are five years before the question can even be considered again. A lot can happen in five years!"

"Yes, it certainly can. However unfortunate this has all been for you, it has worked very well for me. I have been very impressed with what you have been able to do with August's horses. I know that you are free—I wonder if you would consider coming to train for me? As you know, I live in Bavaria. The stables and gallops are round my house. I have a small shooting lodge in which you could live. As for your salary and all those things, we can sort them out later, if you come, but rest assured, I will make sure that you are better treated than I am sure was the case with August."

"I do not have to think twice! Of course I will come. I can come today if you like. Your Cousin has told me I can stay here in my hotel until my future is resolved. When it is fixed, I am to notify Schmidt. He will see that all my effects are sent on to me. Apart from my evening dress and a small overnight case, I have only what I stand up in."

"Good heavens. August will not permit you to return to sort out your affairs?"

"No, not even to collect my clothes."

"Ye gods! I do feel sorry for you. Come then tomorrow. Here is the name of my house. Take the train and get off here." He handed Robert a blank piece of headed notepaper. "You can take a cab from the station. When you arrive, I will show you the house and you can settle in. As soon as you feel ready, you can start your duties."

"Thank you so…"

Emil cut him off. "Don't thank me." He smiled. "I am not being the least philanthropic. I want my horses to beat those of August. You are the person who can make it happen."

CHAPTER 19

Robert alighted from the train the next day in the early afternoon and was soon on his way in the station cab. Emil Zellatel's house, when he arrived, proved to be a large brick built Schloss, with tall slate roofs and round turrets, with onion shaped domes atop each, on the two front corners. Robert paid off the cab and stood uncertainly on the step before a massive oak door. He tugged on the iron bell pull. It peeled at some distance within, provoking a prolonged and savage barking from some heavy hounds. Presently they could be heard bounding to the door. Robert was thankful for the thickness of the massive oak that separated him from the slavering, snarling, barking, from within. Presently a voice could be heard, commanding the dogs to be quiet. The noise subsided. With a venerable creaking, the door slowly opened. He was bidden enter. Cautiously Robert stepped over the threshold. The dogs stood by the fire, at the end of the Hall, eagerly waiting the command to defend the house from this intrusion.

Robert was shown into a small study. Emil was seated at a desk. He got up as Robert entered.

"Hello, it is good to see you again. You managed to get here all right." Before Robert could answer, the two dogs pushed their way in. They started a detailed examination of his every scent. "Oh do not mind them. Go on, lie down. Schnell…Schnell."

"Big," said Robert nervously, as one of them took a slobbering sniff at his ear.

"Oh yes. They have to be big and strong. It takes a strong powerful dog to take on a boar or a wolf."

"Do you still have wolves here?" said Robert, his voice rising to a nervous squeak, as the dog jumped up and placed its paws on his shoulders.

"Get down you great brute. Oh yes, but they do not bother us much except in the early part of the year when the snow is on the ground, when they find it difficult to find enough to eat."

"They must eat a lot of food."

"The wolves? They mostly eat deer, rabbits, sheep and so on. Occasionally they will take a calf or a foal."

Robert was finding it difficult to keep his feet as the two big dogs pushed round him.

"Not the wolves, these great dogs."

"I expect that they do. There is always something to cut up for them. One of the boys, he does that. Now I expect that you would like to see your house and settle in. Come." He put down the papers that he had in his hand. Robert followed him out into the hall, the two vast dogs pushing and jostling between them. Emil pulled a bell-pull by the fireplace. He took up a short Loden cape that had been on a chair by the fire. He selected a bunch of keys off a row of hooks by the door and led the way outside.

"The house is in the park; we can walk across to it." As they walked across in the afternoon sunshine, Emil pointed out the stables and the village, which could just be glimpsed through the trees. After a brisk five minute walk, they came to the house.

It at least was in good repair. There was glass in the windows and the roof seemed to be sound. The big balcony that ran round at first floor level did not look rotten. There were some large deer antlers hung up on the gable end. The key opened the door easily; in fact it looked as if the lock was kept oiled. Inside the house felt dry and warm. It smelled faintly of pinewood. They walked from room to room. There were plenty of wooden chairs and tables and a large table in the dining room. There were no curtains or carpets. There was a large cast iron range in the kitchen, with a hand pump by the ancient stoneware sink. There were some candlesticks and oil lamps in the kitchen and assorted pots and pans and crocks in the cupboards.

There was no furniture upstairs in any of the rooms.

"I am sorry," Emil laughed. "We used this as a hunting lodge. We had no need for beds. I will have some sent over for you straight away with some blankets and linen. Now, what about food? I will ask my cook to prepare you a hamper. This can be sent over too. Milk and butter, you can get from the dairy. Look, it is over there." Emil pointed to a range of tiled roofs, just visible to the side of the Schloss. "Eggs, too. Young pigeons from the er…what you call it…pigeon house, the dovecote.

"The water is good here. It must be pumped up every morning into a tank in the roof, from the well. You can have a boy to do that and do the wood, shoes and odd job, the…what do you call it in England?"

"The back house boy?"

"Yes, the back 'ouse boy. You can have a back 'ouse boy. He can come over with the things in a short while. Is there anything else that you will need for the next couple of days? I am sure that you will soon find your way about. Here are the keys." He handed the bunch to Robert. "I will call for you at 9 o'clock in the morning tomorrow. You can come to see the horses and ride round the Park. I had better go now to get all these things organised for you." He held out his hand and they shook hands warmly. "Until tomorrow morning then, good-bye." Turning on his heel, Emil was gone.

Robert surveyed his new home. It is a lot better than the last time. No need for a night in a rat infested tack room this time. He shuddered at the thought.

He walked round the house again, going from room to room. He sniffed the air. No smell of mice. No mould or damp. In fact, the empty house felt warm, dry and welcoming.

There were three main rooms downstairs and he decided to use the smallest, with a good view out over the Park for his study. The bigger of the other rooms was filed with the great table and had obviously been used for the hunting lunches.

Robert examined the table. It did not seem to have a hole for a handle. If he could take out some of the leaves and make it smaller, it could go in the other room and this room would make a very comfortable drawing room. He found that if he pulled at one end, he could open it up enough to take out the leaves. After a certain amount of heaving and struggling he managed to get it into the other room and set up to his satisfaction, so that it would comfortably seat eight people. Not that he was likely to be entertaining anyone, but he felt that that size suited the room. He was so preoccupied with the table that he did not notice a wagon draw up until there was a loud knocking at the door. He opened the door and in marched a team of men carrying beds, hampers and some easy chairs. One carried a rolled up carpet on his shoulders. They put their loads down and bowed to Robert. One, who was obviously the foreman, handed over a note. Robert opened it and read:

∾

As I walked home, I realised that you had not any easy chairs, so have sent some. If I think of anything else, I will send it. I will send the Housekeeper over tomorrow to organise you some curtains. The men will put all the things where you want them.

With much gesticulation and what seemed like a lot of swearing in German, which he could not understand, the furniture was spread round the house to his satisfaction. He went round all the men, thanking them, shaking them by the hand. The one that he took to be the foreman pushed forward a youth of about fifteen. The foreman pointed at him.

"He Villie. He gout." He grinned broadly and patted Willie on the head. Robert took him and showed him the pump. It was not long before he could hear water splashing into the tank upstairs, impelled by the clanking pump in the back yard.

The beds were carried upstairs and so was the large hamper, which proved to be full of blankets and linen. The other hampers were carried into the kitchen. When all was done, the men jumped onto the wagon and departed.

Robert went to the kitchen to unpack the provisions. His new employer seems to be a man of his word. He spread the contents of the boxes out on the table. There was everything that you could possibly think of. Robert was astonished. Jars of pickles, bacon, eggs. A jar of cream. Flour, salt, sugar. Everything that he might need. Even a big bowl of dripping. There was a large ham, a string of sausages, a joint of pork and a roll of beef and a string of plump young pigeons ready plucked. He was certainly not going to starve. He was suddenly seized with the desire to do some cooking.

He found what looked like a sack of vegetables under the table and opened it. On the top was a hard white cabbage and inside was a mixture of potatoes, carrots and onions.

Villie came in with an armful of sticks and got to work lighting the kitchen range. He filled the kettle and placed it on top.

"We will see how long it takes to get hot." Willie brought in a good pile of wood to keep it going. He lit the fire in the study, bringing in the wood for that. Robert took one of the empty hampers which he put in the corner of the study, to act as a log basket. Willie soon filled it. Robert thanked him and asked him to come back at 7.30 in the morning. Clutching his hat to his chest, Willie bowed and bobbed, then ran out of the door. Robert was not sure that he had understood—the morning would tell.

Robert returned to his stores to consider what he might prepare for his evening meal. It was only then that he realised he was exceedingly hungry. He decided to sort out what we would like to eat and put the rest of the things away, so that he can see what he was doing. The kettle was singing on the stove and a gentle plume of steam was coming out of the spout. Robert put some more wood into the fire. He opened the oven door. It certainly seemed to be getting hot.

Quickly, he put all the stores into the capacious larder. He rolled up his sleeves and, tying a tea cloth round his waist, contemplated the store. After some moments' thought, he decided.

"How does soup, followed by pigeon breasts, followed by pork chops followed by cheese, followed by apple fritters and cream, strike you?" he said out loud to himself.

"A trifle ambitious?" he answered quizzically.

"No, no, nonsense. Nothing to it. All you need do is keep calm and get organised."

Robert put a pan of water on the fire and peeled some carrots and an onion He chopped the carrots and put them into a pan of water, then peeled a couple of potatoes and cut them up and threw them in too. Taking the cabbage, he cut it in half. He put one half away and cut the other into three slices and put that in the pot as well. He finished peeling the onion and chopped it up and put it in a pan on the fire with some of the dripping. Soon the room was filled with frying onion smells. Robert took three of the pigeons and cut off the breasts and put them to one side. He chopped up the remains of the pigeon and quickly browned them in the pan with the onions, then put them into the soup pot, with the vegetables, which was just beginning to boil.

He quickly cut off a goodly slice of the pork and put it in another pan and sprinkled it with herbs, adding, just enough milk to cover it. This he put to the side of the fire; it did not need to cook too fast. Then he looked at the soup, which was simmering away quietly on the fire. He moved it more over the heat. The vegetables were boiling away. The cabbage was tender, so he took it out and, putting it in a dish, sliced it up and placed a little knob of butter on it. He put it in the bottom oven to keep hot.

He put the onion pan back on the fire and as soon as they were sizzling away, he dusted the pigeon breasts with flour and put them on the onions to cook, turning them until they were browned before placing them in to the oven to finish. He decided to abandon the idea of apple fritters and so put some of the cheese and apples onto a plate for the end of his meal. Under the table he espied a cardboard box, which upon inspection proved to be full of bottles of wine. He looked at the German labels uncomprehendingly. The Gothic lettering defeated his attempt to decipher what they might say. One seemed to be a red wine, so he put that on the table. Another, in the midst of it flamboyant text, had the word *Mosel*. This he recognised, so he decided to try it.

Robert looked at the soup. It was reducing steadily and the meat was coming off the bones of the pigeon remains. He added salt and pepper and cut a thick slice of bread and put out the crock of butter.

He carefully ladled the soup into the a bowl without squashing the vegetables, and poured out a glass of the white wine.

"If I might venture, Sir, your very good health, Sir." He turned to his right and bowed.

"And yours, Sir, and yours." He turned and bowed to the left. The wine was excellent—fresh, sharp and fruity. He finished his soup.

Robert brought the pigeon breasts out of the oven and placed them on a bed of onions. He put the pan on the hot part of the fire and put a ladle of the soup into it to make some gravy, with a spoonful of flour sprinkled and stirred in to thicken it. With care he fished out the carrots from the soup pot and served then with the breasts. He then opened the bottle of red wine.

The wine was good, too. Quite unlike any red wine he had ever tasted—soft and fruity, not too tannic. Nice and light. Roberts' pigeon breasts were slightly pink when he cut into them and their delicious flavour, combined with the sweetness of the carrots, was a perfect foil to the light red wine.

"Sir, if I might say so, this is most excellent."

"Thank you Sir," he replied aloud to himself. "Call it beginners luck."

"Are you ready for the next course, Sir?" He stood up and bowed.

"Ah! The pork in milk. I'm not sure that I fancy that, it seems slightly unnatural"

"You are not going to fail me now, Sir. This dish is fit for a king." Even as he spoke he was pouring the milk in which the pork had been cooked onto the meat on the plate. The potatoes were quickly fished out of the remains of the soup pot and the buttered cabbage rescued from the bottom oven. It had started to go a bit curly, so he quickly stirred it with a fork, before placing it, too, on the table.

"Here we are, Sir. Be brave. Try it. You will be surprised at how good it is." He sat and started to eat.

"I have to agree, Sir. This pork is very good, tender and succulent and the herbs lend a nice touch." He laughed to himself and ate his meal with relish.

"I wonder what Elizabet is doing now? Probably the same as me—eating some fantastic meal their French chef has prepared. I wonder if she's thinking of me."

He finished his meal and sat back comfortably in his chair. Suddenly he sat up.

"I say, Sir," he said out loud. "Would you like some cheese?"

"Yes please, Sir," he said to himself. "I have eaten extremely well. If I might say so, Sir, you have performed a culinary miracle, but a little cheese and perhaps an apple would just round it off." He ate his apple and cheese and sat back in his chair, at last satisfied.

"Well, it was excellent. Well done, Sir. Now I suppose we ought to do the washing up."

"I thought you might say that." Stoically he washed up and put everything away. By the time he had finished, it was very late.

"I think, Sir, that it is time to go to bed. I want to be ready to leave the house at 9 o'clock, so I ought to get up at 7."

"Yes Sir. Thank you, Sir. Anything you say, Sir." He laughed out loud. "Silly ass. If anyone sees you, they would think you were stark staring mad. You'd be put away."

With that, taking his candle, Robert went up to bed. When he got to his room, the moon was shining brightly. He went to the window and looked out at the silvery view. What lay ahead? Only tomorrow would tell and that could wait. He undressed and got into bed. For a long time he looked out of the window. Back in Hungary, Elizabet would be looking out at that same moonlight world. He lay awake for a long time, pondering the good fortune that had brought him here, just when everything seemed to be lost. Far away, quavering in the still air, he heard the mournful howl of a distant wolf.

CHAPTER 20

Robert threw himself into his new position with enthusiasm and energy. He found that the Prince was as good as his word. The stables were in immaculate condition. When the horses went out, they were beautifully turned out. The head lad, who had been running the stud on a temporary basis, had a keen eye for detail. He was very thorough.

His horses were a credit to his efforts. Luckily, he had spent some time working in England so his English was quite good. He was very resentful of Robert, as he had hoped to be promoted as trainer. It took all Robert's tact and guile to deal with him. Robert did the best he could to show that he was appreciated. He gave him as much authority as he could. It took several months for Robert to gain his confidence and obtain his willing co-operation.

Robert found that the Prince's office staff were very willing and ready to prove how efficient they were, which took a great load off his shoulders. They saw to all the things that needed to be ordered. They made all the race entries and the travel arrangements, so that Robert was free to devote all his energy to the well-being of his horses.

He finally managed to appoint a cook, not that he didn't enjoy cooking, which was great fun on the odd special occasion. But it was just that he felt he should concentrate on more important things. He found the business of providing regular daily meals irksome. She was a large lady called Anna, the mother of one of the lads. She lived in a cottage nearby. She came in in the morning to prepare the midday meal. She did the baking and made everything ready for the evening. She was a cheerful soul. Robert was pleased and relieved to find his household so well ordered. Anna produced a friend who came in on

Mondays and Tuesdays to do the washing and ironing. She also found a girl from the village to act as housemaid and to cook and serve the evening meal.

One day a note came from the station to say that several boxes and trunks had arrived for him and were awaiting collection. He sent the wagon down to fetch them. That night he spent a happy evening unpacking his few possessions and spreading them about his house. The little brown photograph of Lillian he put on his dressing table.

Robert was happy. His training programme was beginning to bear fruit. He could already see a definite improvement in the performance of some of his horses. His household was well ordered and he felt comfortable and well looked after.

There were two race meetings soon after he arrived. He was very careful to make sure his head lad took the credit for the horse's performance. In one, their horse was second and in the other, their entry came fourth. Robert insisted that he go and lead them in and collect the prizes. Robert was very surprised when, after the race, he had come and shaken his hand.

"Zank you. Not many vood 'ave stood back like zat. You give to me ze credit, for zat I sank you." Robert laughed, but he was inwardly gratified.

"Rubbish. You are the one who has brought these horses to this condition, it is your success. You deserve the credit. I certainly have no wish to take it from you."

After that the head lad seemed to master his resentment. He and Robert struck up an agreeable working relationship.

The autumn wore on. Robert took huge delight in riding out with his horses in the first light of the morning, the autumn colours of the trees firing up as the first rays of the rising sun struck them. As the sun gradually rose up from behind the distant hills, the brilliant light spread over the Park into the surrounding forests, until everything appeared to be aflame with the splendour of autumn. The mornings were frosty. The keen air was a tonic after the dusty heat of Hungary.

The evenings were drawing in. It was often nearly dark by the time they returned from the afternoon rides, to begin the business of rubbing down and bedding down for the night. Robert used to go up to the Office to work till about six o'clock, before going home to wash and change before dinner. Whilst he was very comfortable, he had to admit to himself that he felt very lonely. He developed the habit, after his meal, of walking over to the stables to do a round of the horses. He would spend an hour or two over there, then come home and sit with his feet on the hearth whilst he enjoyed his glass of whisky, procured from England at great cost. He often used to think of Lillian and try to puzzle out what had happened to her, but always her image would become blurred with the ever-present vision of Elizabet.

He thought of Elizabet sitting at her piano in the corner of that blue and gold room, playing to her parents, as they sat on either side of the fire. He thought of her as they had explored the Count's stables, but most all, he thought of her in his arms, laughing with excitement as they waltzed round the Ball room. He was still angry with her for bringing about his sudden exit from Hungary, thus putting so many miles between them, but he had to admit it was probably for the best. He was certainly much more comfortable here. His horses were of higher quality, he was better treated and more comfortably situated. As things were, it was better that he kept as far away from Elizabet as possible. He could not afford to become too fond of her, just in case…Yes, for the time being, his life was good, but he missed Elizabet more than he realised.

The Prince left him alone to find his own feet and he rarely saw him. However, one morning, when he went in to the office there was a note for him, asking him to call at 10.30. When Robert was shown into the study, he was warmly greeted. Also in the room was a little bow-legged wizened man in a wide skirted coat and another taller, clad in green breeches and coat. The latter he had seen round the Park. He had come to know that he was the "Wildhuter"—the gamekeeper. The other he did not know, but was soon introduced as "der Jager"—the huntsman. Speaking alternately in German and English, the Prince outlined his plan for the autumn hunt. He was going to have a party staying at the Schloss for ten days. He wished to entertain them, as he usually did, to some sport. He wanted to have three days of hunting with the hounds and three days of shooting in the woods. The need for horses would be considerable. The huntsman had his own horses and mounts for his servants, but for the household they would need extra horses for the guests. Of these some had to be of sound temperament and trained to being ridden side-saddle. Robert was given a list of the days and numbers.

For the shooting they would need various wagons—two to take the shooting party to their positions, and two to bring the food out at lunch time. Now that he was living in the shooting lodge, there was apparently another that they could use, but they would have to rearrange the drives so that they were at the right place at the right time. They would want the small van to take the staff to serve and prepare the food and they would need two, possibly three, carriages to bring those ladies not in the shooting party out to the lunch. They would need the game cart to collect the slain. Robert made notes of all this on his list. Any of the lads from the stables not being used for anything else would be needed as beaters, so Robert would not be able to work his horses on those days. He would have to make arrangements for them to be fed and watered by a skeleton staff. He should check with the Estate carpenter that all the carts and carriages were in good repair. He must liase with the head coachman to make sure he had all the staff and horses that he needed. If he needed any more coachmen or footmen, Robert was to provide them from the racing stables lads. The Prince then unrolled a large map of the Estate on the table. A long discussion ensued about the sport. Robert could not understand much of what was said, but was amazed at the extent of the Estates. They encompassed several villages. All the spare men, women and children were being called upon to act as beaters. It was like planning a military operation.

The next three weeks were very busy for Robert. All the vehicles needed for the Sport had to be dragged out of their lodges, cleaned and repaired. Robert had to maintain a large stable of light draught horses to supply the occasional needs of the household. He insisted that the teams needed were put together straight away, so that they became used to each other. Each team was to practise driving out together. By the end of the fortnight they were as well trained and disciplined as he could wish. Every morning, too, an observer might have been startled at see a different string of horses filing out across the park. Robert and four volunteer lads each day rode out on five of the most sedate and stayed horses that he could muster, side saddle. Robert put them through their paces stoically, every day. By the time of the first hunt, they were well schooled, as quiet as lambs, as ready as they could be.

Robert was very pleased to receive an invitation to take part in the Hunts.

On the morning of the first, he rode into the Schloss courtyard, smartly turned out in his black hunting jacket, his black top hat carefully brushed and a packet of cold beef sandwiches in each pocket. His flask, filled with whisky, was safely tucked inside his coat. He was not prepared for the sight that greeted him. The Courtyard was filled with mounted people, the men in a variety of hunting liveries and the ladies in their brightly coloured habits. There were crowds of people from the village who had come to watch. The Prince's staff were circulating in the crowd, bearing trays of steaming glasses that were being offered to those taking part. The Prince's huntsmen were in a group together, in striking liveries of blue with red facings, their great brass horns seemingly entwined round them. The Prince himself was in a splendid befogged livery of the same colours and sported a gallant cocked hat with a plume that owed its design to a previous century. Robert guided his horse amongst the throng. He had no idea who they all were, but he doffed his hat gallantly to anyone who caught his eye. This seemed to be the thing to do. It seemed that everyone was slowly circulating, greeting all they knew as they did so. Suddenly his heart missed a beat. *There* was Elizabet! She wore a red habit with generous flowing skirts and had a red hat to match, crowned with a froth of white ostrich feathers that tossed and bounced as she moved. At the same moment she saw him and they both sat rejoicing at the sight of each other. Robert urged his horse forward. Steering through the press, he gained her side. He reigned in beside her and doffed his hat. They shook hands, but she did not let go, so they sat just looking into each other's eyes, storing up that magic moment for as long as they possibly could.

"Robert, how are you? You are looking so vell. It suit you 'ere."

"Elizabet—I am well, and so are you! Look at you, as beautiful as a peach on a summer's morning." She giggled.

"You say the silliest things." But she blushed and gave a little wriggle of pleasure. "I hope that you have made the good huntings for us."

"I have had nothing to do with the hunting. We have just trained and prepared some of the horses. The hunting is in charge of the fellow over there." He pointed with his crop to the head huntsman who, catching his eye, touched the peak of his cap with his whip.

"You train this horse?"

"Yes, we have trained five to side-saddle. You would have laughed to see us all riding round the Park side-saddle."

"Vhy? I ride all day at the hunt on the side-saddle. At home I do not ride side-saddle, but Emil, he like to see his ladies ride side-saddle, so I do it to please him."

"Well, I agree with him, you certainly look very beautiful. So elegant." Again he was rewarded with a breathtaking smile.

"It is difficult. At the end of the day I have very tired."

"Oh, it is not too bad; in fact, I quite enjoyed it, once I got used to it."

"So you enjoy it, yes? You would not enjoy it after the day of hunt."

"Oh, I am sure I would. If you can manage, so too could I!"

"You could manage a day of hunt.? So. Vith you I vill have a small vager, that you vill not a days hunting do!"

"Right, I will—we hunt again on Thursday. I will ride then side-saddle!"

"I vill tell every one, so that they all know, so that you cannot escape." She laughed. "This I vait to see."

"It will be worth it to see you laugh like that again."

At that moment the huntsmen who had gathered together in a group in the middle of the yard, played a long fanfare on their horns, and with a general bussle of excitement, the Hunt moved off.

Robert spurred his horse.

"I will ride with you," he called. She laughed at him over her shoulder.

"If you can keep up!" she called.

The hunt set off at a steady trot. Soon they crossed the Park and entered the forest. Everyone waited, the horses steaming expectantly in the chill of the morning, whilst the huntsman cast forward with the hounds. Presently there was a distant clamour from the hounds and the horns sounded the chase. There was great excitement as everyone set off in pursuit down a long sunlight ride. Presently they came to a fork in the ride and there was some dithering. The party divided into two. In the distance could be heard the baying of the hounds and the occasional blast on the horns. Elizabet galloped off and Robert followed. They turned this way and that. Presently they came to a small clearing from which there was no exit. Elizabet rained in her horse and held up her hand.

"Listen, can you hear the hunt?" she asked.

Robert listened. Apart from the gasping breaths from their horses and a solitary blackbird singing from a tree, he could hear nothing. They waited and listened. Presently they heard the horns. The hunt seemed miles away. Elizabet frowned.

"We have taken the wrong way. The hunt it is lost! Now we shall never catch it up!"

"Don't blame me, I was following you."

"Well, you should have *said!*"

"How could I say? All I could see was the tail of your horse and your backside bouncing up and down."

"Backside? What is backside?"

"Your bottom." Robert stood in his stirrups and slapped his behind to give explanation to his remark. Elizabet looked in astonishment and then blushed.

"Oh!" she scolded. "You are so rude. I do not know why I love you so much."

"Oh? You still love me then?"

"Of Course I love you! You know that I love you. Come!"

She reached out and hooked the rein of Robert's horse with the handle of her riding crop and pulled it towards her. When he was near enough, she leant over and throwing her arm around his neck, she pulled him towards her and kissed him on the lips. Their horses shifted uneasily and moved apart. The two of then leaned further over in their embrace until they both fell off onto the ground. The horses shied and started away. Robert was the first to his feet. He quickly caught the horses. They had pricked up their ears and were looking towards the far off sound of the hunting horn; any second and they would have been off to join the hunt.

"You do not vorry about me then. Off you go for the horses. And here I have to sit."

"If I had not caught them, they would have been off and we would have had to walk home. Come on, we had better see if we can find the hunt. Here, I will give you a hand up." He led the horses over to where she sat in the grass and offered her his hand. She took it and started to rise, then sat again and pulled him down too. They kissed again on the grass. She opened her eyes and looked up to see the horses staring down at them.

"Tie up the horses. I cannot make love to you vith them vatching."

Robert scrambled to his feet. He led the horses over to a tree and tied them up. He returned and sat down beside her.

"Are you hungry?" He took out his packet of sandwiches and his hip flask. He opened the packet. "Oh dear, they seem to have got a little squashed."

"You think more of eating your squashy bread and meat than of giving me a kiss?"

"No, of course not. But you know very well that at any moment Lillian could appear."

"Do not be so ridiculous. 'Ere? In the middle of the forest? How would she find us in the middle of the forest, in Bavaria! You are being too stupid. You told me you think she dead! How she going to be 'ere? Kiss me! You vill forget her."

Robert hung his head. "I know you think me very silly, but I cannot just forget her. I cannot shut her out, as if she never existed. She could still come back. Whilst there is that chance I must be prepared for it."

"But you said that you love me."

"I do. I do love you. Some days, I cry out for wanting you, but don't you see, I cannot allow myself to even think it. She might come back and then what would we do?"

"If she come back, I vill go to the Little Sisters to shut myself avay, never to come out into the vorld again."

"Don't be so silly. We will have to go our separate ways and never see each other again. You will soon find someone else and forget all about me."

"And me—vill you forget all about me?"

"No, I will never forget about you, you know that." He leant over and kissed her, but she did not respond.

"I think we have a very unhappy."

"Let's not think about it. Here we are, together, in this enchanting clearing. There is no one to bother us for miles around. Let's eat my sandwiches and enjoy ourselves." He offered her the packet. She brightened a little.

"I too have got!" She opened the side of her skirt and produced a large bag that was fastened to her belt by a snap clip. "Here, the cook he made this for me." She opened the bag and pulled out a cold chicken leg, some thick slices of a large cooked sausage, two little white rolls spread thickly with butter, some fresh radishes and an apple.

"He did not want you to fade away!"

"Fade avay? What is fade away?"

Robert laughed. "Become so weak that you are in danger of dying."

She laughed and slapped her thigh. "Do I look as if I am going to die?"

Robert laughed. She certainly didn't.

"Come on, let's share what we have got; then we can try and find the hunt."

They sat in the warm afternoon sun, leaning back to back, enjoying their picnic. Suddenly Elizabet spoke.

"How many children shall we have?"

Robert was taken aback.

"For goodness sake, I absolutely refuse to discuss it until we are married. That will not be for a long time yet, if at all. So let's eat up our food and hear no more of this."

"Robert, we cannot go on like this, loving each other. Maybe never able to be together. We cannot go on in this vay. It is too unhappy. I spend many times crying in my bed about it. What are we going to do?"

"Do? We can do nothing. I too spend much time at night trying to think how it will all work out, but I do not know. I dare not think about it, the different possibilities. We can't do anything about it; we cannot change it, we have just got to wait. No amount of worrying will change anything, so let's enjoy our lunch. Here we are together in this truly magic spot. The sun is warm, the bees are humming and the birds are singing. I am here with the most beautiful and desirable women that I have ever met and I intend to enjoy every precious second."

She rolled over on top of him and kissed him long and hard. "Always, my darling, you talk too much." She kissed him again. They lay together enjoying the warm sun. Robert sat up. His voice was husky with tenderness.

"It is better that I do keep talking. Come on, let's have some food."

He opened the packets and spread them out between them. "Come on, let's eat. Don't look at me like that. We simply cannot. We have simply *got* to wait."

"Robert, I think that you are a very strong man."

"No, I am not strong. I am caught between the devil and the deep blue sea and I don't know what to do. It's easier to be stuck in my dilemma than it is to take a decision. When I have waited as long as I have to, according to the law, then I can take a decision—but until then I have to wait..." he hesitated, "...just in case."

They sat together in the afternoon sun and shared their picnic, having to be content with each other's company.

When they finished their lunch they remounted and set off to try and find their way back to the Schloss. Robert had no idea where they were as he had never been out in to this part of the forest before, but taking a lead from the direction of the sun and trying to remember the way they had come, they set out. They kept coming to clearings and crossroads, as the different forest paths met theirs. He had no recollection at all of any of them. Before long it was obvious they were completely lost. Presently they came to a more open part of the forest. There was a small hill with some old trees on the top. They certainly had not passed that place before.

"If we go up there, I can climb a tree to see if I can see the Schloss. We can't be that far away."

They rode over and Robert dismounted. Giving Elizabet his rein to hold, he scrambled to the top of the hill. He found a gnarled old pine tree and climbed up as far as he dared. The view was stunning. The sun was beginning to go down and the mists were rising in the valleys. The rolling distance looked blue. There was forest as far as he could see. He carefully turned round so that he could see the way they had come. The view was the same—forest covered hills rolling away into the blue distance. There in the distance, behind them, he could make out the church of the village and the Schloss. He climbed down and remounted his horse.

"It's that way." He pointed with his crop in the direction from which they had come. "We have been going in completely the wrong direction. It is quite a long way off. It will be nearly dark before we get there."

They set off together.

"Are there wolves, here? I have always the horror of being chased by the wolves."

"I do not know. The people are always talking of them, but I have never seen any." He paused. "But then I have never been into this part of the forest."

"Listen! What is that?"

Far away they could just make out the sounding of the horn. The notes sounded sad and mournful in the distance. They pulled up their horses and listened.

"They have killed a stag," she said. "That is the *Curee*, the salute to the good hunt. They vill make for home now."

They hacked on in silence together. The moon, first a flicker through the trees, gradually rose into the sky, filling the glades and rides with eerie shadows and patches of silver light. A pheasant called harshly as it flew up to roost, "cock cocking" noisily as it flapped up into the branches. Somewhere an owl hooted. In the distance one answered.

Far away a vixen barked, its rasping cry hanging in the frosted air. Robert could feel the heavy cold air almost pressing down on him. Their horses puffed out little clouds of steam with every breath. This was one of those beautiful times of the day—that fragile time between the day and the night when the day creatures were settling down for the night and the night creatures were beginning to be about their business. Robert reined in his horse.

"Listen."

Elizabet stopped a little away from him to see what was wrong.

"Why you stop?"

"Listen," said Robert, cocking his head.

"I hear nothing."

"No, that's just it. Not a sound. Listen."

They sat and listened. Even the horses seemed to be listening. Not a sound. Even the breeze was still.

"Isn't that just perfect, not a sound—perfect peace."

"We must go on. My father, he vill be worried that we are lost. He will be reaching for his horsewhip again." They both laughed.

"Don't remind me. I thought the old boy was going to have a heart attack."

"You need not worry of that. Always, he get so excited."

"You know, I still feel angry with you about that evening. You really managed to ruin everything. If you had planned to spoil his big night, you could not have found a better way."

Elizabet looked at him with tears in her eyes. "Oh, do not have the anger vith me. I did not think. It was said before I knew."

"Well you certainly blew the barrel wide open. Thank goodness for Emil. Were it not for him, I would have been thrown out onto the street there and then with nowhere to go and no prospects. I do not know what I would have done."

"Well, he likes you. He would not like to see the unfair. He is very pleased to have you here. Already, he say you make the vinners. He hope for many more in the spring."

"Well, he has some good horses. With luck we should do quite well."

"Papa vill have the great sad if you beat him."

"I think that Emil has got some better horses than your father and that they should beat yours easily."

"That is impossible. Our horses are the best." She went quite red with her anger at the implied slight of her horses. Robert laughed.

"You must learn to be realistic. Partisan devotion is one thing, but do not confuse it with common sense. If you are going to bet on horses you must not allow your natural favour of your own horses to cloud your judgement. You will take the quick path to ruin if you do."

"'Err 'Enery, you give me a lecture?" She laughed at him as she mocked him.

They rode on in silence. The moon rose above the mist and spread its silver light through the trees, casting heavy shadows that dappled the ride as they rode. Presently they could hear a bell tolling.

"They ring the bell so that we can find our way home."

Robert was glad to have its guiding sound. He was beginning to get a little anxious. He was not at all sure that they were not lost again.

It was almost dark by the time that they reached the Schloss. A groom came running out to take Elizabet's horse and help her dismount. She walked stiffly to the steps and turned to Robert.

"It has been so good to see you again…"

Robert stopped her. "Hurry along or you will be late for dinner. I have been invited, too, so I must go home and change. I will join you shortly."

Elizabet smiled. "All is not over then, I can see more of you?"

"Yes, hurry along, or Emil will wonder where you are."

He turned his horse and cantered away. He rode quickly to his house and handed his horse over to his groom who sat in the tack room, waiting for his return. He too walked stiffly into the house.

Some fifteen minutes later he had managed to struggle into his starched shirt and white tie and, wrapping his cloak round him, he ran out of the door.

He arrived hot and breathless at the Schloss, having run most of the way. After handing his cloak to a footman he mopped his brow with his handkerchief, tweaked his tie in front of an ornate gilt mirror and was shown into the drawing room. It was full of people and hot and noisy, but as he walked in the door he heard a well remembered voice booming out.

"Arr, here is the late Mister 'Enery, always he is late!" The room went silent and everyone turned to look at him.

"Good evening Count, I hope that I find you well."

"Vell? Of course I am not vell, look at this." He stabbed with a heavy walking stick in the direction of a large bandaged foot propped up on a footstool.

"Oh dear, what happened, have you had an accident?"

"No, poor papa, he has the gout."

Robert had not seen Elizabet when he had come into the room, but now she stood beside her father, radiant in a stunning dress of deep red brocade. He smiled at her, too overawed to speak. He was brought to earth by a none too gentle poke in his ribs with the stick.

"What is this I hear that you took my daughter lost in the forest? We vorry when the hunt it return and she is not come. Then one say that they think she is vith you, we vorry more, we know that she vill be late. The late Mister 'Enery." He gave Robert another poke with the stick, but luckily Robert had stepped back out of range. The blow dislodged a small side table, sending glasses crashing to the floor.

"August, you behave yourself in my house. I will have no blood spilt on my drawing room carpet." Emil smiled to try and soften the rebuke. "Come on, everyone, let us go and eat. I am hungry even if no one else is."

Everyone murmured their approval and with a great fuss and commotion the Count was raised to his feet and led to the dining room. Emil smiled at Robert.

"I hear that you had a good day. Pity you weren't in for the kill—we got a fine stag. Would you be so kind to escort Cousin Helga to dinner?" He turned away and quickly paired off everyone else. Elizabet, Robert noticed, was being led on the arm of a tall blond young man with rich curly hair. Robert felt a pang of jealousy.

"Goot evening, Herr 'Enery!"

Robert started "Good evening Countess." He bowed slightly and offered her his arm. "I hope you are well. It is so nice to see you again." *God*, he thought, *just my luck to get lumbered with her.* Of all the people other than the Count that he wanted to avoid, she came top of the list. The Countess, however, apparently was prepared to let matters rest. She chattered amiably about this and that as they went into the dining room and waited their turn to be seated. At last everyone was seated around a vast forest of crystal, silver and candles, surrounding pyramids of fruit and flowers, all born on a gargantuan table. Elizabet was seated opposite him. He could just see her face between the legs of a gilded cherub which was carrying a great bunch of plump grapes. Their eyes met and hers lit up as she giggled to him. The countess was involved in some long tale with her other neighbour and the lady on Robert's other side appeared to have no English at all, so Robert was able to watch Elizabet from behind the cover of the cherub. The soup plates were being carried in, and glasses filled, before they had barely settled. Soon all attention was on the meal. Robert eyed his thin pale soup with suspicion. If you were going to have a soup, he thought, have something that would stick to your ribs! He didn't relish this watery looking sample, but was agreeable surprised by the rich and succulent flavour of the first mouthful, which was also scalding hot. He quickly popped a piece of bread roll into his mouth in an attempt to douse the burn. Quickly, he swallowed some water. His eyes streamed. It was as much as he could do not to splutter all over the table cloth. He buried his face in his napkin to try and hide his embarrassment. He recovered and noticed Elizabet's anxious eyes watching him between the legs of the cherub. He smiled weakly at her. Relieved, she resumed her conversation with her neighbour.

"'Err 'Enery, if you take small seeps off the edge of your plate, the soup it is cooler there. You vill not burn yourself. See, like so" The Countess proceeded to spoon a delicate little droplet from the very edge of her plate.

"Yes indeed, it was very careless of me. I was not thinking."

"Ah Herr 'Enery, if you vant to live, then always you must think. It is not always that I will be there to save you."

"No Countess, indeed. I am very lucky that you are here to give me such good advice. I was the totally innocent cause of spoiling the last dinner that we had together. Emil would not forgive me if I were to drop dead on the table and spoil this one too."

The Countess looked at him without smiling. "Do not mock me, Herr 'Enery, I do not like to be mocked."

"I am sorry, Countess, I did not mean to mock you, I was attempting to make a joke."

"That vas a yoke? It seemed like a poor attempt to be very rude to me."

Luckily the conversation was stopped by a waiter pouring a pale, pale coloured wine into her glass and then his.

"Countess, I would like to offer a toast to the success of your horses next season." Robert, glad of the chance to change the subject, raised his glass gallantly toward her.

"Do not talk of the horses. My husband he is so vorried. He cannot find any one to do the training. He did hope that after last season, he was going vith the luck. He has so much the bad temper, he is make us all mad!"

"I too was very sorry. I had felt that I was finally getting to understand your horses. I too was looking for success." The Countess looked at him searchingly for a while, her soup spoon in mid air.

"Herr 'Enery, I did not want to talk about that night, but as it has now come, I vill speak. We had so much the shock. Elizabet has so much a strong vill, she does not make the think. We see now, that if you have the vife, there is no you marry Elizabet, so vhy do we vorry so much. Her husband he is already. One day they are married and it vill be good for both our families. Now that she know that you have already the vife, she forget her silly idea. Perhaps we have the little too harsh."

Robert could not believe his ears. She had seemed so firm and so adamant, that night, yet now it seemed she was almost giving him an apology. This was too good to be true. She seemed to have forgotten that Lillian was missing. He certainly would not remind her. Perhaps this was the chance for a small olive branch. "Perhaps, if I were to talk to Emil, he might permit me to have one or two of your horses here to train; who knows, they might even be winners."

The Countess eyed him with the slightest smile. "You think that this could be? It vould be so good. Then my husband he might not have the bad temper so much."

"Countess, I can but ask. We certainly have room. The competition would be good." Robert smiled to himself into his glass. *Yes, it would be good. They would have to come and visit them and so he would see much more of Elizabet.* Their eyes met under the chubby gilded leg of the cherub and Robert laughed out loud. Her enquiring eyebrow demanded to know what he was looking so smug about. Luckily the Countess was engaged in some voluble discussion with the man on her other side. Robert smiled and mouthed "Later"—but she did not understand and her look of enquiry turned to a look of bafflement.

The plates were quickly carried away and were replaced by others bearing a large fish steak covered with a thick golden source. Robert eyed the large white flakes with some trepidation. They had a familiar look about them. He immediately could see in his mind's eye the large fish at the Ball given in his honour. This must be its cousin, judging by the size of it! It was nearly as big and doubtless had a similar upbringing. Robert eyed it with some suspicion; but he had survived last time, so why not this time.

"Countess, this is Carp, if I am not mistaken!"

"Ya. Emil he has the goot Karpfen—how you say—"Carp?" They are not as big as the ones we have in our Burggraben." She waved her fork in a circular motion.

"Moat?" ventured Robert. "Water, round your castle?"

"Ya, ya. You call this 'Moat'?" She attacked her fish with zest. "Ist goot."

Robert too tried his and found the flesh to be firm and succulent, with the most delicate sauce.

The carp was followed by a small partridge, and after that a huge roast boar was carried round for them all to applaud before it was placed on a side table. One of the servants set to carving it. Soon great slices were being handed round, garnished with baked onions. Dishes of vegetables followed and these were hardly finished when the plates were cleared and a succession of pastries and sweetmeats followed one by one as each was consumed. The noise level rose and the speed of eating decreased, aided by the continuous stream of wines of different hues that were constantly being poured into the forest of glasses. All the time Robert strove to be as agreeable and ingratiating as he could. This was his chance to show the Countess that he was not as bad as she obviously thought. Whether he succeeded he did not know, but she certainly seemed to become quite jolly and amenable, though this might have been due to the wine. Presently the cheese and desert had come and gone. All the glasses had been cleared away and they were left with a glass of a clear dark gold wine which was as sweet and rich as it was flavoursome. Emil rose to his feet and proposed a long and wordy toast to the success of the hunting. Someone else rose and as far as Robert could tell, proposed a health to Emil, which had everyone cheering, stamping their feet and clapping. Someone else rose unsteadily to his feet and made a long speech, which had every one laughing and cheering. Then Elizabet was swaying unsteadily on her feet, despite the efforts of those sitting on either side of her to persuade her to sit down. The Countess went very tight lipped and hissed at her across the table to sit down and not make a fool of herself, but Elizabeth had drunk deep and was not to be deterred. Robert's mouth went dry and his heart started to thump. He remembered what had happened the last time Elizabet had addressed the company! He wiped his sweaty palms on his napkin.

"I vish to make a toast and a small wager." Her English sounded even more disjointed and laboured than usual, as she was trying to make herself heard above the murmur of astonishment and subdued giggles that ran round the table. Some understood her, but most were enquiring of their neighbour about what she was saying. Nevertheless she continued in English. "Herr 'Enery here…" She pointed at him, "…has made the wager that he can a days hunting do riding side-saddle and that on next day of the hunt he vill ride a whole day side-saddle."

There was an immediate uproar round the table. Those who could understand roared their approval and those who could not were clamouring to know what she had said. Elizabet continued: "Vithout falling off!" She laughed at him and sat down in her chair. Everyone started to laugh, clap and cheer. Robert could see that he was required to do something. Everyone was looking towards him. He felt himself growing red with embarrassment. He had picked up a little "stable" German but the thought of standing up and making a speech drove even the polite bits out of his head. He had to do something—the clapping and stamping were getting louder. Even the Countess had got over the shock of her daughter's presumption and was looking speculatively at him to see what he was going to do. In total panic he desperately thought of a course of action. He rose to his feet and, leaning as far across the table as he could, he wagged his finger sternly at Elizabet. This was greeted with roars of applause from everyone. Even the Countess laughed and clapped her hands together. Elizabet smiled her best and most bewitching smile at him, which made his knees feel weak. He pulled out his wallet and selecting the largest note that he could find, he showed it to everyone and, rolling it up, tucked it under the arm of the golden cherub and sat down. Everyone applauded and cheered and soon a dish was being passed round the table. Presently it reached Elizabet and she removed the grapes from the dish that the cherub was supporting and placed the money in their place. The Countess was looking anxious.

"I hope that you do not fall off. If you do it will cost you a great much." Robert's puzzled look made her pause. "You know that if you loose, you vill have to give one of your monies to everyone who has put money in the dish." Robert blenched. He looked at the dish. Nearly everyone had put in a note. There must be thirty or forty notes in there. He quickly multiplied the marks and converted it into pounds. He felt sick in his stomach. If he fell off, he would be ruined. He would not be able to pay all that. These people were wealthy. The money did not matter to them, but a bet was a bet and betting debts were matters of honour and had to be paid. If he lost, he would have to leave the country because he could not pay all that. He smiled weakly at the Countess.

"I had better not fall off then." He caught Elizabet's eye between the legs of the cherub and gave her his sternest look that said 'just you wait until I get my hands on you!' She laughed again at him.

The ladies withdrew from the room and the men all moved down the table and sat again together round Emil. Decanters of brandy were placed on the table and cigars passed round. There was a great deal of good humoured banter about Robert's wager and much speculation about how long he would last before he fell off. Robert also came in for some considerable comment about how he had allowed himself to be put in that position in the first place. There was much speculation about what might be behind it all. Emil, who had been present at the fateful dinner in Vienna and knew what lay behind it, directed the conversation to the day's shooting that he had organised for the next day. Robert was disappointed that he had not been asked to join in, but he would be needed to look after the carriages and carts that were going to be needed if everything and everyone were to be in place at the right time.

"Mine Got!" bellowed the Count when he heard of Robert's part in the plans of the day, biting the end off a large cigar and puffing it to life from a candle handed to him. "If you leave it to 'Enery, it vill all be late. The late Mister 'Enery, he vill make it late, even if it is not.!" He laughed out loud, puffing acrid clouds of cigar smoke in all directions. "He is alvays late. When he come, everything it is late." He chuckled to himself and thrust his nose into a large glass of brandy.

"Like your three winners, I suppose." Emil looked hard at him from over the top of his glass.

"Vinners? Vhat three vinners? Vhat you talk about?"

"You have forgotten? So soon? In Vienna. At the last meeting. You had three winners, you remember? Henery was not late that day; if you remember, he gave you three winners. None of them was late then!" Emil almost glowered at him. The Count went very red.

"Vhen he give me three vinners, you take him avay from me, so that you have vinners and I have no more."

"I have only got 'Enery here because, if you remember, after that evening, he had nowhere else to go."

The Count stood up noisily. "Arr-rr…" He almost growled like a bear. "I vill go unt joint the ladies. They do not make argue vith me." He drained his brandy and stomped out of the room. Robert had been feeling acutely embarrassed. He did not like being argued over, as if by two dogs with a bone.

Emil stood up. "I think it would be a good idea if we all went to join the ladies"

As they left the dining room, he drew Robert to one side. "I am sorry about that."

"Don't worry. I know the old boy enough to know that that is typical of him and that it means nothing."

"Don't let the old fool get you down. He has never been very well disposed to anyone who thwarts him. He has convinced himself that I have taken you from him so that I can have winners and to prevent him from having any more!"

"Well, if it will make the peace, why don't I have two or three of his horses here. We have got the room and the competition would be good for our training." Emil looked at him with surprised appreciation.

"That's an excellent idea. Mind you, I am not too keen to have the old boy round here all the time, but hopefully, if his gout is bad enough, when he gets home, he will stay there. Yes, I will propose it to him. If he accepts, we will manage somehow, and if he doesn't, well, the olive branch will have been offered and he can not keep growling at me all the time. By the way, are you seriously going to ride side-saddle?" Emil ushered Robert out of the room toward the drawing room to join the ladies.

"Well, it is not quite as daft as it seems. You remember that we spent over two weeks schooling the horses and so I am well practised! Thank goodness!"

They entered the drawing room. Elizabet was at the piano playing an accompaniment to a short fat man who was singing some song in a reedy tenor voice that relied more on the good dinner than on any natural quality. Robert made his way over to her and joined the group of admirers round the piano. One by one they all took a turn at singing. Elizabet seemed to have an endless repertoire of songs and knew them all, happily playing the accompaniment.

"Vell Robert, what vill you sing for us?" She was playing a little air softly, but did not look up. "Every one has sing, it is for you now!"

Robert quite enjoyed singing, but he was seized with panic.

"What can *I* sing? I do not know any of these songs. The only songs that I know are not suitable for the drawing room. In any case they are English songs and you will not have the music."

"If you sing the tune to me, I can play it for you." She looked up at him with a beatific smile. "You vill not escape. All wait to hear you sing."

Robert looked round the room nervously and saw that indeed everyone was looking expectantly at them. He wracked his brain amid a rising sea of panic.

"I know, try this..." He sat on the stool beside her and hummed a few bars of "Drink to me only" into her ear. "Umm, your perfume smells delicious."

She giggled and played on. "Yes, I think that I can play that. If you start to sing, I will play."

"Tell them that it is a very well known song in England. It is an old song of a lover longing for his lady."

Elizabet stood up and, addressing the room, introduced Robert and his song.

"Stop." Emil stood up. "I have the music for that song." He went to the bookcase and produced a small volume. "Here, *Folk Songs of the World*. He quickly turned the index and found the page. "Here it is!" He gave it to Elizabet who quickly looked at it and tried a few bars. She smiled at Robert. Robert, taking courage in both hands, took a deep breath and started.

"No, No. you are wrong." Elizabet played the first note. "*That* is vere you start."

Robert sung the note.

"No, up, up." She played it again. This time he found the right note and so he sung it through to the end. Elizabet played and when he had finished everyone politely clapped. She gazed up at him and their eyes met. She could see tears in his eyes. She reached up and took his hand.

"You sang that song for me. It is so romantic."

Robert pulled his handkerchief out and blew his nose to try and hide his embarrassment. She started to play another piece and everyone drifted off. Robert alone stayed by the piano.

"Yes, I sang it for you." His voice became husky with emotion. He quickly changed the subject to hide his embarrassment. "Emil is going to suggest to your father that we have some of his horses to train."

"This is a goot idea. Papa 'as been so angry since you have gone. He might be more happy if he think that he might have the more vinners."

"Of course, you will have to make frequent visits to see how they are getting on."

"This is more better. Then we shall see more of each other." She smiled up at him. "This is a very goot idea. Did you think it?"

"Yes. I mentioned it to your mother at dinner and she thought it a good idea. Emil, too, thought it good. I think it very good. Do you think that your father will agree?

"Vell, Robert, you are the very clever one. I vill make papa agree; then we can meet many times." She smiled up at him from the piano and blew him a kiss. Robert blushed.

"Do not do that in here, people might see!"

"Och, let them see. If they have not see by now they are very stupid." She finished her piece and standing up took his hand and led him back towards the others.

"Papa, Emil has offered to let Herr 'Enery train some of our horses here. We shall have some vinners again!"

The count who had been dozing, his bandaged foot sticking out on a stool in front of him, jerked awake.

"Vinners? Don't talk of vinners. We had vinners, but now it is all gone, finish!"

He groped for his brandy glass, wiping a drool from his chin with a large handkerchief with his other hand at the same time. "We had a man, but Emil has take him. We shall have no more vinners. Emil vill have them and we vill be always late." Elizabet went and knelt beside him and took his hand. Carefully, as if talking to a child, she repeated what she had said. At last he understood and the first smile that had been seen on his face since Robert left, gradually spread.

"Brandy, Brandy." He waved his empty glass in the air. A footman who had been standing in the dark part of the room for just such an emergency stepped forward with a decanter and poured it for him. "Is this true? Emil, this is very generous."

"Yes cousin, it is true. I shall be glad to take two or three. We will have to come to some arrangement, of course, but otherwise consider it settled."

The Count's face had darkened at the mention of 'an arrangement', but he smiled a happy smile. Before his befuddled eyes he could already see a procession of shining trophies decorated with his racing colours. Elizabet stood up beside Robert and, resting both her hands on his shoulder, put her lips close to his ear.

"Who is the clever boy then?" she whispered, and gave him a little kiss on the cheek.

CHAPTER 21

Robert stood with his back to the mirror with his riding breeches down round his ankles.

Bending down, he squinted between his knees at his bare reflection, to examine the damage on his more private but very tender places. The saddle sores looked red, raw and angry, which was just as they felt! He had in one hand a bottle of iodine, in the other a piece of cotton wool. He did not need to tell himself that this was going to hurt—he knew it. He knew how it would sting and burn when he applied it to the raw flesh, but he felt that it was a necessary treatment. Gritting his teeth he applied a liberal quantity of the pungent brown fluid to the cotton wool, then, shutting his eyes, he dabbed it firmly on the sore. The howl of anguish could be heard all round the house.

There was a knock on the door. He hastily hung his dressing down over his shoulders and opened it. Willie staggered in with two great brass jugs of hot water and a huge grin on his face. Robert pointed angrily to where the bath stood. Willie put down the jugs and left.

Robert walked stiffly over to the bath. He poured in the water. He knew this was going to be hurt too. Tears came into his eyes at the very thought. Dropping his dressing gown in a heap on the floor, he painfully stepped in.

Stiffly, he attempted to sit down, but hesitated at the idea of the hot water on his bare sores. He gritted his teeth. After a nervous pause he sat down with a splash. His cry of pain was heard by the stable lads in the yard and they laughed with glee. Robert dashed the tears from his eyes.

"Ye Gods, there must be easier ways of pleasing a lady than this!" The pain eased as he became accustomed to the hot water.

Robert had contemplated declining the invitation to dinner at the Schloss, but he knew that if he did not show up he would never be able to collect his bets. He had to grit his teeth and be there. And so it was that about an hour later, walking like some stiff marionette, he painfully entered the drawing room.

He was greeted with much applause and jocularity. Elizabet came to him and kissed him on the cheek.

"How is my hero? How is your poor bum?" She hung onto his arm and smiled up at him. Robert was more taken aback than shocked.

"Where did you learn that word?" he laughed in spite of his pain.

"Is that not a good vord?"

"No, it is not a good word. Definitely not a word to use in the drawing room. If your mother knew what you meant, she would be shocked."

"She vould not know what it meant if I said it."

"No, but Emil certainly would and so would your father, so do not use it in here."

Elizabet laughed and took him by the arm. "Come, we have moneys to collect." She took up a big dish from a side table and led him round the room to everyone, to collect the bets that had been placed the night before. There was good-humoured laughter and ribaldry all round, but by the time they had been round the room, they had what appeared to be a very large heap of notes. Even Elizabet's father had produced his wager, not without complaint, but Elizabet had taken it from his hand and put it in the dish with the rest. When they had been round everyone, she quickly shuffled the notes into a neat pile and, deftly folding them, she put them into the top of her bodice.

"Hey, that is my money." Robert vainly tried to prevent her.

"If you want it, you know where it is." She smiled at him. "I vill look after it. One day you vill be glad."

"But it is mine—give it to me. I earned it. I have got the saddle sores to prove it! Hand it over."

"If I give it to you, what vill you do? On some silly bet you vill loose it all again!"

Robert was a little annoyed, but there was nothing he could do. Everyone was laughing. He had to make the best of it and laugh too.

He was too sore to enjoy the dinner. It seemed to go on forever and he kept shifting uncomfortably on his chair. Sitting was an agony and he found the strain of trying to make polite conversation with his neighbours too taxing. At last the meal was over and the ladies withdrew. Emil produced cigars and brandy, but at least Robert could stand or walk about. He was the butt of considerable laughter and much advice about how to get his money back, all of which he had to accept with good grace. At last Emil rose to go to the drawing room and Robert excused himself. If Emil would excuse him, he was going to go home. He shook hands with everyone and went out to the hall to ask for his cloak. A footman brought it for him and helped him on with it.

"So you were going to run away and not say to me goodbye?"

Robert turned. Elizabet stood in the doorway. He walked across and took both her hands in his.

"It would be better."

"Vhy? Vhy vould it be better? You slink off like a cur dog and we do not see each other again!"

"But we shall see each other tomorrow. To night, I am very sore. I cannot sit around any longer."

"But I wanted to play the piano and see you watching me like that, as if I were a little mouse and you ver the great big hungry cat, which want to eat me up."

"I don't think I would be a very good audience to night. I will see you tomorrow." He noticed that her eyes were full of tears.

"No, we go home tomorrow. Mother is not vell—she vish to return, home. We go tomorrow. I shall not see you anymore." She drew close to him and kissed him lightly on the lips.

"No." He stepped back. "No. We cannot do this."

She stamped her foot. "You make me so angry!" She glowered at him. "Your eyes say yes, but your voice it say no!"

"My heart says yes, but my head says no. You know we cannot. What if she comes back? What would we do then?"

"But you feel that she is dead!"

"Yes, my heart tells me she is dead, but my head tells me we must wait."

"Oh Mister cold!" she snapped at him angrily. "So you alvays do what your head it tell you?"

"No! You know that is not fair."

"No, I am sorry. Vill you write to me then?"

"Yes, I can write, but you will never get the letters. Schmidt will give them to your father. You will never get them."

"Write to Gretchen. She makes my clothes. Vhen I go to see her to have the fittings, I can collect your letters. Give me paper and pencil and I will write her name for you."

Robert gave her his pocket book and a pencil and she carefully wrote down the name and address. "We will meet again in the summer, when you come for the race meetings. If I have some of your father's horses to train, I am sure that you will come to see them run. We will be able to meet again then. Goodbye, my little one. Look after yourself."

He drew her to him and they kissed long and gently.

"Goodbye Robert. Write to me many letters. I vish to know everything what you are doing. Then I shall know that I am alvays in your heart."

"How could you possibly doubt it? You know that you are in my heart always and that I think of you every day." He kissed her again and quickly walked to the door. As the unseen footman opened it for him, he turned and waived to her. She stood where she was, lit by the light of the fire, her hand raised in farewell.

He walked stiffly and slowly back to his house. There was a bright moon and though the air was keen, he was not cold, for he was well wrapped in his cloak. Far, far away, in the dark forest a wolf howled, its cry rising and falling, long, distant and eerie. He stopped and lent against the fence to listen to it. There it was again. The hackles rose on the back of his neck. He shivered. It seemed almost supernatural. He walked on wondering about the nocturnal affairs of the wolf. *I bet he wasn't married to one and in love with another!* He had done his best to keep such thoughts out of his head. He had worked hard so that he did not have time to think them, but here in the moonlight, they had come unbidden and he could not push them away. He thought of Elizabet, standing by the fire, her hand half raised in sad farewell. He thought of Lillian. He was alarmed to find she had become a shadowy figure. He could no longer picture her clearly in his imagination. He concentrated harder. Gradually her image cleared. He felt quite disconcerted. It was as if, by losing her image, he had in some way betrayed her. It was as if he were letting go of her, so that she slipped away into the darkness. As he walked her image appeared to fade and flicker, like a dim magic lantern show, with every footfall. He realised with a shock that the image he had in his mind was the sepia photograph that was in his dressing table. Elizabet he could picture in full, real colour. The two images kept fading and interchanging in his mind as he walked. There seemed to be no conflict between them. It was not as if one or other was struggling for suprem-acy, but there was no doubt that Lillian, the sepia picture, was fading. He struggled to bring her face into bright detail, but he could not. What would happen if she reappeared and he did not recognise her? If she did come back now, would he still love her? He could not imagine that they would feel for each other as they had before. That would be impossible. Too much time had elapsed. Too many things had happened. Time would have changed them both. They were not going to be the same people they were when they last saw each other. Being separated, they would have grown apart. And what of Elizabet? If Lillian were to reappear, what could they do? It would be impossible that he should stay here.

He couldn't possibly take up his life with Lillian with Elizabet always on the scene. It just would not work. He would have to leave and probably go back to England. It would not be fair to any of them if he stayed. Perhaps he ought to leave now and go right away. In the end he would forget Elizabet. Eventually she would forget him. In England, if Lillian were to reappear there would not be the complication of Elizabet. Perhaps that would be the best thing. But…he had a good job here. He was just getting his teeth into it. He was looking forward to the coming season, with some excitement, as he would have a real chance to prove himself. Was he just going to give it all up and run away—again? He stopped and leaned on the fence again, banging his fist on the wooden rail in frustration. Far away, across the forest, the wolf howled once more. A cold shiver ran down his spine. It was a very strange unearthly sound. It echoed and swelled round the forest like the cry of a lost tortured soul that has found out that its worst fears of hell have become a present and awful reality. Robert leant on the rail and felt that any manifestation of Hell could not be worse, at that moment. He could not go on like this. He was going to have to go back to England. He could not stay here any longer. He could not exist with Elizabet suspended in limbo for another five years. It was not fair on either of them! It simply could not work! It would not work! It would destroy them both! He walked on, gently swinging his legs, wide, so that his sores did not chafe on his trousers. There was no doubt, they hurt. He never should have allowed himself to accept the stupid bet.

The bet! His Money! She had taken it all! He could see it in his mind's eye, being thrust down the front of her dress. He tried to work out how much it was, but he could not. There was no way of knowing that everyone had paid up as they should. Doubtless some had short-changed him. But nonetheless, it was a large amount. If he were going to go away, he would need it. It was one thing to need it, another to get it. If he told Elizabet that he needed it because he planned to return to England, she would probably throw it into the fire rather than let him have it. He would have to think of some ploy to get it from her. No, he could not do that. It would be a betrayal, to get it from her and then to tell her that he was going to go. He was in a mental turmoil—he could not keep running away. The time comes when you have *got* to turn and face the gremlins that life throws at you. If you run they will be snapping and growling at your heels forever. If you turn and face them, they may hiss and spit at you, but they will back away. What was the likelihood of Lillian returning now? He was a betting man. He could assess the odds, the likelihood, as well as anyone else. She has been away for so long that it is most unlikely that she will return now or ever. In his heart he knew that. So what, then, was he afraid of? If he truly loved Elizabet, was it not worth waiting? The time may seem long, when looked at from this end, but looking back five years, it is nothing. No time at all. It is soon gone. If he walked away now, he would forever regret what he had given up.

CHAPTER 22

Emil held the letter in his hand. He sat at his desk in front of the fireplace. The row of cups and trophies on the mantelpiece testified to his success as a race-horse owner.

Robert looked at his friend and employer with respect and affection. Had they both changed so little over the last five years? Robert had to admit that he had grown fatter. His hair was beginning to grey at the temples, but Emil looked hardly different at all. He still looked as fit as when they had first met. Perhaps he had a few more lines round the eyes, and his hair, too, was beginning to grey at the temples. Perhaps his waistcoat buttons strained more than they used to, but otherwise the years had scarce touched him. They had flown by leaving hardly any sign of their passing.

Looking back, five years seemed like nothing. All that time ago, in his kitchen, when he had felt so low, five years seemed endless. But five years, looking back, seemed to have passed in a flash. As he sat here now, he thanked the heavens that he had not cut and run, as he had intended. He had been right. He would have regretted losing what he had now for the rest of his life. He had not managed to put Lillian's ghost behind him, but, like an old photograph left in the sun, the image in his mind had faded.

He had worked hard. His efforts had been crowned with success, as the row of trophies on the mantelpiece testified. He had also had some success with the Count's horses and had managed to find some winners for him too. He had taken care not to enter them into direct competition with those belonging to Emil, too often, and so had managed to keep both happy. Emil had been surprised and gratified that he had applied himself with such determination to the task, but Robert knew it was only by throwing body and soul into his work, that he could drive the ghosts into the background.

He had derived great strength from his correspondence with Elizabet. He had posted his first effort to the seamstress. After two weeks, he was very heartened to receive a letter back. Elizabet had difficulty with spoken English, but when it came to writing, it was almost a lost art. He laughed and laughed at her scrambled sentences until he had to admit to himself that she was doing a lot better in English than he would be able to do in German.

They had been able to meet at race meetings and at the annual hunt, when Elizabeth and her father had come to stay at the Schloss with Emil. For the last couple of years, Elizabeth's mother had declined to come. She found the long days of sport in the open air and the great boisterous dinners in the evening too tiring. She preferred to stay at home. Robert's reserve had gradually dissolved as Lillian's image faded in his mind. He and Elizabeth were able to derive great strength and resolve from their brief meetings. He began to look forward to them, not as he had at first, to dread them, because they had posed more problems than they solved. But now that was all in the past. Those long frustrating years were over.

Emil looked up. "Robert, thank you for showing me this. I do not know what to say. Do I commiserate with you or do I congratulate you? I do not know what to say to you. I know what I would like to say, but I do not know if I should."

"Say what you like. If it is something that you truly feel, I'm sure that I can't take offence. I know that you would not have said it, if you didn't feel yourself a friend."

"Well Robert, thank God for that! That is what I really feel. I know what this will mean to you and Elizabet and I can only say how glad I am. How the two of you have endured for so long, I cannot understand. I can only marvel at your constancy. Whether you will be able to break down the resistance of August and Helga I do not know, but at least you are free to try at last." He folded the letter and gave it back to Robert who took it and put it in the inside pocket of his jacket.

"Emil, I would like to ask for some time off. Not immediately, but soon. Now that Lillian has been declared officially dead, I would like to go back to England for a short while to hold a memorial service for her. She never had a funeral. She never will have one. But I feel that some kind of funeral service would finally lay her to rest. I would like to do it where we used to live, as that was her home too, our home together. I would like to do it as soon as it can be arranged. With you permission, I will write to the Vicar of the Church there, to try to arrange it as quickly as possible."

"Yes, of course. There is nothing vital happening here and in any event, I am sure that your system works so well that the Stud will run without you breathing on it all the time. Of course you must go. Take all the time that you need."

"Thanks. I'll set it in motion as soon as I can. Now I have one more favour to ask you. I would like some time off now to go to see Elizabet to tell her. I want to speak to her in person. I can't do this in a letter."

"Yes, of course you must."

"I would be grateful if you would tell no one, for the time being. I do not want word of it preceding me. I think this is something she should hear directly from me."

"Yes, of course. My lips are sealed. Make whatever arrangements you need, but please keep me informed so that I know what is going on."

Robert got up to leave.

"Robert, good luck."

The two men shook hands and Robert left the room.

Robert sat on the little seat in the sun. The steamer seemed to be flying along. The Danube was running high and fast with floodwater. The little steamer was surging along with hardly any bow wave, carried by the swift current. Robert was in buoyant mood. After five years of pent up emotions and half-seen fears he was suddenly free. He—they—had been patient for so long, nothing was now going to stand in their way! He was free at last to pursue the girl he loved. He was exhilarated by the speed of the craft, thrilled that it was rapidly approaching its destination.

He could see the landing stage ahead with people waiting expectantly on it. Even as he spoke, the steamer swung in a sharp ark across the river and was being carried along, stern first, heading for apparent doom against the weathered piles of the landing stage. Just as it seemed certain it would be dashed to pieces, the paddle wheels on either side started to churn the water furiously. The boat gradually developed enough power to breast the current, the bow wave mounting to a foaming white crescent as the little boat surged into the flood. With a gentle bump it nudged the landing stage. Ropes were quickly thrown and secured as the still churning paddles held the little boat against the rapid current. Impossible things always look easy when they are done by someone who knows exactly what he or she is doing! The whistle of the little boat shrilled above him. Robert jumped. The ropes were already being cast off. The bow of the boat was swinging out into the currant. He grabbed his bag and ran for the gangplank. He ran ashore, even as it was pulled from underneath him and landed on the quay breathless. He turned to wave his thanks. Already the little boat was being swept downstream. The captain waved from his wheel-house. Two little puffs of steam heralded two shrill toots from the whistle.

Robert walked to the little inn, rattled the door and walked in. He would stay here tonight and hire a horse in the morning. He stood waiting at the rough bar, but no one appeared.

"Hello!" Robert called. "Hello—anyone at home?" In the five years that he had been working for the Prince, Robert had mastered sufficient conversational German to get by.

"Hello!" Robert called again, louder, rattling a wooden breadboard on the counter top. "Hello!"

Suddenly a tousled blonde head popped up from the floor. "Yes, what do you want?" it asked in thick German.

Robert started. He had not noticed that the cellar flap was open. "I would like a room for the night please, and perhaps some supper." For all Robert's mastery of the language, he had not developed the harsh demanding tone that would normally have turned this request into an order. The young girl, now revealed as she climbed up out of the cellar, looked at him in some surprise.

"Yes of course, your honour. I will see to it at once. We have ham and vegetables. Some cheese. Some wine. Bread. Will that be all right?"

Robert was speechless. This was the same girl who had been here when he had first come. Then a girl, now a young woman, but hardly changed.

"You do not remember me, do you?" Robert smiled at her. He was rewarded with a shy smile from her blue eyes.

"Oh yes, your honour. I remember you very well. We do not have many strangers here. Then I remember, you could speak no German. Now I can see that you have found a little!"

"The old man, your grandfather?"

She nodded.

"He was so kind to me. Is he still here?"

"Yes, he is out in the vineyard. He will be in when it is time for his meal. He is never late; he must have a clock in his tummy."

"And your little one. You had a child, I remember?"

"Oh yes, he is outside playing. He will come in with his grandfather. I will prepare some food for you." She smiled and left. Robert noticed that she still had no shoes on her brown feet.

Whilst she was preparing the food he decided to have a look at the village. He went outside into the afternoon spring sunshine and walked along the dusty street. The few houses were small and single storied. The windows were all shuttered and the place looked dead. There was not a soul around. A small group of scrawny chickens dusted in the sun. A dusty cat pretended it could summon up enough energy to stalk a sparrow that was hopping around looking for any small morsel of food that it might find. The usual group of pigeons sat on the rooftops. Robert had the feeling that though he could not see anyone, people were watching him. It made him feel a little uneasy.

He could see a group of children out in the meadow. It seemed that they had been sent to bring in the geese. He stopped to watch them for a while. They were definitely coming this way. Behind the little Inn, the hills rose quite steeply and working between the steep rows of vines, he could see some people. Robert was struck by the evident poverty of everything. The cottages and garden fences were repaired any old how, using whatever came to hand. There was not a lick of paint to be seen on anything. The whole place had a ramshackled and makeshift appearance.

He crossed some small vegetable patches, which made him think of the allotments in his village back in England. There were rows of maize and tomatoes growing in the open and green plants, which he took to be peppers, as well as onions and greens. He wandered past the allotments to reach the riverbank. Here there was quite a well-defined path that followed the river. However, as the water was running very high, the path was soon flooded where it dipped to a lower level. Being unable to proceed, he turned and walked back along the bank to the small landing stage. There was a small skiff tied up there, evidently belonging to some fishermen. They were unloading their catch and Robert stopped to watch. They seemed to have a basket of brightly striped perch. In a wooden tub were some squirming eels. They explained that the river was running too high. Their nets kept on being swept away, clogged with debris. Fishing was no good at the moment. But, they shrugged their shoulders hopelessly—they were fishermen, they had families to feed and must try. It was dangerous work when the river was high like this, but they had been quite lucky, they had a few fish and had not lost their nets. They showed their catch to Robert. Perhaps he would like to buy some fish? Robert was certainly keen to look and to see the fish. They gleamed a wet silvery sheen and their colours looked almost iridescent in the light. He thought of the cold meat and cheese on offer for supper. A baked fish certainly seemed attractive. Perhaps Elly could prepare and cook it…Elly! That was her name. Why should he suddenly remember that, after all those years?

"Yes, I will take that one" He pointed at a large perch that seemed to be the biggest one in the basket.

No, he could not have that one, the fisherman told him. That was for his family. They would make a good meal off that. The fisherman picked up another. He could have this if he wished.

Robert offered a handful of coins and the fisherman selected two. The man then reached over the side of the boat and, pulling out his evil looking knife, cut off a good handful of rushes. In no time at all he had plaited up a small basket and slipped the fish into it.

Robert went back to the Inn, carrying the little basket carefully so that it did not drip on his trousers.

"Elly, Elly," he called as they entered. She stuck her head round the door at the back.

"How did you know my name?"

"I remembered. Suddenly I remembered! After all that time. You see, the little things that stick in the back of your brain. Look, I have bought this fish. Do you think you could cook it for my supper?" He offered the little basket. She stretched out a brown arm and took it.

"You must have paid him a lot. He will not always make a little basket." She disappeared.

Robert called after her. "Do you think that I could have a bottle of wine?"

There was some muttering from the kitchen and after a little clanking her brown hand reappeared and banged a bottle down on the counter. Robert waited a little.

"Could I have a glass please?"

More clanking from the kitchen, and then one appeared in the same way, none too gently beside the bottle. Robert waited.

"Could I have an opener please."

There was a loud crash from the kitchen followed by some loud swearing, from which Robert gathered she had pulled the draw out and it had fallen on the floor. After much clattering, she appeared and banged a corkscrew down on the counter.

"Is there anything else that you would like." She glowered at him. "Shall I open it for you? Perhaps you would like me to drink it for you as well."

Robert took up the bottle, the glass and the opener. "No thank you. I can manage to do that."

He went outside and sat at one of the benches in the afternoon sun. Drawing the cork, he poured the wine. At that moment Elly came out with two buckets and went over to the pump to fill them with water. She was muttering and grumbling as she went past. She came staggering back with two buckets brimming full, splashing over her feet. Robert jumped up.

"Here, let me carry those for you."

She shrank away from him and hurried inside.

Robert shrugged and sat down. Evidently, carrying water was woman's work. In the distance he could see a cloud of dust that was heading towards the village. He could see that it was a coach. He sat in the sunlight, watching its progress as it slowly crossed the plane. It soon became obvious that the children and the flock of geese were going to arrive at the village street at the same time as the coach.

As the coach rounded the last corner, the geese, in a white gaggling tide, flowed out of a gap in the fence, onto the road. The geese and the children scattered in all directions. The Coachman shouted and attempted to stop his horses, but he ploughed through the squawking scattering flock. The geese scattered everywhere. The children ran round shrieking, trying to round them up. Suddenly the street was full of people angrily shouting. They caught the horses and pulled the coach to a stop. The driver stayed on his box clutching his whip. The people were very upset and were angry with him. It seemed that none of the children had been hurt, but two of the geese had been killed. The crowd was becoming angry. Robert recognised the coach. It belonged to the Count! The driver was Joseph. He walked across and pushed his way through the people.

"What are you doing here?"

The look of relief on Joseph's face was obvious. "For you, vee 'aff come. Graffinflein say go, be there tomorrow. You to bring."

"But how did she know I was coming?"

Joseph shrugged. He did not know. She had said go. He was here. By now the crowd had worked out that Robert was in some way connected to the Count's coach so they turned angrily upon him. The dead geese were waived under his nose. It was obvious that blood money was being demanded. Robert pulled out his purse. After a lengthy haggle, he finally handed over some small coins.

During this time the children had rounded up the rest of the geese. They all stood in the middle of a sea of orange beaks as the geese crowded round them. It seemed that with the handing over of the coins, honour was satisfied. The small crowd dispersed. The children drove the geese away and the slain were born off. Robert turned again to Joseph. "But how did Graffinflein know that I was coming? I have told no one? There is not time for a letter to have arrived." Again Joseph shrugged. She did not tell him what she knew or did not know.

He turned to Joseph. "Stable the horses for tonight. We will leave first thing in the morning. Have you got lodgings?"

Yes, Joseph assured him. Whenever he came to meet the steamer, he always stayed the night in that house. He pointed to a run-down little place. He whipped up the horses and moved off. Robert returned to the bench, only to discover, to his annoyance, that the bottle of wine had disappeared. His glass, too, had been emptied. The geese had all miraculously disappeared. So had the children. Robert looked about him in some surprise. Had it really happened, or had he fallen asleep in the sun and dreamed it all? The white feathers blowing around in the wind were testament to what had happened. There was no other sign that anything had happened at all. He was just going to resume his seat when the old grandfather emerged from the door, tying on his white apron. He had obviously just come down from the vineyard. He held out a gnarled and dirty hand. His German was laboured and thick. Robert had the greatest difficulty in understanding what he said.

Yes, he remembered the time when Robert last had visited, years ago. He remembered that he had enjoyed some of his wines. He was very pleased to see him again.

"You must not mind my daughter, she had a great sorrow; we should be sad about it, but no, it was common in these parts; There were many fine young girls who suffered from the same problem. The men of the Count, they come, they go, but always it is the same. The young girls of the place, babies they have. They were good girls. It is not that. It is the men of the Count. They are bad men. There are some, I will not mention names, but they do not stay here anymore, that bring to the Count great trouble. Eef they stay here, I slit them like a pig…"

Robert was taken aback by this outburst. "But I am of the Count."

"Yes, but we can see that you are different, you are not one of the roughs of the Count. I think, Sir, that your food is ready. It is better to come in and eat it now, before Elly becomes more angry. She is a good girl, but she gets very angry if things do not suit her."

Robert allowed himself to be ushered inside and sat at the rough table. The Innkeeper hurried off. Presently he returned with a bottle and glass. The wine, he said, came from the south side of his vineyard. He went to the window and pointed up the hill. It got more sun there and ripened better. He poured out some light red wine. This grape had been growing there since before his father's time. He had no idea what its name was. He hoped that Robert would enjoy it. At that moment Elly entered with a large brown earthenware pot, which she crashed down on the table. She took off the lid and gave the contents a quick stir with a large wooden ladle. She ladled out a bowl full and put it down, none too gently, in front of Robert.

"It is hot," she called back to him as she went back to the kitchen.

He could see that for himself. Great clouds of acrid steam rose from the bowl. The pungent smell of onion, pepper and garlic made his eyes water. He explored his bowl with a spoon, cautiously. Of his fish, there was very little sign. Some evil looking bones protruded in the air, as if to warn against further perils within. Robert had hoped to see his fish, beautifully baked and sitting golden brown on a dish, inviting him to eat. He was disappointed to find that it had been hacked to pieces and boiled up in a stew. The stew was indeed hot and fiery. Hot too, from the peppers that had been generously added. Though the wine did not really go with the pungent mixture he was glad of it to assuage the burning in his mouth. He attacked the rough brown loaf with some determination as it provided some blotting paper for the fiery sauce. Of the fish there was very little sign. The piles of needle sharp bones mounted on his plate, but he did not find much fish. He prodded round in the pot with a spoon.

Elly reappeared to take the plates away. Robert stirred the pot. "There is not much fish in this stew," he said. She looked at him with disdain and swept the pot off the table.

"There is not much fish on a perch. Do you the want cold meat and the cheese?"

"But what I mean is that for the size of the fish there was not much of it in the st..."

She interrupted him angrily. "Do you want cheese or what...?"

"Elly, I do not know what is troubling you, but there is no need to be rude. Yes please. I would like some cold meat and cheese."

She clattered the plates into the bowl and ran out. He could hear her angry voice in the kitchen. Presently the Innkeeper returned carrying a tray with some coarse brown bread, a small joint of cold bacon and a hard cheese. He had also a bottle of red wine. He set the things on the table.

"Please do not mind Elly. She is angry today. I have told her that she can go home. She lives in that house there..." He pointed across the dusty street. "Her husband he is away. He works for the Count. Perhaps you remember him. He is called 'Boy'."

Robert smiled. Yes, he remembered Boy—a big strong blond lad who had been his driver for a little while. So he had married Elly. They must have met when he came down here to bring people for the river boat. The Innkeeper poured the wine.

At the moment 'Boy' was away on some business of the Count. He explained. He would not be back for some weeks. "Elly is always so when he is away. He is away a lot. We have a stormy time and now Joseph is here…" He shrugged his shoulders and left his sentence unfinished. "Try this wine. It is from our own vineyard. It is not the best there is, but it helps the bread and cheese go down."

Robert ate the rest of his meal in uneasy silence. He had liked 'Boy' and did not like the idea of Elly entertaining Joseph whilst he was away, especially as he was the indirect cause of bringing Joseph here. He considered leaving right away and taking the risk of travelling in the dark, but Joseph had presumably driven all day to get here, so he would need some rest, though by the sound of things, he was not going to get much tonight. There was nothing he could do about it and it was not his business anyway.

It was dark by the time he finished his meal, so leaving instructions that he was to be woken in good time so they could get away at first light, Robert went to bed.

CHAPTER 23

❁

Robert leaned out of the window of the coach. On a bare low hill overlooking a bend of the road he could make out a horseman.

"Joseph, can you see? Look over there!"

"Yes, I see. So? Many people must have stopped what they are doing to watch. It is not often that they see a coach tearing along like this."

He was right. Having taken head of Robert's instructions, he was urging the horses along as fast as he could. The Coach lurched and swayed over every rut and pothole, raising a billowing cloud of dust behind them. He was being tossed around like butter in a churn. Had he not been so impatient he would have found the journey most uncomfortable.

He was not certain about the horseman. He felt slightly uneasy. He looked out again and the figure had gone. He called up to Joseph once more.

"There was something funny. He was too far away—I could not see. What did you make of it?"

The unease in Robert's voice was obvious. Joseph pointed with his whip. Robert looked. The horseman was coming down the side of the hill. He had a second horse with him on a leading rein. Robert watched, but he was lost to view behind some trees.

"It is almost as if he were waiting for us. He came down off the hill as soon as we came round the corner. I think we should prepare ourselves for an encounter."

The coach thundered on. Suddenly Joseph trod on the break and pulled in the horses. The coach slid to a halt in a cloud of dust. Robert was thrown in a heap on the floor. He could hear voices.

He disentangled himself. Cautiously he raised his head so that he could peep through the window. The rider, for indeed it was he with the spare horse, was talking quickly to Joseph. He had his back to them. His long fair hair hung down his back. Long fair hair?

"Elizabet?" squeaked Robert, in surprise. "What on earth are you doing here?"

She had turned and brought the horses to the door. She was grinning from ear to ear.

"Vell Robert, are not you pleased to see me?"

"Yes…but…what…?"

"Oh come on, I have come to meet you. Don't you see? Come on, we vill ride back together."

A grin of understanding spread over Roberts face He jumped out and swung himself up on the horse.

"I thought you might be a robber or something…"

Elizabet laughed. "You thought I vas a robber?"

"Well yes, you looked a bit like a robber, standing up on that hill top."

"How can I look like a robber? I am only little, and my long hair." She tossed her head so that it blew in the wind.

"From where we were, we could not see that. You looked just like a Robber."

"Well, I am not a robber. I have not come to steal from you. What I vant from you, you vill give willingly."

She rode her horse close to him and leant over and kissed him. She held his hand. "Robert, it is so good to see you." They sat holding hands, drinking in the happiness in each other's eyes.

"It is good to see you too. I cannot tell you how much I have looked forward to this moment." He choked up with emotion. Hot tears welled in his eyes and he could not speak. She watched him sympathetically. She could see the emotion in his eyes. She felt it too. She was first to recover.

"Come on, we must ride on. There are people coming to the castle tonight—we must not be late for dinner."

The necessity of the moment broke the spell and they set off together at a steady canter.

"How did you know I was coming? How did you know that we would be here this afternoon?"

Elizabet smiled at him. "I knew"

"But *how* did you know? A letter couldn't possibly have reached you in time. How could you possibly know?"

She laughed at him. "I look in my crystal ball! There vas this handsome stranger. I just knew that to meet him, I must go."

"Don't be silly, how could you know?"

"I know. I know all that you do. Where you go. Who you meet. I know all about you, Robert 'Enery."

"But how can you possibly know? Where was I last week?"

"You vere in Prague."

Robert was considerably taken aback. "How can you possibly know that?"

"I know," she smiled at him.

"It was a lucky guess. What did I do in Prague?"

"You vere at the race meeting and had two horses; one it vas second and one vas not in a place." She smiled triumphantly at him. "You see, I know all!"

Robert was considerably disconcerted. He did not like the idea that someone was spying on him. He liked even less the idea that his every move was being relayed to Elizabet. But how? She could see his displeasure and tried to reassure him.

"I was not make the spy on you, I just vant to know all thing about you and know that you were safe."

Robert was considerably rattled. "I think it is the bloody limit!"

"It is not the limit. I vas not the spy. I vanted to learn to love you. How can I love you if I do not know you? Do not use that stable language to me."

"I am sorry, but it is a bit of a shock to find that my every move has been watched as if I were a criminal."

She sought to soothe him. "Do not vorry. If I had not interest, I would not have done this."

"Well, how did you do this impossible thing?"

"Do you truly tell me that you did not know?"

"No, I have no idea how you could have done it."

She grinned like a child that has a secret and is bursting to tell but wants to keep the suspense going as long as possible. "I cannot believe that the so good Captain of the Horse has not found out how I can do this thing."

Robert was getting irritated. Here suddenly had appeared what seemed to be a golden moment. What a romantic thing—to come out to meet him with two horses so that they could ride in together, but now it seemed to be rapidly turning bad. To think that somehow she had been spying on him all that time and that she seemed to know his every move, even as it happened! He did not reply. They rode on for some time in silence. All the while, she kept looking up in the sky. Suddenly she pointed.

"Look, there! Look, there is your answer."

High up a lone pigeon was flying purposefully and straight.

"Pigeons!"

"Yes, pigeons. Vith little messages tied to their legs. They are so quick. In a few hours I can have news from anywhere."

"Pigeons! I never thought of pigeons." Light dawned. He had noticed the flocks of pigeons almost everywhere. It had never occurred to him that some might be kept shut in for messenger service. "But a pigeon will only fly home...."

She laughed again. "Every time one of our coaches go out, it take some of our pigeons vith it. The driver he can use them to send messages back if he has need. Mostly they are put at our houses, so that they can use them to send news to us."

"The lunch basket! Under the drivers seat! I never looked! I assumed that it was the driver's lunch basket."

"Lunch basket?" She laughed out loud. "The Captain of the Horse who inspect everything, think it vas a lunch basket? When you go to the races, one of the grooms has the 'lunch basket'! After each race he send a bird. Sometimes we know the result before you have even left the course."

Robert was dumbfounded. It was so simple! Quick and fool proof! No, not quite fool proof.

"Look," he pointed.

The pigeon was still just in sight, but high above it a black dot was plummeting like a stone. It struck the pigeon in a cloud of feathers, with a force that broke its neck and they both tumbled to the ground. The falcon, for falcon it was, opened its wings and endeavoured to glide down with its prey. It landed some way off.

"That is one message that will not arrive."

They both galloped over to where the birds had fallen. The falcon was crouching over its kill, mantling it with its wing and tail, tearing at the feathers. When they rode up, it stared at them fiercely; then, rising laboriously, it flew off, carrying its prey with it. Elizabeth looked crestfallen.

"We lose many. Some are caught by falcons, like this one. Some are shot by ignorant peasants. Some lose their way. But most of them get home. If we have the very important message, we send two pigeons. One of them will arrive."

Robert had to admit that he was impressed. "But you can only receive messages. You cannot send them."

"No—yes. In our loft, we have the pigeons of other people. They look after our birds, we look after theirs. If we need, we send one of their birds back to them. It is very good. It vorks very vell. So we know always what is happening."

They rode away in silence. The pathetic little pile of feathers scattered in the wind.

"Robert, you have not told me why you make this visit. When the message came yesterday morning, vith my breakfast, it I could not believe. When this morning I had the message from the Inn that you had left, at once I had the horses fetch to set out to make for you this surprise—here I am." She flashed him a radiant smile. "Is not the best surprise that you could have?" She reached across and took his hand. He gave hers a firm squeeze. He was too full to speak. His anger at learning that he had been spied on evaporated when he remembered the reason for his visit. He had come to propose marriage to the girl he loved. Here they were together, riding through this beautiful countryside, the sun warm on their backs. The sky was clear and blue and full of the sound of unseen sky larks singing above them, yet he somehow could not bring himself to say that which filled his heart. Despite the romantic beauty of the situation, the moment was not right.

Just then they crested the hill. Stunned by the view, they stopped. There, spread out below them, was a long valley, nestled in between heavily wooded hills. Below them they could see the coach, a small dot crawling along, trailing its plume of dust behind it. At the end of the valley, on a long eminence, stood the castle, full in the warm sunlight. Beyond it the hills rolled out of sight into the blue distance. Elizabet drew in her breath and let out a long sigh of pride and satisfaction.

"Isn't that so beautiful. One day it vill all belong to me. Then to my children. Then to their children. Then to their children after them. I hope that they vill love and look after it like I do."

Robert was impressed too. He had never seen the castle from this vantage point. It was certainly impressive. They sat and drank in the view. A feeling of well-being welled up in Robert's breast. *This* was the place. *This* is the moment.

"Come on," Said Elizabet, urging on her horse. "We vill be late for dinner."

The moment had gone! Robert followed.

He was going to have to find some reasonable explanation to give to the Count for his sudden appearance. He could invent some tale about wanting to visit the stallion, to see if all the arrangements were made for the planned visit of some of Emil's mares in a few weeks time. At Roberts urging, the Count had bought a young stallion from England. It had produced some very promising foals and he had arranged that some of Emil's mares should come over to visit it, so that they too would produce some of its good foals. The Count had struck a hard bargain with the fee. Emil had demurred about the cost. But Robert saw it as a good investment. It was also a further chance for him to see Elizabet. He had been keen and eager enough to overcome Emil's indecision.

"Well?" called Elizabet over her shoulder. "Why have you come so sudden?"

He drew up beside her.

"Elizabet, will you stop a minute?"

They reined in. They were just by a ramshackled farmyard with a stinking pile of rotten vegetables and manure that was oozing black viscose liquid over the road. On the top a bloated dead sheep, its legs pointing in the air, lent its rotting smell to the throbbing stench. Elizabet looked about her in disgust.

"Look at this filth. No vonder they are peasants. They vill always be peasants if they live like this. Where is he? I vill tell him to clear this up, or he can get off this land. It is disgusting."

"Elizabet!" Robert almost shouted at her. "Elizabet! Will you be still a minute and listen to me!"

She reined in her horse and looked at him.

"Yes, Robert," she said quietly. "I am listening. What is it you vant to say?"

"Elizabet, will you marry me?"

She looked at him without flinching.

"What?"

"Will you marry me?"

"Well, of course I vill marry you. You know that—y ou have known that for five years, but we have to wait."

"No!" said Robert. "The waiting is over. If you will, we can get married now."

Slowly she understood and a huge smile spread across her face.

"You are free and we can get married?" She hardly dared speak.

"Yes. I have had an official letter from England. I am free. The waiting is over."

He took her hand, tears in his eyes. "Now we can begin our lives. I want to go back to England to have a memorial service for her, but when I return, I will be free. We can get married."

"Oh Robert, I do not know if to have happy for me or sad for you. I vill come with you to Eengland. You vill need someone to help you."

"Absolutely No! Out of the question. That is something that I have to do on my own. It would be completely wrong for you to be there. Do not feel sad for me. I have lived through all degrees of sadness and happiness, hope and despair, over the last five years. I do not feel sad anymore. I just want to see it all properly ended. When that is done, then we can get married. That is why I am here. I have come to tell you that I am free and that we can get married at last."

She reached out and took his hand. She started to laugh. She laughed until the tears ran down her face. Robert had to laugh too. Eventually he recovered.

"What on earth is so funny?"

"You," she gasped. "Oh, you Eengleesh! You are so romantic! Of all romantic places in the vorld, you propose to me at a stinking muck hill."

Robert looked about him. He too laughed.

"Come on. If we stay here any longer we will rot too."

They rode on. Robert had felt lightheaded. He had done it. It was said. She had said yes. He was suddenly full of panic. *Had* she said yes?

"I will have to ask you again."

"I hope that it is a more romantic spot next time."

They rode on in silence. She had said yes. That was all that mattered. He smiled happily at her. She reined in her horse and, taking his hand, leant across and kissed him.

"I love you Robert 'Enery"

"I love you too Elizabet."

They rode on again. Despite her happiness, a frown came over Elizabet's face.

"We vill have to speak too, vith my parents. I think that we vill have some big fuss."

"But you are over twenty-one—you can do what you like, surely?"

"That may be so in your country. Here it is different. I am a daughter. I must do what my father vishes. I think that you must get ready for the horse vhip." They both laughed. "It is not to laugh. My mother is not vell. She has become very frail. I do not vant to alarm her. I do not vant to go against the vishes of my father. For all his faults, he is my father and I love him. I vill not go against what he say."

"Oh, might this all make for more delay?" Robert felt an awful pit of anticlimax growing in his stomach.

"Well, after five years, what is a little time longer? If we are patient we vill vin."

"I've…we've been patient. We have endured for five years. The time is past for patience."

"Just a little longer. It vill happen. You vill see."

They had reached the castle and clattered across the wooden bridge over the moat. Robert looked up. The roof, as usual, had a crowd of pigeons sitting on it and there were a few flying round the dovecot. How could he have been so stupid and not worked that out for himself. He would go to the dovecot one day and have a look, to see exactly what was going on in there. A boy came running out and took their horses. Elizabet spoke sharply to him and he mumbled a reply and led them off.

"Something is wrong. One of the grooms should have come. The boy vould not answer me. He just mumbled and ran. Come on."

She almost ran up the steps to the door. It did not open. Robert pushed past her and opened it to let her in.

"Frank?" She called again. "Frank!"

The old man came hurrying towards her.

"Frank, what is going on? Why was there no groom to take my horses? Why was there no one at the door?"

"Have you not heard, Graffinflein?" The old man wrung his hands. "We have had news today. The peasants are not working. They demand more money. The Count is beside himself with rage. He will not give into demands! He will not pay more."

Elizabet listened to him in horror. "Is this true? How can it be true? Where is everyone?"

The old man bobbed in anguish. "I fear Graffinflein that they have gone."

"Gone? All?"

"Yes my Lady. They have gone to tend their crops."

"Their crops? They are not their crops, they are our crops!"

"Not anymore, Graffinflein. They say that they should have the produce from the crops that they tend."

Elizabet went white with rage. "Where is my father? I must speak with him!"

"He is in the breakfast room, Graffinflein."

He went to open the door for her, but she had already burst in. Robert, who had with difficulty followed what was going on, followed her. The Count sat in front of the fireplace, a large glass of brandy in his hand. The fire was not lit, or the hearth tidied and the breakfast things were still scattered over the table.

"Father, is this true what I hear? It cannot be. Tell me it is not true." She knelt down beside his chair. She took his hand. He focused on her with difficulty.

"All the servants have deserted us. What shall we do? How shall we manage?"

He caught site of Robert standing uncertainly in the doorway. "Ha, the late 'Enery. What do you vant? What are you doing here?"

Robert started on his carefully prepared speech about the Stallion.

"Do not talk to me of horses! We can have no more the horses. Without my servants and my crops, I am ruined. I have nothing. The horses they vill have to go."

"But papa, we still have the farms and the Estate."

"The manager of the Estate he has not yet come, but I know what he vill say. They are all peasants who vork there. They will leave their vork and go home to vork on the land, and take my crops! We shall have nothing. Everything it vill be gone. You must not tell your mother. We do not vant to alarm her. We vill have to do the best we can until it is clear what vill happen." Elizabet got up and kissed her father and marched to the kitchen.

The French Cook was busy working on his own. He threw his hands in the air in a gesture of hopelessness when Elizabet appeared.

"'Ow can I work on my own?" he demanded angrily. "I need someone to 'elp! To fetch theengs, to carry, to prepare the vegetables, to make the dough. I cannot cook eef I have not people to 'elp me!"

"Cook," Elizabet said. "Everyone seems to have gone. We are going to have to do the best we can." She threw her coat onto the kitchen chair and tied an apron round her. She took up a tray. "I vill clear the breakfast room. Robert, if you could bring sticks to light the fire in the blue room, that would be most good!"

Robert made for the back door. "I will check the horses first. Then bring some wood in for the fire, when I come back."

As everyone departed, the cook realised he was still on his own.

"And who is going to 'elp me?"

Elizabet, who had heard him as she went out with the tray, stuck her head round the door. "You 'elp your bloody self!"

Cook gaped open mouthed. He had never been spoken to like that before and certainly not by the lady! He leapt into action as if prodded by a needle.

When Robert got outside, he found no one in the yard. The two hounds, which were in their kennel, jumped up, winning against the bars as he appeared. He went over to them. They had no water and no food. They obviously hadn't been seen to recently. He hunted round and, finding a bucket, drew some water for them from the well.

"You will have to make do with that for now, lads."

Leaving them happily slavering away in their bowl, he looked in the stable. The horses tethered in there were uneasily stamping in their stalls. A quick look confirmed that they had no water or feed. He threw off his jacket, undid his waistcoat, rolled up his sleeves and set about fetching them water. He found some hay and filled their racks.

"You will have to make do with that for the time being."

He walked round to the front of the Castle. The coach and horses still stood there, just as Joseph had left them. Robert climbed on the box. Slowly, he drove the coach round to the back. It was a long time since he had driven a coach and four in hand, but he took it slowly so that he had time to gauge the width of the turns. He drew the coach into the furthest corner that he could find. There was no way that he was going to be able to manhandle it into the coach house on his own. The best he could do was to leave it as much out of the way as possible. He unhitched the horses one at a time and put them in their stalls. He gave them feed and water and hung their harness up in the tack room. They would have to manage without being done down tonight. They were dirty and dusty but they would have to wait. He would have dismissed any of his employees if they had put a horse away un-groomed and cleaned, but these were exceptional circumstances. He found the two horses that he and Elizabet had ridden in a loose box, with their harness still on. He took this off and watered and fed them both. They, too, would have to wait until later. Having settled the horses as well as he could, he found a bin with some corn and so he fed the poultry and collected the eggs. He brought these to the kitchen.

The cook was in despair. He could find no asparagus. He must have asparagus. The young pigeons that had been promised had not arrived. There were no fresh vegetables. There were no flowers for the table. What was he going to do?

Robert went out to the dovecote. He had never seen inside and so he was mildly curious. He opened the door. He was almost overwhelmed by the smell. The inside of the wall was lined with little pigeonholes, most of which were occupied. This was obviously not the place where the messenger pigeons were kept. As soon as he opened the door the flying adults took to the wing and flew round inside, stirring up the dust and feathers. They could come and go through the louvered lantern at the top and most fluttered up and out of that. There was a large post in the middle, reaching from floor to roof. Fixed to this was an angled ladder that could be pushed round so that it was possible to climb up and reach into every pigeonhole. Everything was covered with droppings and the floor was piled high with droppings and feathers. Cautiously, he picked his way to the ladder and climbed up. It was not long before he found in the pigeonholes enough fat fledgling pigeons to meet the demand of the moment. The first ones he found were too young and small, but there were enough that were nearly ready to fly that were fat and big enough. He took them to the kitchen. The cook took one look at them and immediately started to rave and shout.

"'ow can I cook them, they 'ave still their 'eads and feet and feathers!"

Robert took them to a back house. He quickly plucked and dressed them, then took them back to the cook. He threw the little corpses down on the kitchen table.

"Here you are. Would you like me to cook the bloody things as well?"

Taking up a basket, he went down to the kitchen garden to see what he could find. To his surprise, as he picked his way through the rows of beans and young carrots, he found he was actually enjoying himself. This was quite fun. He gathered an enormous selection of vegetables and staggered back to the kitchen with his overflowing basket. There was something satisfying, therapeutic, about bringing in the produce. He brought his basket triumphantly into the kitchen and put it on the table. The cook descended on it and started to throw the vegetables out.

"What ees thees? I cannot use this. Thees ees no good."

Robert snatched the basket from him and tipped all the vegetables out onto the floor.

"If they are no bloody good, go and get your own!"

He thrust the empty basket into the startled man's hands and stormed out. He found the barrow for the firewood and went to the Stick lodge. The logs were large, but there was a heavy splitting axe near by.

He set a log on the block and with one hefty swing of the axe, split it in half. He put the two halves in the barrow.

"The next one is that arrogant Frenchman's head!" He set it on the block and cleaved it in half with a mighty swing. By the time the barrow was full, he had exhausted his anger with the cook. He trundled it round to the French window of the dining room and rattled on the glass. Elizabet was busy laying the table. She ran over to let him in.

"Where have you been? We must get this fire lit or the room vill not be varm."

Robert quickly explained and told how he had enjoyed working off his anger.

She laughed. "It is time someone told that silly man off. He terrorise the whole household vith his anger. When you have finished vith the wood, you must change. You vill have to carry your own cases up. It cannot be helped. You can have the tower room again. It is always kept ready. I do not know how we are going to manage. We have only Frank and the cook. You vill have to help me vith the serving. Do not pour soup into anyone's lap."

Robert went and opened the window in the blue sitting room and then trundled round with the barrow and carried in the wood. He laid the fire and lit it and placed the guard in front to catch the sparks. He put the wood barrow away and came back into the kitchen. As he entered he could hear raised voices. There was Elizabet. She had a large kitchen knife and had forced the cook back against the hot cooking range with the point sticking in his ribs.

"I am Graffinflein!" she shouted at the cowering man, who did not know whether the sharp knife in his ribs was a worse peril than the hot stove burning his backside. She prodded harder. "I am not one of the little kitchen maids to be bullied. You do not speak to me like that. I am mistress in this house. You speak to me like that again and I stick this in you and throw you in the moat to feed the Carp. Do you understand?"

"Yes, yes Graffinflein. I am very sorry, Mistress. Owwee." He squirmed as the hot stove burnt his behind. Elizabet kept him pinned there until he cried out again and then released him.

"Do not forget." She flung the knife down on the table. She saw Robert in the doorway. "Bloody cooks," she said and stormed out. Robert was hard put to keep a straight face. He followed quickly after her.

"They are vegetarian."

"What are you talking about?" A slight flash of irritation sounded in her voice.

"Carp. They are vegetarian. If you throw him in the moat they won't eat him. Oh, and by the way, don't use that kitchen language in front of me."

She looked long and hard at him and then laughed. "Touché," she said and laughed again. "I think I burn his bum." She giggled like a schoolgirl. "Serve him right. Take that bucket of flowers and put petals in the fingerbowls. They is on the sideboard there. Put some vater in each from that jug."

She took a great handful of flowers and, breaking them off short with her teeth, quickly arranged them in the gold ormolu centrepiece on the table. Robert scattered the petals in the fingerbowls. She came over to see.

"More than that." She took up some flowers and threw in handfuls of petals. "That is better. It vill hide the water when it get mucky. Come. We go and change. The guests vill be here soon." She turned and quickly looked round the table. "Pretty," she said with some satisfaction. "I like doing this. I like the table to look nice. I like my guests to see that we have for them, made the effort." She dusted her hands together. "Come on. We vill race. I vill be changed and down again before you are."

She ran for the stairs. Robert grabbed up his case and ran after her, but he was considerably hampered by the weight. She had disappeared by the time he got to the top of the stairs. He hurried to his room and opened his case. Eventually he found all he needed.

He struggled into his stiff shirt and with much cursing threaded his studs and cufflinks.

Eventually he had his tie tied, his hair brushed and his coat on. Whilst he was giving a final tweak to his tie, he noticed his fingernails were still black from his foray in the vegetable garden. He quickly found his pocket-knife and cleaned them. He poured some water from his jug into his basin and gave them a quick scrub. Good as new! Then he noticed that whilst scrubbing he had sprayed soapy water all over his jacket. He quickly took it off and sponged it down with his face flannel. Grabbing it up, he ran out of the room, struggling into it as he ran down the stairs. He paused at the door of the blue drawing room to collect himself, then entered.

"Ah, it is the late Herr 'Enery again."

"Good evening, Count. Good evening, Countess. It is kind of you to receive me and I am pleased to see you looking so well."

She sat by the fire. He took her proffered hand and raised it to his lips, in the way that he had learned.

"I am pleased to see you 'ere again, Herr 'Enery. It vill be nice for you tonight. We 'ave some guests coming to us for dinner. We shall have a happy evening. After dinner, perhaps our daughter vill play on the piano for us. Where is she? August, where is Elizabet?"

"She is still upstairs changing," said Robert with some satisfaction.

"No she is not," said Elizabet. She played a chord on the piano. "I am here." She played two or three other chords. Robert turned in astonishment. He was sure that she had not been there when he came in. She smiled coyly at him.

"Well, Robert, who won?" She played a few more chords. She wore a pale blue gown that left her shoulders bare. Her hair was piled casually up on her head and held at the back by a silver comb which had some small yellow rosebuds threaded through it.

She smiled smugly as she played. Robert was puzzled. She looked so pretty sitting there, the soft light glowing on her shoulders. How could he have not seen her when he came in?

Frank was teetering round with a tray of drinks. He paused in front of the Countess.

"Do you wish to wait, Countess, or will you begin dinner?"

"Wait? Why should we not wait? Of course we vill wait. They are not late are they?"

Frank bowed slightly. "I understood, Countess, that they were to arrive an hour ago."

"An hour? You say an hour? Something must have delayed them. Are there floods? Has there been a gale? Perhaps a tree is blown down and blocked the road. Perhaps they have had an accident! August! August!"

The Count woke with a start.

"August, send a boy out at once to see if they are stranded on the road somewhere."

The Count fumbled for words.

"Shall I go?" said Robert. "From which way are they coming? What are their names? I do not want to bring in any waifs and strays that I find on the road!"

"No, no, you cannot possibly go, Herr 'Enery. My husband he vill send out a boy to look for them."

"It is no trouble Countess."

Robert made for the door. At that moment a loud knocking could be heard. Frank put down his tray and excusing himself, left the room and went to open the front door. They could hear voices in the Hall and presently Frank returned.

"Count and Countess," he announced formally, "Doctor Hoffman!"

The Doctor was a short and energetic man, dressed in evening clothes, but with his riding boots. He strode briskly into the room. He bowed to the Countess and kissed her hand. He shook hands with the Count, who was still struggling to stand up. He quickly moved to the piano and kissed Elizabet's hand. He returned to the fireplace, shaking hands with Robert as he passed.

"I am the bearer of bad tidings, I am afraid. I expect that you know what is going on. It makes it impossible for us to come tonight. We have no grooms to drive the coach and attend to the horses. My phaeton is too small for all of us and I could not ask my wife and daughters to ride over. The return journey in the dark would be too much for them. I alone have ridden over to say to you we are very sorry, but we are unable to attend. I would have sent a boy, but I do not seem to have any at present and so I have come myself, so that you are not inconvenienced." He took a drink from the tray that Frank proffered. The Countess looked puzzled.

"But why 'ave you no people? What is happened?"

Before they could stop him the Doctor had launched into an explanation.

"Have you not heard? All serfs and peasants have stopped work for more money. They are going to take the crops off the land that they work. The simpletons, they think that they will be rich. Most of them will hardly be able to produce enough to support their families, yet alone have surplus to sell. Even if they do, it will be in such small quantities that they will not find a good market for it. The only people who might buy it will be other peasants. They will not want it, because they will be trying to sell their own."

"But this is terrible. You mean the peasants are going to take the crops off the land? But this is terrible." The Countess went quite white. Elizabet hurried over to her.

The Doctor swallowed his drink. "Thank you very much, just what the Doctor ordered." He laughed. "I am sure that you will understand, but I must return home to look after my family; as they are alone, we have no one left there now." He quickly shook hands with everyone and Frank showed him out. The Countess was distressed.

"This is terrible. What shall we do? Have our servants gone as vell?" She knew the answer from their silent faces. "We cannot possibly stay 'ere without servants."

"Mother, do not vorry, the cook is still here and Frank. Robert has been helping too, we vill be all right." Frank was hovering near and said something quickly to Elizabet.

"Yes Frank, please, we vill come through before Cook throws the food into the moat. Come on Mother, Papa, come on, we vill go in for dinner."

She shepherded them through to the dining room. Robert put some more wood on the fire and set up the guard and followed them. He arrived in the dining room to find a bit of a family dilemma going on. The Count and Countess had taken their usual places at either end of the table, but this would not do for Elizabet.

"This is ridiculous. We cannot sit so. Mother, come and sit here beside Papa. I vill sit next to papa on the other side. Robert, you sit next to my mother."

She pushed them all into place. They sat down and the Count, squinting uncertainly at the person on his right, found that for the first time in thirty years of married life, he was sitting next to his wife. The meal was served by

Frank. As it progressed, Robert was pleased to see that most of the vegetables that he had gathered from the garden did in fact appear. Obviously Elizabet's threat with the carving knife had been enough to stop the histrionics and inject some realism into the situation.

They spent the whole meal discussing the turn of events and what they were going to do. In the end it was decided that they would return to Vienna the next day. The castle would be shut up and Frank and Schmidt would be left behind to look after it until the situation resolved itself. The Count felt that once the people had found that their freedom was not the wonderful thing they had supposed, they would be eager for their old jobs back. In fact, it was a blessing in disguise for there would be the chance to make some much needed changes.

Robert felt that he could handle the coach with two horses, so he would drive them to the steamer and bring the coach back. The next day he would ride out to the Stud, to see that things were alright there. Most of the people there lived in the Bothy and had no land, so they should still be there. They should be able to provide the basic care to the horses until a decision about their future could be made. That would depend on the turn of events. He was then to return to Bavaria. Someone from the Stud would have to come with him to the Inn by the ferry to take the horse back.

CHAPTER 24

"This is not what I had wanted for you." Elizabet's mother carefully adjusted the veil, so that it hung in neat folds down her daughter's back. "I had so wanted you to have a beautiful wedding in the Cathedral. The Bishop would have come, it would have been so lovely."

Elizabet bit her lip. She had heard this non-stop since it had been finally agreed the she and Robert could get married. Her mother had been unwilling to accept the situation, but when faced with Elizabet's bombshell she had quickly given in.

Robert's request to the Count to marry his daughter, now that he was free to do so, had been flatly turned down. He was quite unsuitable as a husband for the future Countess and father of the next Count. Besides, Elizabet was already betrothed! Even when it was pointed out that the proposed suitor had long ago given up any idea of a liaison and was married to someone else, he would not give in. Despite many hours of discussions, he was adamant and would not be moved. He would not relent.

Elizabet had stayed very calm despite the hours of obstinate refusal. In the end she had to admit defeat. Even though she had waited five years and refused many other offers of marriage that had been made to her, her father still would not relent.

"You do not marry the trainer of the race horses—that is the end."

Nothing would change his mind. She appealed to her mother, to intercede for her but to no avail. Nothing that anyone could say would change his mind. Robert was desperate. Elizabet, despite his cajoling, would not go against her father's wishes. She was adamant that the only way forward was to make him change his mind. Robert was exasperated.

"You might as well try to stop the flow of the Danube with a tea strainer as to get him to change his mind."

"Do not be so weak. The trouble with you, Robert, is that you give in too easily."

"Give in too easily?" Robert was angry and showed it. "You have had five years in which to persuade him to change his mind! Still you have failed. It would be better for us to go away and get married, then let him know afterwards." She had looked at him, tears in her eyes.

"I could not do that. It would break his heart. He may be an obstinate old ass, but he is my father and I love him still. I could not make him break his heart. Be patient still, my darling, I have a way which will make him change his mind. Trust me, you will see. Next week it is his *Namenstag*. I will ask Mother to let me arrange a dinner for him. He will change his mind then. He will be so angry with me, but it will not break his heart."

Robert was intrigued. After five years, what was going to suddenly make him change his mind? He did not have to wait long to find out.

Elizabet obtained permission from her mother to arrange the dinner for his *Namenstag*. She got out and cleaned the best silver. The table was decorated with the racing trophies and extravagant arrangements of flowers and fruits amidst a veritable forest of candles. The meal was endless in its variety and delicacy. The wine flowed through a regiment of glasses in bewildering abundance as each course progressed. It was not until after dinner, when he was settled in his chair by the fire in the blue drawing room, with a glass of his best brandy in his hand, sated with fresh crayfish, clear beef consome, pate de frois grois, grilled mountain trout, roast wild boar, wind torte and ripe figs and peaches from the garden, that she tried to raise the subject again.

"You think that you can fat me up like the goose for the slaughter. You are wrong. I say always no! Always no it vill be!"

Again she got the answer that she expected. She smiled at Robert. Reaching across to where he sat beside her on the sofa, she squeezed his hand.

"Trust me," she whispered.

"Papa, I am very sorry to tell you this: Robert and I vill have to be married. I am have a baby."

There was a deathly silence. The Countess who was usually very pallid went whiter still. She stifled a little cry with her lace handkerchief. The Count struggled to his feet. He glowered at Robert.

"You bring this disgrace on us?" he roared. "You come into my house! Drink my wine. Eat my foods, then you bring this disgrace upon us! This shame! How can you sit there? It is the horsewhip that I should have given years gone."

Robert was completely taken aback. He tried to protest his innocence, but Elizabet signalled to him to keep quiet.

"Be silent!" roared the Count. "I do not vish to hear what you have to say." He took a large gulp at his brandy and sank back in his chair. "We cannot this scandal have. There is nothing to do. You must get married straight away, so that no one know. You vill have to put up vith being the vife of the race horse trainer. We shall not be able to hold up our heads, when people know!"

The Countess had dissolved into silent tears but between sobs and recriminations she finally agreed that that was the only course open.

The count banged his glass down on a side table. "Vith you, my daughter, I have much anger—you vill go to bed. How could you shame us so? It is too terrible. We vill call the priest to talk about the quickest arrangements we can make, tomorrow. To you, 'Enery, I have nothing to say but disgust. I do not vish even to speak vith you."

Robert saw that retreat was the best course. "If you do not want to hear what I have to say, I will retire. I will wish both of you goodnight." He bowed to them both and left the room. Through the closed door he could hear the sound of a loud and acrimonious argument. He waited outside, feeling that he should go back in to defend Elizabet, but whilst he was still undecided, she emerged, looking slightly white, but with a triumphant smile on her face.

"Well?" she fell into Roberts arms. "Did I not say that I would get them to agree?"

"How could you!" Robert scolded." How could you treat them like that?"

"Well, they have treat me like a little girl. They would always have found the way of saying no. Mother was hinting the other day that it might be best if I went with the Little Sisters after all. Now I have made this too late."

"Well, there must have been another way. Now they think that I have seduced their daughter. They will think even less of me than they do now."

"Well, so what! At last they have agreed to us getting married. We vill not have to wait any longer."

The priest for the village Church was summoned the next morning. The arrangements were quickly made. The Countess was, however, adamant that it should be a quiet affair. The Count, too, was all for haste before the real problem should become apparent. The Countess insisted the wedding should be quietly conducted in the village Church. Any ideas that she had had of having a grand wedding in the Cathedral were abandoned.

"You cannot marry the Captain of the Horse in the Cathedral. Everyone would at us laugh. We would become the laughing stock of the neighbourhood. If you persist in getting married, it will be a quiet service, in the village church, with just a few friends and close family."

Elizabet and Robert had not argued. As far as they were concerned, the sooner it was over and done with, the better. They had no wish to have the bother of a large wedding in the Cathedral with the Bishop. Elizabet's mother, though she had insisted on the arrangement, was far from happy with it. The priest from the village tried his best to make her change her mind. He could see his chance of officiating in the Cathedral before the Bishop fading away.

"It will mean that you will get few presents. Many of your friends will turn their backs on you."

"Mother, we do not need presents. Robert is established in his house. We have nearly everything that we need. As for my friends who shun me, let them. We will soon find out who are our real friends. They will stick by us. The others, poof, good riddance!"

"You will find that Society will shun you too, especially when all can see that you are with child"

"There has been no trouble up to now. Everyone has been very kind. I am not the first person to have a baby."

"Yes indeed. When he has been the Eengleesh trainer, he is the curiosity, but you will find that when you are his wife, it will change. Everyone will notice when your child is born. You will be shunned, even despised by everyone."

"Oh mother, you are so old fashioned. We will be all right. We shall be so happy together that we will not be bothered by other silly people." The argument and discussion had raged on for days, but as the preparations for the wedding proceeded her mother had finally decided to make the best of the bad job. She had looked out her own wedding veil and was now tenderly arranging it on her daughter.

"Come, or we will be late!" the Count called from outside the bedroom. Elizabet's mother kissed her daughter.

"Good luck, my daughter, may God be with you. Here is your father come to take you to the Church." She smiled at the maid. "Please let him in."

The Count stomped into the room when the door was opened for him. He already had his coat on and carried his hat and stick.

"Come on! Come on! Always you women are late. We must leave or we vill be late." He stopped at the sight of his daughter. She did a little pirouette.

"Will I do, papa? Will you be proud of me?"

He looked at her speechless. At last he fumbled out his handkerchief and blew his nose loudly whilst he overcame the lump in his throat.

"Yes, my dear, you will do very well, very well indeed, but I shall not be proud. You are the bad girl. You go against our vishes." He blew his nose again. "But for all that you are the bad girl, you are still my daughter and I still love you. This is not what I would vish for my daughter but I hope that you vill be very happy. Now come, it is time to go, or we vill be very late."

Elizabet's mother accepted her cloak from the maid and, kissing her daughter one last time, hurried from the room. The Count shuffled in embarrassment. He had rehearsed many times the advice he was going to give his daughter, but now it just did not seem appropriate.

"Are you sure you vish to go ahead with this? It is not too late to change your mind?"

Elizabet smiled at him. "Yes Papa, quite sure. We have been through this many, many times. We shall be very happy." She took his arm. "Come on," she smiled up at him, "or we vill be late! Come. Lead your little daughter to the Altar."

When they reached the front door, the carriage with Elizabet's mother in it was just leaving the Courtyard and their coach was just drawing up. It was bedecked with ribbons and Joseph had a white ribbon tied to the end of his whip.

Frank hastened forward to open the door of the coach so that they could enter. He was getting very old and stooped and found his extra work very tiring.

Most of the people had returned to work at the Castle once the euphoria of working for themselves had died down and the realities of their true situation had been forced upon them, but they were still short handed. Many of the Count's people found that their crops did not provide much surplus for sale. They were soon desperately short of money and not able to buy the things they needed. Many of them found that they were worse off then they had been before. They worked harder and they earned less. This had caused much bitterness, which was aggravated by the Count taking a much firmer and more dictatorial role in the way that the land was managed. Many were forced to sell their land back to the Count in order to survive. The Count would not re-employ those who were not good workers or with whom he had some difference. Some people were left without work or any means of support. Several families had thus been forced to move away to find work. This further added to the discontent the people felt.

It was a rather sullen little crowd that had gathered at the Church to watch everyone arrive. Had it not been that Elizabet and Robert were quite well liked by everyone, there would have been no one there at all. Inside there was a very small congregation. The village choir sung the Mass and led the Hymns. The incumbent was a young curate who was completely overawed and kept loosing his place in the Service.

Eventually Elizabet and Robert walked out of the Church, man and wife. They rode back together to the Castle for the wedding breakfast, in the blue landau normally only used by the Countess. The reception and the wedding breakfast, too, were fairly subdued with only a few friends present. There was no grand ball arranged for the evening and they had decided that they would leave in the afternoon to spend their first night together at an Inn. They planned to spend a week at a resort on the Black Sea before returning to Robert's House in Bavaria.

Elizabet soon found that her mother's predictions were true. She found that the little House in Bavaria, provided for Robert, was very small after the space of the Castle. One day when she was riding with Emil in the Park she tackled him on the subject.

"That lovely house down by the lake, that stands empty. Would it not be possible for us to move in there? The Lodge is very small for a family and if we have children we will be very cramped."

"Elizabet, my dear, that house is for members of my family who might have need of it."

"But I am a member of your family and my need is great."

"Yes, but you are also the wife of my Captain of the Horse! It certainly would not do to put the Captain of the Horse there. The house that you occupy is provided for him because of his office. It is convenient to the stables and the park. It is very adequate for one in his position."

"But it is not adequate for me. It is very small. We are so crowded."

"Well, there it is. I do not want to say to you 'Told you so,' but you should have thought of it before. We all warned you enough about how things would be different if you were to marry Robert."

"But you like Robert."

"Yes, I do like Robert. He is good with my horses. I consider him a friend and hope that he thinks the same of me, but when it comes down to it, he is the

Captain of the Horse. That is why he is here." He paused. "That is why I pay him."

They rode on in silence. Elizabet knew there was no point in pursuing the matter further. Emil had very quickly put his finger on the divide that existed between them, one that even the ties of family marriage would not bridge. She was sensible enough to resign herself to the situation. She soon adapted to life in 'her little cottage' as she described it.

However, she did find it quiet. She was not able to attend the "season" in Vienna and Prague, as had been her habit, for Robert could not take that amount of time away from his horses. She went to stay with her friends in Vienna to attend some of the concerts and the opera, but things were not the same. Her friends were unmarried and full of chatter about their romantic liaisons. She was married and so very much out of it. She was fed up, too, with fending off the question, 'Where is your husband?' and the astonished look of the faces of those who replied, 'Oh, he works, does he!' She tried to ignore news of events to which they had not been invited. She had a small circle of friends who lived near them so she was able to assuage her social urges through them.

There was still the racing season. She and Robert were welcome guests at parties in connection with the races. At least with racing Robert was an important part of the scene. Training horses both for Emil and for her father had earned him considerable status in racing circles. This she could enjoy. She had to be content.

The word had soon gone round that they had had to get married, which was why it was such a small wedding, done in such haste; but when, after due time, it became obvious that she was not pregnant, the whispers became more confused. At last her father tackled her about it. He was furious when he realised how easily he had been duped and would not speak to them for months. However, he relented when Elizabet finally was able to tell her mother she was expecting. He was certain that the child would be a boy, to be the heir that he so desperately wanted, even if it was the son of the Captain of the Horse.

Robert had continued his habit of visiting the stables after his evening meal and sometimes he would be gone for hours. She had a small piano brought over from her parent's home and contented herself, in the evenings when she was alone, in playing it.

Her time, however, was soon filled with the care of her firstborn child and the others that followed. Their first three children were all girls, and were born fairly quickly—Maria, Helen and Olga. Though Robert delighted in them, he did not give up hope of one day producing a son. The Count, having got over his initial disappointment, pinned his hopes on the arrival of the second, but when this too was a daughter he became more and more agitated. When the third child, too, was a daughter, he was beside himself.

"What do you expect, if you marry the Captain of the Horse. He is always late! He cannot now make the sons. What vill happen to all these girls? They vill have to go to the Convent. No one vill vant to marry the daughters of the Captain of the Horse. It is ridiculous making all these girls." Elizabet had long given up worrying about his grumblings. She could turn a deaf ear to all his complaints. Had it not been for her mother, she would not have made the effort to go to visit him. The Countess had always been in a slightly delicate state of health, but though she delighted in her little granddaughters, they soon tired her. She would take herself to bed when Elizabet came to stay, only permitting the children to visit her one at a time. It soon became apparent that this was not an act and that her health was declining rapidly. The Doctor Hoffman made his best efforts, but none of the many potions that he proscribed seemed to have any effect.

One autumn Elizabet was again staying at the Castle on one of her periodic visits. She was sitting with her mother whilst the children were downstairs with their nanny doing some mornings lessons.

The Countess stretched out a hand and stayed Elizabet's sowing.

"Tell me, child, are you happy?"

Elizabet was startled by the question. She hesitated in her reply. It was not something she had ever really considered. When they were first married she had been ecstatic. She had enjoyed their little house and their new baby. She felt that the house was far too small. There were so many things in her past life that she missed that she shut them out of her mind. She did the best that she could to content herself with the present.

"Yes mother. I am happy. Life it is different. I have to content myself with different things. There are many things which I miss, but then there are many things that I have. I have my darling daughters, they keep me very busy. It is good now. Emil has engaged a Governess to teach his children. He has said that she can teach our children as well, so they go to her every day for lessons. This they can do until they are older and go to the Eengleesh School. It is good. They learn well. It gives me the chance to have a rest."

"You need to rest, my child?"

"Yes mother. The girls are so exhausting; besides, I have again the little visitor." She patted her tummy and smiled at her mother.

"You are with child again, my daughter?" The Countess could not hide her look of surprise. "Perhaps this time it will be a boy."

"No, mother, it is another girl, I am sure."

"Well, do not tell your father anymore the disappointment. He will be more cross than he is already. I wish you well of it my dear. But I fear that I will not be here to see it."

Elizabet looked at her mother, fear in her eyes.

"Do not look at me like that," her mother continued. "I am not afraid. I know that soon I will be passed from this place to be with my maker."

Elizabet took her mothers hand. "Mother, do not say such things. You will soon be better and well again. I will not hear such talk."

"Do not distress yourself, child. I am not sad. Why are we here on this earth? Why? So that we learn to love God, so that when we die we are ready for heaven with Him." She held up her hand to stop Elizabet's protest." I am old. I have lived long on this earth. I have seen many things and done many things too." She smiled quietly to herself. "Now it is time for me to face my maker. But I have learnt that he loves me. He will forgive all the silly little things that I have done wrong in my life. He will welcome me. I am ready for Him when 'e calls." She lay back on her pillow. "I shall be sorry that I do not see the little one, but I will watch from on my cloud to see how it is going. I am sorry to leave you with the care of your father. He becomes more and more the trouble with every day, but it cannot be helped."

Elizabet stood up. She gathered the bedclothes round her mother. "Shush, shush, mother. This is silly talk. We will be here for Christmas. We will make many happy times. It will be lovely to be all together again. Then the winter will soon be past. The spring will come. You will feel better again. Rest now. I will bring you some broth presently."

"No, you will not come for Christmas. I can not receive you for Christmas. I will find it too much. Besides, Robert will have the duties with his horses. He will not be able to be away for Christmas."

"Always he is with his blessed horses. Every Christmas since we have been married, the blessed horses have to come first! Just for once, surely someone else could look after them at Christmas."

Elizabet's mother smiled weakly. "Do not say we did not tell you. He is the Captain of the Horse. That is what they do; you had five years to find out all about that."

"But that was before we were married. I thought that once he was married things would be different." She left the room but as she passed through the door, sad tears rolled down her cheeks.

She left the castle a week later, with the children and her nanny, to return to Bavaria.

The winter seemed long for her, as she feared every day that news would come from her home. The snows were deep that year; they lasted through into the spring. For the most part, heavy with child, she was confined to the house, not wishing to risk a fall in the snow. She became very fractious and irritable with her enforced imprisonment in the crowded confines of their small house. It was almost a relief when Robert came in one evening in April with a small scrap of paper in his hand.

"Elizabet, I have some serious news for you. Here, sit down in this chair. Emil gave me this note. A pigeon has arrived from your father. It seems that your mother is failing fast."

Although Elizabet had been fearing and half expecting this news all winter, her hopes had raised with the coming of spring. It was a great shock to her.

"I must go to her at once and be with her." She stood up. Robert caught her shoulders.

"It is completely out of the question. You cannot make that journey now. The baby is due at any time. I will not hear of it. I am very sorry, but you simply cannot go!"

"Robert, of course I must go. I cannot not go. I vill make the short journeys each day. I shall be all right."

"Listen to what I say, Elizabet, you are *not* going."

Elizabet was angry and there were tears in her eyes. "Why always must I fight for everything? I tell you that I am going and that is that. The children vill be all right 'ere. There is Anna, and the maid and the nanny to look after you all, you vill all be all right. I am young and strong and I too vill be all right. I vill leave in the morning. Please order the coach for me to be ready to leave at 9 o'clock."

Robert knew that when her chin stuck out like that, there was no changing her mind. She was much like her father. Once she had decided something, nothing would change her mind. He knew that there was no point in prolonging the argument.

"Well, you must take your maid with you. She can look after you. Whatever you do, make short journeys each day so that you can get a good night's rest in between each stage. If you feel any discomfort at all, you must stop on the way for a day or two of rest before going on. Do you understand? You must not do too much to tire yourself out. You do not want the baby born by the roadside, like some gypsy child under the hedge!"

She looked at him defiantly. "Do not be so ridiculous. I shall be all right. I can take care of myself. The train is good, the boat is calm, the coach journey is not too long. Send a message to have Joseph meet me off the boat in three days' time."

She set out the next morning with her maid, well wrapped up against the cold, charcoal warmers packed round her feet. By the time she reached the boat, she was already beginning to wish she had obeyed Robert. The baby was turning and kicking in her stomach. She was sure labour would begin at any minute. The long journey from the boat to the Castle in the Count's rickety, ill sprung coach proved too much for her. She caught her maid's hand.

"I am sorry, but the pains are starting. Please call out to Joseph to make haste!"

In panic the maid leaned out of the window. She shouted to Joseph: "Quickly, quickly, Joseph, the mistress, she start in labour."

Joseph took a long second to digest this news, then, gathering the reins up in his hand, he let out a yell that startled the horse. With a couple of thunderous cracks of his whip over their heads, he set them flying along as if the slavering jaws of hell were at their very heels. The coach lurched forward, creaking and protesting at every joint. It bounced and swayed sickeningly over every pothole. Elizabet and the maid hung on inside as best they could, perched on the edge of their seats to try and mitigate the jolts and bumps. The maid leant out of the window again.

"Oh hurry, please hurry! Quicker! The pains are coming quicker, please hurry."

Joseph reached for his whip and cracked it with renewed desperation over the horses' heads. "Schnell, Schnell!" he yelled at them. They renewed their flagging efforts and pounded along, sweat and foam streaking their heaving, sweating sides, their gasping breath wheezing and rattling from their straining lungs.

"Oh be quick!" called the maid again. "The baby will soon be come. Can you not alarm them at the Castle? Do something—let them know we are coming." They clattered over the river bridge.

"Not long now. We nearly there!" shouted Joseph over his shoulder. "Yow, yow!" he shouted to the horses. "Horn, horn, blow the horn!" he shouted to the postillion, who was using both hands to hang on. At the peril of being thrown off the coach, he took up the horn and blew for all he was worth.

A maid in the castle, dusting one of the rooms, had a window open and heard the sound. She looked out and saw the coach coming in the distance, a cloud of dust billowing behind it. She quickly ran downstairs.

"Mr Frank, Mr Frank!" she called out frantically. She ran round looking for him. "Oh, Mr Frank!" At last she found him in the pantry.

"Catch your breath, child. Whatever is the matter?"

"Mr Frank, I was upstairs, and I heard this horn blowing and I…"

"Calm down, child, calm down! Just tell me what it is you want to say."

"There's a coach coming at an 'ell of a lick and its blowin' its 'orn. I think it's Joseph. There must be something wrong!"

"Good girl, thank you. Go quickly to the back door and ring the big bell. Wait there till the men come, then tell them to come to the front door. I will speak to you about your language later."

Frank ran to the front door and out onto the step. The big bell started to toll as the maid threw her weight onto the rope.

As it rang out, men working in the stables and the garden ran into the house, bidden by its imperative call. At that moment the coach came crashing round the corner over the bridge and clattered and slithered to a halt in front of the steps, showering sparks, dust and gravel in all directions.

Some of the men appeared on the steps. Frank was hovering about uncertainly.

"It is Joseph. He has been to fetch Graffinflein. There must be something wrong."

They all ran down the steps to the coach. Joseph jumped down.

"Am I glad to see you! Quick! It is Graffinflein—she has started with the baby."

Frank opened the door of the coach. Elizabet was convulsed with pain. The maid was white with panic. He called up two of the men.

"Quickly, you two, help her out and carry her up to her room." He grabbed the young footman who had also come running." You go with them and show them where to go."

The little maid, flushed with the excitement of being allowed to ring the bell, appeared.

"You run to the house keeper and ask her to attend Graffinflein in her room at once." He grabbed one of the other men. "You run to the kitchen and get them to make hot water. Lots. Quickly!" One of the stable lads appeared. "You run to the stable. Take a horse—go to the village. Ask for the Doctor to come as quickly as he can." He mopped his sweating brow and straightened his wig. "Thank you, Joseph, you have done very well." He turned to Elizabet's maid who was standing in a dither, too dazed to follow when Elizabet had been carried away. "Go with your mistress and attend to her. I will send up someone to help you. Go, go now, they will come. Quickly, go in the front door and up the stairs—you will see them."

He re-entered the front door. The Count stood outside the door to his study.

"Vhat on earth disturbs my household upside down when we are in mourning?"

"Excuse me, Excellency, but it is Graffinflein, who has started in labour. She does not yet know about her mother and forgive me, Sir, this is not the moment to tell her."

"Frank, were it anyone else but you who tell me what to do in my own house, I vould kick him out. Where is Graffinflein? Why has she not come to see me?"

Frank quickly told him what had happened. He was somewhat mollified. "Yes I have sorry. You have done the right thing. I vill go up and see her now."

"Perhaps now would not be just the right moment, if I might say so, Sir. I will have word sent to you as soon as it is convenient for her to receive you."

The Count stood uncertainly for a while. "She is being looked after all right? Has the Doctor been sent for? Very well then, I vill be in my study. Call me as soon as she is able to see me. Do not tell her about her mother. I will tell her that. Tell the others as well. They are not to tell her about her mother. If she asks, say that she sleeps and will come to her as soon as she wakes."

The doorbell clanged. "Excuse me, Sir, that might be the Doctor." Frank opened the door. It was indeed the Doctor.

"Right, quick, show me to the patient. Time and new born babies wait for no man. Hello Count. This is exciting! I will report shortly. Lead on, Frank."

At that, they both set off up the stairs. The Count was left suddenly on his own, in a state of some agitation. He went to the decanter in his study and poured himself out a good measure of brandy. He sat at his desk but could not settle. He wandered around, waiting for news. He poured out another good glass of brandy and stood it on the mantelpiece. After what seemed forever, the Doctor came down the stairs again. He had a wide grin on his face.

"Congratulations, Count, you are again the grandfather."

The Count gave him the brandy that he had poured out for him.

"This is all very exciting. Thank you very much for coming so quickly. Mother and child are well, I hope. Is it a boy or a girl?"

"Yes, yes, both doing very well. It is a girl." He could see the look of disappointment on the Counts face. "Well, the mother is in fine shape. She could have many more children yet. Plenty of time for a boy."

"It is that Captain of Horse. We did all we could to prevent her from marrying him. We said that no good would ever come of it. Do you know she tricked us into allowing her to marry him? She told us that she was pregnant by him. So of course they had to be married as quickly as possible. But she was not pregnant at all."

The Doctor smiled. "She was always headstrong, that one. I am sure that if she wanted it, the world would stop turning."

Even the Count had to admit a grudging smile. "She can certainly turn the world upside down. Thank you very much for coming so quickly. Thank you for all your help last week. What with births and deaths, we are taking up rather a lot of your time lately."

The Doctor looked at him. He placed a sympathetic hand on his arm. For all the Count's irascible nature, he was fond of the old man.

"I cannot say how sorry I am about that sad news. You know, she had been ill for a long while. When she first spoke to me about it, it was already too late. There was nothing I could do for her, apart from doing the best I could to alleviate her symptoms. I am sorry. Though she was a gentle woman there was a thread of steel that ran through her. Have you made any plans for the funeral yet?"

The Count had a misty look in his eyes. "No, not yet. The priest and the undertaker are coming up this afternoon and we will discuss the arrangements then. I am glad that Elizabet is here. She will be able to help me with things. She will know what hymns and so forth that she would like us to sing, though what good they will do her now, I do not know."

"Well, they will help you. They will be a fitting tribute to her and a suitable farewell. Anyway, we must not get maudlin. Please let me know the arrangements. Frau Hoffman and myself would certainly like to attend."

"Yes, thank you, Doctor. I will send word. Would you like some more brandy before you go?"

"No thank you, I must be on my rounds. It would not do for me to turn up smelling like a still. I will call tomorrow to make sure that all is well with your patients. About this time, I think?"

"Yes, that will be fine. Thank you Doctor. Thank you, too, for what you did last week."

Dr Hoffman took up his hat and coat. "Think no more of it. Goodbye, Count, goodbye."

The Count showed the Doctor out and shut the great door. He turned and found Frank hovering at the foot of the stairs.

"Graffinflein is ready to see you now, Excellency. Perhaps you would ask her; the ladies of the household would love to see the baby. Perhaps, sometime soon, they could come up for just a little peep."

The Count looked at him. "Why, Frank, I think that you would like to see the child too."

"Yes, Sir, I would. I think that it is very exciting. It is the first child to be born here since Graffinflein herself and after the sadness of this week, it would be a great fillip to everyone."

"I will go to her and will ask her. I am sure that she will be only too pleased to show her off."

He climbed up the stairs and knocked on the door. Her maid opened it and let him in.

Elizabet lay in bed, her fair hair loose all around her on the pillow. One hand hung out and she gently rocked the little cradle that was just beside her. She was deathly pale and looked completely exhausted. She smiled weakly at her father.

"Hello papa. I am sorry to arrive in such a turmoil! I felt for sure that the baby would be born in the coach. How is mama? I would like to go to see her as soon as possible."

"You must stay in bed. You cannot get up and start walking about the place. What nonsense is this?"

"That is an old wive's tale. I am perfectly fit and strong. I could certainly walk as far as her room to see her, even if I need my maid to help me."

The Count walked over and took her hand and kissed her pallid cheek. He looked in the cot at the tiny little face that was tightly screwed up, as if trying to shut out the world into which it had been thrust too early. He sat on the side of the bed.

"This is your cot! I remember you in there, just like that. When I came in the room and saw you lying like that, I was reminded of your poor mother. I never thought that you were much like her, but seeing you lying like that, I could see a striking likeness—quite disturbing." He took her hand tenderly in his. "My dear, you must be brave and console yourself with your new baby. I am afraid that your poor mother is with us no more. She died two days ago."

Elizabet looked at him and slowly her eyes filled with tears that ran down her cheeks. She gripped his hand.

"Why did not you send for me sooner? I could have come sooner. I would have been here."

"I sent for you when I thought that the time vas right. If it vas the wrong time, I am sorry. I did what I thought was best. If you had been here, what could you have done?"

"Well, probably nothing, but I would have been here. Is she still here? Can I go and see her? I would like to see her."

"It is better if you do not see her. Remember her as you knew and loved her, a treasured person, full of warmth and life. You do not want to see her now."

There was a knock at the door. Elizabet's maid came in. She dropped a littler curtsey.

"Excuse me Frau 'Enery, your Excellency, but Frank says that begin' your pardon, but the Reverend and the Undertaker is here. He says that he has showed them into the breakfast room."

"Yes thank you. Tell him that I will come at once." Elizabet was still shaking with silent grief, the tears running down her cheeks.

"Do not fret, dear. Your mother had been ill for a long time and knew that she was dying. She was well prepared and had made her peace with her maker. She had only the life of an invalid before her."

"Yes, I know." She wiped the tears from her eyes. "She told me in the autumn, when I was here, that she had not long to live. I chided her and told her not to be so silly. Now she is dead and I was not here." Her eyes filled with tears of sadness and remorse.

"I am sorry, my dear, I must go down and see these people. Will you be all right? I will send your maid into you. I will come back up again as soon as they have gone." He bent and kissed his daughter's wet cheek and left the room. He paused by the door. "The women of the household seem to want to see the baby. When you feel like it, send for them. They would like that." He smiled at her and left. Her maid slipped in quietly and sat on a chair by the wardrobe.

Elizabet shut her eyes and lay still for some long while. The tears flowed steadily down her cheeks. She thought of her mother in a kaleidoscope of images that spanned their life together. Even in the age of domestic servants and governesses, she had, being an only child, been unusually close to her mother. Though she had had some pre-warning last autumn, it seemed inconceivable that she was now gone. At least she had her husband and her children to fill that hole in her life. She sat up in bed.

"I wish to go and see my mother. Please pass me my house coat and help me."

"But Frau 'Enery, you cannot. You cannot get out of bed and walk around. The Doctor said that you had to remain in your bed for a month. You must not get up."

"What rubbish! How many babies has he had? What does he know? If I feel strong enough, I can do it." She swung her feet out of the bed and stood up.

"Help me on with…" The room went grey and she fainted on the floor.

"Frau 'Enery, Frau 'Enery! What the 'ell am I going to do now?" The maid patted her face and tried to move her.

"Just help me up and stop making a fuss." With the maid's help, she struggled onto the side of the bed and sat, with her head in her hands. "For goodness sake, stop fussing. I will be all right. Just give me a minute. I will be all right. I stood up too quickly, that is all." She sat upright and stretched her arms up above her head. She was still deathly pale. "You see, I shall be all right. Just put my housecoat over my shoulders and help me on with it."

"Madam, you really must not. The Doctor said you must not and not, you must!"

"I shall be all right. I can lean on you. In a moment, I will be right as rain. Come and support me, I am going to stand up."

"No Madam! You must not!"

Elizabet slowly stood and started to sway. The maid grabbed her.

"There, you see, I am all right—let me lean on you."

"Get back into bed at once. You must not do this. If the Doctor knew, he would be very cross. If your father knew he would stop you. He would not let you."

"That is why I want to go quickly, before he comes up to stop me." She took a couple of unsteady steps. "Here, let me hang onto you."

The maid still stood uncertainly.

"Look, I am going to go, even if I have to crawl on my hands and knees. You can either help me, or you can refuse and pack your bags and leave this instant!"

The maid hesitated no longer. Being a personal maid was a lot better than any of the other positions that she might find in a household. On the whole, she liked her mistress. This was the first disagreement that they had had. She was not about to lose her good job. She took Elizabet's arm and helped her through the door.

"We go this way. My mother's room is that one, the third door."

They reached the door. Elizabet would not admit that her knees felt weak. She was very glad she had her maid to lean on. The door was locked. However, the key was in the door. She turned it.

"My mother, who died two days ago, lies in here. Even now, my father is downstairs arranging her funeral. I wish to go inside to see her. I will quite understand if you do not wish to come in too. You can wait outside here."

There was a look of horror on the poor maid's face. "You mean that there is a dead body lying in there? I'm not going in there. Not now I'm not."

"No, all right. Calm yourself. I quite understand. I will pass you out a chair. You can sit on it until I am ready to come out again. Perhaps you would look at the baby from time to time."

Elizabet went into the room. She passed out a chair for her maid to sit on. She shut the door. The curtains were closed but admitted a thin chink of light. She crossed the room to open them a little so that she could see. She sat on the side of the bed and looked at her mother. At first, she was quite shocked. Was this really her mother? The face looked gaunt and pallid. The cheeks and the eye sockets had shrunken, leaving the bones, the forehead, the cheekbones, the jaw, prominent. Her skin had the look of cold, cold marble. Her hair protruded in untidy wisps. Elizabet stood up quickly. Immediately she felt faint again. She had to sit on the bed until she had recovered. She sat on a chair. She wanted to sit with her mother. She did not know what she wanted to say or do. She just felt that by sitting there, she could somehow communicate her love for her and her sorrow. She wanted to re-live things of their life together, but she could not. Somehow she could not see in this cadaverous object, the mother that she had loved. The door opened slowly and her father came in. He came and stood beside her. He put his hand on her shoulder. She leant her face on his hand. She sobbed and sobbed. He lifted her up.

"Come, my dear. Come away from this sad sight. Come back to your room." He put an arm round her and gently led her back to her room. He gave her to the care her maid.

"Put her back into her bed. I will return when she is settled." He went downstairs and rung the bell for Frank. "Would you please ask Schmidt to come to me and come yourself, so that I may discuss the funeral arrangements. Will you please have some hot milk and honey sent up to Graffinflein. She has been sitting with her mother and is a little weepy. I must go soon back to her."

Frank and Schmidt came to his study. "Please sit down, the two of you, and make such notes as you need. I have spoken to the Doctor. He says that as the weather is cold at the moment, we can leave the funeral for another week. I have seen the priest and the undertaker this afternoon and have set the funeral for seven days from now. The service is to be at eleven in the morning. Schmidt, if you can engage the orchestra and choir to come. I wish for the requiem of Herr Mozart to be sung for her. Write to the bishop asking him to officiate. Offer him and his secretary a room for the night. I have made a list of those who should be informed. Send out to them as soon as possible. This list is of our family and close friends. They are all to be offered to come to lunch afterwards or to stay the night if they wish. Frank, you had better be prepared to make up all the beds. Lay on a cold buffet in the great hall. I have no idea how many people will be coming, but keep in close touch with Schmidt for numbers. Graffinflein will certainly still be here. I expect her husband will come, I do not know about the children. I think that is all at present. Oh yes. Tell Joseph to get out the coaches and carriages and clean them. Make sure that they do not squeak or fall to pieces. I have no idea how many we will need. Presumably, those that come here will use their own carriages. Make sure that you have a good supply of black plumes. On our carriages, one on each corner and one on each horse should be enough. Ah! There is the milk for Graffinflein. I will go to her. If you think of anything else, let me know. Yes, yes, flowers in the Church. The Countess liked white lilies. Fill the church with white lilies." He refilled his brandy glass and went upstairs behind the maid with the tray.

Elizabet was sitting up in bed. She gratefully accepted the hot mug. The maid put the tray down and left. The Count peered at the baby.

"It is a good little baby. It does not make the cry."

"Well, she is content and fed. Perhaps now she will sleep."

"You can feed her all right?"

Elizabet laughed. This was as near her father had come of ever asking her a 'personal' question.

"Yes, you know me. I am like the good farmyard cow."

He nodded thoughtfully. The awful truth was dawning on him. No! He did not know her. As a baby and a child she was kept at arm's length. If he saw her once a day, that was enough and that was usually to kiss her goodnight. He had not really taken much notice of her until 'Enery had appeared on the scene. He was pleased to see that she had confidently taken over the role that his wife fulfilled in running the affairs of the castle, but when 'Enery had arrived, she seemed a changed person. She became much more confident. Her natural competence had flourished. He was surprised to see her obstinacy when the question of her marriage to 'Enery first reared its ugly head. He had assumed that she would give up if she had to wait five years but was a bit taken aback to see that the longer she waited, the more determined she became. He had done everything he could to put her off but secretly admired her constancy.

It had been a real shock to him when he had walked into the bedroom earlier, to see her lying there with such a look of her mother. He sat and talked with her for a long time. He was amazed that his relationship with her had changed. She was no longer the little child that needed to be humoured and corrected if necessary. Suddenly she had grown into a mother and a woman. He found that they talked as equals. They could derive great strength and companionship from each other.

Later, the staff all filed through the bedroom and peered at the little face in the cot. He had sat on the bed, holding her hand and glowing with a subdued paternal pride.

Elizabet was absolutely adamant that she was going to attend the funeral. Dr Hoffman could wring his hands as much as he liked. Nothing and no one was going to keep her away. Robert was able to make a flying visit, too, to be there, but it was felt better for the children to stay in Bavaria with their Nanny.

The church was packed and there was a crowd outside. They stood stoically in the chill wind, only able to catch snippets of the singing from inside the little church. After the requiem the coffin was carried to the grave, and after a short sorrowful service, Elizabet's mother's mortal remains were laid to rest in the cold earth. They sorrowfully returned to the castle.

The castle was packed. It seemed that everyone who had been at the Church had called to pay their respects to Elizabet and her father. The kitchen staff were hard put to produce enough food. Frank and his men were kept busy filling glasses. Elizabet's father was getting more and more grumpy.

"Who are all these people? I do not know who half these people are. What are they doing here? I am sure that they have only come for a free meal." People kept coming up to him to shake his hand and offer their condolences. He became more and more confused.

Elizabet's maid came to her to say that the baby was crying. It needed feeding. When she had finished and the baby was clean and changed again, she brought it down for people to see. Many took this as a sign that they should be leaving so made their goodbyes and departed. Only those who were staying the night remained.

Dinner that night was a long and formal affair. Though it had been prepared with the accustomed care, no one was in the mood for a gastronomic extravaganza. Everyone was glad when it came to an end. They made their excuses early and went to bed. Breakfast was a rolling meal, as some had to be away early. Robert, too, had to leave at first light, as he had some horses running the next day. He had to get there on time to oversee the event. He left Elizabet in bed and kissed her as she slept. She stirred and woke.

"Are you going now?"

"Yes. I must go straight away, or I will not catch the boat. Stay here as long as you like, we are managing very well at home. Do not try to do too much. You need to get your strength back. Stay as long as your father needs you. I think that the baby is beautiful, just like its mother." He kissed her tenderly. "Goodbye my little one. See you home soon." Taking his coat and his bag, he left.

Elizabet felt that she had let her mother and her father down when she was most needed, by not being at the castle when her mother had died. She walked every day to the little Churchyard to tend the flowers on her mother's grave. At first there had been a huge mountain of blooms, but gradually they withered until only a few remained. She took fresh ones from the garden.

"Papa, you do not come to the grave," she said to him one day.

"No, my child. I do not like graves. They are nasty mournful things. I do not like to think of her lying dead under all that earth. I would rather remember her in my heart, alive and warm, as she used to be. Her body will not after all run away and her spirit it is not there. Her body it is now a dead thing. Her spirit it is, that is still alive. It is to that which I would rather talk."

Elizabet stayed at the Castle for two months to regain her strength and to help her father sort out her mother's affairs. He had become more and more irritable with her prolonged illness and very few of the people who came to work at the Castle could endure to stay very long. Frank continued to run the household, more out of habit than devotion to his master. Even he found his situation strained to the limit. The persistent Schmidt continued to administer the Count's Estates. There is no doubt that without his efficient administrations the Count's affairs would have collapsed in chaos long ago.

It was with some reluctance that Elizabet set off, with her maid and the baby in the arms of a young girl who had been retained as nanny, to return to Bavaria. Her father had been very reluctant to let her go. He had made all sorts of excuses to prevent her, but she was determinedly adamant that she should go. She wished to see her other children and to be reunited with Robert. After engaging a housekeeper to assist Frank and a new valet to look after her father, she persuaded Schmidt to make the arrangements for her. After a prolonged farewell, she finally set off to return home in the rickety coach.

When she finally arrived, exhausted after the long journey, she was greeted by Robert who as in a highly elated mood.

"We have had some new arrivals whilst you were away!"

"New arrivals—what new arrivals?" She took off her hat and sat wearily down on a chair.

"Well, I am not at liberty to say, but three horses have come to be trained."

She looked at him with some anger. "I have been away for two months and all you can talk about is horses?"

Robert was not put off. "They came in a special horse box. They had purple blankets. They were guarded by a troop of Cossacks." The excitement shone in his face. "They have come a long way, from the North. The owner is important, very, very important—he speaks Russian."

She looked at him in surprise. "You mean the Ts..?"

He stopped her before she could say it. "We have all been sworn to secrecy. No one must mention it. Apparently, he has seen my horses run and has been so impressed that he asked Emil if I could train some for him. When he asks, the thought is the deed and so here they are. They arrived two weeks ago."

She listened to him almost without reaction.

"I think you might be just a little excited," he admonished her. "This is a wonderful chance for me. I might say a great honour. If I am successful with them, there is no telling to what it might lead. I might even become the Imperial trainer one day"

"Well, I am glad for you. I think that you might be just a little excited too. I have been away for over two months! That girl, standing there, holds the little daughter that you have not even looked at yet! We have spent three days on the journey and we are very tired. I shall have some hot milk brought up to me and will go to bed. You can tell me about your stupid horses in the morning."

Ushering the nanny and the baby before her, she went upstairs. Robert was dumbstruck. He realised he had been less than solicitous, but she might have seemed a little interested.

Whilst Elizabet had been away he had spent most of his time with his horses. The three children that had stayed behind were in the charge of a nurse. He was out in the morning before they were got up and back in the evening after they had gone to bed. He had hardly seen them. During the day they went to the Schloss and spent the day with the governess and Emil's children. They had been wildly excited when Elizabet returned late in the evening and had come charging downstairs, whooping with excitement to see the new baby when they heard the coach arrive. Eventually they had all gone upstairs together with their mother. Robert sat by the fire with his customary glass of whisky, feeling both annoyed and happy. He was pleased to have Elizabet back home again, but he felt disgruntled that she did not show more interest in his new horses.

Their life soon settled down into a pattern. With the older children out of the house all day, Elizabet was able to devote all her attention to the new baby. Eventually the baby was christened Cornelia. Robert was at work all day, leaving early in the morning, He returned for his breakfast before she got up. The only time she saw him was for the evening meal. When this was over, he used to return to the stables to look over the horses. Often he did not return until after she had gone to bed.

CHAPTER 25

Robert looked down into the little grave. The coffin seemed so small. Elizabet stood beside him. Between them, Maria and Helen wept silently into their handkerchiefs. Cornelia, it had been decided, was too young, so she had not come to the funeral, but stayed at home with her nanny.

Robert stared at the little wooden coffin and in his mind's eye he could see his little Olga lying inside. So pale and still, dressed in the white dress that she was to have worn for her first communion. His eyes misted over.

As if in the distance, he heard the priest droning on in Latin. It was bitterly cold. The snow lay thick on the ground. His feet were freezing cold. He wiped the tears from his eyes and looked at Elizabet. She was deathly white, her lips set in a harsh thin line. She had an arm around each of her two daughters. She gathered them protectively to her. Robert reached out and put his arm round her shoulders. It was surprising how different the girls were. Maria was the studious one. She always had her nose in a book. She was content with her own company. Helen was tough and resilient. A complete tomboy, she had a forceful personality. She was never happier than when she was bossing everyone about.

Olga was a gentle dreamy child. She loved the flowers and butterflies in the garden. She was always out looking for new buds or flowers to bring in for her mother.

Robert shuddered, for he could picture her bloody face as she lay on the kitchen table whilst Elizabet tried to clean her up. Robert had heard the screams from the stables. He had run home to find them all grouped round her inert body on the table. The backhouse boy had been sent to run to the stables, to take a horse to go and fetch the doctor. Robert had carried the little body up to the bed room. He left her in the care of Elizabet and the maid, who as gently as they could, undressed her, cleaned her up tenderly and put her into her bed. Maria and Helen where weeping hysterically and were being consoled by the maid. Anna the cook was hovering about, wanting to help, but not knowing quite what she could do. Robert took her aside.

"What on earth happened?"

"As far as I can gather, Sir, they were tobogganing. She flew down the slope straight into a tree. I heard them crying and ran out. I carried her in. She was completely unconscious. I feel quite sick, Sir. The poor little body has never moved." There was a loud knock at the door. Robert quickly went to open it. The Doctor hurried in.

"'Err 'Enery. I am shocked to 'ear this news. I 'ave come as quick as I could. Where ees the leetle girl?"

Robert quickly shook him by the hand. "Thank you, Doctor. Come this way, she is upstairs." He led the way at the run. The Doctor followed. "In here, Doctor." He ushered him into the little bedroom. "I will wait downstairs." It was obvious that he would only be in the way. When he arrived downstairs, Maria and Helen were still weeping hysterically. He gathered them into his arms to try to soothe them.

"Shush, shush, my darlings, all will be well, she will soon be all right again."

"But we have killed her," they wept onto his shoulder. "We have killed her." They wailed inconsolably.

"Of course you didn't kill her. What a silly thing to say. Of course you did not kill her. Tell me what happened."

Maria recovered herself enough to tell him between sniffs.

"We were playing with the toboggan on the little hill at the back of the orchard. We were having such a good time. The snow was packing down tight. The toboggan was flying down. We were taking it in turns to fly down the hill and drag the toboggan back. At the bottom you had to fall off so that you did not go into the trees. Olga was watching from the top; she was afraid to go, so she missed lots of turns. We tried to persuade her, but she would not. In the end she plucked up courage, but she begged us not to push her so that she would not go too fast." Maria cried again. "But we did not listen, it was such fun. We ran and pushed her as fast as we could. She screamed at us not to, but it was too late, she was flying down the hill. She screamed with terror, she was going very fast. We shouted to her to roll off, but she dare not. The toboggan flew straight into a tree and she shot off and hit the tree with her face." Maria burst into tears again. "She just crumpled in a heap and never moved. Helen ran for Mummy and I tried to cover her with my coat. Then Anna came and Mummy too and they carried her in. Then you came. And now the Doctor has come and she is going to die and we killed her." She burst into tears again. Robert did his best to comfort her.

The maid came hurriedly down the stairs.

"Herr Meister, the Doctor has asked for you to come upstairs. I will stay with the girls." She gathered them to her like a hen comforting her chicks. Robert quickly ran upstairs. Elizabet was sitting on the bed holding Olga's hand. The Doctor stood at the foot of the bed, packing his bag.

"Herr Henry, Frau, I am afraid that I must tell you to prepare yourselves for the vorst. Her pulse is very veak. Unless she regains consciousness soon, she vill slip avay. Call me if there is any change, any at all and I vill at vonce come. The next 24 hours vill be critical."

Robert looked at Elizabet's white face, the tear streaks showing on it. He put his hand on her shoulder and gave it a squeeze. She briefly rested her cheek on it.

"Thank you doctor, for coming so quickly—let me show you out." He took the Doctor downstairs.

"'Err 'Enery, I vill call again in the morning. Make sure that your vife has some rest. This has been a big shock for her. Two patients ve do not vant."

"Yes Doctor, thank you Doctor." He shut the door and came in, to be met by Maria and Helen.

"Papa, how is she? Will she be all right? Tell us that she will be all right. Can we go up and see her?"

"The doctor says that she must have complete rest and quiet. She is sleeping now. Come up quietly and see her, but do not wake her. Then my dears, it is time for you to go to bed. There has been quite enough excitement for today and you must be tired. Have you been given any supper?"

"Yes papa, we have had some hot bread and milk and Anna has been reading a story to us." The three of them went upstairs into Olga's room. Elizabet looked up when they came in and smiled weakly at them.

"Shush, shush, do not disturb her. Just kiss her gently and then go to your bed. I will come and tuck you in, in a minute."

They gently bent down and kissed the little face in the bed and then kissed their father. He could feel their little tears on his cheek.

"Come on, I will pop you into bed. You see, when she has slept, she will be right as rain in the morning." He ushered them out and took them to their room. "Come, my children, let us say a little prayer, especially for Olga." The three of them knelt by the bedside. "Dear Jesus, please look after our little Olga and make her well soon and bless us and mummy so that we can help Olga to be better quickly." Tearfully they got into bed. Robert sat on the side of the bed and took both their hands in his.

"Listen, my little ones, you must not reproach yourselves. You were all playing together and it was an accident. You did not intend any harm. You just wanted her to have a good ride."

He wiped way the tears on Maria's face with his hand.

"Darling, it was just an accident. Accidents happen. You cannot change them. They happen. They have happened before you even think that they could happen. Just pray that Olga will soon be well again. Now go to sleep both of you. In a little while your Mother will be here to tuck you in. Goodnight Maria, goodnight Helen. If you want anything, call out, we will be here. Good night, my little ones." He kissed them both on the cheek and went out of the room.

Elizabet was still sitting on the bed holding Olga's hand.

"Come downstairs for a while and have some supper, you will be tired."

"No, I will sit here. If she wakes up, she will want me here."

"Shall I bring you up some food then? I will see what I can find."

"Yes, thank you, a cup of soup or something would be good. I will sit with her tonight. You must go to work in the morning—you must have some sleep."

"No I will sit with you. I have sat up many a night with a mare that is going to foal; I can sit up with my own daughter when she needs me. I will go and see what they can produce in the kitchen and bring it on a tray. Cheer up Darling, she will recover, you see. She may be little, but she is like her mother, tough."

Elizabet smiled wanly, but said nothing. Robert went down. He found Anna the cook sitting anxiously in the kitchen with the maid and the nanny.

"I must tell you all that things do not look good. The doctor has told us to be prepared for the worst. The next twenty-four hours will be crucial."

They chorused their sympathy.

"Thank you, thank you, all we can do now is pray. The Mistress is going to stay by her bedside. If you would be kind enough to prepare a bowl of soup and some bread, I will take it up to her."

Robert and Elizabet sat together hand in hand, by the bedside, into the night. Elizabet held Olga's hand all the while, almost as if she hoped that. thus linked, their combined strength would flow into the little girl and give power to her recovery. Robert must have dozed off, because he was woken by a violent shake and Elizabet's urgent call. She was standing by the bed gently shaking

Olga. He was instantly awake and by the bedside. He looked down at the little still face on the pillow and urgently called her name, but in the dark of the dawn, the little soul had slid quietly away from its earthly body to find refuge in the arms of its maker. Elizabet had fallen into Robert's arms and wept great sobs of grief. Robert had gently lowered her into the chair.

"Sit here, my dear, I will call your maid to come to you and then ride for the Doctor."

He had run out of the room and banged on the maid's door. "Quickly, go to the Mistress in Miss Olga's room. Ask cook to make some coffee." He ran downstairs. Grabbing his cloak, he ran across to the stables. With shaking hands he lit the hurricane lamp. Collecting his tack, he had hastily thrown on the bridle and reins onto his horse. Not wanting to waste time he had grabbed a handful of the horse's main and swung onto its back. He clattered out of the yard bareback. It had seemed no time before he was banging on the Doctor's door. The doctor's head had appeared at an upstairs window.

"Wer da?"

"It is me, Doctor," Robert called up. "Robert Henery."

"Oh ja, 'err 'Enery. Ze leettle girl?"

"Yes. Please come quickly."

"Ja, ja, I come at vonce." Presently he came running out of his house, still in his nightshirt, struggling to do up his trousers. He had run to the stable. Being used to being called out in the night, he always had his horse saddled up and ready. The two of them had galloped back, with the tails of the Doctor's night-shirt streaming in the wind.

Robert was jerked back to the present by a none too gentle prod from the verger. He looked around him. The verger was offering him a small shovel with some earth on it. He looked at it uncomprehendingly, then at the priest. The priest motioned him to take some in his hand to throw in the grave. Robert looked at him uncertainly, not understanding what was required. The Priest stretched out an arm and, taking a small handful, threw it down on the coffin and motioned that Robert should do the same. Robert took a handful and threw it. The tears filled his eyes. He could not see where it went, but the hollow rattle of the earth on the wood told him he had succeeded. The girls had made some little posies of some early snowdrops they had found in a sheltered corner of the garden with some sprigs of rosemary. They stood either side of their mother, tears streaming down their faces and threw them into the grave. Elizabet, too, took a handful of earth which she threw into the grave. Sorrowfully, they turned away to walk back to their coach. Once in the coach, the girls clung to their mother and sobbed uncontrollably. Robert, too, sat, holding Elizabet's hand and wept bitter tears.

The girls went to bed early but they could not sleep. It was not long before they came down again to the drawing room to find their parents. They curled up together in the sofa with a cup of hot milk which Elizabet made for them with a spoonful of honey.

"Mummy, you are always telling us that God loves us. If he loves us, how can he be so cruel?"

Elizabet's first reaction had been one of shock, but her heart went out to her poor daughters, burdened with such tragedy.

"My darlings, God is not cruel. He too weeps for the sadness of his people. All He want is that people learn to love Him, so that when they die they want go to heaven to be always vith Him."

"But how could Olga learn to love him—she is only little? She will not be able to go to heaven."

"Of course she will go to heaven, do not worry yourself. She is young and little. In her heart she vas born to love God. She has not been old enough to forget how she should love Him."

"But Mama, if we are here to learn to love God, how is it that people when they grow up, forget about Him?"

"Their lives become full of moneys and wars and loves and hates and the things that worry us now. They forget that they must look further for the real purpose in their life."

"It would be easier if God had made us all in Heaven straight away, then we would not have the sadness of life and death."

"But He did that and look what happened."

"What happened?"

"One of the archangels, the most powerful of the angel, wished to be like God Himself and he made with his friends, rebellion. There was a terrible struggle. The rebellious angel was throwed out with his friends and they fell and fell to that place which we call hell. There they stay for ever, trying always the best they can to turn people away from God, so that they too will go to hell. God saw that to put people straight into heaven was not good. He wants people in heaven who have learnt to love Him and want to go there, because they wanted for ever to be with Him."

"But why did he take Olga? If He can do every thing He could have stopped the toboggan. He could have made her not to die."

"It is very hard to answer. We do not know what God want or think or do, or why. We know that He has made the earth and everyone on it. He has give to all, the free will, so that they can choose to love Him. If He interfere on the earth with what is going on, He at once interfere with the free will of someone. If He interfere, He take away the free will. He make of people puppets, who do not have any longer the free will, but dance to His tune like a puppet. When people die and come to Him in heaven, it is not a great sadness for Him, it is a great joy, for they have come to Him because they have learned to love Him while they are on this earth. It is only for us a sadness. We forget why we are on earth and have great sadness that we no longer have the one which we love. We forget that the one we love is gone to heaven, which we all strive for all our lives. So we are sad that we have lost one we love. We should remember that she is now in heaven and that the day will come when we too will be reunited with her and Grandmama and all people who are no longer with us." She took up her daughters in her arms.

"Mummy, when I go to heaven, will I see my rabbit?" Helen asked. She had stopped crying and was listening intently to what her mother was telling her. Despite her sorrow, Elizabet could not help smiling.

"No my darling. You will not find the animals in heaven. They do not have a soul, that invisible part of us that is together our spirit and our will and our understanding, which lives after our body is laid to rest. The animals are here to help and comfort us whilst we are on the earth. When we are in heaven we do not need such comfort, because we are in the presence of God. Now it is time for you to go to your bed, but do not be sad for Olga, my little ones, for she is now in the place where she will find the most happiness." She kissed them both and led them upstairs to their beds.

Robert had sat and listened to all this in impressed silence. He had never given any thought to such matters. Death was inevitable and not talked about. When people that you loved died, you were cast into an agony of grief and sadness. It made a great impact on him, hearing and witnessing so unexpectedly this straightforward faith of Elizabet. He had never really thought of the reason for his existence. He had taken it all as a matter of fact. Here he was. He had a wife and children and a good job. He was a trainer of racehorses and quite a good one at that. Such basic facts had been sufficient for him. It had never ever even occurred to him that his life on earth might have some divine purpose.

The weight of Olga's death pressed heavily on them for many weeks. It was only with the coming of the spring that the sound of the girls' laughter could again be heard in the house and garden. Elizabet, for all her strength used to buoy up her other daughters, felt Olga's loss with a great and heavy sadness which weighed heavy with her for the rest of her life.

CHAPTER 26

That summer was a busy one for Robert. The demands of his work preoccupied him almost completely. Emil had some useful horses entered for racing in the year so they had high hopes of some good winners. The Count also had some likely horses. Robert was particularly keen to provide some winners for him. Apart from his desire to ingratiate himself with his father-in-law, since Elizabet's mother had died, he was aware that the Count was very much on his own. Indeed, the Count rarely went to the castle, spending most of his time in hotels, attending the different race meetings, always hoping to find those elusive winners.

In addition, there were the three horses with the purple rugs that had mysteriously appeared in the stables, one night, with their Cossack guards about which they must not speak. The guards lived in the Bothy. Whenever the horses went out on exercise, the Cossacks went with them armed to the teeth with rifles, pistols and bandoleers bristling with bullets. Robert had protested to Emil about this. Any attempt at concealment and anonymity was completely destroyed by their presence, but it was insisted that they stay. Robert found it quite unnerving to ride out on exercise with this barbaric looking armed guard. When the three horses were exercising out on the gallops, the Cossacks insisted in racing along as well. Unfortunately, their horses, for all their bloodthirsty cries and fanatical enthusiasm, could not keep up with the best race horses from their master's Stud. They soon lagged behind. This had a detrimental effect on the training of the race horses, as they, seeing the bigger number trailing behind, began to assume that this was the pace. Their inborn herd instinct made them slow down so that the slower members could keep up. In vain did Robert try to explain this to the captain of the small detachment. He either did not, or would not understand that his enthusiastic efforts were actually teaching his master's horses to run slower. Robert gave up. No one would listen to him. He would just have to make the best of a bad job.

All these horses had been entered for a full programme of racing, so he was often away from home for days on end. Elizabet, since Olga's death, had no wish to do the circuit of hotels, race meetings and endless dinners. She preferred to stay at home with her children so that she could live every moment with them. She had bitterly reproached herself for missing so much of Olga's short life because she had often been away, leaving the children at home in the care of the nanny. It was not going to happen again. She was going to be a part of and share in everything they did. She missed Robert when he was away, longing for him to come back. She was not lonely—she had the children and the servants—but his absence still left a great emptiness. She always looked forward to his return. She had enough money so could just manage, though she had to be careful. She used to extract whatever money she could from Robert and hide it away. She knew that if she did not, he would as likely lose it all in some ill considered bet. He was an incorrigible gambler. He would have a bet on anything. He would lose as much as he won, often more! Unless she could get his winnings from him whilst he was still flushed with his success, he would as like as not lose them the next day. She tucked it away with the money that he had won, which she had taken from him on the night when he had spent a day hunting sidesaddle. She had determined that she would not spend this unless she had to. She would keep it for a rainy day.

It was a great relief to them both when, with the approach of winter, the racing season came to an end. Robert was able to settle down to a period of life at home with his family. The three horses with their purple rugs and their fierce guards disappeared one night as suddenly as they had come, much to Robert's relief. It appeared that, with the onset of winter, they were to return to their home stables before the roads became impassable with snow.

One evening, shortly after they had gone, there came a loud rapping on the door. Robert and Elizabet were sitting by the fire.

"Good gracious, what can that be at this time of the night!" Elizabet put down her sowing in alarm. Robert took the lamp from the Hall table and went to the door.

"Yes?" He opened the door enough to see out. He was brushed aside by a fur-clad figure, who marched in, scattering snow in all directions as he shook off his great coat. Thus revealed, Robert recognised the Captain of the Cossacks. He swept off his hat and made an exaggerated bow. From a big bag that hung across his shoulder, he produced a package. This he thrust at Robert.

"For you!"

In surprise, Robert took it. The man threw his coat over his shoulders again and, looking like some great furry bear, marched out into the snowy night. Before Robert could stop him he had ridden off into the dark. Robert watched his figure riding away; then, closing the door, he returned to the drawing room.

"You remember the Cossacks who were here in the summer with the 'visitors'? That was the captain. He thrust this package into my hands then marched out into the night." Robert shook it speculatively.

"What is it? Who is it from?"

"I do not know. Shall I open it?" Robert turned it over and examined it.

Written in purple ink was the scrawl: "Herr Henery." Robert took out his pocket-knife to cut the string and break the heavy wax seals. He opened the packet.

"If it is from whom I think that it is from…" He quickly unwrapped the papers, letting them fall to the floor. Inside was a small glass breadbasket prettily enamelled with yellow and blue pansies. Inside that was a small grey box fastened with a press-stud. Robert handed the breadbasket to Elizabet and opened the small box. Nestling in a bed of grey velvet was a gold tie pin with a small horseshoe studied with diamonds and sapphires. A small card was enclosed. In purple ink it said: 'With thanks for all you have done for our horses.'

"Well, I am blessed. Do you suppose that Cossack had to ride all the way here to deliver this to us?" Robert looked at his tie pin. He was thrilled. "Fancy him going to the trouble of sending us these gifts." Robert stuck the pin into his cravat and studied the effect in the mirror hanging over the fireplace. When it was adjusted to his satisfaction, he took the glass dish from Elizabet to have another look at it. Elizabet was scowling.

"Smile, darling. Look, it is lovely."

"After all the work that you put into his horses! The late nights! The worry! The care! He send you a glass dish that anyone could buy at a fair, with a silly little pin!" Elizabet was angry. "What good are these things? We can not eat them? I cannot feed the children with them. For all the effort and work that you have given to him, he give you these trinkets in return."

Robert had been excited by the gifts so was considerably crest fallen by her attack.

"It is not what the gifts are that is important. It is from whom they have come; that makes them important—that he even bothered to think of sending them in the first place. I am very pleased, so do not you spoil it by being a sour cabbage."

"Oh, you are so stupid. You are like a child. Pleased with little baubles. How can we live on such things? This is so mean for all the effort that you have made. All he can send you is these little things."

"But darling, I am already paid by Emil. If the three horses had belonged to Emil I would have given them the same attention."

"Oh, you are worse than a child! He get some secretary to send you these..." She was lost for words. "...these things, and you are happy. You know that you are worth much more than this; it is not a just reward for what you have done."

"But I am happy." Robert was getting a little annoyed. "I am pleased that he thought enough of me to even bother to send anything at all. My reward has been to see his horses run well. I am glad to accept these gifts as a token of his recognition of that. I am not going to hear any more about it." He picked up the bowl and took it into his study, where he placed it on the mantelpiece. The tie pin he put back into its box and put it inside the bowl. Elizabet took up her sowing again. She could not hide her disappointment for him. This was poor reward for all he had done. She was annoyed too that *he* was pleased with the gifts and would not see how undervalued he was.

Robert and Elizabet determined that they would make the first Christmas after Olga's death as happy as they could for their daughters. On the feast of St Nicholas they prepared little presents for them all which they hid all round the house. This year they all felt her absence very keenly. Cornelia insisted that if she was in heaven and watching them, they ought to hang up a stocking for her, so that she could see that she had not been forgotten. Nothing would dissuade her, so accordingly, four little stockings hung by the fireplace on the eve of Saint Nicholas feast day. Elizabet and Robert were able to laugh this off, but made sure they put in the one for Olga three homemade sweets and three sugared almonds and three apples, so that the children could share them out between them.

There were presents, too, for the maid and for Anna the Cook and for Nanny. Anna prepared a special lunch for them all, which was served in the candlelit dining room. In truth they had a happy family day. In the evening, they gathered round the piano to sing and play together, until it was time for the children to go to bed. It was not until Christmas that the healing seemed to crack.

As was their custom to go to Midnight mass on Christmas eve. They set off in the coach with the children all bundled up in their thick coats, bursting with excitement at being up at Midnight. They had been put to bed after tea, to be woken up to go to Mass. The servants came behind in a separate coach. The church was lit by what seemed like hundreds of candles and was packed full of people. The mass celebrating the birth of the risen Christ was a joyful but solemn occasion. The choir sung and the congregation joined in with enthusiasm and conviction. The air was heavy with the smell of incense. A blue haze of it hung round the altar, which was lavishly decorated with splendid white lilies especially grown in the hothouse at the Schloss. The priests wore their best vestments. They made a vibrant splash of colour in the church which, despite the many candles, was quite dimly lit. The organ thundered out its well-known tunes and the congregation sang as one, with a gusto that threatened to raise the roof. The soaring descants of the choir filled the church and echoed round the dark rafters. It was a truly uplifting celebration, filled with happiness. For the children it was a powerful and mystic occasion, one that would stay in their memory for the rest of their lives. After the Mass was over, everyone hung around outside the church to greet each other and wish each other a Happy Christmas, instead of, as usual, scuttling home. When they finally returned home, there was cold meat and fruit set out for anyone who wished. The children had a cup of hot milk sweetened with honey and went off to bed.

The next day was the servants day off so there was prepared a table of cold meats, cakes, sweetmeats, fruit and nuts with wine and apple juice and, as the centrepiece, a great glazed and decorated cold fish. This cold repast was set out in the dining room. They could help themselves as they fancied. Robert had hardly got to bed before it was time to get up and attend to the horses. It was the stable hand's day off as well. He and the head lad were to see to all the horses—Robert in the morning, the head lad in the afternoon. They had tossed a coin to see who was to do which. Robert was thankful that he had won the morning shift. At least, when he was finished, he could go home and forget the horses until the next day. He could go home at lunch time to enjoy lingering over the cold buffet that was prepared and waiting. In the evening, after they had lit the candles on the Christmas tree, they gathered round the little wooden crib with its set of hand carved wooded figures depicting the scene in the stable in Bethlehem where the Saviour of Mankind had been born. Elizabet told the children the story of the carpenter who had had to take his wife to

Bethlehem and could not find anywhere to stay so had ended up sleeping in a stable with the animals. She was heavy with child, she explained. The baby had been born that night so he had been laid in the manger. The child, it had been revealed to the parents by angels, was the son of God. He had come to earth to be born as a man so that everyone would be able to go to Heaven.

They concluded their prayers in front of the crib. When the candles on the tree were blown out, they gathered round the piano to sing carols. They always started with 'Silent Night', sung first in German for Mamma, then in English for Papa. It was whilst playing this that a lump came into Elizabet's throat. She could not sing. A great feeling of sadness and melancholy overwhelmed her. Hot salty tears filled her eyes, then splashed down onto the keys. She had to stop playing. Hiding her face in her hands, she was wracked with great sobs. The children all clustered round.

"What is wrong Mamma?" "Please do not cry." "Why are you crying?" Cornelia started to cry too. Maria ran to her father. "Papa, Papa, quickly. Come, Mamma is crying. You must come to her!" She pulled him up to drag him to the piano. He disentangled Elizabet from her weeping daughters and led her to the sofa in front of the fire. He sat dawn beside her and cradled her in one arm, with his daughters in the other. Presently she recovered enough to sit up. She took out her handkerchief and blew her nose. Robert kissed her wet cheeks and she reached out to the children.

"I am so sorry, my little ones. I have tried to be so strong for you all, but it is so hard, so hard." She took out her handkerchief to wipe her eyes as they again filled with tears. "When I play 'Silent Night', I think of my poor mother playing it for me when I was a little child; then I think of my own child, my little Olga and I can no longer hold back my tears." Again she was compelled to stop as her eyes filled with tears. The girls crowded round to hug her until they were all piled on the sofa. Robert did his best to comfort them all.

Maria looked at her father, round eyed, tears streaking her cheeks.

"Does this mean that Mamma does not believe all that she has told us about Olga and Grandmama going to heaven?"

"No, of course not. Of course your mother believes that she has gone to heaven. She is very happy for her because she has gone to heaven and is in a place with God, where she will be happy for ever and ever. Of course she will. It is wonderful for her. But though we know that, it does not make it any easier for us. Though we know that she watches over us and will always be with us in spirit, we do not have her here. We cannot touch her or hear her laugh or see her funny little face. In that way she is lost to us. It is for us a great sadness. Do not be afraid. When we are sad, it is good to cry—the tears will wash our sadness away. Why don't you go to the piano to play some cheerful music to make mamma happy again?"

Maria wiped her tears away and, kissing her mother, went to the piano. She began to play some Mozart. Elizabet sat up and regained her composure. Robert left her in the care of her daughters. Going to the kitchen he prepared a great jug of hot milk and honey.

They sat round the hearth in the firelight and talked about Olga. All of them had their own precious little memory of her which they had up till now kept to themselves, but now in this most intimate of moments, they were able to share, laugh and enjoy together. This helped greatly to unburden their secret grieves. When the children finally went to bed they went with a lighter heart than they had had for a long time. As Maria left Robert caught her hand.

"Thank you my darling. You are such a help to your mother and to us all."

Maria looked both surprised and pleased.

"You played the piano tonight so well that it has cheered us all up. Look how sad we were, yet now we will all go happy to bed. You are such a good girl, such a help to your mother with the other children. I am afraid that you might feel that we take you for granted, but we do not. We are much blessed with a wonderful treasure and you are it." He pulled her down so that he could kiss her cheek. "Good night my treasure, sleep well, knowing that your Mamma and Papa love you very much."

Maria was completely overcome. "Good night Papa. Thank you. I love my sisters. I will always help to look after them. Good night Mamma. Do not be sad, for we all love you."

Robert and Elizabet sat in the flickering firelight, watching the flames, holding hands. At last Robert got up to put some more logs on the fire. They watched the sparks that this disturbed, as they flew up the chimney.

"Come on, my dear, we have work to do." He reached out a hand and, taking hers, pulled her up. She stood up and put her arms around his neck. He held her tenderly.

"I've been there too, darling. I know how you feel. For the most part you can put it behind you, but the moment comes when some chance happening catches you unawares. You cannot stop it all coming out." He kissed her tenderly. "Come on, we have got work to do. We do not want to be at it all night."

The day after Christmas was the feast of St Stephen. He was the person who was chosen to help the Apostles of Jesus of Nazareth with their work in the early church. They had traditionally kept the feast day by providing a great

meal and party for their staff—the people who helped them. Elizabet went to
the kitchen to prepare the vegetables whilst Robert prepared the table. He went
outside to cut some holly. He managed to find some berries that the birds had
not yet eaten; also some fir branches with cones still on them. He scrabbled in
the snow under the wall and found some Christmas roses. These he brought in
to decorate the table to give it a festive air. He set out the knives and forks and
the glasses. When he had finished, he, too went to work in the kitchen. It was
late at night before all was ready. The vegetables all washed and prepared, in
bowls of water, stood in a neat row. The ham skinned, painted with honey and
dusted with breadcrumbs, was placed in its dish. The great joint of boiling beef
was placed in a pan on the stove with onions and spices to boil slowly overnight. The great fish had been washed, cleaned and was ready to go in the oven.
The stock pots and the pot of soup were filled and placed on the fire to stew
slowly overnight. The red cabbage had been cut up. It was put in the bottom
oven so that it too would slowly cook. The bread rolls were rising under a
white cloth, ready to be baked at the last minute. The jellies and aspic had been
placed in the larder to set and the white wine, the butter and the cream had
been put in a bucket and had been lowered down the well to cool. Everything
that could be done, was done. The fat chickens were stuffed and ready. The
fruit had been piled into dishes and placed on the sideboard in readiness for
the morning. Robert also brought a small fir tree into the dining room. He
decorated it with painted fir cones, coloured ribbons and sweets. He cut some
holly and, shaking off the snow, brought it in and placed a small sprig behind
each of the pictures. At last all was prepared. Robert and Elizabet could go to
bed. Robert, who would be getting up early in any case to see to the horses, was
to put the meat on to cook so that it would be ready for the dinner.

At one o'clock the next day, Anna the cook was seated at the head of the
table, presiding over the feast. The rest of the servants and their families, all
dressed in their best and feeling very self-conscious, were seated round, waiting for the feast to begin. The children, dressed in traditional costumes, waited
on them. Robert acted as wine waiter. At first the atmosphere was very tense as
everyone was quite embarrassed at the reversal of rolls, but as the meal progressed and course followed course, tongues were loosened. A happy atmosphere prevailed. Finally the meal was finished. The people sat back with that
happy glazed look on their faces that told more eloquently than words that
they could eat no more. Anna rose unsteadily to her feet. She proposed the
health and good fortune of Robert and Elizabet. There was a burst of clapping
and cheering which went on until Elizabet finally appeared from the kitchen,

with her sleeves rolled up and one of Cook's aprons tied round her. She was red in the face from the heat and she had a long wisp of her fair hair hanging down. With the children happily standing round her, she took her bow. Robert put his arm round her waist and when the hullabaloo had died down, thanked them for all they had done throughout the year. The table was cleared except for jugs of beer and cider, the bottles of wine and trays of warm Mehlspeisen—sweetmeats and pastries that Elizabet had been making whilst the meal was being eaten. Tied to the little Christmas tree were little presents for everyone. The children now took these and gave them out. The children then sang some carols whilst Elizabet played the piano. They had an upright piano in the dinning room, so that the children could practise without driving the rest of the household mad! Once the singing and playing started, Robert and Elizabet were able to withdraw to leave their staff to enjoy the rest of the evening in their own way. The sound of the singing, music and merriment could be heard until well into the night.

On New Year's Eve, Emil gave a big dinner and ball at the Schloss to which Robert and Elizabet were invited. At midnight, they put on their cloaks and all came out onto the terrace to hear the village clock strike midnight. Whilst they listened to the Church bells being rung glasses of hot gluevine were handed round. Emil called them all inside again. They continued dancing until the dawn. Robert and Elizabet walked home across the park in the snow, the moon casting deep purple shadows all round. Far away in the distance they could hear a wolf howling. They stopped by the gate to listen. The night was deeply still. Not a sound could be heard, not even the rustle of the leaves. Then again, in the distance, the silence was broken by the solitary howling rising and falling, on and on. A shiver ran down Robert's spine.

"Ooh," he shuddered," it's an eerie sound. I remember on the first night that I was in Hungary, when I stayed at the castle, I heard wolves howling for the first time. I was very frightened. What is wrong, dear—do not cry." Tears were running down Elizabet's face.

"It makes me think of my home. My Mamma, God bless her. My poor Papa living in the castle in the winter on his own. We always had the wolves. In the winter they sing like this. People used to make big fires in the village when they hear wolves make sing close by. The fires were lit to keep the wolves away. When the wolves come too close, they put on the fire, branches of dry holly, which make loud crackling and bright flame. This frighten away the wolves." Robert put his arm round her and held her close.

"It's quite a frightening sound. I'm glad it's a long way away, though it somehow has an unearthly beauty to it."

"You would not say that if you had just found the remains of your young foal or calf that the wolves had eated, or had your geeses killed. When they are very hungry in the deeps of the winter, they will even kill the children if they catch them. They are easier to catch than deer, when there is deep snow."

"Come on, let's get home, we will catch our death of cold standing around here."

They walked on together, arm in arm and were glad of the warmth of the house when they finally shut the door. Elizabet went round to each of the children. She tucked them in and kissed them all lightly on the cheek. Robert looked at his watch.

"Come on, let's get to bed. At least with this snow, we will not be riding out in the morning, so I do not have to get up till six o'clock."

"What on earth do you do at that time of the day? I think that you go out then to get away from me."

"Is that what you think? Well, I will show you different!" He chased her upstairs to their bedroom.

CHAPTER 27

Spring was slow in coming that year. The snow hung around until the beginning of April. Robert was getting increasingly anxious. Because of the frozen ground and the slippery conditions, he had not dared to take the horses out onto the gallops so his training schedules were falling badly behind. He had made some lunging circles on the park with straw. The horses were exercised on these as much as possible. The lads, understandably, hated this work! Robert had constantly to keep an eye on them. They complained that they felt cold and dizzy as they endlessly turned in the centre with the horse alternately cantering, trotting and walking round them on the end of a long rein. However, Robert persisted, as it was the only exercise he could give the horses until the snow and frost went. He had to regulate the horse's diet carefully, too, as he wanted to keep them in the best possible condition. He was very anxious that they might, because of their lack of exercise, put on too much fat.

He was exasperated by the futility of fuming against conditions out of his control, and because of it, became irritable with Elizabet and the girls. He found it a strain, living in a home environment completely dominated by females. All the talk was about ribbons and fabrics and about what could be made with this piece of material, or how the drawing room might look better if it were redecorated in a different colour. He had been happy with it as it was. If he had been suddenly blindfolded and asked what colour the walls were, he probably would not have been able to answer correctly. What did it matter? As long as the colour was not obtrusive, what did the particular shade matter? He felt his home had been taken over! He felt he was being increasingly excluded. He spent more and more time at the stables or in the Estate Office. When he was at home he shut himself in his study.

It was something of a relief when a letter came from Schmidt informing Elizabet that her father had not weathered the winter well and was in poor health and spirits. He suggested that if she were able to make a visit, this might help restore him to a more cheerful mood. Robert was ready and willing to agree that she should take the children to stay with him for a while, so it was planned that they should go, to be there for Easter, then stay as long as seemed necessary. By then the racing season would be in full swing. He would be away from home quite a lot anyhow, so it would hardly matter if they were not there.

It was with a mixture of sadness and relief when, one April morning, he waved them goodbuy as they set out. They went in two carriages—Elizabet and her maid, with Cornelia, in one, and the nanny, Maria and Helen in the other, with a governess, who had been retained to come with them—as Elizabet planned to stay for at least two months. They were to be taken to the station to catch the train. They would be met at the other end by coaches sent down from the castle. The girls were very excited since this would be the first time that they would be on the train. Robert stood on the step and watched the little cavalcade drive across the Park.

One of the stable lad's wives had agreed to come in to cook for Robert whilst they were away. Robert was a little concerned about being alone in the house with the live-in maid, but he need not have worried. Her mother could also see the problem. She insisted that her daughter come home to live until the household returned to normal. She could come over in the morning to fulfil her duties but there was no question of her staying overnight alone with the Master. Robert was relieved. For the first time since he left England he could settle down in the evening, in front of the fire in his study, with a glass of whisky in his hand and enjoy the peace and solitude. He thought a lot about England and Lillian, but she had become just a name to him, rather than a person. He thought of Lord Shotley too and the other people he had known. They must be getting quite old by now. It was, after all, twenty years since he had left England.

It was whilst he was deep in this reverie, one evening, that there came a loud knocking at the door. He opened it. Too his surprise, he found Emil standing on the step. He ushered him into the study and sat him in a chair, in front of the fire. He soon had a large glass of whisky in his hand.

"What on earth brings you here at this time of night? Not bad news, I hope?"

"Yes, Robert. It is bad news! Very bad news—news that will affect us all!" He paused and drank. Robert waited expectantly.

"Ferdinand has been assassinated!"

"Ferdinand?"

"Yes, the Archduke Franz Ferdinand of Austria. He was in Sorojevo and he has been shot. He is dead!"

"My God! Assassinated! That is terrible! What is the world coming to? Terrible though this is, it will not affect us though…will it?"

"Well, who knows what will happen? It could affect us. The Austrian Government has issued the most impossible ultimatum to the Serbs. If they do not accept, the Austrians will declare war."

"It won't come to that, surly?"

"It almost certainly will. The Serbs are not going to accept the ultimatum. It is ridiculous. No one would accept it. It is just being used as an excuse to go to war with them and take revenge."

"That will not affect us though, will it?"

"Well, it depends how the situation develops. If it is beyond the strength of the Empire, Germany will throw its lot in with them; then there is no telling what might happen. I am on the military reserve and I have already had unofficial warning that I might be called up."

The next few days were very tense. Everyone was on tenterhooks. No one could talk of or think about anything else, other than what might happen. They did not have to wait for long. The Serbs flatly rejected the ultimatum, as it had been inevitable that they would. Austria consequently declared war on Serbia, as had been widely predicted.

It seemed that the matter was going to be settled on a local level but immediately the Russians mobilised to come to the defence of Serbia. Germany, wanting to settle some old scores and hoping to put pressure on the Russians by attacking her main ally, implemented the Schlieffen plan and marched across Belgium to attack France. Belgium immediately called upon her ally, Great Britain, to come to her aid. Britain, who was also a party to a tripartite alliance with France and Russia, declared war on Germany. In a matter of a few hectic weeks, the whole of Europe was at war.

Many of the stable lads enlisted. Robert suddenly found that he had to do their work, despite pleas in the village for older men to come and help. He found that as an Englishman he had suddenly become the 'enemy'. No one would talk to him; no one would come to work for him, or to help out. He was shunned as if he personally was responsible for the catastrophe in which they all found themselves. One night just as Robert was going to bed there was an urgent knock on his door. Robert opened it cautiously. Emil was again standing there. As soon as the door opened, he pushed in past Robert, quickly shutting the door behind him. Robert, somewhat startled, stepped back. Emil was dressed in a military uniform over which he had thrown an old loden great coat. He was out of breath. He had obviously been hurrying.

"Robert, pay attention to what I have to say. I have to join my regiment tomorrow, so I have no other chance than now. Listen. I have heard this evening that tomorrow all English citizens living in Germany are to be arrested and interned. You must escape tonight or you will spend the duration of the war, however long that may be, behind bars in some Godforsaken prison camp." As he was speaking, Robert ushered him into the study. He poured out two large glasses of whisky.

"Escape? How can I escape? What about the horses? I cannot just go and leave them. We are desperately short handed as it is. I cannot just go."

"Do not worry about my horses," Emil said bitterly. "I no longer have any horses. The Kaiser needs them. They have been requisitioned."

"Requisitioned? All of them?"

"No. I am allowed to keep enough for the use of the household."

"But they are race horses. They are not war horses. They are too good for that."

"Oh, don't worry, no doubt some prancing staff officers will make sure that they are allocated to them. It will just tickle their fancy to ride around on some of the best horses in Germany. The Commission is in the stables already counting them to make sure that I do not spirit any away. The lads have all been conscripted into the army. They will ride them all away tomorrow morning. All the draught animals of the estate are to go too. They will be rounded up tomorrow to follow on as soon as they are all assembled."

"But they cannot just take your horses! They are valuable."

"Yes. That is why they are taking them. They are going to give me a receipt, though quite what good that will be, remains to be seen. Now, enough of this. You have your own situation to consider. The Burgermeister has orders to arrest you in the morning. He is to put you in the cells until you can be moved to a camp. You must escape now."

"But how do you know all this?"

"Never mind how I know. Someone who felt he owed me a favour has given me the tip. You must go now. There is no chance of your escaping, unless you go at once!"

"I can't go now. I'm not ready. What about Elizabet and the children? I cannot just run away and leave them!"

"Do not worry about them at the moment. They are quite safe where they are. In any event, she is a Hungarian in Hungary. It is very unlikely that the fighting will be near them."

"But if the Russians invade to relieve Serbia, they will be right in the middle."

"Well, what are you going to do about it? Are you going to stand in the road with your beautiful sporting gun and hold up your hand when the Russian's cavalry comes to tell them that they cannot pass?" Robert had to laugh at the absurdity of the notion.

"If I go, I ought to go to them, so that at least I can be with them."

"Robert, do not be ridiculous. How can you get to them? Forgive me, but the minute you speak, your accent is so bad, you would be arrested. The roads and rails are under military control. There are guards everywhere, checking people's papers. You would be picked up at once."

"Well, let me take a horse. I will go across country."

"Even supposing that you make it, how are you going to get across the Danube? There are guards on all bridges over the major rivers; you would be picked up at once."

"There must be a way. I cannot just go and leave them! They could be in real danger."

"Supposing, just supposing that you managed to get through, they would be worse off with you there. You would be putting them into danger. You would be arrested as an English person. Very likely they would be arrested too, for no matter what Elizabet claims, she is English by marriage, so of course all the children are English. Do you want to see them all arrested?"

Robert could see the reason behind this. "Well, what am I going to do? Perhaps I could take a train…"

"No! Look, I have already thought what to do. Pack a light bag with as much food as you can carry and any portable valuables, then put this on." He offered Robert a chauffeur's coat and hat. "I will take you to the Swiss boarder in my car. You will have to make your way over the boarder on foot, but once you are in Switzerland, at least you will be free of the threat of internment. You will have time to work out what you are going to do next."

"But I must tell Elizabet. I cannot just disappear."

"For goodness sake, Robert! You have not got time. Unless we go now, you will not make it. You have got to cross the boarder into Switzerland in darkness, otherwise you will be seen and arrested or shot! Unless we go now, you will be too late. Now stop prevaricating! Come! When you are in Switzerland you can send as many letters as you like. For now, quickly write out a little message. I will have a pigeon sent first thing in the morning, but be quick, for we must go now."

"I cannot possibly allow you to do this, You are bound to be found out and you will be accused for helping an enemy of the Country escape. It is quite out of the question. I will go on foot and walk to the next station. No one will recognise me there. I will be all right if I only move at night."

"Do not talk such rubbish. How far do you think you would get? You will be behind bars before the day is over! They will not be able to prove anything against me and even if they do, I am to join my regiment tomorrow, so I will be gone also!"

Robert decided. He could see that everything that Emil said was sense. He quickly ran upstairs to collect some extra clothes. Snatching up Lillian's photo, he ran down again. He took the money that he had in his desk. He stuffed the glass vase with the tie pin into his bag. He went quickly into the larder. He filled a game bag with all the cold meat and cheese he could lay his hands on. Pulling on his boots he returned to the study. Emil stood in front of the fireplace, a glass of whisky in his hand.

"Are you ready? Take this as well. You might be glad of it, if the nights are cold." Robert took the half-empty whisky bottle and stuffed it into the top of his bag.

"Yes. Just a minute, whilst I do these notes." Robert tore a piece of paper in four and after some thought wrote on one: 'Gone to visit Lillian's grave. Stay where you are. See you when the wind changes.' He gave it to Emil. "Please make sure that this is sent off to Elizabet tomorrow, without fail. I will write to her when I get to Switzerland."

"Yes, of course, without fail—but now we must hurry. Come on."

Robert locked the back door and ran back into the study. "Right, I am as ready as I ever will be."

Emil put down his glass. "Come on then. You must walk across the Park to the South gate. Keep in the shadows of the trees. I will pick you up in the car. Be as quick as you can. It should take you twenty minutes or so. I will be there in twenty minutes' time. Blow the hall lamp out before you open the door. Technically, you are enemy now. It would never do for me to be seen leaving here. I might be shot for aiding the enemy! Leave the other lamps burning—they will go out when they run out of oil. I do not want it to look as if the bird has flown tonight!"

They left the house in silence. Robert locked the front door. Emil reached his hand out for the keys.

"You had better give them to me. Just in case. I will hang them in the office in the Schloss. See you in twenty minutes." He walked quietly away, keeping to the shadows of the hedge.

Robert set off across the Park, his bags over his shoulder. He too went from shadow to shadow, keeping as much out of the bright moonlight as possible. He was aware of the need to hurry. By the time he reached the South gate he was sweating heavily. There was no sign of Emil, so he dumped his bags on the ground and waited in the shadows of the wall. Presently he heard the puttering of the engine. Emil was coming down the drive without lights. He stopped just inside the gateway. Robert stepped out.

Emil saw him. "Quick! Change hats and coats. I forgot. You do not know how to drive, do you? I will be the chauffeur, you sit in the back. If we get stopped, whatever you do, do not say anything."

They quickly changed. Robert climbed into the plush seats at the back. Emil slid back the glass partition so that they could talk and set off. Robert had never been in a car before—this was a new experience for him. It was a lot faster than the coach. Not as fast as a train, but by the very dim light given off by the two hissing lamps, it seemed to be very fast indeed. It was very plush and comfortable but the springing was no better than a coach. They lurched and jolted along as Emil did the best he could to avoid the worst of the pot-holes. They were stopped three times by guards on the river bridges, but Emil's curt explanation that he was taking the General and that all these questions were preventing him from getting there, soon had them on their way again. They drove hard all through the night but as dawn rose over the still distant Alps, Emil stopped.

"We are not going to make it. We will arrive in the middle of the day. That is just going to be no good at all. You will have no chance if you try to cross the boarder in daylight. We will have to hide up in a wood or somewhere to wait until this evening…" He drove on for about half an hour, by which time it was quite light. Suddenly he swerved into a gateway and drove deep into a wood. Presently they came across a small clearing. He drove into it and backed the car as far into the trees as it would go. Quickly cutting off some leafy branches, he gave some to Robert.

"Come on." They ran back to the road to do the best they could to brush out the wheel tracks. When they got back to the car, they covered the front with the branches. At least it was hidden from a casual observer, should one happen by. Emil opened the trunk and took out a big basket of food.

"I threw these in the back, just in case we should have time for a bite; we might as well avail ourselves of it now. We are going to have to wait here for the rest of the day."

He spread out the contents, half a ham, some cold beef, bread and cold potatoes, some hard cheese and a bottle of wine. They sat in the morning sun, with their backs against a tree and ate their fill. When they could eat no more, they packed the things away. Curling up on the mossy ground, they went to sleep. It was late afternoon when they awoke. Emil sat up listening intently.

"Listen!" From the road they could hear the sound of many horses and wheels rumbling.

"It sounds like a military convoy. As long as they don't see our wheel tracks, we should be all right." They waited, hardly daring to breath. The column took a long time passing. Eventually the sound of it faded away into the distance. Emil heaved a sigh of relief.

"I do not think that they saw anything. We will have to wait for a while, now. We do not want to catch up with them." They waited for the rest of the afternoon. It was dusk before they were on their way again. Presently Emil called over his shoulder.

"We will soon be at the Austrian boarder. I will take a side road. I do not know if there will be a Guard post there, but hopefully we will be able to bluff our way through. Whatever you do, do not speak." In the event the boarder had no guard. They were soon heading towards Switzerland in the gathering dark. The hills were getting steeper. The car was finding it more and more difficult to climb them. On occasions they slowed to a crawl. Little puffs of steam came out of the bonnet. At last Emil pulled into the side of the road. There was a wide grass verge. He turned the car round and turned off the engine.

"Bring your things. The boarder is just over the top of this hill."

Robert swung his bags over his shoulder and they set off up the hill.

"It's very good of you to take this enormous risk for me," Robert said with sincerity.

Emil smiled. "Think nothing of it. I would do it for any of my friends and so would you."

"But if you get caught, you will be shot."

Emil shrugged his shoulders. "I do not plan to get caught! You had better give me your uniform. If you get caught in a German military uniform you will be shot as a spy."

They stopped and Robert gave Emil his coat back. They reached the top of the hill. Cautiously they looked over it.

"Look, the boarder is down there."

Robert stared into the dark but he could see nothing.

Emil pointed. "You will have to go across country. You cannot go down the road—you will be arrested at once. See that pointed hill on the skyline? Keep that in front of you. Go round to the right-hand side of it. If you keep going steadily, you should be well inside Switzerland by morning. Keep well away from the guard posts. Be as quiet as you can. They are bound to have dogs. You do not want to start them barking. The moon should be out again soon and it will give you enough light to see by, but keep in the shadows as much as possible." He placed a hand on Robert's shoulder. "Well, this is it. Good luck, Robert. I hope that we will meet again soon. God be with you. Think of me, your friend, from time to time, with some kindness."

Robert was not very good at 'goodbyes' and could feel a lump coming into his throat. "Goodbye Emil. I cannot thank you enough for what you've done for me. You've risked your life to save me from prison."

The two men embraced.

"Goodbye, Robert."

"Goodbye, Emil."

Still they clung together. Emil gave Robert a shove.

"Go on, be off with you—God speed."

Robert started off down the hill, but he stopped and turned.

"Godspeed with you too, Emil." He waved his hand. Slowly he walked off down the hill. Emil sat down on a rock and watched him until he disappeared. He sat on the rock until dawn, but heard no dog bark, no shout, no shot, no sudden alarm in the night. As the sun rose over the hills, he stood up stiffly. Climbing back into the car, he drove away.

CHAPTER 28

Elizabet held the pieces of paper in her hand. The messages had been brought in from the pigeon loft at tea time. Emil had also put a short message into the tiny container. It was just as brief.—"Join regiment tomorrow. All horses requisitioned. Lodge closed down. Robert safely in Switzerland. Stay where you are until further news. E."

Elizabet had been wracked with anxiety ever since she had heard about English people being interned. A very precocious, unpleasant little official had come to the castle demanding to know where Robert was. He had openly sneered when he had been told he was still in Germany. "He will be arrested very soon there. He will be locked up, safely out of the way," he had jeered.

At least these two messages confirmed that Robert had escaped to Switzerland safely. She was mindful of her children's safety. She felt that personally, here, she would be all right. She was, after all, Hungarian, surrounded by her own people, even though she had married an Englishman. But she was taking no chances with the children. Their father was English, so presumably they were too. It was possible they might be interned as well, though what threat they posed to the safety of the Central Powers, she could not see. However, she was going to take no chances. She did not take them out of the Castle grounds. She made sure that there was always someone with them watching over them.

She found, as Schmidt had warned her, that her father was in very low spirits when she arrived. He had however cheered up when he saw her. He was content to know that she had taken charge of the running of the Castle again. The continual stream of small demands irritated him. Schmidt was always bothering him with some trivial matter or other. He had become so exasperated with the man, that he would start shouting at him on sight, not even waiting to hear what he had to say. Schmidt was forced to resort to making all the decisions himself. He soon found he could do nothing right and in desperation he had written to Elizabet. He was thankful she had come. At least the Count was in a happier frame of mind. He could unload all the problems onto her. However, there was one problem he would have to deal with himself.

He toyed with the brown envelope in his hand. He decided to speak to Elizabet first.

"Graffinflein, I have here a letter from Germany. From the War Office. I have been called to join the army. I must report on the twenty-third." He consulted a calendar. "That is next week. To arrive there on time, I will have to leave straightaway." He had thought for a long time about what he should do. His first reaction was that this presented the golden opportunity to leave the Castle with all its problems and the irascible Count, but news of heavy casualties was filtering in from the Front. He was not so sure. It might be that his work here would protect him. When the choice was between being blown to bits in a muddy, water filled, stinking, rat infested trench or putting up with the Count's unpredictable humours, it did not take him long to make up his mind! He would need Graffinflein to endorse his application for a Reserved Occupation.

She took the letter from him and read it. *Thank God!* she thought to herself. *At last I shall have this loathsome person off my back.* She handed the letter back to him.

"I am very sorry, Herr Schmidt. Of course you will have to go. We will miss you here and all that you do for us, but the call of your country must come first. I will come to the office later this morning. You can tell me everything that I need to know; then you can leave as soon as you are ready."

"But Graffinflein, you will not be able to manage everything. There are so many details. So much to remember. So many people to consider. There are the Estates and the Stud, the Mills. The peasants, every thing. It is not just running the affairs of the Castle, you know."

"Herr Schmidt, if you have been as efficient as you make out, I am sure that I will find everything in good order. I am sure that I will be able to manage."

"But Graffinflein, there are so many things. I think that I must apply for 'Reserved Occupation' so that I can stay here to see that everything runs as efficiently as it can."

Elizabet's eyes narrowed. *So that was what this was all about. He was hoping to avoid going to fight. He was afraid he was a…* She stopped short of thinking the word 'coward'.

"No, we could no possibly stand in the way of you and your duty. We will manage, have no fear." She sounded more confident than she felt, but if it meant she would get rid of the dreadful man any sacrifice was worth taking. They would manage somehow. She decided not to tell her father just yet.

Later on in the morning she went to Schmidt's office. She spent the rest of the morning going through all his records and accounts with him. It was hot and stuffy in the little office. The smelly paraffin lamps added an oily airlessness to the room. She felt slightly faint and sick. Soon after she arrived at the Castle she realised she was pregnant again. Now she was going through that time when it did not take much to make her feel queasy. However, she bit her lip and did the best she could to pay attention to Schmidt as he droned on, explaining the significance of this column of figures, this list, that set of records. By lunchtime she felt quite dizzy. She was glad, when the gong sounded, to escape from the close confines of the oppressive little room.

It was decided that Schmidt should leave after breakfast the next day. Elizabet resolved that she would not tell her father until after he had gone.

The next morning, after breakfast, she met Schmidt in the hall. His one small bag was packed. He stood uncertainly with his hat in his hand. He had said little at breakfast, and now stood looking for all the world like one going to the gallows.

"Goodbye, Herr Schmidt." Elizabet shook his limp hand. "Good luck. Good fortune go with you. Go with a proud heart, knowing that you are doing your duty. Have no fear, we will be all right here. Thank you for all that you have done for us."

A small tear came into his eye. He had worked for the Count for so long that any other existence seemed alien and threatening. He had been so long in the security of the Castle, that the outside world with all its likely dangers seemed terrifying. Elizabet could see the fear and uncertainty in his eyes. She realised that he was loathe to go.

"We will remember all that you have done for us here. We wish you well in your new career as a soldier."

Schmidt could say nothing. He picked up his bag and walked out of the door. He had arranged for the coach to take him to the river steamer. It stood ready for him outside. He climbed in. As it drove off, he did not look back. Elizabet came in from the front step and shut the door firmly behind her and leant back on it with a sigh of relief. Thank goodness he had gone! She felt as if a weight had been lifted. Horrid man! He made her flesh creep. She was sure she could manage very well without him.

She determined that she would ride out to the Stud later on to see what was afoot there. She went to the kitchen to ask the cook to prepare her a picnic. The French cook had disappeared one night as soon as the war had started. His was a very precarious position. He had felt the real hostility of his situation. He knew that he must get away to some neutral country, for as an 'enemy' he would be arrested. No one saw him go, or had heard anything of him since. Franc had managed to find a woman from the village who came to take on the task. Whilst her food lacked the finesse of the Frenchman, it was good and wholesome. She prepared it without the histrionics that had accompanied almost everything that had previously come from the kitchen. She cheerfully prepared the picnic in a basket. When it was ready, she sent it to the front door. Yes. She would prepare a special little dish for the Count and the children for their lunch. She would make a proper dinner for the evening.

Feeling that she had begun to take control of things, Elizabet set off in her little gig for the Stud. In a bag she had the Stud book that Robert had made, which Schmidt had maintained, based on information given him by Soldo. She was just about to cross the bridge over the moat when a young man dressed in a military uniform, riding towards her, blocked her way. She reined in her horse and waited for him to come. He stopped beside her and saluted.

"I seek the Count Ramoskie. Will I find him here?"

"Yes, he is here, but he is old and frail. I am his daughter. I look after his affairs. If you have any business with him, you must speak with me." He looked at her uncertainly for a moment, then handed her a letter.

"In that case, Frauline, I will give this letter to you. Good day." He turned his horse and rode away. He stopped on the middle of the bridge and turned back to her.

"It must be obeyed." He rode away. Elizabet quickly opened the envelope and read:

From the German War Office—to the holders of numbers of Horses.

∾

> You are required to make your horses available for the War Department forthwith. All horses are to be delivered to the railway station [this was crossed out and under it was written 'the River steamer'], five days from receipt of this letter. An officer in charge of the Muster will be there to receive them. He is authorised to issue a receipt.

> You may only keep those horses that are essential for the running of your needs.

Any person not delivering up all the horses that he has, will be regarded as a traitor and will be forthwith subject to the full penalties of Military Law.

Signed…General in Charge of Requisitions.

She was shocked. All their horses!? She was damned if she was going to hand over all her horses! They had carefully followed the breeding programmes that Robert had set out. They had some very promising horses. She was just not going to hand them over. She whipped up her pony. Presently she was spinning along at a smart pace whilst she wondered what to do. Whatever she handed over had to be a realistic sample of what they might expect. She would have to close down the Stud. If she did not they would think that there were still horses out there. What would happen to all the people who worked there and their families? Were would they go? What would they do? They would not get paid anymore. How would they live? There was a small farm attached to the Stud that provided the men and their families living there, with all the vegetables, eggs and poultry that they needed. It also produced milk, cream, butter and cheese. It grew enough grain, straw and hay for the horses and cattle and beans for the pigs and sheep. It enabled the Stud and the people who worked there to be self-sufficient. If the Stud was closed down and the farm handed over to the people who lived there, to sustain them, some huge problems would be taken off her shoulders. All the problems of sending horses to race meetings would also disappear. Presumably if people had to surrender their horses, there would be no racing. Well, it didn't matter. If their horses were gone, the question of racing was purely academic. They certainly would not be taking part. All these questions and many more kept buzzing round in her head and she hardly noticed the journey at all. She arrived, it seemed to her, before she had barely left.

It was not long before she found Soldo. Taking him into the tack room, she explained what had happened and her plan. Between them, they selected six of the mares, all of which were in foal and the young stallion. These were to be brought to the castle. The six coach horses would be sent in their place. All the other horses except the four Lipizanners that were used to pull her mother's coach were to go too, except for the pony that she was using today and two riding horses. On second thoughts, she decided that the four Lipizanners were too conspicuous. It would be better to surrender them and to keep four of the other coach horses. No doubt some dandy officers would be glad to commandeer the Lipizanners to pretend that they were little Napoleons. They were welcome to them. They looked very fine, but had been selected because they were very sedate and steady, most suitable for her mother's stately progress wherever she went. Half of the draught horses attached to the Stud were to be retained, so that the people living there could use them. She told Soldo to send the oldest. The rest of the horses from the Castle and the Stud were to be rounded up to be taken to the collecting officer at the steamboat on the next Wednesday. Soldo nodded that he understood.

Elizabet then asked him when it would be convenient to assemble everyone from the Bothy so that she could speak to them. She wished to speak to them altogether. Soldo said they were usually all there at about 6 o'clock in the evening for their meal—that would be a good time. She asked him to go round to tell everyone that she wished to speak to them. She would like representatives from each family to gather in the courtyard then, as she had something important to say.

With the time that she had spare, she decided to go and look at the house. She had not been near it since she had been over it with Robert all those years ago, when he had first arrived and it was being prepared for him to live in. Taking her picnic basket, she walked through the inner arch. The garden was completely untended. She again had to push her way through shoulder-high stinging nettles. At least the windows and the roof were sound. She tried the door. It was locked. The key? She had not thought to bring the key from the Office. There must be a key here somewhere that she could use. The key was rather large, she remembered. When they were preparing the house, rather than carry it around in his pocket, Robert had hidden it behind—that brick! Carefully, and after a little struggle, she eased the brick up from the floor. There, underneath it, was the key. It must have lain there since Robert put it there last. Schmidt must have used the key from the Office when he had come to collect Robert's things. She cleaned it on her skirt and then, fitting it into the door, turned the lock after considerable effort.

The door creaked open, but this time it did not fall off its hinges. She walked in. Everything was as it had been left. The furniture that had been sent from the Castle stood together in the hall, just where it had been left when it was unloaded off the wagon. The vase of flowers still stood on the floor, just a few dead stalks surrounded by a circle of dead leaves and petals. She walked round the house. There was a thick coat of dust everywhere. Cobwebs hung in festoons from the beams and doorways, but it was otherwise sound. In the kitchen, the hamper of food that she had had sent was still on the table. She opened the lid, but the chewed papers and chaos inside told that the mice had long ago eaten all the contents. She dropped the lid shut with a bang. Mice ran out in all directions and disappeared in every corner. She let out a little scream, quickly gathering up her skirts as they scurried around in panic.

She decided to sit outside in the sun to eat her picnic, so taking a chair from the hall, she settled down in the sun. As she ate, she remembered the first visit to the house with Robert. She had been overwhelmed by the neglect of it all then. She felt overwhelmed by the pathos of it now. Here it was, just as it was left then. Nothing disturbed. Half prepared, nothing finished. Even the bed that had been sent was dragged into the side room. Robert had obviously slept on it there. He had not bothered to have it carried upstairs. Now where was he? What had happened to him? She had spent all last night tossing and turning, worrying about him, not knowing. She had sent a pigeon back to Emil asking for more information. Robert's message said that he was going to visit Lillian's grave. When she first read it, she had had a shock. Was he still hankering after her? But after some thought, she realised that it could only mean that he was going to try to reach England. But what chance had he? He spoke German so badly—the minute he opened his mouth he would be arrested. Then what would happen to him? Would he be put in prison? Would he be put in a labour gang? She did not know. It did not bear thinking of. Suppose he had been captured already! He might even have been shot trying to escape! Tears ran down her face. Not knowing anything was worse than knowing that he was dead. If he were dead, that was a finite thing. She could eventually come to terms with that. Not knowing was terrible. By not knowing, you could imagine all kinds of things, all kinds of alarms and horrors could fill your mind. But then there was Emil's note. He had gone to the army. What would happen to him? Would he be safe? How did he know that Robert was safe in Switzerland? How could he be sure? Unless he had some hand in his escape! That would be like Emil. He liked Robert. He would help him if he could. What was going to happen to her and the girls? At least they were safe here. They could stay here with her father until the situation changed. Robert knew where they were. He would surely find a way of getting in touch.

She shivered. The sun had gone in. It was getting cold. She looked at her watch. It was time, anyway. She walked back to the Courtyard. There was quite a crowd gathered there. She found Soldo.

"Are there many more to come?"

"A few more I think, Graffinflein; perhaps we wait a little."

They waited another ten minutes. A few more people gathered round. Elizabet looked at the faces surrounding her. Some she recognised, but most she did not. Women, children and old men.

"Where are the men? There are only old men. Where are the men?" She climbed up on the water trough so that she could see better.

"There are no young men. Where are they?"

Soldo avoided her eyes, but did not answer. Elizabet jumped down and faced him. "Listen, you silly man! I am trying to help you. Where are they?"

"They have gone, Graffinflein."

"Gone? Gone where?"

"I do not know, Graffinflein." He was clutching his hat to his chest and wringing it miserably in his hands.

"Why have they gone?"

"They had their papers to go to the army. They did not want to go. They have gone to the mountains."

"But that will make them deserters. If they are caught they will be shot."

"They would rather take the risk than go to the army and be blown to bits."

"But the army is winning. We are having glorious battles. The German army is invincible."

"If they are invincible, let them fight. We do not want to fight for them in their wars. If we fight, we will fight here, to defend our own. The Russians are attacking from the North and our men will go and fight them in the mountains. They will not go and fight in a German Army."

"But we are allies of the Germans. Their fight is our fight."

"Forgive me, Graffinflein, but we have no quarrel with the French or for that matter with the English. We do not wish to fight them. If we fight, we fight for our homes and our own peoples." Elizabet shrugged. They had to make their own decisions, she could not compel them. She jumped up on the water tank again.

"Gather round and listen. I have very important things to say to you. I have had a letter—a letter from the German High Command, commandeering all the horses. They have to go on Wednesday, to help with the war effort. I have spoken to Soldo. He knows what is to be done. Because there are no men here, the work will fall on you older men and you woman; those that can, will have to help. Everyone who works until Wednesday, will be paid in full. Soldo will keep a list and give it to me. I will make sure that monies are given to him for that, according to his list. After Wednesday the Stud will be closed. There will be no more horses here, so there will be no more work. This is not of my choosing. It is because of the war."

A murmur ran round the group. Several shouted out. "What about us?" "What are we to do?" "Bloody typical! Use us as slaves when we are wanted and dump us when we are not."

"No, listen." Elizabet raised her voice so that she could be heard. "Listen. I do not want to do this. I do not want to give away my horses. Would you? No. Would any of you? Of course you would not! We are Magyar! The Magyar do not give away their horses! But I have no choice. They know we have horses here. I have been commanded to hand them over. I cannot refuse. If I do not hand them over, I will be accused of hindering the war effort. Perhaps shot." A murmur ran round again. "Listen. I am not dumping you. Listen! You are all free to go if you wish. I cannot hold you here. If you have anywhere else to go, then go there. But until the war is over and we are able to reopen the Stud, you may stay here. You may continue to live in the Bothy. I will turn over to you for your use the farm with everything on it, free of rent. It is up to you to cultivate it. Run it in a way that produces enough food for all of you. If you can produce a surplus that you can sell, you can keep the money. Use it to buy things that you need. When all this is over I will take the farm back again, but until then, I can only wish you good luck. I am sorry. I am not dumping you, but that is the best that I can do for you." There was silence in the crowd. She jumped down from the tank and hovered uncertainly. No one said anything, so she climbed into her gig.

"Soldo, are you clear about everything?"

"Yes Graffinklein. I think we are all clear."

She cracked her whip and drove away. No one moved. No one waved. She felt annoyed, sad, let down. She had done for them more than most would. She had tried to make provision for them in the most generous way that she could. Many would have simply told them there was no more work and that they should leave. She had left them with a roof over their heads, and the farm would support them. They could consider themselves a lot luckier than most. Someone might have said something. Anything would have been better than that hostile silence. She shuddered. It was cold. She wrapped her shawl round her. It started to rain, a drizzle soon turning into a downpour. She stopped to pull up the hood, but she could not.

"Damn, damn, damn!" she shouted at the obstinate thing. She gave up and, sitting in the pouring rain, she drove home as fast as she could. When she arrived home she was shivering and blue with cold, absolutely soaked through.

She went straight into the kitchen and had cook make her some hot milk and honey. She asked Frank to organise a hot bath for her, but that was going to take some time. The copper had to be heated. It would be a while before there was enough hot water. Cook put some blankets in the oven to heat them up. Posting a maid at the door to keep people out, she stripped off her wet clothes in front of the warm kitchen range and wrapped herself in the heated blankets.

"I shall be in the blue drawing room. Call me as soon as the water is hot." In her bare feet, with her wet hair hanging down and wrapped in blankets, she went into the blue room where the children were reading. Maria was playing the piano. Her father was asleep in his chair. When they saw her they ran shrieking to her.

"Mamma, what are you doing! Are you being a witch? Are you being the wife of Saint Nicholas bringing us presents?"

"No, you silly little things, I am not. I am being your poor mamma, who has got soaking wet and is freezing cold and who is trying to get near the fire so that she can be warm." The noise woke the Count who demanded to know what on earth was going on.

"Why are you walking about looking like the wet bear?"

She rolled a log onto the hearth and, sitting on it as near to the fire as she dared, she told him of the developments of the day.

"You give away my horses!" he gasped in horror when she had finished.

"No papa, I did not give them away. The Government has took them."

"Took them? How can they just took them?"

"It is for the war. They need them for the war." She showed him the order "They will give a receipt for them. Maybe, we get paid."

He was slightly mollified, but the shock was deep. "My beautify horses. All gone! Given away!" he kept muttering to himself.

Elizabet gave up trying to tell him. He had got the idea into his head and it was not to be lightly shifted.

"Schmidt would not have let them be given away. Why did you not speak with him?"

"Schmidt has gone, papa."

"Gone? Schmidt gone too? Why he gone?" he demanded cantankerously. "Where he go?"

"He has gone to the army. He has had papers telling him to go. He had to go at once."

"Gone to the army? God help us all. Schmidt in the army! He cannot go. He is needed here. He would not have let my horses be given away."

Luckily at that moment the maid came in to say that Graffinflein's bath was ready, if she could come whilst it was still hot. Elizabet got up from her log and, wrapping her blankets round her, bent down and kissed her father.

"I love you papa, but sometimes you can be very difficult." She left the room.

"What, what, what was that which you say?"

After Elizabet's bath, she did not dress for dinner but came down in her housecoat. She was very tired and still chilled through after her soaking. She felt that she would go to bed early as soon as dinner was over. She would ask Frank to see that a warming pan was put in her bed. Before coming downstairs she looked in on Cornelia, but she was already fast asleep, so she went to the top of the stairs and called for Helen to come up. She tucked her into bed and kissed her goodnight, then went down to dinner. Maria was allowed to stay up to have dinner with her mother and Grandfather, so the three of them went to the dining room together. Elizabet had had the table made smaller. It seemed ridiculous that they should be spread round the huge table, having to shout at each other to be heard. The smaller table had been moved to a position in front of the fireplace, so at least they could all be reasonably warm. Once the soup was eaten and they were enjoying the main course, Elizabet put down her knife and fork.

"Papa, Maria, I have something to tell you."

"What, you have more to tell us? What is it this time? You will say that you have given away my house next."

"No papa. It is about Robert. You saw in the paper that they were going to arrest all Eengleesh people to lock them away. I have had a message from Emil. Emil has gone to join the army too, but he say that Robert has escaped and is safe in Switzerland."

"Emil in the army? Robert in Switzerland? What has the world come! What has happened to my horses that Emil has? You will tell me next that they have been given to the Germans as well!"

"Yes, I suppose they have. He said in his message that his horses had all gone and the Stud was closed down!"

"Mine Gott! The world will come to an end!"

"Is papa all right?" Anxiety was etched on Maria's young face.

"I do not know, my darling. Emil says that he is safe in Switzerland. I had a message from Papa too. He say that he will try to get to Eengland. I do not know, my darling, where he is, or if he is all right or not. We just have to wait until we hear." Her lip quivered as she fought to hold back her tears. She pushed her plate away. "I do not want to eat. Too many things have happened today. I am not hungry. I will go to bed." She got up and kissed her father. "Goodnight, papa. I will go to bed. I am very tired. Do not worry about these things too much, it will not change them. Goodnight Maria, my dear, do not be too late to bed."

Maria jumped up. "No, no, I will come to bed too, I am not hungry."

"No my dear, you stay and finish your meal; you do not eat enough for a mouse as it is."

"No, no, mama, I will come up. Goodnight Grand Papa" She kissed him lightly and followed her mother.

The Count shook his head woefully. "First the horses, then Schmidt, then Robert, then Emil, now Elizabet and then Maria. Am I the only one who is left?"

CHAPTER 29

The next morning, Elizabet went round the stables in the castle with Joseph the coachman and the head groom to decide on the horses to be handed over. She felt a certain unease. Both of them had been working at the Castle for several years, but since the servants' strike, in which they had both taken part, she was not so sure of their loyalty. The horses that she handed over had to be convincing, or the German authorities would come round to see for themselves. If they came to the castle to inspect, she was not at all sure that some of her staff might not betray any extra horses that she had hidden away. She had thought of sending the best horses away. There was a small farm, isolated in the forest, that she could use, but she felt so sure that she might be betrayed if she did so, that she decided against it. She had always lived a happy and secure life and this feeling now, that there were people upon whom she had to rely, but who might not be entirely trustworthy and loyal, was unpleasant, disquieting and unnerving. She had to show confidence, even if she did not feel it.

She carefully inspected everything. In the end, she stuck to her plan. Only the four best coach horses were to be retained. She would keep her pony for her gig and one young carthorse for duty around the place. She would also keep four riding horses. Everything else was to go with the horses from the Stud. The mares and the young stallion from the Stud were to come here. She would try to pass them off as coach horses, if she had to. Neither Joseph nor the groom had been called to the army, as they were too old. The under grooms had gone already, some to the mountains, some to obey their Call-Up papers—and in the latter case had gone to the Front. The two of them had been doing their best to look after the horses but were finding the task beyond them. The stables were not cleaned out. The horses had not been groomed for a long time. They were relieved that their work was going to be lightened and saw the whole thing as a blessing. They enthusiastically tried to persuade Elizabet to get rid of every horse that they came to. Their obvious glee at the lessening of their charges irritated Elizabet, who was feeling as if she were consigning her best friends to a firing squad with every horse that was selected.

Elizabet was very moody that night. She felt she had betrayed those that trusted in her, but she could see no realistic way of avoiding sending any of the horses. The children, catching her mood, were particularly quarrelsome and squabbled incessantly over everything. In the end she could bear it no longer.

"Oh, for goodness sake, you children, that is enough. You go all to bed!"

Their chorus of protest only stiffened her resolve. "No! I have had enough. Off you go at once to bed. I cannot stand any more of this stupid, stupid quarrel. Maria, go and call your Nanny. She can put you all to bed now. Hurry, hurry, be quick."

Maria shot off, wiping the tear from her eye. Presently she returned with the Nanny.

"Please to take the children to bed at once, They do nothing but squabble."

The nanny bobbed a little curtsy. "Yes Mam, but please Mam, the children ai'nt 'ad no supper. If you please, mam." She bobbed again.

"They will not have any supper. They are too naughty. Take them off. Goodnight, children. I hope that you behave better in the morning."

"But mama," ventured Maria, "it is not fair. Cornelia was taking our things."

"Silence! You all go to bed. I will hear no more. Goodnight. Off you go. And take all your things with you."

Sheepishly they gathered up their books and dolls. Kissing their mother and grandfather goodnight, they went sadly to bed.

"Elizabet, you must not be too hard with the children. It is very bad for you. I know that you have worry about Robert. It is so difficult for you. You are only little. At once all these heavy problem are on your shoulders. Half the men have gone. Schmidt he is gone. The horses they are all to go. The Stud it is no more. The house and all, it has to be run. These are heavy, heavy things for one so little. And your papa, he is old and tired out. He is no more the use to you. He has become only a burden. He knows that it is much, much for one to carry, but it is not fair to take it out on the children."

Elizabet felt chastened. Her father had become more and more garrulous as he had become more and more incapacitated. She had had nothing from him but grumbles and complaints every since she had returned to the castle. She was taken aback that he still had a spark of perception in him. She wiped away a tear that had unbidden rolled down her cheek.

"Of course you are not a burden. We are a burden to you, with the noisy children. But they try to be good."

"What rubbish! You are not a burden to me. What would have happened to me these past few weeks, if you had not been here to take all problems? I just know what a burden it is to you. I am sorry it is so, when I am helpless to deal with all. The children are a delight to an old man. They have brought joy and happiness to him. They bring light and laughter into an old man's life. When there is only the cold grave to look at, they are like the rays of the sun." Elizabet knelt down on the floor by him and took his hand.

"Sh-sh, papa, you must not talk like that. You will live to be a hundred." He smiled at his daughter.

"God forbid that I should live to be a hundred! You must call for the vet and have me put down long before then. But no—I shall not live that long. I know that my time it is near. I am sorry that I shall leave your when the world it is upside down. But I know that my time is soon. I thank the Almighty for give me the warnings, so that I have time to prepare my soul to meet its maker."

Elizabet stroked his hand. She could not speak. She had been distressed to see the deterioration in him when she had returned to the Castle. She had watched with growing alarm, the obvious decline, since she had been there. She had called Dr Hoffman to see him, but he was not hopeful. Now he too had been called to the army, and there was no one left that she could call. She was on her own. His life was in her hands. It was so unfair. What did she know about medical matters? With her children, she could cope. She could rely on her mother's instincts, but with her father, it was different. The threads that joined them were different. More vague. More ephemeral.

"Come, come, Papa, you must not talk like this. You see, when the spring comes again, you will feel stronger and be like the spring lamb."

He shook his head and smiled faintly.

Elizabet got up. "You are right. I vas unfair with the children. I will go to them."

She went to the kitchen and made a big bowl of bread and milk and, taking three bowls and spoons on a tray, went up to the children. Cornelia was asleep, but from the room occupied by Helen and Maria could be heard a gentle sobbing. She pushed open the door and, feeling her way in the dark, she found the table and put the tray down. She went to the window and drew back the curtain. The moonlight flooded in, bathing the room in it's soft light. She went softly to the bed and peered at the two girls. The moon glinted on their eyes that looked uncertainly up at her.

"My darlings, I am so sorry that I vas angry with you. It vas not good of me, to take my worries out on you."

Maria propped herself up on her elbow. "Mamma, I am sorry that we were so noisy. But we are worried too, you know. It is our father who is lost. Anything could have happened to him. We are very worried too. This war it is terrible. Any thing could happen. He could even now be caught and in prison. He could even be dead—shot." Her voice trailed away.

Elizabet kicked off her shoes and climbed into the bed with her and hugged her tight. "My darling, you are very young. These are terrible things that happen to one so young. You must be brave. When all that is bad, seems near, you must have courage, the world it is an angry place. Terrible things happen, but you must never, never give up hope. Remember that if God is on your side no one can ever stand against you. We, my darling, must face whatever lies ahead of us with this spirit. Terrible things may happen, but whatever happens nothing, nothing can come between us and the love of God."

Maria stifled a sob. "But it is so unfair. Papa, what has he done? Now he has to run and hide, so that he can be safe. We are here. Grand Papa is not well. There are no Doctors left to help him; they have all had to go to the war. It all makes you so angry and then we are naughty and you are angry with us."

Elizabet hugged her. "Poor Maria, we put such weights on your shoulders. Such a heavy load for one so young."

"Mama, when will we see Papa again?"

"I do not know, my darling, I do not know. We must pray for him, that he will be guided safely. We must hope that he get safely to England. When the war it is over, then he will be able to come back to us. Come now. I have made you some bread and milk. Sit up and eat it."

She got out of the bed and pulled up the pillows so that they could both sit up. "Here, this is nice and hot. I will put some honey on it for you."

The girls sat up and gathered the bedclothes round them. They realised that this was something of a treat and that their mother was trying to make amends.

"Mama, when can we go home?" Helen took her bowl with a happy smile.

"I do not know, Darling; we will stay here for the time being. I do not know. Perhaps we will never go. I do not know."

Helen looked alarmed. "But we must go home. What will happen to Bo-bear if we do not go? He will be all on his own. He cannot stay all alone."

"I do not know, darling. He is a big boy. He can look after himself. I know, perhaps if we stay here a long time, I can write to Anna and ask her to send him in the post."

"He will not like that. He will hate it. And when the postmaster puts the postmark on his nose, he won't like that."

"I will ask Anna to put him snugly in a box and pack him up. When the postmaster goes stamp, stamp, he won't feel a thing. Now come on. Give me your bowls and go to sleep."

She kissed them both and tucked them in. When she went to the window to shut the curtains, she could hear a wolf howling in the forest. The sound of it made her shudder. It seemed to her as if it were mourning the lost past and all the people who would be killed in the war. She remembered walking home with Robert in the snow after the New Year's Ball and hearing then the distant howling of the wolves. She sat down suddenly on a chair; a big tear welled up and rolled down her cheek. So many people were going to die; it was almost as if the wolf were howling a lament for them. She stood up and sadly shut the curtains.

"Goodnight my little ones. Sleep tight." She kissed them both and slowly went downstairs.

The rest of the week passed in a sort of limbo. She was apprehensive about handing over the horses. She had given instructions that all the stable people who were to come, were to wear their National costume. The Germans were taking horses off the Magya and they were going to know it. She decided she would go too. She simply could not sit at home whilst her horses were driven away.

On Wednesday morning she was up before it was light. She dressed carefully in a white brightly embroidered blouse and a full red embroidered skirt. Her hair she shook loose and tied it up in a brightly coloured scarf. She pulled on her red boots. She looked at the result in the looking glass. She looked as if she was going to a fair! Well, at least the Germans would see this was something special.

Frank had got up early and made breakfast for her. He realised that this day was of great significance. He had asked if he could come too, but Elizabet said no. He was too old. It was not fair to ask him to ride all that way and back. Besides, he was needed to keep things running at the castle. She had not told her father or the children what she was doing. They were to be told simply that she had gone up to the Stud and that she might not be back until the next day. When she had had her breakfast, she threw a shawl over her shoulders and, taking a horsewhip off the hook by the back door, went out to the stables. Joseph and the Head Groom were there already. Their three horses were saddled up, ready. The other horses, those that were to be handed over, were penned together, loose, in the yard. They had discussed many times, how they were going to do this. At first it was thought that they would put all the horses on leading reins and take them between them, but there were too many for that. In the end they decided they would take them in a loose herd and drive them along. The only problem was that once the horses realised they were free, they would go charging off and could scatter all over the place. In the end it was decided that the road gate should be shut and that when the horses were let out, they could go careering about in the Park. Once they had calmed down, they could be driven together in a herd to the rendezvous with the horses from the Stud. That was likely to precipitate another stampede, so she had chosen a large field surrounded with thick woods. Once the two herds had met and settled down, they would drive the whole lot to the river. They would have more help then, being joined by the people from the Stud, so they should be able to manage.

As predicted, when the horses were let out together, they shot across the courtyard and out over the bridge, over the moat, as if they were in a race. By the time Elizabet and the others had mounted up and followed them, they were chasing across the Park. By the time they had ridden down to the gate, the herd had quietened down enough to follow them. Elizabet rode in front with Joseph. The head groom dropped back behind to keep them all together. Once they had formed into a tight group, they were content to stay that way, so they moved on at a steady trot. It took them an hour to reach the rendezvous point. When they got there, the sun was just rising behind the trees. The horses from the Stud had not yet arrived. Elizabet was quite glad of the rest. She realised woefully that she was going to be exhausted by the time they got back to the Castle.

After three-quarters of an hour, she was getting anxious. There was still no sign of the horses from the Stud. Time was getting on. She was on the point of sending Joseph to look for them, when he shouted and pointed. A cloud of dust was coming. Presently, she could see it was the herd of horses coming at a good pace. The three of them mounted up and placed themselves to block the road, so that the horses would go into the field. They poured in, raising a great cloud of dust as they streamed past. Soldo reined in beside her with a great grin on his face.

"Here we are. All come, as you say."

"You are late! What happened?"

He shrugged and said nothing.

"Have you got all the horses?"

"Yes, they are all here."

"How many people have you to help?"

He shrugged and waved his hand around. Quite a number of horsemen had joined them, now that the herd was in the field. Several old men in white shirts and black hats and waistcoats and six, seven, eight, nine women in bright traditional costume.

"You can have half an hour to eat your breakfast, then we must go."

For Elizabet, who had already been waiting nearly an hour already, that half-hour seemed like an eternity. When breakfast was finished the herds were rounded up. They set off to drive them to the River. Elizabet knew that they would have to keep moving to keep them together. They planned to stop once at the pond, so that the horses could get water, but apart from that it was going to be a long, long day in the saddle. By keeping them going at a steady pace the herd kept well together. Two of the hands were sent ahead to make sure the road was clear. Elizabet did not want the horses scattered all over the countryside by the sudden appearance of a coach or whatever suddenly charging through them. They completed the whole journey without any problems and it was with great relief that Elizabet turned in her saddle to watch the whole herd pour into the field by the river. She was dusty, thirsty and tired and she ached in places that she would rather not think about. Though the evening sun was beginning to lose some of its heat, she was still hot and sweaty from the ride.

There was no sign of the German officer, so telling Soldo and Joseph that everyone must wait, she rode up to the Inn. Tethering her horse outside, she went in. The fire in the heath was out and there was not a sign of anyone. She ached all over and was in no mood to be kept waiting. There was a heavy jug on the counter and so she banged this vigorously.

"Hello, Hello!" she shouted angrily. "Anyone about?"

There was a commotion in the room above and presently a tousle headed young woman came running down the stairs. She had bare feet and was buttoning up her dress.

"Yes?"

"Are you not Elly? Did you not marry Boy, who works for us?"

"Yes." She looked at Elizabet, daring her to make any comment about her dishevelled appearance.

"I take it Boy is not here?"

"No. He has gone to the fighting. I do not know where he is." Elizabet looked straight at her. *And don't care either*, she thought.

"I need to see the German officer who is supposed to be here to receive our horses." There was a slight creak from the top of the stairs. Elizabet could see his boots on the top step.

"He is not here," Elly lied. "He has gone out."

Elizabet looked at her and then up at the top of the stairs.

"Perhaps you could ask him to come back in and to come here. Now. If he is properly dressed." She turned her back on the stairs and looked out through the grimy window to where her horses were milling around in the field. It was a small field and there were rather a lot of horses. They were getting restless. She heard footsteps quickly coming down the stairs. When they reached the bottom she turned back.

"Ah,—Herr SCHMIDT!" Her astonishment was real. "Herr Schmidt, what are you doing here?"

"Herr Leutnant Schmidt, if you don't mind, Elizabet Ramoskie." He tried to draw himself up to his full height, but he just looked sleazy in his ill fitting uniform. He clutched at his trousers as they threatened to fall down. His greasy hair had been cut in a short military style but stuck up in all directions. Elizabet had to suppress a giggle for he looked like a wet gosling.

"Well, Herr Leutnant, I would be more impressed if you were to put your belt on and tuck in your shirt."

He bit his lip in frustrated anger as he hastily tucked in his shirt. About his belt he could do nothing. It was still upstairs. He had recognised Elizabet's voice when she had come in. He felt humiliated and embarrassed at being so caught out. He had hoped he could have sneaked down, if she had gone outside, but the stupid girl from the inn had not got the whit to decoy her outside under some pretext or other. Now instead of having the upper hand and being able to represent the face of authority, he could see that she was despising him, now that she had got over the surprise of finding him here.

"Herr Schmidt, why are you here? I thought that you had gone to join the army."

"Frauline, as you see, I am in the army. They thought that with my...er..." he paused, "local knowledge, at this moment, I would be more useful here."

Elizabet could sense the implied threat. *Thank God*, she thought, *I have brought the horses as I should. He will know exactly how many there should be.*

"I have brought my horses as I have been requested. You will please come outside and count them, then oblige me with a receipt." She went to the door and waited for him to open it for her. Schmidt yearned to refuse, but he could not. This was, after all, why he was here. He picked up his hat and a notepad and pencil and dived forward to open the door for her. She swept out. He followed sheepishly, clutching his trousers. His hat was far too big for him and sat on his ears like a drooping mushroom.

They walked across the road. Schmidt climbed up on the gate to get a better view. He started to count. After three goes, he gave up. The horses kept moving about so much that he quickly lost count.

"This is impossible. Be so kind as to tell them all to stand up and keep still."

Soldo looked at Elizabet. She shrugged slightly and motioned towards the gate. Soldo climbed up and shouted.

"Stand up, you unfortunate animals. Stand still." Some of the nearer ones pricked up their ears at the sound of his voice, but on the whole, his shouting had no effect whatever.

"Try counting again," Elizabet urged. She was getting impatient. It was getting late and she wanted to be on her way home. Again Schmidt started to laboriously count. It was no good. After a short while he lost count again. Elizabet was getting impatient.

"Climb up on the gate. Perhaps you will get a better view from there."

Schmidt tried but he could not manage to hold his notebook and pencil and climb, and at the same time hold his trousers up. He slipped and fell. His trousers, large and ill fitting as they were, fell round his ankles and he stumbled and fell over. Elisabet's people laughed and jeered at him. He struggled to his feet and, pulling his trousers up, ran for the inn, his dignity and authority lost for ever. Shortly he returned. He had retrieved his belt and walked across the road, trying to look as if nothing had happened. Elizabet tried not to laugh and looked at him solemnly.

"Perhaps you could try again," she said sweetly. He successfully climbed the gate this time and started to count. He presently gave up and started again.

"It is no good. They keep moving about. It is impossible to count them. You must make them march past me and I will count them as they go by."

"For goodness sake, Herr Schmidt. They are horses, not soldiers. They have no idea about marching."

"If they cannot march, they will be no use to the army." Elizabet looked at him in disbelief.

"I assure you they cannot march. They have no idea about marching. If you had said that they needed to march, I could have told you that they could not and it would have saved everyone an enormous amount of trouble. If they are no use to you, we will take them home." She stood up in her stirrups. "Soldo, they are no use to the Leutnant. They cannot march. We will take them all back home."

"No, wait." Something like panic seized Herr Schmitt. He had been ordered to collect them and collect them he would. It was not up to him to say if they were suitable or not. "I know how many horses that you should have. All I need to do is to be sure that I have them all here." He scribbled on his pad. "This is how many horses there should be at the Stud." Elizabet moved her horse closer so that she could see.

"No, we have sold some since you left. You can cross 19 off that number."

"Sold them? Why have you sold them?"

"Herr Schmidt, you know very well that that is what studs do. We breed horses and sell them. That is how we make money. If our horses are good and win races, people think that they are good and pay more money for them. You well know that that is what it is all about." Schmidt reluctantly altered his figure.

"The two stallions. They are both here?"

"Yes," lied Elizabet. "Walk through them and you will find them." She was confident that he would not.

"The horses from the castle. Are they here? I can see the white ones, the ones your mother used. Are all the other ones here?"

"No we have kept four of the coach horses and my pony. We have kept ten of the heavy horses for the farms and one for the Castle. Everything else is here."

Again he scribbled some figures on his pad. "Look then, this is the number of horses that should be here. Is that correct?"

Elizabet looked at the figure. "Yes. That is correct. They are all here. You can count them yourself and check. Will you please give me a receipt?"

Schmidt reluctantly filled in a form.

"I have entered the number here as being correct. Will you please sign it." He handed it to Elizabet, pointing to where she had to sign. She hastily did so and gave it back. Schmidt signed the receipt and gave it to her. She quickly read it and, folding it, put it safely in her small saddlebag.

"Herr Schmidt, do not expect me to thank you. I do not enjoy handing over my horses and have only done so because of the order that I have had. Frankly I am disgusted with your behaviour with the girl Elly. She is married to one of our most trusted men and you are taking cowardly advantage of his absence, away at the fighting. If I were you I would not sleep tonight for fear that someone will slip in and slit your throat. We have a long ride ahead and we wish to start."

"Ride? On what will you ride?"

"Well, on these horses, of course."

"No Frauline. I have counted those horses as well."

"Don't be so ridiculous. You do not have these horses. These we need."

"The Kaiser, he needs them too. His need is greater than yours."

Elizabet laughed in his face. "If he wants them, he will have to come and get them."

Schmidt drew his revolver. "If you do not hand over those horses at once, Frauline, I will shoot them from underneath you."

Even as he spoke rifles miraculously appeared in the hands of the men from the Stud and pointed at him. Elizabet look at him without flinching.

"Herr Schmidt, where do you wish to start?" She rode her horse up to him and took the revolver from him and thrust it into her belt. "Just wait until I tell the Kaiser that you drew your revolver to intimidate an innocent woman."

"Give me that back at once. At once, do you hear, it is government property."

"No. It is too dangerous for you to have a thing like that. I will keep it safely. You might hurt someone with it. Goodbye, Herr Schmidt. I hope that we never meet again."

She wheeled her horse and galloped off. "Come on, everyone!"

They clattered off together, leaving Herr Schmidt fuming impotently in the road.

It was beginning to get dusk so they maintained a steady canter. Eventually they reached the watering hole and gave the horses a much needed rest and drink. The men busied themselves with the fires. The women prepared some strips of bacon to fry over the fires. Each fatty slice was cut in several places down to the rind. Both ends were impaled on a stick so that it was impaled like some succulent cock's comb. The rasher was cooked over the fire and eaten hot off the stick with some bread. By this time it was dark. They sat round in a circle in the firelight, eating their simple food. One of the men from the Stud produced a balalaika. Softly, he began to play a sad little tune as they ate. Elizabet leant against a tree and tears rolled down her cheek. Joseph was the first to notice.

"Graffinflein, you all right?"

It was some moment before she could reply.

"Yes, Joseph. I am all right. It is so sad, that music. It brings tears to my eyes. Here we all are. It is a beautiful evening. We are sitting under the stars by the fire. He is playing that music, which makes me so sad. Many of our young men have gone, to we know not where. We have just handed over all our horses. We do not know what the future will hold. I have done all I can for you all, but I do not know what will lie ahead, or what will happen to us all. I feel so helpless. Things are happening to me and to you which I cannot change. I cannot defend you or me from their consequences. I feel responsible for you all, yet there is nothing that I can do to change things or make them better. We are all going to have to be very brave and strong if we are going to face what is to come."

"Don't worry, Graffinflein. We have been through worse than this before. Your care for us has allowed us all to stay at the Stud and to use the farm. We will be all right. When better times come, there will be horses back there again. Now that you have got the big pistol of the Herr Schmidt, no harm will come to you. No one will dare hurt you for fear that he get his head blown off." Every one laughed.

"Thank you all for backing me up. I do not know what would have happened if you had not, he was in an ugly mood. He was very embarrassed."

"Don't worry, Graffinflein. We will look after you."

Elizabet stood up. "I am going to press on. My father and my children will be wondering what has happened to me."

"You cannot go now. It will be morning before you get home. You are better to camp here with us for the night, then go on in the morning." Elizabet stood uncertainly. She was certainly tired. She did not relish the idea of riding home alone in the dark on her own, but her anxiety for her children was greater.

"No, I will be all right. I know the way. I would rather go on." She went round the people from the Stud and shook all their hands. "Thank you for your help and for your loyalty. Soldo will come tomorrow with a list of what I owe you all. It will be paid to you. Good luck to you all. Look after each other." She turned to Joseph and the head groom. "Come on, you two. You come back with me now. We will leave now, if you please."

Joseph protested. "Please Graffinklein. We would be better to stay here for the night. We are all tired. If we rest and move on at first light it will be better."

"No, come on. Look, the moon will be up soon. Come on, let's go. I will go now."

Grumbling, the two of them mounted up. Together they set out for the castle in the dark.

Elizabet was not worried about riding in the dark. She knew that her horse could see a lot better than she could. Her prediction was right. The moon soon came out and bathed everything in its silvery light. In a way it made the journey more difficult, because they were going from quite bright light to deep shadow as they passed under trees. The contrast was stark and confusing. However, they made steady time. The dawn was just breaking as they clattered over the bridge at the castle. A very welcome light was burning in the front hall. Stiffly, she slid off her horse. She was cold, sore and stiff. For the last few miles she had hardly been able to keep her eyes open. Several times, she had nearly fallen off her horse as she had nodded off to sleep. She gave her reins to the head groom and calling "Goodnight" to the two men, stiffly climbed the steps to the front door. The door was open. She went in as quietly as she could, shutting the door behind her. The figure of Frank, draped in a blanket, lurched up out of the chair in front of the fire.

"Graffinflein? Is that you?"

"Yes Frank, it is me."

"Thank goodness. We have been so worried about you. I said I would wait up for you." He shuffled over to the door and lifted the great iron bar that secured it. With a clatter, he dropped it into the slot.

"Thank you for waiting up for me. You should not have done that. You go to bed to get your rest. Do not worry about the morning. We will get up when we wake up. I will see to the children and to my father. You sleep as much as you like."

"Yes Graffinflein, thank you—I will not be sorry to get to bed."

CHAPTER 30

❀

The weeks passed and there was still no word from Robert. There had been no message from Emil either. Elizabet's feeling of alarm and distress increased with every day. They were virtually cut off from the outside world and only small scraps of news filtered out to them. The war seemed unreal and remote. They produced all the things they needed at the Castle and so they could survive very well without much contact with the outside world.

Elizabet, however, had had to drive into the town to buy salt and nails and so she was able to hear some news of what was going on. It appeared that Germany had attacked Russia and that terrible battles had taken place. Russia by way of a counter diversion was trying to attack Hungary through Slovakia, but was being held up in the mountains by the troops of the Empire. If the Russians broke through, they would all be in danger, but it did not seem likely. The defenders were confidant that they would be able to hold out, provided that they had enough food. The fighting in France seemed to have reached a stalemate and was too far away, too remote to threaten them. Nearly everyone with whom she spoke, however, had sons, or brothers, or husbands who were away fighting. No one had had any news from them and everyone was in a high state of anxiety for their loved ones.

Elizabet went and sat in the Church for a few minutes. It was so different to the little church by the Castle. It was tall and dark. The stone pillars stretched up into the dark vaults of the roof. The air was heavy with the smell of incense. And far away by the Altar the little red Sanctuary lamp burned brightly. She sat for a while, a tiny figure in that huge place. Was Heaven going to be like this? Enormous, tall and gloomy? She laughed to herself. No, of course it would not. Heaven was a place of light and happiness. This gloomy edifice was an attempt by the feebleness of men's minds to express something of the grandeur that must be due to the Creator. She stood up and walked up the isle to where there was light. In the side isle there stood on a special altar, a statue depicting the Virgin holding the infant Jesus. There were many votive candles burning in front of the statue. Elizabet took one, too, and dropping some small coins in the offertory box, lit it and placed it with the others.

She knelt down and silently prayed to the Virgin, whose statue helped to focus the thoughts of the faithful upon the special position she must have in Heaven as the chosen mother of the Son of God. She thought of Robert trudging through the mist in Switzerland. She thought of her children, so young. What sort of a world would they find when this was all over? She thought of her father. She thought of all the other women across Europe, all beseeching the Blessed Virgin to ask her Son to send their men folk back safely to them. She knelt and a feeling of total despair came over her. How could it happen? Both sides were praying for deliverance, yet many, many would be killed. The world had gone mad. God in heaven must be weeping in frustration. She felt herself saying, *I don't care about all those others. Just please keep Robert safe. Please protect my children. Please guide me so that I know what to do to look after them.* She walked sadly out of the Church. Before going home she drew enough money from the Bank so that she could pay off the people from the Stud according to Soldo's list.

The summer passed quickly. She busied herself with the affairs of the Castle and with her children. In the mornings they had lessons and in the afternoon they could play in the grounds or help with the work with the animals or in the gardens. Joseph and the head groom had long since gone to the fighting. She was left with Frank and an equally old gardener. Between them, they grew enough vegetables for their needs and the litter of pigs that they raised were growing to a good size. Elizabet enjoyed working in the garden and helping with the animals. She even learnt to milk the cow! The geese that lived on the moat were fattening quite well and so it looked as if the household would be well supplied for the winter.

Elizabet found as her pregnancy progressed, that she could do less and less and easily became very tired. She had to rely a lot on the children. Luckily they were willing and happy to work with the animals. It was a relief when her baby was born and she could resume her normal active life. Her father was delighted—a boy at last! He had lived long enough to see his grandson! The baby was christened Christopher in the little church by the castle. Her father wanted it to be called after him, but Elizabet was adamant it should be called

Christopher. St Christopher was the patron of travellers. He would look after Robert and take him safely to England. If the boy was called Christopher, it would remind her to pray to the Saint every time she thought of the child.

That winter was cold and long. The wolves became very bold and with no men to keep the fires burning at night to keep them away, they came down into the Park and attacked the sheep. Three were killed and eaten. The next day Elizabet and the children managed to drive the survivors into the stable yard. They put straw in the empty stables and the sheep were shut up in there at night. The children were told that under no circumstances were they to go outside at night. If the wolves could not find any more sheep, they would be just as pleased with a fat child! Whenever Elizabet went outside, she stuck Herr Schmidt's heavy revolver in her belt, just in case. Every night the wolves could be heard howling in the Park. At first the children had been very frightened by them, but they soon got used to them. They could even recognise the different wolves by their voices and gave them names. They used to make up stories about them and their antics. The geese on the moat were not so happy with their new neighbours and spent many restless nights safely on the moat, watching in silent fear as the wolves prowled up and down on the bank. Gradually the moat froze over and the wolves became bold enough to venture out on the ice. The geese's refuge shrank alarmingly. Elizabet watched with consternation. Two or three more cold nights with hard frosts would see the water completely frozen over and the wolves would be able to catch the geese! She and the children tried to drive the geese off the moat so that they too could be shut up in the stable, but the stupid creatures, not understanding the reason for this sudden assault on their dignity, just swam round and round under the bridge. Soon it became obvious she could not drive them to safety. She resolved that she would not let the wolves have them. They were being fattened up for the household. She tried feeding them on the bank, in the hope that whilst they were feeding, she would be able to go round behind them and frighten them away from the moat, so that the children could drive them into the stable yard—but to no avail. Even when they were feeding, there was always one that was watching and as she approached, it would let out a squawk and the whole flock would flap back in panic to the safety of the water. It was obvious that if there was any more frost, the moat would freeze over and the wolves would get them all. She had not fed them all summer so that the wolves could be well supplied! If any one was going to eat them, it was definitely not going to be the wolves.

That evening, she settled the children in front of the fire with a book. Telling the nanny that on no account were they to be let out, she went to the gunroom and, taking a shotgun and a handful of cartridges, she went back to the moat. At the first shot the window of the blue drawing room flew open and the children's three heads popped out.

"What are you doing, mama?"

She was very cross with them. "Just go back in at once and shut the window! You will fill the house with cold. Go back in at once."

Reluctantly the window shut. She took aim again. Again the window flew open at the sound of the shot.

"What are you doing, mama? Are you shooting the geese? Look, Mama is shooting the geese! There is a dead one there. Mama, don't shoot the geese! You are so cruel." They all started to wail and cry.

Elizabet who was feeling very miserable herself was very angry. "Go back inside this minute! Nanny, you are not to let the children open the window again, do you understand? It is better that we eat the geeses than let the wolves eat them! Go inside. I will shoot some more."

The nanny shut the window, but every time she shot, the little faces appeared at the window again. In the end Elizabet could commit no more murder. She did not know how many she had shot and the survivors were huddled up in a group under the bridge. She felt sickened at what she had done. She counted. There were five geese floating on the water, but she was no better off. She still could not get them. She put the gun away and went to look for a long pole so that she could poke them to the side and collect them. However, she could not break the ice so that she could reach them. Back in the shed she found a big old apple basket and some rope and with this she was able to go onto the bridge and scoop them out of the water beneath. They were extremely heavy and by the time she had scooped them all out in this way, she was exhausted. She dragged them one by one into the kitchen. When she had finished, she went up to the blue drawing room. She was greeted with a chorus of horror from the children.

"Murder!" they shouted at her. "How could you be so cruel? The poor geese! What have they done to harm you? Mama, I hate you! Our lovely geese, you have murdered them!".

Elizabet, who was feeling like a criminal anyway, was very angry with them "Stop it at once, you silly children," she scolded." Why do we have the gooses? We *eat* them! That is why they are there. They make very good food and good grease to make our shoes waterproof. That is why we have them."

"But you just went out and murdered them!"

"How do you think that they get off the moat and into the oven? They do not walk there!"

The children went very quiet.

"But they do not get shot."

"No, that is true. But you saw for yourself, we could not get them off the water and into the yard. If we leave them there and it freeze more, the wolves will eat them all and we will have none. Now come down all of you and help pluck them. The feathers will come off easy if they are still hot. Once the birds get cold it is very difficult to get the feathers off."

The children were a little hesitant at first, being reluctant to touch the dead birds, but Cornelia pulled a few soft feathers off the breast of one and blew them up in the air. They settled on her head and her nose. Soon the kitchen was full of flying feathers and down as the children blew them up in to the air.

"Stop. Stop. Put these aprons on, or you will be covered with fluff. Now put all the little fluffy feathers into this pillowcase. The bigger feathers into this box. The big feathers on the wing are too strong. You will not be able to pull them."

"Why do you want the little soft feathers?"

"To make stuffing for a pillow. It is very good for that. It is soft and warm."

"Do you mean to tell us our pillows are full of feathers?"

"Why yes. What did you think was in them?"

"I do not know. I had never thought."

"They have to be cleaned and baked in the oven to dry them and kill any germs, but then they make lovely soft pillows, until you horrid children bust them and all the feathers fly out!"

It was not long before the air was full of feathers flying in all directions. They had all got feathers in their hair. But the geese had so many feathers. When the first layer came off, there was another layer underneath. They soon got very tired and carried on in silence. Nanny proved to be something of an expert at plucking geese and she soon showed them how to do it so that they took both layers of feathers off together. They laboured all afternoon and eventually had all the geese more or less plucked, apart from the wings. These Elizabet cut off with a sharp knife.

"We will put the geeses in the larder for now. In this cold weather, they will keep for many days before we need to worry about preparing them. Thank you, children. Thank you, Nanny. You have all work very hard; now let us clear up and have some tea."

Helen held up the neck and head of one of the geese. She opened its eye.

"Mama, it looks so alive. Its eye looks still alive, the poor thing."

"Come on, put it down, let us sweep up these feathers."

They had to sweep round the kitchen several times before the last of the feathers was cleared up.

That night the frost was severe and the little safe haven that the geese had became smaller and smaller. The wolves stood on the bank and waited. The next day the ice had spread further and there was very little water left. The geese were managing to keep swimming round and thus stop a small patch from freezing under the bridge. Elizabet was horrified to see from the footprints in the snow that the wolves had been out on the ice on the moat. The geese had very little chance of lasting a couple of more nights. That evening, she went again to the gun cupboard. Her shoulder was still black and blue from the recoil of the shotgun and was very painful if she lifted her arm. She did not normally have anything to do with the guns, but she knew that the one that she had used for the geese would not be heavy enough for a wolf. She bore the wolves no ill will—they were, after all, only following their instincts. If she must shoot one in an attempt to protect her geese, she wanted to make sure it was dead. She could not bear the thought of the animal running away injured. She looked at the row of guns and selected the one that seemed the biggest. It seemed enormously heavy. She put it to her shoulder and practically toppled over with the weight. Well, if she leant out of the window, it might do. She looked in the cupboard for some cartridges that might fit it. She found some in a box, as big as plump sausages. She weighed one in her hand It was exceedingly heavy. That should knock a wolf over. The trouble was, the explosion would probably knock her over as well! She put them back in the cupboard. They were too mighty for one so small. She looked along the shelf and knocked over a small box. Some heavy bullets in brass cases fell out. Ah! They were the things! Now all she had to do was to find the right gun. After several tries, she found one that seemed to be the right size. The bullet fitted. She tried the bolt action and it seemed to work all right. *Right, Mr Wolf. This evening, you are going to have to watch out.* When the children had gone to bed, she collected the gun and the bullets and went up to one of the spare rooms. She opened the window a little and poked the rifle out. She had a good view of the moat and she settled down in the dark to wait. A cold draught blew through the open window and in no time, her teeth were chattering with cold and she was shaking all over. She shut the window and, going downstairs to the kitchen, she made herself some hot milk. She took it into the dining room and poured into it a liberal measure of brandy. She collected her big fur coat and returned to the bedroom. With the hot drink inside and wrapped in the warm coat, she felt better prepared. She opened the window again and, pulling her fur hood over her head, she settled down to wait. Presently the moon came out, bathing the whole countryside in a magical white light that reflected off the snow, making it almost as bright as day. The countryside looked so beautiful in the strange ethereal light. Her eyes started to water from the cold draught that blew in through the open window. Despite her warm coat she was beginning to shiver again. Quite a lot of cloud had blown up whilst she waited and occasionally the moon would be covered. A wolf howled from the park and another answered from quite close. The geese cackled nervously from under the bridge. Elizabet thought she saw a movement. She hastily wiped her eyes and stared again with fierce concentration. Yes! There was something there, just by that small bush. Yes, there it was again! Definitely something moved. She aimed the rifle at it. At that moment the moon went behind a cloud. She could not see the sight. Wait! Wait! Wait for the moon to come out again. Presently it again bathed the scene with brilliant light. There was a wolf! Right on the edge of the moat. It stood looking straight at her. She fancied she could see its eyes glinting in the moonlight. A shiver ran down her spine. She took aim and pulled the trigger. Nothing happened! She pulled again. Nothing happened. Fool! There must be some kind of safety device. She angrily pulled the gun in and banged it against the window. The wolf vanished in an instant. She quickly examined the rifle and found a little leaver that turned back and forth quite easily. Beneath it was engraved the letter "S". This must be a safety catch. Pushing it so that the "S" was covered, she poked the rifle out of the window again and settled down to wait. She waited, until she could not stay any longer. Despite the freezing cold, she kept falling asleep. She waited for the next two nights. On the third night, she was just about to give up when she saw a wolf. It appeared by the moat and sat looking at the geese. She took careful aim and squeezed the trigger. The deafening crash shook the house and a tongue of flame leapt out into the darkness. The rifle slammed against her shoulder, nearly knocking her over. It jumped in her hand and jammed her thumb against the underside of the open window. It slammed against her chin and she bit her lip. She peered out into the night. Of the wolf there was no sign! They certainly would not come back tonight, so she shut the window and put the rifle away.

The next morning, when she went to feed the geese, she tucked Herr Schmidt's pistol in her belt. She looked to see what she might find. There was no sign of a wolf. There was a little trail of blood from the edge of the moat and out in to the Park, but there was no sign of a wolf anywhere. She was sorry. She had hoped to find a dead wolf. But there was nothing. She had a big bruise on her chin and her shoulder ached. Her thumb throbbed painfully and she knew that she would have a black nail before long; but she was still sorry at the thought that she might have injured one of the wolves.

She did not try to shoot a wolf again for spring was coming and the remaining geese managed to keep their little patch of water under the bridge free of ice. Gradually the snow and ice melted. The spring flowers began to appear and the Missile thrush could be heard shouting his song from the top of the tall elm tree. The wolves gave up their attempt to catch the geese and returned to the forest.

Elizabet's father had spent the winter in his chair in front of the fire or in bed, but as spring came, she had hoped he might venture out into the garden for a while. Instead, he remained in bed and did not even come down to his chair in the evening. He remained thus for several weeks, existing only on brandy and soup that Elizabet patiently fed him with a spoon. He became progressively weaker. Elizabet found it exhausting nursing him all the time and attending to her children and the needs of the rest of the household.

As the first daffodils were blooming under the shelter of the wall, he died. He was buried in the little churchyard in the village. Frank and the old gardener had wheeled his coffin down to the church on the old four-wheeled bier that was kept there. A simple requiem was said over his body in the little church and then, sorrowfully, he was wheeled out into the churchyard and silently committed to the family grave. Apart from the household, there was no one else at the funeral. Elizabet had not had the energy to write to all and sundry to let them know and there were no men to carry messages. She had written out some little messages and taken them to the pigeon loft. She did not know which pigeons belonged to whom and so she took one out of each pen and sent them on their way. She had found a little box of the canisters and after considerable difficulty, finally managed to tie them to the birds' legs. She remembered the loft man telling her that they had to be let out one at a time, or they might go off together, so this she did. She wondered what to do with the remaining birds. Those belonging to other people could not be kept for long. They could not be let out for exercise, because they would fly off to their own homes. In normal times, they were used often enough, so this was not a problem. They were simply replaced with other birds, sent over on the coach, so none of them were shut up in the loft for long. But these were not ordinary times. The loft man had gone off to the fighting and so had most of the people who might expect to receive a pigeon from her. She certainly had no wish to come and attend to the loft every day and it clearly could not remain like this. She decided to let the pigeons out and let them return to their owners. She watched them as they flew round in a flock and instantly regretted what she had done. She now had no means of contacting the outside world. Ah well, it was done. She would go next week and enquire about one of those telephones that people were talking about. They certainly sounded amazing. If she could get one, she would.

In the event no one came to the funeral and when she returned to the Castle she felt very low. Her father had insisted that people were not to be sad at his funeral. Champagne was to be provided. She had instructed Frank to put some out in the hall with some glasses. She had asked Cook to prepare a cold luncheon, in case anyone came. This was all set out on the big table. But there was no one there. She went to the kitchen and found the staff seated round the fire.

"Please come, all of you, to the hall. My father wished to have a party and as there is no one here, we all will have to do the best that we can."

She sent Maria up to the nursery to ask Nanny to come down with the children. They too could join in. They stood round in sombre mood and dutifully drank the champagne and ate the lunch. Conversation, such as it was, was stilted and awkward. Elizabet was glad when Frank finally shuffled to his feet.

"Countess, thank you for entertaining us all to lunch. It has been an honour and a privilege to work for your father and you have our deepest sympathy on this very sad day. With your permission, we will clear these dishes and things away."

"Yes Frank. Thank you. That would be very kind. You children go to the blue drawing room and play. I will be there soon." She wanted to think.

She felt so restless that she had to pace around. She soon found that she was wandering round the empty house, going from room to room. She lingered in her mother's room—completely untouched since her mother had died. All her mother's things were there, just as they were when her mother last used them. Her father's room, too—still untouched as well. Then the guest rooms. The beds were ready, but unused. She wandered to the tower room and lay down on the big bed. Robert had slept here. He had stayed here on his first night. She covered her face with her hands and great sobs shook her. Where was he now, when she desperately needed him? What had happened to him? It had been a year since he had escaped and she had heard nothing from him. No letter! No message! Nothing! For all she knew, he was dead. It was most likely that he was dead. If he was alive she would surely have heard from him in a year. She was all alone. Both her parents were dead. Her husband had disappeared and must be presumed dead. Emil, the one person in whom she felt she could confide, had gone to the war. Goodness knows what had befallen him. What was she going to do?

Countess?

She sat up with jerk. Frank had called her Countess. He always called her 'Graffinflein'—little Countess. Her father had become fairly unpopular in the neighbourhood. He was irascible and autocratic with the people on the Estate. They were reluctant to bring their problems to him as he was often less than sympathetic, but he was always there, the final arbiter, the one who represented authority.

She realised with a jolt that this roll had now fallen on her shoulders. She knew that she was more popular then her father. She had taken an interest in the well-being of her people and had done what she could to help them, but in the end, the problems could always be passed on to her father. Not any more! All the problems of their little world were going to land in her lap. More than ever, now, she needed her husband by her side. She sat on the bed, her head in her hands, rocking back and forth. It was so unfair, so unfair! How was she going to manage? She had her children to look after and to educate and bring up. Was that not enough problem on its own? She had the house and estate to manage and now she was going to get all the problems from the surrounding countryside landing in her lap. There was no one to help! No one!

CHAPTER 31

She had bought the telephone. A spotty young man in an ill-fitting suit had showed her several instruments and she had chosen one. He had allowed her to try his in the shop. She had telephoned her Cousin Maria, the wife of Emil, having, after much difficulty, found the number from the exchange. Maria was amazed when she realised who it was who was calling her. She had not heard from Elizabet since she had left to go and visit her father before the war had started. No, she had heard nothing from Emil since he went away. Robert? No, she had heard nothing of Robert. He had disappeared the day before Emil went to the war. There had been some trouble about it. She did not know what it was. But some officers had come to the Schloss looking for him and seeking Emil, but Emil had gone by then. They made a great deal of fuss when they realised that Robert had disappeared. They tried to accuse her of aiding the enemy! But she soon sent them packing! Why was she phoning? Elizabet explained that she was thinking of buying a telephone. She was trying this out in the shop. She had to bite her lip to stop the tears. She had hoped she might have had some news about Robert...

Yes, yes, she would buy the phone. It did not seem to be all that expensive, when you could talk to anyone with it, wherever they were. She signed the paper promising to pay the charges for the calls. It was then that the young man asked her where she lived. It appeared that the nearest line to her was several miles away. It would be necessary to erect new poles and hang a new line to connect her to the system. She shuddered when he told her how much extra this would be. At first she had refused out of hand. It was a ridiculous sum! The young man had suggested to her that if other people on the way could be persuaded also to have a phone, then the cost would be shared, so substantially reduced. She had brightened at this. She could see the advantage of having a telephone. She was keen to see it installed. She had agreed to make some enquiries to see if she could find some more potential subscribers.

It took her two weeks to find enough people willing to share the cost of the line to make the whole project worth while, but there was no doubt it had been worth it. She no longer felt so isolated. She could talk to others without the business of going to visit them. It did mean that her social occasions were considerably reduced. She did not have to go out for tea or to play cards to hear the latest gossip. She could simply pick up the telephone to hear all the news in her own home without the bother of having to get out the pony and trap. It also meant she was better informed about what was happening in the war and the world outside, generally.

She soon found that, in fact, her role and her life did not change. For a long time she had been running things for her father, but he was always there to advise her. Now it was she who had to bear the final decision. After a while she became quite used to this. She was pleased to be able to do small things that helped her people, of which her father would never have approved. She found that this had a reciprocal benefit. Whereas before it had been difficult to find people to help in the house and garden, she could now find plenty who were willing. Granted they were all older men, those too old to fight, but what they lacked in speed and vigour they made up for in knowledge and loyalty.

It was a pleasure for her to go round the stables—to see everything clean again. The horses well groomed. It was not possible to exercise them properly, as she had no stable lads to ride out in the morning. Despite restricting the horse's rations, they were fat and out of condition. But at least she had them still. Herr Schmidt had never returned to enquire about the six missing mares and the young stallion. The mares had all produced their foals. It was with some pride that she sat at her desk, looking out over the Park, watching them gallop round in the early spring sun. How Robert would have enjoyed that. He would have been proud of her to know that she had been able to retain a nucleus of the Stud and that it was growing again.

She chewed the end of her pen. It had been three years since he had disappeared. She hadn't heard anything from him at all. No telephone call. No letter. Nothing. It was the nothing that was the worst. Her eyes filled with tears. Angrily, she wiped them away with the back of her hand. Surely, even with the war on, he could have sent some kind of message somehow. She felt confident that he was still alive. She felt that in her heart she would know if he were dead. When the war ended they would be able to be together again. She prayed for that moment every day. She worried daily about where he was and what had happened to him, as well as about her own fate and that of her children. She was feeling depressed and weighed down with worry.

She jumped when the telephone rang. It did not ring very often, but when it did, its jangly bell always made her jump.

She picked up the instrument, one piece in each hand and, leaning back in her chair, gazed out over the Park. It was a friend that she had in Pressburg—and she was in a high state of excitement.

"Have you heard? There has been a revolution in Russia! They have arrested the Tsar and they have formed a provisional Government." Elizabet could not stop her friend's words that poured from her like steam from a boiling kettle. Eventually her friend hung up in a flurry.

A revolution in Russia? Arrest the Tsar? That was indeed a desperate and dangerous step! To arrest the Tsar was tantamount to sacrilege! It was well known that the Tsar was extremely autocratic and ran a ruthless and cruel regime. He had established the 'Okhrana', the Secret Police, to seek out troublemakers. Any potential subversive, real or imagined, was arrested, to be sent in servitude to the salt mines in Siberia. Though he had allowed a parliament to be formed, only the landowners had any voting rights. If the Parliament went against his wishes, the Tsar simply closed it. There was considerable discontent throughout Russian Society. The Parliament and those who could vote for it, were continually frustrated in many of their ideals, for the Tsar would not allow any reforms with which he did not agree. They felt that they were nothing but puppets—powerless to prevent the Tsar's rule lurch from one disaster to the next.

The Tsar was much influenced by his wife who was a strong, resolute woman, but she in her turn was influenced by the monk Rasputin. He was universally hated by everyone, but because he had been able to cure Alexis, the Tsar's son, who was a haemophiliac, he had gained a powerful influence in the Royal Court. He began to assert this influence upon the affairs of government. In the end, his influence and interference became intolerable. Some officers murdered him. His body was thrown in the river. But for the Parliament to arrest the Tsar! They must be mad! How could they do such a thing! The Tsar was the father of the people, the anointed, sacred ruler. He could not be arrested! She contemplated this momentous event, but could not imagine the outcome. If the people had risen up against their anointed King, there might be no limit to the awful things that could happen. She considered her own position. After all Russia was only just over the border of the Austro-Hungarian Empire! What would happen if people remembered that Robert had trained some of the Tsar's horses, in Bavaria? Would it be possible that revolutionary fervour might spread to engulf them all? She did not think so. The Emperor in Vienna, though he had been crowned King of Hungary as well, had allowed a Hungarian government to be formed. It had considerably more powers than had been allowed the parliaments in Russia, so there was far less discontent from the members.

All through that spring and summer, there were rumours and counter rumours about the Russian Government. The progress of their war with Germany was not going well. Several different attempts to overthrow the properly formed assembly, by frustrated people who thought they could run it better, were attempted and failed. There was considerable disquiet, spread by a political party called the Bolsheviks, who were trying to persuade the workers and peasants to form local workers committees in the factories and villages. In some of the villages the peasants were even dispossessing their landlords to take control of the land. The Bolshevik committees and their activists, the Red Guard, as they called themselves, were occupying the houses of the landlords—throwing them and their families out, with nothing. Their houses and possessions were being requisitioned as the property of the people. The landlords lost everything, their houses, their possessions, their money. They had to make shift as well as they could. This news was the most alarming, in case this idea should spread southwards into the Empire. Ideas and ideologies could spread on the wind. Russia was only just the other side of the mountains. Elizabet felt very vulnerable and exposed. She worried daily about her safety and the safety of her children.

There were rumours that deserters from the army had returned to the area. It was said that some of them had joined the Red Guard and were spreading the Bolshevik ideals, spreading sedition and unrest through the region. Elizabet felt that in her situation she was at particular risk. She went to the gun cupboard and took out some of the guns. She hid these round the house, where she felt they might be readily accessible, with some cartridges by them. Her own 20 bore shotgun she hid under her bed.

A small detachment of militia was sent to the area to try to root out the deserters so that they could be returned to their regiment. The manpower situation was becoming critical. They would be shot by a firing squad as a warning to others in an attempt to stop the flow of desertions.

One day, the officer in charge came clanking up to the Castle in his military motorcar. Elizabet received him in the hall. She had a tray of tea brought from the kitchen. He was polite and courteous. He was most anxious that Elizabet should be aware of what was going on. He urged her to advise him of any rumours that she might hear. Elizabet was at pains to assure him that as far as she knew, at that moment, there were no deserters in her villages. News would surely have reached her. She would certainly be watchful. She would definitely let him know of anything that might come to her attention.

He made it plain to her that she herself was under suspicion. He had been told that her husband was an Englishman who had somehow managed to escape those who went to arrest him for internment. Did she know how he had escaped? Where had he gone? What had happened to him? Who had fore-warned him of his impending arrest? Where was he now? Who had helped him escape? Was it possible that her sympathies were not with the Central Powers at all? Perhaps she was not as firmly committed as she might be! Could it be that she might even have some sympathy for any deserters that might come back to the area? Perhaps, even, she was in the pay of a foreign, enemy power? Elizabeth laughed in his face. What could she possibly tell anyone, stuck here hundreds of miles away from any fighting, that would be of the least use to them? Elizabet was completely flustered by his barrage of questions, half formed suspicions and accusations. She explained to the officer that she knew nothing whatever about her husband's departure. She did not know how or when or where. She had heard nothing from him since she had left their home to come here to stay with her father. She did not know anything about his escape to Switzerland, until after it had happened. She had heard nothing from him since the one small pigeon message, saying that he was going. As for her allegiance to the Central Powers, it was not something she had even thought of in any serious way. She was Hungarian. The fact that Germany had dragged them into a war with England was an accident of politics. She had no quarrel with the English. The fact that she was married to an Englishman had no bear-ing on her feeling towards Hungary or to Germany.

The officer was incensed. How could her husband escape and she know nothing of it? She was concealing things from him. She explained how it came to be that she was here, whilst he had remained in Bavaria, but he plainly did not believe her. It was not possible that she should know nothing of such a plan. The English were the enemies of the German people! The peoples of the Austro-Hungarian Empire were the allies of Germany! It followed that any Hungarian person who had any sympathetic feelings towards the English at all would be thought of as a traitor, an enemy of the great German peoples! They would be treated with the severity that they deserved.

Elizabet was furious. She jumped up, knocking over the tea tray, scattering cups, biscuits and sugar lumps all over the floor. The officer too, jumped up as milk and tea cascaded over his breeches.

"Get out, you stupid little man!" She pushed him towards the door. "How dare you come into my house and imply that I could be a traitor! What impertinence! Just you wait until your husband is missing without any word for three years. See how you like it. This war is nothing to do with me! I am not a German! I will not have you, by false innuendoes and threats, embroiling me in it. I have already given all my horses to the War effort, yet you come hinting that I am a traitor because of my husband, who is an Englishman, has disappeared and from whom I have not heard a single word for three years. This is not our war. We breed racehorses. We do not make wars. Now our living has gone. When we were married there was no war. It is not of our making or of our choosing. Now it has come into our lives and forced us apart. Because of it we will probably never see each other again! Get out! Leave me alone and do not come bothering me with your despicable innuendoes again!" She was so angry that she pushed him out of the door, shutting it with a crash behind him and throwing the great bolt.

She held her head in exasperation and stamped back to the fire. "Stupid man! Does he not realise that if deserters came back here and any of them had joined the Red Guards and started stirring up troubles, I would be the first one to be in danger. Traitor to Germany? I could not care less about Germany. All I want is for the war to end so that my Robert can come back, if he is still alive!" She collapsed into the sofa and wept bitterly, disregarding the broken and scattered china.

There was a loud knocking at the door.

"What does the stupid man want now?" She looked up and saw his hat sitting on the hall table. She jumped up, grabbed it and ran to the door. "You stupid little man! How can you arrest me when you cannot even keep yourself properly dressed!" She shouted at him. She was about to open the door, but decided against it. She ran to the window and flung it open. "Here!" She threw the hat out. "Make sure that you are properly dressed next time you come to see me."

"You be careful, Frau 'Enery, ve vill be vatching you."

The hat, caught by the wind, sailed in a graceful ark and fell into the moat. She laughed at him and slammed the window shut.

She sat by the fire and pondered his visit. When Frank came in to collect the tray she stopped him.

"Frank, please sit down."

"Sit down, Lady? What about this china?"

"Leave it for now. I need to talk to you. Sit down please." He still hesitated. "Frank, please sit down."

"Talk to me, Lady?"

"Yes please. Frank, please sit!" She was getting exasperated. "Listen. What do people say about me?"

"Say about you?"

"For goodness, Frank, stop repeating everything that I say!" She stamped her foot angrily. Broken china scrunched into the carpet. "That German officer was hinting that I might be a spy. Because I have an English husband, he suggested that I might not be unsympathetic to any deserters from the army that might come here. Do the people think of me as a spy?"

"No, no, of course they don't, Lady. What could you tell the English about things that are happening here, that would help them in the war with Germany."

"That is exactly what I said to him. But he thought that because I was sympathetic to the English, because of my marriage, that I might be prepared to turn a blind eye on deserters from the army." The old man looked at her.

"And would you?"

"Would I what?"

"Turn a blind eye to any deserters that came here." Elizabet thought for a little: *It is me who is supposed to ask the questions—what impertinence is this? Has Frank been persuaded to spy on me?* That was a disquieting thought. Frank was the one person she thought that she could trust. To be as cautious as possible, she decided not to answer that question.

"Frank, have you heard what is going on in Russia? These Red Guards?"

"Yes Countess. The kitchen talk is full of it."

Elizabet sat up in alarm. "How do they know. How have they heard?"

"Newspapers and pamphlets and the word?"

"The word?"

"Yes. In the taverns at night, in the marketplace. The talk in the Taverns is full of it. There seems to be a person called Ulyanov, a self-styled leader. He calls himself Lenin. He seems to be urging the people to rise up and take power from the Government. He has some powerful slogans that appeal to people. It seems that he has a great deal of popular support. He is urging the soldiers in the Russian Army to desert, to disobey their officers. The peasants in the country are to expel their landlords and take over the land for themselves. He is urging the peasants and workers to form what he calls, 'Soviets'.

"Soviets?"

"Yes. They are to be committees that will take control of everything in their area so that all can be run for the benefit of the people there."

"What about these Red Guards? What of them?"

"As far as I have heard, Lady, they seem to be striking workers, peasants and deserted soldiers. They are forming gangs, Lady. They are evicting landlords and taking over their houses and lands, for as they say, 'the good of the people'. They say no one is to own anything anymore. Everything is to be held by the 'people'. All production is to be shared equally by everyone. Everyone is to be paid the same, no matter what they do." He paused and laughed softly to himself. "I look forward to the day when I am paid the same as the Prime Minister!"

"Such talk needs to be stopped at once. It is very dangerous."

"It is too late to stop it. It is common talk everywhere. People can talk of little else. These are simple slogans. People who are starving and have to grub for a living quickly catch hold of them."

"Is there any talk of forming such a 'Soviet' here?"

"I do not know. I cannot say. I do not hear everything that is going on."

"Thank you, Frank. You would tell me if you heard of any such thing, wouldn't you?"

"Yes Lady. I am an old weak man. They do not take any notice of what I say, so I say nothing, but I keep my ears open."

After Frank had cleared up the mess and taken the tea try out, Elizabet threw another log on the fire. She sat for a long time, curled up in her chair, in its flickering light, pondering the news that the visit from the German officer and her talk with Frank had yielded. She was not too worried about the threat to accuse her of being an English spy. She decided it was simply calculated to frighten her, but this other business was of much more concern. What would happen if the people decided to form one of those 'Soviets' here?

What would happen to her? What would happen to the children? She could find no answers to these questions. But it was very disquieting. Russia was a long way away, it was true. But Revolution was a very infectious thing. How would her people react to the idea? Especially in view of their connection with the Tsar, albeit remote? Was she popular enough to withstand such a challenge? She did not know. Could she rely on Frank to tell her what was going on? She doubted it. Of all her people, she would trust him the most, but he was old and frail. He could be easily bullied or intimidated by some one younger and stronger. She was going to have to be very watchful in future and take careful note of what was going on. She sat in the chair, hugging herself in anxiety, heightened by this latest news. Since she had heard of Robert's flight she had been consumed with worry. The concerns of looking after the Estate, her land, constant anxiety about their safety, had worn her out. She felt desperately tired, yet she could not sleep, constantly awake to the least sound in the night. She had lost her appetite and only picked at her food. She had become pathetically thin. Her fair hair had become lank and grey.

That night, when she went to bed, she retrieved Herr Schmidt's revolver from where she had hidden it and tucked it under her pillow. In her closet, she found an embroidered shoulder bag, which was big enough. In future she would keep the revolver in that and take it wherever she went. No one would suspect that it was in there. At least, she would be prepared.

The autumn passed uneasily with rumour and counter rumour flowing freely around. Every day, Frank would come to her with some new tale, often contradicting the one that he had brought yesterday. In the end, she began to suspect he was being fed with all these conflicting stories simply to keep her guessing.

She found that the people working at the Castle, if anything, were falling over themselves to be helpful. The woodpile for the winter was completed, the vegetables were safely gathered and put in clamps in readiness for the winter. The pigs had been slaughtered. The bacon, hams and chaps cured. They were even now hanging in the smokehouse, as they gradually matured. The jams and bottled fruits had been prepared, to be put away in the larder. The honey had been drawn off the hives. It now stood in golden jars in serried rows in the larder. The wines had been racked off their lees into bottles and stored away in the cellar. The barrels had been cleaned. This year's grapes had been picked and pressed. The juice was even now fermenting in the freshly vacated barrels, in preparation for next year. Joints of beef and pork had been salted down in the big barrels in the cellar. The geese were being fed with boiled maize to fatten them up for the winter. Piles of cut holly branches had been placed in preparation to light fires to keep the wolves at bay. She did not want a repeat of last winter's experience. They had never been in such a state of readiness for the coming winter. Last year had been a disaster. She did not want it to happen again. She was mistress of the household. She was determined to show everyone that she could manage. She even stopped carrying her big revolver around with her. It was a very heavy, awkward encumbrance. She hid it in the piano stool under some sheet music.

She had a considerable shock, then, one Sunday morning, as she was having a cup of coffee, before going to Mass, when Frank placed a newspaper in front of her.

"I found this in the kitchen last night," he said. "I thought you ought to see it."

WORKERS REVOLT IN RUSSIA

The headlines screamed to the world. She took it up. She quickly read it. It seemed that striking workers in Moscow had revolted, led by the Bolshevik party. They had overthrown the Provisional Government, setting up a "Revolutionary Committee" to take charge. She read on with horror. The Committee, led by Lenin, had declared an immediate end of the war against Germany. It then announced that all land in Russia was to be confiscated from the landowners to be given to the peasants. All titles and acknowledgements of rank were to be abolished. Everyone was to be equal. When she had read it she got up and threw it on the fire.

"On no account must anyone see this. Not a word must be spoken about it, do you understand?"

"Yes, my lady, but I think it is a little too late! That paper has been here for quite some time, I gather."

"Why was I not told about this immediately?"

"I am very sorry, my lady. I did not know. I only found it myself this morning. I asked Cook where it had come from. Apparently Boy brought it here a few days ago."

Elizabet was shocked.

"Boy? Boy has come back? Boy is here? What is he doing here? Why have I not been told? Have you been keeping things from me?" Her anger and anxiety cowed the old man.

"I am sorry, my Lady. I did not know. It was only when I found the paper and questioned Cook this morning that I heard about it."

"I am very glad to know that he is safe, but he cannot stay here. It is out of the question. It is far too dangerous for us. If he has deserted from the army, I shall be accused of harbouring a deserter. I might even be thrown into prison. If the German officer hears about it he will welcome the excuse to arrest me. We must go to Mass now. If we do not go quickly, we will be late, but get word to Boy. Tell him that I will see him as soon as I return. Now please go and tell the children to hurry, or we will be late."

They hurried down to the Church. The Mass had already begun when they arrived and so instead of taking their usual seats in the front, they slipped into seats by the door. Maria leant over to her mother.

"Where is everybody?" she whispered.

Elizabet looked round. The church did seem unusually empty.

"Ssh. I do not know. Attend to your prayers." Elizabet found it very difficult to concentrate. This new situation was extremely difficult. Whatever happened, Boy must go away. He could not stay at the Castle. He must go at once. Everyone must be sworn to secrecy. It must not be know abroad that he had even been there.

"Et cum spirit to tuo," she answered automatically to the response. She was not paying attention at all. She made a great effort to bring her mind to the here and now. After Mass, as they were leaving the Church, the priest took her to one side.

"I have the gravest news. I have heard that the revolutionaries in Russia have taken the Tsar and all his family and....," he hesitated, he hardly knew how to say what he had to tell her, "...they have taken them and shot them!"

"*Shot* him?" Elizabet squeaked, too shocked to speak.

"Yes! It has been announced that they are all dead. It seems they have just taken them and shot them."

"And The Tsarina?"

"Yes, Lady, and all the children."

"Little Alexis?"

"Him too. May God have mercy on them." He crossed himself.

Elizabet was too shocked to speak. She felt faint with shock and her stomach churned.

He caught her arm. "Are you all right Lady?"

At last she found her voice. "How could they do such a terrible thing? How could God allow such a terrible thing to happen?"

"God does allow or not allow. He has given man free will. If He did not allow people to do what they wanted, there would be no free will. We would be just puppets."

Elizabet was weeping with shock. She quickly pulled out her handkerchief and blew her nose. "This is terrible. Shocking. What is the world coming to? Those poor little children, Olga, Maria, Anastasia, Alexis, Tatiana. They are the same age as my own children. How could anyone be so barbaric as to take them and shoot them?"

"You must take the greatest care, Lady. Many soldiers have deserted and have gone to join the Revolutionaries. Apparently they are forming what they have called the Red Guard to help enforce the revolution. If that situation were to spread here, I need hardly tell you that you would be the first to be in the greatest danger. I have also heard that some of the people who have been in the hills with the irregular fighters, from here, are returning home. Some have been seen around. As technically they are deserters from the German army, the authorities are making an attempt to round them up. They will obviously go into hiding. What support they get from the local people remains to be seen, but I am warning you to take the strongest possible measures to protect what is yours."

"Yes, thank you, Father. I will do what I can." She was dying to tell him about Boy, but she dare not, in case he should inadvertently betray the fact to the German authorities.

"My dear, please take the greatest care. If they come here I fear that you might be the first person that they might bother. Be very careful."

She shook his hand.

"Come on, children, let us go home."

They walked together across the Park. The snow was quite deep and Cornelia kept falling in it. She became cold and wet. By the time they reached the door she was wailing and grizzling. Elizabet became quite exasperated.

"For goodness sake, Nanny, take them in. Give them some hot bread and milk to warm them up. Stop that crying, little one. You will soon be warm and dry again. Take them to the nursery afterwards. They may come to the dining room for lunch."

They climbed up the slippery steps and entered the front door. She stopped in the Hall and looked around her in surprise and horror. There were about twenty people standing in the hall round the fire. She stood there and could not move. She felt the blood draining from her face. Any minute, she felt she would faint. She must get a grip. No, no, she could not faint here in front of them.

"Who are you all? What do you want? What are you doing in my house?" A cold feeling of dread ran through her. "Nanny, quickly, take the children." She handed over the baby Christopher. "Quickly, take them!"

Nanny shepherded the children out. Elizabet turned to face the people. There were men and women. They were armed with rifles and with pistols thrust into their belts. She froze with horror. A cold vacuum was paralysing her whole body, immobilizing thought, freezing reason.

"Well, who are you? What do you want of me?"

She tried to sound braver than she felt. No one moved. No one spoke. She looked more closely at them. "Boy. What are you doing here?"

He was thin and gaunt. His face had lost its boyish good looks. He looked lined and grey and desperately tired. His eyes had lost their happy twinkle. He had an indifferent cruelty that sent a shudder through her. To look on him was like looking into the face of a dead man.

"I am glad to see you safely returned from the fighting. I will do what I can to help you, but you cannot stay here. The German officer has already been here looking for you."

She looked round. "Joseph! You have returned safely too." She recognised some of the other men as being stable hands from the Stud. They had disappeared when the war had started, but now had returned. Some of the women were those that helped in the house. She felt slightly less alarmed. Most she recognised. These were her own people! She could feel the blood begin to course through her veins again. The fog of fear was beginning to lift; she could feel her limbs tingling with the return of sensation, the return of control.

Lolling in a chair by the fire was a young woman with fair tousled hair. She wore a pair of long black boots over a pair of men's trousers. She had a black leather jacket thrown over her shoulders. Her shirt hung carelessly open. Round her arm she had tied a wide red band. Elizabet looked at her. At last she recognised her. "You are the girl from the Inn by the river! You are Elly! You are the wife of Boy! What are you all doing in my house? What do you all want?"

"It is not your house." Elly did not look at her, but stared at the fire. She swung her leg up and down over the arm of the chair.

"What do you mean, 'it is not my house'? Of course it is my house. It has descended through my family for generations, to my father, and now that he is dead, it is mine. You will be kind enough to stand up when you address me."

Elly stared at her in disbelief, but did not get up.

"And who paid for it?" Elly sneered. "Who paid for it?" she repeated, spitting the words out as if they were bullets. "*We* have paid for it. Us peasants. We who must stand up when we speak to you! By our sweat and our labour. We have paid for it. Our fathers and their fathers back through the generations. With our sweat. We paid. You took."

"That is not true. You know that. We provided you with houses and farms. Work and food. We have set up care for your children. We have provided for a doctor to look after you when you are ill. For any work that you have done, we have paid. There is work for anyone who wants it. We have supported you all."

"How many of us have a house like this? How many have a fire like this to keep us warm?" She got up and kicked the logs with her foot so that sparks flew in all directions. "How many of us have pretty things like this?" She picked a china figure off the mantelpiece and let it drop to the floor. It smashed to fragments. She ground them with her foot. "You and your children live in a house that is big enough for a whole village. Most of these people have only one room for their whole families. Here you have a separate room for each of your children and many to spare. You have enough food in your larders to withstand a siege. None of us has more than will last us until the end of the week."

"You have been searching round my house?" Elizabet's voice shook with indignation. "You cowardly people, you wait until I have taken my children away to Mass and then you come in here. You go through my whole house? Is that why you were not in Mass? Instead of being in Mass, where you should be, you were here, behind my back, rummaging in my house! You have not the courage to come when I am here, but must come like thieves as soon as my back is turned. If you have any complaints or grudges I will hear them now, otherwise I am ordering you to leave my house. Leave it at once! Do not have the impertinence to enter again without my invitation." She had got over her shock at finding them all in there. Now she was seething with rage. If a wild tiger had sprung through the door at that moment, she would have strangled it with her bare hands. No one moved. No one. Elly laughed at her.

"Elizabet Ramoskie, we are not leaving. We are taking this house over on behalf of the Committee of the People. Property no longer belongs to individuals. It belongs to the people. All the food in the house has been produced by the peasants, so it belongs to them. We will take it. We are taking it all back!" She almost spat the words at Elizabet.

"You have been reading the rubbish that has come from Russia. What has happened in Russia has nothing to do with us! This is not Russia! We are Magyars! We do not do what some ignorant peasants in Russia have done." Elly's eyes flashed with anger.

"That is half the trouble. You see that most of your world is full of ignorant peasants. You do not see us as people who feel and dream, just as you do. We are only ignorant, as you put it, because we cannot afford to buy people to teach us. We cannot afford to go to visit other places, other towns. And why can we not afford this? Because we have to work hard, our noses to the ground, to scrape a living. We can only scrape a living, because you pay us so little. You keep the crops, the results of our labours, and in exchange you give us pennies. This has come to an end. We have seen what has happened in Russia. Power has been given to the people. They are no longer peasants. Everyone is equal. None will have more than any other. The age of the greedy landlord is over. From now on all land, all crops, all produce will be held by the people." Her eyes flashed as she unfolded her utopian dream. "We will not be ruled anymore by superstition or priests. What has God done for any of us? There is no use for fairy tails and faith in the modern world. We will believe in what we can see and understand. The priests will no longer be able to keep the people in control with the threat of Hell. We have seen enough Hell here on earth. We do not want to look forward to Hell in eternity."

Elizabet was incensed. "What about Heaven in all eternity. The Son of God came down on earth. He suffered torture and death to save everyone from their sin. He rose again from the dead. He showed that there is hope after death. We have no longer the fear of the grave, because He has shown us the way to everlasting happiness. All we have to do is believe in him. He will save all who want to be saved, no matter what they have done wrong—even you, Elly."

Elly went white. She struck her with a vicious backhand blow that knocked her to the floor.

"You are so gullible!" Elizabet sneered at her, picking herself up off the floor. "You think that you will all be equal. You think that there will be fair shares for all. You will soon find out that this will not work. There will always be those who manage to gather a bigger slice of the cake than others." She realised the hole that she had dug for herself.

"Well at least we will see it happening. We will be able to do something about it—like now." Elly sat down in the chair again, suddenly aware that she had won the fight. "You must leave this house by sunset. You can take with you whatever you can carry. If you have not left by then, you will be thrown out. You and your children."

"This is ridiculous. I will not be put out of my own house by my own people." Elizabet stamped her foot in rage and frustration. "You are my people—where is your loyalty. Your gratitude? You have been our people for generations. We have done the best that we can to look after you. Are you now going to turn and bite the hand that has tried to help you, like rats from the sewer? I will have you thrown out. You, Joseph, you and you. If you want you positions back, put this person out. The rest of you go with her." No one moved. "Joseph, do what I say at once! You can have your position back as coachman. I will forget your part in this."

Joseph looked at her. "No Graffinflein. I will not do that. There is nothing left that you can offer me. All that you had, has been taken over by us, the people. You cannot bribe me or persuade me or order me. I am no longer one of your servants. You are no more my mistress."

She looked at him in disgust. "All the things that we have done for you. For your family and children!"

"That is in the past, Elizabet Romoskie. We are not talking of the past. It is only the future that counts. We will no longer accept to be peasants, depending on the goodwill of our landlord."

Elizabet was incensed that he had called her by her name.

"How dare you address me by name! Where are your manners, or is it too much to expect manners from someone who runs away from his duty? One who hides while others are killed for his freedom?" She thought he was going to hit her too! She braced herself for the blow.

"No!" shouted Boy. He stepped between them, forcing Joseph back. Elizabet grabbed his arm.

"You! You throw them out. You know that they should not be here."

He turned to her. His face was gaunt, like one from the grave. His tired cruel eyes bored into her like smouldering red hot gimlets.

"No. It is ended. I fought to win the war. We were out there in the freezing cold—c old that would turn your blood to ice. It was so cold that our fingers froze to our rifles. We had no bullets. We had no food. All we had was the snow to eat. If we could catch a rat we could eat it. We had no fuel, no matches. We ate the rats raw. Ten men fighting over a raw rat!" A tear ran down his cheek from his cold eyes. His body started to shake, his hands trembled. "Then the shells came. We had no warning. First there were ten of us. When we picked ourselves up there were only three of us left!" He hesitated, his eyes sightless as his mind was filled with the horrors he had witnessed and experienced. "We had meat then. We gathered up what we could find. We had to keep it inside our coats to stop it freezing solid. Our officer had been killed. We did not know where we were. We just walked away. We walked. We walked without hope. We walked through the snow and the blizzard. We walked in the dark. We walked because there was nothing else to do. We walked until we reached home. I have seen suffering, horror, that I hope even you do not dream about in your worst nightmare—and why? To keep you and your blood sucking people in comfort? If you wish to live in comfort, you go out there and fight for it. I have been there. I have done the fighting. I did not do it for you, I did it for me!" He shouted in her face. "For me! For my wife, for my children. Now Lenin has showed us how this is not a dream. He opened our eyes. Fair shares for everyone. Everything owned in common, all to the greater good." He glowered at her. "No longer will whole villages slave to keep one family in comfort. We who work will share the fruits of our labour."

Elizabet recoiled from his venom. "You fought for your children, did you? How do you know that they were yours?"

Boy stared at her, his eyes burning like coals in a black smith's forge. All his dreads, his suspicions, his fears were realised in that moment. He turned to Elly. She was shrinking in horror into her chair before his wrath. He threw his fist at her, driven with every ounce of wounded, defeated and disgusted manhood that had blindly driven him through those blizzard wracked wastes, where his body had given up, where only that small flicker of hope had driven him on, had kept him staggering from beyond the edge of endurance. He hit her full in the face. The force of his anguish knocked her and the chair in which she sat, backwards to the floor.

Elizabet had sense enough to realise that no matter what happened next, no one in the room would help her. They were a group together. No one would break ranks. She would have to pretend to accept the situation. There was nothing else that she could do. If she could get to the telephone she could denounce them to the German officer. He would arrest them.

Those nearest ran and picked up Elly. Her lip was cut and her nose was bleeding. She could not look at Boy. She was struggling to hold back her tears—tears of hurt, tears of remorse.

Elizabet, her nerves strung to breaking, saw a small chance. "I cannot possibly leave by nightfall. I have my children to look after. You cannot just turn us out at night in the dark. What would we do? Where would we go?"

Elly had resumed her seat in the chair by the fire. She wiped her face on her sleeve. "No. You will not be thrown out in the dark. Be gone at two o'clock or you will be thrown out. If you are still here when it gets dark, then you will all be shot! The Tsar was shot. We are not afraid to shoot his lackeys and lickspittles."

Elizabet was horrified. "It is half past twelve now, we cannot be ready to go by two o'clock. What about all my things? How am I going to take them?"

"You take what you can carry. The rest stays here. They are only things." She got up and, picking up a chair, smashed it against the edge of the table.

Elizabet cried out. "No! Stop that! At once! Those chairs are valuable!"

"Are you going to take them all with you? Can you walk out of here with all these chairs?" She picked up the pieces. "Wood! That is all they are. Wood!" She threw them on the fire.

Elizabet ran to her. "Stop. You cannot burn them It is a sacrilege!"

"The people's committee can do what it likes. You will not stop it."

Elizabet saw nothing but contempt in their eyes. She knew she was defeated. Hot tears started to well up in her eyes. *I will not let them see me cry, I will not!* She ran out of the room to the kitchen.

CHAPTER 32

Elizabet raced to the kitchen. This was her worst nightmare come true. What was she going to do? She must get away with the children. Get them to some place of safety. Where could she go? Wherever they went, she would be known. What could she do? Sobbing with anxiety and frustration, she burst through the kitchen door.

"Maria, children, nanny!" She leaned on the big table, breathing deeply, her hand shaking, her knees trembling, ready at any moment to let her down. Maria was carrying Christopher in her arms. The other two girls sat at the table with a big slice of bread and jam each.

"Where is nanny and cook and the others?"

Maria shifted Christopher on to her other hip. "They have gone. There is no one here."

"Gone? Where have they gone?"

"I do not know! Nanny put on her hat and coat and ran out of the back door. We have not seen the others. They must have gone before we came in."

"Here, give me the child." Elizabet took Christopher. "Sit down Maria. Now all of you listen to me. This is not a joke. This is not a game, this is very deadly serious." Cornelia started to giggle. Elizabet glowered at her in fury. "Stop, stop that silly laugh at once. This is not a time for laugh, it is a time of great danger. The peasants from the village have come with guns. They have taken over the house. They want us to go. We have to take whatever we can carry, then we must go. We have to go now." She fought back her tears. "We have not choice." Her voice faded to a whisper. "If we do not go now, as they tell us, they will shoot us. Maria, take the children upstairs. Put them in their warm clothes.

Bring them back here, then put their winter coats and hats and gloves on. Make sure that they put on their warm boots."

"But mama, they cannot just take the house or throw us out. Tell them to go back to their business."

"I have tried that! There are twenty of them. They have guns. They have the idea that everything must belong to everyone, so they can have our house and things. We can only take what we can carry."

Maria was crying. "They cannot just throw us out. It is our home. They cannot just take it."

"Listen, my darling. They can, and they have done. There are twenty people with guns out there. How can I defeat them? If I defy them more, they will shoot us. They have shot the Tsar of Russia with all his family. If we do not do as they say, they will not hesitate to shoot us. Now come on. Take the children up the back stairs. Go quietly. Be as quick as you can. When you have dressed them, wait in here, till I return. If anyone comes, hide in the laundry room. Come, you children—quickly. Do as Maria says! No arguing."

She chased them all up the back stairs. She put Christopher down in the large laundry basket, then ran to the linen cupboard where she gathered up a handful of pillowcases. She would put the valuable things into them. There was no point in taking any glass or china things, they might get broken. There was all the silver and the jewellery. There were the bankbooks in the office, also the money in the safe. She ran up the back stairs to her mother's room. She emptied her jewellery box into a pillowcase. She crawled under the bed to open the little safe in the wall. Everything that was in there, she put in the pillowcase. She went to her father's room. She took his watches, cufflinks, studs and his cigar case. She opened his safe behind the back of his wardrobe and took out everything that it contained. Running back to her mother's room, she swept up all the photographs, with the clock, off the mantelpiece into the pillowcase. She went back to her room. She took her jewellery, her photographs and her fur stoles. She collected up her warm clothes. She pulled out the middle draw of her dressing table. From behind it she took the envelope which she had taped on to the back, which contained the money that she had collected from Robert, from all his silly bets. She kissed the bulky packet and thrust it into the front of her bodice. Thank goodness she had taken it from him.

Herr Schmidt's pistol! She must take that! It was in the piano stool in the blue sitting room. She ran to the window, to the secret door in the window recess. Making as little noise as possible, she felt her way in the dark along the secret passage that went to the blue sitting room. She had not used the passage since she and Robert had had a race to see who could change the quickest! She had slipped into the room to the piano stool to pretend that she had been there all the time! She felt the door with her hands. It opened into the side of the window recess behind the thick curtains. If they were open, the door in the window recess would be hidden. She could slip into the room. She carefully turned the wooden catch. The door opened a fraction. She held her breath and listened. Her heart was thumping in her chest. She was sure that anyone standing in the room would hear it! There were no lights on in the room. She could not hear anyone talking. Carefully she opened the door. Thankfully the thick folds of the curtain hid it from view. She slipped through to stand behind the curtain, her heart pounding. After a minute she was sure there was no one in the room. Carefully, she moved the curtain so that she could see out. There was no one there. She quickly went to the piano stool and took out the bag with the pistol. She heard voices outside! She was hardly back behind the curtain before some of the 'Committee' came in. She did not dare move. They came into the room and went over to the fireplace. Silently, she slipped through the door. Carefully, she shut it, silently turning the catch. She hurried back to her room. There, taking up the pillowcases, she ran down the back stairs. She had got all that she could from the bedrooms. She went to the laundry room. The children were there. They all clamoured round her when she came in.

"Be quiet. All of you, be quiet. Helen and Cornelia, go upstairs to the blanket chest outside my bed room. Bring two blankets each. Do not fight. Do not squabble. Do not make a noise. Go upstairs quietly. Bring them down here. Maria, go to the larder. Get as much bread and ham as you can. Put it in this basket. Bring some apples, the bowl of butter and a knife. Bring it back here. I think there is some cold beef. Bring it too. And a pot of honey."

She took up some of the pillow slips and went into the pantry. Packing as much of the silver as she could into the pillow case, she took it back to the kitchen. Hastily going to the office she took the bankbooks and the money from the safe. She returned to the kitchen. The children were all there.

"Now listen, my children. We will take the sledge. I will drive it with one horse. I will tie two other horses on the back with halters. The other horses I will turn loose. They will follow us or not. I cannot help it, but I will not leave them here for those peasants to have." She spat the words out as if they were some new terrifying poison. "We shall have to cross the bridge. They might see us. We need to make all ready. Then we make a distraction—it might be they do not see us go."

"Mama, can I bring my box?"

"Yes dear, you can bring it, but do not tell the others or they will all want to bring something. We have not got room for any more. Be quick. Run and get it."

Maria shot off up the back stairs. The box had been carved by a young man in Bavaria, for whom she held a special affection. He had given it to her for her birthday. It was her special treasure. Presently she was back.

"They are all up stairs in our bedrooms, going through all the draws. They did not see me."

"Good. While they are up there, perhaps we can escape. You children all come with me. Bring all that you can carry!"

Picking up her bulging pillow cases she led them all out to the stable. The sledge stood in the yard, with a tarpaulin over it. They loaded all their things on it. She tucked the children in with the blankets, then pulled the tarpaulin round them to try and make a hood. She tied it round with a length of rope, which was far too long and kept getting tangled. Finally she had all secured and the spare rope pushed under their luggage. With Maria's help she harnessed up the horse. They tied the others at the back. Then they opened all the stables to let all the other horses out.

"Quick, get that fork and bring the biggest load of hay that you can carry." Elizabet also took a great forkful of hay. They dragged them into the kitchen, then piled them against the door into the hall. "Go and get on the sledge and make sure that the others are safe. When we go, we go fast."

When Maria had gone, she ran into the larder. She collected the large bowl of dripping and threw it onto the hay. She lit the oil lamp and threw that onto the hay too. It burst into flames which rapidly set fire to the fat and the dry hay. The draught from the open back door fanned the smoke and flame through into the hall. She waited until she heard someone shout, then running out, she locked the back door. She threw away the key. She untied the horse and, jumping on the sledge, she cracked the whip over its head. It started off with a jerk, which knocked her over. By the time she had struggled up again, her horse was doing its best to race the free horses. They were all going pell-mell for the bridge. She shut her eyes and hung on. Somehow they got over the bridge. One of the loose horses was pushed into the moat and was swimming for the shore. She snatched a glance backwards. There was a column of smoke coming out of the front door, but she could not see anyone. She had a quick count. As far as she could see, all the loose horses were following them. The two on the halters were cantering along behind. They crossed over the bridge, over the stream toward the fork in the road. Which way? She had not thought! She was so anxious about getting the children safely away that she had not thought where she might go!

She turned towards the village. As the snow was thick they made no noise as they cantered along, but the bells on the sleight were ringing loudly. Anyone would hear them come. She tried to stop the horse, to do something about them, but she could not. The loose horses would not stop! The horse pulling the sledge was not going to be left behind. They careered through the village. A dog ran out barking at them as they sped through, but apart from that they saw no one. They came to a sharp bend in the road. The loose horses, unguided, went straight on, jumping the ditch and on over the field. The horse pulling the sleigh, suddenly finding itself on its own, slowed down. Elizabet was able to get it under control again. She slowed down to a walk. Standing up, she looked behind her. She fancied that she could see a red glow in the sky where the castle stood. But she could not see anyone following them. Once the fire was out and it was discovered that they had gone, the hunt would be up. She had to put as much distance between her and the people as she could. At least they would not have any horses that they could use to follow her. They could telephone, of course. They could get others to set up a road block to stop her. She looked at the wires sagging down, with the weight of snow. If she could cut them, they would not be able to do that either. How could she? She had no cutters. She could not climb up the pole even if she had cutters. She looked at the wires. They were not so high—the heavy snow made them sag down. She had an idea. She had used a length of rope to tie the tarpaulin over the sledge. It had been very long and troublesome to tie. She had tucked the unused end into the sledge. Quickly looking round, she found a piece of fallen wood from a tree. Pulling out the end of the rope she tied the wood to it. Swinging it round her head two or three times, she threw it up to the wires. At the fourth go she managed and the wood sailed over the wires. Catching the end she untied the wood and tied it to the sledge. Quickly climbing back on, she cracked her whip over the horse's head. "Hey, Hey!" she shouted and cracked the whip again. The horse leapt forward. The rope tightened with a jerk that dragged the sledge suddenly sideways. The children screamed. She thought she was going to tip everything over. "Ho, Ho!" she shouted again. The horse pulled. Suddenly the wires snapped with a twang and came snaking down. She drove on until the wires pulled out of the loop of the rope, then she stopped and tucked the rope back again into the sledge. What was she going to do now? Where could she go? If she could contact the German Officer, she could denounce them as deserters. He would go to arrest them. She did not know how to find him. He roamed around the country, staying in the local inns. It was impossible to know where he was. Meanwhile, where was she going to go? What was she going to do? She thought of going to the Stud, to the house there, but that would be exchanging one hornet's nest for another! No doubt, if they had occupied her house, they would have occupied the house at the Stud long ago. She stood in the sledge, not knowing what to do and becoming more and more panic stricken. She expected at any minute to see horsemen coming after her! The Doctor's house? Since the doctor had gone away to the war, his wife had remained in her house. She ran a clinic where she could help with the simpler problems of the village people. Elizabet had helped her. The two of them had become good friends. It would mean going back to the village. She would have to risk it. She could not just wander the countryside in the dark with the children. Sooner or later she would be stopped and caught. She had to have a plan. She pulled the sleigh onto the side of the road and, turning round, headed back to the village. They reached the Doctor's house, but the gate to the yard was shut. She gave the reins to Maria. Jumping down, she yanked the bell pull. In the house, in the distance, she heard the bell ring. At once a dog started to bark. Elizabet stood in the street, anxiously looking up and down. Any minute someone might come! They would be discovered!

"Oh come on. Come on. Be quick!"

At last the Doctor's wife came out onto her front porch with a lamp. She was quite used to being called out at all hours of the day and night to attend to some medical emergency or other.

"Who is it? What do you want?"

"It is me—Elizabet. Quickly! Open the gate. Let us in. Be quick. Oh please hurry!"

"Elizabet? Is it you, Elizabet?"

"Yes, quickly, quickly! Open the gate and let us in!"

Her urgency was apparent in her voice. The Doctor's wife ran to the gate and, lifting the heavy bar, swung them open. Elizabet led her horse in but unfortunately cut the corner too fine. The sledge wedged against the gatepost. She tried to push it free, but she could not.

"Quickly, you children, jump off! Help push. Christopher, you stay there—you are too small." Suddenly finding himself alone, he started to wail. "Quickly, push, push, before he wakes the whole village!" Their combined effort freed the sledge. They pulled it inside and quickly shut the gate.

"What on earth are you doing here at this time of the night? What is going on?"

"Let us come in, then I will tell you. Can I put my horses in your stable?"

"I have only got one empty loose box; you can put them all in there."

"Thank you. Will you take the little children inside? Maria, will you help me with the horses?"

They took the sledge as far into the Doctor's yard as they could. They unhitched the horses, then put them into the loose box with some hay. Without them on it, the sledge was quite light. They pushed it into the corner of the yard. There were lengths of wood standing against the wall. They laid these down in front of the sledge and covered it all with the tarpaulin. Anyone taking a casual look might think that it was just a woodpile. They brushed snow over the tell-tale tracks and went into the house.

The doctor's wife had made a big saucepan of hot milk. She gave Elizabet and Maria a big mug full each. Into Elizabet's she poured a liberal shot of brandy.

"Now, tell me what on earth is going on! I could not make any sense of what the children were saying. Do you want some food? Something hot to eat? I have put on a gulyas, to warm you all up."

It was only then that Elizabet remembered that they had not eaten anything at all, all day. Normally they would have had a big breakfast when they got home from Mass, but that had not happened. In her anxiety to escape safely with the children, she had not thought about eating. She was shaking violently both from the cold and from the anxiety of the moment. She had not had time to feel the shock of the events. Suddenly it hit her. She sat down on a chair and, burying her head in her hands, burst into tears. She sobbed and sobbed. The children jumped up from the table and ran to her, hugging her. They too all started to cry. The sight of their mother's distressed state was too much for them. The Doctor's wife did not know quite what to do. She flapped around indecisively.

"Maria, take the little ones."

Between them, they prised them off Elizabet. They huddled together on the big kitchen chair whilst she did the best she could to comfort Elizabet.

"I am so sorry. I am so sorry!" Elizabet sobbed. She sat up and blew her nose on her handkerchief. Between sobs, she explained to the doctor's wife what had happened and what she had done. "But what could I do? I did not know what to do. I just panicked. I did what I could. The house may be burnt to ashes, for all I know, but I was not going to let them just throw us out and take it!"

"You were very lucky to get away. I have heard that this has happened to other people. Some who have resisted have been shot. They are not being content to just turn people out and take everything; some people are being locked up and treated very badly. Stay here for tonight, but it is too dangerous for you to stay longer. They are bound to start looking for you. I do not think that the fact that I am the Doctor's wife will protect me if they find you here."

"But what am I to do?" Elizabet wailed.

"First you all sit and eat some of this gulyas. Come on, children, sit round the table." She served them a steaming bowlful each. "My goodness, you are hungry! Who would like some more?" They all offered their bowls. Even Christopher pushed his bowl hopefully forward.

When they had eaten, she took the children to bed. "Come on. It is late now. You can all sleep in the big bed. You will be warmer there. You do not have to worry about getting up in the morning. You can sleep all day if you wish."

Elizabet came up too, to get them ready and tuck them all into bed. She kissed them all goodnight, last of all Maria.

"Mama, you won't cry anymore, will you?" Her anxious face peered up at her mother. "It makes us so sad when we see you cry!"

"No my darling, I will not cry anymore. I was just hungry and cold. Even mummies have to cry occasionally." She kissed her softly on the cheek. "Sleep tight, my darlings. You have been so good today. I am so proud of you all." She blew out the lamp and went downstairs.

The Doctor's wife had made a pot of her precious coffee so they sat by the hot kitchen stove.

"Elizabet, I am so sorry for you. What a terrible thing! What you must do is to stay here tonight and tomorrow, but you must leave tomorrow night after it is dark. If they come here enquiring, I am sure that I can stall them for one day. If you travel by night, you should be able to get clear away. It will be the last thing that they would expect you to do. I am afraid that you cannot stay after tomorrow. If they do not soon find you, they will know that you are hiding somewhere, then they will start searching."

"Yes, thank you. That is very kind of you. Have you heard that they have shot the Tsar, the Tsarina and all the children? Can you believe that anyone would do such a thing?"

"*All* the children!?" The Doctors wife gasped in horror. "I do not believe it! Who told you?"

"The priest. After Mass. He took me aside and told me. He warned me that I should take great care."

"He is right. This is terrible! Terrible! What will come of it all. Elizabet, you must take great care. If they catch you, they might shoo…" Her voice trailed away as she realised the enormity of what she was saying.

"It is worse than you know. Robert has had some of the horses of the Tsar to train in Bavaria. For goodness sake, do not tell anyone. I think that they know. That girl called us the 'lickspittles' of the Tsar. I am putting you at great risk! Our being here is putting you in great danger. You have been very kind to help. I don't know what I would have done, or to whom I might turn. But what about you? Will you be safe?"

"Oh, do not worry about me. They need me. Who else is going to deliver their babies and lance their boils?" Elizabet sat shaking her head.

"All is lost. First my husband. Then the horses. Now my home! Now My clothes! All our family pictures and furniture. All the beautiful china and glasses. The Stud and the horses are no more. I was going to win such races for my Papa, for his memory. Now all is gone. Everything is gone. How shall I live? What shall I do? Where shall I go?" Silent tears ran down her cheeks. "What will happen to us if they catch us?"

The Doctors wife came to her and put her arm around her. "I think that you must make sure that they do not catch you. Try not to think about what might happen if they do. What about your place in Bavaria? Where you husband was working, could you not go back there?"

Elizabet considered this suggestion. "Do you think I would be safe there? Would not the troubles have spread there as well?"

"No, I do not think so. Germany is still an enemy of Russia, even if the war between them is now over; but I do not think those ideas would have spread that far yet."

"Because we were allies of Germany, technically we were enemies of the Russians, yet their ideas have spread to us."

"Yes, but we are a lot closer than Germany is."

"But I am still the Englishman's wife. The children are English. Will they let me pass?"

"I think that you could persuade them that you are Hungarian, one of their allies. You will have to pretend that your husband is dead if they ask about him. I have got some of my husband's Government forms here. I can make out some papers for you. If I cover then with rubberstamps and smudge them a little so that no one can read them, you could probably get through to Bavaria without being questioned. We can change your papers slightly. I am sure you will get away with it! 'Enery we could change quite easily. No one will notice.

You can be Hungarian going to visit a sick Aunt or something. No one need know that you are married to an Englishman."

Elizabet smiled ruefully to herself. "I might not be, for all I know. He might well be dead, I do not know. Do you know I have not heard anything from him since the war began? I did not even know that he had escaped to Switzerland, until after it had happened." Tears again started in her eyes.

The Doctor's wife hugged her. "I think your best plan is to go to Bavaria. You will not be safe anywhere here."

"But how can I get there? The river boats will be watched. I will not be able to use them. Do you know that the ringleader of the gang that came to my house was the girl from the inn by the river steamer landing? She is called Elly. If I see here again without her thugs round her, I will kill her with my bare hands if I have to!"

"Her? Is that what her name is? Is she their leader? She is a right madam, she is. I think all her children are by different fathers?"

"How many children has she got?"

"Three, I think."

"She will spread her legs for anyone, she will. If you could get as far as Pressburg you could take the train from there. If you can go quickly enough you should get there before they can send word to stop you." She frowned. "But the telephone. Can they not telephone?"

"No, the telephone is not working."

"No?"

"I have pulled the lines down!" She nodded. "That is what I will do. I cannot think what else I can do."

"Good, that is decided. Now go to bed. Get some rest! Do not come downstairs unless I come up to get you. Keep the children upstairs. Make sure they keep away from the windows. People are in and out all day with their little ailments. It would not do if anyone saw you. I will make you a hot meal in the evening, before you go."

"Thank you so much. You are risking so much for us."

"Oh, go on! Get some rest."

Elizabet went to bed, but in spite of her tiredness, she could not sleep. For a long time she tossed and turned, going over in her mind all that had happened.

It was midday before she awoke. She felt stiff and unrested. She ached all over. It took her a few minutes to realise where she was.

"My God, the children!" She jumped out of bed and ran to their room. They were all still asleep. She left them sleeping and went back to her room to get dressed. The Doctor's wife must have heard her moving around, because she came running up the stairs with a large tray with bread and hot milk.

"I have been thinking. It might be better for you, safer, and make things easier, if you were to be dressed like a man. I still have some of my husband's clothes here. I know he was bigger than you, but if you were to wear trousers and a coat, with a hat pulled well down, you might pass as a man from a distance. It might be a good idea to dress Maria in his cloths as well—she is quite grown now. It might save her from unwelcome attention."

Maria came into the room, looking tousled and sleepy.

"Hello darling. Did you sleep all right? Are the others all right?"

"Yes, thank you. Except the others kept tossing and turning all night Christopher says he wants his potty. I told him he had to wait."

"I had better go to him quickly, or he will wet the bed. The Doctor's wife has just suggested that we dress up in her husband's clothes, so that we look like men. We might be safer." She went to attend to Christopher.

The Doctor's wife took Maria to her wardrobe.

"Look, here are my husband's clothes. Take whatever is any use to you. When your mother is ready, she will come. But please stay up here. Do not come downstairs. There is some bread and milk on that tray for your breakfast."

They had some excitement trying on all the doctor's cloths. Later, as it got dark, three very odd looking little men in badly fitting clothes came downstairs, with a small girl and a child. After they had had their tea, they all went outside and with the help of the Doctor's wife, dragged the sledge out and turned it round.

"What on earth have you got in those pillowcases?"

When Elizabet told her that they contained all the valuables that she had been able to hastily grab together, from her house, she laughed. "You can't go clanking around the place with a load of pillowcases. I have some suitcases that you can have. Bring all that stuff inside. We will pack it up properly."

As Elizabet was unloading the things she suddenly stopped. "The horses! I have not fed the horses."

"Do not worry, I attended to them before breakfast."

"Thank you. What would we have done without you? I will just see to them now, then come in."

She quickly fed the horses and went inside. They packed the cases with all their things, putting some clothes on top of each one. They would not pass a search, but they would deceive a casual inspection. When it was all done they ate the meal that the Doctor's wife had prepared for them. Then it was time to go.

They embraced all round. Elizabet had to fight down her tears.

"I cannot thank you enough," she began. The Doctor's wife would hear none of it.

"Be on your way. One day we will meet again, who knows. Here, take this, you may need it." She took out of her pocket a small gold medal on a chain and hung it round Elizabet's neck.

"What is it?"

"It is a St Christopher medal. He protects travellers. He will look after you."

Elizabet bit her lip to try to stop the tears. "Will you accept the two spare horses? They are slowing us up. It makes things more difficult with them behind. You can always say they wandered into the yard so you shut the gate if anyone asks you about them!"

She thankfully agreed. Soon they had the biggest and strongest harnessed to the sledge. Elizabet borrowed a pair of pliers and after a prolonged struggle, some cut knuckles and a broken nail, managed to pull all the bells off the sledge harness. At least now they would be able to go along silently. The children made a nest in the blankets. Maria and Elizabet covered them with the tarpaulin as best they could and climbed up onto the seat.

"Goodbye. Thank you so much."

The Doctors wife opened the gate. She looked up and down the street. There was no one in sight, so she waved Elizabet out into the dark of the night.

Elizabet's eyes soon got used to the dark and in fact because of the snow, it was really quite light. She could see quite well. The children were very restless under the tarpaulin. They kept squeaking and arguing. Helen wanted to know why she could not sit on the seat as well as Maria. It was not fair. Maria always had the treats! She was treated as one of the children. Elizabet had to get quite cross with her to make her stop. Someone had to be with the little ones to make sure they were all right. It was not long before Maria began to feel the cold and was glad to get under the tarpaulin, but by then Helen had gone to sleep. Elizabet kept going at a steady trot. They made good time.

Once in the middle of the night, she saw the lights of a coach coming towards them. Elizabet pulled off the road into some bushes and waited, hardly daring to breathe. The coach passed by without seeing them. Just after dawn, they came across an old barn. By the look of it, no one had been near it for years. She drove round behind it and tethered up the horse. She went inside to explore. It was full of hay. There was no sign that any had been taken, so it would be just their bad luck if someone came today. They opened the door and drove the horse inside. At least he would have enough to eat.

It was one of those barns with a door either side, so that the wagons could be drawn in from one side, unloaded and driven straight out through the door in the opposite side, so that the wagon did not have to be turned round. She found some branches and did the best she could to obliterate the sledge tracks in the snow. When they had finished, the snow looked almost worse than when they had started, but hopefully it would pass unnoticed. She unlatched the door on the opposite side of the barn, so that they could quickly drive straight out and get away if they had to. They spent the day in the barn, resting and sleeping. They made a good meal off the stores that they had brought with them. That evening they set off as soon as dusk fell. They passed through several villages, but no one challenged them. They made good time in the night and when dawn broke she pulled into a small wood to hide up for the day. She could see the spires of Pressburg in the distance. If they left in the mid-morning, they should arrive just after everyone had gone home. With luck they would be able to get down to the railway station without attracting too much attention. She gave the children a picnic from their stores but then they had to wait for the time to pass. They were very fractious. They wanted to run around and play, but she would not let them. She made them get back on the sledge into the nest that they had made with the blankets. She did not want to be caught out by anyone coming and not be able to move off quickly if she had the need.

In the early afternoon, they set out again. They met several other carts and wagons coming out of the town. As they got closer, so the road became busier. Despite every nerve-wracking encounter, no one bothered them. She became more nervous as they approached the bridge over the Danube.

"Maria, you must go with the little ones and keep them quiet. They must not make a sound. Helen, you come to sit by me. There are bound to be guards on the bridge. Keep your collar up and your hat down and whatever you do, do not speak!"

The traffic became thicker, then slower, until they were slowed down to a walk. They were behind a wagon with a big load of hay, so they could not see in front of them to see if there were any guards on the bridge or not. However, even though the traffic slowed right down, they kept moving. Suddenly they were on the bridge. There were guards on both sides of the road. They seemed to be German and Empire soldiers and a party of Red Guards. Elizabet drove slowly on. She could feel her hands sweaty on the reins. She gritted her teeth.

She felt that they were staring at her. They were so close, she could have stretched out her hand and touched them. She felt like screaming. She bit her lip, expecting any one of them to shout out for her to stop. She would have to, for she could not get past the wagon in front.

"Do not look at them. Look straight ahead." Out of the corner of her eye, she could see them looking at her. She waved her whip in a half salute but kept driving steadily on. The bridge seemed to go on for ever. There were several guards on the bridge, lounging on the parapet, but they took no notice of them. There were more guards at the other end of the bridge, but they waved them through.

She was through! She let out her breath in a big sigh. She did not know that she had been holding it in. She felt quite dizzy with fright and relief.

Though she had been to the station several times, she had never driven there herself and she was not sure of the way. However, after driving round for a while, she suddenly came across it. She hitched the horse and taking off her man's hat, she threw a cloak over her shoulders and went to the ticket office to enquire of trains. It seemed the only train was at eight o'clock in the evening. She paid for the tickets and asked about a porter. There were no porters. There was a war on. All porters were away fighting. If she had luggage, she could take a barrow. He pointed to where they stood. She pushed the heavy barrow out to the sledge. With the children's help, she loaded all the luggage on it. Between them, she and the children managed to push it onto the station. She looked at the horse. What was she going to do with that? She could not just leave it standing there. Guards would soon be alerted to the fact that something was up if she just left it there.

"Now you children, you must sit here. Sit on the luggage. Do not go away. Do not make a noise or draw attention to yourselves, do you hear? Maria will be in charge. You must do as she says. I will come back as soon as I can." Immediately they broke into a chorus.

"Where are you going? We want to come too. Do not leave us here."

"Sh, sh, my little ones. I have to do something about the horse. I cannot just leave it standing there. Promise me that you will be good. I do not want to leave you here. I will be as quick as I can. Now huddle together so that you keep warm. Maria, if anyone bothers you tell them that the children have got chicken pox. They will go away and leave you alone." She was very apprehensive about leaving them, but what else could she do? She pulled on the Doctor's hat again. She drove round until she found a livery stable and pulled into the yard. She was greeted by a wizened old ostler.

"Can you take my horse for the night? See that he is fed and watered. I will want him ready at eight o'clock in the morning. I will pay you when I collect him."

"You won't get 'im back if you don't," he grumbled.

She hurried back to the station. At least the horse would be looked after. When she did not come back for him he would probably be sold.

When she got back to the station, her heart stopped. The children and the luggage were surrounded by a group of soldiers! Damn! Damn! The bag with the big pistol in it was in the basket with the picnic things! Whatever was she going to do? She ran over and pushed her way through them. The children were in a frightened huddle on top of the luggage.

"What on earth is going on here?" Her outrage made the soldiers stand back. Maria and Helen flew into her arms.

"Oh mama, mama, these soldiers want to kiss us."

She turned on the soldiers with such venom that they cowered back. "You cowardly swine! You think it amusing to frighten little girls. How dare you treat young people in that way!" Her anger was so intense that they retreated down the platform, Elizabet after them. "You are supposed to be the gallant heroes defending the nation, but all you can do is bait young girls! If I had a gun I would castrate the lot of you with one bullet! Where is your officer? He will know how to deal with evil gutter louts like you. What regiment are you?"

"Forty ninth foot regiment, Lady," one of them muttered. "We didn't mean no 'arm, Lady."

"If you did not mean harm, why did you make it? Could you not see how you were frightening them?" She drew herself up to her full fierce height. "What very bad luck for you. I am the wife of the Leutenant General of the Forty-ninth Foot regiment. You have not heard the last of this." They looked at her in horror. "Are you travelling on the Munich train?" she demanded. They all nodded. "When the train comes in, you will please put all that luggage into the guard's van for me and unload it at our station when we arrive."

The one who seemed to be the senior stood to attention and saluted. "Lady, I would like to apologise. We didn't mean no harm. We will put your luggage on the train. You leave it to us."

"Perhaps you will be kind enough to stand someone on guard, so that I can take my children out of the cold into the waiting room, until the train comes." She turned to the children. "Come on, children, we will wait inside. Maria, bring the picnic basket. We can eat whilst we wait." She shepherded them into the warm room. "How did they find you out?"

"I am afraid it was me. I took my hat off to scratch my head. They saw my long hair. I hate it. I shall cut it off and never have long hair again." Maria sobbed.

Elizabet put her arm round her. "They were only boys. Some of them not much older than you."

"Boys or not, I was very frightened. I do not know what we would have done if you had not come back at that moment."

"You must be on your guard all the time. You must not take any chances. Luckily no harm is done. Now let's have something to eat. I am very hungry."

"Mama, Papa is not really a Leutenant General, is he?"

"No, of course he is not, but they did not know that. Nothing impresses a soldier more than rank!"

The train was only half an hour late. The soldiers, who had been stamping up and down outside the waiting room, not daring to come in, soon loaded the luggage. Elizabet took the children to board the train, but standing on the platform was a group of rough looking men with rifles. They had red arm-bands. They were checking everyone's papers. She gathered the children closely to her. When her turn came, she flapped the papers under their noses.

"I should stand well back. Them children 'ave got 'orrible chicken pox." She spoke to the one who seemed to be the leader in her best village accent. He looked through the papers and studied the Doctor's rubber stamps. *I bet he can't read*, she thought to herself. He gave the papers back and waved her on without speaking.

Eventually the train drew out of the station. It stopped at the Austrian frontier. Presently inspectors came round examining the tickets. They inspected papers and passes and questioned everyone. Everyone was ordered off the train. They were lined up against the wall of the building.

"What is happening, Mama?" Maria asked.

"I do not know, darling. Do not talk in Eengleesh." She bent down to the other children. "Whatever you do, do not talk in Eengleesh." People were being shepherded through the office. After what seemed forever, when they had been standing on the cold platform so long that their feet were numb, it was their turn to be ushered in.

Elizabet's heart sank. There were some men and women in there. They all had red armbands.

"Papers!" The one at the desk held out his hand. Elizabet said nothing but handed them over. "Search them." Immediately the other people descended on them and made a quick search through all their pockets.

"Strip them!"

Elizabet was frozen in horror. "No! No! Not the children! They are only little. Leave them alone."

"Everyone. Be quick."

"No, you will not strip the children. I will not permit it." The leader got up from behind the table. He came round to face Elizabet.

"You either strip so that we can search you, or we take you outside, put you up against that wall and you are shot. Which is it to be?" Even as he spoke a shot rang out from outside. They flinched. The children started to cry. Elizabet tried to comfort them.

"Sh, my children. Quickly, do what he says." She helped them off with their clothes. They all stood shivering, in a row, in their underclothes.

"Everything—and be quick," the leader growled. "You are wasting my time."

"No! No! You can see that we cannot possibly have anything hidden."

"Everything, and be quick about it."

"No! I absolutely refuse! You will not treat my children in this way. I demand to speak to your commanding officer."

"I am my commanding officer. Take them outside. Shoot them." He walked over and opened the door.

"No! Stop! Stop crying, children. Quickly, take off your clothes." They stripped off their clothes and stood there naked, shivering with cold and terror, frightened and humiliated. One of the women guards came forward. She subjected each of them to a humiliating, personal and invasive search. They hung their heads and cried in shame, indignation and hurt. The guard walked round behind them.

"Bend over!" They did not move. "Bend over!" she screamed. Completely cowered and demoralised, they bent over. Again she searched them painfully and personally, with a prying finger.

"All right, you may go. Take your clothes. Get out. Take your papers." They grabbed up their clothes to hide their shame and were bundled out of the back door.

"Next!" they heard the Guard call as they were pushed naked out into the bitter cold of the street.

"Quickly children, put your clothes on." Elizabet was shaking so much that she could not do up their buttons. Maria was the first to get dressed. She helped the others. She hung Elizabet's blouse over her shoulders. When the children were dressed, Elizabet got herself dressed. The wind was freezing cold. She could feel herself getting numb by the minute. The children hung together until she was ready. They were cold, frightened and completely demoralised. They said nothing. Olga and Cornelia clung to each other, crying softly. Maria tried to comfort Christopher. At last they were all ready.

"Come on, children Let us get on the train." In silence, they dumbly followed her. They walked round the shed to the train. It was very full. They had to push their way practically to the front to find some seats. Eventually they found three seats together so thankfully took them. Christopher sat on Maria's lap and Cornelia sat on her mother's. The children snuggled to their mother, still too traumatised to speak. The train waited for what seemed like hours in the station, but eventually it started to leave. It made its slow way across Austria, stopping many times in sidings as other trains rushed past in the dark. None of them slept. They felt tired, dirty, abused and depressed when the train stopped at the German frontier.

German police and soldiers boarded the train. Systematically, they inspected everyone's papers. When they came into Elizabet's compartment, the children clung to her in terror. They started to cry with fright.

They took only a cursory look at Elizabet's papers. She held them up showing the big Hungarian stamp and her maiden name, carefully keeping her thumb over her married name. They seemed satisfied and passed on. Eventually the train set off again. It was three o'clock in the morning before they stood on the station surrounded by all their baggage as the train disappeared into the night. The young soldier had been watching out of a carriage window. When he saw them alight, he had jumped down too and helped unload all their things. Elizabet was relieved to see that the picnic basket with the bag containing the big pistol was still there. Thank goodness it had not been discovered. There was no telling what might have happened if any of the guards or soldiers had found it.

At least Elizabet felt safer here. She was far enough away from the Red Guards. It was unlikely that the doctrines of Lenin would have spread this far. The Station Master was hovering about wanting to get to bed. He had waited for the train to come. The gap between this one and the next, at seven in the morning, was lessening. He wanted to get to bed whilst it was still worth going.

"Excuse me lady, but are you being met? There is no one waiting in the yard."

"No, we will take a cab and send down for the luggage tomorrow."

"Cab? Cab?" He laughed. "There's no cabs, lady. There won't be any cabs 'till nine o'clock in the morning."

"But what are we going to do?"

"Well you can either walk, or you can wait."

"It is too far to walk. We will have to wait in the waiting room until a cab comes."

He unlocked the door for them. The fire had died down. "Can we have some more coal to make up the fire?"

"Well, lady, I don't know about that. There is a war on. Can't get coal for love nor money. Coal is like gold dust, coal is."

"Well, we will just have to make do. We have slept in colder places. Come on, children, curl up on the benches; you will have to sleep here, now. We will go on as soon as a cab comes."

The benches were hard and uncomfortable. About every half-hour they were woken by trains thundering past. At last it was light. Elizabet could give up pretending that she was asleep. Christopher had gone to sleep on her lap. Her legs were numb. As gently as she could, she moved him and stood up. Her feet were an agony of pins and needles and she nearly cried out. By wiggling her toes and stretching her legs, the circulation was gradually restored.

"Come on children. Let's have something to eat. We may have to wait for a long time till a cab comes."

"Oh mama, I could not eat anything. Specially if it is bread and ham." Helen pulled a wry face. "I don't want to see ham ever again."

"What about some bread and honey? There is a pot of honey here that we have not opened. Here, hold this." Elizabet handed her the loaf. She produced the honey. They were soon all breakfasting off bread and honey. The world did not seem quite such a hostile place.

At last a cab came down to the station. Elizabet ran out and stopped it. Quickly they packed all their things and loading as much of the luggage as they could on to the cab. They all squeezed in and headed for the Schloss.

CHAPTER 33

It was eleven o'clock in the morning when they arrived at the Schloss and pulled up outside the great front door. They unloaded from the cab in a stiff, dishevelled and dispirited group. The children were exhausted. Elizabet was no better. She sent the cab back to the station for the rest of their luggage; then, ushering her weary children before her, she banged on the great knocker. For a long time nothing happened. Suddenly the hatch door opened with a rattle and a sour looking woman peered out.

"Yes?"

Elizabet did not recognise her. "Would you please tell your mistress that her cousin Elizabet 'Enery has arrived with her children to call upon her."

The face disappeared. The shutter snapped shut. Elizabet felt wretched. She was cold and exhausted from lack of sleep. Her hair was undone. It blew in wisps in all directions. Her clothes were creased and dirty. The children looked like urchins from the street, crumpled and dirty, their faces tear-streaked, puffed up from fatigue and stress. She felt totally demoralised by the supercilious eye that had peered at them with such hostile disbelief from behind the small shutter. They were kept waiting several more minutes. At last they could hear the bolts being drawn back. The door opened just enough to admit them, one by one. They stepped into the Hall. A short dumpy woman in a black dress with a white apron and cap had admitted them. She said nothing. She had no need, for her haughty disdain said it all. They shuffled inside.

"Come this way, please. My mistress will see you at once."

Her disapproval needed no interpretation! They followed her in silence to the drawing room. She bade them enter.

Maria Von Zelletal was sitting by the fire. She rose to greet them. Hard though the war had been on them all, Maria had lost nothing of her impressive stature and she stood, majestically in front of the fireplace like some mighty floral marquee. She met Elizabet in the middle of the room and embraced her in a benign hug. Elizabet's strength gave way. She sank into a chair and burst into floods of tears. The children immediately flocked to her. They too dissolved into tears. Maria von Zellatel did not know what to do. She tried her best to console them all. Eventually, Elizabet managed to compose herself and calm the children. She spoke to Maria.

"We have had the most terrible time. We are lucky to be alive."

She quickly told of their misfortunes and their terrifying experiences. Maria heard her out in silence, waiting for her to finish.

"I see now why you arrive here looking like a tramp, with your children looking as if they have just been picked up off the street! Not one word of this must be spoken in front of the servants. They must not hear of it. You see we live in very reduced circumstances. Apart from some who are really too old, all my men have gone off to the War. Even the older men have been called to fight. I have only women in my staff. Some of those have gone to the munitions factory. I will help you all I can but we must think what is to do."

Elizabet interrupted her. "Have you heard anything from Robert?"

Maria looked at her. "Robert? Robert who?"

"My Robert! My husband, Robert!"

"Oh, yes, I am sorry! No. Nothing! Nor from Emil. I do not know what has happened to him, or if he is alive or dead. It is very worrying."

She in her turn took out a handkerchief to wipe the tears that had all unbidden filled her eyes. Elizabet stretched out a hand of sympathy towards her.

"We are two desperate wives together then. I have heard nothing from Robert since I left here. I do not know anything about him either. For three years, I have heard nothing."

Maria was in some agitation. "I am very sorry for you, but why have you come here?"

Elizabet was a little taken aback. "We had nowhere else to go. I was going to go back to our house, but felt that I should call upon you to tell you that we had returned."

"Elizabet, you cannot possibly stay here. The war is going badly for us at the moment. There is such a strong anti-British feeling, you could not possibly stay here. No one will serve you in the shops. You will find that no one will talk to you. Your children will be bullied by the local children. You will find life impossible. When news reaches the authorities, you and the children will almost certainly be arrested to be interned. Goodness knows what will happen to me, for harbouring you. It is without question! You cannot stay here! You must go at once! What you need is a plan!"

"But what I am going to do? Where shall I go!"

Elizabet, who's nerves had been at full stretch for the last week, felt devoid, helpless. She could not think what she could do. She felt lost. She had lived through desperate days by her wits, driven by her determination to look after her children, but now when she thought she was safe, it was all going to start again. She was exhausted, hungry and spent. She could think of no plan, she could think of nothing. She buried her head in her hands and wept tears of frustration and exhaustion. Maria felt sorry for her.

"Excuse me, lady." The maid stood there.

"Yes? What is it? Will you please knock before coming in like that!"

"Excuse me lady, but I did knock."

"Well, knock louder next time, then do not come in until you are bidden! What is it you want?"

The maid looked at her sullenly. "There's a cab wot 'as brought some luggage from the station. 'E wants 'ees money."

Elizabet got up. "Yes. Excuse me. I will go and pay him." She blew her nose and left the room. When Elizabet returned her cousin Maria was hatching a plan.

"Look, go back to your house, for now. When you are rested, you can think what to do. No one has been in it since you went away, so I do not know how you will find it. I will have cook prepare you a hamper, which I will send over, so you will have enough food for a couple of days. After that we will see. But I do not think that you will be able to stay here. I will call the staff together. I will swear them to secrecy but you must keep inside. Do not burn any lights, or people will start asking questions. There is a four-wheeled trolley in the coach house; you can use that to take your luggage across to the house." She smiled at the children. "You girls are big and strong, you can help your mother push. Is that all the luggage that you have brought?"

"Yes. That is all. We had very little time and we could only take what we could carry."

"It does not look very much!"

"It is not very much. It is very little, when you think that that is all that we have left of our home!"

"If you need anything, send one of the girls over to ask for it, but do not come in daylight. I will come over to see you tomorrow and perhaps we can think of a plan. I believe that we have the key to the house in the office. Whilst you are loading your luggage, I will find it for you."

Between them they loaded up the cart, which they had collected from the stable. Together, they pushed it over to their house. Maria had found the key. She handed it to them.

Elizabet had never expected that the day would come when she would be pleased to return to the little house, but when she turned the key in the lock and the door swung open, she could have wept. The children rushed in to find all their things in their rooms. It was like stepping back in time. Everything was as it had been left. There were cobwebs about, dust on everything. The air was musty, and there was a strong smell of mice, but it still had all their things, which were just as she remembered them. She wandered into the kitchen. There were dirty plates in the sink, the mould on them, long dead through malnutrition. There was no sign of Anna the cook or the maid. She should have asked Maria about them. She could hear the children running about upstairs. They were excited at being back home. Perhaps they would forget their ordeal now that they were amongst their own precious things again.

She called up the stairs.

"Maria, Helen, come down here please." At last they appeared, and she was heartened to see something of the sparkle in their eyes returned. "Will you please go to pump up the water? You can take it in turns." They chorused their disapproval. "What have you done?" She caught hold of Maria's arm. "Come here, child. Let me look. What have you done?"

Maria hung her head, then lifted her head defiantly. "Well, it is done now," she said.

"But your hair! All your beautiful hair! You have cut it all off!"

"I will never have long hair again. Never! I was so frightened on the station! I had given the game away. I had let you all down. By my one thoughtless act I had placed us all in terrible danger! I thought that those soldiers were going to hurt us. Thank goodness you came. I will never have it long like that ever again."

Elizabet put her arm round her. "You poor, poor darling, never mind. You are safe. No harm was done. Your hair will grow again."

"No mama. I will never let it be long again! We will go to pump up the water."

"I am sorry, dears, but it has to be done. There is no one else."

Grumbling, they went off. Before long she could hear the clank of the pump from the yard. She set about lighting the fire in the kitchen stove. Presently the girls returned.

"Mama, the tank is full. It is running out of the overflow in the yard."

"The tank must have been nearly full. That water must have been up in that tank for three years. Do not drink any unless it has been boiled first. It may not be very nice. It might be full of dead bats, dead flies, all kind of horrible things. On second thought, it might be wiser to drain it all out and pump up some fresh."

"Mama!" the girls complained. "After all our effort!"

"Never mind dears, it is better to be safe than sorry." She turned on the tap in the kitchen sink to let the precious liquid run away. "Will you go to the back door? There used to be a box there with sticks put there ready to light the fire. Will you bring me some?" They went.

Presently they came running back.

"Mumma, look, look what we have found!" They held out a piece of paper and some money. Elizabet took the paper. It was a hastily written note from Robert, for the cook.

> 'Dear Anna,' it read, 'I have very suddenly had to go away. I do not know when I will be back, or when Frau Henery will return from Hungary. I must therefore say goodbye to you. Thank you for your devoted service to myself and my family. Please find here money for a month's wages. I am very sorry that I cannot give you proper notice, but I have no doubt that by the time you find this note, you will know why it has been written in such haste. I hope that you will not think too badly of us, who have been privileged to count you as a friend. I will never think of all our friends here as enemies. Remember that wars are not made by ordinary people, but by those who would lead them.'

Tears filled Elizabet's eyes. "He had time to write this, but he has not been able to send even a word to me." She covered her face with her hands and wept bitterly.

There came a knock at the door. She dried her eyes and opened the door. A boy stood there. He had a wheelbarrow with the box of food that Maria had sent. He did not say anything. He just picked the box up and put it on the kitchen table.

"Thank you. If I were to pay you, would you be so kind as to pump up the water for us, please?"

He looked at her with a mixture of disgust and loathing. "I would not take your stinking English money for anything."

"It is not English money. It is German money. I am not English. I am Hungarian."

"You are the wife of the Englishman that escaped?" he demanded.

"Yes, I am."

"That makes you English."

At that moment the children came clattering back into the room.

"They are English," the boy said. "My father is dead because of an English bullet. I would give one back to all English." He turned on his heel and ran out. The children gaped after him in astonishment.

"Oh dear, children. I think that we might find things difficult. You must not go outside. Is that clear? You heard what cousin Maria said. They do not like us here, because of the war."

The last of the water drained out of the tank and the tap in the kitchen stopped running. She sent Maria and Helen out to pump up some more. She unpacked the food that Maria had sent and prepared some supper. At least it would make a change from bread and ham. Wonderful—fresh eggs. She would make omelettes for them all. When their meal was finished, it was nearly dark.

"I am sorry, children, we cannot show the lights. We must not advertise to everyone that we are back here again. We might as well go to bed. It is not good making a fuss. We have had the hard time! An early night in a comfortable bed will be good for us all. I will come too, to make the beds."

She went up with them. The blankets did not seem damp. She found some clean sheets from the cupboard. They smelt a little musty, but they were not damp. She made up beds for the girls and the cot for Christopher, which she put in her room.

The children were asleep almost as soon as their heads touched the pillows, Helen clutching Bo-bear to her. Elizabet went downstairs. Opening the door of the kitchen stove, she drew up the kitchen chair and sat in front of its warmth in the dark. If she could not stay here, what on earth could she do? She did not feel that there was any chance of going back to Hungary. Even if she could get back to her home, she would not be allowed to enter. She never should have left. She should have stayed and defied them. They would not have dared shoot her and the children. Would they? Would they? She should have called their bluff. If she had stayed, she could have negotiated. Having left, she was lost, they would never let her back. She remembered the look in Boy's eyes. She knew that she was deluding herself. She was one small woman against twenty armed and resolute people. They would have thrown her out, even if they had not carried out their threat to shoot her. One day when all this madness was over and people came back to their senses, she would be able to go back. But what was she going to do now? She could not stay here and she could not go home. What the hell was she going to do?

She looked at the heavens and shook her fist. "How could you do this to us? We have been to church as we should, we say our prayers, I have brought the children up to love and know you. I have done the best that I can to look after my people. They have turned against me and taken from me everything that we have. It is so unfair!" She wiped the tears from her eyes and curled up in her chair. She awoke with a jolt. The fire had died down and she was cold and stiff. With some difficulty, she groped her way upstairs in the dark. She looked in at the children—they were all sound asleep. She kicked off her shoes and, falling into bed, was soon asleep, still in her clothes.

She was awoken by someone hammering on the door. She struggled out of bed and looked out of the window. A boy stood there. A different one to last night, she was glad to see. He had a large milk can. She opened the window.

"Put it down there—I will collect it in a minute, thank you." The boy looked up at her, then, putting it down, ran off. She decided to leave the children to sleep as long as they would. She could give them some breakfast when they woke up.

She tided herself up and re-did her hair. With a shock she realised she had not done it for days. She went downstairs and made herself some coffee. She sat at the kitchen table and tried to take stock of what she might do. She could not go home. The Red Guards would catch her, or worse. She could not stay here. It was obvious that there was strong feeling against her. Plainly the news had got out that she was here so she could expect only trouble. There was another knock at the door. She was surprised to find her Cousin Maria standing there in some state of agitation. She quickly came inside and gratefully accepted a cup of coffee.

"I am sorry, Elizabet, but it seems that news is already out that you are here. Apparently some people from the village wanted to come for you to arrest you straight away, but they were persuaded to wait for the Chief of the Police. He will be here this afternoon. When he comes, you can be sure that you will be arrested. Luckily that gives us a little time. You must go at once. I will help you. Get the children up. Take your things and depart. I have ordered a cart to be here in half an hour. Go to the station. Take the first train."

"But where can I go?"

"It does not matter, just go to somewhere where no one knows you. You can say that you are Hungarian. There will be no one to denounce you. You must hurry so that you are well away, before they arrive."

"But what about you? If I am gone, they will know that you have helped me. Will not you be in danger?"

"Well, I expect that there will be some anger and some shouting, But I am a big girl, I can shout too!" She laughed. "Come on. Let's get the children up and ready." They woke the children and quickly gave them some breakfast.

"Now listen to me, children. This, it is serious, as it vas before. This is not a game. We have to go away from here. We have to be quick. Some peoples come to catch us. If they do they will put us in prison, which is a horrible, damp, dark, smelly place, full of hairy spiders and great scaly tailed rats! We must be gone before they come so that this does not happen."

Maria went quite pale and her lip started to tremble. "They will not search us again, will they?"

Helen started to cry. Cornelia's chin started to pucker.

"No my darlings, if we are quick, we will be gone before they come. Now quickly. Collect the things that you want to take, then we must go."

They were packed up, ready when the little cart arrived. It was driven by an aged old retainer, whom Elizabet remembered as one of the Coachmen. She smiled at him, but he looked straight through her with a scowl on his face. They loaded everything on and put the children in the cart. They tied a tarpaulin over them. Elizabet climbed up on the box beside the driver.

"Goodbye, Maria, thank you for what you have done for us."

"Goodbye, Elizabet. God go with you. What will you do?"

Elizabet hesitated. The tiny seed of an idea that had lodged in her half-asleep brain last night suddenly burst into life.

"I will go to England."

"England? Are you mad?" Maria squeaked. "England! You can't possible go to England. Don't be so ridiculous! There is a war on. You will never get there!"

"What else can I do? Wherever else I go, some one will think me an enemy. At least in England I will have the legal protection of being married to an Englishman."

"How on earth do you think that you will get to England? For goodness sake, be serious. There is absolutely no way that you will be able to get to England. Even to say it will get you arrested. How are you going to get there, the trains are all at sixes and sevens. Even if you get as far as the coast, which you will not, how are you going to cross the sea? There is a war on, in case you have forgotten. No boat will dare to even to think of trying to get to England. What will you do in England if you do manage to get there? You do not know even if Robert is there."

"If he is there I will find him. If he is not there, I can claim protection as his wife."

"But they are our enemies. They will lock you up."

"They are not my enemy. I am the wife of an English person. They will not lock me up. Drive on driver, we must go."

"Goodbye. Good luck, you stupid, stupid, hopeless girl! God be with you and protect you."

"Goodbye Maria, remember us."

The little cart set off and made its way across the Park towards the station. Elizabet wiped the tears from her eyes. After all the perils of their arrival, she had thought they were safe, but now they were on the road again, fugitives. They were going to flee to England. Who knows what might await them there. She lifted the corner of the tarpaulin.

"You children stay out of sight. I will let you out when it is safe to come out." She turned to the driver. "I can see that you do not like doing this. I am sorry to embarrass you but thank you for your help."

He looked at her bitterly. "I have three sons. Two are dead. One is missing, presumed dead. Were it not for my grandchildren I would have nothing left."

"My husband is missing. I have lost my house and home. Here I run and hide like a criminal to protect my children. I am very sorry for you. This war is terrible. It has done terrible things to civilised people. We have all had to pay so much. We are like the wheat at harvest time. We are cut down and bundled up and then we are thrashed. Our best is taken away and we like the chaff that remains are thrown to the wind and blown away."

"I am sorry, lady. It is terrible for both sides. For the ordinary people like us that get caught in the middle. I have no quarrel with you. If I were to take my anger out on you, it would not bring my sons back." A tear rolled down his cheek. "I will take you round to the back of the station and you can there unload, unseen."

They made good time to the station. Elizabet could not bring herself to speak to the man anymore and so their journey passed in silence. He drove round the back of the station and stopped the cart by one of the luggage bays. They quickly unloaded their luggage and placed it in a square on the platform.

"You children, get inside. Maria, you come with me." She threw the tarpaulin over the cases. "You children, stay there until I come back. Whatever you do, be quiet. Helen, look after them and do not let them fight. Whatever you do, do not let anyone hear you speak any Eengleesh!"

"Mama, we are not really going to England, are we?" Maria's alarm was real.

"Yes. We are going to find your father. It seems that for some reason or other, everyone else hates us."

"But do you know how to get to England?"

"No, but I expect that we can find out."

"Do you know how to find papa?"

"No, but I expect that we can find him too." Maria was not encouraged by these answers.

"Look, there is a map. Perhaps that will show us the way." Elizabet had no idea about how to reach England. She went to have a look at it. It proudly displayed the rail network urging its readers to take a holiday by rail.

"Look, that island bit is Eengland. I suppose those dotted lines across the sea are where the ships go."

"But mama, they all go from French ports. Germany is fighting the French. We will not be able to enter France from here; they will arrest us. Even if the trains can cross the border."

"Look, Darling, there is one that goes from Holland. We will go to Holland and catch a boat from there. I will go to see if I can buy tickets." In the event she could not buy a ticket all the way, but managed to get them for a train as far as Cologne. There she would have to get another ticket. She handed over her money. So much! The cost of all these train tickets was going to use up all her money. The train had been signalled and was just pulling in. If she wished to catch it, she must be quick. There was not another until this time tomorrow. She and Maria ran back to the luggage. They could hear the children squabbling half way down the station.

"For goodness sake, you children, I thought that I told you to be quiet! Come quickly, this is our train, now coming in. Leave the tarpaulin. We cannot manage that." Between them they dragged their luggage to the guard's van and piled it in. The station became alive with people. Many got off the train, some just to stretch their legs, others to be about their business. People arrived as form nowhere, all running and pushing, trying to get onto the train which was already packed.

"Come, let us find a seat. Where is Christopher? Where is Christopher?" she cried out in alarm. "He was here, right beside me just now!" Frantically, she looked up and down the platform. "Quickly Maria, run down the station. See if you can find him! Helen, hold Cornelia's hand. Do not let her go! Stay here."

Elizabet ran the other way, but there was no sign of him. She could see that the guard had his whistle in his hand. Any minute now he would blow it.

"Where is he?" She stamped her foot in desperation. Maria came running back, breathless.

"There is no sign of him that way. Look! There he is!" She pointed. His little face was peering at them from the guard's van. The Guard blew his whistle. The train began to move off.

"Quickly, girls, in there with him!" They all ran and climbed into the van. It was full of luggage and boxes of all kinds. The guard jumped in. He shut the door behind him.

CHAPTER 34

❀

"What are you doing, you cannot ride in here. Have you got tickets? Show me your tickets. Let me see them."

The guard was astonished at finding them in the van. Elizabet, much to his surprise, produced her tickets. She handed them over.

"I was quite sure that you had not got tickets, that you were trying to get a free ride." He clipped them, handing them back. "Look, I know the train is very full. I will go to see if I can find you seats, then you will have to get out of here. You cannot ride here. This is for baggage, not for passengers." He was gone for about an hour. When he returned, he said, "The train is full. They are standing in the corridors. If you can put up with it in here, I expect that I can put up with having you. Just don't tell anyone that I let you stay, that's all."

Elizabet thanked him. She did her best to settle the children down. There were no windows, so they could not see out. Presently the train slowed down and stopped.

"Is this Cologne, yet?"

"Bless you no, lady. We won't get there 'till tomorrow morning!"

The children groaned, "But that is not for hours!"

"Try to get some sleep. Our journey will be very long."

"Excuse me!" The guard looked agitated. "You are English! You were speaking English!"

"No Mr Guard, we are Hungarian. The children have had an Eengleesh nanny," Elizabet lied, "and so I speak in Eengleesh to them so that they do not forget what they have learnt."

"Oh, Hungarian, 'eh. Must be nice to be able to afford a nanny. I never 'ad no nanny. What is a Hungarian lady doing over here, if I might make so bold as to ask?"

"We are going to see my sick cousin in Holland," Elizabet lied again.

"Going to see a sick person in Holland?" The guard looked incredulously at her. "You can't just go travelling about—there is a war on."

"Shall I write to my cousin and ask her to postpone her illness until the war is over?"

The guard had the good grace to smile. The next time that he left the van Elizabet scolded the children.

"You must *not* speak in English! You must not! It is very dangerous! If people hear you speaking in English, they will think we are spies and we will be arrested! You must take care! We were lucky. The Guard, he is a nice man. We will not always be so lucky!"

The train rumbled on. Because there were no windows in the van, they could not tell if it was night or day.

The journey was long, tedious and slow. The train seemed to stop at every town. Every time it stopped the door would be flung open. Some of the luggage was passed out whilst more was passed in. Every platform was crowded with soldiers, waiting to be taken to the Front. Many of them seemed to be little more than boys. Elizabet could have wept. All these young men. Most likely going to be slaughtered! It was terrible, terrifying. What madness had gripped the world? What sacrifice would the Gods of War demand before peace, so dearly bought, would be allowed to return? The train rattled on, it seemed, for ever. Eventually in the morning they arrived in Cologne and disembarked on to the station. They dragged their luggage out onto the platform where they huddled dejectedly, surrounded by it all as the train drew away into the distance. The children were tired, aching and hungry. Elizabet found a seller with rolls and coffee, so she brought some for them. They sat on their luggage to eat this simple breakfast.

"Maria, you stay here with Helen and the two little ones. I will go to see about ticket to go to 'olland. Now, all of you—you must not talk in English. You must not! It will bring only danger!" Though they always spoke in English together, they all could speak German. They just had to remember to do so. Leaving them, Elizabet went in search of tickets.

Yes, she was told, there were trains that went into Holland. There was usually a considerable hold-up at the frontier. They would have to disembark to get into a Dutch train that was usually standing ready. It was not possible to maintain a timetable. The next train was supposed to depart at nine hundred hours the day after tomorrow, but there was no telling if it would or not. The man could not tell her when it would arrive in Amsterdam. It was in the lap of the Gods. Well, if she did not want to go to Amsterdam, she should change, but she would have to ask. They could not tell her about trains from here. Yes, she could put her luggage in the Left Luggage. No, he did not know where she could stay. She would have to go into the town to see what she could find.

Elizabet returned to the children who were sitting anxiously, in a huddle, waiting for her. Between them, they dragged their luggage to the Left Luggage Office. Having handed it safely inside, they set off into the town to try to find some lodgings for the two nights.

Cologne was seething with people. There were groups of soldiers on their way to the front. There were soldiers who had returned from the front with every kind of disfigurement and injury, begging for pennies as they passed. Over all towered the twin spires of the huge cathedral. Its bell was tolling dolefully, calling the faithful to Mass.

"Come on children, we will go to Mass to pray that we get safely to England." They joined the throng of people entering the massive iron studded doors. From the outside, the cathedral looked huge and forbidding; inside, it was massive! Gigantic pillars stretched, it seemed, to the heavens. Enormous windows, filled with brilliant stained glass, illuminated the interior with rainbow brilliance. In the distance, some remote choir, as yet unseen, was signing the Introit to the Mass. The chords rose and echoed through the massive vaults of the cathedral, like some fleeting dove that swirled around inside, seeking the hand of the Redeemer. The Cathedral was packed with people of all kinds, all here at that moment in time, seeking consolation and comfort from their hidden God, trying in their re-awakened beliefs to seek some solace from the horror of war that touched everyone.

Elizabet led the children down the isle. She found a pew that had enough space for them all. They huddled together, the children daunted and cowered by the huge vastness of the place. The soaring arches directed the thoughts of the faithful towards the heavens. The air was blue with the smoke of candles, redolent with incense. Elizabet was overwhelmed. Tears welled up in her eyes. She remembered her simple marriage in the village church and the baptisms of her children. She remembered Maria and Helen's First Communions, with Emil's children in the great cathedral in Bavaria. How much had happened to them in the short years between.

She led them all to the Altar for communion. When the Mass was over, she went in search of a priest. There were several by the big doors greeting the people as they left. She spoke to the first.

"Father, I am a refugee from Hungary. Is there anywhere here where I can stay with my children for two nights? I have to wait until I can take a train."

He smiled at her kindly. "How well you speak German."

"In Hungary everyone speaks German."

"Oh, I see. Do you have any money?"

"Enough."

"Frau, Frau." He called to a woman standing talking. "This lady needs a room for two nights; do you know where she could go?"

The woman looked at Elizabet and the children. "If it is only for two nights, she could stay with me. I have no food to offer her, but a bed she can have for a small consideration."

Elizabet took an instant liking to her. She seemed kind and genuine. "Thank you so much. You are so kind. Of course we cannot eat your food. I will buy enough food for us and bring it. Just to have somewhere to sleep is indeed a miracle."

"Come with me then. I will show you where I live. We will pass through the market, so you can buy some food, if there is any. It has been terrible since the war started; everything has been in short supply. All the men have had to go to fight and there is no one left to work the land. The old men and the women are doing what they can, but everything is in short supply. Life has been very difficult. I am so glad to help you and your children. My men, my husband and my two sons, have gone to the war. I have heard nothing from them since they went. I am so anxious. I do not know what regiment they are in, or where they have gone. I question all the wounded soldiers that I meet, but they do not know. Many of them are so dazed by their experiences, they can tell me nothing. What they can tell me sounds very different to what we read in the newspapers. It sounds to me that we are not being told the truth. I am very worried for their safety. I come to mass every day to pray that they will come home safely." She shrugged, as if to shake off her worries. "Come, my house is big and empty. I would be very pleased to hear the cry of children again. Come." She led them out into the sunshine.

"Thank you father. You have been such a kind help."

"Bless you my dear. I am glad to be able to help. You will help her too. She has been very anxious and anguished since the war started. It will be a great tonic to her to have someone else to worry about, even for a short while."

They managed to find some small potatoes, some withered beetroots and a scrawny shinbone in the market.

"Well, it will not make a feast, but will keep us going for a while. Perhaps, if I come here early in the morning, I might find something more."

The woman led them to her house. She showed them the rooms she could offer. She had two rooms, her sons', that the children could use. Elizabet could have her bed. She would sleep on the sofa.

"I will absolutely not hear of it," insisted Elizabet. "It is quite out of the question. The boys' room will be ample for us. I would not dream of turning you out of your bed. We will only be here for two nights. We are very grateful just to have somewhere to sleep!" The woman reluctantly agreed.

They made a stew with the shin and the vegetables. The woman produced half a loaf of hard dark bread. She also disappeared into the cellar. She returned with a slim dusty bottle. This she would open when their supper was over and the children had gone to bed. She was sorry that there was no hot water, but she was without coal. If you wanted coal you had to take a bag to the depot to fill it yourself. She could not do that. Elizabet offered to go in the morning, with the two oldest girls, if she would look after the two little ones, to collect some coal for her.

The stew, when it was ready, was a rather thin odd red colour, but it was hot and nourishing. The children were glad to have a hot meal after so many days of cold food. They were glad, too, to be able to get into bed and sleep. Cornelia and Helen slept in one bed, one at either end. Maria had the other bed. Elizabet was going to share it with her later. Christopher was put to sleep in the large draw from the bottom of the wardrobe.

Maria and the woman sat talking until late into the night. She opened her bottle of sweet rich wine. She was interested to hear all Elizabet's story. Elizabet was only too pleased to be able to unburden herself to someone else, to tell of all her misfortunes. The woman must have sensed this, for she kept her glass filled and let her talk on uninterrupted, until she had finished. When Elizabet finally finished, she sat there, exhausted, emotionally drained with the tears running down her face. The woman had the good sense to sit quietly with her, softly stroking her hand until she was able to compose herself.

Elizabet slept well that night. It was quite late when the noise of the children wakened her. She quickly dressed the children and they all went downstairs. The woman had been out earlier. She had managed to buy a loaf of bread with a small lump of butter. She had also been able to buy some small sausages, which would do for their lunch.

After breakfast, following the woman's directions, they went down to the coal depot with some canvas shopping bags to collect some coal. On the way, they found an abandoned pram with a bent wheel, so they took it with them. They were able to put in it more coal than they would have been able to carry. With its bent wheel, however, it had a mind of its own. They had a long, tiring struggle to push it back to the house. They were hot and exhausted by the time they arrived. The woman was thrilled. Enough coal for a little hot water! What a treat! They went to bed again early that night, as Elizabet wanted to be up early in the morning so that they could go to the station to collect their luggage and be on the platform in readiness for the train.

Awaking in good time in the morning, she quickly dressed the children. The woman had again been to the bakery early. She had managed to purchase a big loaf. She had cut it all up and with a smearing of jam, was preparing sandwiches for them to take with them. They breakfasted off the crusts in a little milk. Elizabet was sad to part from the woman, who had been so kind to them and kissed them all goodbye. Elizabet had the greatest difficulty in persuading her to take any money. Eventually, she reluctantly accepted the proffered notes without counting them. The woman insisted on coming with them. She looked after the two little ones whilst Elizabet and the other two found a trolley, collected their luggage and took it to the platform. The train was already there. Most of the seats were already taken. They loaded their luggage into the van. Eventually they found enough seats. The woman realised they would loose their seats if they did not stay in them so she proposed to leave them sitting in the train. She would not wait with them until it left. Who knows, she might be there all day, waiting. They wished each other God speed and made great promises that they must write to each other after the war. She left them and returned to her house. As the priest had predicted, their visit had been like a tonic to her.

They sat all morning in the train. It hissed and clanked, but did not move. The children did nothing but demand to go to the toilet. Elizabet delayed them as long as she could, but when it became obvious that they must find relief or burst, she reluctantly sent them one at a time with Maria. Eventually, in the late afternoon, hours late, the train, without any warning, set off. Thankfully, they had all returned from the toilet by then. She shuddered to think what would have happened if any of them had been absent at the time! The train clanked through the night, stopping several times at different towns. At three in the morning it arrived at the frontier and pulled into a siding. Everybody was ordered out. They ran and collected their luggage out of the Van and dragged it into the large shed into which all the passengers were being herded. Gradually, they were all passing through the German check-points.

"They are going to search us again," Maria said between her teeth, clutching her coat round her and hanging onto Elizabet's hand. "I shall scream if they as much as look at me." She was shaking violently. She had gone ashen white. Her fear was infectious. Already Helen and Cornelia were beginning to cry. Elizabet did the best she could to calm them, but she too was beginning to feel the dread of anticipation.

"No, my dears, they will not do that again. Come on! There is no need for this fear." She sounded braver than she felt. Eventually, they passed through. The guard quickly looked at their papers and passed them through. He did not ask to see their luggage. He had no interest in a woman and her scrawny kids. They were just part of the human flotsam that was flowing out of Germany. Elizabet sighed with relief. She could not believe their luck. They passed on and round the corner. There stood two more officers.

"The luggage. Open it. Put it all up on this table." Elizabet did not know what to do. She could not refuse. The big revolver was in the shoulder bag, under the sandwiches. She could not let them find that, whatever else they found. She would be arrested at once. She lifted all the cases onto the table, letting the shoulder bad fall off her shoulder on to the floor as she picked one up. The guards began to open the cases. It did not take them long to discover the contents. They said nothing, but hastily covered up the valuables so that no one else should see them. From each case they both took one item, which they placed in a box of their own on the other side of the tables.

"Taxes. These are export taxes. Good. You can go. Fasten your bags and go. What is in the shoulder bag that you have put on the floor?"

Elizabet felt herself going red. She pretended that the exertion of bending and picking it up caused it. She tucked it under her arm in such a way that she held the pistol between her arm and body. She stood up and opened the bag so that the guard could see inside.

"See, it is just some sandwiches that we have brought for the journey."

"Ha! How kind. We have had nothing to eat all day. Thank you for being so thoughtful." He reached into the bag and took them out. "Go on! Clear off. Take your brats and your antique shop and go. Be thankful that the taxes are not higher."

They were shepherded across the station to where another train stood waiting. This, it seemed, was the Dutch train. Officials were checking everyone's papers and questioning them about their journey. It took ages. They queued for hours in the freezing cold. A biting wind was blowing through the station, so they all huddled together to try to keep warm.

"It is no good crying because you are hungry. I have no food. The guard took our sandwiches. I cannot see anywhere where we can get food here. When I can get food, you will have it. Now listen. If they ask you, you must say we go to see our Aunt Maria. You do not know where she lives. Mama knows. We go with Mama. Understand, all of you? That is what you say. You do not say anything more. Understand? Now we are out of Germany, do not talk in German. It is better to talk in Eengleesh."

Maria looked at her. "But mama, that will be telling a lie. You have told us we must not tell lies."

Elizabet smiled. "You are right. I should not ask you to tell lies. But it will help us to get there safely. I tell you what. I have that photo, still, of Cousin Maria, that she gave me. When we get to where we are going, I will show it to you. So it will be true that you will see her when we arrive."

She smiled at them encouragingly. When it was their turn to be examined, the officials were as bored with the whole process as she was. They were not the least interested in where she was going, her luggage, or where she had come from. They were however suspicious of the big German rubber stamps all over her papers. In the end she had to produce her marriage certificate to prove that she was indeed Hungarian, as she claimed. Eventually, they let her through. She was able to shepherd the children on to the waiting train. They had to wait for a long time whilst the rest of the passengers were examined. She was hard put to pacify the children. Cornelia and Christopher grizzled and complained all the time, much to the annoyance of the rest of the passengers crammed into the compartment. She did the best that she could to keep them quiet.

At last the train moved off, but it seemed to progress at the pace of a snail. It was dark when they finally arrived at the junction where the line for Rotterdam split off.

It seemed that they had been in the slow moving train for ever, though it had only been a day and night. They ran to the guard's van and sorted out their luggage. The guard blew his whistle whilst they still had a case in the van. Elizabet pushed it out and jumped after it as the train slowly moved down the station. She stumbled and fell on the platform. The children ran shrieking after her and helped to pick her up. Luckily she was not badly hurt, though she had torn her stocking and grazed her knee. She sat on the ground looking at her bleeding knee, weeping tears of annoyance, hurt and frustration. She picked herself up, helped by the children.

They gathered their luggage together. Painfully they sought out the ticket office. Elizabet enquired about the train for Rotterdam. There was not going to be one for two hours. Just outside the station there was a stall selling coffee and pastries. She bought some rolls and two cups of coffee to share with the children. It was little enough, but it revived their flagging spirits. Eventually the Rotterdam train arrived. They loaded all their things onto it and climbed in. They could not find any seats, so they had to stand in the corridor. It was dark when they finally reached their destination. They put their luggage into the Left Luggage Office and set out to find a little café or somewhere where they might find something to eat. Eventually they came to a square. There were several small cafés round it. Elizabet selected one that looked more warm and inviting than the others. They all went inside and settled at a table, glad of the warmth. She ordered bowls of soup and rolls for each of them and enquired about the possibility of finding a room for the night. She was directed to a street where there were many boarding houses. Someone there would surely find her a room.

After finishing their meal they set out to find the street, Elizabet and Maria taking it in turns to carry Christopher. It was very dark. The streets were deserted, except for the cats that yowelled and spat at them as they passed. They seemed to be wandering half the night. Eventually they found the street that they sought. It seemed that the people living here nearly all took in lodgers. Most had little signs in the window saying that they had no vacancies, but at last she found a rather shabby looking house, at the far end of the street, that had a sign saying 'Vacancies'.

With some trepidation, she knocked on the door. Eventually, it was opened by a scruffy woman who was wearing a well worn pair of slippers with a large hole through which protruded a big toe. She was smoking a hand rolled cigarette. Her hair writhed in yellowed grey wisps round her head, for all the world like some modern day Medusa.

Yes, she had a room. Only one. They could have that if they liked. Yes, she could give them a meal in the morning—rolls and coffee, or at least, what Elizabet thought at best would be something approximating coffee, hot and black. No, they need not see the room. They could take it or leave it. Oh, and money now, if you please. Elizabet had had enough. She would have slept in a dustbin if she could have found an empty one that was not occupied by some of the many cats that seemed to be everywhere. She paid the money and allowed herself to be shown the way. The toilet apparently, was 'out the back', wherever that might be. At the very mention of the word, the children all clamoured to go. The lady of the house shouted directions to them as they groped their way in the dark. It turned out to be a dilapidated old shed in the back yard. The children were frightened to go on their own, so the visit turned into a communal family affair. They all returned to the house as quickly as they could. When they were inside again, Elizabet complained to the woman of the house.

"There was a rat in your closet. We could hear him squeaking and splashing about."

"Ow, you mustn't mind 'im—'e can't get out and bite you."

Elizabet shuddered. By the look of the house, the rest of his brothers were lurking around, just waiting their chance to mount a rescue bid. The stair carpet was threadbare and loose underfoot. The walls felt damp.

"Be careful, children, that you do not trip on the carpet. If you go to the toilet in the night, be very careful."

"Do not worry mama, I will burst before I go out there again, without an armed guard." Maria shuddered at the thought.

They spent a restless night. The noise from behind the wainscoting kept them awake—c constant gnawing and scurrying behind the wall and in the roof. The people in the next house had a loud, fierce sounding argument, which went on half the night and kept them all awake. Elizabet was very glad when morning came and it was time to get up. The children by then were all sound asleep. They were very reluctant to get up.

After they had breakfasted, she set out with them to find the dock to see about a boat to England. It seemed that Rotterdam was a City of docks, but eventually they were directed to a grubby office on a waterfront. The superintendent laughed.

"A boat to England? Did she not know that there was a war on? The German Submarines and motor gun-boats would attack any boat going to England! She had as much chance of getting a boat to England as of flying there herself. She might get a fishing boat to take her. They go out and fish all night. Some take their catch to England to sell. It was fine if they could get into English waters whilst it was still dark. The fish fetched a good price there. The boats fished their way back the next night, under cover of darkness. "Find them? Oh, you will have to go to Den Haag to find them. They do not come up here. This port only handles the deep-water trade and there has not been much of that, with the war! You will have to get the train." Elizabet's heart sank. Not another train!

She was sick to death of trains, of loading and unloading heavy luggage. For two pins she would abandon the lot, were it not for the fact that they might be able to sell the contents when they arrived in England. Though they were her family treasures, she was hard headed enough to know that in England she might find things very different. She did not know what her money was going to be worth. She might find that her treasures were worth more than her money. She did not know for how long she would have to support herself before she found Robert.

She thanked the superintendent and took the children back to the station. She found the train and bought a ticket. The exchange rate was horrific. She was forced to pay an enormous sum in her German marks. The train was not going until the next morning. She did not know what to do. Whatever happened, she was not going to go back to the house of last night. The children were tired out and dispirited with walking about. They were hungry too and fractious. She decided to stay on the station and sleep the night there, waiting for when the train would come. Between them thy collected their luggage and, piling it up as a sort of stockade against the wind, they curled up on the floor and settled down to wait. The children were restless, cold and could not get comfortable. They continually whined and grizzled with each other. Elizabet was exasperated with them and felt tired and wretched herself. The day dragged by and eventually, long after darkness had fallen, the children fell asleep. Elizabet could not sleep. In the dark she could hear the local rat population scurrying around. Some of them seemed to be very close. Once she saw one, silhouetted in front of a distant light. It seemed as big as a cat. She found a pile of coal and, arming herself with a selection of handy sized looking pieces, she returned to the children and sat up the rest of the night in watch, in case any rats should venture too close. Several times she threw a coal and once the clatter of her missile was answered by an indignant shriek from what had obviously been a prowling cat. At last dawn came. She sat shivering with cold and fatigue. It was well into the morning before the train arrived. She roused the children and after loading all their luggage again, they found a draughty carriage. The children were in very low spirits after their restless and fitful night. Elizabet was very hard put to keep patience with their continual clamour that they were tired and hungry.

Den Haag was a cold, windy place. A small harbour was surrounded by a cluster of low salt streaked buildings with a stone mole projecting into the yellow surging North Sea. There was a trot of fishing boats tied up in the harbour, straining uneasily at their mooring ropes. Apart from a few raucous gulls being tossed in the wind, there was not a living thing in sight. By the quayside, there was a low inn, cowering, as it were, from the onslaught of the incessant wind.

There appeared to be a light inside. Smoke was blowing from its chimney, in wind shredded black smudges, blown away before they had hardly emerged. Crouching against the wind, they made their way to the door and hastily went inside. The air that hit them, if it could be called air, was hot and thick, pungent with blue tobacco smoke, rank with the smell of wet clothing, sweaty people and stale beer. The low room was packed with the roughest collection of rugged people that Elizabet had ever seen. As she hastily shut the door behind her, their noisy conversation stopped. To a man, they all turned to look at her. They stared in silence. The children shrank to her. She put her arms round them protectively.

Elizabet stared back nervously. "I wish to be taken to England," she ventured. "Is there one of your fishing boats that is going to England, that would take us?"

A large be-whiskered fisherman turned and roared with laughter. His blue reefer jacket hung open to show a huge belly that hung over his wide belt. He had a small salt stained blue peaked cap on the back of his shaggy head. He wore a large pair of sea boots, turned down below the knees.

"So you want to go to England?" He laughed again with a sound like thunder rolling down a drain pipe. "What do you think we are? The drivers of the Ferry?" His comrades laughed too. Elizabet felt very uncomfortable. She felt her courage failing her.

"I was told that if you went fishing at night, you might land your catch in England in the morning. We could land as well. I will pay." She added nervously: "I will pay you whatever I might have to pay if I went on a ferry!"

"Ha, lady, but there is the problem. There is no ferry. So no one knows what you might have to pay. You might have to pay an enormous sum of money. There is no telling."

"No telling," echoed his mates. They all looked at her.

Elizabet felt like turning and pushing her children before her, to run out of the door, away from these fierce looking people. She opened her shoulder bag and pulled out the big pistol. Everyone dived to the floor. The man behind the bar disappeared like a puppet.

"As well as paying a proper fare, I will give this." She brandished it in the air. The big fisherman climbed to his feet.

"You be careful where you point that thing, it might go off."

Elizabet pointed it more purposefully at him.

"It might indeed go off. I think it is you that should be careful."

"If I did agree to take you, are you brave enough to come?"

"What do you mean?"

"It is a small boat. There is no room for passengers. The night is dark and rough. We go to work, not to take the air. We have no room for passengers. You would have to stay below and be out of the way; it will be very uncomfortable."

"You will take us then? And our luggage?"

"Luggage? Let me see this Luggage. You did not say anything about luggage."

Elizabet led him outside and along the quay to where their luggage stood. She felt foolish brandishing the big pistol, so she put it back in her bag.

"What have you got in your luggage that is so precious that you must take it to England? Open it and show me."

Elizabet opened the cases one by one and showed him. He examined everything. In the end he took out the silver samovar.

"For this and the pistol, I will take you to England. You can keep your worthless money. If we are stopped and searched by the Germans, I will hand you over, saying that you are stowaways. I cannot risk my crew being in trouble with the Germans. If we are attacked, you will all have to take your chance with the rest of us. In the dark, we are as likely to be attacked by the English as by the Germans!"

Elizabet knew that if she were going to go, she would have to agree. She held out her hand. He shook it with his massive paw. He held out his other hand for the pistol.

"No! I will give you that when we are safely on our way."

He smiled. He admired the courage of this little woman with her four children. She certainly had pluck! He took her back to the Inn and persuaded the innkeeper to find some food for them all. They all sat round a small table by the fire and enjoyed a bowl of hot stew and bread with some glasses of milk.

The fishing boat's crew carried all their luggage aboard, for they were ready to sail on the evening tide. She could not believe it. After everything that had happened, they were actually on their way to England this very night. She hugged the children. "We are on our way tonight, to England to find papa! Be brave, my children. The night will be long and frightening, but God willing, tomorrow we will be in England."

The little boat certainly was no luxury liner. The wheelhouse was only just big enough for a man at the wheel and another. There was a minute galley just beside the engine and in the fo'c'sle there were four bunks, squeezed in to the bow of the boat. The rest of the space in the boat was taken up by the fish hold.

The children were put into the bunks and told that that was where they were to stay. The smell of dead fish and hot engine oil was indescribable. They protested loudly about being shut in that terrible place. There was no light except that which came in through the porthole. That rapidly dimmed as the light faded. The Skipper relented. They could be on deck until they started fishing, then they would have to go below to be out of the way. It was too dangerous for them on deck when the nets were being worked.

Three of the boats went out of the harbour together, just as the sun set. The children watched with great interest as they set off out of the harbour. Once they reached the open sea they became frightened. The boat rose and pitched to the short North Sea swell. They became cold and wet as they were being continually drenched by the spray that flew over the bow. Presently the skipper called for them to go below. It was completely dark and he was going to shoot his nets. It was far too dangerous for them to be on deck as all the assorted ropes and cordage snaked across the deck and disappeared over the side into the sea.

Elizabet hustled them below and put them into the bunks. They had to lie down, as there was not enough headroom to sit. She put Christopher in the bunk with Maria, so that she could stop him rolling out. She lay on the other bottom bunk. She stayed with them in the hope that they might go to sleep. The noise in the cabin was very loud. Every timber creaked and groaned, as if at any minute the little boat would burst apart under the strain. The sea kept smacking against the bow, just a thin plank of wood away from their heads. The engine noise echoed in the empty wooden boat and when the nets were shot, the winch rumbled and grumbled. The children were very frightened. They complained that they felt queasy. The smell and the motion were upsetting them. Elizabet left them and went to see if she could find a bucket, in case they were sick. The skipper was none too sympathetic.

"Sick? They are sick already? We have not started yet. We are still in the shelter of the land. It will get worse when we get out in the middle." He poked his head out of the wheelhouse and shouted. Presently one of the crew arrived with a bucket and a big grin on his face. Elizabet took the bucket and went back to the children. After the keenness of the open deck the little cabin was stifling. Helen and Cornelia had thankfully fallen asleep. Christopher had woken up and wanted to play, but Maria was feeling very sorry for herself. The motion of the boat was working havoc on the meal that she had eaten at the inn. She was sure that at any minute she would be sick. Elizabet took Christopher onto the other bunk so that she should have some peace. Presently Maria was very sick into the bucket.

"Oh mama, I think that I am going to die." She groaned and was sick again. Elizabet did the best she could to soothe her. She was feeling queasy herself. Luckily Christopher had got tired of playing and at last he, too, had gone to sleep. The winch started to groan again.

"I think they must be hauling in their nets."

"Mama, I must go outside for some air. If I could get some air, I would be better."

"All right. I will come with you. I think some fresh air will do me good as well. Just outside the door, though. We must not get in their way."

They quickly slipped outside the door and stood on the deck. The spray was continually blowing over the fo'c'sle and the freezing wind fluttered their thin clothes. In a minute they were shivering with cold. The nets were indeed being hauled in and at that moment the bulging purse was hoisted over the deck and the tie released. A torrent of silver fish cascaded over the decks and, flapping and swirling, washed over their feet. Maria screamed as the silvery flapping tide flowed round them. They were pressed against the fo'c'sle bulkhead. There was no escape—the door was held firmly shut by the weight of fish. In with the fish was a mass of seaweed, sea urchins and little green crabs that were running everywhere. Maria screamed again as one scrabbled against her legs, and then another and another. They seemed to be everywhere. Two of the crew came to them and threw the fish away with their bare hands. When the door was clear they opened it and pushed Elizabet and Maria inside and slammed it behind them. Maria lay on here bunk, sobbing and shivering. Elizabet lay with her, to try and warm her up. She put her coat over them both.

Elizabet sat up with a start and banged her head on the bunk above. What had happened? She must have fallen asleep. The engine seemed to have stopped. The boat was silent, but it was rolling and tossing in a most uncomfortable way. She put on her coat and went on deck. She picked her way through the seaweed and dead fish that littered the deck towards the wheelhouse. There was no one in there. The crew was gathered at the stern of the boat. The big skipper was there, pushing for all he was worth on a long pole and chewing in anguish on a black cheroot.

"What is happening? Why have we stopped?"

The Skipper grunted. "Look! We have caught a mine. Thank all the gods we spotted it before we pulled it on board."

Elizabet could see in the nets trailing astern a large round object, only feet away from the stern of the boat.

"What are you going to do?"

"What am I going to do? I do not know what I am going to do. Right now I am praying like mad, but that does not seem to be doing much good."

"But what will happen?"

"If we hit it, lady, we will all be in the clouds with the seagulls."

"Why don't you start your engine and go away from it?"

"I can't start the sainted engine. The propeller would catch the net and wind it all up. If the mine did not go off and blow us all into cod fish bait, we would jamb the propeller and then we would be sitting here unable to move in the daylight. The German motor boats would soon find us."

"If you let the net out again, what will happen? Will the net and mine sink?"

"Yes. It will sink and when it hits the bottom—BANG! Right underneath us!"

"But if you started the engine as soon as the net sank and let it out as far as it would go, whilst you ran away as fast as you could, you would not be sitting on top of it when it went bang."

"And what would happen to my net, if it went bang?"

"It would be full of holes I suppose."

He looked at her and spat the stub of his cheroot into the sea.

"We are about to be blown to kingdom come and you make jokes. You are a cool one, that is for sure. It is full of holes already. They just would not be joined together any more!"

Despite the very real and obvious peril that they were in, Elizabet had to laugh.

"I was not wanting to make a joke. I just meant that it would be spoiled. Ruined!"

"It would be that all right." He pushed with the pole again as the swell threatened to wash the mine onto the stern.

"It is only a net."

"Do you know how much a good net costs?"

"More than a boat?"

"No, of course not. Not more than a boat."

"Mr fisherman, it seems to me that you have a choice. Net or boat." Another surge brought the mine perilously close. "If you do not make up your mind soon it will be net and boat and us as well."

He looked at her in some awe. None of his crew would have dared to tell him what to do in his own boat. But she was right.

"Ja. You are right. Start the engine. Let go the winch." He ran back to the wheelhouse and banged the telegraph to full steam ahead. The net and the mine disappeared into the dark sea and the little boat surged forward. The net warps flew off the winch as it was dragged out behind them. The boat jerked as they came to the end. They all held their breath.

Nothing happened. They waited more. Nothing happened. The Skipper stuck his head out of the wheelhouse.

"We are going too fast. The net is not going to the bottom. I will gradually slow down. I do not think that it is too deep here. We will know when it hits the bottom."

They did. None of them was prepared for what happened. There appeared to be a bright flash in the water astern and a huge column of water shot up into the air and hung there like some over-towering frozen fountain. The crash that followed was ear splitting. Then the column started to fall. All those tons of foaming water cascaded onto the deck. Elizabet clung to the rail as the water poured over her and threatened to wash her away. The cascade seemed to go on and on, then suddenly, it stopped. The air stank of the burnt smell of the explosion and of fish. Indeed, there were dead fish swilling around on the deck. The wave caused by the shock of the explosion hit the stern of the boat and swept Elizabet off her feet. She was washed into the angle of the wheelhouse and clung on for dear life. At last it subsided and she struggled to her feet. She was soaked through to the skin. Her hair had come down and was hanging in lank locks all round her. The Skipper had been knocked over by the blast and had only with difficulty managed to get up onto his feet again in the confined space of the wheelhouse. He stuck his head out of the window.

"You are still here then! Have you got any more bright ideas?" He looked at her bedraggled soaked state. "Here, come in here out of the cold. You will catch a death out there."

"No, I must go to the children. They will be frightened." She made her way forward. She could see three white anxious faces peering out of the fo'c'sle door. She went to them and shepherded them inside.

"What happened?" they clamoured. "It woke us up. Are we sinking?"

"No, we will be all right. We caught a mine. It went off. But we are all right." Elizabet was shivering violently and she could not stop here teeth from chattering.

"But mama, you are soaking wet!"

Elizabet laughed. That was an understatement. She could feel the water still running down her back. She platted her hair and let it hang in a pigtail. At least she was out of the wind in this little cabin.

"I shall be all right. We are all right now. We will be safe. You children go back to sleep again."

"I could not go to sleep, mama, I still feel sick."

"Come on. Go to sleep and you will not feel sick anymore."

She settled them down and went out on deck again. The cold wind cut through her wet clothes. The crew had recovered the remains of the net and were busily bending on a replacement. She made her way to the wheelhouse and went inside.

"The little ones are all right? For goodness sake, woman, come here, you will freeze to death."

Indeed, she was blue with cold and shaking uncontrollably. He opened his sea coat and enveloped her in it. She did not protest. She was glad of the heat from his body and gradually she warmed up.

"Thank you. That is better. I am warm now." She was reluctant to leave the warmth and the shelter of his coat and she snuggled against him.

"Here, come on, you do not want to get too cosy." He opened a locker and pulled out a large woollen jersey. "Put this on."

She struggled into the enormous garment in the confined space. It swamped her completely and reached down below her knees. She laughed.

"I must look ridiculous."

"Who cares about what you look like. Are you warmer?"

"Yes, thank you. That is much better."

She watched the crew on the deck, working by a shaded light. The replacement net was made ready and they waved to indicate that it was ready to shoot. She watched with some interest as it was thrown over the side, followed by the two doors that would hold it open against the force of the water. It disappeared into the sea and the hawsers ran out. It seemed a perilous process. It was amazing that no one was caught up in the ropes and things and dragged into the sea.

"What happens now?"

"We will trawl the net for an hour and then haul. We should get one more shot before it gets light. By then we should be in English waters. We cannot fish there, but at least we should be safe from the Germans. They will not chase us in English water. Here, you steer the boat, I will go and get some coffee."

"Steer it? I could not steer it. I would not know what to do."

"Look, this is the wheel. Just keep it like it is. That is all you have to do." He put her hands on the wheel and went out.

"But wait. I do not know what to do!"

But he had gone. She gripped the wheel and stared into the darkness. *What happens if we bump into something?* She stared through the window. To her surprise, though it was dark, she could see the sea around the boat. She could see the foaming crests of the waves as they hissed past, flashing the blue green fire of the phosphorescence. She had never seen it before and was fascinated by its colour. She gripped the wheel with grim determination, terrified that she should deviate even half a degree from the chosen course. She looked at the compass. It swung gently back and forth as they rolled over the waves, but it told her nothing. Every now and then, the wheel would kick wildly in her hands. She could see how people fell in love with their boats. It felt alive. It was like a horse. You could feel it moving underneath you. It was almost as if it was living and breathing, doing its best to please you. The wheelhouse door slid open and two steaming mugs were thrust in, followed by the skipper.

"Well, it was not so bad. We are still here. You have not sailed onto any rocks."

She took the mug. The coffee was hot, sweet and black. She cupped the tin mug in her hands and welcomed the warm liquid.

"Do you know, I actually enjoyed it. I felt a real thrill from driving your little boat. It is like riding a horse. You can feel the life of it under you."

"Stupid dumb animals. I have never ridden a horse, nor do I want to. But when I go to heaven, I hope that I shall have a little boat like this to sail."

"I got you wrong. When I first saw you, I was very frightened. You seemed so big, so strong, but I can see that you are really a very kind man and that you too have a soft heart." She smiled at him. He roared with laughter.

"We were both wrong then. I could not believe this little person that came into the inn, looking so frightened with her small children. I felt sorry for you. You seemed so lost and vulnerable. But you are not like that, are you?" He looked at her. "You may be little on the outside, but you are very big on the inside. In that little shell is a tough little nut."

Elizabet laughed. She had been called many things, but never a tough nut.

"Tell me, little nut, what on earth are you doing running away to England?"

Elizabet told him the whole story, from the day she first met Robert until the present. He listened with rapt attention until she had finished.

"My God, these Red Guards. I have heard tell of them. Stupid fools. If they think that everything will be shared out equally, they are blind, or stupid. They are ruining the country for an ideal. I work hard, but I work for me. If all that I earned was going to be shared out with everyone, with those who could not work and those who would not—and there will be plenty of them, parasites who are prepared to grow fat off the sweat of others—I would not work so hard. I would say why should I bother? Then everyone would be worse off. Well, your Robert is a very lucky man. I am very jealous of him. He is very lucky to have such a one to love him. I would like to take you back to Holland and keep you for myself, but I will not. I know that you would find a way of getting back to your Robert."

Elizabet blushed. She did not know what to say.

"You are very kind. I cannot thank you enough for helping us. I will never forget you and your kindness to us. I will go back to my children. They will be wondering what is happening. At least it is calmer now. They should not be feeling so sick."

"Yes, we are across the widest part. It is more sheltered here and the sea is calmer. Because of the delay with the mine, I will haul the net here and then make a run for it. It will soon be light and I would not want to be caught by a German patrol."

"I will go back to the cabin and get out of your way then."

She opened the door and slipped out. She picked her way back to the cabin and was glad to get inside out of the cruel wind. The children were all asleep and so she quietly lay on the bunk, listening to the noises of the boat. She heard the winch start up and the creaking and clattering as the net was hauled in. She heard the catch cascade onto the deck. She could hear fish flapping against the door. She tried to think what she would do when she got to England. She knew nothing about England. She knew of London and that there was a famous race place called Ascot and another called Epsom. The headquarters of racing where the famous Jockey club was, was called…She searched her memory for the name…Newmarket! Perhaps that would be the place to go to. At the headquarters of racing, someone might be able to tell her of the whereabouts of Robert. Yes, she would go to Newmarket. What would happen if she could not find Robert? She would have to keep on looking, however long it took. She fell asleep.

The door slid open. The skipper poked his head inside.

"My God, there is a fug in here like the inside of my sea boot on a hot summer's day. No wonder the children are feeling sick! Come outside and look, we are arriving in England. Hold on tight. It is going to be very rough when we go over the bar into the harbour."

They all came out on deck and stood huddled together under the shelter of the fo'c'sle. There was less wind here, but in the chill of the dawn it cut through their thin clothes with a penetrating keenness. Astern, the first pale rays of the sun were shining up over the horizon and streaks of pink and yellow were gradually mounting up into the sky, pushing back the dark of night. Ahead, they could just make out the loom of a low coastline. A small lighthouse that appeared to be on the end of a mole flashed out briefly. The crew were busy gutting the fish and throwing the entrails overboard. The boat was surrounded by a cloud of raucously squawking seagulls, wheeling and diving to catch what they could. The skipper stuck his head out of the wheelhouse and shouted to them.

"Hold on tight, it is very rough now, as we go over the bar."

Even as he spoke, the boat began to plunge and swoop, until it seemed it would dive headlong to the bottom of the sea. The children screamed pitifully as they were thrown about and held on for grim death. Just as suddenly, it was over. The boat slipped past the mole and entered the harbour and everything was suddenly calm once more. The skipper called to them again. "I will unload the fish first. When that is done, the crew will unload your luggage and you can go ashore. Just keep out of the way, until I tell you." Even as he spoke, boxes of fish were being handed up from the hold and stacked on the deck.

The boat crossed the harbour and moored against a long quay in front of a long open shed. Even as the mooring ropes were being secured, cranes were lifting the fish boxes off onto the quay. In no time at all, all the boxes were laid out on the quay. The skipper went ashore and was immediately surrounded by a crowd of men. There seemed to be a lot of shouting and smacking of hands. Already the fish were being wheeled away to a train that stood waiting. He came back on board a broad grin on his face. "That is very good. I have made a good price for my fish. I need not worry about the loss of the net."

Elizabet had been watching with some interest. "You have sold all the fish already?"

"Yes. They were eager to have them." He held up a handful of chits. "I will take these to the office shortly and get paid. It has been a good night's work. Now, that train will have all the fish in London in three hours' time. There will be fresh fish on the menus by lunchtime. We will unload all your things and you can get on the train. You can be in London, too, by mid morning if you get on that train."

"But do I not have to see some officials? I cannot just arrive—can I?"

"There are no officials about at this time of the day. I am just a fishing boat. They do not expect any people; this is not a passenger port. When you get to London tell the police that you are here and how you came. That will be all right."

"But I do not want to go to London. I want to go to Newmarket. Will this train take me to Newmarket?"

"I do not know. I will ask. Come on, the train will go soon. Your luggage is being put in the guard's van and you will have to buy tickets."

He took them to the ticket office and asked about tickets to Newmarket. Yes, she could have tickets. She had to change trains at Ipswich. She might have to wait there a while. But there would be a train to Newmarket from Ipswich. It would be the train for Cambridge. She must not go as far as Cambridge. Get off at Newmarket. She listened to this all, nodding uncertainly. She proffered some money. The ticket clerk looked at it in some disgust.

"What is that? Us don't take no foreign money. Yew'll hev to give we proper money. Us don't take that there."

The skipper looked at her. "Have you got no English money?"

She shook her head. What was she going to do?

"Hold on. I will go and get my fish money. That will be in English. I will change some of your Marks for you, so that you have enough cash for your journey."

Presently he returned and changed some money for her. She handed a handful of the unfamiliar notes to the ticket clerk. He took what he needed and gave the rest back to her.

"Get yew on quick, Missus, that owd train be about to goo."

The Skipper hurried them along the platform and ushered them into a carriage. The train had no corridor. They were in a small compartment on their own. He slammed the door shut. Elizabet found how to open the window and, tugging the strap off its button, she let the window slide down. She leant out.

"I do not know how to thank you. I…" Tears filled her eyes and her voice trailed away. She could not speak. She shook her head and, reaching out, took his hand. "Thank you, thank you," she whispered. He was completely taken aback by this show of emotion and, caught unawares, a tear came into his eye too.

"You do not have to thank me. It has been a pleasure to be of assistance to such a bold lady. But do you not forget something?"

"Forget? What?" She noticed the rough woollen sleeve. "Oh, yes." She laughed. Stepping back from the window, she peeled off the great jersey and handed it to him. "I am sorry. I nearly went away with your big jersey!"

He laughed and took it from her. "No. That is not what I meant. There is still part of our bargain to be fulfilled."

"Bargain?"

He made a pistol of his fingers and made as if to shoot her.

"Oh! Oh yes, the big pistol." She grabbed her bag and, taking the pistol out, gave it to him. He very quickly wrapped it up in the jersey, hastily looking round to make sure that no one else had seen him.

"They do not like pistols here. I must keep it hidden. Ah, here they come." He pointed with his free hand. The two other boats were just entering the harbour. "They will be too late to catch this train." He laughed. "It is always I that get the best prices." The train started to move. "Goodbuy, little nut. Good luck. I hope that you find your Robert. If you do not, do not despair. Come back here and I will take you back to Holland and look after you. I am a very kind man. You would have nothing to fear from me." He was walking along the station to keep up with the train. Elizabet did not know what to say. For all that he was a rough fisherman, she knew that he was a really genuine man and she would be forever grateful to him.

"Thank you. Thank you. You have been so kind. I can never repay you. I will never forget you."

By now the train was moving too quickly for him to keep up. He stopped at the end of the platform and raised his hand to her. She leant further out of the window. "Goodbye, good bye…What is your name?"

If he heard her, she did not hear his reply. She watched and waved until he was out of sight.

CHAPTER 35

❀

They stood on Newmarket station in a little huddle, surrounded by their luggage. The train slowly disappeared in the distance, leaving a trail of little white puffs of steam in the sky. Elizabeth watched it disappear and suddenly felt very alone. She did not know what she had expected, but it certainly was not this. She looked about the desolate little station in some dismay. There was no one else about. No one else had got off the train. There was no one on the station. The station itself was little more than a large canopy over a short section of the platform supported on top of a small grubby waiting room. There were two sets of railway lines and a similar, though slightly larger building on the other side of the track. At the end of the platforms there was a crossing gate which was, even as she watched, being reopened by a man who had come down from the signal box. Of the town, there was no sign. Apart from a coal yard beyond the crossing gate, there seemed to be no other habitation in sight. Elizabet stood uncertainly on the platform, not knowing quite what to do next. A man in uniform came out on to the platform opposite. She called across to him.

"Is this Newmarket?"

He looked at her for a while and then pointed to a large blue enamelled sign that proclaimed in large white letters "NEWMARKET." Elizabet read it carefully and felt very embarrassed. The man said not a word, but the look on his face was enough. Elizabet screwed up her courage.

"How far is it to the town?"

He took off his hat and made a wide gesture with it, indicating the direction behind him. Elizabeth looked in the direction of his gesture but could see no sign of anything. She tried again.

"Is there perhaps a cab?"

The man replaced his hat and pointed to a cart being pulled by a small white pony that was even now crossing the line at the crossing gate and turning into the station yard on her side of the track.

Eventually they had their luggage piled precariously on the back and all the children seated.

"Were to, lady?"

Where to indeed! She had no idea what she was going to do next. She was tired and weary of travelling. She felt like Mr Wagner's Flying Dutchman—condemned to wander the world for all eternity.

"Well, to Newmarket, please, wherever that may be."

"Bless yer, lady! This *is* Newmarket."

"Is there anywhere vhere we can stay? An Inn, a hotel?"

"Why, bless you lady. There is plenty of places wot yer can stay in. There's the Rutland Arms, wot is posh." He looked at their dishevelled clothes and untidy hair. "Or there is the Greyhound, or the White 'art. Or there is the Star, or the 'alf Moon, the Black Bear, the Black Bull, or the Black 'orse. There's any number, lady."

Elizabet did not know what to do. Her hesitation was obvious.

"Tell you wot, lady. I'll take yer to the Star, wot is abart middle. If it aint no good, yer can go somewhere else."

Elizabet nodded her agreement uncertainly and they set off, back over the crossing and down into the town. Elizabet was considerably cheered. The way went past some substantial houses and presently they came into the long high street. This seemed to be full of horse traffic of every kind. There seemed to be some kind of market going on, as there were stalls lined up all along the side of the wide road where a number of people were selling their different wares. There was a large variety of shops, mostly clean and brick built, of fairly modern appearance. In between the market throng, threading their way through the press, there were several strings of racehorses returning from morning exercise. She was pleased to run an approving eye over them.

They arrived at the hotel and were soon installed. The landlord promised to move in some extra beds for the children and was able to provide them with a hot meal. If they would eat their meal first, they could have a bath in about an hour. He had to have the bath carried up to their room and the water heated. Yes, she could have a second bath, if she liked, if she really wanted to bath the children, though in his experience it was not a thing that children usually worried about too much. Whilst the water was being heated they had the first decent cooked meal that they had had for days. They found the food bland and uninspiring, but they were all hungry enough to eat whatever was put in front of them. After their meal, she took the children upstairs and gave them their bath. After she had had her own and redressed her hair and put on some clean clothes, she felt a new woman. She went through all her luggage, collecting her money that she had hidden. Whilst in the house in Cologne she had put as many notes as she could into the lining of her case and the rest she had folded up into a silk scarf that she had had tied round her waist. Her jewellery she had carefully rolled up into her spare socks and stockings. This she decided to leave for the time being. She carefully locked her cases and put the keys round her neck on a ribbon. She thrust her accumulated bundles of notes into her large shopping bag.

"Come on, children, put on your coats. We will go out and see the town."

They walked up the street and were curiously interested in everything that they saw on the stalls. They came across a bank and so she went inside to see if she could change the notes that she had into English money. When she had finally made the clerk understand what she wanted, he asked her to sit and eventually she was ushered in to see the manager.

His office was as brown and gloomy as had been the reception room and she felt more and more apprehensive. Yes, he would be very pleased to open an account for her. She had only to make a deposit and he would arrange for her to be able to draw on it straight away. She handed over the remaining notes that she had—still a substantial amount.

"These notes are German. Are you German, then?"

She carefully explained her whole situation. He nodded his understanding. No, he had not heard of a Mr Henery, but he would make some enquiries for her if she wished. It might be as well for her to go the Police station and make herself known and the circumstances of her arrival. It was best to be on the safe side. He would report her presence. She must understand that there was a war on and one could not be too careful.

He counted the money. Indeed, it was a very large sum. She was lucky to have been able to escape with such a large sum. Unfortunately, the German mark had been drastically devalued again. He would not be able to offer her a very good exchange rate. He would confer with his head office in London by telegraph and offer her the best that he could, but she must understand that the German Mark was not a currency of much value at the moment. He gave her some English money to meet her immediate needs and asked her to return in the morning. No, he did not immediately know of anyone who had any houses to rent, but he would enquire for her.

Elizabet left the Bank, feeling very uneasy. If the Mark had been seriously devalued, she might very soon find herself short of money. Then what would she do?

She walked on down the street, ushering the children before her. She came across a large and imposing red brick building with a large gilded sign—The Jockey Club. She stood on the pavement and looked at it. Was this the famous Jockey Club, the headquarters of racing, of which she had vaguely heard? Surely, if anyone knew about Robert, he might be found here. She ushered her children uncertainly into the imposing hall, but here she faired even less well. Ladies were not admitted unaccompanied and only then on special days. No—no one had heard of a Mr Henery. He certainly was not a member. Yes, if they heard anything of him, they would send word round to the Star Inn for her.

She next walked to the Church. She could see the tower from the High Street and found her way to it. It was a handsome building with a tall imposing tower. She went inside and hesitated. It did not smell right. There was no smell of incense. There was no sanctuary lamp. There was no tabernacle. On the Altar, there stood a simple cross. The atmosphere felt cold and void. There were no Stations of the Cross on the walls. There were no statues, nor was there an altar to Our Lady. She gathered her children round her.

"I do not think that this is a Catholic Church. I remember Papa saying that in England they do not have the Catholic. All the Churches are Church of Eengland. We must look somewhere else for the Catholic Church." As they went out of the door, there was a Clerical gentleman changing the notices on the notice board in the porch.

"Excuse me Father. I vas looking for the Catholic Church."

"Ah yes. You need to go into the Main Street." He gave her directions of how to find it. "It is a very small building. It looks like a tin shed." He saw the look of surprise on her face. "I gather from your accent, that you are not a native of these parts?"

"No, I am from Hungary. These are my children." They all solemnly shook hands. "We are here to find my husband. His name is Robert 'Enery."

"I am the vicar in charge here. I am not a 'Father'. This Church is of course of the Church of England. Henery? No, I do not recall anyone of that name. However, if I hear anything, I will let you know. Where are you staying?"

"I am at the hotel called the Star. My name is Frau…Mrs 'Enery. If you were to hear something, you could leave for me there a message."

They made their way across the town and eventually found the Catholic Church in a side street. It was, as the Vicar had told them, a small tin shed. Elizabet looked at it with considerable misgivings.

"This is a Church? At home we have such sheds. They are used to keep cattle. We do not use them as Churches."

She opened the door and looked in. It was as poor as the outside. There was a little red sanctuary lamp glowing in the corner, in front of the tabernacle on the altar. Round the wall, there were displayed small plaster Stations of the Cross. There was a large plaster statue of the Virgin standing on a small side altar. They went inside and knelt down.

"Children, it is good that we pray and give thanks to St Christopher and to Jesus and to Our Lady for guiding us safely here."

As they left, she noted the times of the Sunday Masses. She took the children back to the hotel and after giving them an evening meal, they all went thankfully to bed. Never had white fresh sheets seemed so inviting. The children went to sleep almost at once, but despite her overbearing weariness, sleep would not come to her. She spent the night tossing and turning, in fitful catnaps, with all her problems churning around in her head. Would she have enough money? Would she find Robert? What was she to do if she could not? Through it all she could smell the smell of the little fishing boat and see the receding figure of the big fisherman standing at the end of the platform as her train drew her away from him.

She awoke the next morning feeling jaded and tired. After breakfast she left the children in the charge of Maria and returned to the bank manager.

"Ah, Mrs Henery. Please, take a seat. I have mixed news for you. I am afraid that the Mark has fallen dramatically in value, yet again! We can only offer you this amount in pounds sterling for what you deposited yesterday."

She looked at the figure. She had no idea of the value of a pound or of the cost of living here, but it seemed very little. It would depend what it would buy. But judging by how much she was having to pay to stay at the Star, she would very soon have no money left. Then what would she do?

"This is terrible. You have taken all my money and give me nothing. What am I to do? I cannot afford to stay at the Star. If I stay there, I will have no money at all. There must be another Bank in the town that will give me more pounds for my monies."

"Dear lady, you are welcome to go to visit any of them. Rest assured I have done the best I can for you. I should be very surprised if they will even consider accepting the money at all. You are welcome to go and see what you can do. I will hold my offer until this evening for you. If you do not come back today, the offer will lapse."

Elizabet thanked him and left. It was not long before she returned.

"They will not take my money at all. I will have to accept your offer. But what will I do? This is very little money. It will soon be gone. To think what I have had to leave behind in 'Ungary. Would it be possible to bring any of that here?" She wrung her hands in agitation.

"I am afraid that there is no chance of getting anything transferred here from Hungary. Technically, as part of the Austro-Hungarian Empire and ally of Germany, it is an enemy state. However, it is not all bad news. One of my clients has a row of little cottages. One of them is empty. You can rent that if you wish. It is a very small cottage, and consequently very cheap. You could live there for a lot less than you're having to spend at the Star. I know it is small, but it might serve for the time being."

Once again Elizabet felt herself being forced into a situation she could not accept.

"Let me look at this cottage, as you call it. It may be that it will be all right for the now."

"Yes, yes of course. Just allow me to collect my hat and coat and I will walk round with you now. I will just tell them that I am going to be out for a while, then we will go."

They briskly walked through the back streets, twice having to step aside to allow strings of racehorses to come past. At last they reached the cottage. It was one of a row. It had two tiny rooms and a kitchen. There was a water closet outside in the yard. There was a tap at the kitchen sink. This gave mains water. There was no need to pump up every day. The water was there at the turn of the tap. There were three tiny rooms at the top of the steep narrow stairs. Elizabet looked about her in horror.

"People live in a place like this? This whole cottage would fit into one of my servant's room at home!"

"Well, it is very cheep to keep warm and you will not have to spend much time cleaning it. Hold a duster in each hand. A quick pirouette in each room and the job is done." He smiled at her encouragingly.

"Duster? I do not do dusting! I have servants who do dusting."

He smiled at her sympathetically. "Not any more it would seem. In your present difficulty, it might perhaps help you a little, with a certain economy of scale."

Elizabet could see that it would be a lot cheaper than the Star and it had the advantage in that she would be her own master, able to come and go as she pleased. It would do for the short term. When she found Robert, she would be able to go back to live in his house with him.

"I will take it. These furniture is very poor and ugly but it will do now."

"Good. I am sure that it will be a help for you. Let us walk back to my office and I will draw up the lease. If you like you can pay a month's rent in advance, then you will not have to worry about it for a while."

They walked back to the Bank and finally she returned to the Star, with the lease in her handbag. When she arrived, she found the children very subdued and Maria in tears.

"Oh, mama. The police have been here. They stayed for ages. They kept asking me questions about where we had come from and what we were doing. They wanted to know where you were and what you were doing. They are going to come back tomorrow to talk to you. I was terrified that they might want to search us all again!"

Elizabet hugged her. "I have been able to rent a tiny cottage. It is like a little doll's house. It is very small, but it will be for us our house until we find papa. We can go there tomorrow. The police will not know where we have gone."

The next morning Elizabet paid the Star for their rooms and, having ordered a small cart to collect all their luggage, they moved into their little house. It took the police until the afternoon to find them and they were not best pleased with Elizabet when they finally spoke to her. They spent the best part of two hours questioning her, but finally they seemed satisfied and left, only asking her to notify them if she went away from Newmarket. No, they had heard nothing of any Mr Henery, but if they heard anything, they would let her know. There was going to be a race meeting shortly and race people would be coming to Newmarket from all over England. He might be in Newmarket then.

They settled into their little house and were pleased with the freedom that it gave them, though it was very cramped and the children were constantly squabbling over trivial matters. It was soon obvious that they were going to run out of money and something drastic had to be done. Maria managed to obtain a position at the Post Office as a junior clerk and brought in a small wage that sustained them. Elizabet, who liked sowing and was quite good at it, went round all the dress shops and tailors in the town, looking for work that she could take in, doing alterations and jobbing tailoring for them.

The race meeting came and went and there was no news of Robert. The summer wore on. Elizabet worked late into the night to complete her work and

Maria worked whatever extra hours that she could to earn as much as possible. By being as frugal as they could, they managed a precarious living. One night Maria came home late from the Post Office and found Elizabet at the kitchen sink, weeping pitifully. She had been preparing a swede to stew for the next day with some beef bones that she had managed to beg from the butcher. Her knife had broken in the hard vegetable and cut her hand. She was holding the cut together to stop it bleeding.

Maria put her arm round her waist and kissed her. "Come mama. Stop crying. I will bandage it for you." She tried to lead her mother away from the sink, but she would not move. Her skinny shoulders heaved with her sobs.

"If I had known it was going to be like this, I would not have come. We live like peasants in a foreign land. I have nothing to give you children. It is as much as we can do to pay the rent and live. Look at us. We are thin like strings. All our clothes are shabby and mended. It would have been better to have stayed with the big Dutch fisherman. He at least was kind. He would have looked after us."

Maria hugged her mother. She too was in tears. "Come, mama. Let me bind your hand." At last she managed to make her sit on the kitchen chair. "You must not talk like this. If we were not here, we might never find papa."

"Do you think that we will find him? We have been here all this time. No one has heard of him. I thought that if we came here, it is the centre of horse racing. If he is in Eengland, one day he would turn up and we would find him. But now I begin to lose hope."

Maria had finished binding the finger. She put the kettle on the stove to make a cup of tea.

"If we went back to the Dutch fisherman, we would never find papa. You must not give up hope. You say yourself that if he is in England, one day, sooner or later, he will turn up in Newmarket. Well, that day has not yet come. We cannot go away. We must wait. We must keep our hope alive. Next week is the big race meeting. It is the most important of the whole year. Who knows, Papa may come to that."

Elizabet reached out and took her hand. "You are so good. You have been such a strength to me. I have had to lean on you so much. It is your strength that has helped me to carry on. You are so right. We must wait. It is just that sometimes I get so low. It all seems so hard. Such a struggle. It just go on and on and on and I feel so helpless and so tired."

The kettle had boiled and so Maria made a cup of tea for them both. They had adopted the English habit of tea drinking. They both preferred coffee, but it was easier and cheaper to get tea.

"Here, drink this, it will warm you," Maria said. "You work too hard and do not eat enough. Look at you! You are as thin as a broomstick. Drink this up and then you are going to go to bed. You need to have a good sleep. In the morning you will feel better."

"I cannot go to bed. I have the hem on that dress to finish. It has to go back tomorrow."

"I will finish it for you. You are not going to do anymore tonight. Look at your hands. Your fingers are raw from sowing. You must go and have a good sleep. Do not worry about the others. I will make sure that they go to bed properly. Go on. Up you go. I will bring you a hot water bottle."

Reluctantly Elizabet allowed herself to be packed off to bed. Presently Maria went up with the hot water bottle.

"Here you are, mama. Snuggle down with this. Do not worry about the others—they will be all right." She kissed her mother on her forehead and went downstairs.

The next day Elizabet felt much better. She had slept without a break all night. She felt rested and restored in spirit. She finished some other alterations she had to make to a ball gown, which took her all day. At teatime she put the children into their coats and took the dress down to the shop to give it back. Then they all went down to the Post Office, so that they could meet Maria as she came out of work and walk home with her. They all walked back up the High Street together, looking in the shop window and chattering about everything that they could see in the windows. They were fantasising about all the wonderful things. If only they were rich, they would buy nearly everything that they saw. Maria was carrying Christopher who, though he was four, found the journey up the High Street on his short legs rather tiring.

"What would you buy, Christopher, if you were rich?"

"I would buy that funny little white dog." He pointed up the road. Looking in the next shop window was a small man in a shabby suit and a large trilby hat. On a lead, he had a scruffy lively little white terrier that was busily sniffing round.

"Christopher, don't point like that, it is rude!"

The man heard her and turned. He doffed his hat and smiled at Christopher.

Maria went deathly white. Her voice caught in her throat. "*Papa?*" she whispered, unable to speak. "Mama, mama!" she whispered urgently.

Elizabet turned to her. "Yes dear. What is it?" She noticed the man and the colour drained out of her face. "Robert?"

Robert stood, his hat still held in the air.

"Elizabet? Maria? Helen? Cornelia?" He gaped at them, thunderstruck. "What the bloody hell are you all doing here?"

Elizabet stood rooted to the spot. She could not move. Robert stepped forward and caught her in his arms. "I don't believe it, I don't believe it." He hugged her to him. He reached out and hugged his daughters as well and the little white dog jumped up and down, barking excitedly.

THE END

0-595-32925-X

Printed in the United States
48739LVS00007B/5